BRIGHT SEGMENTS

Nominations due: August 28, 2024
http://bit.ly/SohoPressIN

Nominations due: October 1, 2024
http://bit.ly/SohoPressLR

ALSO BY THE AUTHOR

THE LEW GRIFFIN NOVELS
The Long-Legged Fly
Moth
Black Hornet
Eye of the Cricket
Bluebottle
Ghost of a Flea

THE JOHN TURNER SERIES
Cypress Grove
Cripple Creek
Salt River

THE DRIVER SERIES
Drive
Driven

OTHER NOVELS
Renderings
Death Will Have Your Eyes
The Killer Is Dying
Others of My Kind
Willnot
Sarah Jane

NONFICTION
Difficult Lives: Jim Thompson—David Goodis—Chester Himes
Ash of Stars: On the Writings of Samuel R. Delany
Gently into the Land of the Meateaters
Chester Himes: A Life
The Guitar Players

POETRY
Sorrow's Kitchen
Rain's Eagerness
Black Night's Gonna Catch Me Here
Night's Pardons
Ain't Long 'Fore Day

BRIGHT SEGMENTS

THE COMPLETE
SHORT FICTION OF

JAMES
SALLIS

Published by
Soho Press, Inc.
227 W 17th Street
New York, NY 10011

Library of Congress Cataloging-in-Publication Data

TK

ISBN 978-1-64129-554-3
eISBN 978-1-64129-555-0

Interior design by Janine Agro

Printed in the United States of America

10 9 8 7 6 5 4 3 2 1

*The title of this book is in homage to and
the book is dedicated to the memory of
Theodore Sturgeon*

BRIGHT SEGMENTS

CONTENTS

Kazoo 1

A Few Last Words 5

Letter to a Young Poet 20

The History Makers 26

Front & Centaur 33

Slice of Universe 38

Winner 42

The Leveller 45

D.C. al Fine 51

Faces, Hands 55

53rd American Dream 75

The Creation of Bennie Good 80

Jim and Mary G 83

Bubbles 89

And then the dark— 96

At the Fitting Shop 103

The Opening of the Terran Ballet 108

The Anxiety in the Eyes of the Cricket 115

Jeremiad 123

Marrow 139

Récits 142

Doucement, S'il Vous Plait 153

Insect Men of Boston 157

Free Time 160

Jane Crying 164

Hope: An Outline 167

The Very Last Days of Boston 174

Enclave 179

Syphilis: A Synopsis 184

Only the Words Are Different 188

European Experience 194

My Friend Zarathustra 200

Delta Flight 281 203

The First Few Kinds of Truth 205

Second Thoughts 209

Under Construction...211

Attitude of the Earth Toward Other Bodies................................215

Intimations...224

The Invasion of Dallas..227

Driving..232

Need...236

Old Times...238

Becoming..240

Three Stories 248

The Western Campaign...254

Octobers..257

Upstream...260

I Saw Robert Johnson...264

Others...267

Blue Lab..272

Oblations...278

Men's Club...281

Allowing the Lion...283

Impossible Things Before Breakfast..285

Potato Tree..288

Finger and Flame...291

Walls of Affection...295

Changes..298

Miranda-Escobedo...303

Dogs in the Nighttime...306

Wolf...308

Memory...312

Joyride...317

Pure Reason..320

Hazards of Autobiography...327

The Good in Men...333

More Light..335

Bug..339

Moments of Personal Adventure...343

Breakfast with Ralph..347

Ansley's Demons...350

Echo..358

Notes...363

An Ascent of the Moon 365

Autumn Leaves 368

Dawn Over Doldrums 373

Powers of Flight 382

Stepping Away from the Stone...386

Roofs and Forgiveness in the Early Dawn.........................389

Dear Floods of Her Hair...392

Vocalities...397

Ukulele and the World's Pain..402

Drive..405

When Fire Knew My Name 420

Get Along Home..426

Blue Yonders..430

Christian 432

Concerto for Violence and Orchestra................................439

New Life...464

Venice Is Sinking into the Sea...468

Pitt's World 472

Flesh of Stone and Steel 480

Up 483

Day's Heat 492

The Monster in Midlife 504

The Museum of Last Week 507

The Genre Kid 510

Telling Lives 513

Your New Career 517

Blue Devils 520

Shutting Darkness Down 526

Among the Ruins of Poetry 532

Good Men 535

Bleak Bay 542

Career Moves 546

Saguaro Arms 548

How's Death? 551

Alaska 554

How the Damned Live On 560

Miss Cruz 563

Ferryman 571

Freezer Burn 577

Bright Sarasota Where the Circus Lies Dying 582

The Beauty of Sunsets 585

What You Were Fighting For 588

Dispositions 595

Billy Deliver's Next Twelve Novels 597

Figs 599

Sunday Drive 604

The World Is the Case 609

Zombie Cars 612

Net Loss 615

Season Premiere 618

As Yet Untitled 623

Comeback 626

Beautiful Quiet of the Roaring Freeway 628

New Teeth 632

Scientific Methods 639

Annandale 642

Bury All Towers 647

The Cry of Evening Birds 650

Big Day in Little Bit 653

Lying Down 657

Revenance 664

Quilts 668

Getting in Shape 670

When We Saved the World 673

Old Gifts 684

Schools of Thought 687

Subtraction 691

The Way of His Kind 695

Well Met 699

Blood Draw 703

Silver 706

Out and About 713

All My Grendels in a Row 719

Billy Deliver's Last Twelve Novels 724

Doom Patch 727

On Hunger Street 731

Rivers Bend 735

Parkview 741

How the World Got to Be... 748

How I Came to Be 752

Abeyance 757

Acknowledgements 825

KAZOO

Walking down the street on my way to see The Leech, I'm attacked by this guy who jumps out of the alley shouting *Hai! Hai! Feefifofum!* (you know: bloodcurdling) over and over, cutting air with the sides of his bands. He says *Hai!* again, then *Watch out, man! I'm gonna lay you open!* He's still assaulting the air, battering it too.

My, I think, *an alley cat.* Then I stand off and kind of watch this little dance he's doing. Dispassionately in front, you see, but I get to admiring it. I mean, he's cutting some great steps, beating hell out of the air. I snap my fingers for him, clap a little.

You watch out, man! he says. *You get cute, I'm gonna hurt you bad, put you through that wall there.* Then he goes back to his *Hai!* and *Feefifofum!* He's standing off about three yards from me, jumping around, chopping his hands back and forth, looking mean, a real hardankle. He's about five foot and looks like he might have modeled for Dylan Thomas's bit about the "bunched monkey coming."

By this time there's quite a crowd piling up. They're all standing around clapping, snapping their fingers, digging the action. Some guy in like black heads in to sell *Watchtowers* and this Morton pops up and starts passing around stone tablets and pillows of salt. There's a guy out on the edge of the crowd, he's picking pockets, got three arms. Deep Fat Friar passes by, frowns, goes on down the street flogging himself with a vinyl fly swatter. And there's this cop on the fringe giving out with a mantra of dispersal. *Ibishuma, go go; Ibishuma, go go.* (Don't think he had it quite right, you know?)

One guy pulls out a set of plastic spoons and commences to make them go clackety-clack, clackety-clack between his thumb and great toe. Another guy has a kazoo. Someone else is trying to get them to do "Melancholy Baby." *Take your clothes off and be adancin' bare,* this smartass yells out of the back of the crowd. He *is* kinda hairy, this guy.

Come on, Ralph, he shouts at me. *Come on, man, we're gonna tangle. Hai! Feefifofum!* But you can tell he likes it, the attention I mean, because he goes up on his toes and pirouettes.

I stand there looking at him, frowning a little, dispassionate again. I mean, I'm getting kind of tired of the bit by now. Some guy comes by about then with a monkey on his back, grinding at a nut-chopper. Another one's hunkered down on the corner to demonstrate his Vegamatic; his buddy's scraping bananas. And there's this like arthritic wobbling down the sidewalk with a Dixie cup, begging green stamps.

Hai! Hai! Hing! (that last one way up in the nose).

He stops and drops his hands, looks down at the concrete, shuffles his feet. *Aw come on, Ralph* . . . Then he's *Hai!*-ing and *Feefifofum!*-ing again, going at it like mad, jumping around.

And by this time I'm beginning to get *real* tired. I mean, I put up with his bag through here but now I'm gonna be late to see The Leech, so I—and let this be a lesson to all of you—I move in for the kill. I've been watching Captain Conqueroo on the morning tube, you see, and I'm like eager to try this thing out. So when this guy sees me coming and charges in, I just step ever so casually to one side and with a sudden blur of motion I get him with the Triple-Reverse Elbow Block, lay it right on him. He folds up like a letter that's getting put in an envelope that's too small for it and he falls down in like slow motion. His tongue's hanging out and a fly's walking up it toward his teeth.

Name's not Ralph, I tell him. Then I stand there humming along with the spoons and kazoo till he can breathe again. Which doesn't take him over twenty minutes or so—we'd only got through "Black Snake Rag," "Mountain Morning Moan," and part of "America the Beautiful" (raga form).

Anyhow, he starts coming back from violet toward the pinkish end of the spectrum, and he looks up at me and he says, *Aw gee, Algernon. Look, give me a chance. Sorry I bugged you.* Saying that reminds him of something and he stops long enough to spit out the fly. *Wasn't my idea,* he goes on. *Nothing personal against you, guy told me to do it . . . Bartholomew?*

I shake my head. I kick him a little. *Who.*

Guy just came up to me at the bus stop, told me you were on your way to the bank, don't know who he was. Said if I beat you up I could have the money and if I didn't he'd send his parakeet out to get me . . . Chauncey?

I kick him again. *Big guy? Southerner? Hair looked like a helmet? Scar where his nose should be, cigar stuck in it?*

Yeah . . . Look, you wouldn't be Rumpelstiltskin by any chance?

Sorry. I tell him that as I'm kicking him.

Didn't think so.

I reach down to help him up, since he's obviously going to need help. *That'd be Savannah Rolla, a friend of mine,* I tell him. Savvy's a film-maker and I know he and a poet-type by the name of Round John Virgin are hassling with a love epic called *Bloodpies*—in which the symbols of the mudcake, the blood bath, the cow patty, and innocent youth find their existential union—so I look around for the cameras. But I can't spot them.

I'm on my way to the blood bank, I tell the guy. *He's got a funny sense of humor, Savannah does. Do anything for a friend, though.* And since his hand's in mine anyway since I'm helping him up, I shake it.

Ferdinand Turnip, I introduce myself—*Ferdinand. My wife is a Bella, name's Donna.*

Percival Potato, he says, and gives me this big grin like he's busting open. *Mad to greet you.* He's giving me the eye, so I take it and put it in my wallet right next to the finger someone gave me the day before.

We talk a while, have lunch together in the laundromat, then it's time for me to split. We notice the band's still going at it so Percy cops a garbage can and heads over to blow some conga drum with them. I walk a mile, catch a camel, and rush to the blood bank. I realize I've left all my beaver pelts at home again, so I take off one of my socks (the red one) and give it to the driver. He blows his nose on it, thanks me, and puts it in his lapel.

At the blood bank Dr. Acid tells me The Leech is dead from overeating. Dr. Acid has three friends: Grass, who's rooting around in the drawers; Roach, who looks like a leftover; and Big H, who rides a horse—Joint has the bends and is taking the day off. They're all eating popcorn balls and scraping bits of The Leech off the wall, putting the pieces in a picnic basket that has a place for bottles of wine too. They ask me to stay for a potluck dinner, but I say no. I cop some old commercials with them for a while, then I dive out of the window and swim to my studio. Someone's dumped Jell-O in the water, and it's pretty tough going. The crocs are uptight today, but the piranha seem placid enough.

At the studio, reverently, I apply the sixty-fifth coat to my *Soft Thing*—four more to go. I've carefully calculated the weight of my paint, canvas, medium. The last brush stroke of the sixty-ninth coat, and my painting will fall through the floor. It will be a masterpiece of aesthetic subtlety.

By the time I've drunk all the turpentine and finished burning the brushes, it's willy-nilly time to dine. But the lemmings are bad in the hall so I'm late catching my swan and I have to wait on top of the TV antenna for over an hour. Then by the time I get home, the vampires are out. They wave as I pass. Everyone knows you can't get blood from a Turnip.

I go in and Donna comes up and kisses me and puts her arm around me and tells me she doesn't love me anymore. I look out the window. Sure enough, the world's stopped going 'round.

So I go in the john and find my kazoo and I play for a long time.

A FEW LAST WORDS

What is the silence
a. As though it had a right to more
—W. S. Merwin

Again:

He was eating stained glass and vomiting rainbows. He looked up and there was the clock moving toward him, grinning, arms raised in a shout of triumph over its head. The clock advanced; he smelled decay; he was strangled to death by the hands of time ... He was in a red room. The hands of the clock knocked knocked knocked without entering ... And changed again. The hours had faces, worse than the hands. He choked it was all so quiet only the ticking the faces were coming closer closer he gagged screamed once and—

Sat on the edge of the bed. The hall clock was ticking loudly, a sound like dried peas dropping into a pail. This was the third night.

The pumpkin-color moon dangled deep in the third quadrant of the cross-paned window. Periodically clouds would touch the surface and partly fill with color, keeping it whole. Dust and streaks on the window, a tiny bubble of air, blurred its landscape; yellow drapes beside it took on a new hue.

He had watched it for hours (must have been hours). Its only motion was a kind of visual dopplering. It sped out into serene depths, skipped back in a rush to paste itself against the backside of the glass, looking like a spot of wax. Apogee to perigee to apogee, and no pause between. Rapid vacillation, losing his eyes in intermediate distances, making him blink and squint, glimmering in the pale overcast. And other than that it hadn't moved. Abscissa +, ordinate +. Stasis.

This was the third night.

His wife stirred faintly and reached to touch his pillow, eyelids fluttering. Hoover quickly put out his hand and laid it across her fingers. Visibly, she settled back into blankets. In the hall, the clock ticked like a leaking faucet. The moon was in its pelagic phase, going out.

The third night of the dreams. The third night that lying in bed he was overcome by: Presence. In the dark it would grow around him, crowding his eyes open, bunching his breath, constricting—at last driving him from the bed, the room. He would pace the rugs and floors, turn back and away again on the stairs, wondering. He would drink liquor, then coffee, unsure which effect he wanted, uneasy at conclusions—certain only of this sense of cramping, of imposition. In the dark he was ambushed, inhabited, attacked again from within.

His wife turned in bed, whispering against sheets, taking her fingers away.

Hoover lifted his head to the dresser, chinoiserie chair, sculpt lamé valet, to glazed chintz that hid the second, curiously small window. A simple room, sparse, clean, a room with no waste of motion. And a familiar room, intimate and informal as the back of his hand, yet his eyes moving through it now encountered a strangeness, a distortion. He cast his vision about the room, tracing the strangeness back to its source at the window: to pale plastic light that slipped in there and took his furniture away into distances. It occurred to him that he was annoyed by this intrusion, this elusive division of himself from his things. He watched the moon and it stared back, unblinking.

Hoover fixed his chin between his fists, propped elbows on knees, and became a sculpture. His face turned again to see the window, head rolling in his hands, ball-in-socket.

A cave, he thought: that was the effect. Gloom, and moonlight sinking through cracks: pitch and glimmer. A skiagraphy of the near and foreign. Quarantine and communion, solitude and confederation. A cave, shaped in this strange fight.

And bruising the fight's influence, he walked to the chair and stared down at the suit he'd draped over one arm—looked at the hall clock—ten minutes ago. It was happening faster now . . .

The suit was pale, stale-olive green and it shined in a stronger fight. The coat barely concealed the jutting, saddle-like bones of his hips; his wrists dangled helplessly away from the sleeve ends like bones out of a drumstick—and Cass hated it. Regardless of fit, though, it *felt* right: he was comfortable in it, was himself.

He took the coat from the chair, held it a minute, and put it back. Somehow, tonight, it seemed inappropriate, like the man-shaped valet that no one used. As with the room, the furniture, it had been taken away from him.

He turned and shuffled across the rug to search through the crow-black corner closet behind the creaking, always-open door, discovering a western shirt with a yoke of roses across its breast and trying it on, then jeans, belting them tightly, and boots. The clothes were loose, looser than he remembered, but they felt good, felt right.

Stepping full into light at the door, he shattered strangeness, and looking back saw that the moon was now cockeyed in the corner of the pane.

Ticking of a clock, sound of feet down stairs.

He assassinated death with the cold steel rush of his breathing . . .

The night was pellucid, a crystal of blackness; hermetic with darkness. He moved within a hollow black crystal and up there was another, an orange separate crystal, bubble in a bubble . . . And quiet, so quiet so still, only the ticking of his feet, the whisper of breath. He pocketed his hands and wished for the coat he'd left behind.

Hoover turned onto the walk, heels clacking (another death: to silence).

A sepulchral feeling, he thought, to the thin wash of light overlaying this abyss of street. A counterpoint, castrati and bass. Peel away the light and you: Plunge. Downward. Forever.

Another thought . . . you can tell a lot by the way a person listens to silence.

(Sunday. It was evening all day. Over late coffee and oranges, the old words begin again. The speech too much used, and no doors from this logic of love. We go together like rain and melancholy, blue and morning . . .)

At the corner, turn; and on down this new abyss. Breath pedaling, stabbing into the air like a silent cough, feet killing quiet—

I am intruding.

Darkness is avenging itself on my back.

(And I, guilty realist, dabbler at verses, saying: There is no sign for isolation but a broken spring, no image for time but a ticking heart, nothing for death but stillness . . .)

Light glinted off bare windows. Most of the houses were marooned now in a moat of grass and ascending weed. Driveways and porches and garages all open and empty, dumbly grinning.

(Evening all day. World out the window like a painting slowly turning under glass in a dusty frame. Rain in the sky, but shy about falling. The words: they peak at ten, pace by noon, run out to the end of their taut line . . .)

The shells have names, had them. Martin, Heslep, Rose. Walking past them now, he remembered times they were lit up like pumpkins, orange-yellow light pouring richly out the windows; cars, cycle-strewn yards, newspapers on steps. The casual intimacy of a person inside looking out, waving.

(And I remember your hair among leaves, your body in breaking dew, moonlight that slipped through trees and windows to put its palm against your face, your waist; bright and shadow fighting there . . .)

Darkness. It moves aside to let you pass. Closes, impassable, behind you.

(Four times: you came to bed, got up, came back to bed. You turned three times, you threw the pillows off the bed. Michael, never born, who had two months to live, was stirring in you and stirring you awake.

Your hair was on the bed like golden threads. The moon had pushed your face up into the window and hidden your hands in shadow. You were yellow, yellow on the linen bed; and opened your eyes.

—If I weren't afraid, I could leave and never look back.

You say that, sitting in a hollow of bed, knees tucked to your flanneled breasts, arms around yourself.

—Would you follow, would you call me back?

I watch your steps track down the walk to the black, inviting street. And later, when I open the door, you're there, grinning, coming back; coming back to make coffee and wait for morning. And another night, another day, saved from whatever it is that threatens at these times . . .)

Hoover looked at the streetlight shelled in rainbow and it was ahead, above, behind, remembered. Darkness shouldered itself back in around him. Snow hung in the air, waiting to fall. The dead houses regarded him as he passed, still, unspeaking.

(October, time of winds and high doubt. It comes around us like the shutting of a light: the same thing is happening to others. And the people are going away, the time has come for going away . . . It all boils up in a man, and overflows. His birthright of freedom, it's the freedom to be left alone, that's what he wants most, just to be left alone, just to draw circles around himself and shut the world out. Every man's an island, why deny it, why tread water. So people let go . . .)

Hoover picked the moving shape out of the alley and was down in a crouch, whistling, almost before the dog saw him. It raised its nose from the ground and walked bashfully toward him, sideways, tail banging at a drum, whining.

"Folks leave you, fella?" A brown shepherd with a heavy silver-studded collar; he didn't bother to look at the jangling nametags. "Take you home with me then, okay?" The shepherd whimpered its agreement. Hoover rummaging in his pockets.

"Sorry, fella, nothing to give you." Showing empty hands, which the dog filled with licks and nuzzles, snuffling.

"Bribery, eh. Sorry, still no food." He stroked his hand into the dog's pelt, found warmth underneath. It sat looking up at him, waiting, expecting, its tail swishing across pavement.

When he erected himself to full height, the dog jumped away and crouched low, ready to run. Hoover walked toward it and put out a hand to its broad, ridged head.

"It's okay, fella. Tell you what. Come along with me to see a friend, then I'll take you right home and see about getting you something to eat. Think you can wait?"

They punctured the night together, down the walk, heels clacking, claws ticking. Hoover kept his hand on the dog's head as they walked. The nametags threw bells out into the silence.

"Or maybe he'll have something for you there, come to think of it."

Click, clack, click. Staccato tattooed on the ponderous night. The sky is still ambiguous.

(Remembering a night we sat talking, drinking half cups of coffee as we watched stars sprinkle and throb and fade, then saw dawn all blood and whispered thunder. I remember how your eyes were, pink like shrimp, pink like the sky when it caught the first slanting rays and held them to its chest. And as morning opened around us we were talking of Thoreau and men who sailed the soul, of ways and reasons to change, the old orders, and of why things break up. Outside our window it was growing between them, people were letting go, were wanting their Waldens, their Innisfrees, their Arcadias, they were falling away from the town like leaves, like scaling paint, by twos, by ones. Even in our house, our hearts, it moves between us. Between us. We feel it turning, feel it touching. But we care, we love, we can't let go . . .)

Hoover drew up short, listening. The shepherd beside him cocked its ears, trembled happily.

It happens like this . . .

A drone, far off. Closer. Becomes an engine. Then a swelling of light blocks away. Then a rush and churning and soon two lashing white eyes. Loudest, chased by a dog. A roar and past, racing. A thrown thing. Neil's car . . . and silence again.

And minutes later, the shepherd's body went limp and its head fell back onto his lap. Hoover took it in his arms and walked out of the road, its head rolling softly along the outside of his elbow. In the streetlight his face glistened where the dog had licked it.

Crossing the walk, kicking open a gate that wind had shut, Hoover surrendered his burden into the lawn. Ten steps away he looked back and saw that the dog's body was hidden in deep grass, secret as any Easter egg.

Three hundred and some odd steps. Two turns. Five places where cement has split its seams, heaved up, and grass is growing in the cracks. Pacing this map . . .

(The sea grew tired one day of swinging in harness, ticking in its box of beach. One spark in the flannel sea, possessed of fury, gathering slime like a seeded pearl, thinks of legs and comes onto a rock, lies there in the sun drying. It seeps, it slushes, it creeps, it crawls; it bakes to hardness and walks . . . All to the end: that I am walking on two feet down this corridor of black steel and my hand is turning like a key at this found door . . .)

The door collapse-returned. He looked around. A single light cut into the café through a porthole of glass in the kitchen door; powdery twilight caught in the mirror. In the dim alley before him, neon signs circled and fell, rose and blinked across their boxes like tiny traffic signals. Profound, ponderous grayness, like the very stuff of thought . . .

Decision failed him; he had turned to go when he heard the door and saw light swell.

"Dr. Hoover . . ."

He turned back.

"Didn't know for sure you were still around." Nervously. "About the last ones, I guess."

Hoover nodded. "Any food, Doug?"

"Just coffee, sorry. Coffee's on, though. Made a pot for myself, plenty left." He stepped behind the counter and knocked the corner off a cube of stacked cups, burn scars on his hands rippling in mirror-bemused light.

"Sugar, cream?" Sliding the cup onto crisp pink Formica.

Hoover waved them both off. "Black's the best way."

"Yeah . . . No one been in here for a week or more. I ain't bothered to keep the stuff out like I ought to."

Hoover sat down by the cup, noticing that Doug had moved back away from the counter. "Like you say, I guess. Last ones."

Doug scratched at his stomach where it depended out over the apron. Large hands going into pockets, rumpling the starched white.

"Reckon I *could* get you a sandwich. Or some toast—then it don't matter if the bread's a little stale."

"Coffee's fine. Don't bother."

"You sure? Wouldn't be any trouble."

Hoover smiled and shook his head. "Forget it, just coffee. But thanks anyway."

Doug looked down at the cup. "Don't mind, I'll have one with you." His penciled monobrow flexed at the middle, pointed down. It was like the one-stroke bird that children are taught to draw; the upper part of a stylized heart. "Get my cup." Over his shoulder: "Be right back." Light rose as the kitchen door opened; died back down, leaving Hoover alone. He turned his eyes to buff-flecked white tiles; let them carry his attention across the floor, swiveling his chair to keep up. Light picked out tiny blades of gleam on the gold bands that edged Formica-and-Naugahyde. A few pygmy neons hopscotched high on the walls. The booths were empty as shells, humming with shadow; above them (showing against homogenized paint, rich yellow, creamy tan; sprinkled among windows) were small dark shapes he knew as free-painted anchors.

(All this shut in a small café, sculped in shades of gray. Change one letter, you have cave again . . .)

Doug came back (light reached, retreated), poured steaming coffee. He squeezed around the end of the counter and sat two seats away.

"Neil left today."

"Yeah, I saw him up the street on the way here."

"So that's whose car it was. Wasn't sure, heard it going by. Going like a bat out of hell from the sound." He drank, made a face. "Too hot. Wonder what kept him? Said he was going to take off this morning." He blew across the mouth of his cup, as though he might be trying to whistle, instead breathing vapor. He tried another taste. "Will came through, you know . . ."

Hoover's own cup was sweating, oils were sliding over the surface. It was a tan cup; the lip was chipped. They weren't looking at each other.

"That big cabin up on the cape. His grandfather built it for a place to get away and do his writing, way the hell away from everything. Now it's his."

"I know. My sister called me up last week to say goodbye, told me about it, they thought it was coming through. Wonder when she's leaving?"

Doug looked up sharply, then dropped his head. "Thought you knew. She left about three, four days ago." Doug belched, lightly.

"Oh. I guess she went up early to get things ready, he'll meet her there. You know women."

"Yeah. Yeah, that's probably it." He went for more coffee, poured for them both. "Coffee's the last thing I need."

"You too."

"Yeah—lot worse for some, though. Been over a week for me, lost about twenty pounds. Catnap some . . . Thing you wonder about is, where'd they find a lawyer? For the papers and all. Didn't, maybe, guess it don't make much difference anymore, stuff like that. Anyhow, they're gone."

(And the wall's a wedge. Shove it between two people and they come apart, like all the rest . . .)

Hoover shrugged his shoulders, putting an elbow on the counter and steepling fingers against his forehead.

"Almost brought a friend, Doug . . ."

The big man straightened in his chair. His mouth made "Friend?" sit on his lips unspoken.

"But he was indisposed, disposed, at the last minute."

Doug was staring at him strangely.

"A dog. Neil hit it. I was going to see if I could talk you out of some food for it."

"Oh! Yeah, there's some stuff, meat and all I'm just gonna have to throw out anyway. What isn't spoiled already's getting that way fast. Didn't know there were dogs still around, though? Whose is it?"

"There aren't now. I hadn't seen it before. *Was* it: it's dead." Extinct.

"Oh. Yeah, Neil *was* going pretty fast. Dog probably wandered in from someplace else anyway, looking for food after they left him." Gazing into the bottom of his cup, Doug swirled what coffee was left against the grounds, making new patterns, like tiny cinders after a rain. "Always been a cat man myself. Couldn't keep one, though, haven't since I was a kid. Sarah's asthma, you know."

"You do have to be careful. Used to have hay fever myself, fall come around I couldn't breathe. Took an allergy test and they cleared it up."

"Yeah, we tried that. Tried about everything. You oughta see our income tax for the last few years, reads like a medical directory. Sarah got so many holes poked in her, the asthma should have leaked right out. Wasn't any of it seemed to help, though."

"How's Sarah doing? Haven't seen her for quite a while. She's usually running around in here helping you, shooing you back to the kitchen, making you change your apron, talking to customers. Brightens the place up a lot."

Doug tilted the cup to drain an extra ounce of cold coffee off the grounds.

"Not much business lately," he said. "Boy I had working for me just kind of up and left three-four months ago and I never got around to looking for help, no need of it, specially now."

"She's well, though? Doing okay."

Doug put his cup down, rattling it against the saucer.

"Yeah, she's okay. She—" He stood and made his way around the counter. "She went away a while. To get some rest." He dipped under the counter and came up with a huge stainless-steel bowl. "Think I'll make another pot. This one's getting stale. Better anyhow if you use the stuff regularly, easier on it, works better—like getting a car out on the road to clean her out."

He started working at the urn, opening valves, sloshing dark coffee down into the bowl. Hoover watched Doug's reflection in the shady mirror and a dimmer image of himself lying out across the smooth Formica.

So Doug's wife had gone away too; Sarah had gone to get some rest . . . Hoover remembered a song he'd heard at one of the faculty parties: *Went to see my Sally Gray, Went to see my Sally Gray, Went to see my Sally Gray, Said my Sally's gone away—only this time Sally Gray had taken everybody else with her . . .*

Doug was chuckling at the urn.

"You know I gotta make twenty cups just to get two for us, I mean that's the least this monster here'll handle. Ask him for forty, fifty cups, he'll give it to you in a minute. But you ask him for two, just two little cups of coffee, and he'll blow his stack, or a gasket or something." He went back to clanging at the urn. "Reckon you can handle ten of 'em?" He started fixing the filter, folding it in half twice, tearing off a tiny piece at one corner. "Hell, there ain't enough people left in town to drink twenty cups of coffee if I was giving it away and they was dying of thirst. Or anywhere around here."

He bowed the filter into a cone between his hands, climbed a chair to install it, then came down and drew a glass of water, putting it in front of Hoover.

"That's for while you wait."

"I need to be going anyway, Doug. Have to get some sleep sooner or later."

Doug reached and retrieved Hoover's cup, staring at the sludge settling against the bottom. "One last cup."

"All right. One more."

One for the road . . .

Doug bent and rinsed the cup, then got another from the stack and put it on the counter. He stood looking at the clean empty cup, wiping his hands against the apron. He lit a cigarette, nodding to himself, and the glowing red tip echoed one of the skipping neon signs on the wall behind him. He put the package on the counter and smiled, softly.

"You know, you could've sat right here and watched the whole thing happening. I mean, at first there'd be the usual group, but they were . . . nervous. You know: jumpy. They'd sort of scatter themselves out and every now and then the talk would die down and there'd be this quiet, like everybody was listening for something, waiting for something. Then a lot of them stopped coming, and the rest would sit all around the room, talking across to each other, then just sitting there quiet for a long time by themselves. Wasn't long before the regulars didn't come anymore—and you knew what was going on, you knew they were draining out of town like someone had pulled the plug.

"That was when the others started showing up. They'd come in with funny looks on their faces, all anxious to talk. And when you tried to talk to 'em, they'd be looking behind you and around the room and every once in a while they'd get up and go look out the window. And then they'd leave and you'd never see them again."

Hoover sat with his legs cocked back, toes on the floor, regarding the glass of water (the bubbles had nearly vanished). He nodded: he knew, he understood.

"For a while I got some of the ones that were coming through. I'd be in the back and I'd hear the door and come out, and there'd be this guy standing there, shuffling his feet, looking at the floor. He'd pay and take his coffee over in the corner, then the next time I looked around, he'd be gone—lot of them would just take it with them, to go. Then even that stopped."

(The people: they drip, trickle, run, pour, flood from the cities. They don't look back. And the ones who stay, try to fight it—they feel it growing in them worse than before. Turning in them, touching them, and they care they love they can't let go. But the harder they fight, the worse it is, like going down in quicksand, and the wall's a wedge: shove it between two people and they come apart, like all the rest, like all the rest of the world . . .)

Doug found something on the counter to watch.

"One time during the War, the ship I was on went down on the other side and a sub picked us up. I still remember how it felt, being in that sub, all the people packed in like sardines, stuffed into spaces between controls and motors. You'd think it would be full of noise, movement. But there was something about being under all that water, being closed in, something about the light—anyway, something that made you feel alone, made you want to whisper. I'd just sit in it and listen. Feel. And pretty soon I'd start wanting them all to really go away, to leave me alone . . ."

Doug stood looking for a moment out one of the small round windows past Hoover's shoulder.

"Yeah. Yeah, that's the way it is all right." Then his eyes switched back to Hoover's cup. "I better go get that coffee, just take it a minute to perk."

He picked up his cup and walked down the counter toward the kitchen, running his hand along the Formica. The door swung back in, wobbled, stopped (light had reached, retreated).

Hoover felt suddenly hollow, empty, squeezed. He looked around. The room was a cave again.

Out in the kitchen, Doug moved among his stainless steel and aluminum. Hoover heard him banging pots on pans, opening doors, sliding things on shelves out of his way. Then the texture of sound changed, sank to quiet, became a silence that stretched and stretched. And seconds later, broke: the back door creaked open and shut with a hiss of air along its spring, clicking shut.

(So now the quicksand's got Doug too, for all his fighting. Now he's gone with the rest, gone with Sally Gray . . .)

Outside in the alley angling along and behind the café, Doug's Harley Davidson pumped and caught, coughed a couple of times and whined away, one cylinder banging.

Hoover sat looking at the abandoned cup as silence came in to fill his ears. Then he heard the buzzing of electric wires.

The last grasping and their fingers had slipped.

The wedge was driven in, and they'd come apart . . .

He stood, digging for a dime and finding he'd forgotten to fill his pockets, then walked to the register and punched a key. "No Sale" came up under the glass. There were two nickels and some pennies.

He fed the coins in (ping! ping!), dialed, and waited. The phone rang twice and something came on, breathing into the wires.

"Cass?"

Breathing.

Again: "Cass?" Louder.

Breathing.

"Cass, is that you?"

Silence.

"Who is this? Please. Cass?"

A small, quiet voice. "I'm afraid you have the wrong number."

A click and buzzing . . .

After a while, he reached up and flipped out the change tray. As the lid slid away, a tarnished gray eye showed there: someone had left a dime behind.

Nine rings. Cass's voice in the lifted phone. Sleepy; low and smooth; pâté, ready for spreading.

"Cass?"

"Is that you, Bob? Where are you?"

"Doug's place. Be right home." The space of breath. "Honey . . ."

"Yes?"

"Get your bags packed, we're leaving tonight."

"Leaving?" She was coming awake. "Where—"

"I don't know. South maybe, climate's better. But maybe that's what everyone will think—anyway, we'll decide. Just get your things ready, just what you absolutely have to have. We can always pick up things we need in towns. There's a big box in the bottom of the utility closet, some of my stuff, some tools and so on I got together a while back. Put that with the rest—there's some room left in it you can use. I'll be right home. Everything else we'll need is already in the car."

"Bob . . ."

"Just do it Cass. Please. I'll be right back, to help."

"Bob, are you sure—"

"Yes."

She paused. "I'll be ready."

He hung up and walked into the kitchen, came out again with a ten-pound sack of coffee under one arm. He started over the tiles toward the door, then turned back and picked up the cigarettes lying on the counter. He stood by the door, looking back down the dim alley: stood at the mouth of the cave, looking into distances (he'd seen a stereopticon once; it was much the same effect).

The tiny neons skipped and blinked dumbly in their boxes; the kitchen light glared against the window, fell softly along the mirror. Shadows came in to fill the café; sat at tables, slumped in booths, stood awry on the floor; watching, waiting. At the end of the counter, the blank tan cup silently surrendered.

He turned and switched the knob. Went through the door. Shut it behind him. The click of the lock ran away into the still air and died; he was locked into silence . . .

Cautiously he assaulted the street's independence, heels ticking parameters for the darkness, the motive, the town. The sky hung low above his head.

(I walk alone. Alone. Men don't run in packs, but they run . . . Death at the wheel expects his spin. Dark seeps in around the edges, winds rise in the caves of our Aeolian skulls, five fingers reach to take winter into our hearts, the winter of all our hearts)

And they came now in the darkness, they loomed and squatted about him, all the furnished tombs: this dim garden of rock and wood.

(Bars of silence. Score: four bars of silence, end on the seventh. See how they show on my white shirt among the roses. Bars and barristers of silence)

The quick blue spurt of a struck match. A cigarette flames, then glows, moving down the street into darkness.

(There is no sign for isolation but a broken spring, no image for time but a ticking heart, nothing for death but stillness . . . and the wall, the wedge, is splitting deeper but we'll hold, for a while we'll hold on, you and I.)

He stood still in the stillness that flowed around him and listened to the hum of insects calling through the black flannel. As if in answer, clouds came lower.

(At the mouth of caves, turning. We can't see out far, in deep, but the time has come for going away, the time has come for becoming . . . At the mouth of caves, turning, and time now to enter the calm, the old orders. At the mouth of caves. Turning.)

He walked on and his heels, talked, and the night came in to hush him.

He shouted out into the dark, screamed once out into silence—and it entered his heart.

He passed a pearl-gray streetlight, passed a graveyard lawn.

("Sudden and swift and light as that the ties gave, and we learned of finalities besides the grave." Is this how it feels, the instant of desertion—a vague epiphany of epochal stillness, primal quiet?)

Around him, scarcely sounding his echo, stood the shells of houses, like trees awaiting the return of dryads who had lost their way.

(The instant of desertion, the instance of silence)

The cigarette arced into the street and fell there, glowing blankly.

He bent his head and began to hurry.

And with a flourish, the snows began.

LETTER TO A YOUNG POET

Dear James Henry,

This morning your letter, posted from Earth over two years ago, at last reached me, having from all indications passed through the most devious of odysseys: at one point, someone had put the original envelope (battered and confused with stampings and re-addressings) into another, addressed it by hand, and paid the additional postage. You wonder what word suits the clerk who salvaged your letter from the computer dumps and took it upon himself to do this. Efficiency? Devotion? Largesse? Gentilesse?

At any rate, by the time it finally reached me here, the new envelope was as badly in need of repair as your own. I can't imagine the delay; I shouldn't think I'd be so hard a man to find. I move around a lot, true, but always within certain well-defined borders. Like Earth birds that never stray past a mile from their birth tree, I live my life in parentheses . . . I suppose it's just that no one especially bothers to keep track.

For your kind words I can only say: thank you. Which is not enough, never enough, but what else is there? (Sometimes, as with our mysterious and gracious postal patron, even that is impossible.) It makes me happy to learn that my poems have brought you pleasure. If they've given you something else as well, which you say they have, I am yet happier. You have expressed your joy at my sculpture. That also makes me happy. Thank you.

In brief answer to your questions, I am now living in Juhlz on Topfthar, the northernmost part of the Vegan Combine, though I don't know how much longer I shall be here. Political bickering breeds annoying restrictions and begins to throw off a deafening racket— and after four years the Juhlzson winter is at last creeping in (I'm sitting out on my patio now; I can see it far off in the hills). The two together, I'm afraid I can't withstand.

The hours of my day hardly vary. I rise to a breakfast of bread and wine, pass the day fiddling at my books. I rarely write, sculpt even less, the preparation is so difficult ... Night is a time for music and talking in Juhlz cafés, which are like no others. (The casual asymmetry of Juhlzson architecture always confounds the Terran eye. The people are like the buildings, off-center, beautiful. You never know what to expect.) I have taken up a local instrument— the thulinda, a kind of aeolian harp or perhaps dulcimer, fitted to a mouthpiece—and have got, I am told, passably good. I play for them and they teach me their songs.

(The sky's just grown gray cumulus beards and a voice like a bass siren. It should snow, but won't. My paper flaps and flutters against the table. Darkness begins to seep around the edges. This is dusk on Juhlz, my favorite time of day.)

As to your other questions, I was born on Earth: my first memories are of black, occluded skies and unbearable temperatures, and my parents fitting filters to my face when, rarely, we went outside (my poem, Eve Mourning).

My father was a microbiologist. Soon after I was born, he became a Voyager; I remember him hardly at all, and his hands mostly, at that. My mother, as you probably know since one of my publishers made a thing of it quite against my wishes, was Vegan, a ship's companion, a woman whose gentle voice and quiet hands could do more than any medic to soothe a hurt, salve a scar. They met during a Voyage my father took in place of a friend—his first—and were together always after that. One of my early sculptures, Flange Coupling, was realized as a memorial to my parents. I don't know if you've seen it. The last I heard, it was in a private collection on Rigel-7. But that was years and years ago.

My early life was spent in comfort, in my grandparents' home on Vega and other times in crèches on Earth. When I was seven, my parents were killed in Exploration; shortly after, I was sent to the Academy at Ginh, where I passed my next twelve years and for which the Union provided funds and counsel. My *Letters Home*, which I've come in past years to misdoubt, was an attempt to commemorate that time, at least to invest it with private worth.

I don't know what command you have of Vegan history; I suppose when I was a young man I cared nothing for history of any sort.

But these were the years of the Quasitots, who supposed themselves a political group and spent their time and talents in metaphorical remonstrance against the mercenary trends of Vegan-Outworld affairs. (If I am telling you things you already know, please forgive me, but what looms large on my horizon may be unseen from yours; I have no way of knowing.)

In one of the "Letters" I quoted Naevius, an early Roman poet (my interest in Latin being perhaps the sole solid tie I have with my father's world): "Q. Tell me, how was your great commonwealth lost so quickly? A. We were overrun by a new lot of orators, a bunch of silly youngsters." I believe we thought that fitted us. We answered their declarations and old speeches with avant-garde aesthetics; we thought we would be the "silly youngsters" who'd usher in a new order. I suppose, vaguely, we believed that artists should inherit the universe.

One of my friends at the Academy took to composing symphonies of odor, the foulest odors he could find and produce, dedicating each work to the two governments. Another created an artificial flower which would wilt if touched; yet another gathered dung and baked it into likenesses of the Heads of State. My own contribution (half-hearted at best, I suppose) was the sculpting of single grains of sand, using the tools of my father, then scattering my invisible beauty in handfuls wherever I walked.

I'm not certain any longer what we really thought we were accomplishing. In our own words we were reacting, we were speaking out, we were being ourselves, we were caring. At any rate, this activity channeled our energies, brought us to work, made us think, let us live off of each other's various frenzies. It taught some of us, a few, that words and gestures get nothing done. Maybe somewhere, somehow, it accomplished something larger; I don't know. (I understand, by the way, that microsculpture is quite the thing in the academies today.) Such, anyway, was the temper and tempo of my youth.

When I was twenty, I left Ginh with my degrees and came to live in a small room up four flights of stairs here on Juhlz (my poem, "Crown of Juhlz"). I worked for a while as a tutor, then held a position at the old Empire Library, but came very soon to realize that I was unable to fit myself to a job of any sort.

I fled to Farthay, where I wrote my first novel and married. She was a young, small thing with joy in her heart and light in her eyes, a Vegan. Two years with me, and without the comfort of a child, was all she could bear. She left. It was best for both of us. We had already spent too much of our separate selves.

The rest of my life (I am eighty-four) has been spent in forming and breaking idle patterns. I travel a lot, settle for short periods, move on (your letter retraced, and made me remember, many years of my life). What money I have comes through the kindness of friends; and from other, distant friends who buy my books.

My books: you ask after them. Thank you. Well, there's *Letters Home*, which I've already mentioned and which you've probably read. Quite against my own preferences and wishes, it has proved my most popular book; I've been told that it's taught in literature and sociology classes round about the Union.

There are the novels: *Day Breaks*, *Pergamum* (a sort of eulogy for my marriage), *A Throw of the Dice*, *Fugue and Imposition*, one or two others I'd just as soon not admit to.

Essays: *Pillow Saint*, *Halfway Houses*, *Arcadias*, *Avatars and Auguries*. Two volumes of letters between the Vegan poet Arndto and myself, concerning mostly Outworld poetry, entitled *Rosebushes* and *Illuminations*.

A collection of short stories, three volumes, *Instants of Desertion*.

And of course, the poems . . . *Overtures and Paradiddles*, *Misericords*, *Poems*, *Negatives*, *Abyssinia*, *Poems* again, *Printed Circuits*, *Assassins of Polish*. Some while back, I received a check with a letter informing me that a *Collected Poems* was to be issued through Union Press. I can't recall just how long ago that was, and can't know how long the message took to find me, so I don't know whether the book is available.

And coming at last to the poems you've sent, what am I to say? All critical intent is beyond me, I fear. I've been constantly bemused and confounded by what critics have found to praise and damn in my own work: I was aware neither that I had "narrowly ordered my sensibilities" nor that I "struck out boldly into the perilous waters that lie between a poetry of device and the poetry of apocalypse" (which another renders as aiming between "a poem of sentiment and one of structure"). Give me always the Common Reader, the sensitive ignorance.

("The perilous waters". . . had I known there was danger of drowning, I might never have begun to write.)

You want Authority; I can give you none. Let me instead look up at these winter-blurred hills and say this: the poems you've sent, and which I return with this letter—they are not unique, but they speak of something which may come, something which may become yours alone. Perhaps you have it now. But two years is a very short time.

They are direct, compact, all the flourishes are beneath the surface—things greatly to be praised in a young writer. In one line you are content to give shape, in another you pause and form; always something comes easy, to the ear, the eye, the tongue, the mind, the heart. Also to be admired.

You evidently achieve control with little struggle, effective structure with somewhat more difficulty (precision and accuracy are often separate things). But you have patience, and this will come. Your diction draws crisp, sharp lines around a poem, while imagery and resonance make what is contained soft and yielding. This is at least a proper direction. And I think you are right to work from the outside in, the way you seem to do.

Two years ago, when you wrote the letter, you were looking for an older, wiser, gentler voice than your own. I am sorry that I have been so long in admitting that I cannot provide it. Perhaps you've already found one, in some academy, some café. Or perhaps you no longer need it; edges have a way of wearing off. Peace, calm—but what I can give you is closer to a stillness.

I was quite moved by the Betelgeuse mood poems in particular: I should say that. I envy you these poems. Because of a late-developing nervous disorder, a clash in my mixed parentage, I am confined pretty much to Vega. I've not been outside the Combine since the day I came here. Something in the specific light complements my affliction, and I can go on in good health. But I believe I shall have to return to dark Earth before I die, that at least, in spite of all.

It occurs to me that you obviously know about writing, and I think you must have known the worth of your poems, so I can only assume that you are really asking about living. And I have one thing to say, a quiet thing: Ally yourself to causes and people, and you'll leave bits of yourself behind every step you take; keep it all, and you'll choke on it. The choice is everyone's, for oneself.

The day is wearing down, burning near its end. Lights have gone on then off again in the houses around me. Everyone is feeling alone.

So as darkness and winter move in, hand in hand, let me wish you the best of luck in your ambitions, apologize again for the delay, and bring to a close this letter, longer than any letter has a right to be.

And in closing, please accept again my thanks for your kind words. They are given so easily, yet can mean so much.

Night now. Juhlzson birds have come off the lakes and out of forests, and are throbbing softly around me. The moons are sailing in and out of clouds. In a moment I shall move off the patio into the house. In a moment.

Yours,
Samthar Smith

THE HISTORY MAKERS

In the morning (he wasn't sure which morning) he began the letter.

Dear Jim,

The last time I saw you, you advised against my coming here.
You were quite insistent, and I don't believe the perfectly
dreadful beer we were drinking was wholly responsible for
said adamance. You virtually begged me not to come. And
I suppose you must have felt somewhat duty-bound to sway
me away. That since it was yourself who introduced me to
the Ephemera, you'd incurred some sort of liability for my
Fate. That you would be accountable.

I remember you said a man couldn't keep his sanity here;
that his mind would be whirled in a hundred directions
at once, and he would ravel to loose ends—that he would
crimp and crumble, swell and burst, along with this world.
And you held that there was nothing of value here. But the
government and I, for our separate reasons, disagreed.

And can I refute you now by saying that I've found peace,
or purpose, or insight? No, of course not, not in or with this
letter. For all my whilom grandiloquence, and accustomed
to it as you are, such an effort would be fatuous and absurd.
What I *can* do: I can show you this world in what is possibly
the only way we can ever know it, I can show you where it
brims over to touch my own edges. I can let you look out
my window.

The Blue Twin. That was . . . three years ago? Close to
that. ("Time is merely a device to keep everything from
happening at once." Isn't that wonderful? I found it in one
of the magazines I brought out with me, in a review of some
artist's work about which I remember only the name of one

painting: *A Romantic Longing to Be Scientific*.) Three years
. . . I miss Earth, dark Earth. I miss Vega.

(I remember that you were shortly to be reassigned to
Ginh, and wonder if this letter will find you there among
the towers.)

The Blue Twin, which we always insisted was the best
bar in the Combine at least, probably the Union, agreeing
that bars, those hubs of silence and lurching conversations,
those still harbors, are the emblem of civilization itself.

And the two of us sitting there, talking of careers and
things. Quietly, with the color-clustered walls of sky-bright
Vega around us and the massive turning shut out. You dis-
suading. And bits of my land slaking into the sea. Talking,
taking time to talk.

My work had soured, yours burgeoned, I envied you,
though we always pretended it was the other way around.
All my faces had run together like cheap water-color.
My classes had come to be for me nothing but abstract
patterns, forming, breaking, reforming—while the faces
around you were becoming distinct, defining themselves,
going solid.

I envied you. So I took this sabbatical: "to do a book." And
the sabbatical became an extended leave of absence, and that
became a dismissal. And no book.

We spoke of dissent and resolution, the serpentine ways
of change, ideas that fell by the way with no Samaritan in
sight—and you mentioned something you'd seen in one of
the Courier bulletins crossing your desk: which was my
introduction to it all, to Ephemera. (Ephemera. It was one
of those pale poetic jokes, the sort that gave us Byzantium
and Eldorado and Limbo and all the others, names for
out-Union planets, for distant places. You wonder who was
responsible.)

How many weeks then of reading, of requesting infor-
mation, of clotted first drafts? How long before the night
I collapsed into my bed and sat up again with the line
"Hold hard these ancient minutes in a cuckoo's month" on

my lips—days, weeks? It seemed years. Time, for me, had broken down. And I came to Ephemera . . .

The Ephemera. My window looks out now on one of their major cities, towered and splendid, the one I've come to call Siva. It is middle season, which means they are expanding: yesterday the city was miles away, a dark line on the horizon; tomorrow it will draw even closer and I'll have to move my squatter's hut back out of the way. The next day it will swell toward me again, then in the afternoon retreat—and the collapse will have begun. By the next morning I'll be able to see nothing of Siva, and the hut will have to be relocated, shuttled back in for the final moments.

They live in a separate time plane from ours—is that too abrupt? I don't know how else I might say it. Or even if that makes sense. They are but vaguely aware of my presence, and I can study them only with the extensive aid of machines, some I brought with me, a few I was able to requisition later. The government always hopes, always holds on to a chance for new resources. But all I've learned comes down to that one strange phrase. A separate time plane.

When I first came here, I was constantly blundering into the edges of their city, or being blundered into by them; I was constantly making hasty retreats back into what I started calling the Deadlands. It took my first year just to plot the course of the cities. I've gotten little further.

It's a simple thing, once you have the key: the cities develop in dependence to the seasons. The problem comes with Ephemera's orbit, which is wildly eccentric (I'm tempted to say erratic), and with her queer climate. Seasons flash by, repeat themselves with subtle differences, linger and rush—all in apparent confusion. It takes a while to sort it in your mind, to resolve the year into particulars.

And now I've watched this city with its thousand names surge and subside a thousand times. I've watched its cycles repeat my charts, and I've thrown away the charts and been satisfied to call it Siva. All my social theories, my notes, my scribble-occluded papers, I've put away; I became a scientist, then simply an observer.

It's always striking and beautiful. A few huts appear, and before you can breathe, a village is standing there. The huts sprawl out across the landscape and the whole thing begins to ripple with the changes that are going on, something as though the city were boiling. This visual undulation continues; the edges of the village move out away from it, catch the rippling, extend further: a continuous process. The farther from center, the faster it moves. There's a time you recognize it as a town, a time when the undulation slows and almost stops—then, minutes later, endogeny begins again and its growth accelerates fantastically. It sprawls, it rises, it solidifies.

(A few days ago while I was watching, I got up to put some music—it was Bach—on the recorder. Then I came back and sat down. I must have become absorbed in the music, because later when the music ended, I looked up and the city was almost upon me. I keep thinking that someday I won't move back, that I'll be taken into the city, it will sprout and explode around me.)

Siva builds and swells, explodes upward, outward, blankets the landscape. Then, toward the end of the cycle, a strange peace inhabits it: a pause, a silence. Like Joshua's stopping the sun.

And then: what? I can't know what goes on in the city at these times. From photographs (rather incredible photographs) and inspection of the ruins, I've gathered that something like this must occur: some psychic shakedown hits the people in full stride; most of them go blank, fold themselves into insensible knots—while the rest turn against the city and destroy it. Each time, it happens. Each time, I'm unable to discern respective groups or any abiding *raison*. And each time, destruction is absolute. The momentary stasis breaks, and the city falls away. No wall or relic is left standing; even the rubble is greatly consumed. It happens so quickly the cameras can't follow it; and I walk about for hours afterward, trying to read something in, or into, the scarred ground.

Three years. Amusing and frightening to think of all I've seen in that time, more than any other of us. And what have I learned? One thing perhaps, one clear thing, and this by accident, poking about the ruins. I found one of their devices for measuring time, which had inexplicably survived the relapse, a sort of recomplicated sundial—and I guessed from it that this race reckons time from conclusions rather than beginnings. (I leave it to you to decide whether this is a philosophical or psychological insight.) That is, their day—or year, or century, or whatever they might have termed it—seems to have been delimited by the sun's declension rather than its rise; and I assume this scheme, this perspective, would have become generalized, or itself simply expressed an already prevailing attitude. There's a part of the mechanism—a curious device, either rectifier or drive control, possibly both—that seems to work by the flux of the wind, I suppose bringing some sort of complex precision into their measurements: a kind of Aeolian clock.

And since that last sentence there's been a long pause. As I sat here and tried to think: what can I say now . . . Hours ago, when I began this letter, I had some vague, instinctive notion of things I wanted to tell you. Now it's all fallen back out of reach again, and what remains for you and for myself are these pages of phatic gesturing: Look. See. That, and an old song from the early years of Darkearth: "Time, time is winding up again."

And so I sit here and look out my window, watching this city build and fall. I stare at their clock, which no longer functions, and have no use for my own. I am backed to the sea, and tomorrow Siva will spread and extend out onto these waters. I'm left with the decision, the ancient decision: shall I move?

I put on my music—my Bach, my Mozart, my Telemann—and I beat out its rhythms on chrome tiles. For a while I lose myself in it, for a while I break out of the gather and issue of time.

Outside now, the sky fills with color like a bowl of strung ribbons, the ribbons fall, night billows about me. Twelve times I've begun this letter over a space of months, and each time faltered. Now at last, like the day, I've run through to a stammering end. I've filled hours and pages. Yet all I have to offer you is this: this record of my disability. Which I send with enduring love.

John

In the evening he finished the letter and set it aside and felt the drag of the sea against his chest.

He sat at the empty table he used for a desk, looking up at the opposite wall. On it, two reproductions and a mirror, forming a caret: mirror at the angle, below and left *The Persistence of Memory*, one of Monet's Notre Dame paintings across from that. Glass bolted in place, stiff paper tacked up—time arrested, time suspended, time recorded in passing. And about them depended the banks of shelves and instrumentation which covered the hut's walls like lines and symbols ranked on a page.

He rose, making a portrait of the mirror, seeing: this moment. Behind that, three years. Behind that, a lifetime. And behind that?

He ambled about his room, staring at the strange, three-dimensional objects which surrounded him, not understanding. He picked up the Ephemera chronometer, turned it over in his hands, put it back. Then, four steps and he stood by the tape deck. Making sound, shaping sound.

(All of this so vivid, so clearly defined.)

Bach churned from the speakers, rose in volume as he spun controls, rose again till bass boomed and the walls rattled.

And then he was walking on the bare gray ground outside his hut.

(Feet killing quiet. No: because the silence hums like a live wire, sings like a thrown knife. Passing now a flat rock stood on end, leaning against the sky. Another bit of poem remembered: Time passes, you say. No. We go; time stays . . . And on Rhea there are a thousand vast mole-like creatures burrowing away forever in darkness, consuming a world.)

He stopped and stood on the beach in the baritone darkness, with the pale red sea ahead and the timed floodlights burning behind him. Three yards off, a fish broke water and sank back into a target of ripples.

Looked up. Four stars ticked in the sky, an orange moon shuttled up among them.

Looked down. The city, Siva, swept toward him. He thought of palimpsests, of Saturn devouring his children.

The Bach came to his ears then, urgent, exultant. The night had gone basso profundo, the moon boxed in stars. He sat watching a beetle scuttle across the sand, pushing a pebble before it, deep red on gray.

Later he looked up and the music was over. He turned and saw Siva at his penumbra's edge, turned back to still water.

Turned back to silence . . .

Then the lights went off behind him and he was left alone with the fall and the surge of the sea.

FRONT & CENTAUR

So they went to London and they got a flat together on Portobello Road and they wrote.

Down in the street dogs shoved their snouts into tin cans, scraping them along the pavement; babies waited for mothers outside the shops in prams; the pubs burned brilliantly. One of them had observed: "My urine steams in British bathrooms!" Also, they had discovered that plugs of linoleum would appease the electricity meter.

Dave Dunder was the tall one, the thin one with a voice like vanilla pudding, and he wrote westerns. Bill Blitzen was short, with legs like two huge bolognas, eyes that jumped on you if you came too close, and a burning red bush of a beard; he turned out true confessions, four a week, and ghostwrote poetry (by a machine he had invented) on the side. Seeing them at opposite ends of a bench in Regents Park, a man would automatically tilt his head to one side, trying to get the world back to a level. When they walked together, Dunder leaned out over Blitzen from behind, sheltering him from sun and rain. They wore two halves of a six-foot muffler, ripped in two by Dunder one evening in "a moment of excessive charity." And they were in love with the same girl.

Tonight, after their customary mutual reading from the *Ulysses* nighttown sequence, they had boiled up the day's left-over coffee and gone to work at their desks, which faced one another across the length of the room. A stein of soupy coffee steamed on each desk. With the flat they had inherited an electric heater. It had two filaments, one of which Blitzen had removed, extending it on wires across the room and hanging it from the ceiling directly before his face.

It was in the general order of things that Blitzen would sit down, ringed by sweets and smoking apparatus and small jugs of beer, and set immediately to work. For the next several hours, until he was through for the night, his typewriter would cluck away furiously, steadily, one hand now and again snaking out to light a cigarette on the heater—while Dunder would be ripping sheets off his pad, balling them up and throwing them toward the corner; jerkily spurting and halting toward the end of a story; rewriting, trying to find some pattern in it all; revising and banging away angrily at his desktop.

So Dave had fallen to work tonight, laboring, like a man constipated for weeks, at the final revision of a short-short, and was soon lost to the ordered confusion of pages, inserts, scribbling and deletion. An hour later, suddenly noticing the silence at the other end of the room, he looked up. There was a walrus sitting in Bill's chair, smoking a meerschaum pipe.

"I say," he said. "You're looking rather odd tonight, Blitzen."

The walrus glanced up, then looked back down at his work. "You should talk," it said. "That's the silliest red nose I've ever seen—and I've seen a few in my time." Then, almost as an afterthought: "Now is the time, you know." At these words, Dave's desk became a hippopotamus and went galloping off toward the bathroom. The floor creaked threateningly.

Dave sat for a moment staring at the little circles on the linoleum where desk legs had been. As he watched, they suddenly started moving and scuttled away into a dark corner. He uncrossed his leg and his hoof clattered on the floor.

"Now that *is* strange," he said. "Blitzen, do you think you could take a minute off? I really think we should talk this over." Having finished its pipe, the walrus was methodically going through all the drawers, eating every scrap of paper it could find. There was a small but growing pile of paperclips on the desk before it.

"Now is the time," the walrus said again. It bent its head and its tusk scraped along the desk, scattering paperclips: one pinged into the wastebasket. Minnesota was never like this.

"Yes, it would appear to be, wouldn't it?"

The papers were turning into doves, which flapped away from the walrus and out the window. Dunder ducked to avoid one and caught a glimpse of print on its wing as it went wheeling frantically past him. A moment later it came back to the window with an olive leaf in its beak.

"But I really think we should put our heads together and give this a bit of thought. What are we going to eat, for example? I'll wager there's not a bale of hay in the house . . . Is that right: hay?" As he said this, the rug began to grow. "And what will Berenice say if she comes and finds us like this?" The rug was now three feet tall, a thick field of grass. Not far away, Dunder could make out his beaded belt lying like a snake across the top of the greenery, sunning itself. The rug rustled with the movement of many small things scurrying to safety. He jumped to his feet just as his own chair went hopping off into it; for several seconds he could see its back, bobbing up and down—then the grass was too high.

Dunder stood poking gently at the grass with his antlers, trying to decide what to do. What was needed was organization, some careful thought, a system. They could cope.

And with a *pop*, flowers began growing off the wallpaper, small bunches of orchids, slowly drooping toward the floor under the weight of their heads as the stems lengthened like spaghetti. Feathers from the pillows had gathered in cloudy masses high in the room, and when they parted for a moment, Dunder saw things like water bugs skimming across the surface of the blue ceiling.

He heard a snuffling at the base of the kitchen door; a rather foreboding growl issued from the bedroom. And then the walrus came crashing through the grass and yellow blossoms, muttering to itself: "Berenice . . . I don't know what we saw in her in the first place. She's awfully *thin*, you know." It looked up, saw Dunder standing there, and went running, terrified, back into the growth. After a bit, Dunder could hear it far away, gamboling in bucolic splendor. Then there was a mighty *splash*—

And a knock at the door. It was getting dark; Dunder's nose began to glow.

And another knock.

And another knock.

And another knock.

"Go away," a voice gurgled from across the room.

A key rattled in the lock and the door opened. Berenice stood there naked, clothes and the makings for a late tea under her arm. Her hair was done up in a honeycomb and a silver disk hung against her chest, like the moon sighted between two hills.

"Cut it out, fellows," she said.

"Glug. Glug."

"Now is the time," Dunder told her. That was all he could think to say. Minnesota had certainly never been like this.

"What does this *mean*?" she asked, coming a few steps into the room. "Are you trying to get rid of me? Don't you think you owe me an explanation at least? You don't want me to come around to see you anymore."

"Oh, no," Dunder said. "It's just—"

"That's what always happens. They always do this, it always turns out like this in the end."

"Go away," the walrus bellowed from deep in the weeds.

"See? See? God knows I try to make them love me; it's not my fault. I do everything I can—"

"Now is the time." Dunder. He was rapidly running out of words.

"—and in the end it's always like this, this always happens."

Far away, they could hear the walrus dancing a softshoe and singing "America the Beautiful."

"I'm pregnant, you know . . . We used to be so happy. Damn you. Want accretion, the James-Lange theory of emotion. I thought you would *amount* to something. What happened to us? Epithesis, existentialism. I love you."

It was beginning to rain. "It's raining, deer," she said, then giggled horribly. They huddled together in the fireplace, warm and talking quietly, watching the rain come down outside. "What will become of little William David now? That's what I decided to call him, see." Together they nibbled at chocolate biscuits. She fed him, offering each biscuit on her open hand after taking a few bites, and he chewed them daintily. He ran his tongue along the soft skin at the base of her thumb. She thought it was the walrus' dance which had brought on the rain. "Or do you think David William sounds better?"

There was a polite cough at the door: Dunder and Berenice turned together. A handsome young unicorn stood outside in a shaft of sunlight, tossing its head so that the mane swirled down around its horn.

"Come live with me and be my love," it said.

Dunder was aware of the walrus standing behind him, peering furtively out from the bushes. "Minnesota was never like this," it whispered.

Berenice stood and with one last look at Dunder, a look full of scorn and contempt, walked to the unicorn and leapt onto its great ridged back. "*Americans!*" she said.

The unicorn nodded and swung its tail to brush away a fly that had settled on her bare bottom, in the dimple at the top of her left buttock. They turned and rode off together down the hall toward Cheshire . . .

And nothing's been the same since.

SLICE OF UNIVERSE

The guidebirds beat their tiny wings and moaned to one another across the ceiling of the flightroom. (Fright, complaint, confusion, fear: *Where was home, where was home? So far, so far.*) Half sunk in the suckweed, Merler floated under the blister-cages. The birds' cries crept and rolled on tandem oscilloscopes: the ship took up those lines, tossed them out to the void, moved along them.

Loved Merler, I come to report—and Whorlin stofted into the room, trailing suckweed, upper of his twin external tongues clucking in the "most important" quadrant. Unnecessary, since he was using one tongue—but Whorlin was a stylist, with a reputation to consider.

Merler inhaled, bloated, came up partway out of the suckweed. Then bestupt his tongue in a perfectly chosen reply: *I wish your words to my heart.*

For a moment Whorlin paused. He envied such a natural, easy style. His own tended toward artifice, abstraction: too careful, too considered. He couldn't match Merler's vitality, and that vitality seemed almost effortless.

(*Poor, o poor birdies. Took our homes away. O poor poor birds.* And fluttered their useless wings.)

Whorlin vurked *I have just found* and the stylistic device *Borgman furfth at leisure* in harmony on his external tongues, threading it throughout with a rhythm-of-discovery clicked in paradiddle on his internal tongues, finally adding the odor complex that signified *I seed my words in your heart and pray for their growth.*

Merler tipped sideways on the sand. *Schlupp!* his roots shot up into their sheaths. He rolled back upward and came off the pool. Wetness flowed down him, staining the sand.

Whorlin accepted respect; slipped his tongue into out-phase and began to fugue on discoveries. Almost casually, Merler broke in with a haunting, improvised counterpoint on the theme *My heart is fast, things are slow*, simultaneously chiming his nether tongue several octaves higher and in discord on *Words words words, they breathe and breed.*

Whorlin furled a root out toward the wetness and kurthed his apology in one of the more difficult standard études. Merler, complying, beat out the motif *My heart waits* . . .

Whorlin listened for a moment, then complimented Merler on his attacks.

Yes, regard, obligation. Inner tongues, obligatto: *My words can never approach your fineness.* Throat-tongue, motif repeated, beating: *My heart waits* . . .

(*Home, home, where is home? Where are they taking us poor, poor birds? Where are they taking the birdies' ship? Hurt. Hurt the poor poor birds.*)

With some regret, Whorlin clicked the rhythm-of-directness on his internal tongues, overtoning that they must sometime ensemble together.

A man on Earth, he vurked, and caught a rhythm-of-wonder from Merler. He developed a theme for Earth; halfway through, Merler harmonized acceptance. Then: *My heart waits*, throbbing.

I have just borged.

Acceptance.

A man.

Rhythm-of-wonder.

Whorlin introduced the motif for science, then overtured discovery, improvising on it until Merler rhymed him.

The universe is finite, he went on, developing this theme, concluding with an obligatto *Most important* on his upper external tongue.

Merler motifed the rhythm-of-wonder. Each time his tongues found a beat, Whorlin could feel the seeping life within him; his roots fell away from the wetness, crept back over the sand toward their sheath. Merler paused, then rhythmed completeness.

The work is correct, Whorlin responded. *I have borged the symbols closely.* He buzzed his throat-tongue and added a sketchy odor complex, transferring respect back to Merler.

(*Home, home. Birdies will die away from home. So far, so far. Dead ship, away from home. Where is home? Pity us poor poor birds.*)

This means we shall run out of worlds, Merler vurked.

It borges so.

We shall have no new worlds to find. Image and accompaniment began to rise behind his words.

Acceptance, limitation. *So far ahead it has no meaning. Far, far ahead. Even for us, the two of us.*

Rhythm-of-wonder, swelling. *We shall have no new worlds, new wonders, new voices. We, whose only work and purpose is discovery, whose only love is the voyage. We who have made empty space our friend these million years . . .*

So far ahead we have no symbols for it.

Rhythm-of-wonder. The phase of sadness. *It is enough to know someday there will be no more.* The words dropped onto his tongues and lay there, gathering things—emotion, image, resonance—about them, and then, just before it seemed they must die, escaping. His eyes drooped. His roots lay limply out on the sand.

Whorlin beat out completeness in unity against his palates. And then he listened as Merler built a poem of loss about them in the room of pools and weed and sand: a warm hollow thing, filled with sadness and covered over with wonder and love: a small thing, strange with fur, that broke the heart. And for the first time Whorlin understood the beauty and power of Merler's vurking, the limits of his own trained precision. As Merler's tongues clicked and fluttered and sang . . .

He told of a people which had come from the sea onto the orange plains and rolling, wine hills of a huge double-sunned world; had come and carved the land to their likeness. Then when the land was filled and familiar they had felt again the drag of that sea against their chest and had, some of them, returned. And when even the sea was known, when there were no new things, the people had looked above them and found new worlds, had sailed out to larger seas, seas they believed would never end. They had stepstoned on stars to step among these worlds: quietly, reverently, always listening for new musics, new life. And this in turn became *their* life, the way and beauty of their lives: to be always searching for new things, to be close to beginnings, eavesdroppers to the wonders of a universe. With their birds they had tied world to world, sun to sun, had begun to fill space itself with the paths of their traveling. They were a long-lived people, and one man could in his time be a part of many worlds . . .

And he spoke of things that end. Of the birds. Their ship. The two of them, Merler and Whorlin, away from home a thousand years. And someday the birds would die, the ship be useless, the two of them marooned, alone. Alone—and all the worlds waiting. But not enough: someday there would be no more. Even worlds had their end . . .

His words resounded in the room. Image dropped away and only the sounds were left; then those too were gone, lost in the sand and the weed-crammed pools. The room was quiet with the breathing murmur of controls. Odors drifted, fading, in the air.

It is sadness, Whorlin vurked after a while. Then, respectfully, he reversed his head and departed the flightroom, leaving a patch of wetness behind on the sand.

Merler stood looking after him for a moment, then rolled back onto the suckweed and sent his roots deep down into the living fluid below. He exhaled and his body collapsed around him, sank into the weed. He looked at his bank of controls, at the two dark spots of dampness out on the sand. He spun his eyes in concentration. The guidebirds whined.

(*Poor, o poor birdies. Took our homes away. So far, so far. O poor poor birds.*)

And outside, the darkness that somewhere, someday had an end—this darkness touched softly at the front of their ship, stroked along it, and fell off into the vacuum behind.

WINNER

We're going in at the same time and only one of us is going to come back out. Ten in the morning. No dinner tonight, no breakfast. It's all set. I've told him that but he won't believe it. He just lies there groaning every few minutes saying We're gonna make it Joe, we're both gonna make it. And then a fit of coughing hits him and the nurse comes running.

Three, four times a day Bill goes through the ward taking the bets. They've picked up a lot in the last week or so. More of them, and higher—the coughs and the special nurse, I guess. There's only one guy in the ward now who hasn't kicked in, and we finally figured out he was deaf. Every night just before lights out, Bill comes round to tell me how much is in the pot. When he brings the pills. It's up to $348.83 now. Not bad. I've done worse on the outside in my day, a lot worse.

Bill's a grad student at Columbia. He's on scholarship, maybe a grant or two, but he's working nights as an orderly to help finance his Panther block. He's got light skin and fine features and he could pass for white a lot of places I know. First day I was here, back about a month ago, he told me he was black, just worked it into the conversation, maybe four times.

The guy next to me. He's a little guy. Pushes a hack, and he got torn up pretty bad by two young Negroes up near Harlem. They brought him in about a week ago and it looked like he wasn't going to make it for a while there, but they stuck some tubes in him and he had needles all in his arm the first two, three days, and some kind of oxygen mask with a bag on it. Bill used to go over and snatch whiffs from the mask and come back with a big grin on him. Anyhow, they had to wait this long for the cabbie to get his strength back, like with me. First thing he said the day he came around was, I been shoving that damn cab for fifteen years now, I oughta know better. He doesn't talk much, I don't know if he can, but there's something about him I like. One thing is he's got guts, he's tough. You can see that when the pain hits him and he clenches his teeth, holding on. He's not the kind that gives up easy—it's a long way from the Bronx, but he'll never forget it. And I like that, I know how it is.

Right before lights out tonight Sanders comes over. He makes sure to wait till Bill's gone first, though. They don't have much use for each other, I don't think they even talk. Sanders never got through high school. He had to come up the hard way. And then there's the whole black thing of course. Seems a couple of his buddies on the force got gunned down by blacks a year or so back and he can't forget that, not for a minute. But he's a good guy. He knows what's going on, all about the pot Bill's holding I mean, and he's cool.

He stands by the bed a while looking around the ward, then asks how I'm doing tonight. I don't figure he needs an answer, he knows I'm slated for tomorrow morning. Either way he'll be back on the streets. But word has it he's got a promotion coming up.

"You're looking pretty good."

"I'm okay."

"Look, I'm sorry, Vic. Never intended to shoot."

"That's okay too."

He smiles and looks around again. I don't know what he thinks he's looking for. He knows every crack in the wall by now.

"You need anything? Anything I can get you?"

"I'm good."

"Look, I want you to know, when the trial comes up. I'm on your side. I'll be pulling for you all the way."

"Great. We can say it was a hunting accident. I forgot to wear my red cap."

He's watching my face very closely, finally says "Right" and starts away, but I stop him.

"Sanders . . ."

"Yes."

"Do me a favor?"

"Sure, Vic. Anything."

"Ask Bill to come back in here for a minute. I have to see him."

"Bill . . . ? Yeah, sure. Why not." He goes out through the door and he's gone for a few minutes. Then I see him coming back and he takes up his post just outside the door, in a folding chair out there. A minute or two later Bill comes in. God knows where Sanders might have found him this time of night.

I cut him off before he says anything: "Got something for you, Bill." I reach around under the pillow, take out the roll and hand it to him. The bandages get in the way and it takes a while. "Put it with the rest." When he looks back up at me I shake my head. "No questions." It's not like I have anything else to do with it, and there's a few hundred there.

Bill takes out a little notebook and makes an entry. He knows how to do it right. Then he puts the money in his pocket and leaves. He doesn't say anything more to me but I notice he stops outside and talks to Sanders for a minute, maybe two. Sanders turns around in his chair and glances at me.

I hope I was right about the promotion.

THE LEVELLER

He came out of the city (out of the smell, out of the steel, out of the squatting suburbs) over a hill and fell into morning: it opened around him.

Bouncing on cement seams, the little red Fiat moved slowly along the two-lane highway. On the narrow shoulder, tiny pools of water from last night's rain glinted in the gravel like bits of metal; and water lay in gleaming bands at the bottom of ditches off either side of the road. Beyond these were fences, long fields of corn and grain, a cluster of red barns with houses and sheds, and occasional dirt roads marked only with letters and numbers.

Larry smiled and reached above him to pull back the leather sunroof. Light spilled into the car; he could smell the freshness of the air, its purity.

He slowed, braked gently, stopped. To his right lay the blacktop that passed through Center Junction and led back to the city. Belying the careful grid of all the other roads, it wandered and rolled through the countryside, swinging this way and that, making its own way—a much longer route than the way he'd come. He considered for a moment, letting the car idle, then turned. The Fiat bounced off the highway onto scattered gravel, came down onto the smooth blacktop, and settled into a chugging throb.

Around him now, corn ripened up the stalks wrapped in green corduroy. The farms were farther apart, their colonies of buildings set off from the fields by hills, small orchards, or fenced chicken runs with manure piles steaming in the back. Windmills rose out above the plain white houses and sheds and, in many of the fields, cows grazed together in slow-moving, slow-changing groups.

Larry slowed to pass a tractor which was pulled off to the side of the road. Its driver stood talking with a man who held a hammer. Behind them, a fence sagged. They looked up and waved as Larry drove by.

A bit farther along, he passed an open buggy with bags stacked crisscross in the back. The young Amish driver, wearing what looked to be a new beard, smiled and nodded. Larry eased around the Clydesdale, came back to the right, and started picking up speed again. Around the next curve, he passed a single lone house sitting back off the road. An elderly man, looking somewhat awkward in oversize overalls, was crouched down, clipping grass along the side of the walk. As the Fiat went by, he dropped onto one knee, shaded his eyes, looked up, and waved, his garden tool flashing as it crossed out of the shade of an elm into sunlight.

Larry pulled off to the side and sat for a moment with the engine idling. Three motorcycles passed by him, girls clinging to the cyclists' broad backs, and swept up over the hill ahead. Their sound faded slowly to the drone of hornets in a hollow tree and vanished. Larry shifted into first gear and pulled back onto the road. Ahead lay a dip, another long curve, a new hill.

Bllaarrreee—then the screech of tires.

Larry's eyes jumped to the mirror and he saw the huge green Pontiac. Its driver, red hat pulled down to meet wraparound sunglasses, was leaning on his double horn and blaring away. The car had shot from a side road as though it had been waiting there for him. Larry could see the rolling dust, looking like huge brown feathers, where it had come sliding and skidding out of the dirt onto the blacktop. The driver had one arm in the window; the other laid casually across the top of the steering wheel. His teeth were sunk into a cigarette. Smoke rolled about him.

Bllaarrreeee! Bllaarrreeee!

Larry straightened from the curve, pushed down on the accelerator until he was doing the limit, and started up the hill; but he lost speed and had to drop back to third gear. Behind him, the Pontiac raged. An old Ford pickup with splash guards came down off the hill ahead of them. Its driver was waving his hands and shouting something out the window, but Larry couldn't hear him over the blaring horn.

Bllaarrreeee!

The Pontiac swerved into the space between the back of the pickup and the Fiat, fishtailing, kicking up dirt and rocks. The driver sped up and came around Larry just as a school bus appeared at the top of the hill, then cut back in abruptly, making Larry hit his brakes hard to avoid piling into him.

Through the rear window, Larry could see what looked like a salesman's portfolio and sample case on the sun ledge, as well as a half-filled bottle of bourbon, its amber liquid splashing inside as the car swerved again and shot forward. The driver threw his hand up and poked his middle finger at the Fiat's reflection, moving it up and down and grinning as if the Fiat, its driver, and the whole disobedient world were being triumphantly violated. The Pontiac disappeared over the hill, with the school bus still blatting its warning. When Larry topped the hill, he saw that it had gone around another curve.

He leaned forward, reached under the dash, and pulled a small switch.

A low whine began deep in the car and climbed in pitch to a scream. Needles of sound pricked at his ears; shock waves passed through the chassis and shuddered along his spine, snapping his head to attention, clamping his hands hard on the wheel. All around him, auxiliary engines came to growling life. Larry brought his seat belt down over his shoulder, across his chest, and buckled it. Thin blue smoke rose inside the cab. The taste of metal was in his mouth, the smell of octane sharp as a razor. Under him, the car bucked and rumbled. Gently, he released the clutch.

The Fiat shot forward like a thrown stone, engines bellowing. Larry swung easily through curve after curve, topping the small hills. The sun ducked under clouds.

And there was the Pontiac ahead.

Larry cut sharply to the right, dove around a truck, and streaked across the shoulder, kicking up gravel. Back on the road, running smooth and lean, he rapidly closed the distance. He came up short behind the Pontiac, tailgating, and hit his horn.

Bllaaarrrrat!

It sounded—was made to sound—like a raspberry.

The Pontiac's driver looked up at his rearview mirror, out at the sideview, then jerked around and stared. He raised a trembling hand and threw down his cap. Then he turned back, hunched over his wheel, and swerved just in time to miss a bridge railing. The Pontiac increased its speed and opened road between itself and the Fiat; soon it was out of sight.

Larry drifted for a while, then caught the Pontiac again without difficulty. He came up behind it, hit his brakes, and leaned on the horn. Then he swung in front, pulled to the shoulder, fell in behind, came abreast, and repeated his maneuver. He could see the driver quaking with fury; he noticed that the Pontiac again and again swerved from the center of the road and had to be hauled back. The driver raised his fist and shook it violently. Then his mouth moved in the mirror, making ugly shapes. Larry hit the horn again.

Ahead was Center Junction. Five miles—then ten more to the city. Larry played cat-and-mouse for another two, then shifted to overdrive and pulled away. The Pontiac vanished into a dot behind him.

He slowed as he approached Center Junction and pulled into the combined gas station and grocery store there. He got a Coke from the machine—one of those old-fashioned small bottles—and leaned against the Fiat, drinking it. Looking up, he saw the motorcyclists standing off a bit, watching him. Behind them, by the store, their girls sat on the big Harleys. Two of the cyclists were bending down, trying to see into the car; but the windows were now opaque. The others looked at Larry and grinned.

"Hey, you were really cuttin' out in that thing, man. Must of been doin' one-twenty, one-thirty easy."

Larry just hunched his shoulders. "Sometimes you need to."

"That some kind of custom sports job?"

"Yeah, I guess you could call it that."

"Thought so. Some buggy—and some righteous driving, too. You ever been on a bike? Looks to me like, you know, a guy like you—*Man!* What *was* that thing?"

The Pontiac had just come tearing down the street past the store. Still leaning against the car, sipping the Coke, Larry had raised his hand and waved. "Friend of mine," he told the cyclist. "A real hot dog." He finished his Coke and handed the bottle to the cyclist. "Later," he said, climbing back into the Fiat and buckling the seat belt around him. The guy stared into the car, eyes wide, trying to take it all in.

"Yeah man, later," he finally said. "Hey, you want some help?"

"Thanks. But not this time." He swung the door shut and moved out of the parking lot. By the time he reached the highway connection he was already pushing a hundred.

Larry caught up not too far outside the city, where the flat mud was staked out for a new housing development. He shot in behind the Pontiac; then, on a sharp, climbing curve, he turned abruptly off into the fields alongside. To the Pontiac's driver, it must have appeared that the Fiat simply vanished; but, when he leveled off at the top of the curve, he could see the little car coming across the field, back toward the road ahead of him. He must have known he couldn't get there first, but he tried; at the last minute, Larry eased off and let him slip in ahead. Larry dogged him for a while, then hung in close on his bumper, hitting the horn from time to time. The other driver kept looking up in his mirror every few seconds, letting the Pontiac run off to one side or the other. He almost missed three curves in succession; gradually, by increments, he was slowing down.

At the next hill, Larry repeated his abrupt turn into the fields; but, this time, he pushed the Fiat almost to its maximum, then sat near the top, waiting, as the Pontiac came into view. The driver hit his brakes and the Pontiac skidded out onto the shoulder, into the fields. It went up on its right tires, balanced that way precariously for a moment, then slammed back down. The driver instantly floored it and cut back out onto the road, tearing huge ruts in the field, fishtailing wildly.

Larry let him pull ahead, then closed the gap. He fell back again, gained, and hung on his tail. Then twice he passed him, slowed, and swung off to the shoulder to let him by. The Pontiac was down to about 50 now; they were on a straightaway and would soon be getting into traffic.

Larry braked and sat with the engine pounding, letting the Pontiac pull out far ahead. Then he slowly brought up the speed, popped the clutch, and shot away toward the bigger car. He drew abreast, looked over and waved, and fell behind. He braked again to repeat the maneuver; but, this time, he shot out around the Pontiac—running out yards ahead, gaining speed steadily—then abruptly hit the accelerator and brake simultaneously, in precise, measured touches.

The Fiat swung full circle and came round, heading directly toward the oncoming Pontiac. Panicked, its driver tried to cut into the other lane, but lost control. Larry threw the Fiat into reverse as the big car came skidding and sliding across the highway. It plowed down the embankment; stood for a long moment, improbably, on its nose; and tumbled into the sludge and moss of a deep ditch. It lay there upside down, buried to the door handles. The wheels spun and the horn was stuck, blaring dully, muffled in the mud.

Larry reached over and disengaged the toggle under the dash. With a series of coughs and shudders, the auxiliary engines cut out. Larry shifted into first and pulled away slowly. He passed a church, made a right, and was soon back on the side road, heading toward home.

He passed a farm with dozens of bronze-backed turkeys gobbling and waddling, a rare outside stack of hay, and a half-built barn with *Brenneman 1967* already painted above the place where the doors would be.

He slowed still more and looked around him, enjoying the landscape, the last of this quiet farmland. He began to whistle tunelessly. The sun was up there smiling now.

Just outside the city, the motorcyclists came up behind him and sat very straight and still in their seats, eyes forward, hands held to their caps in silent salute, as they slowly passed. Larry smiled and waved. The cycles throbbed and shot away.

Larry guided his way among intersections, traffic lights, school crossings, and driveways. Finally, he pulled into his own driveway, turned the Fiat off, and sat looking for several minutes at the closed garage door. He started the car again and pulled it over to one side, to the edge of the grass, out of his way.

Tonight, he thought fondly. Tonight he'd take the Morris Minor out, the one with all the switches on the dash. The one with all the lights on the front.

D.C. AL FINE

It was a bad day. A year full of them, in fact. Or three, if you got right down to it. And I did. Way down.

The corporation was going like wildfire, sure—we'd been getting so many government contracts, we kept expecting a grand jury to descend on us—but when I took the suit off at night there just wasn't much there, not much left inside. The whole thing was like a series of snapshots in which I saw my life fading off into the distance, hopscotching away from me. And even then, the snapshots were out of focus, blurred, indistinct. Snap: Mary and the kids were gone, moved back to Boston. Snap: I started drinking too much, couldn't get anything together with another woman, either. Snap: Long discussions with my partners. Couldn't sleep at night, lay there terrified, put away handfuls of Librium, stayed away from mirrors. And then the money was gone and I was in debt.

But this one was the worst yet. I'd stayed on late at the office—it had been dark outside for several hours—trying to catch up on work I should have finished months ago. The figures kept blurring, and the contracts sounded like gibberish, and when I looked back at my day's letters they sounded like lecture notes for some course I didn't have a chance in hell of passing.

Finally I got up and walked across the carpet to the window. Looked at all the little lights crawling along down there, going somewhere, going away.

I don't think I ever made the decision consciously. It's just that I was suddenly standing there with the window open and I was leaning out, looking down. I felt my belt buckle sliding slowly across the sill and I was thinking, of all things, about my swimming coach back at Yale. Keep the legs together, boy, and your whole body rigid, taut, and don't be too quick off the board; you'll go in without a splash.

"Don't do it," someone said.

I looked around and there was a guy sitting on the ledge about two feet away, smoking a cigarette. Twenty-eight stories up.

"You know your trouble, man? You want to be a goddamned statistic."

"Well . . ."

"I know. Wheels within wheels. It'll drive you mad, just watching them." He swung a leg onto the ledge. "Mind if I come in?"

I pulled back out of the way, and he did. "Got a drink? Oh, that's right, you're off the stuff." He paused. "Look, I'm supposed to give you this big philosophical hype now—how knocking yourself off is a cop-out, how it doesn't take guts, that it's sticking it out, dealing, that takes guts. But if you don't mind, we'll just skip that part of it." He glanced around the room. "Frankly, it bores the hell out of me."

He walked across the room and sat down in the chair he'd selected with that first glance.

"I'm from Suicide Control," he said after a moment. "And no, you never heard of it. And we're government, not police. Trained by America's top psychologists to deal with potential suicides, some like you, some quite different. I've been at it for about eight years. For four or five of those years, we've been watching you. I was pretty sure I had the event pinpointed." He gestured toward the window. "Guess I was right."

He sat for a while watching me from across the room. I was still standing by the window.

"Look, man, the point's past and you won't do it now. So why don't you shut the window, it's getting cold in here. Not as bad as out on that damned ledge, but cold. You sure there's not something to drink around here?"

I grabbed the bottle and a couple of glasses from the bottom drawer of the desk, and we settled back with the drinks.

"Have to give it to you, you do make an entrance," I said.

"Precisely why it's effective."

"I see . . . So I'm to understand that you, your group or agency, whatever you call yourselves, maintain surveillance of potential suicides and intercede to restrain them from doing so?"

"Close. But *control*, the word, comes a bit closer."

He finished off his drink.

"A meticulously programmed system of propaganda. Quite subtle, insidious—as it has to be. And utilizing every available media resource. The program's been in effect over a decade now. Results have been excellent."

He held up his glass and looked through it at the window, closing one eye. "Every one of us has his own ghetto, sir. Something inside us. Each of us is *enclosed* by something—background, color of his skin, psychological kink, rotten childhood—something that contains us. We find that and we use it."

He got up and walked to the bookshelves, idly looking over titles, souvenirs.

"There are, of course," he continued, "those—professional men in medicine and law, scientists, technicians, top-level administrators—who must be saved. Protected from the indoctrination propaganda, or from themselves. We guide them away from propaganda, keep propaganda away from them, insofar as we can. There are programs of counter-propaganda, of course. What Kenneth Burke would call 'a symbolic action.' Shock tactics—which is why I was out on that damned ledge." Then, almost as an afterthought: "Need I mention that you're one of those under our protection?"

"A washed-out alcoholic failure. Fine choice."

"Personal ghettos, and breaking out of them. You've a considerable genius for organization and executive function, proven again and again. Whatever interferes with that, one way or another, can be eliminated."

"What you're talking about is genocide. Regulated, scientific genocide."

He turned toward me.

"If you wish. But efficient. And necessary. Or would you, as a humanist, prefer the alternatives? Famine, panic, the dissolution and eventual collapse of any order within the boundaries of *our* country, and then most others. Plagues, an uninhabitable landscape, retreat to underground shelters which can't sustain us. That's the road we were headed down, full speed."

"Who decides? Who says which ones get a chance to go on living?"

"That's classified. Top Security."

I was standing by the window again. "Come here."

He crossed the carpet and stood beside me.

"Look down there," I said. "What do you see? Those are people. Same hopes and dreams, same fears, same hopelessly absurd little lives as you or me. Or anyone else. They hurt, they get hurt, they lose, they get lost. It's not much but it's what they have—till you take it from them."

"Such is the difference between us, sir. I'm younger than you; I truly grew up in a different world. Those lights down there, those tiny things moving around? What can they matter, what can a hundred of them matter, a thousand, when there's an entire country, quite possibly a world, at stake?"

I walked back to the desk and poured new drinks. "And where do you stand in all this?"

"Not among the elected, if that's what you mean." He took the drink from me and had a long draw. "I'm a specialist, largely immune to the propaganda. But when the time comes that I'm no longer essential, I'll go the way of the rest."

"One way or another."

He nodded, and came up beside me at the window. "It's done, sir. It is working."

I don't think I made the decision consciously that time either: I just pushed, and he was there, then not. I threw the glasses out after him. After a while, the bottle as well.

Nothing ever came of it, naturally, and I've been all right ever since. I stay away from newspapers and radios; the thought of another drink never occurs. Business has picked up incredibly, and there's more work than I can do since my partners died (one slit his wrists in a cheap hotel down on the Strip, the other went out the window next door) and the firm fell wholly into my hands. Government contract after government contract, they just keep coming in, and I may be taking on a new partner soon. It's been a good three years. Sometimes late at night I remember that other night by the window and can't help but wonder how much of this was a part of their plan, whoever they are, and if, even while the man was sitting out there on the ledge, he knew what was going to happen. I keep meaning to go down to the library and look up Kenneth Burke, too, but I'm busy and never get around to it.

FACES, HANDS

Kettle of Stars

A lot of Couriers are from academic backgrounds, everything from literature to energy mechanics, the idea being that intellectual hardening of the arteries is less likely to occur if you watch what you eat and keep the blood flowing. You have to stay flexible: one loose word, one unguarded reaction, and you've not only lost respect and a job, you've probably thrown an entire world out of sympathy with Earth. In those days a Courier was a kind of bargain-lot diplomat/ prime minister/office boy, and we were playing most of it by ear; we hadn't been in Union long enough to set standards. So when they started the Service they took us out of the classrooms, out of the lines that stood waiting for diplomas—because we were supposed to know things like unity being the other side of a coin called variety. Knowledge, they assumed, breeds tolerance. Or at least caution.

Dr. Desai (Comparative Cultural) used to lean out over the podium he carried between classrooms to proclaim: "All the institutions, the actions, the outrages and distinctions of an era find their equivalent in any other era." He said it with all the conviction of a politician making the rounds before General Conscript, his small face bobbing up and down to emphasize every word. I took my degree at Arktech under Desai, and in my three years there I must have heard him say that a hundred times: everything else he—or any other instructor—said, built back up to it like so many stairsteps. A zikkurat: climb any side, you get to the top. Some early member of the Service must have had Dr. Desai too. They had the same thing in mind.

For me it was June, on a day like yellow crystal. I was sitting in an outdoor café across from the campus with my degree rolled up in a pocket, cup half full of punjil, myself brimful of insouciance. It was a quiet day, with the wind pushing about several low blue clouds. I was looking across at the towers and grass of the Academy, thinking about ambition—what was it like to have it? I had no desire to teach: I couldn't get past Desai's sentence. And for similar reasons I was reluctant to continue my studies. An object at rest stays at rest, and I was very much at rest.

Distractedly, I had been watching a small man in Vegan clothes work his way down along the street, stopping to peer into each shop in turn. When finally he reached the café he looked around, saw me in the corner and began smiling. I barely had time to stand before he was at the table, hand stuck out, briefcase already opening.

Like Desai, he was a little man, forehead and chin jutting back from a protruding nose.

"Hello, Lant," he said. "I was told I could probably find you over here." He sat down across from me. He had small red eyes, like a rabbit's. "Let me introduce myself: Golfanth Stein. S-T-E-I-N: stain. I wonder if you've heard the Council's organizing a new branch." I hadn't. "Now that we're in Union there's a certain problem in representation, you know. Much to be done, embassies to establish, ambassador work. So we're beginning the Courier Service. Your degree in anthropology, for instance . . ."

He bought me a drink and I signed his papers.

Ten years . . . Ten years out of school, ten years spent climbing the webwork of diplomatic service—and I found it all coming back to me there on Alsfort, as I sat in the wayroom of the Court.

There was a strike in effect; some of you will remember it. A forced-landing had come down too hard, too fast, and the Wagon had snapped the padbrace like a twig, toppling a half-acre of leadsub over onto the fire squads. So the Court workers were striking for subsurface landings, for Pits. My inbound had been the last. They were being turned away to Flaghold now, the next-door (half a million miles away) neighbor, an emergency port.

And if you sat in a Court and sweated at what was going on a Jump-week behind you on Earth and two ahead of you, on Altar; if you cursed and tried to bribe the crews; if you sent endless notes to both ends of the line you were knotted on; or if perhaps you are a history student specializing in the Wars . . . you'll remember the strike. Otherwise, probably not. Alsfort isn't exactly a backyard—more like an oasis.

Two days, and I'd given up insisting, inquiring, begging. I'd even given up the notes.

So I sat in the wayroom drinking the local (and distant) relative of beer. The pouch was locked into my coat pocket and I was keeping my left arm against it. I spent the first day there worrying what might happen on Altar without that pouch, then I gave it up the way I'd given up trying to surmount the strike, to curtail my immobility and its likely disastrous consequences. I just sat and drank "beer" and punjil and watched the people.

There was a short, wiry man of Jewish blood, Earth or Vegan, who limped from a twisted back, as though all his life he'd been watching over his shoulder. He drank tea saturated with grape sugar at ten and four and took his meals as the clock instructed: noon, six. He wore skirts, and a corduroy skullcap he never removed.

There was a couple, definitely Vegan. The woman was old (though only in profile), dressed in Outworld furs and wearing a single jewel against her emphatic and no doubt plastic bosom—a different jewel each time I saw them. Her companion was young, beautiful and asthenic, always precisely dressed in a fine tight suit, and quite often scribbling in a notebook he carried. They came irregularly and drank Earth brandy. By the third day, too much sameness had taken its toll: she sat with her face screwed into jealousy as he smiled and wrote in his book. When she spoke, there were quiet, gulping rhythms in her voice, and her only answer was the boy's beautiful smile and, once, a hand that held hers tightly—too tightly—on the table. He waited in the halls while she paid; she kept her face down, an older face now; they went away.

A Glaucon, a man I knew from Leic, but his ruby robes signaled pilgrimage and forbade us to speak. I watched him at his evening coffees. A recent convert, he was not at all the craftsmanlike politician I had come to know in those months spent on his world, in his home. He had been quick, loud; now he plodded, and his voice followed softly in the distance, muttering at prayer.

And there were others, many others.

A Plethgan couple with a Vorsh baby, evidently returning home from the Agencies at Llarth. They came to the wayroom just once, to ask about Vorshgan for the child, and were told there was none.

The mother was already pale with fear, the father raging and help-less; the baby screamed and was turning blue. They went out talking quietly to themselves under the child's cries. I never saw them again.

A Llyrch woman, alone and wearing only a formal shawl. It was brown, showing midcaste. A single green stripe and a small silver star proclaimed that her husband was dead; that he died in honor, in a duel on Highker, away from home. Once she turned in her seat and the shawl fell partly open, exposing, beneath her hairless head, exorcised breasts and the carvings in her belly. She took nothing but water, and little of that.

And there was a man who came to the wayroom as often as I and sat as long, sipping a pale violet liquid from a crystal cup, reading or simply sitting, hands together, staring at the wall and moving his lips softly. He was short, with a quick smile and white teeth, hair gathered with ribbons to one side of his head. I wondered what he was drinking. He carried it in a flask to match the cup; you could smell it across the room, a light scent, pale as its color, subtle as perfume. Outworld, probably: he flattened his vowels, was precisely polite; there were remnants of a drawl. Urban, from the way he car-ried himself, the polished edge of gestures. His mien and clothes were adopted from the Vegans, but that was common enough to be useless in reading origin, and might have been assumed solely for this trip. Vegan influence was virtually ubiquitous then, before the Wars. I generally traveled in Vegan clothes myself, even used the language. Most of us did. It was the best way to move about without being noticed.

The Outworlds, though. I was fairly sure of that.

Lying out along the fringe of trade routes, they were in a unique position to Union civilization. Quite early they had developed a more or less static society, little touched by new influences spreading outward from Vega: by the time ripples had run that far, they were pretty weak. There was little communication other than political, little enough culture exchange that it didn't matter. The Outworld societies had gone so far and stopped, then, as static cultures will, become abstracted, involuted—picking out parts and making them wholes. Decadence, they used to call it.

Then the Vegans came up with the Drive, the second one,

Overspace. And suddenly the Outworlds were no longer so Out, though they kept the name. The rest of us weren't long in discovering the furth's fur, shelby, and punjil, which for a while threatened to usurp the ancient hierarchy of coffee and alcohol on Earth with its double function as both stimulant and depressant. Under this new deluge of ships and hands (giving, taking) the Outworlds were at last touched. They were, in fact, virtually struck in the face. And the Outworlds, suddenly, were in transition.

But there's always an Orpheus, always those who look back. Under the swing of transition now, decadence had come to full flower. Amid the passing of old artifice, old extravagance, dandyism had sprung up as a last burst of heroism, a protest against the changing moods.

And there was much about the man I watched—the way his plain clothes hung, something about his hair and the subtly padded chest, his inviolable personality and sexlessness; books held up off the table, away from his eyes—that smacked of dandyism. It's the sort of thing a Courier learns to look for.

There were others, fleeting and constant. Single; coupled; even one Medusa-like Gafrt symb in which I counted five distinct bodies, idly wondering how many others had been already assimilated. But these I've mentioned are the ones I still think about, recalling their faces, the hollow forms hands made in air, their voices filling those forms. The ones I felt, somehow, I knew. These—and one other.

Rhea.

Without her, Alsfort wouldn't be for me the vivid memory it is. It would be a jumbled, distorted horror of disappointment, failure, confusing faces. A time when I sat still and the world walked past me and bashed its head into the wall.

Rhea.

I saw her once, the last day. For a handful of minutes we touched lives across a table. I doubt she remembers. For her now, there will have been so *many* faces.

It was mid-afternoon of my fourth day on Alsfort. The strike was beginning to run down; that morning, perhaps from boredom, the workers had volunteered a bit of light, routine work away from the Wagons, just to keep the Court from clogging up beyond all hope. I watched them unpack, adjust, and test a new booster. One of the men climbed into it and with a hop went sailing out across the pads, flailing his arms violently. Minutes later, he came walking back across the gray expanse, limping and grinning. He went up to the engineer and began talking quietly, shaking his head and gesturing toward one of the leg extensions. They vanished together, still talking, into the tool shop, hauling the booster between them.

I had gone from lunch at the Mart to coffee from the lobby servicors. Settling into a corner I watched the people wander about the arcade—colors, forms, faces blurred by distance; grouping and dissolving, aimless abstract patterns. Going back to my room had been a bad experience: too quiet, too inviting of thought.

The landscape of Alsfort . . .

You can see it from the rim in the top levels—though *see* is inappropriate. *Study* would be better: an exercise in optical monotony. Brown and gray begin at the base of the Court and blend to various tones of baldness, blankness. Brown and gray, rocks and sand—it all merges into itself. Undefined. You walk out on the floating radial arms, trying to get closer, to make it resolve at least to lines. But it simply lies there. Brown, gray, amorphous.

So, after the briefest of battles, I wound up back in the wayroom. There was a booth just off-center, provided with console-adjustment seats and a trick mirror. Sitting there, you had the private tables in front of you; quick-service counters behind. You could watch the tables and, by tilting your head and squinting, dimly see what went on behind you, at the counters. Through the door you could watch people wandering the corridors. I had spent most of my four days in that booth, washing down surrogate-tablets with beer and punjil. Mostly Energine: sleep was impossible, or at least the silent hours of lying to wait for sleep. And somehow the thought of food depressed me almost as much. I tried to eat, ordering huge meals and leaving them untouched. By the fourth day my thoughts were a bit scrambled and I was beginning, mildly, to hallucinate.

The waiter was bringing me a drink when she came in. I was watching the mirror, hardly aware of his presence. Behind me, a man was talking to a companion who flickered in and out of sight; I was trying to decide whether this was the man's hallucination or my own. The waiter put my drink down with one hand, not watching, and knocked it against the curb. Startled, I felt the cold on my hands. I turned my head and saw what he was looking at.

Rhea.

She was standing in the doorway with the white floor behind her, blue light swelling in around her body. *Poised* was the word that came to me: she might fly at the first sudden motion.

She was . . . delicate. That was the second impression. A thing made of thinnest glass; too fine, too small, too perfect. Maybe five feet. Thin. You felt you could take her in your palm: she was that fine, that light. That fragile.

Tiny cameo feathers covered her body—scarlet, blue, sungold. And when light struck them they shimmered, threw off others, eyefuls of color. They thinned down her limbs and grew richer in tone; her face and hands were bare, white. And above the small carved face were other feathers: dark blue plumes, almost black, that brushed on her shoulders as she walked—swayed and danced.

Her head darted on air to survey the room. Seeing my eyes on her she smiled, then started through the tables. She moved like leaves in wind, hands fluttered at her sides, fingers long and narrow as blades of grass. Feathers swayed with her, against her, spilling chromatic fire.

And suddenly karma or the drugs or just my loneliness—whatever it was—had me by the shoulders and was tugging, pulling.

I came to myself, the room forming out of confusion, settling into fullness. I was standing there away from the booth, I was saying, "Could I buy you a drink?" My hand almost . . . almost at her shoulder. The bones there delicate as a bird's breast.

She stood looking back past me, then up at my face, into my eyes, and smiled again. Her own eyes were light orange beneath thin hard lids that blinked steadily, sliding over the eyes and back up, swirled with colors like the inside of seashells.

"Yes, thank you," in Vegan, "it would be very nice. Of you." She sang the words. Softly. I doubt that anyone but myself heard them.

I looked back at the Outworlder. He had been watching; now he frowned and returned to his book.

"I was tired. Of the room," she said, rustling into the booth. "I said. To him. I could not stay there, some time ago, much longer. I would like to come, here. And see the people."

"Him?"

"My . . . escort? Karl. That the room was. Not pretty, it made me sad. The bare walls, your walls are such . . . solid. There is something sad about bare walls. Ours are hammered from bright metals, thin and open. Covered with reliefs. The forms of, growing things. I should not have to. Stay, in the room?"

"No. You shouldn't." I moved my hand to activate the dampers. All sound outside the booth sank to a dull, low murmur like the sea far off, while motion continued, bringing as it always did a strange sense of isolation and unreality.

I ordered punjil. The waiter left and returned with a tall cone of bright green fluid, which he decanted into two small round glasses. His lips moved but the dampers blocked the sound; getting no response, he went away.

"I'm Lant."

"Rhea," she said. "You are, Vegan?"

"Earth."

"You work. Here."

"No. Coming through, held up by the strike. You?"

She sipped the punjil. "It is, for me, the same. You are a, crewman? On one of the ships then."

"No. I'm with a travel bureau. Moving around as much as I can, keeping an eye out for new ports, new contracts." Later, somehow, I regretted the lies, that came so easily. "On my way Out. I think there might be some good connections out there."

"I've heard the cities are. Very beautiful."

"This is my first time Out in ten years." That part, at least, was true; I had gone Out on one of my first assignments. "They were beautiful, breathtaking, even then. And they've done a lot in the last few years, virtually rebuilt whole worlds. The largest eclecticism the Union's known—they've borrowed from practically every culture in *and* out of Union. They're even building in crystals now. It's said the cities look like glass blossoms, like flowers grown out of the ground. That there is nothing else like them."

"I saw a picture of Ginh, a painting, once. Like a man had made it in his hand and put it, into the trees. A lot of trees, all kinds. And sculpture, mosaics. In, the buildings. The trees were, beautiful. But so was. The city."

"We've all been more or less living off Outworld creativity for years now."

"A beautiful thing. It can take much . . . use?"

I supposed so, and we sat quietly as she watched the people, her eyes still and solemn, her head tilted. I felt if I spoke I would be intruding, and it was she who finally said: "The people. They are, beautiful also."

"Where are you from, Rhea?" I asked after watching her a while. She turned back to me.

"Byzantium." She set her eyes to the ceiling and warbled her delight at the name. "It is from, an old poem. The linguist aboard the Wagon. The first Wagon. He was, something of a poet. Our cities took, his fancy, he remembered this poem. He too was. Of Earth."

"I'm afraid I don't know the poem."

"It is, much. Old. Cities they are hammered of gold and set, in the land. All is. Beautiful there, and timeless. The poem has become for us. A song, one of our songs."

"And is your world like that? A refuge?"

"Perhaps. It was."

"Why did you leave?"

"I am going, to Ginh. To . . . work." She moved gently, looked around. I noticed again the tension in her face and hands, so unlike the easy grace of her body.

"You have a job there."

"Yes. I—" The mood passed. Her feathers rustled as she laughed: "Guess."

I declined.

"I sing." She trilled an example. Then stopped, smiling. We ordered new drinks, selecting one by name—a name she delighted in, repeating it over and over in different keys. It turned out to be a liqueur, light on the tongue, pulpy and sweet.

She leaned across the table and whispered, "It is. Nice." Her breath smelled like new-cut grass, like caramel and sea breeze.

Long plumes swept the tabletop and whispered there too. "Like the other, was."

"What do you sing, Rhea?"

"Old songs, our old songs. Of warriors. Lovers. I change the names, to theirs."

"How long will you be on Ginh?"

"Always."

You have been there before, then? No.

You have a family there? No.

You love Byzantium, you were happy there? Yes.

Then why . . . ?

"I am . . . bought. By one of the Academies. I am taken there. To sing, for them. And to be, looked at." She seemed not at all sad.

"You will miss Byzantium?"

"Yes. Much."

I cleared my throat. "Slavery is against Regulations. You—"

"It is. By my own, my will."

A long pause . . .

I see.

"My race is. Dying. We have no tech-knowledge, we are not in, Union. Byzantium can no longer, support us. The money, they give for me. It feeds us for many years. It too buys machines. The machines will keep us. A part of us, alive."

She drew her knees up into a bower of arms and dropped her head, making the booth a nest. After a moment she lifted her face out from the feathers. She trilled, then talked.

"When I was a child, Byzantium was, quiet and still. Life it was easy. We sang our songs, made our nests, that is enough. For a lifetime, all our lives, lifetimes. That is, enough. Now it is not longer easy."

"Perhaps it seemed that way. *Because* you were a child."

An arm hovered over the table. A hand came down to perch on the little round glass. "We took from her, Byzantium, she asked nothing. Our songs, love. Not more. Our fires, to keep her, warm. The sky the earth it was. In, our homes."

"But you grew up."

"Yes and Byzantium, much old, she grows. Old-more than my

Parent. Once it sang, with us. Now its voice broke. The souls left, the trees. Our homes. The rivers it swelled with sorrow, too burst. It fell, fruits from, the trees, too they were. Already dead. The moons grow red, red like the eye. Of a much-old man."

"You tell it like a poem."

"It is, one of our songs. The last poem of, RoNan. He died before it was. Finished."

"Of a broken heart."

She laughed. Gently. "At the hands of, his sons. For to resist coalition. He spoke out in his songs, against the visitors. He thought, it was right Byzantium, to die. It should not be made to go on to live. He wanted the visitors, to leave us."

"The visitors . . . Outworld?"

She nodded. The plumes danced, so deep a blue.

"They came and to take, our fruits, too our trees. They could make them to grow-new on Ginh. They took our singers. They . . . bought, our cities, our unused nests. Then they to say, With these can you to build a new world. RoNan did not want, a new world, it would be much-wrong, to Byzantium."

"And no one listened."

"They listened. Much, them. The younger ones to not, who wanted too a life, their own, a world for it. They learned, about the machines. They go-much to Ginh and learned in, the Academies, there, they came, back to us. To build their, world. Took it, of the machines, like too bottomless boxes."

"Ginh. They went to Ginh . . ."

"Yes, where I am. Going. I am with our cities, too our trees on Ginh, in a museum, there. I sing. For the people. They to come. To look at us, listen, me."

The ceiling speaker cleared its throat. I looked up. Nothing more.

"He must have been a strong man," I said. "To stand up so strongly for what he believed was right. To hold to it so dearly. A difficult thing to do, these days."

"The decision was not-his. He had, no choice. He was, what he believed. He could not-go, against it."

"And so were the others, the younger ones, and they couldn't either."

"That is, the sad part."

Someone blew into the speakers.

"You knew him, you believe what he said?"

"He was. My father."

And we were assaulted by sound:

ATTENTION PLEASE, ATTENTION PLEASE. THE CHELTA,
UNION SHIP G-47, BOUND OUT, IS NOW ON PAD AND WILL
LIFT IN ONE HOUR STANDARD. PASSENGERS PLEASE REPORT
AT ONCE TO UNDERWAY F. UNDERWAY F.

So the strike was over, the workers would get their Pits.

A pause then, some mumbled words, a shuffling of papers:

WILL CAPTAIN I-PRANH PLEASE REPORT TO THE TOWER-
MAIN. CAPTAIN I-PRANH TO THE TOWERMAIN. THE REVISED
CHARTS HAVE BEEN COMPLETED.

And the first announcement began again.

Rhea uncurled and looked up, then back past me. Her face turned
up as he approached.

"Hello, Karl," she sang. "This is, Lant." My Outworld dandy. I
reached over and opened the dampers.

He bowed and smiled softly. "Pleased, Lant." Then added: "Earth,
isn't it?"—seeing through my Vegan veneer as easily as he'd made
out her words through the dampers. His own voice was low and
full, serene. "Always pleased to meet a Terran. So few of you get out
this far. But I'm afraid I'll have to be rude and take Rhea away now.
That was the call for our ship. Excuse us, please."

He put out a white hand, bowing again, and she took it, standing.
Feathers rustled: a sound I would always remember.

"Thank you for talking to Rhea, Lant. I'm sure it was a great
pleasure for her."

"For me."

A final bow and he turned toward the door. She stood there a
moment, watching me, feathers lifting as she breathed.

"Thank you for, the drinks Lant. And for . . . to listen." She smiled.

"You are going, Out. You will be on this ship. Perhaps I will. See you, on the ship."

She wouldn't, of course.

And she went away.

Most of the rest you know.

I Jumped the next day for Altar, where I got down on my callused knees and went through my bag of time-honored politician tricks. Money bandaged the wounds of insult, outrage was salved by a new trade agreement. The Altarians would withdraw troops from Mersy: the wars were stayed.

But not stopped. The Altarians kept their sores and when, several weeks later, one of our writers published a satirical poem attacking Altar for its "weasel colonialism, that works like a vine," the wound festered open. The poet refused to apologize. He was imprisoned and properly disgraced, but the damage was done.

War erupted. Which you don't need to be told: look out your window and see the scars.

War flashed across the skies, burst inside homes. Which doesn't matter: look in your mirror for the marks that tell, the signs that stay.

I don't have to tell you that the Vegans, victims of too much sharing and always our friends, sided with us. That they were too close to the Altar allies. That they were surrounded and virtually destroyed before our ships could make the Jump.

I don't have to tell you that we're still picking up the pieces. Look out your window, look in your mirror.

That we have the bones of Union and we're trying to fatten them up again.

I was one of the sideways casualties of war. One of the face-saving (for them) disgraces (for me). I believe I would have left anyway, I might have. Because there's something I have to say. And here I can say it, and be heard.

The Union gives a lot. But it takes a lot too. And I'm not sure any more that what it takes, what it shoves aside, is replaceable. Maybe some things *are* unique. I know one thing is.

Which is what I tell my students.

I sit here every day and look out at all these faces. And I wonder,

Will this one be a Courier, or that one in the front row, or the one in back—the girl who swings her leg, the kid who brings sandwiches to class in his briefcase? Will they be the disciples of Earth's ascendance?

I wonder.

And I tell them that a society feeds off its people. That the larger it is, the more it consumes. That you never know what effect your words will have a hundred million miles away.

You never know. But you try. You try to know, you try to balance things out on your own scales. Utility; the best for the most; compromise and surrender. Your smallest weights are a million, a billion, people.

But I tell them something else to go with that.

I tell them that there may be nothing new under the sun. But there *are* new suns, and new faces under them. Looking up, looking down . . .

The faces are what matter.

The Floors of His Heart

The little animal went racing up the side of its cage, made a leap to the top, climbed upside-down halfway out—then dropped back onto the floor. It did this over and over, steadily tumbling, becoming each time wilder, more frantic. The last time, it lay still on its back in the litter, panting.

And she was lovely below him, beside him, above him. Was lovely in dark, lovely in shadow, lovely in the glaring door as she fingered the bathroom's light.

(She is sitting on the bed, legs crossed, one elbow on a knee, darkness around her. The window is a black hole punched in the room, and for a moment now when she lifts her arm, light slants in and falls across her belly, sparkling on semen like dew in dark grass; one breast moves against the moving arm.

Light comes again, goes again. It strikes one side of her tilted face and falls away, shadows the other. She looks down, looks up, the small motion goes along her body, her side moves against yours.

There are two paths of glowing where light touched her skin, here on her belly, here on the side of her face, a dull glowing orange. Already it is fading.

Outside is darkness. This kind of darkness: it can fill a room.)

She came back and sat on the edge of the bed. The light was off, her skin glowing softly orange all over, darker orange for month-old bruises on her breasts and hips. "Strong. He hadn't been with a woman for three years," she had said when he touched one of the bruises. "A real man." He had beaten her severely, then left twice what was necessary.

"You're really from Earth . . ." (Silence breaking, making sounds. The little animal moving slowly now in its cage.)

"Naturalized. During the Wars."

"Oh. I see." She was thinking about ruin, the way it started, the roads it took. Her skin was losing its glow. "Where were you born?"

"Here. Vega." (She turned to look at him.)

"In Thule." (She waited.)

"West Sector."

She turned back to the window. "I see."

"I was signed Out. It was a Vegan ship, we were getting the declaration broadcast when communication from Vega stopped. Captain turned us around but before we hit Drive, Earth told us it was too late. We went on into Drive and stayed in till we could find out what happened. Altar had ships jumping in and out all along the rim, grabbing whatever they could, blasting the rest, a big Wagon like *The Tide* was no match for what they had. We came out near Earth. Captain's decision, and I don't envy his having to make it. Anyway, the ship was consigned and the Captain pledged to Earth. Most of us went along, enlisted. There wasn't much to come back to."

The room was quiet then with the sound of her breathing, the rustle of the animal in its litter. Light from outside crept across the floor, touching her leg on the bed with its palm.

"You're not Terran. I thought you were."

"I'm sorry. I'm sorry I didn't tell you. I didn't realize—"

"It doesn't matter."

"But I didn't mean to—"

"It doesn't matter." She smiled. "Really."

He lay watching her face above him, a quiet face, still. And the room itself was quiet again, was gray, graying, dark . . .

Later: her hand on his shoulder, her lips lightly against his and his eyes opening, something warm for his hand.

"I made coffee."

He stared at the cup, breathed steam and came more awake. The cup was blue ceramic, rounded, shaped into an owl's head. The eyes extended out at the edges to form handles. "You shouldn't have. Coffee's hard to get, I know, you sh—"

"I wanted to."

"Thank you."

He got up and walked to the cage, hands wrapped around the mug. The little animal was leaning down on its front legs, hind-quarters up, paws calmly working at something, an insect, perhaps. Done, it carried what remained to the back of its cage and deposited it there, then returned to the front and sat licking at the orange fur that tufted out around its paws.

"What is it?" he asked after a while.

"A Veltdan."

"Vegan?"

She nodded.

"I've never seen one."

"There aren't many left—none around the cities. Dying out. They're from Larne Valley."

He thought a moment, remembered: "The telepaths." The colony of misanthropic sensitives.

"Yes. That's where the colony is. I was born there, came to Kahlu after the Wars. Not much left, even that far out. The colony was wiped out."

"Are you—"

She shook her head. "My mother. Mostly I was born without their physical deformity or their talents, though I guess I got a little of both." She came up to the cage, thumped her fingers against the side. "The telepathy . . . some of it filtered down. I'm an empathist." She grinned. "Helps me at my work."

An insect came in through the window, skittered around the

room hitting the ceiling again and again, finally found the window and flew back out. It was neon, electric blue.

"Veltdans are supposed to be the deadliest things in the universe. Four inches from nose to tail, altogether seven pounds—and you can put them up against any animal you want to, any size, any weight."

He took his hand off the cage and put it back around the mug. The Veltdan was over on its back in the litter, rolling from side to side, square snout making arcs. Watching this prim, almost exquisite little animal, he found it difficult to accept what she was saying, to put the two facts together.

"It registers external emotion. Whatever made the telepaths got into the Veltdan too. You get something coming at it with a mind full of hate and killing, the Veltdan takes it all and turns it back on the attacker—goes into a frenzy, swarms all over it, knows what the attacker is going to do next. It's small but it's fast, has sharp claws and teeth. While the attacker is getting battered with its own hate and fury, the Veltdan is tearing it to pieces. They say two of them fighting each other is really something to see, it just goes on and on."

He looked down at the little orange-cerulean animal. "Why should they fight one another?"

"Because that's what they like best to eat: each other."

He grimaced and walked to the window. A shuttleship was lifting. Its light flashed against his face.

Every day just past noon, flat clouds gather like lily pads in the sky, float together, rain hops off to pound on the ground. For an hour the rain comes down, washing the haze of orange from the air, and for that hour people come together in cafés and Catches, group there talking. And waiting.

They were sitting in an outdoor Catch, drinking. Minutes before, clattering and thumping, a canvas roof had been rolled out over them. Around them now the crowd moved and talked. Rain slammed down, slapped like applause on the canvas roof.

"This is where the artists come," she said, pointing to a corner of the Catch where several young people sat grouped around a small table. Two of them, a young man with his head shaved and a girl with long ochre hair, were bent forward over the table, talking excitedly.

The others were listening, offering occasional comments. When this happened, the young man would tilt his head away from the speaker and watch him closely; the girl would look down at the floor, a distant expression on her face. Then when the speaker had finished they would look at one another and somehow, silently, they would decide: one of them would reply. Cups, saucers, crumpled sheets of paper were piled on the table. One of the girls was sketching. Rain sprinkled and splattered on the backs of those nearest the outside.

"The one talking, that's Dave," she went on. "A ceramist, some say the best in Union. I have a few of his pots at home. Early stuff, functional. He used to do a lot of owls; everything he threw had an owl in it. Now he's on olms. Salamanders. They're transparent, live in caves. If you take one out into the sun it burns. Turns black and dies." She took a drink from her cup. "Artists and such all come here every afternoon. I have a lot of their work."

"You like art quite a lot, then?"

"I feel it—what they think, their appreciation. It's in what they do, what they make."

Smiling.

"It's a tradition, coming here. This Catch was built where the *Old Union* sat before the Wars; Samthar Smith came here when he was on Vega. It's called *Pergamum* now."

"'All Pergamum is covered with thorn bushes; even its ruins have perished.' The epigraph for the novel he wrote as eulogy for his marriage."

"Yes." She stared out at the rain. "Dave tells me they've taken the name as a symbol. The ruin of the old, the growth of a new art."

A disturbance near the center of the Catch caught his attention. Holding a glass of punjil, a fat middle-aged man was struggling to his feet while the others at his table tried to get him to sit back down. He brushed aside their hands and remarks, came swaying and grinning across the floor. Halfway across, he turned around and went back to put his drink on the table, spilling it as he did so.

"Hi," he said, approaching the table, then belched. "Thought I'd come over and say that—Hi, I mean. C'n always spot a fellow Terran." Another belch. "William Beck Mann, representing United

Union Travel, glad to meet you." He leaned on the table with one hand, shoved the other out across it. "Coming in from Ginh, stuck here while the com'pny ship gets a tune up. You heading home too?"

Others in the Catch, Vegans, were staring toward their table in distaste.

"No."

"Mind if I sit 'own?" Which he did, swiveling on the tabled hand, plopping into the chair.

"I don't mind. But we're about to leave."

"I see." He looked at the girl for the first time and grinned. His teeth were yellow. "Guess you got plans. Well. That case, s'pose I'll get on back." The fat man hauled himself out of the chair and went back toward his own table. Two of the young people were leaving and he tried to walk between them, knocking the girl against a table. Hatred flared in the boy's face.

"No, Terri, don't," the girl said. "He's drunk."

The boy reached and pulled her to him. Then, just as suddenly as it had come, the hatred vanished from his face. He and the girl went on out of the Catch, holding hands. The fat man goggled after them until someone from his table came and took him back.

"Remember, in *Pergamum*, when the woman pours coffee and says 'That's everything else,' then drops in two rocks of sugar saying 'And this is us' as the sugar dissolves?"

"Of course."

After that, they sat quietly. The rain was over, but winds were rising now.

A shuttleship was lifting.

Against the darkness, bands of pearl spread in layers and deepened, swelling into rainbow colors. They flashed on his face. When he turned from the window, her skin was glowing rich orange.

"Will you stay here? Have you come home now?"

"I don't know."

"It would be good. If you stayed." The Veltdan was making muted, moaning sounds. "That's one of Dave's cups you're drinking from," she said.

He turned to look at her. The orange glow was fading. "Do you remember how *Pergamum* ends? 'Wherever we are content, that is our country.'"

She nodded.

The Veltdan again was hunkered down, working at something with its paws.

"There's an insect. On Earth," he said. "It dies when you pick it up. From the heat in your hand."

He walked toward the bathroom.

A moment later: "The switch isn't working."

"There's a power ration. This area's cut off for several hours, another gets to use the power. The peak periods are shifted about."

He came back.

"You don't know how ridiculous that is, do you? You don't realize. There's enough power on my ship—one ship—to give this place electricity for years. You don't see how absurd that is, do you?"

He picked up the cup and threw it across the room. It struck the wall and shattered; one eye-handle slid back across the floor and lay at his feet, staring up at him.

"I'm sorry," he said.

"It doesn't matter. I can get another from Dave. An olm, one of his olms."

"I'll leave you money. For the cup."

"It doesn't matter." She bent and began picking up the shards. "I have others."

He walked back to the window and stood looking out. He could hear the Veltdan pacing in its cage.

When she spoke, her voice was quiet. "You're not staying."

"No."

"I knew, from the first."

He took the blue shards from her hands and put them in the empty waste-bucket. Then he put money on the cage and left.

Pearl spread outward and shelled the sky.

She stood at the window watching. The colors deepened, flared to a rainbow. Her skin glowed orange.

Behind her the little Veltdan sat very still in its cage and blinked at the light.

53RD AMERICAN DREAM

Sunday and just like all the other Sundays: clouds hung in the sky like jowls or wattles, sky gobbled up air, its feet moved in the grass, it was going to rain. The children had already eaten by the time they got up.

In housecoat (brown check, Neiman Marcus) and slippers (gray plaid, Penneys) Mr. More walked into the living room (he looked like a Viking departing his ship) kicking aside the scattered bones as he came, noting on them the marks, the scrapings of teeth.

"Damn," he said at last, standing in the center of the room, shaking his great sleepy head. (He looked like a bull's-eye surrounded by the rings of furniture bones children.) "I wish you kids could understand how hard it is to get good help these days, then there wouldn't be any more of this. You're using them up at an awful rate, you know: do you realize this is the third time this month? Bedford Hills, Children, is running out of maids." And then because the speech was over, because it was nine in the morning, because he'd run out of words, because he looked like a Viking, he said it again, "Damn."

"We're awful sorry, Pop," Tom, the oldest, said. A trickle of blood ran down the hinge of his chin. Always a slow eater, little Tim was crouched under the coffee table, gnawing at a knuckle-bone. "But we were hungry, awful hungry. And we got tired of waiting for you and Mom to get up."

Mr. More rubbed thoughtfully, sleepily, at the Brillo-stubble of his cheek and chin; his hand came away scratched to a red rash. "Well, I suppose that's understandable," he said. "But get this awful mess cleaned up before your mother sees it."

An exemplary team (one envisioned now the yapping pursuit, the bringing down, the snarled devouring) the children set to work, piling bones onto a red wagon, mopping at the blood with

Scott towels. Tim, the youngest, leaned in a corner with the towels jammed onto his arms, going *click-click* each time one of the others pulled one off.

Mr. More turned around three times and went back into the bedroom. The book she had been reading last night was lying open on the bed (stories Jewish and Zen, yang and yin, fat and thin) with a broken back, but his wife was nowhere to be found. He walked around the room, opening drawers and doors looking for her, climbed up on a chair to look down into the light fixture (king-of- the-hill on a pile of bodies and pieces of body, a single live cyclops fly stared back at him and waved one of its eyelash legs frantically: *j'accuse, j'accuse*). Finally, catching a glimpse of taffeta foot from his maple perch, he realized she was sleeping under the pillow. He jumped flat-foot over the foot rail and came down in a crouch on the Beautyrest, lifted the pillow. "The children ate the maid," he said, and dropped the pillow back.

Minutes later it suddenly lurched and fell to the floor. His wife stretched slowly and turned over. "Poor Griselda . . ." she said to the suspended ceiling with all its many sound-absorbent holes.

"No, Dear. They ate Griselda last week. This was Olga."

"Poor Olga . . ." She pulled the covers up over her and he could hear her sobbing down in her dark warm cavern. He dived head-first onto the pillow, got up and went to the closet, which perforce *yawned* open. (A thin slice of darkness being overtaken, now, by irregular white boxes ranked on the shelf above, the line of clothes anchored with clothespins to the adjustable bar below.) He thrust his hand, quickly, in and out: jaws of clothespins snapped, a hanger fell rattling out of the bundle in his hand. (The closet was now in need of a new lower-left bicuspid.) His hand braved the depths of a box, emerged with a pearl-white shirt. He began dressing, diagonally, from the imported clockwork left sock to the hand-stitched right cuff and the tortoise-shell elephant.

He was standing at the mirror, filing down his teeth, when Tim came and stood in the doorway behind him. Tim was dressed in balls of bread which he had glued all over his body after slicing off the crusts. He looked like a renegade dandelion.

"Okay, Pop, it's all cleaned up," he said. "We saved some for you, though—it's in the fridge."

"Right . . . look, I'm not too hungry. Why don't you kids have it later? You can make a sandwich or something." (Page 119: "Parents must sacrifice for their children.")

Tim looked dubious. "We got ketchup?"

"Sure thing."

He tilted his head. "Pickles?"

"Big sweet ones." (Page 143: "Often the child is reluctant to accept this sacrifice; a careful air of nonchalance on the parent's part is the most satisfactory, and the most effective, response at these times.")

"It's a deal!" and he shot away, out into the living room to tell the others, leaving a trail of breadcrumbs to find his way back.

In the mirror Mr. More saw his wife bound out of Her bed (36x72: the covers flapped like brown bats), race across the cold Montina squares like a cowardly Queen, and dive like perhaps Ty Cobb beneath His (40x80: the floor was 3D, no goggles required, sparkly pearls in yellow phlegm). "Kamikaze cantcatchme!" she yelled in transit. Then, sweetly, from under the bed: "You remember when the kids brought that puppy home last week . . . ?"

He opened a drawer and replaced his toothpick-file in the case among the rest, just below the rat's tail and just above the camel-hair navel-lint brush, slipping it into its loop like a toe into Indian sandals. (His pride was the two-foot-long emery board he'd bought off an elephant manicurist when the circus was in town.)

"Sure do," he said. "And a sweet, soft little thing it was, too."

"Yes, it was, wasn't it?" Her hand crawled out from under the bed, crept across the linoleum—then went scuttling back sideways, back under the bed, leaving behind something that looked like a misanthropic butterfly: her rainbow bra. The games were beginning, the Sunday games. "But they wouldn't eat a thing afterward, remember? They're just going to have to start eating regularly, Bruce." She always pronounced his name to rhyme with *cruise*. "Three meals a day, no snacks, get their vitamins, get their iron. Can't let them wreck their health." Again the hand came creeping out only to dash back to safety. But it left behind, this time, two sharp rubber cones with plastic warts on the ends. The warts, Mr. More thought, were like hard pink raisins. Or like, perhaps, Bing cherries impaled on the ends of ice-cream cones.

"I think you're right," he said to his wife. "I'll talk to them about it this evening." He opened the velvet-lined jade-and-ivory case which squatted with springy S legs on top of the dresser, as though it were about to hop off. He took out his Sunday eyes and put them on. They were made to resemble the eyes of a potato ("The potato is an innocent fruit") and were gold, twenty-three carats fine (the twenty-fourth part being constituted of tiny silver stars). They stuck out from his face like mutant, misshapen corkscrews. He turned his face from side to side, admiring himself in the mirror. "Yessir," he said, "first thing this evening." (Page 654: "The casual ease of early evening is the most propitious time for family conference, and the dinner table perhaps affords the most comfortable and accessible opportunity.")

This time the hand *rushed out* (nails clattering on the floor) and *crept back* (dragging its thumb). A *tempo* was being established. Smack in the center of one of the Montina squares now, floating in the phlegm, were two mounds of collapsing flesh. Two dimples with Scripto erasers inside, Mr. More thought. Or demitasse saucers with little prunes on them inside the darker cup-ring. Or a plastic dog dish. A pale smear of blood tracked back toward the bed, mixing already with the phlegm, thinning the fluid, which then overflowed into the room, bearing chunks of pearl that whirled and spun like leaves, clicking against the doors pipes bureau bed shoes.

"And they'll listen, too," Mr. More said. "Or no more TV." (Page 4: "The simplest punishment is often the most effective.") He removed hair eyebrows ears and put on his skullcap. Then stood staring into the mirror for several seconds. Finally, he reached up and removed his nose, moving it to the tip of his chin. Much better. *Much* better. A *timbre* to match the *tempo*.

Again the hand: the dash, the creeping retreat. So bold, so coy, so like a Restoration lady. Lace pants this time: a small pile of cobwebs on the floor. As he watched, they dampened, dissolved, joined the blood and phlegm, strings of stuff like seaweed. The floor was yellow going orange, of a starchy consistency. That is to say, *sticky*.

"I think that's enough, don't you, Dear?" Mr. More said. "Shouldn't you stop now?" He walked back to the mirror and, one by one, unsheathed his teeth. They clicked, one by one, into the porcelain sink, almost invisible. White. White.

"Are you ready then, Darling?" his wife said. And then the surrender, the sweet surrender, ahhh, as one by one her legs came sliding across the floor and bumped with soft thuds (like huge spaghettis) into the waterpipes, splashing the orange blood-phlegm up onto the base of the walls to water the orchids blooming there. Sucking sounds. A toe fell off, and the toenail off that. Mr. More picked the nail up and put it in his pocket; it would make a good pick when, later, he played his harp, plucking the strings one by one.

He kicked the legs aside.

"Yes, Darling, I'm ready," he said.

"Then call the children." (Page 456, right before the good parts: "Whenever and wherever possible, satisfy the children's curiosity as to what goes on behind closed, adult doors; at all costs, avoid deepening this curiosity, this wanting-to-belong.")

Mr. More called the children and together they hauled her body up onto the bed—it was covered with cobwebs—and he beat her with the olive branches and peeled willow wands he kept in the cupboard while the children watched and applauded. She screamed magnificently this time; her body oozed phlegm and later gave out great clouds of dust that looked like brown feathers.

Later he played the harp with his teeth and the children applauded again. And after that, with toothpicks and red wax off Gouda cheese, they put her back together again. However. That is to say, all but one hand and a toenail. Mr. More kept the toenail and had a ring made out of it. And they finally found the hand when, late that night, it crawled into bed with one of the children (Tom, the oldest).

That night at dinner (veal in ketchup and chowder in powdered milk) he gave them all a stern talking-to (op. cit.). And the next day, Monday (which was, incidentally, Columbus Day), he hired a new maid. She had white white teeth and flat nails, her hips were like a saddle, her nipples like Chianti corks.

Genevieve was her name and the children loved her.

THE CREATION OF BENNIE GOOD

"Do you like my foot," putting it on the table. There, between the chipped saucer and candle; you have noticed how carefully I avoid the marmalade, the box of salty butter. "Will you accept it as a token of my affection? For you? It is, as they say, a good foot." Earlier, I have deftly undone the laces with my toes, grasped the sock between piano-key toes and foot and slowly drawn it off, like peeling a willow wand. "The arch is long and graceful, with the springy delicacy of a light man. The toes curl in as though to embrace the foot; the nails are flecked with color. And pink is the color of this foot." Pink, with the bright red crescent at the top of the curve: pimple on one side, in the curve, and dimpled on the other. "I am offering this, should you want it, my dear. It is all I have."

Her attention is arrested by my foot. This is true of most. At parties my friends will group together talking, and glancing occasionally with great expectation toward the corner chair where I sit calm, unmoved, unmoving. As the evening advances, their glances are more frequent and begin to form a rhythm; then finally, beginning as a low moan among the women, gradually swelling up through the groups until it becomes a steady, hard, syncopated shout, and bursting at last out of the crowd, the call comes: *Foot! Foot!* Then slowly I lift it to the level of their eyes and one of them, a woman, the chosen, comes forward out of the group wearing shyness like a belt and starts softly to undo the pale pink shoe, dropping it to the floor, where it lies on its side in the carpet pile. You have seen the way a snake is skinned—first the skin is slit away from the mouth, then rolled gently down along the body: this is how my sock is removed—then thrown to them. A few are unable to stand the pressure and must be sent away. Others on the edge near me remove their own shoes and socks and sit staring sadly at the pale uncovered feet. I tell her all this.

"It's all I have, it's yours." But this one, this Sally, is more moved than the rest. Already the tight black circles around her eyes are smearing, becoming less distinct; eyelids covered in green sequins are flashing like tiny chandeliers. Her little hands are perched on the rim of the cup and soon one will creep out across the ceramic dishes to shyly, lightly touch my foot. She is overwhelmed at the size of the occasion, the depth of my offer.

Perhaps I will make conversation; I've found this sometimes helps, especially in the initial slight embarrassment. I will discuss various projects.

Such as . . .

Last year I had a large number of foam-rubber genitalia prepared for me by an advertising firm. These were bright pink and varied in size from two feet to six in length, and from a few inches to several yards in circumference. The order was placed on a Monday after a weekend of planning and sketching; on Thursday the genitalia were ready; and on Friday I set out for Niagara Falls with them packed away in my trunk. When I opened the trunk later, at the hotel, the genitalia expanded—virtually exploded—out in my room, filling it. Some had got tangled together, like fingers in doughnuts. That evening I fought my way through the foam to go out and walk among the people, talking to many and asking questions. And the next morning, when the sun was gleaming on the water, I walked with my trunk to the top of the Falls and floated my collection of vast foam genitals down toward all the people below: they bobbed and raged on the water.

Or. I will have a simulacra head made of intelligent clay—in my image precisely, though perhaps a touch more worldly, without the elusive pale delicacy of my own features. With great patience I will teach this head to say Yes, and I will keep it in a wooden box, a box of dogwood, on my left shoulder. Whenever I am asked a question requiring response, I will reach up across my chest and open the door to this box. The head will open its eyes, say Yes—and I will shut the door.

I will train crickets to function as metronomes and place one with every violinist in the world, thus restoring natural order to contemporary music.

By lies and deceit I have caused the Atlantic and Pacific Oceans to become jealous of one another; already they are creeping across America toward a confrontation. Frantically I have this morning cabled the Dead Sea, entreating it to intervene. Which it will.

And she listens. Even as lorries load cans in the alley and roll away, scraping long grooves in the bricks on each side, as the photographers shyly cover their lenses with their hands, as the waiters come and go, replacing dishes, bringing fresh flowers in vase after vase, the clack-clack of them in their rubber shoes. She listens.

And I tell her again, does she understand: "I am a ruined man. This is all I have left. And this, I offer to you." We sit for several minutes listening to corks pop off bottle after bottle around us, like children pulling fingers out of puffed cheeks. They have worked a long time for this; we are at last together. When I look at them, they raise their glasses toward us in celebration. Quickly, more bottles are brought in. A serving cart full of jangling green and clear, that hums and glides too slowly in front of the trotting waiter. More corks, soda, bubbles cascade into glasses, cubes of ice pop up like fish heads and the bubbles resemble their eyes. Me straight in the chair with a high head talking. Admiring how she maneuvers the delicate machinery of eggcup and spoon.

When I am finished she calls softly for the table to be cleared. With a wave of her hand, and light winks in the rings. The band stops and all is quiet as the waiters come and depart with full arms. I am finished. The lights go up, a few people stand for a better view.

She sits straight. So straight like a Cezanne cypress, and hardly anyone breathes now as, smiling, she moves back in her chair and adjusts the top of her body. We hear the gentle, crisp sound of her skirts . . .

Finally I lift my head out of my wet hands. There is little energy left, in me.

And now there are cheers, calls of approval, relief. She is smiling. Staring straight into my eyes and nothing moves. The green folds of her skirt are pulled back, arranged around her waist and legs like a monster lettuce, and there on the veined marble table, square in the center by my own, she has put her foot. Her tiny foot is offered, there.

And on it, the most exquisite black shoe.

JIM AND MARY G

Getting his little coat down off the hook, then his arms into it, not easy because he's so excited and he always turns the wrong way anyhow. And all the time he's looking up at you with those blue eyes. We go park Papa, he says. We go see gulls. Straining for the door. The gulls are a favorite; he discovered them on the boat coming across and can't understand, he keeps looking for them in the park.

Wrap the muffler around his neck. Yellow, white. (Notice how white the skin is there, how the veins show through.) They call them scarves here don't they. Stocking cap—he pulls it down over his eyes, going Haha. He hasn't learned to laugh yet. Red mittens. Now move the zipper up and he's packed away. The coat's green corduroy, with black elastic at the neck and cuffs and a round hood that goes down over the cap. It's November. In England. Thinking, The last time I'll do this. Is there still snow on the ground, I didn't look this morning.

Take his hand and go on out of the flat. Letting go at the door because it takes two hands to work the latch, Mary rattling dishes in the kitchen. (Good-bye, she says very softly as you shut the door.) He goes around you and beats you to the front door, waits there with his nose on the glass. The hall is full of white light. Go on down it to him. The milk's come, two bottles, with the *Guardian* leaning between them. Move the mat so we can open the door, We go park Papa, we seegulls. Frosty foggy air coming in. Back for galoshes, all the little brass-tongue buckles? No the snow's gone. Just some dirty slush. Careful. Down the steps.

Crunching down the sidewalk ahead of you, disappointed because there's no snow but looking back, Haha. We go park? The sky is flat and white as a sheet of paper. Way off, a flock of birds goes whirling across it, circling inside themselves—black dots, like iron filings with a magnet under the paper. The block opposite is lined with trees. What kind? The leaves are all rippling together. It looks like green foil. Down the walk.

Asking, Why is everything so still. Why aren't there any cars. Or a mail truck. Or milk cart, gliding along with bottles jangling. Where is everyone. It's ten in the morning, where is everyone.

But there is a car just around the corner, stuck on ice at the side of the road where it parked last night with the wheels spinning Whrrrrrr. Smile, you understand a man's problems. And walk the other way. His mitten keeps coming off in your hand. Haha.

She had broken down only once, at breakfast.

The same as every morning, the child had waked them. Standing in his bed in the next room and bouncing up and down till the springs were banging against the frame. Then he climbed out and came to their door, peeking around the frame, finally doing his tiptoe shyly across the floor in his white wool nightshirt. Up to their bed, where they pretended to be still asleep. Brekpust, Brekpust, he would say, poking at them and tugging the covers, at last climbing onto the bed to bounce up and down between them until they rolled over: Hello. Morninggg. He is proud of his g's. Then, Mary almost broke down, remembering what today was, what they had decided the night before.

She turned her face toward the window (they hadn't been able to afford curtains yet) and he heard her breathe deeply several times. But a moment later she was up—out of bed in her quilted robe and heading for the kitchen, with the child behind her.

He reached and got a cigarette off the trunk they were using as a night table. It had a small wood lamp, a bra, some single cigarettes and a jarlid full of ashes and filters on it. Smoking, listening to water running, pans clatter, cupboards and drawers. Then the sounds stopped and he heard them together in the bathroom: the tap ran for a while, then the toilet flushed and he heard the child's pleased exclamations. They went back into the kitchen and the sounds resumed. Grease crackling, the child chattering about how good he had been. The fridge door opened and shut, opened again, Mary said something. He was trying to help.

He got out of bed and began dressing. How strange that she'd forgotten to take him to the bathroom first thing, she'd never done that before. Helpinggg, from the kitchen by way of explanation, as he walked to the bureau. It was square and ugly, with that shininess peculiar to cheap furniture, and it had been in the flat when they moved in, the only thing left behind. He opened a drawer and took out a shirt. All his shirts were white. Why, she had once asked him, years ago. He didn't know, then or now.

He went into the kitchen with the sweater over his head. "Mail?" Through the wool. Neither of them looked around, so he pulled it the rest of the way on, reaching down inside to tug the shirt collar out. Then the sleeves.

"A letter from my parents. They're worried they haven't heard from us, they hope we're all right. Daddy's feeling better, why don't we write them."

The child was dragging his highchair across the floor from the corner. Long ago they had decided he should take care of as many of his own needs as he could—a sense of responsibility, Mary had said—but this morning Jim helped him carry the chair to the table, slid the tray off, lifted him into it and pushed the chair up to the table. When he looked up, Mary turned quickly away, back to the stove.

Eggs, herring, toast, and ham. "I thought it would be nice," Mary said. "To have a good breakfast." And that was the time she broke down.

The child had started scooping the food up in his fingers, so she got up again and went across the kitchen to get his spoon. It was heavy silver, with an ivory K set into the handle, and it had been her own. She turned and came back across the tile, holding the little spoon in front of her and staring at it. Moma cryinggg, the child said. Moma cryinggg. She ran out of the room. The child turned in his chair to watch her go, then turned back and went on eating with the spoon. The plastic padding squeaked as the child moved inside it. The chair was metal, the padding white with large blue asterisks all over it. They had bought it at a Woolworth's. Twelve and six. Like the bureau, it somehow fit the flat.

A few minutes later Mary came back, poured coffee for both of them, and sat down across from him.

"It's best this way," she said. "He won't have to suffer. It's the only answer."

He nodded, staring into the coffee. Then took off his glasses and cleaned them on his shirttail. The child was stirring the eggs and herring together in his bowl. Holding the spoon like a chisel in his hand and going round and round the edge of the bowl.

"Jim . . ."

He looked up. She seemed to him, then, very tired, very weak.

"We could take him to one of those places. Where they . . . take care of them . . . for you."

He shook his head. "No, we've already discussed that, Mary. He wouldn't understand. It will be easier this way. If I do it myself."

She went to the window and stood there watching it. It filled most of one wall. It was frosted over.

"How would you like to go for a walk after breakfast," he asked the child, who immediately shoved the bowl away and said, "Bafroom first?"

"You or me?" Mary said from the window.

Finally: "You."

He sat alone in the kitchen, thinking. Taps ran, the toilet flushed, the child came out full of pride. We go park, he said. We go see gulls.

"Maybe." It was this, the lie, which came back to him later; this was what he remembered most vividly. He got up and walked into the hall with the child following him and put his coat on. "Where's his other muffler?"

"In the bureau drawer. The top one."

He got it, then began looking for the stocking cap and mittens. Walking through the rooms, opening drawers. There aren't any seagulls in London. When she brought the cap and mittens to him there was a hole in the top of the cap and he went off looking for the other one. Walking through rooms, again and again into the child's own.

"For God's sake go on," she finally said. "Please stop. O damn Jim, go on." And she turned and ran back into the kitchen.

Soon he heard her moving about. Clearing the table, running water, opening and shutting things. Silverware clicking.

"We go park?"

He began to dress the child. Getting his little coat down off the hook. Wrapping his neck in the muffler. There aren't any seagulls in London. Stocking cap, Haha.

Thinking, This is the last time I'll ever do this.

Now bump, bump, bump. Down the funny stairs.

When he returned, Mary was lying on the bed, still in the quilted robe, watching the ceiling. It seemed very dark, very cold in the room. He sat down beside her in his coat and put his hand on her arm. Cars moved past the window. The people upstairs had their radio on.

"Why did you move the bureau?" he asked after a while.

Without moving her head she looked down toward the foot of the bed. "After you left I was lying here and I noticed a traffic light or something like that out on the street was reflected in it. It was blinking on and off, I must have watched it for an hour. We've been here for weeks and I never saw that before. But once I did, I had to move it."

"You shouldn't be doing things like that."

For a long while she was still, and when she finally moved, it was just to turn her head and look silently into his face.

He nodded, once, very slowly.

"It didn't . . ."

No.

She smiled, sadly, and still in his coat, he lay down beside her in the small bed. She seemed younger now, rested, herself again. There was warmth in her hand when she took his own and put them together on her stomach.

They lay quietly through the afternoon. Ice was re-forming on the streets; outside, they could hear wheels spinning, engines racing. The hall door opened, there was a jangle of milk bottles, the door closed. Then everything was quiet. The trees across the street drooped under the weight of the ice.

There was a sound in the flat. Very low and steady, like a ticking. He listened for hours before he realized it was the drip of a faucet in the bathroom.

Outside, slowly, obscuring the trees, the night came. And with it, snow. They lay together in the darkness, looking out the frosted window. Occasionally, lights moved across it.

"We'll get rid of his things tomorrow," she said after a while.

BUBBLES

D——, where are you now?

I've searched for you down in the cove, by the little sandstone temple that the Greek built when his daughter married, where a wild cat lives, all butter and ginger; in the Soho pubs and Hampstead house parties; down by the docks where the air smells of banana, oil floats out on the water (Ophelia's gowns), and spiders crept across the top of my black shoes that stood like open graves on the whitewashed boards.

Once, I asked after you at the small café on the bridge by Paddington Station and a man in the corner, overhearing, paused with a forkful of soft dry cheese in front of his mouth (his forefinger nicotine-stained halfway down between the joints) and spoke across the room through already-parted lips: "Kilroy, you say? Ah yes, he was here. Remember him well; almost like my own son, he was. Yes, he was here"—then delivered the fork and chewed: a mouthful of crumbling custard. On the brown table beside him sat his teeth, pound notes clenched between them, a pink money clip in the morning sun.

("Love, hate indifference," you used to say in your flamboyant way, "they can work wonders, miracle. If you have belief." And—flamboyantly, extravagantly—I believed. In you. And now have only this, all this need and guilt, that bangs away inside me.)

Outside the café now, four men point in four directions and step backwards until they come together. A delivery boy in white pedals along the bridge and stops before me, returning undelivered another of the cables by which I have tried to reach you:

Yesterday the cows came
home stop Bailey expected
later today stop Where
are you stop

On the opposite wall of the bridge someone has spray-painted *Kilroy the saviour.* "Is it true, sir?" the delivery boy asks. "Can he really do all they say he can?" I go over and scrape the white letters off into an envelope, marking it *near Paddington Station, 4 Jan, 6 AM.* Does this mean he has left the city? A lorry comes by, killing the delivery boy, who has tried to follow me across the street.

And so I go walking down Westbourne Grove where teddy bears hang by their ears on clotheslines, where marzipan elephants lounge in the palms of children and American Indians camp in the dust-bins, their salty teepee smoke spiraling up between the Queen Anne houses. Leaning against one of the spear fences, a flop-hatted old man blows his nose into a tiny rag of flannel then holds it out away from his eyes, looking to see what he's brought up, like a fisher, from the deeps. "Hey, got a sixpence?"—and his huge nostrils hang there in front of my face like two black holes in the morning. As always, walking—its regularity, the rhythm of it—brings me to another kind of rhythm; I always end up singing or, in busier parts of the city, humming quietly to myself. So now as I walk (hopefully toward you) over the gobbets of paint and the heelspores of crushed orange chalk, past the walls and fences painted with six-foot flowers and diminutive Chinese dragons, past the bakeshops with their pastel facades, I'm singing softly to myself *Jesus wants me for a sunbeam.*

Who would have thought it. When we squatted together in piles of dust behind the books upstairs, sharing the last disposable yellow paper robe (luckily a forty-four, so it fitted us perfectly) and nibbling at the cake of vanilla seaweed we found in a drawer when we took the flat? That you should leave, and months later the realization of what had happened would come so suddenly upon me, and with such force, that I would sit for days without moving or speaking, until friends came at last and bore me away. That finally, obsessed with the depth of my loss, I should come searching for you, asking everywhere, sending these messages out ahead of me (cables, phone calls, bits of paper thrown out the window to passers-by), out from my tiny room in Clapham Common, and following these signs across all of London: chalk on brick walls, letters sprayed from cans, empty chocolate wrappers which could be yours . . .

On the street in front of a fish shop two children are killing one another with wooden swords while all the silver-bubble fisheyes watch them calmly and dogs sit across the street quietly looking on. Farther down, where wind has rattled windows, a burglar alarm clangs. In this amazing new stillness a young man enters a nearby dentist's office ("Half a pint, sir? Three bob, please; just put this over your face") and emerges giggling. The window is filled with old dental tools toppling in lines off the velvet-covered shelves and looking like instruments for exquisite torture: relics of orbicular inquisitions.

In Notting Hill Gate (I wonder if you remember this) the buildings catch the wind and lay it like a ribbon down along the pavement; it swirls about my ankles, clinging, resilient, as I tramp through. Three one-man bands glare at one another from the corners of an intersection, waiting for the light. The flowerseller's black Alsatian is wearing a chain of daisies at its neck; it can catch pennies on its tongue. Remembering the old man's nostrils on Westbourne Grove, I make for the tube station. One wall is covered with telephone numbers; vast 69s scratched into the cement with belt-buckles or penknives; a poem in red shoe polish:

> During the raids
> the lost plane
> reported
> the war over
> the pilot missing

On the other, in a tiny, elegant script, is penciled: *When Kilroy returns.* I stop and with people staring over my shoulder scrape the minute gray flakes off into an envelope.

The third level is deserted. I stand alone by the track, hearing the far-off rumble of trains and the dim, flat voices that float after me, tangling together, down the corridors behind. I turn to look down the rails and when I turn back, a cleaning machine is rushing toward me, its tiny mechanical arm erect out in front like a bull's horn. Quickly I step back against the wall, into the leering two-dimensional arms of a Chinese prostitute. "*Look out! Mind!*" the little machine shouts—penny-sized speaker rattling, distorting under the load—then pulls to a stop just past me and comes slowly backwards.

"Who," it asks (the arm quivering), "are you" (arm stabbing out toward me). "I" (arm bending back to point dead center to itself from above) "am The Machine. *Look out for The Machine!*" A pause. "I'll get you, you know; going to take your place, replace you, do away with your sort." (The arm stabs out again, almost to my knee.) "And about time, too. *So look out!* I'm giving you fair warning now!"

It starts away; then stops, purrs a moment and returns, the little treads lugging sadly backwards.

"What are you doing here!" it demands. "Let me see your passport! Would you like your shoes shined. They need it. I have some nice red polish."

I back away from the arm.

"Kilroy," I say quickly. "Have you seen him; has he been here?"

"Kilroy! You know Kilroy! Yes, he was here!" The little machine pauses, waving its arm thoughtfully. "*He* listened to me. We used to sit here for hours, talking over philosophical problems—mostly ethics, I remember. That was before he went away." The arm droops. "A good man. Sometimes, thinking about a man like that, it almost makes me want to forgive you for everything. Almost." The arm suddenly springs back to life, full of excitement. "Do you know where he is!"

"I'm afraid not. I'm trying to find him."

The arm wilts again. "The only one who ever had enough sense, enough compassion, to listen. He knew I was right . . ."

"When I do, I'll let you know, and tell him that you asked after him." I turn and start back up the corridors, but the little machine shoots around in front of me.

"Just a moment," it says. "I'm supposed to give you a riddle, you know, before I can let you go." It sits for several minutes, the tiny arm flopping and waving, in deep thought. "But I can't think of one just now. Would you like to hear me clap my hand. I suppose it's all right for you to pass, since you know Kilroy. But I should have something done about those shoes if I were you."

I walk up the tunnel. Behind me the little cleaner shouts: "You don't have much time left, you know. *Watch out for the*

Machines!"—and goes zooming away down the concrete beside the tracks. The last syllable blurred, rattling like a cough; apparently the speaker had finally been too much strained and the diaphragm had cracked.

I climb back up past all the posters of women in yellow swimwear and the ticket machines into the crowds. It's five now, and the streets are full of dogs. As I walk past a row of phone booths outside a Wimpy Bar, one of the phones rings. I beat the others there and pick it up.

"Yes?"

"We've found him." Outside, it's raining; this booth contains me perfectly, with water breaking on the gray glass, destroying the world outside.

"Where?"

"There's been an accident. Mercy Hospital. He's asking for you. Hurry." The rain is washing cigarette butts up under the door and into the booth. On a minicab sign someone has written on the cab's window: *He slept here.* Not bothering this time to collect the message, I ring for a cab.

At the hospital I'm greeted by a nurse in layers of diaphanous white that slide over one another, with pink somewhere underneath. She's painted black rims around her eyes, and has a pink-white mouth.

"This way, hurry. He's been asking for you. It may be all that's keeping him alive, making him hold on."

We go down white tile halls where everyone else walks near the walls; the center is new and clean. Then into a room full of soft murmurs and liquid sounds. Five surgeons squat in one corner talking together quietly. A nurse kneels by the bedside crying. Outside the window four young girls stand still and straight, and sing.

He lies on the bed under a clear plastic tent, with the sheets pulled up to his chin. All around him the air is filled with tubes and small, pumping engines. Fluids run bubbling through the tubes; go slowly down, and more quickly up, along them. It's as though his blood system, lymph system—all the delicate soft machinery of his body—have been brought out into the world, redirected through glass and plastic. He is larger than the rest of us. (I remember the long months I lay still and dazed, recovering from the loss of your leaving. Perhaps it was here that I lay sustained.)

When the nurse folds back a flap in the tent he opens his eyes, and I hear the soughing of the pumps more distinctly.

"You . . . came." When he speaks, the fluids run faster in the tubes, gurgling in time with his voice. Bubbles forming, bursting, passing slowly, like fisheyes, along the tubes.

"I . . . told them . . . you would." His eyes are gray, pupil and iris barely distinguishable from the rest. It occurs to me now that he can see nothing; I could be anyone; it wouldn't matter. (And how you smiled and brought coffee and talked to me quietly. Your face was always so different, so changed, in the dark.)

"I . . . knew you . . . would." There is a gentle hissing as the nurse opens the oxygen valve a degree wider. (The way I stood at the window, watching, not yet understanding. Afterwards, the room seemed . . . larger.)

"Bless . . . you."

Fluids jumped in the tube (*bubble bubble bubble*: the rhythm of a laugh) and now are still, as the pumps shut off. There is only the hiss of oxygen coming into the tent, out into the room. One huge bubble hangs motionless at the bend of a tube, watching.

"Is he dead?"

The nurse goes over to speak with the doctors. They listen carefully, tilting their heads toward her, and nod. The nurse returns:

"Yes."

So I go into the hall and stand there looking out at the polished green grass and flowers in the hospital lawn. A vine which has climbed the building is now blossoming, scattering leaves down into the yard. It looks like the veins in a hand. Flowers climb along it toward the roofs.

"I'm sorry . . ." She comes up behind me.

"You needn't be. It wasn't him."

"Then who?"

"I don't know." I turn to face her. The pink-white lipstick is smudged at one corner of her mouth. Should I tell her? How much she resembles his wife; that this may have made it easier for him, near the end? "I don't know who he was. I've never seen him before." I start down the hall and she comes after me.

"Please, just a moment. This." She holds out a large manila envelope: bulky, jangling. "His personal effects, what he had in his pockets. I wonder . . . could you take them? Please." I take the envelope from her and leave. Hardly anyone in the halls now. The sun is slanting in through the window, moving out across the tiles. When I turn my head to look back at the vine, it almost blinds me. But the flowers are spilling up over the edge of the roof.

Later, on the street, I open the envelope and spread the contents out on top of a low wall. It contains: thirty-nine ha'pennies, two sixpences marked *EM* in red ink, a child's gyroscope top, and a number of small white envelopes containing bits of paint and graphite, each with a place and date scrawled on the outside.

Farther along the wall in black chalk: *We shall be reborn*. Conceivably. But I've used all my envelopes. The only unsealed one I have is the one with the dead man's things—so I scrape the chalk off into that and mark it *Mercy*. (Tomorrow I will have to return to the phonebooth.) And go walking softly down the street toward home. With a song in my mouth.

Like eyelids, all the windows are open, rolled up on their cords. And night blooms over the heads of the buildings.

AND THEN THE DARK—

"Good evening, Mr. Davis."

He lifted his head to peer into the dimness outside the influence of his lamp. (*Two shapes, men in coats. Fog on the window. Lights outside.*) He put down the pen; moved his hand out across the desk, out across the leather-framed blotter.

"No. Don't move the lamp, Mr. Davis. And I'm afraid we'll have to ask you to keep your hands where they are."

One of the men shut the door and stood with his back to it, eyes on the window. The other walked across the room (*in window light: tall, thin, dark eyes, pale; heels soft in the carpet*) and slumped into the padded chair. Reaching under his coat he brought out a cigarette, matches—struck a match and held it near his face (*yellow, shadows, cavernous eyes*). He leaned out across the desk to drag the ashtray toward him (*it was full; ashes spilled around it*), then sat in the chair smoking quietly.

And Davis sat staring out over a slab of white light at two men and a window.

Three o'clock. And the leaves are afraid, they tremble on the trees.

He is sitting in a dark room, a room of orange and green, smoking. Outside the window the limbs of trees move ponderously, like the legs of huge dying insects. A forgotten radio blats late news from the white-tiled kitchen.

(*How to escape this sense of darkness, filling?*)

He hears the sound of feet on the stairs, and the door from the stairway opens into the room. "Darling . . ." She is gray-eyed with sleep, holding a gown close against her breasts.

"I couldn't sleep."

"Again."

There is a sudden thrust of wind and one branch dips violently, scratching along the glass. He lights another cigarette and, hand shaking, reaches out toward his cup. Cold, gray coffee and grounds like tiny cinders run out across the table's mirror top.

("We'll have to put on a new shift: twenty-four-hour production."

"I believe Goodrich has a breakdown on the new figures."

They all look down the table toward Goodrich, who now stands, shuffling papers, his meerschaum pipe smoking away like one of the plant's chimneys.)

She is bending down to the table. The loose skin at her stomach swings gently, showing in outline under the gown; her breasts, still enlarged, move against her arm. She stands, damp rag in one hand, cup in the other, and goes out to the kitchen; comes back with a drink.

"They've doubled the order," he tells her. Her hair is disarrayed, tangled down around her face. The gown falls just above her knees and her feet are bare, toes curled against the cold.

(*When thoughts turn sour and refuse to stick; the whole thing shatters across like struck glass.*)

"Darling . . ."

Upstairs the baby wakes crying, frightened by the wind.

Finally: "Working late aren't you, Mr. Davis?"

"End of the year. Lot of paperwork to clear up."

The man smiled, looking over the things on Davis's desk. "But you're not working on that, are you?" He nodded toward the blotter, where Davis's arm covered a much-corrected sheet of paper. "A statement, perhaps? For the press?"

Davis started to stand and the one at the door jerked his head around to watch him. "Please sit down, Mr. Davis," the thin one said.

"Who are you? How did you get in here?"

"Sit down."

He sank into the chair. The man at the door turned his head away again, stared back at the window.

"Now, it doesn't matter who we are, does it? You remember that—someone working late, like you. Just a visit; we just came to have a little talk with you. That's all."

"If this is a robbery, I'm afraid your timing is off. The vault's sealed for the night. And the payroll doesn't come in until tomorrow. Afternoon."

The thin one snubbed his cigarette out, pushing more ashes over the edge onto the desk. "Really, Mr. Davis, I did expect better of you." He laid his hand on the leather arm. His fingers were long and thin; they trembled slightly. "Don't make our little talk difficult, any more difficult than it has to be. Please." Now Davis could make out the features of the man at the window. A nondescript face: chinless, balding, ordinary. He was heavy, and stood solidly on his feet, like retired military who, standing in place, come automatically to attention.

"As for how," the thin one went on, "shall we just say that certain of your employees came to you with quite outstanding records and . . . recommendations." He smiled again, and the skin tightened across his face. "There won't be any record of our visit, of course."

"I see."

The man lit another cigarette and tossed the match into the ashtray. Ashes puffed up where it hit. When he raised the cigarette to his face, Davis noticed again the odd contrast, the slackness of the man's body and the nervousness of his hands.

"Good." Blue smoke spiraled toward the ceiling, drifted into the lamp's light, from the cigarette held motionless in front of his face. "Like to talk now, Mr. Davis?"

Davis shook his head.

Silence. Smoke.

"No? And I'd heard you had so very much to say."

The man settled lower in the chair, put out his legs and crossed his ankles. A daub of ash fell onto the front of his coat, sparking for a moment before going out. Only his arm moved, carrying the cigarette up to his mouth, away from his mouth, up to his mouth . . .

Finally: "Sedition, Mr. Davis. Shall we talk about sedition?"

His wife moves about in the room above, comforting the child. He hears her footsteps, her soft voice, the child's subsiding cries. Sometimes he fears they are spoiling the child; it meant so very much to them, having her, and she was so hard to conceive. And he fears the fault was somehow his, borne on the failure of his first marriage.

He hears the mobile start up as the baby is put back into her bed, and as the music winds down, he sits quietly thinking. He was seven. His mother went away and brought back the new child . . .

(The child was sleeping: this was the whole house.

He lay in bed, watching the motion of car lights on the ceiling, until his parents were in bed. Then, quietly, he crept down the hall into the nursery and stood before the cot, looking down at the fragile, strange little body, infuriated at its helplessness. He raised one hand and hit it, hit it again, again—until the baby's screams woke his mother and she came running across the house.

By the time she got there he had the child in his arms and was cradling it and crooning and crying softly.)

When his wife came back down into the living room, he was thinking of small dark bodies lying strangely on fields, their arms and legs at odd angles.

"She was just frightened," his wife told him.

"Jane," he said, "I can't do it. Not any longer. No more."

"Your calls, your . . . arrangements . . . were naturally relayed to us, you see. You understand: patriotism. A going thing these days."

He looked down at the paper under Davis's arm.

"You're a practical man, Mr. Davis. You understand how things work, how things get done, otherwise you wouldn't be where you are now." The smile again, the tightening skin. "And you're an important man, a very important man." He came up straight in the chair, leaned forward. "But you know that, don't you? That's why you're here tonight. It works both ways. But ask yourself: *How* important?"

He leaned farther forward, putting out one hand to the silver frame. He turned it around and looked at it closely for several moments. "Your wife." Then put it back on the desk, facing Davis. "A beautiful woman. Let's see, how old *is* your son now—Dave, isn't it? Nineteen? History at Yale, if I remember right."

Davis nodded.

"You're quite fortunate that he hasn't got himself involved with the Secessionists, you know: it's a cancer that claims more and more of our young minds. The government's tolerated them up till now." He punched his cigarette into the ashes, pushing it forward as though he were closing a switch. "Domestic strife. That's bad for a country. Splits it up, drains its energy. The Black riots, the Coalition, now this so-called Secession. Silly protests, all of them, but they demand attention needed elsewhere."

He forked another cigarette out from under his coat, lit it.

"I'm sure you'll understand that."

There were several moments of silence, in which Davis sat looking at the photograph the man had replaced square on the blotter. Light from the lamp glared on the glass, obscuring the faces of his wife and son, the shape of their house behind. Smoke rose, heaving softly, into the light.

"There's even a rumor going around to the effect that the Secession might be indirectly funded by your company. An outright lie of course. But if the story got out . . ."

"Headlights, Carl," the man at the door interrupted.

Then: "Gone. The watchman."

"Time?"

"Twelve."

"On schedule."

The yard lights went off as the watchman's car passed through the west gate. Lee would be sitting in the booth now, radio on against regulations, eating the sandwiches his wife packed up in polyethylene. Davis looked out the window, blinking.

There were clouds the color of ashes.

Evening climbs the towers, tanks, derricks. From the window he can see only the plant and a slab of gray sky that seems to him now pendulous, impending. He knows that the tiny shapes moving among the scaffolding far away across the concrete, and against that sky, are men.

Father—

A product (as you say) essential to the security of the nation. "The chemical reaction melts the flesh, and the flesh runs down their faces onto their chests and it sits there and it grows there. These children can't turn their heads, they are so thick with flesh. And when gangrene sets in, they cut off their hands, their fingers, or feet."

"Their eyes are gone, melted away, and their ears are lumps of raw flesh, fused shut; they resemble nothing so much as huge pink cauliflowers, rotting."

"Twenty civilians for every soldier."

—Some relics of our past.

We are committing a crime of silence. That, at the very least.

How much does the individual owe to his society, and how much can that society reasonably, ethically, demand of him?

I have my answer. Do you?

Love,
David

Gradually it grows dark outside, sinking from steel-gray to plum to black, and finally he is staring at a vague reflection of himself and the office in the glare of the overhead light.

He withdraws and crosses the room to shut off the light; sits at his desk and touches the intercom.

"Betty, before you leave, could you get my wife on the phone?"

"Yes sir."

"And then Jim Morrison at United Press."

"Yes sir."

Waiting, he turns on the desk lamp and sits in a small circle of light.

"Now, you take Santos at Allied, there's a good man—and he's just been given a grant to expand operations. A small plant, but quite efficient. Something about a new thickening agent, better than polystyrene, some say. Worked his way up from a technician. Now he's got a fine home, a beautiful wife, three sons—all of them draft age, as it happens."

The man's arm went up to his mouth, away from his mouth. It reminded Davis of blinking neons. He looked down at the papers under his arm; he'd spent hours on them and now they seemed so distant, unreal.

"Is it strong enough, Mr. Davis?" He reached out, took the papers and, squinting in the dim light, read them.

The man at the door put his hand on the knob: "Twelve-twenty, Carl."

"Then that's about all, Mr. Davis. I hope you'll remember our talk tonight." He put a hand on the desk and stood, rolled the papers up, stuffed them into his coat pocket. "We'll be in touch."

The other was already in the hall. The thin one walked slowly across the room and turned back for a moment at the door.

"The papers would never have printed it, you know."

And then they were gone, the door closed.

Davis sat listening to their footsteps fade away, loud and hollow in the hall. Then the clank and whirr of an elevator descending. Then silence. He noticed how the top sheet of the pad was covered with pressure marks.

(*For God's sake, Dave, don't give up. Don't let go.*)

He stood and walked to the window. Looked out on the towers, tanks, derricks erecting themselves against the sky; at the clouds that moved among them. His breath made circles of frost on the glass. Below, the two men came out of the building and got into their car. Its domelight went on-off, on-off, with the two doors, then headlights came on and lay out along the field of concrete. Dimly, Davis could hear the engine. As he spoke softly to the room, something remembered from college long ago, the circle of frost from his breath spread, deepened, tugged at the light.

> *"But that was his duty, he only did his duty—"*
> *Said Judy, said the Judy, said poor Judy to the string.*

Davis stood staring at his own breath, at his face in the circle of frost. The edge darkened and began to recede, quickly, vanishing into its own center.

When the pane cleared, the car was gone. And then the dark was absolute.

The darkness that surrounds us.

AT THE FITTING SHOP

Can I help you sir; you seem to have lost your way?

Why yes, thank you, I'm looking for the plumbing shop.

Certainly, sir. That would be, let's see, department fifteen-bee. Up this aisle, turn right, right again at Canned Goods, left and keep bearing left around Magazines till you get to Needlework, go through Hobbies and Crafts and take the corridor down through Exotic Foods, then aisle eighty-three—and you're there. Simple. You might want to pick up a compass at Sporting Goods. That's on your way, swing back right just past Suspenders, big stuffed bear, you'll know it when you're there. Makes things a little easier . . . You *do* have a map?

Uh yes. Yes, thank you very much.

Matson.

I beg your pardon?

Matson: my name. My card. Give me a ring if you need any further help. Number's down there, use one of the house phones.

Thank you very much.

No thanks necessary, son, it's my job.

Ah, pardon me. Is this the plumbing shop—down there?

Ha. Sorry, kid, you're in the wrong wing. Up that way. Garden Tools—next floor up. You can take the escalator at Stamp Redemption, elevator at Cosmetics, or walk up just past Archery. Me, I'd prefer the walk—takes you right smack through Tupperware, that'll put a smile on your face.

Sir . . . Sir? Could you tell me, is this how I get to Garden Tools?

Afraid not, Sonny. You're way off course. Look, you go down there and ask that guy in the pink shirt. He'll show you the way to Power Tools and from there you're okay, got a straight shot. Sure thing.

Ah . . . Sporting Goods? Can you tell me which way to go—right, or left?

Well, I'll tell you. You could take that right down into Tall-n-Slim, then come back around Canned Goods Imported till you get to Stationery and pull another right there. Or you could follow that left fork there on to Belts and Neckties, work your way over toward Lavatories and go down on the Autolift. But if *I* were you, I'd go back along this aisle till I got to Stamp Redemption, then I'd make straight for Lay-Away and cut across Carpets-and-Draperies to Complaints. That's the quickest way to get to Hardware, from here anyhow.

Hardware? That's what I want to ask for, then—fifteen-bee?

You bet.

Sorry, but you gave me a fright. You the new helper?

Ah, no. I'm looking for Hardware. Fifteen-bee.

I see . . . well, you're in the basement, you know.

No, I didn't.

Well, you are.

I see. Could you tell me how to get to Hardware, then?

That'd be fifteen-bee, right?

Yes sir.

Well son, I'm not sure; haven't been up there for months myself. Since last Christmas as a matter of fact. Had to go up for some shopping then, though. Waited till late at night 'fore I'd go up. Near as I can recall . . . you got a map?

Yes sir.

Let's have a look then . . . yeah, that's it. Look, somehow you gotta get back up to Coffeepots-n-Cannisters—that's on Level Four about halfway down aisle twenty-eight-cee, next to Lingerie, see? You can find that by yourself now, can't you, just look for the nekid women. I mean, you can get there with the map?

Well, I *think* so.

Good boy! Sure you can, that's the spirit. I reckon you'll make out okay; you've got lots of spunk for a youngster, and that's what it takes.

Yes sir. Thank you very much, you've been very helpful.

Don't thank me, son—you'd do the same for me. We gotta help

each other out, don't we. I mean, what else is there? Man can't help a guy that's in a jam, what else matters?

Won't you take a seat, son? You look a little tired. Here, this one, with the pink arms. Gives you a good view. Notice how the indirect lighting sparkles on all the chrome fittings—it took four engineers and two interior decorators ten weeks to get that effect. You really do look tired, you know. Shouldn't push yourself that way; there'll be time enough for that when you're older. Take care of yourself, enjoy your youth while you've still got it.

I'm sorry, thank you. I had some trouble getting here.

No wonder, either: that's last week's map you've got there.

O. But this *is* Hardware?

Right!

Department fifteen-bee?

You bet!

Where they sell the penises?

Sure thing!

Finally . . .

Ah, you'll pardon my asking, son, but you do have a certificate? From your parents, I mean, testifying to your age—and of course notes from your teacher and minister . . . I'm sorry: rabbi. The law requires it, you see, and . . . ah yes, that's right, everything seems to be in order. Now. Just what style did you have in mind?

Well, I really hadn't given it much thought. I don't know a great deal about all this, I'm afraid. Uh, what would *you* recommend?

Well sir. Of course it's difficult to form an *accurate* judgment without knowing the person, I mean *really* knowing him, if you get my meaning. That is to say, the *essential* him—all the little qualities and quirks that make up his whole, his personality. But judging from your *apparent* physique, and from certain mannerisms which I've noted already, I would go so far as to suggest that one of our *Sassafras Tangles* would not be *too* terribly amiss. And it *is* one of our more *popular* models, quite a *serviceable* style . . . a hunch, of course—but intuition is often to be relied upon, especially when it comes of long experience, familiarity with the product. The shape of the face and buttocks is a particularly useful indication. And the hand of course.

I see. Uh, would it be too forward of me to ask a more, uh, *personal* recommendation?

Ahhhh. Of course, I understand. Well, *personally* I go for the *Polish Sausage*. Quite stylish, never out of vogue, the upkeep isn't as demanding as some. Also, formally, I find it compelling: a certain purity of line, simplicity, an essential *honesty*. The floor manager would swear by the *Mushroom Arrow*, though, and that's one of the best recommendations you can get—I mean, from a man who really knows his trade, knows what is available. The *Arrow* particularly fits the jauntier, dashing sort, I feel.

Uh, could I, do you suppose . . .

Certainly sir!

Yes . . . that *is* very nice.

We have one of the finest fitters in the trade. It is exquisite, isn't it? Truly exquisite. A man feels proud, with a product like that, the result of a totally *committed* craftsman. Exquisite.

It certainly is. A *Polish Sausage* . . .

Shall I measure you for one then, sir?

Well, I'm not quite sure, I mean I haven't seen any others. Do you suppose I could see a few modeled? Perhaps that would help in the final decision?

Why certainly, sir. *Keiris*: the models!

You are most kind.

A fine choice, sir. The *Mandrake Special*, in red, with full attachments. Possibly the best-tooled model we make, and we make the best in the business. Each one finished by hand—an absolute *triumph* of craftsmanship. No: of *Art*!

I believe that I'll be very happy with it.

Yes sir, you'll be *most* happy with it. I can personally assure you of that. You'll find it quite durable, and with care it will bring you many years—even a lifetime!—of pleasure. Simply return it once a month for adjustment; and should anything go wrong—the least malfunction—we will repair it free of charge or, in more serious cases, replace it entirely, just like a Zippo.

Zippo?

A cigarette lighter, sir. Like our *Mandrake Special*, the best available.

Ah. I'm too young to smoke, you know. Though perhaps I'll take it up now . . .

Yes sir, that might be nice. Well, I believe that's everything, then. You'll find lubricant, spare screws and washers—also instructions relating to cleaning, maintenance, minor repairs and adjustments—in the complimentary kit that comes along with the *Mandrake Special*. And the usual instructions on how to use it to full advantage, of course. Your parents will be billed; and if you don't mind, sir, I'd like to add that I think they'll be very proud of your choice, very proud indeed.

I hope so. Thank you very much, again, for your advice. You've been *most* helpful.

My job, sir. More than a job: my calling. *Keiris!* My assistant will show you out, sir: he knows a shortcut. And I believe you will be passing Wine Cellar and Smoke Shop on your way, should you like to stop in there for a quick purchase or two before we close.

Yes, perhaps I will.

It's been a pleasure to serve you, sir.

Yes, thank you. I believe you have made me a very happy man this afternoon.

I hope so, sir. We do our best.

THE OPENING OF
THE TERRAN BALLET

Barii Volk is of course Jordon Ligochee's son. Just ten years after Jordon's publication of his five-page *Design for Loving* established him as our finest contemporary poet, sixteen-year-old Barii echoed his father's success with *Shadows*, a collection of lyrics ("antiques") in the demanding Rilkash stress-control manner. It was, however, to prove more than an echo. The shadows were to pass under relentless examination and Barii was to carry his lyricism and formalism to its logical, though unanticipated, limits; besides his *Floors of My Heart*, the next year saw a number of uniquely instrumented chamber works and the debut of his *First Symphony (The Whilom)*, played by the New Union Ensemble and conducted by the young composer himself, who came to the console rather like a skinny bird and departed it, after the final drawn beat of his baton and the hammer-blows of thundering ovation, in a heap of sweaty clothing, his hair unkempt, his face drained and weak—happy with the reception afforded this return of his to ancient forms.

In months to come, though, Barii was to move on to newer forms of expression; indeed, one critic remarked that Barii Volk was by himself encompassing the full range and development of contemporary art media. He was to pioneer in the growth of sound crystals, work that finally resulted in the delicately beautiful *Mauve Necklace* now housed at the Kahlu Museum, sprinkling out impromptu sonatas as the light strikes it, molding its tones and structure to the shifting patterns of light in the room and to the movement of viewers. He was to be one of the first to experiment with energy sculpture, the best-known example of his work being *Waiting Room* commissioned by Councilhome. Walking through it, one experiences every neural nuance of anxiety and anticipation. He was to introduce the fraloom to Larnian music and train young performers in the technique of this many-voiced instrument. Everything he took up seemed transformed; critics remarked his insight into essential structures. We all waited to see where his interests would next fall.

And then, five years ago, came the startling news of his renunciation of Larne citizenship. Barii was not available for comment, and for evidence or explanation we had only three poems published a month later—anonymously, yet bearing the unmistakable stamp of Barii's lyricism.

One was in French, the others were translations, one from the Rilkash, one from ancient Anglaise . . .

> *jamais revoir face à vous dans la glace*
> *en arrière de moi*
> *où dans les ans nous trouvons content*
> *à nous*

The tree goes on
Into the sky; branch, leaf, twig

Do not stop it.

One lifts
a foot, and puts another
in front of it to claim

the generous sky.

Some time later, a small privately printed volume made its appearance. Entitled *Occasion: Départ*, it consisted of a number of short, inter-related fragments, "occasions of single moments, arrested in time." There was great disputation among scholars as to whether the piece could actually be considered a single, integrated poem, or if it might finally be seen as nothing more than a collection of fragments, of notes *for* poems. (I trust that I have made clear my own position on this matter, both here and in several earlier monographs which were in fact among the first studies effected.) There was further debate over the volume's intentions and significance. Suffice it to say that reactions were mixed.

Nothing more was heard from the young poet, then; no amount of inquiry, however intrepid or privileged, could discover any clue as to his whereabouts or current activities. Later we learned he had left the planet. Shortly after, Jordon Ligochee, who had been deeply hurt by his son's action, died.

Years passed. Gradually rumors began: Barii had left Union, had left the system, had gone to Earth. We all smiled at the image of young Barii there on our dark, exhausted world. At which point the announcements arrived, each one personally signed by Barii Volk and posted from Earth.

It is rumored that the Director of the Council of Arts, upon receiving his invitation, responded: "What the hell is a ballet?" (It is also rumored that he responded: "Where the hell is Earth?" But I believe we may safely accept that as apocryphal.) Perhaps so. At any rate, the response communicated, as well, his intention to attend.

In due course I received my own invitation and secured passage on one of the Earthbound wagons. At the suggestion of this magazine's editor I approached Barii for an interview, which, to our mutual surprise, was granted, it being arranged that I should meet him at the theatre in New Rome upon my arrival, on the afternoon before the first performance of his ballet.

I found him just off the heart of the theatre, in a small room crowded with books and unfamiliar musical instruments. He was slumping on a couch, bent over a large six-stringed instrument, performing some minor adjustment while another, much older man—doubtless the musician—stood by waiting. Barii had put on weight in the past years, and had come to resemble less the skinny bird with which I'd always compared him. Also, he had abandoned his familiar flamboyance of dress and was now attired in the plain, rough clothing I'd noticed on others about the theatre; but when, moments later, he looked up, I perceived again those familiar dark eyes, the sharp face, that quick and slightly mocking smile. His hair was gathered with a ribbon to one side of his head.

He must have heard my approach for, just as I lifted my hand to knock at the doorsill, he sprang from the chair and came striding toward me across the room. "James? I've followed your work with a great deal of interest and admiration. Your article on Arndto I found particularly helpful . . . and your own *Third Cycle*, of course. I'm pleased to meet you at last; anticipation of that pleasure was the reason I responded so happily to your note about an interview."

I must admit to surprise at the esteem he afforded these small contributions of mine. I smiled and said, "I thought you should like the opportunity to talk about your new work, after these many years of silence."

"I would prefer to let the ballet speak for itself." He turned and held the instrument out to the waiting man: "Here, John, I think that should take care of it. If there's any further trouble, bring it back." The man came across the room and took the instrument. "Fotra, this is James. He's come from Larne for our little performance. James—my concertmaster, Fotra Bramin."

My face doubtless betrayed my mystery at the term, for Barii quickly explained: "The concertmaster is the first violin. The most important single member of the orchestra."

The man tucked the instrument under his arm, walked away in a slow, stooping gait. Others met him just outside the door and they walked off together, chattering. Something which had earlier registered subliminally sprang to the fore of my mind: that Barii, like the people here, was noticeably shorter than the rest of us.

"Please sit," Barii said. "And perhaps you would like to try some beer." He crossed to a shelf and brought back a large jar, the top of which he unscrewed and put aside, handing the jar over to me. It was half-filled with a yellow-brown liquid in which light swam and rolled. "Don't worry, it's quite sanitary. I produce it myself, in small quantities. That extra space is necessary to obtain full body and flavor: it should be just about right, now."

I took the jar and drank. The world was sudden, amber, in the brass-bright depths. It was heavy—fluid rather than liquid—with a sweet but somehow quite satisfying taste. I expressed my approval.

"I don't think I have it *quite* right yet, but it *is* refreshing, isn't it? One of the small pleasures we lost when we gave Earth up for dead."

We sat for several minutes talking of Larne and what the younger artists were engaged in there. I told Barii about the new odor symphonies, which owed so much to his early work, and spoke to him of Heinreid Flant, who seems to me the most brilliant and inspired of the new generation of energy sculptors. Barii inquired briefly about microsculpture, something with which he professed he had always wanted to work yet had never found the opportunity. "The journals always give a prejudiced view of what's really going on," he remarked, then flashed a smile, remembering the auspices under which I'd initially approached him.

"You called that instrument a violin," I finally asked. "Would you care to tell me more about it?"

For the next hour or so I was offered up what must surely be one of the most comprehensive surveys of musical history existent. Barii told me how he had traced the evolution of our own instruments backwards to the ones I would see utilized in the ballet later that night; how he had been forced to reconstruct the peculiar musical scale of ancient Earth then, from books and the memory of a few of the older Terrans, reconstruct the instruments around those concepts. "I have undoubtedly made many mistakes," he said at one point. "The violin for instance: should it have six strings tuned E-A-D-G-B-E, or four tuned E-A-D-G? I settled on six."

There was a light knock at the door and Barii sprang to his feet. It was a young woman.

"Barii, I'm sorry to bother you, but there's a problem in the score. Movement Seven. The choreography and accompaniment are out of synch."

Barii took her hand and led her into the room. She was very young, smaller even than Barii, her hair short and colorless. She had huge green eyes. "Nonsense, Verity, you musn't be always apologizing. James: my leading lady, Verity. James, from *Lyric Quarterly*. On Larne." He squeezed her hand gently, turning her toward the door. "I'll be with you in a few minutes, darling. You mustn't worry, everything will be all right."

She left, and Barii continued his explanation, much of which I have reported in the second part of the present article. Frequently people came to the door with last-minute troubles and were politely turned away with assurances that he would be along soon, they mustn't worry. I kept trying to steer our conversation toward the ballet itself but Barii resisted every attempt, mentioning only that the work was dedicated to his father.

Even when he had reconstructed the scale and instruments, he went on, his work was far from finished. He had then to learn the Terran language perfectly ("It was incredibly idiosyncratic"); to make a deep study of Earth myth and legend; and to train his performers—to make artists of a people who had sunk to a virtually pre-agricultural society. "I saw it as a moving outward," he intimated, "by returning to origins. I felt, I was sure, that a vitality existed here—a vitality I needed. In the course of my study I discovered the ballet and I felt that here was the perfect medium for me: at once personal and formal. A pure lyricism, combining myth and language and music and motion . . . plus a rigorous form. It was the end of all my previous work and, at the same time, possessed much that previous work had lacked."

He waved aside my objection to that final remark.

"I'm sorry, I felt closed in. That I had exhausted the possibilities. This may have been the explanation for my peripatetic courting of artistic forms toward the end, before I left Larne. I tried to make that clear in translations I published anonymously. I was looking for something I could never have found, something which no longer existed there. Here, I think, I may have found it."

Our conversation continued for some minutes, but I could get Barii to say no more about the ballet. Eventually I could see that he was tiring of our talk—becoming anxious to be again among his musicians—and excused myself, once more expressing my anticipation of the performance to commence in a few hours' time now.

Barii stood and shook the hair back away from his face. He took my hands between his own.

"It's been truly wonderful to meet you, James," he said, looking into my eyes. "I hope you'll not be too terribly disappointed with our little ballet . . . Good-bye."

I took my leave and walked on the hills above the theatre to wait for the performance.

The sky was gray, impending, with streams of ochre and maroon on the horizon. Leaves like the husks of sigflees on Larne covered the hills. Wind tumbled in the leaves as I walked among them. They crunched beneath my feet.

The ballet was titled *Jordon*, and was dedicated to Barii's father. Would it achieve that union of lyricism and formalism he hoped for? Had he found an answer to the exhaustion of our forms, found the vitality he wanted—or was his love for this world and its people blinding him, obscuring his critical senses, causing him to delude himself and accept mediocrity as vital? There had been clues, certain words in his conversation, certain gestures, which could indicate his awareness of the ballet's failure. But he placed great faith in it, had devoted to it so many years of his life . . .

These were the thoughts that crowded my mind as I walked alone on the hill through the leaves, all scarlet and mud-brown. The streams of color on the horizon were flattening, disappearing. There was a sense of dampness in the air and in my lungs, too, as I breathed.

I sat on the stump of a tree and looked down at the ramshackle theatre far below. As I watched, two tiny figures came out and looked up toward me. One raised his hand and waved; the other hesitated a moment then waved as well. They started off together away from the theatre and from me, holding hands.

The darkness, the dampness, was drawing closer around me. I sat on the hill for several minutes more, then went down to wait with the others for the opening of the ballet.

THE ANXIETY IN THE
EYES OF THE CRICKET

Afterwards, they sat together on the terrace patio smoking.

Behind them on the steel slab, the house, with its forty rooms separate as the chambers of a nautilus, stood like something grown up out of the hill. The steel extended several yards down into gray ash-like soil, steel scaffolding still farther, to the baserock. Behind the house, for more than a mile, the ground was pitted into a bare colorless canyon, scooped out and pushed forward to form this hill.

Jerry had just come from the East, with his arm torn loose from the socket and one eye half-closed on itself. Passage was difficult these days. He had come on impulse; felt the pull one morning and responded to it as he had so many times before. In China now, and certain portions of India, at least one small part of the economy would be finding itself empty and crippled.

"How is it there now?" his friend had asked as he smoothed on the salves, wheeled the square white machines, tables, glass chambers across the floor in the bare white room, pulling Jerry's body, wrecked by disease, malnutrition, and damage, back into a single organism. For Jerry, accustomed to the tonal languages of the East and its strange, inverted thinking, the rough, assonant rhythms of his friend's speech, its somehow Parnassian starkness, were oddly disturbing: a disorientation which was to continue, in fact to grow ever more persistent. English, which had become the French of the last century, then a kind of mirror-image Mandarin—sparse and subtle in its rhythms but yielding great resonance, a quality first noted by mid-century mystery writers and exploited by certain American poets—was now atrophying, dying in upon itself. Words tumbled readily off the tongue, too readily, in brief economical strings like a kind of verbal semaphore, and increasingly had relevance only to themselves. Poets, Jerry knew from personal experience, were having a hard time of it. Simultaneously, the tone-rich Chinese language was bursting open, becoming rich and resonant in substance as well, coming more to resemble the evocative, implicit poetry of its written form, now in turn increasingly linear and stylized. What was the precise relationship of language to society, of spoken to written language? English, with its truncated bursts of energy; the flow of Mandarin. Did entropy in one predict, or establish, entropy in the other? Which way did the influence flow? Jerry wondered.

"Better," he had answered his friend.

"You have a perverse love for ambiguity, Jerry. Better than before, or better than here?" He selected a scalpel from the tray and moved behind Jerry with it. The shoulder was anaesthetized, but Jerry could feel warm blood running down his ribs.

In answer, he had simply smiled.

Now two Drambuies sat on the red enamel deck-table between them and the taste of the thick, sweet liqueur was still in Jerry's mouth. Another glass, a tumbler, was partly filled with cigarettes of strong black tobacco—perique, Jerry thought, from the smell—wrapped in meerschaum papers. His friend held one of these, hand cupped against his ear and elbow on the chair arm, violet smoke pouring out around his bleached white hair. He was dressed in black silk pajamas, and Jerry wore a similar pair; his own Western clothes had been spattered and torn when he arrived. Near the center of the table, almost touching the pole which suspended a Union Jack umbrella out over them, sat a wineglass left out overnight. It was half-full. A delicate crust of ice skimmed the deep red surface and, thinner still, ran up the side of the glass along which, yesterday afternoon, Jerry had sipped the wine. Its gold stem was as thin as a flower stalk, the glass itself as large as a man's cupped hands, the base formed of three long, twisted gold tendrils, like roots or the foot of a bird. Jerry, newly aware of color, sat staring for some time at the form all this took, then reached out and shifted the glasses. His right arm and shoulder, the damaged ones, were in the sun, and ached slightly. No use—just another form. The umbrella's gold-braid fringe was still. There was no wind, no movement.

Far below, a small private boat slid through the black water, lugging a makeshift barge—actually more a raft—behind it on a single thick cable. There were still those who cared. The barge was filled with the bodies of the suicides, stacked randomly crisscross on the flat deck like matches in an ashtray. Miles away down the river, where the boat was headed, the flames showed dim in the sun. Jerry imagined for a moment that he could hear the popping of flame within flame as it reached out and ran across the bodies, choosing eyeballs which would explode into gray sizzling mush, lips which would burst and let out fresh pink meat, soft swollen testicles. The chaos, he knew, was apparent. An illusion. The real problem was over-organization, entropy, the seeming confusion only the final struggle against that imposition. Fact and metaphysics were, finally, the same thing.

Looking back to the barge he thought of Gericault, and only then noticed the words stenciled in bright red letters across the boat's prow: *The Medusa*. Irony or humor? He wondered. Was it form or quality that separated them—if, indeed, the distinction could exist anymore, if any could. A defense, he supposed, but what sort of man—

"It's a question of guilt." Michael snapped the cigarette away from him and it tumbled through its own smoke out into space, down along the cliff and into the water, to collect with the refuse and bodies which floated several feet out from each bank.

Jerry shrugged. "For some." Pain stabbed into the socket of his shoulder and twisted, then quickly withdrew, leaving behind a dull throb. He lifted his Drambuie and looked across the rim to the city far below beyond the water. The city was completely still; nothing moved inside it. "You?"

"Perhaps . . ."

"You told them the city would kill them. You predicted that much." Jerry found it difficult to look at his friend. Difficult, too, to speak in the old language: he had no right here, he didn't belong. Not any longer. He was intruding.

"I predicted everything. Save for the end . . ."

"They struck first."

"And the city is dying. Like the rest." He took another cigarette from the tumbler. The remaining ones toppled, like jackstraws, into a new pattern. "But do they know? If they knew . . ." His hand stopped in mid-wave and fell back onto the chair—too much effort. And no reward. It didn't matter. Too late.

He struck a match and for a moment Jerry shrank back in his chair, then overcame the reflex. But when Michael pushed the tumbler toward him, he shook his head violently.

Jerry said, "They might do something?"

His friend sat smoking, staring out across the water. Finally he spoke, only his lips moving.

"The boats. From the States. They are coming in at the rate of ten, twelve a day now. The holds are full, the decks as well. The bodies are stiff as boards. They say the crews have learned to walk across them without noticing they're there. Or what they are. As though they *were* boards. Southampton is packed with them, miles out to sea, the Pool of London filled months ago."

"And you began it? By telling them—"

"Jerry. That was after I came here, after all this was built. You should understand. You've been here a week now." (That morning as they lay side by side in bed, exhausted, Michael had said, "Jerry, you are the most religious person I know. I'm in awe of that, it frightens me.")

"And tomorrow I leave."

Michael looked up at the sky. It was choked with smoke from the burning bodies, smoke that hung motionless in dense, shapeless clouds, like clots of blood. "Where will you go?"

Jerry paused. "Into the city. I'd like to borrow your boat." Suddenly he caught the smell of cabbage from the gardens beside the house. There were a dozen varieties—it was one of the few things which would grow from the soil now—and the smells of each mingled together, though Jerry felt, if he wanted, he could separate every one, like picking out individual strands of seaweed. A small plot of artificial flowers stood beside the cabbage, their bright red and yellow heads lost to the sheer mass of greenery. "I have a family there."

Michael said nothing for several moments, then looked down at the river; away from the smoke. The boat was almost out of sight; only the barge showed. "You never mentioned that before. You knew—"

"That it would be against your principles? Yes, but I care more for you than for your principles. I haven't seen them for years. But now . . ."

"You're amused, Jerry? That I hold to my own morality, even in all this?" He sipped at his Drambuie, then suddenly threw the glass away from him out over the cliff. The liquid spilled, spinning in a flat disc and, while the glass plunged downward, seeming to hesitate before it followed, breaking into a loose shower. "No. Of course you're not. I had the boat destroyed. Burned. I'm sorry."

"I'll find a way."

Michael looked at Jerry, opened his mouth, then shut it again and turned away.

"A wife," Jerry said. "And a son."

Michael nodded. He reached up to the monogrammed pocket and took out a boiled egg, already peeled, put it on his palm then returned to the pocket and brought out a small silver spoon between his first two fingers. The spoon dangled loosely between them; the hands were pale, bloated white, the fingers perfectly straight, joints hardly creased at all. He knew from experience that offering one to Jerry would be a futile gesture. But a gesture these days, however futile . . . He looked across the table at his friend and Jerry shook his head. His hair was short now, shorter than Michael had ever seen it. He had arrived with hair filthy and tangled; repairing him, grooming him, Michael had no choice but to cut it. He remembered how Jerry had sat staring into the mirror, very still, watching the fine, tangled black strands fall onto his shoulders and tumble down across his chest and arms as his friend moved behind him, manipulating the scissors.

Michael lived on eggs (difficult as they were to obtain) and Drambuie, but had been unable to discover what kept Jerry going. He had never seen him eat. It seemed to him that Jerry grew thinner every day, and there had been, these past few days, a weakness in his movements, one all the more remarkable for its contrast to Jerry's strong, deep voice. What strength he had left seemed to have gathered in that voice, and in his hands.

Michael lifted the egg in his palm and looked at it against the smoke-swaddled air. So simple, symmetrical. Egg and hand barely distinguishable. His friend's voice came across the table to him, soft now, and low.

"It's not the effect, but the *fact*, that one finds intolerable."

Michael made no response.

"They are there. Inexorable, ineffable, intolerable."

"If such things as facts exist."

"The absence of fact, in effect, *becomes* fact."

"Yes. I suppose . . ." What had he begun to say? It was lost, whatever. "Don't try to help me, Jerry." He stabbed spoon into egg and a plug of white flew off into the air, landing just past the patio and throwing up a fine cloud of ashy dust. Jerry watched as he scooped out a daub of dull yellow on the tip of the tiny spade the size of a fingernail and lifted it to his mouth. A pink tongue met it, rolled back into the mouth. Jerry wondered idly how the egg would taste on top of Drambuie. He lifted his own glass, empty now, and a drop of the thick liqueur which had gathered back to the bottom slid slowly down it to his tongue.

Jerry looked toward the garden. He found himself unable to watch the eating. For the first time he noticed a sign there, a hand-painted square on a short stick, almost lost in the rolling folds of cabbage: *Keep ceaseless watch for COLORADO BEETLES. They can destroy our potato crops.* He remembered seeing the same sign, years ago, printed then and neatly designed, in every London post office. When he turned back, two more private boats moved slowly down the water, pulling cluttered barges. A body toppled off one and fell into the wake, drifting, slower still, toward the base of the cliff below.

It was getting dark. Michael had finished the egg and now wiped his palm on his leg, smearing the bits which were left into the dark silk pajamas. He looked down at the barges.

"A question of guilt: is it real? Can it ever be real? Or is it just a word, something conjured up, manufactured, to hide something else we're afraid to face?" He walked to the edge of the patio steel and looked down. (Associations, Jerry thought. I can't stop making associations, not even me. It's the place, I have no right to be here. Mallarmé said that poetry was made from words, not ideas. And Goethe said that whereas an idea was one thing, a word could always be found to replace it. Associations. I can't stop them.)

Ten feet out from the base of the artificial cliff, the body, propelled by the lazy euphoric wash of boat and barge, collided with the outermost of the bobbing refuse, disrupting it. Finally it came to rest alongside another body, this one gray and bloated from long exposure to the water, and there was only the slight synchronized rippling of movement among the whole. Final remnants of the boats' passage.

Michael turned back to Jerry. There was a gentle wind from downriver, where the bodies were burning. The umbrella fringe leaned into it, the cabbage swayed all together, its complex leaves rippling lightly backwards, backwards, backwards again. Jerry suddenly remembered something from Wallace Stevens: "All of our ideas come from the natural world: trees equal umbrellas." Was that true?

"To bed now, Jerry?"

"But—"

After a moment he got up and followed his friend. Associations. He thought of the cabbages, of his marriage.

Later that night he woke alone in bed. Michael was standing naked at the window, looking out, with a cigarette in his hand. There was a bright erratic light outside. The radio was on low. Michael seemed to know instantly that he was awake.

"Jerry. Come to the window."

The city was burning.

The fires were steady, slow, borne in every building, every house, every street: there was no violence to them, and Jerry, watching, felt a strange sense of peacefulness. Even at this distance, climbing slowly, quietly toward the top of the city, the flames showed on their faces. The black water was full of fire.

Without turning from the window Jerry said, "Put that out." Michael stared at him for a moment, then dropped the cigarette and ground it into the carpet with his bare foot.

They stood watching. Neither moved. It was a single fire now, and as it rose, smoke fluttering upwards, the cloud of black settled down onto the city. They could hear the crackling, explosions, the steady rumble of buildings tumbling back into themselves, pushing the flames higher through the empty corridors.

When Michael spoke, his voice was like the click of a revolver rolling onto the next chamber, a beetle shutting its wing case.

"You'll still—"

"Tomorrow," Jerry said. "When the fires have died down."

The fire's light showed on the bodies and refuse against the far bank, making each thing a different object, something apart from the rest. People stood on the bank and looked down into the water. They stood completely still.

"Your wife and son?"

Jerry nodded, and the flames were in his hair. Rubble began to fall into the water, pushing bodies and refuse out away from the bank. They began to drift slowly across the river toward the cliff. Finally, beside him, Michael broke the silence.

"We'll go together."

Jerry cut him off, nodding again, then walked away from him through the doors and onto the patio, where he sat down at the edge of the steel. Michael would know enough not to follow.

He sat there all night, alone, watching the city burn.

JEREMIAD

And Jerry left the burning city behind him, returned to the East—to Calcutta, to Burma, Peking, Mashhad. Would he now feel as out of place here as he had in London before he sat on the hill and watched the city burn, the people who stood so still on the harbor and stared into the violent water, the rubble and bodies drifting on the black water toward him?

In Cambodia he was assaulted by a gang of youths, his arm torn loose again in the struggle—and woke to find himself in occupied Vietnam. Days later, with a select group of fellow laborers (Jerry and a Buddhist South African, escaped just before the overthrow, were the only whites among them), his arm hanging limp and useless at his side, he fought his way across the border into the Republic. Only Jerry made it. The others died and the South African surrendered. Women soldiers found Jerry wandering beside the Nhi Ha; in his delirium he thought they were American Indians and, when they approached him, turned and began to walk steadily out into the river. (There had been a time when Jerry recoiled from water; now he embraced it, opening his arms to take it to him. A fire in his shoulder.) One of the soldiers crossed herself and dived after him, dragging him by his hair, grown long again now, back to the bank. They took him to their general.

Weeks later, a white face above him, Jerry woke. The light struck his eyes like fists and he quickly shut them again. He heard a voice. English. It sounded far away; it came down long hollow corridors filled with the buzzing of flies.

"Mr. Cornelius?"

Jerry moved his head weakly. There were thorns in his neck, knots of thorns. (Who was it—Schumann? Someone. Dead. Mad, from hearing a constant hum in his ears, and killed himself. A high F. Jerry's was E7, the full chord. In an echo chamber. In his skull.)

"Mr. Cornelius?"

He opened his eyes and shut them even more quickly. They were full of flames.

"You will be all right. My medic—"

Then the buzzing swelled, the flies settled down onto slabs of raw red meat. And then it was inside him, swelling inside him, and it blotted out all the rest.

At night the flames would come back to him, filling the walls of the general's green room. Dark green, deep as the grass at night, bright red and yellow. Among them he could see the faces of his wife and son, Cass and Dylan (Dylan, he thought, Welsh for *water*), their faces black, dissolving, hair afire and eyes staring out at him. Her brown eyes wide, empty, as the fire (or was there fear in them?) picked the flesh off her body and Jerry remembered himself how soft each part would feel to the fire's rough hands. The child would open his mouth, scream, scream, but there would be no sound over the roar of flames and collapsing buildings, only his mouth open round and the flames leaping inside it. Their faces behind the flames now. And then, at the edge of the flames, he would hear the gentle, quick laughter of Michael, his friend. The sound of Michael saying: Guilt.

General Lee was a mercenary—or had been, until he found every regular soldier above him dead or wounded, the other mercenaries crossing the border, and the people here in Haiphong (women, children, the crippled and insane) looking to him for leadership. Secretly, he had made arrangements to leave the country; then the Republic was proclaimed and, inexplicably, supported by the League of Nations. That night a man was found dead in his small boat anchored just off the harbor, and the next day General Lee had assumed official control of the border sector, "Lee County." Weapons were requisitioned, and supplied. They were mostly .22s of American make. In the weeks which followed Lee's assumption, the few South Vietnamese soldiers who crossed into the North, and several mercenaries who tried to return, were quickly shot and torn apart by Lee's squads of women. They had no idea what force hatred, combined with loss and near-Messianic devotion, could have.

The General was small, like the people he "looked after," with slick black hair gathered behind his head with a blood-red ribbon. Beneath his thin, sharp face there were only the dense robes, blue, rising high on his neck and dropping over his hands and bare feet, giving no indication whatsoever of a body within them. He was an American, born in Louisiana and escaped just before the revolutions and final secession. He was Cajun, and still spoke with a slight French accent. "The bayous for the rice fields," he would say, the dark blue robes swaying ponderously as he gestured toward the lands beyond the patio. "It was not a difficult exchange."

Jerry remained with the General for several weeks, during which time he was given the best care and medical attention possible to the city, now little more than a village, though all the rubble had been cleared long ago and everything within Haiphong was clean and neatly ordered. The man who cared for him was in fact the General's own specially imported physician, a large, vague man with hands that reminded Jerry of palm leaves, who never spoke and never met Jerry's eyes. Most likely German, Jerry suspected, though few were left after the '38 crisis in Ostrava and Jerry, having never seen one, couldn't be sure. "*Du är ein Deutsche,*" he said one day as his bandages were being changed. That was the best he could manage. He knew a little Danish, and he dimly recalled struggling through Rilke as a child, but that was long ago; still, he thought the man would understand. But he made no reaction. He continued unwinding the soiled gauze and cotton, carried it carefully across the tiles to the disposal unit, then took fresh wrappings out of the sterilizer and bound them tightly across Jerry's chest and arm. When he had finished, he turned and left the room. Jerry's shoulder stung where he had pulled the mats of cotton away from the new, forming skin, following it with a gentle pressure of his fingertips to ease the pain.

Though it was rumored he had once been Taoist, the General had no religion, a rare thing these days; Jerry couldn't in fact remember ever having met another person—aside from himself, of course— who had been able to make his way through the welter of ancient and ephemeral codes of belief which the world offered now. The General was an ascetic, however, and this presented something of a problem. Still, love of a sort was possible between them, and in its own way, slowly, that love developed. When Jerry was better, the General sent women to his room several nights in succession. Jerry's turning them away (kindly and, once, regretfully) somehow cemented the relationship between the General and himself. They settled into a smooth, pure love, expressed in the many nights they spent alone together drinking local tea and talking (the General smoking rice-hulls in a briar pipe; this and the tea were the only concessions he allowed himself), fed by one's guilt and the other's gratitude, or by some curious combination of the two which existed in each. Soon they were speaking in French, falling back onto English when Jerry occasionally found the General's distorted Cajun French impenetrable.

The night he left, the General signed a safe passage for Jerry and escorted him to the boat which was to take him on the first lap toward Calcutta.

The sun was almost down, its maroons and ochres lying out flat along the river, filling it with color. Birds skimmed low to the surface. In the distance their wings, the size of Jerry's hand, appeared to be single feathers and their long legs, dangling down into the clear water, looked like lengths of thin bamboo.

"You'll come back, Mr. Cornelius?" the General asked, in English. His brown eyes were very still, and caught none of the light from the water. It occurred to Jerry that they had never touched.

"Would there be something to come back to, General? When the time came?" From across the city he could hear the sound of gunfire as the women's army practiced on targets. Jerry had seen the targets; they were roughly drawn outlines of small men, with the heart, genitals and brain carefully drawn in.

"There is only peace here, Mr. Cornelius, and that will not change. Nor will our values. Trouble and strife have done with our land. Now they have gone elsewhere, as you are about to do."

"Calcutta . . ."

"Perhaps. But not, I think, for the moment."

"And perhaps if I did return, I would bring the wars back with me?"

The General turned and looked out over the river. "It is possible. You are a most exceptional man."

The boat's motor coughed twice and caught. General Lee held out his hand to give Jerry the safe passage.

"Good-bye then, Mr. Cornelius."

Jerry took the papers and his fingers for just a moment touched the General's palm. Impulsively he reached out to the blue robes, then dropped his hand. He turned and stepped quickly into the boat. Only when it was far out on the water and Jerry looked back to see the General standing there alone on the harbor did he begin to cry.

He was still weeping when the boat docked at Haing Nhu Khan.

The burning city. Brown eyes. An open soundless mouth.

Jerry lay on one of the Persian carpets, staring into the empty fireplace. The words, remembered, were inside him: guilt, loss, denial, fear. Michael's words, above the burning city.

It was all locked in his childhood. London, Simla. But wasn't the house, London—

Gone. It was no use; Jerry was confused. There seemed so many childhoods when he tried to recall them, and all of them gone. Perhaps there was one for every change his body had suffered, the world filled with the broken childhoods of Jerry Cornelius. If that were true . . .

It would all be over soon.

London, Simla, now Calcutta, Mashhad. He had to get it all outside him; that was the only way.

He tried to shake his head but the movement wasn't right. He knew what he meant to do but, for several moments, the words for the intent wouldn't come. This had happened quite a lot recently; Jerry suspected he was suffering aphasia—slight, but on several levels. Words eluded him, almost there, the concept firm but the words would fail to congeal around it, would be inaccurate, distorted. Other times, the words themselves would evoke no response. His gestures, too, were impaired, contradictory, inadequate.

He squeezed his right hand hard into a fist and managed to regain control. He rolled over in the carpet and got up, walking toward a small shelf of books beside the fireplace. Ran his finger slowly along the books, stopped at one, slid the finger up along the spine and tilted it out. He took it down, turning it over and over in his hands, the stiff coolness of it.

It was a small, thin volume, foolscap 16mo, bound in black. The spine was bare. *Abyssinia*, in deep blue on the front. And below, in tiny silver letters: *Jeremiah Cornelius*. This, to the best of his knowledge, was the sole remaining copy now, after the city's burning. He opened the book, at random, saw first lines and had no need to read further. He remembered.

The murder

I shall never,
never kill you, no. You will always
be there
on the headstone of morning . . .

Living with you

Another year and the ground
pulls harder,
the heart
on its intricate stalk succumbs again . . .

He was sixteen, married, happy, and afraid. "A man of independent means." There had been this, a novel called *Moth*, then the scientific treatises destroyed with his father's house, the unified field theory . . .

Jerry pushed thoughts away.

The epigraph was on the page opposite the dedication, in Tempo, bold small capitals. Camus. "There is only one liberty, to come to terms with death. After which, everything is possible." His voice soft, Jerry read it aloud. When he finished, the words remained in the room.

He looked around at the bare walls, the matched Persian carpets, the colonial cane furniture he'd brought here. The fireplace he never used. Her painting above it: soft-bodied women in groups, bleak, with hollow mouths and weak orange hair. Christ, he thought. Christ. It was true. Everything was water if you looked long enough.

—Sorry to bother you, General Cornelius, but New Olgayte is bombing us again.

—Where the hell is New Olgayte?

—That new South American republic, sir. The one—

—Oh, them. Again! With our own goddamn bombs, I suppose.

—Yes sir. What should we do, sir?

—Do? Don't be an ass, Brunner, you know we can't do anything. They'll get tired and stop eventually. More likely run out of missiles in an hour or so, anyhow.

—They've wiped out Denver, Louisiana's hit bad. Most of the Midwest. Mexico too, but we think that was a miscalculation.

—You've got to admire the little bastards.

—Yes sir.

Jerry was walking through the Mashhad streets, his light-weight black boots pushing through mud and garbage, fine black hair flapping behind him like a tiny cape. He was wearing a scarlet Edwardian suit that made his face look even paler than usual. He hadn't eaten for weeks, and was thinning back down from the influence of General Lee's rich food and drink.

The architecture here—baroque cotyledon pods looped and grooved with gold, occasional jade, makeshift concrete bunkers left from the war and taken over by the new government, wooden-slat houses—suited Jerry's mood perfectly. It was March, it had been raining for five days, and now it was very hot. Sweat gathered in Jerry's thick eyebrows, ran down his back inside the clothing. It collected, also, in his rough new mariner's beard. He took the clay pipe out of his mouth in sudden disgust and threw it onto the street, then immediately wished he hadn't. The smell was terrible.

The markets were closed and no one else was about. A pack of dogs came out of one of the houses, spotted Jerry, and went running off together down the street away from him; only one stayed behind, nuzzling at the garbage and snorting as water went up its nose. One of its legs was chewed almost to the bone. Jerry had been locked away inside his house for some time. He had no way of knowing why the people had left the city—or, indeed, if they all had. He noticed that there were no flies. On one of the bunkers a wet flag sagged against the pole. Like the buildings it was curiously hybrid, stillborn. In the center of a grass-green field an orange lion stood facing left, a sword in its paw. Yellow words in Farsi—probably a Sunni slogan—spilled from its mouth. Behind it, a fierce red sun emblem raged, diminishing the rest.

Jerry passed close to a doorway and felt a pressure on his shoulder. He looked down and saw a ruined brown hand, looked back up and saw an old woman standing there. Her teeth were gone, the lips and skin around them little more than loose, leather-like flaps. She had been fat once, but now there was no flesh under the skin, and it had fallen into sags, slack and baggy like ancient breasts, covering her face. Which was probably just as well. He shouldn't have liked to see what was in that face. One ear was torn off, the eye on the same side half-closed and running; the thick gray fluid had dried in several of the creases down that side of her face, weeks or months old. The bones were bending, fusing, pulling the body in toward them. She was naked, and her hand trembled on Jerry's shoulder. Even in the garbage-filled street, she stank.

"Jerry," the old woman said. She spoke in Kurdish. "Don't you know me?" He could barely make out the words—pick them out of the mumbling—but he knew. Her hair was still violent red.

"Miss Brunner! Why, I haven't seen you since—"

"No. You haven't." She pulled the hand away and it fell limply to her side. She raised her head, and that seemed to take all the strength she had left. "I've missed you, Jerry."

"Aristophanes and all that?"

"*Like* that, yes. I've changed, haven't I, Jerry?"

Jerry was full—of contempt or impatience, he wasn't sure which.

"Not significantly, Miss Brunner." Contempt, then.

"Ah, but I have, Jerry, and so have the times. Things get back to normal so quickly."

"Normal? My God "

"Change requires death and destruction, Jerry. And change is normal."

"'We are conceived in our conceits.'" Jerry shook his head. "No. You haven't changed. That's the same old Miss Brunner saying that."

Suddenly she stood up straight and almost made a smile out of the flaps of skin around her mouth. "We stopped too soon, Mr. Cornelius."

"We didn't stop, Miss Brunner. We were stopped."

She collapsed again, her arms hanging out in front of the stooped body. She looked down and closed her eyes. Finally she said, "In the East. It was the East, wasn't it, Jerry? They stopped us in the East."

"Kuwait."

She was quiet for several minutes. The dog started hesitantly toward them and Jerry kicked out at it, spattering muck against its side. It turned and ran away, limping and, a little farther on, falling. It didn't get back up. Jerry could hear it whimpering.

"Have you read Firbank, Miss Brunner?" he said, impulsively. "Firbank feared that serious talk would always become sober tosh. Firbank was right."

"There is a word . . ."

"Rodomontade. There are always words, Miss Brunner."

"Yes."

"We should have that one tattooed on our chests."

He turned and started away but the hand, somehow, managed to find his shoulder again.

"Jerry. I've missed you, Jerry. Where are you staying?"

He grinned. "Hilton."

She shrugged her body down out of the doorway into the street. He thought for a moment she was going to fall, like the dog.

"That's a lie, Jerry." She stared away from him down the street.

"Yes. Of course."

She began to walk away, ponderously dragging her feet through the clogged, clotted streets, dragging the legs and then the body above them. She would die, he thought, unless she found someone soon.

"Good-bye, Miss Brunner."

"It's 'Mrs.' now. Good-bye, Mr. Cornelius."

Jerry stood watching her walk away. She reached a corner and turned, staggering against one of the bunkers. She rested a few seconds, then pushed herself back upright and went on. Jerry realized he was muttering to himself—

> Out of the ash
> I rise with my red hair
> And I eat men like air.

He shivered, and a tear ran down the crease of his cheek into the corner of his mouth. He reached up and brushed the hair back away from his face, felt the wetness on his fingertips now. He went over to the whimpering dog, raised a foot, and crushed its skull with the heel of his boot. It never moved.

The next day, he left the city.

He searched the house methodically. He went through every drawer, every cupboard, gutted all the furniture. He opened the back of the toilet and let out the water. He pulled off ventilators. He climbed to look down into light fixtures. He rapped on the walls, the floor. He took the tops off the stairs. He blew both safes—nothing but gold. He looked up the chimney—never used. He paced off the floors, walked outside and paced along the sides of the house. Nothing.

It wasn't here.

The floor was already covered with stuffing, rattling paper, splinters and slabs of wood, bricks, plaster. Furious, he tore the colonial cane furniture apart and threw it across the room. He ripped up the rugs with a knife from the kitchen. He dumped the books onto the floor and smashed the bookcase against a wall. After that it was more difficult, but he did what he could.

Finally he stood at the door and looked back, pleased.

There. That would give the bastard something to think about.

He was going to die.

There was a cable waiting for him when he reached his house off Holland Park Avenue. There were also quite a lot of newspapers. He caught a glimpse of the headline on top of the four-foot stack, a *Daily Mail*: SADISTIC SKIPPER DROWNS PARROT. Chuckling, he opened the yellow envelope.

He had cabled, "What is the exact nature of the catastrophe. Don't know. Don't know. Back soon." And Michael answered, *Another collaboration, Jerry? I love you. I miss you.*

Another collaboration . . . yes. But with whom—Michael? There wasn't enough of Michael left. Miss Brunner? He didn't know where she was, even if she was alive, after Kuwait. The General, the girl?

Then he noticed the last line of Michael's cable. *Come home. I fear for your life, Jerry.* He went inside and began to laugh, and went on laughing, wildly, beyond control—then collapsed among the wreckage, still laughing, rolled over and passed out.

They lay side by side, on their backs, in the bed. His heart beat irregularly; he put his hand over it and watched the fingers being pushed away from his chest. The fingers were pleasantly thin.

Aside from the bed, a framework of hollow brass tubing and a mattress, there were only two low bamboo tables in the room. On one of them lay a small two-stringed instrument with a gourd body. On the other there were teacups without handles which would fit perfectly inside cupped hands, an alcohol burner, a loaf of rice cake. The windows were bare. Outside, a tear-shaped . . . kite. That was the word. (The aphasia again?) A tear-shaped white kite with a short white tail drifted steadily, slowly, across the cloudless sky. The afternoon sun showed on the side of one sill and the wall opposite. Outside, it would be hot; here everything was cool, even her body beside him.

"You're rather sentimental, Mr. Cornelius."

"Yes, I know. Hell, isn't it?"

He reached out, very gently, and touched the bruise on her thigh, laying two fingers on the aureola. (He was amazed at his capacity for tenderness now, this moment.) It was beautiful. Almost perfectly round. There were three distinct colors, with bits of rainbow hue between them. The center very small, a spot of deep blue the size of the pupil of an eye and almost as dark; then the aureola of purple-brown, like another color for skin; a narrow penumbra outside, brown becoming yellow—and then the smooth whiteness of her skin. Her body was familiar to him, painfully so.

"You don't mind, then?" he asked.

She sat up and tossed the short brown hair back away from her face. Her eyes, too, were brown. Her breasts were so small they hardly moved; they were little more than the large, still puckered nipples. Her stomach rubbed against her thighs as she shook her head.

"Names don't matter, Mr. Cornelius. They are only words, they mean nothing. Only gestures matter, between people." She watched the kite as it began to bounce, riding the corridors of wind. "My last . . . the last man I was with. He would have me take emetics before sex. When I climaxed—" She looked back at Jerry and grinned. "And sometimes he would join me."

"Without benefit of the emetics, I suppose?"

"Yes." She touched his hand, which still lay gently across the bruise. "He put that there, at first. But I thought it was beautiful, and I wanted to keep it. Every few days it begins to fade and then I—"

"This man. It was in London? I think I know him."

"I believe you do." She rolled to get a joint and Jerry's hand slid off her leg. The breeze was steady now. The kite throbbed on its string, a cloud behind it. It began to rain, and the kite struggled as it was pulled toward the ground. Rain spattered on the sill. Jerry lay quietly for several minutes and watched the rain, the new water. The girl sat beside him smoking. Hash, from the smell. He studied the casual white symmetry of her back, amazed at it.

"Words," he said after a while. "Mallarme said that poetry was made from words, not ideas."

"It would take a Frenchman to say that. But I didn't think anyone used French anymore."

"I've been to America," Jerry said. "Louisiana. And long before that . . ."

She waited for him to go on. When he didn't, she took the last drags of the hash into her lungs, held them, and said, "At any rate, it's true." She exhaled, coughing slightly, then rolled on her buttocks and took a meerschaum-colored ceramic ashtray off the floor. She stubbed the cigarette out with deliberate concentration, squeezing the filter together and pushing down till the end crumpled like a drinking-straw wrapper. When she took her hand away, the end was smashed into the ashtray, the rest angled, tip tilted thirty degrees or so up from the bottom. (The associations, Jerry thought. They're starting again.) The filter was oval now, and there was a thin line of stain across it. It looked like a tiny mouth, precise and perfect as the fingernails of a newborn child. The kite was gone from the window.

"Do you know the work of Miroslav Holub, Mr. Cornelius? He is a countryman of mine, a Czech. In 'The Root of the Matter' he wrote:

> There is poetry in everything. That
> is the biggest argument
> against poetry."

"No. The Russians . . ."

"Yes. The Russians. I suppose the world hated us for that. Still, we had much to lose, either way. We cannot all be as fortunate as the Americans; we can't all remain neutral."

"The world recovered, dear. The world always recovers. It has an amazing capacity for muddling on through." Enough, then, of that. Jerry got up and began to dress. He noticed a tiny red sore, an eruption, like a pimple, on his penis. He shrugged and pulled on the scarlet suit, sat on the bed and pushed his feet into the boots, still filthy from Mashhad. He stood and turned back to the girl.

"I'll find him in London, then?"

She nodded.

"Why are you telling me this?"

She paused, her pale face tilted to one side, staring at him. The nipples were relaxed now, small orange cylinders against her flat chest. The lipstick glistened slightly. "Perhaps . . . perhaps it is because I am sentimental too, Mr. Cornelius."

Jerry went across the room and opened the door. "I'll see you again. Soon."

She smiled. "Be discreet, Mr. Cornelius."

"Thank you, but I'd rather be dead."

"Good-bye then, Mr. Cornelius."

Jerry went out, closing the door gently behind him. Out into the rain. Where the thin fabric was soon soaked and it looked like blood.

The door was heavy teak. Grooves had been cut into it and filled with bronze, resembling the whorls and veins of various leaves. When he knocked, it opened and a slender, tall man stood there blinking. The room was dark behind him, dark and warm. He wore scarlet trousers and a bright yellow shirt. The top button was undone, the broad flowered tie tugged partly away from his neck. His black hair was fine, falling onto his shoulders. His face was pale, his mouth ascetic.

"You're Cornelius?" He pushed his way in and shut the door. The man backed quietly away and made no move to resist.

"Yes . . ." Then he smiled and said, "I've been expecting you." He raised his hand and pushed the hair together behind his neck. It had just been washed; it was still a bit wet and stood slightly out from his head. There was a copy of *Farewell, My Lovely* spread open, face down, on the bed. The pillow was damp where his head had been, the orange bedspread vaguely hollowed from his body.

"Yes, I suppose you have, haven't you." He took the revolver out of his pocket. It was American make, a .32 built on a .45 frame, the only one of its kind.

"I see you found your gun."

Yes, he had, finally, in an empty house in Mashhad. After a great deal of searching.

"And you didn't."

Instinctively, the man backed against the desk.

"Justice," Jerry said, very slowly. "Freedom. Truth. Love." With each word he moved his finger gently against the hair-trigger and the other's body jerked back against the desk, his back arching, as the bullets slapped into him and their soft heads spread like tiny hands across his skin and penetrated.

"Words—" he said, and died for them. His body rolled and fell forward onto the desk, then slid slowly backwards off it. He dropped onto the floor, sat there looking at the window with dim eyes, and finally collapsed against the side of the desk. Very slowly, his shoulder moved toward the corner, downwards, into open space.

His head dragged against the edge of the desktop, bent without resistance, and he hit the floor, lying halfway under the desk, staring up at it.

Jerry went over and looked at him for the last time, then reached down and closed his eyes. There was chewing gum stuck all over the bottom of the desktop. Things were back to normal.

Jerry looked around. Nothing else in the room but the book and the coat that matched the trousers. It was hung on the back of a reading chair. He walked over and checked the pockets, taking out the safe passage stamped *Republic of Vietnam* and signed *General Lee*, which was all they contained. There was probably money and identification in the trousers, but Jerry had no use for either.

"Good-bye, Mr. Cornelius," he said. He supposed it was bound to happen sooner or later. He went into the hall and shut the door behind him. It was like advancing to the next chamber of a nautilus. The lights were very bright.

"'I fear those big words which make us so unhappy,'" Jerry said for the dead man.

There was one thing remaining.

Jerry returned to his house off Holland Park Avenue and searched through the rubble and mess the dead man had left behind. Finally he found it at the bottom of a heap of papers and stuffing. He threw it into the fireplace, piling loose paper and stuffing on top of it—madly, frenzied—until the fireplace was filled. Then he struck a match, held it a moment and tossed it in. The pile caught at once, bursting into flame with a sound like that of the wind, expanding, all the bits exploding away from one another.

Jerry stood watching. Balls of burning paper and cotton wool rolled out into the room and he kicked them back. The flames, the poems, rose gently into the chimney.

That night Jerry dreamed of the burning city. Buildings tumbled back into themselves, pushing the flames higher through the empty corridors; people stood still in the harbor and stared; bodies and rubble and refuse drifted on the black waters toward him; and then there was only the fire, in the water, in the buildings—only the flames. But the woman and the child were no longer there inside them, and he wasn't sure now what the flames meant.

By morning American planes were overhead. The bombs falling slowly, slowly, tumbling down into London . . .

When the first ones struck, Jerry was thinking of the girl, the kite, the fingernails of a newborn child.

MARROW

(*Il fait beau*, the sea is calm. Earlier, snow was falling, *dans la mer*. To vanish. The ocean taller in its coffin, rising. A few single notes, and the air sustains them—fall of snow falling, no girl for my arms. Gulls tiptoe along the railing. Want to be skua searching the Arctic, white across miles and miles of white tundra, human heads to defecate on. They are riding with the ship to America: immigrants with tiny passports tucked beneath their wings. After disgorging us, the ship is scheduled to return the Statue of Liberty to France; and perhaps, disillusioned, disheartened and disappointed, a few of the gulls, a few friendly pigeons, will return as well. Now the holds are closed on thousands of copies of old *Encounters*. Ballast. And behind us, in London, the bear and deer are moving slowly inward toward the heart of the city.

I am talking to an Indian woman; her clothes stitched full of mirrors, returning a sense of separate selves. Each tiny mirror lightly tinted, each a different color. She is smoking a pastel-orange cigarette, the base of her fingers imbedded in a ruby, holes drilled through to form a ring. Smoke now, like a momentary veil among her fingers. My breath on the glass. Gray in the gray of mirrors, and the green of the sea. While round and round the deck rides a cripple, shouting military commands. His legs are missing from the knees down, and the pedals of his bicycle are fitted with clamps into which the tips of his crutches are inserted, then strapped. He has been cycling around the deck since I boarded at Southampton. It's a child's bicycle. Just the steady thrust and drag of his shoulders against the crutches, and the shouts. The chest of a wrestler. And my breath in the mirrors.

—And your father?

—Yes. Military adviser after he was captured by our troops. He was much respected.

—A prisoner of war.

—Yes . . . that, at least.

I break off conversation and a solitary gull falls quietly into the sea from the top of the mast; seconds later, a melancholy cry, as another plunges after it. The two white bodies float peacefully together on the surface of the water, gently moving away from one another in the wake of the ship. Her hip against the railings.

—I'll see you for dinner, I say. Though I won't. And I have never seen her in the dining hall.

Perhaps she eats alone in her room; there is some religious, possibly a medical reason, for this; that I am intruding? On her privacy, her faith.

She smiles, and the pale cigarette goes over the railing. The ring moves slightly along her fingers toward the knuckles and settles back as she raises her hand, slides it once across the space between our eyes; a cutting edge of softness.

—I am afraid I must dine with my husband. To see then my confusion: she moves her hand toward the cyclist, who is just now coming into sight around the contoured corner of the deck. That curves, like the thickest part of a bird's wing.

—But he . . .

—Yes. He is like that. A man full of power.

I realize now how loosely her gown fits her, that the ring at one time would not have moved on her fingers but fit them perfectly. I smile and start away as she lights another cigarette, this one ochre. And then in the hallway outside my room, to stop and read the letter again.

J,

I received your gift this morning. Something of a shock, but a welcome one. And lovely. I suppose this letter will finally find you in some country neither of us had ever heard of—if it finds you at all, if the postal services are indeed still functioning, as they say—and I hope you find what you need there, or have found it already. *I* was never able to discover what it was—I realized that this morning, sitting in the early light, pressing your gift against my cheek—and for that I'm sorry. Perhaps, in time, you will be more fortunate. Probably.

It's gone terribly cold now. Clouds with horrible bloated

bellies. All the surrenders to a winter that's finally come. I sit and listen to the grass that grows inside the walls. I found a shirt of yours today in one of the cupboards.

C'est la calme qui m'étonne. So here I am. With nostalgia, for the comfort of lies.

I keep remembering something you once said, about the bones, "my little monument not quite complete."

That's what we all are, isn't it? Monuments not quite complete.

Me

The room is hot and dark, but empty. I take off my clothes and lie on the top bunk, staring up at a faultless steel ceiling. I think of the woman standing up there above me, waiting. What color cigarette would she be smoking now? Violet. Like her eyes. Lanterns. She would have turned a little further toward the rail. And others—others would be talking to her now. And all the time that little man going round and round on his cycle. And gulls, dropping off the mast, one by one, alone and in pairs. I look for a moment at my white suit hanging strangely on the back of the door, so light that it moves gently, rippling, in the air that issues from the grill close to the floor beside it, below the dressing mirror.

I lift my arm and the stump extends an inch above the buttoned sleeve, as though severed by the light from the window. *La main coupée.* I raise the other and put it behind, to pretend the hand is still there. And move the fingers, light glinting in the rings which cover each one. *Je suis l'homme qui n'a plus de passé,* I say quietly. I am the man with no more past. And laugh, at what follows.

We're a hundred miles out from New Orleans, where the statue lies waiting. Through the porthole I see even now the first signs of land—birds, shaped clouds, a ship—and hear the boat just beginning to lug in the backwash. After a while I get down and open the cupboard by the mirror. Far off there is the sound of a foghorn, like the cry of one enormous gull. I take out the small metal case and slowly begin to assemble what it contains.)

RÉCITS

I used to live with a woman who looked like you. She had large breasts that hung down and rolled across the top of her stomach and she always supported them, the weight of them, with the flat of her arms, hugging herself like a toy bear. Her teeth were even, like tiny ceramic tiles, the color of milky amber. Getting in, out of bed she always kept her legs together.

Afterwards the room seemed so much . . . larger. As I stood looking at the closed door. I was aware for the first time of the space between things.

Her proportions were always astounding; each day, I discovered them as though for the first time. Her buttocks, the short firmness of her legs, the shallow back and small shelf there—these were not the ones expected, my wife's. They startled.

She disliked my smoking in bed. So afterwards, I would sit in the chair across the room by the window, watching her. The electric heater glowed against the wall and sparkled when I lit cigarettes off it. She wore shiny, round-toed shoes, wrinkled on the top, with buckle-straps going across. And tights, always—I never saw her without tights.

At two or three we would reach up in the dark and it was like shutting doors. I would lie watching her dress, then dress myself. Walk four blocks and find a cab. Back to her husband, who wouldn't ask questions. On the street: You don't take care of yourself, you know. On the street: I'm an abstraction, to you, I could be anyone. I am woman. The thing—perhaps even the quality.

When she was gone, the knives would come out of the mirror like sharks.

Some of us who come to London never drink coffee again.

We are sitting in a Lyons, having tea in the middle of the morning. Somehow (the way I chew my toast?) the talk has got onto the subject of camels.

"One hump or two?"

You will want to know
how I am making
out here in this
city of penetrating light.
I should write you letters
explaining that I am in
fact doing well; how pleasant
it is here, how good jobs
are easily come by, how
beautiful the children are.

These letters would make
you smile, know how I miss
you, make you go look
out your window and looking
for men. In your hands,
with all the scribbling
and erasure, my pressured
hand, they would have
the texture of lettuce leaves.

When we make love she turns her face to the wall, where
blond and gray stripes resemble an abstract cypress forest. She
puts a knuckle in her mouth, hears my watch ticking by her ear.
The heater glows against the wall. Only in the final moments
does she turn her face up and open her eyes, watching me.
There is a spring coming up through the sheet. And then she
says Hmmmm.

Later, we fold a torn sheet several times and lay it like a bandage,
a compress, over the spring.

PS Indubitably.

Locust husks! Summers (he thinks it was summers) they'd hang
askew all over trees, fences, even the side of the house. Light and
fragile as fallen leaves, dead spurs caught in the bark, burst in a split
along the back. He collected them; he remembers one summer when

a whole wall of his room was covered with them. Lined perfectly, all climbing upward, row by row.

Also: figs, fireflies searching for an honest man, the red veins in shrimp.

1. What is the exact nature of their relationship?
   Changeable.
   Is there a word?
   Weighty.

   And is he weary?
   Yes.

   Of?
   Explanations, digressions, rationalizations, endless nights of discussion—what should she do?

2. A quality of hers: to live in a maze of possibilities.
   A quality of his: to accept as what he *can* occur, only that which *does* occur.
   The first allows great freedom of movement and excludes responsibility; the second, similarly, makes guilt impossible. More and more, it is this that sustains him.

3. Him, aware of himself—and her, of him moving within her.
   He has said in his allusive way that together they are long-legged flies. He tries to explain country music to her.
   Finally, as so many times before, he falls back to Creeley: "It is only in the relationships men manage, that they live at all."

4. Where does it end?
   On the 52 bus, halfway between Notting Hill Gate and Marble Arch.

Were there prior signals?
Cabs, for them, assumed a large importance. They began
to read the names on bus panels and wonder about those
places, where they might be.

How did it end?
In argument over the respective merits of various
shampoos.

—Across this page of his notebook (as well as many others, and all
the poems) he has scrawled *HA* a number of times, *H* rolling lightly
like a valley into the *A*'s hill.

They trade stories about shells.
   She used to find in the Florida ocean, floating branches which,
removed, proved to be covered with clam shells, tiny and white and
perfect as teeth.
   He once came across a huge pile of shells on the bank of a bay.
Chalky white and crunching to bits when he walked into them.
Bending to look closer, he discovered that each shell was punched
full of round, button-sized holes; what remained were the narrow
spaces around the holes, looking like a patchwork of nose septums.

PS I love you.
PS I miss you.
PS I enjoy mispelling and singing.

She swears that roaches live in the Swiss cheese at this delicatessen;
you can see their heads popping out on the hour for a look 'round.
At night they chew the soft cheese like the wax in your ears. She
points out how very much this cheese resembles sponge—and how
roaches, like many deep-sea fish, haven't changed in thousands of
years. But he doesn't believe her.

He was ill. She learned this from friends and came walking down
Portobello Road with cheese and apple juice early one morning.
That was the first time they tried to end it.

• • •

He has said: It's your freedom makes me do this.
And she: You contain me.

He has a knack for aphorism and she, for conjuring disappointment. Often, sitting beside her, he feels he has been in some
obscure way defeated. Her preparation of meals for him, or his
for her, has somehow come to be like the running-up of flags.
Each morning she goes and brings him things: food, cigarettes,
soup, soap, shower attachments. You don't take care of yourself,
she says.

At night, in the dark room, they open doors to a few more
monads; advance to the next chamber of the nautilus. He begins to
perceive new relationships everywhere. An evening sky is the color
of kazoos, his brown shoes on the floor are abandoned tanks.

He asks her, What do penises look like? And she answers: mushrooms. One of his favorite foods.

Later she is asleep and he suddenly exclaims, The fish are not
afraid!

She starts awake and when he repeats it, this delights her. But he
didn't want to repeat it.

—They are in the cab.
They are going home.

—He to his, her to hers.
With?

—Platitudes, gratitudes.
But the age demands an image.

—True.
Well?

Days later: "The residue of each in all the others." A warm day, with
pigeons in the corners, and rain.

• • •

PS I got your letter today and will write again when I can.

I shall answer rage with outrage; expect you to collect my words in little wood boxes of parsley or sawdust; require that you follow behind, obligatto? No.

Outside, standing by the cab, I hear his shouts, the clatter of things thrown at the floor. The driver and I talk about last night's rain; how it took him two hours to cross town, generally a fifteen-minute trip; how he got a fare to Brighton, ten quid. You come out the door when streetlights are turning from orange to yellow, you are wearing your cantaloupe-color coat, the cab's blue light glints in your glasses.

Now, in the cab, you begin to talk.

"Selling pieces of my life. Am being, in a sense, auctioned off—but this is of course no truer for me than for others. Just that my bids are recorded.

"Publishers, contracts, agents, a grant here, a fellowship there, royalty statements, letters; half for my wife, son, friends.

"There is ten percent left. That, I offer to you."

My speech, too much used: Je me retournerai souvent.

Memory is a hunting horn
It dies along the wind

Books, papers and typewriter, flowers in a beer bottle—on his desk.

For him: the texture of the moment, objects in disarray.

For her: a pattern of abstractions.

"I think my period is starting, you may get blood on you."

"That's fine."

"I didn't know. Whether it would matter."

Later, waking in the night, he realizes how participation in the present is always diluted—by memory, by anticipation. He resents this. Against the window and light outside, the flowers are transformed. He is becoming confused. He is terrified of hurting her.

• • •

Believe, please, that I understand and appreciate your concern but feel it, upon this occasion, somewhat a waste. By actual count there were fifty-seven people directly concerned with my affairs yesterday; and from every indication the number has risen considerably today.

At the top of this page you'll find a small rendering of two cows facing one another across a field of watercress; this is in the nature of a bonus, on your stock in me.

PS All the flagpoles have bloomed to flowers. The air smells of eggshells and coffee grounds. There are meringue nativity scenes in all the eggshells. I am yours.

"The goddamn hot-water heater only heats three cups of water at a time."
"Yeah."

Things in the world: a series. A drawing.
  1. Mozart
  2. Watermelon
  3. Oil derricks
  4. Puce
  5. Drambuie

Why, he asks, this urge toward capitalization?

She wants to answer but all she can think is *epithesis*—a nonce word. He gives her *micturation* in return and for days, at every opportunity, they are rehearsing one another's words. They often make these trades.

Smoking American cigarettes in London. A bit of chauvinism to contrast his adoption of a British accent, British clothes, British mannerisms, always saying "Sorry." (When she brings an American penny out of her purse he laughs; dollars, though, he can still accept as authentic, unsuspect.) Five bob a pack: made in Switzerland under American license. To buy them he puts on his best voice, assumes a business air, gets it over with as quickly as possible. He is embarrassed; she loves it.

She begins to recognize lines from Creeley.

> Love comes quietly,
> finally, drops
> about me, on me,
> in the old ways.
>
> What did I know
> thinking myself
> able to go
> alone all the way.

Or:
> Everything is water
> if you look long enough.

His favorite:

> What
> has happened makes
>
> the world.
> Live
> on the edge,
>
> looking.

Conversation becomes for them a kind of verbal semaphore. Sentences need never be finished. A word, a pause—and the other is smiling, responding, thoughtful. Perhaps the sentences *couldn't* be completed; perhaps they were begun—formed—in this certainty of communication. Sometimes she wonders. She considers holding back her response, to see.

• • •

Toys.

As a child she slept in a bed full of stuffed animals, contorting herself to fit in among them. He once began a poem: We lie down, the menagerie invades our bed.

She doesn't know about gigging frogs, so he tells her. The miniature trident; how he went gigging toads when he was ten, not knowing the difference; how difficult it is to kill a toad (one, he stabbed fifteen times). Then he explains how you can milk a toad using two matchsticks, something his grandmother taught him. She used to find frogs the size of her thumbnail in her backyard in Florida; sometimes they would cover entire limbs. Once, his lawn mower turned up a nest of baby rattlers.

Finally he remembers the plastic cow. It had a balloon udder you could fill and milk. The teats, bucket and tail (which worked the udder) were white. The rest of the cow was brown.

More and more, the word *guilt* enters his conversation.

Outside, it is getting dark.

Like a marble trapped in a single chute he slides back and forth through the hall between his rooms. Kitchen: milk bottles lined on the floor in one corner, apples and cheese on the table; teapot, strainer, cups and bags, all used, in the sink. Sleeping room: flowers (tulips) in a cup on the desk, returnable bottles stacked like wine bottles (a honeycomb) in the cupboard. Window obscured in a haze of blue lingerie-curtain. On a trunk, two small brass sculptures from a series called *Joy of the Unborn*. They are fetuses entangled in their cords.

As he walks back and forth—pouring beers down the drain, poking at the tea machinery with two fingers—someone traces his steps in the room overhead. Heads and shoulders cant out of windows across the street. Across the street a man stands poking at his belly in the mirror.

Night is falling, filling: he tries various phrases, like strings across his tongue, and abandons them, standing by the window finally, speechless.

The doctor, a woman, Pakistani, arrives and asks what he's on: Meth, pep pills ... There are several in her list that he's not heard of. Taking his pulse, she pulls his arm down and glances at the inside of his elbow.

One morning when it is raining a letter arrives. He wonders, Did he know she would write it? Has he been expecting this letter? Her name is typed in the corner, with a brown ribbon.

By the time he gets it back to his room there are spots all over it from the rain, like an unevenly ripe fruit. He props it against the bottle of flowers while he changes clothes, hanging the damp ones on a chair in front of the electric heater. Then he makes tea and sits on the bed to read the letter.

It is badly typed, on blue paper. There are many x-ings out; words break off arbitrarily at the right edge of the page and continue a full inch-and-a-half from the left on the line below. This is the first writing of hers he has seen and he looks over the page with interest, thinking how strangely this refutes her general sense of form and order, how easily the typewriter has confounded her.

Her signature is in pencil at the bottom of the second page—a row of bold printed letters, lightly connected—and he quickly turns to see what remains on the last page. It is half-filled with PSs

1. The sky is bruised with light.
2. I have to save us from abstraction.
3. The knives come out of the mirror like sharks.

Can one's obsessive guilt be cancelled by another's innocence?

He thinks so; he tries.

What qualities does she find common in him and her husband?

A certain shyness, which leads him to such ends as falling off chairs to gain attention; a precise inability to mount stairs; in bed, preoccupation with the cleft between her buttocks; a penchant for leaping through the barriers between rooms.

And he, in her and the other?

The sound of their breath in the dark.

How much has he predicted, to himself?

All but the end. That, like regret, would be against his nature.
Lying here now in the dawn, alone, how does he see the city?

As a thing composed of pale, obscene, gone-off neons. Water trucks sailing slowly down the streets. Milk carts gliding and jangling down the streets. And cats. Cats walk along the sidewalk beside them in utter silence.

DOUCEMENT, S'IL VOUS PLAIT

They're forwarding me on to Versailles now. At least I think it's Versailles. I watched the postman's lips as he readdressed me, concentrated on the stammering pressure of the pen as it darted across my face—the *a*'s and *e*'s, unaccountably, in small capitals, the rest properly in lower case—and tried to ignore, to block out, *faire taire*, the dragging accompaniment from the side of his hand. And I think the word he printed, with his felt-tip pen, was V*ersailles*. I felt the four strokes of the *V* and *l*'s quite distinctly; they were rapid, hard. That I am being forwarded is certain, for I saw the stamp descending like a dark sky and was able to read quickly, and backwards through the smear of ink before it moved away, leaving my eyes blotched with black, the words *priére de faire*. And if the next were *renvoyer*, there would have been no need for the postman's pen, for the additional letters among which I was able to discern only (I think) the single word *Versailles*; a simple circling, an arrow, should have been sufficient to send me on my way back to 1, Petherton Court, Tiverton Road. It must have been, then, *suivre*. So at least, for another day, another few weeks, perhaps my abiding fear—that I bear no return address and will end among the dead letters—this fear is allayed.

I am dropped from a box into a hot canvas bag. The smell of paste and ink, of dry saliva and, somewhere deep inside us, perfume. Apparently, while sleeping I have gone astray and been returned—to travel to some scrawled new address, to be set aside for inspection and at last referred back—to the post office collection box. It was the shock of falling through the slot onto hard edges and sharp corners, no doubt, that awakened me. The other letters will have nothing to do with me; they sense difference. And their language is unfamiliar now. Something guttural, that might be German. My questions go unanswered. Deep in the canvas (the perfume?) I can hear a British accent, a soft weeping, but am unable to make out the words.

• • •

I wait in a cold hall, propped against the frosted mirror of an ancient oak wardrobe near the door, for a week before someone finally scribbles *Not at this address* in a cramped, small hand, afterwards retracing several of the letters and scoring beneath them, four heavy lines which feel at first like rips then like deep bruises, and drops me in the corner mailbox on his way somewhere. The mailbox is round. British.

Why do they move about so much? How are they able; where does she get the money? And is there the faintest remain of a familiar perfume in this box . . .

I am being forwarded again. I have no idea where.

It is Christmas, I think, and I am lost in the deluge of mail. Crushed with parcels, shuffled like a card but never dealt. High in my solitary forgotten pigeonhole now, I observe the functioning of our postal service. It never before occurred to me how astounding, what an efficient, essential instrument of society, this service is. Or the complex problems dealt with each day as little more, actually, than part of the routine. I watch with fascination. Perhaps this is the work I was meant for.

I was a writer. More and more, my attention centered about the mail: my correspondence, the possible arrival of checks or hopeful word from my agents, rejected manuscripts that must be sent back out at once, copies of my books or magazines containing some small piece of mine, perhaps a foreign translation of something I'd done long ago and almost forgotten, packets of books about which publishers hoped I would be inclined to say something complimentary, a note of praise from some editor of a non-paying quarterly. The post was delivered twice daily, nine in the morning and just after noon. I would sit on the steps in the hall with a cup of tea, or the worst times, days I was definitely expecting something, with a drink, waiting. My wife and I got into shameful screaming fights over this, and once I struck one of the children who raced out of the flat before me and grabbed the mail from the postman's hands.

(I always waited, looking away, until he had deposited it in the box and left the building; then forced myself to walk slowly to it, whistling, and to every appearance completely uninterested. I believed that somehow this outward display of unconcern would influence what was there.) After we left the States and came to live in London, things became much worse, my expectations more desperate. And while my wife was conscientious about collecting it from the box, that having been done, mail lost all importance to her, as though for some reason she could not accept it as a real thing, part of the daily discourse of our lives. Forced to be away from the flat during the time of delivery, I would return to look hopelessly into the empty box, and then to spend untold minutes searching the flat—for she could never recall just what she had done with it. Often I would find an important letter leaning against a dirty cup among stacked lunch dishes, forgotten. Others would finally appear in my oldest son's wastebasket, the stamps having just been torn away for his collection. Generally, considerable portions of the message were torn away as well.

Faces bend down and leer at me where I lean in the boxes. Shade light from the small window with their hands so they can see my diagonal cutting through the stream of fluorescent light from behind. Breath frosts the glass. Finally I'm removed between two fingers, crushed with others in a gloved hand. The thumb of the glove is empty and flops against us.

Later a man stands over me. All the others have been opened. They are lying, torn and empty, at one side of this table, and he is turning me over and over again in one hand, mumbling to himself, a pink plastic letter opener in the other hand that I see periodically, rising jerkily toward me as though by its own will, then retreating again from sight. Minutes pass, and the next time the hand appears, the letter opener has been replaced by a pen; then a rapid scribbling. He puts me down, goes away. From beside me, among torn bodies, comes the scent of familiar perfume. It is fading.

It would seem that I am in Poland. Or perhaps Yugoslavia.

I always wanted to travel. Jane and I would lie for hours in bed with car lights sliding in sheets across the walls and ceiling and talk of all the places we should go—making plan after plan and abandoning each in turn, as some consideration of my work intervened. Departures were postponed time and again, applications for visas were canceled, passports expired. Jane collected a sizable library of travel guides, two cardboard boxes full of travel folders. She became well known in the lounges of airports, ticket agents, foreign consuls. Soon she read nothing else, thought of nothing else.

"How were the children today?"

"They were in Hawaii."

Other places.

They're forwarding me on to Rhodes now. Ailleurs. Gdzies. I have no idea where. And my sole, my only consolation, is that somewhere, at the end of all this, somewhere my wife and family wait to receive me. I imagine how they will discover me one morning on the floor by the door, beneath the mail slot—perhaps they will have heard the outside door, the brass lid swing shut as I'm pushed through, even the sound I make striking and sliding out onto tile or wood, a few inches—and how then they will prop me up lovingly on the table between them; between, perhaps, the cornflakes and Billy's strained fruit.

INSECT MEN OF BOSTON

Like a man at breakfast who looks up at his wife, Darling why is there a razorblade in my orange juice?

That wife on the living room floor with *The Times* spread out all around her. I just heard Beethoven's Pastoral Symphony on the radio he says, coming into the room, I cried.

"Penn Central is bankrupt."

"Why are they doing this to me?"

Communication then has again proved impossible oh well. I shall go for a ride on the bus he thinks into Roxbury. And wear a white sheet. Do we have any other kind. Will my body to the university hospital and if she wants me she'll have to go through seven years of medical school. I'll deny that I'm married to her. Say I don't know this woman. I think I've seen her in my building. I think I've seen her with a child. It was probably stolen. Why can't they just leave me alone.

He has a ham sandwich for lunch. There is no bread and he uses a bagel. She comes into the kitchen for coffee. She is on a diet and has been eating toothpaste again. You're disgusting she says. "Yes would you like to go to bed with me." And that was the last cup in the set. Oh well. He goes to the window and pushes her plants out.

She is taking a bath. Yesterday, driving back from Concord, they saw a Madonna standing up in a tub among trees. The whole thing was painted blue. Would you like me to read you something? "Hand me my comb the big one." He looks down at the pile of clothes she took off. No there's nothing he wants to wear.

She is doing a new painting. But the subject she's chosen, a huge bottle with ferns, is too large for the canvas. And she paints on the walls. One fern touches a window: she takes the brush away, to step back and look. He raises the window. She paints on the screen.

When she moves the canvas, ferns and leaves remain behind on the wall and screen. A friend has accepted the canvas (which has become a Madonna with child) as cancellation of a debt. The friend frequently brings people over now to "see the whole painting" or "experience the totality." She is generally working, since it is the weekend and this is her only free time, and he makes coffee for the friend and his companions (remember that this is *her* friend, not his, he hardly knows the man) while they sit with crossed legs discussing the relevance and impact of this temporal disruption. The tension generated in the suspension of time between seeing the canvas and this, the rest of the painting. A valid and heretofore insufficiently explored concept. One says. The friend manages this skillfully, often contriving to let them pass hours in aesthetic discussion before escorting them into her "studio" to reveal the rest of the painting. She has added apples and grapes to the limbs of the fern. References to Ovid are inevitable. So is running out of coffee. And the "fern" is becoming a mad horizontal tree. The friend has to move her aside to show his companions the rest of the painting. He is increasingly embarrassed, uncertain how much of the tree he may now fairly consider "his."

Why don't you ever write about me?

I write about your paintings don't I?

You can't write about paintings.

Of course I can. You're standing there. We've been married for six years. Your jeans are spattered with paint. It seems to be mostly green. Your hair is tied back out of your face. You're on a diet. You have two brushes in your hand, one wound in the last three fingers, I guess it's for detail, one between your finger and thumb. That's the one you're using now. You're not wearing shoes and you have on one of my T-shirts. Your breasts are hurting. You keep touching the left one with your hand. There are brown fingerprints all around it.

She drops the towel and begins flushing the toilet wildly, again and again.

What is your name? she asks. He shrugs and tries to cry, but he's forgotten how. They do *The Times* crossword together.

They go swimming. She looks like a turtle lying on the beach in the sun. Children are diving off the dam.

He meets her at the trolley stop and carries thirty pounds of mushrooms she bought at the Haymarket up the hill. She cuts off the stems and glues mushrooms all over the ceiling and walls of the bathroom.

What does this mean? he says. Holding a piece of bacon on a fork over the pan. Nude.

She stacks plums in the medicine cabinet. She puts her blond wig on a cauliflower. She stuffs the toilet full of spring onions and closes the lid. She fills the bathtub with small pieces of cardboard that say "Frog." The other rooms with popcorn.

Last night they went to a movie. It was a very bad movie called *Mainspring*. An inhabitant of which kept saying Why are you trying to kill me I've seen you in the other room waiting to kill me. As that inhabitant changed its diaper his child talked about thermodynamics. And in the dark he put his arm around her, touched her breast with his fingers.

I will put itching powder in her bra. I'll go out at night and make obscene phone calls to her. I'll put blood on the toilet seat.

She picked up his wallet and threw it out the open bedroom window. "Frisbeeeeeee."

When she finally came back he ignored her. She stood in doorways but he outwaited her. She took off her clothes and danced for him. She passed out on the floor in front of him. She put rubber bands around her breasts. She got a carrot from the kitchen and lay down on the couch, throwing one leg over the back. Hello he said.

What a sad thing, that tear in her pants. Where I could put a hand in her sleep now. Never know how kind I was.

She punches the paint out of the holes in the screen with a pin. It's Sunday.

As a man might say I've found relief here, a harbor.

"It was an accident," she said.

FREE TIME

Sometimes I become quite certain that I shall go mad from this preoccupation with women. The rest of me sink in this obsessed mind for good, as in a swamp. I'm passing a shop, a girl is looking into the shop window and I can think of nothing now but her legs and the way her skirt fits over her hips. Want to see her breasts. Will she turn and smile, caught a flash of thigh there, the top of stockings. Walk up the steps. Always so lonely here. And on the trolley devastated, a ruins, all these women I must watch. There doesn't seem to be anything else. Just have them smile for me, feel their skin. Lie by this one, hand on that bare waist. How gentle I would be. Whenever I was going, what I was doing. That doesn't matter now.

I can remember my father. He is coming up the stairs which lead down by stages from our yard here to the street far below. He is carrying something. A paper bag, under his arm. It was taped shut at the store and he has ripped open the side. A flapping, gaping dark gash. He is holding one of the beers in his hand, drinking it as he climbs. Toward me on my first real bicycle.

From my window here I see gulls that have wandered in from the harbor. They drag themselves along above trees, drop to the ground and try to understand what that is. Only once before, in London, have I seen gulls in the middle of a city like this.

At night I lie here listening to country music that comes up from the bar below my room. I've written a song:

I just kind of ran out
Of money and time and friends
And then I ran out
On you.

• • •

I work during the day, in a department store. At five I sit down with
mv first martini, away from the windows, and I sing that. Gulls pay
no attention, neon signs just go on flashing, traffic does not abate.

You used to meet me downstairs in the street after your Women's
Lib meeting. Sometimes I would wait for hours.
    I am reworking my destiny with a freedom, I said.
    But why do you want to make people ashamed of their existence?
    I'm sorry. But love is a process like decompression, for the diver.
    Like manumission for the slave.
    Who is always drowning.
    Or already drowned.
    And we would walk by the lake.
    "If two people love each other there can be no happy end to it."
    ... Yes you said.
    All my friends are killing themselves.
    You said: a boy I used to go with read about territorial impera-
tives. I came home late one night and there he was on my porch
pissing on the front door.
    Really, I said. They are.

With profits from my first book I had companies in all the major
cities print thousands of matchbooks with the words "Father where
are you?" and my phone number. These were distributed free
by diners and truck stops, newsstands, pipe shops, laundromats,
sporting goods stores. I got no reply.

_____ has always played a large role in my life. That is to say,
whatever I did, it was some memory or occasion of _____ against
which I measured it.

Finally, pushed to the wall, I quoted Jung.
    As a result of the ego's defective relation to the object—for a
will to command is not adaptation—a compensatory relation to
the object develops in the unconscious, which makes itself felt in

consciousness as an unconditional and irrepressible tie to the object. The more the ego seeks to secure every possible liberty, independence, superiority, and freedom from obligations, the deeper does it fall into the slavery of objective facts. The subject's freedom of mind is chained to an ignominious financial dependence, his unconcernedness of action suffers, now and again, a distressing collapse in the face of public opinion, his moral superiority gets swamped in inferior relationships, and his desire to dominate ends in a pitiful craving to be loved.

I went to see Marc in his hospital room. He hadn't done a very thorough job of it. Some broken bones, low on blood, collapsed lung, colitis. After three one would have thought serious tries. We watched TV on a set that hung from the ceiling.

Leaving the hospital and walking down Portobello Road, I saw a double pram on the pavement outside a shop. One child sat erect with a smile, banging two rattles together. The other had slumped forward on its face. A brightly colored arrow protruded from its back.

My father was not so much absent as irregular: from time to time he would appear with his bags newly covered in customs stamps and claim checks, and those times, for a week, two, a month, he might be with me every waking hour (I seem to recall there were even occasions upon which he came and lay beside me at night); but always would arrive the morning I woke to my mother telling me he was gone, and it then could be a year, or more, before I again saw him.

I have to confess, no, I really must tell you this, that I have no conscience in regard to posterity, absolutely none. For despite the most specific instructions from my translator, and I received a letter just this morning describing exactly what he wished and wished not, indeed would refuse, to see in my future work (I tacked it to the wall above the chair where I work), I go on letting these "stories," these things of mine, have their own way. (As I did, finally, you.)

• • •

My next book will be called *The Collected Love Poems of Adolph Hitler*. The one after that, *Krafft-Ebing I Love You*.

One memory of my mother. She is laughing with the rest at my father who is very drunk and men keep bringing her drinks.
   I am five, standing by the wall a room away, listening.

Last night I came home from work, set my martini alongside, and copied this into my notebook. From Cocteau:
   Sexual vice reflects one of the most intriguing forms of aesthetics.
   It is not from taste, as a collector might group furniture and fabrics, that this septuagenarian arranges the smallest details of the scenario without which he cannot satisfy his senses when daylight comes. If he disguises himself as a Louis XV soubrette, if he wears chains and submits to the insults of a telegraphist, and finally opens an obscene telegram signed by his daughter, this occurs after researches and obscure preparations which leave him no choice and end in a masquerade where his senses desperately construct an equivalent, more baroque, but in fact hardly less individual than any other, for beauty.

My strongest impressions are of my father sitting across the table with a book. I would look at him, his eyes would slide up from the page, he would smile. Then return to the book. One evening as he drank with my mother in the front room, I slipped into the study and examined the stack of books on the table beside his reading chair; I touched each title, mouthing the words to myself. *Traitor Within*, *The Cry for Help*, *Man Against Himself. Probleme des Selbstrmordes.* Each volume was a study of suicide.

JANE CRYING

This is my wife in the blue window crying. And my son in the room behind her playing with his Christmas toys. As you can see, she is wearing only a delicate yellow bra and even at this distance you can tell how soft and smooth her brown skin will be. When you touch it. That first time.

As I recall, we met while skydiving. I came out of the plane after her, fell free until I was just above the silk mushroom of her parachute, then pulled the cord of my own kit. I believe we discussed Kant on the way down. That is to say, the categorical imperative.

But she is not crying. She is laughing. They are all laughing. Jane, Pam, Barbara, Pat, Chris. They are all together in bed. Happy and laughing. They are drawing straws tonight. Pam draws the short one. The others use their own straws to tease her erogenous zones, of which she has more than her fair share. This is to excite her sexually. So she will be ready. When I come. At the height of her passion.

My wife is sitting in an expensive Danish chair. It is her parents' chair. In her parents' home. She is sitting before the fireplace in which they burned the gift wrappings last night but there's no fire now. Only the light on the snow. The light of the moon, a clean cold light. She is trying to keep from thinking about thinking about crying. About me.

For years then I didn't see her. Till one day, skindiving off Bermuda, and a shark approached. As we had been well taught, we swam together directly toward the shark and thumped it on the nose, whereupon it fled. Naturally this shared experience created an instant bond between us. She invited me to her cabana for a

JANE CRYING • 165

drink and we talked over old times. Later we dined together and she introduced me to my son. The following day we were married.

This is my wife at a party with someone. She is wearing a dazzling low-cut Neiman Marcus gown and has somehow contrived to have breasts. Her hair is blond and she is wearing a fall, piled and twined into an intricate coiffure atop her head. There are pink pearls resting against her skin, the soft brown skin at the base of her neck. She is smiling and slightly drunk on Brandy Alexanders. Perhaps this is not my wife at all.

Kate. Joanna. Hilary. Pam. Carol. Crystine. Renee. Wynn.
    56 Ridgemount Gardens. 141 East 13th. 6 rue de Tournon. 221 Camden High Street.
    Houston and Delancey. Cracow. Juarez. Harlem. Rio. Milford.

She hasn't heard from me for several years and received this morning a copy of *Certains*, a collection of poems written in French published last year in Paris and dedicated to her. *Á Jane, á jamais.* The first section is titled "Poésies pour la mort." She has been trying all day to read it. Now she is reading one of the books I gave her. *L'Écume des jours.* She reaches the end, cries, reads it again. She is reading the last chapter with her eyes closed. Tears are coming out from under the lids.

Marc. Gary. Ted. John. Terry. Andre. Marek. Bob.
    5430 Wateka Drive. 331 Harvard Street. 18 Orchard Street. 6918 Philadelphia Avenue.
    Dallas. Cambridge. Boston. Mexico City. Washington. Dallas.

Now she is crying because she is in a white gown at a wedding. Because we are being married again. My son is the best man.

She is crying again. Our son has left to find me. He believes I am in Paris and has flown there to bring me back. He is twelve.

This is my wife at her first one-man show in a Boston gallery. She has lost weight and is wearing a trousersuit. Her hair is black. She is wearing glasses. She is beautiful. She is crying because they are buying all of her paintings.

Jane. Gail. Cambridge.
  Jim. Julio. Argentina.

She takes the news quite well. *Missing in action.* This is my wife in the blue window crying. It was the least I could do.

HOPE: AN OUTLINE

I haven't named any of you. I never shall. And they should know that, by now, but keep asking. With their mouths and bright tools outside the small circle of light, and this chair.

Can I help it if your answers come walking out of dark subways at night. Alone, in white coats.

"What do you want from me, no, what do you really want."

(Just to get up every morning with the same body beside me.)

That was one exchange.

Another:

This morning I found a cup of coffee three weeks old in the kitchen.

I want to go back to the doctor and say why did you give me dark eyes.

I want to return my left foot because the socks you gave me don't fit.

That—then letters addressed to postmen, knees of women that won't stay together. Some things I have to tell you because I'm sick of being loved and you'd better listen. (They won't understand.)

That you tore me out by the roots etc. and I pressed my lips against one kind of wound, a female organ.

That the body will not go out of itself. Like the mind. But try.

That planes are arriving from London so fast the men on the field who wave them in have got their arms tangled together into knots.

That I threw your luggage out of the window.

Remember walking up out of the subway at night, holding his hand, afraid to ask his name, and does he have one. And so on. Thirty-six cigarettes a day, more, three nights and the desk clerk's nervous. A man torn to shreds by wind on the streetcorner one afternoon. Some souvenirs.

The second day, and I still won't talk. No, there was no one else involved. I was alone.

They are drinking tea now, crossing off the questions already asked, rewording others to fit. The first one's thirteen-year-old daughter is pregnant, the second is worrying about athlete's foot. Brushing ash off the white socks he despises.

"What do you want from me, no, what do you really want."

No, there was no one with me. I was alone.

They are playing back the tape from our last session.

The first one is tall and sad; he dislikes doing this. He watches my face from outside the small circle of light—and, then, there are brief silences. He knows that soon now the second will kill him.

They are playing the tape. They have forgotten me. And the first one is watching the second closely.

Go on.

Tell a story. It doesn't matter which, because you know a lot of them; and those you don't know, you make up. Don't give the characters names, because they might not like the ones you choose, and they could have had so many other adventures anyhow. Don't be too specific about places because wherever you look we've been there before. Give the characters proper motivation and be suitably mysterious about your own. Put your name at the top of each page and enclose sufficient return postage.

With the change of season your Snomobile converts easily and quickly to a lawn mower. Simply disengage *hasps* 1-5 and remove the Cab. (See Diagram 1.) This unlocks Blade W, which may then be lifted from its cradle (see Diagram 2) and replaced by Blade S. Tighten *bolts* 1-8. (See Diagram 3.) Your mower may be adapted to particular lawn conditions either by tightening *lugs* 1 and 2 (see Diagram 4), or manually, with the internal Lift Selector. (See Diagrams 5 through 7.) With the Lift Selector at full *Open* (see Diagram 8), your mower will easily handle inclines of up to 110°.

A concentration camp. It might be 1999, it might be Poland, it is December. There are two men alive. A German. A Frenchman. The Frenchman is a member of the Resistance. From time to time he walks to the small window and looks out at the snow still falling, says to himself very quietly *Non!*, then returns to sit on the bunk. The bunk is a slab of steel welded to the steel wall. The snow has been falling for as long as he can recall. Then he gets up, walks to the door and shouts out into the hall: *Non!* echoes in the hollow chambers of the building. It has the sound of a blank going off in a revolver. The German is bringing his dinner. Kosher salami tonight, Grenouille. It's kosher salami every night. He looks at the food, two translucent slices like congealed, pale red grease on a single slide of bread, and says to himself quietly *non*. They refer to one another as Gerald and Grenouille. Possibly this is because they have forgotten their names. Gerald sets the tray on the bunk. It, too, is steel. The ragged sleeve of his uniform touches the solitary wool blanket.

—You will eat your meal, Grenouille.

—Non.

—You must eat your meal, Grenouille, or you will die.

—Non.

—But you have no choice.

—Non.

—Please eat your meal, Grenouille.

—Non.

Gerald picks up the tray and starts to leave. Grenouille will never eat; he is afraid Grenouille will die. He does not understand that Grenouille would die only if he *did* eat: that this is all that keeps him alive, this choice of saying Non.

—Gerald.

—Yes Grenouille.

—Where am I, just tell me where I am.

—Where you were before. We have not moved you, I have received no orders to move you. You are where you were before. You know that.

—Then . . . I've forgotten. I . . . don't remember.

There is a pause. Gerald stares sadly at the food.

—Please eat, Grenouille.

He waits for an answer, then moves again toward the door.

—"I am a man, Jupiter."

—What Grenouille.

—Nothing.

Today:

1. ~~Take bookback to library check out Neruda "Heights"~~
2. Call dr re blood type
3. ~~Letters~~
4. ~~Ms to BReview~~
5. ~~Have lamp repaired~~
6. ~~Shop food (mushrooms)~~
7. ~~Pick up tree at D's~~
8. Call J
9. ~~Go over to Hyannis P and bail water out of the gdmn boat~~
10. ~~Tape, cigarettes~~
11. ~~Movies~~

Tell her that yes you will stay away from other women and question-able situations. You will try, yes, to become a better person, but you can't be sure; how much of this is after all a lie. Imply that it may all be. You will do anything of course, but does she really want you to, to stay with her. She knows very well what you need from her. Will she give it and can she, without damage to herself. And naturally you can't live without her, nothing makes sense that way but you don't have enough however massive love for both. Amazing. Can she, and tell you, decide what she wants, what she really wants. Then go to bed with her. If that doesn't work, go away.

I am working in my room. I've got up early and there's much to be done. Still, the sheets of paper are slowly making their way from the stack on the left of my desk to that on the right, near the lamp. From time to time the phone will ring. An editor will ask is that poem ready. The one ... And no, I will say; there's this comma ... Ah yes, commas. Troublesome things. There follows a brief discussion on the role of the comma in contemporary writing, and the advisability of my foregoing their use; the example of Apollinaire. Finally I hang up the phone and continue work. A few more sheets move from the stack on the left, into the space before me, go away to join those on the right. This time it is the doorbell which rings.

A stout small man with a red face stands there smiling at me. In his hands he holds a bundle of papers which, upon my admitting to my name, he begins to disassemble. What I thought a bundle is actually one large, stiff document. It hangs from his outstretched arms now, swinging in the wind like a bedsheet set out on the line to dry. It is a summons, the printing in script. Your postal expenses, he says. Your rent, the typewriter, the tape recorder . . . I pay him—I can't afford the loss of more time which this document promises—and together we search for the line upon which I am to inscribe my name, having already admitted to it. This accomplished, I return to the study. It is ten. The stout little man drives past outside my window in a metallic-blue MG. The phone sounds, unanswered. I hear the morning post drop through the slot onto the kitchen floor but do not go down to retrieve it. I resume my work. The sheets of paper are now sorted by color. There are four stacks: top copy, carbon, drafts, notes and commentary. White, yellow, blue, pink. The doorbell rings again.

I open the door to find a sheaf of papers beneath my nose. They issue from a small feminine hand attached, in turn, to a tall blonde in bellbottoms and tank top. Moonlighting, she says. Overtime, trying to catch up. I know it's Saturday and I do hope I'm not disturbing you at your work but. Well, these bills, you see. They have to be paid. We have coffee together and with a pad of my yellow paper, the paper used for first drafts and carbons, we detail the items rendered on the bills. I make a token payment and sign an agreement. The rest will be paid within the fortnight. It is, after all, so easy to sign one's name. One has done it so many times; it requires no thought. We kiss and the blonde rides away on her Honda. I return to my study. The stacks of paper have grown in my absence.

The postman rings twice. It is a special delivery letter. Again I sign my name. I have accepted this letter, I am liable to its content. We gave you service when you needed it now we need money please see that we get it. This is scrawled in ballpoint on a formal bill dated three months ago. The bill, at the top, reads *Plumbing and Heating*. I have never heard of the firm listed there.

The next is a mild-mannered representative from the utility companies. He has had the kindness to come out on this Saturday morning (though it is now afternoon) to inform me that, unless the companies receive payment within the week, my telephone, electricity and water will be taken away from me. The water, I assume, carried away in ponderous, elephant-like trucks, the electricity lured into bell jars and trapped there. I offer to exchange the phone, which I am quite willing to do without (it is ringing even as we speak), for maintenance of the other services. I will even surrender my water, as there is a lake nearby. But the electricity. I own an IBM, surely he must understand, my source of income, etc. He laughs at these little jokes of mine and descends the stairs to his gray Lincoln. I go upstairs and rip out the telephone wires from the wall, then into the basement to shut off the water main. I am complying to their requests, I am adapting myself to the demands of my society, to its norms.

The left-hand stack, the unworked material, approaches the ceiling. There are other callers. I listen to their demands, their explanations, their requests, I comply, I will meet my obligations. Yes. I sign my name again and again until, at last, it begins to look strange to me, foreign and new. That signature racing across scored black lines. I pledge my arms, my heart to science. My body, upon death, to the local University Hospital (thereby meeting the bill for my child's birth). They tattoo the sole of my foot.

I am in my room working. They arrive between stanzas, lines, in the caesurae. Each time I go down to talk now, I carry with me papers from that increasing left-hand stack, which I burn in the garden as they talk.

Then for several hours I am alone. The telephone will not function, there are no callers, I have crushed the clockwork of the doorbell and pay no attention to repeated poundings at the doors downstairs. I work. And the stacks are exhausted. They go into various envelopes and files and one, the top copy, distributes itself among a number of envelopes which I will mail when I am able to secure money for postage.

It is six. I am eating dinner in the kitchen when I look up from the table and discover a man standing at the window looking in at me. I go to the door and dismantle the locks, which I have bought on credit, just this afternoon, at the hardware store.

It is seven. He stands silently at the door and watches me. He is holding only an old envelope. On the backside of the envelope he has scribbled numbers and words. Our records show, he says. He has on his list every art exhibit to which I have been, every concert I've attended, the title and performers of every record I own, the genus and size of each tree in my lawn. Yes, I ask. Yes.

He is silent. And silently continues to stare into my eyes and judge, with one sideways glance, the shape and size of my ears. He stares back quietly at my eyes. The light is on his face now. Yes?

And I wait.

THE VERY LAST DAYS OF BOSTON

That requires an answer.
Something.

Mason Terrace, where we all came afterwards—après coup, he says.
Where the leaves this fall are skeletons. Where everything seems to
have happened before, in that past we can't admit. Where the wind
sounds like gills ripping out of the flesh of fish, and it rains. Where
this morning the charred bodies of all the women I've loved come
floating down the stream outside our window. Where women's
remains go thump-thunk in the heart banks as we pass. Etc.

And don't think I haven't seen you waiting in the next room to
kill me.

With this turtle staring.

Its blunt head is pushed against one side of the glass cube that
contains it, at the center of the room. Its nose flattened against the
glass and it never moves. Each time I cross the direct line of its
vision, it blinks; nothing more. The shell has been expertly cut away,
something I never knew was possible, and hangs on the wall above
a Mexican cane chair. At the party tomorrow night it will become
an ashtray. You have painted a Madonna-like self-portrait inside it.

Your hair is long in the portrait.

1. A man was cut in half by a window. But not to worry: his wife
contrived a system of straps and replaceable cellotape by which
he is capable of functioning normally; only in such acts as seating
himself and sex does he experience difficulty, and must he proceed
with caution. But there's more. One night when he put his dentures
in the glass alongside the bed they dissolved, and the next morning
he found a goldfish in the glass, which is of course in reality a jar.

He carries it with him from bar to bar now that his wife's left him, and drinks only with the jar and the fish on the counter beside his beer, cigarettes, good intent; beside the hand that is open and holds so much memory.

One of them finds divorce papers in a drawer of the desk. 6. *The said Plaintiff avers that in violation of his marriage vows and of the laws of this Commonwealth, the said Defendant did: Offer such indignities to the person of the Plaintiff as to render the condition of the Plaintiff intolerable and life burdensome.* The part after the colon has been typed in. The date of marriage has been left blank; neither of them knows. Folded into the legal document is a scrap of brown notepaper on which her mother has detailed, step by step (and they are numbered), just what she is to ask the lawyers, just what she is to do. He corrects several minor inaccuracies and signs the papers. He puts them back into the drawer. One of them answers the phone and says that No, Jane is not home to a confused male voice which will not leave a message. One of them finds a letter to her on the letterhead of his publisher. The answer to this letter is filed away in the same envelope, never mailed or perhaps later revised. What I want to know is why did you feel it necessary to lie to me and tell me you weren't sleeping with anyone else, when I never required such a statement from you. I tried to call you last night and again at 6:30 this morning—needless to say, you weren't there. Living with him for six years has given me a very low tolerance for lies. Perhaps if you were first, things would be different—but that's how it is. And it ends: I need you more than two days out of fourteen. One of them is the husband.

2. He's an electrician. He keeps sticking his hand into appliances and so on and getting shocked, and he discovers that this stimulates him. (Background on flagging interest in wife, poor relationship, affairs.) So he hooks himself and the woman up to batteries and a series of induction coils: they receive a steadily increasing flow of electrical power—which ends in a high-amperage shock at the exact moment each comes. Over the months he rigs more and more voltage into the circuits; they need more each time, to come at all.

Months pass. One night when they come, and it's great, the lights go off outside. The window dark. They unhook the wires, tear off the taped electrodes, walk to the window, look out. They have just blacked-out New York City.

"Another month just left
        Its umbrella in the hall
And I can't get used to your apartment. (Just *in* it, you say.) I've taken a room across the street, where I'm obliged also to take weak tea each afternoon with the landlady and to have cheap gauze curtains on mv windows (as though they were wounded). At night I watch you return to your apartment with other men. The shapes in your window, against the shades."

3. Women.
Women in boots to their knees or slacks and sandals. Women in Neiman Marcus gowns, women who know how to say no, women with green eyes, with small feet, with stockings that have elastic at the top and no garters, women with narrow hands.

Women met in elevators, you hold the doors open for them, women who look like Edna Millay, like Virginia Woolf, women turning back to look while they wait at the corners for traffic, women in windows. Women with things inside them. Women bleeding, women eating, women standing in front of a Stella painting. Women with their hands on pianos, arms, something else.

Women watching you through the doors of a State Hospital.

Women waiting.

4. "Pandora tells Jordan about kudzu. Back home. Arkansas: a small town cupped up against the river by hills, and a problem of erosion. From Japan officials imported a green vine but failed to bring along the vine's natural enemy, a pale red beetle. The vine now covers the hills—a cushion of green several feet deep, leafy pads like the ears of small stuffed elephants—and climbs the radio towers, kills all flowers, chokes the trees. People must go out every week and chop it back away from their lawns."

"There are twenty people living in the apartment now. Pandora writes in the bathroom, as this is the only quiet place. She has a shelf above the sink where she keeps her books and notes; on the door facing the toilet is a sketch of her done by Jordan, the breasts amazingly detailed, showing the stretch marks and the single long hair that curls down around her left nipple. Sitting here with all the others moving about out in the other room, she fills exercise books with poems and letters, using every part of the page. These are all addressed to men she has known—farewells there was no time for. Occasionally there is a knock at the door and she must surrender, for a few moments, her room."

"Jordan had always thought crocuses were insects, small, unseen things that clicked away far off in the bushes and trees. Once, just before the end, Jordan tried to leave the city. He went out into the country where one night the streetlights failed to come on at dark. He ran back to his cabin, turned on all the lights and wrote Pandora a letter, in which he questioned the ideas that had brought him there. He looked up at the hills then and suddenly remembered what Pandora had told him about kudzu. Terrified, he fled back to the city—back to Pandora—arriving before his letter. When it came he threw it into the fire and sat for hours with the flames in his face, shaking with fear. Pandora never saw the letter. The next day, it began."

I wander through your flat, looking for pain, assurance. There are times we've been happy. The way your skin goes over your hips. A letter from you one day in rain. And waiting for me at the airport. When we met by mistake in town. But that was before all this. Before it was possible to have nothing outside your window. And I've given the windows away. Some will be interested in trying to rebuild, even now. Let them.

5. They are moving the city again. For the third time this year the men arrive in their trucks and brown trousers, smiling. They drive their vehicles wildly, like dodgem cars, against the buildings. Walls, windows, doors fall into the backs of the trucks and the trucks begin

to move away, out of the city, to take them somewhere else. The remains are washed away by torrential rains, which follow.

Till someday I'll be found in a small dirty room in the North End (which they've put back together). Their heads will be lined up on my bookshelf—all those men, necks crusted to the bare wood—and when they open the door—it won't have a lock and their approach will be silent—I'll look up and say, You've come back.

And the water will be coming into Boston Harbor, carrying French ships.

(Something about fish.)

Where it never rains.

Women waiting.

ENCLAVE

A bright yellow room. The room is empty save for a table and two chairs, a bed, a small animal cage beside it, books. The bed is steel-framed, the headboard and base composed of slender steel rods; it creaks with every movement in the room, whether or not the bed is itself occupied. The cage is of the same steel rods, but painted a chrome-bright green (those of the bed are white), and is approximately two by three feet. It appears to be empty; but harsh, metallic sounds (gratings, clicks) issue from within it throughout the play. The cage is supported, at the level of the bed, atop a stack of oversize books like those which contain reproductions of paintings, or like "coffee-table" books. The stage is in fact literally overwhelmed by the *presence* and the *fact* of books; filled with them; they are piled on the floor, the bed, against the walls. They are of every possible size, yet each is either scarlet or sky-blue. Some are neatly, squarely stacked; others lean in disorder against the walls and bed; some are in precisely swirled columns, like spiral staircases, and reach as high as eight to ten feet. In one corner there is a pile of them, hundreds of books, paperbacks, magazines, dumped there at random and looking as though the entire mass would collapse were one to touch it, even come too close.

A woman is standing at the blank, yellow wall stage-right, dressed in formal eveningwear, staring *out*, as though a window existed there. A man is on the bed. He is naked, books piled under and around him. (Because of the books we cannot actually see that he is naked.) After several moments, during which the tableau is held, the man speaks. Even then, there is no movement.

—Well?

The woman continues to stare *out*. Finally he speaks again.

—What color uniforms?

She parts her lips. Begins slowly, quietly.

—Pink . . . ? No. No, they're naked. They're naked this time.

—Students.

—No . . . No, they look too young.

—Soldiers then.

—Some of them have painted the top of their bodies brown . . .

—Or veterans.

—Some of the children are wearing armbands . . .

—The old woman, is she still out there?

—She's making a speech. She has to stop every few seconds to put her teeth back in. They keep falling out.

Pause. The woman continues to stare fixedly at the wall. The man picks up a book, thumbs through it, tosses it back onto the bed.

—The bombs?

—Of course. You can't hear them? They haven't stopped for weeks now. Not for a moment, a second.

The man shrugs. Books shift on the bed, slide down his body.

—You get used to them I suppose. Don't notice. After a while.

—Do you think it's really America?

—Don't be silly. Who else would it be.

As he speaks these lines the man is pushing books away from him, struggling out of the bed. Several books fall on to the floor— the greatest quantity at the exact moment his feet touch the floor. Simultaneously the rest, those remaining on the bed, collapse together into a heap. The man rises and walks distractedly among the stacks of books, vaguely toward the tea table. (He contrives to remain partially under cover of the books, so that we never in fact see that he is naked until play's end.) The woman is still standing at the wall, motionless, looking out.

—There's a priest . . .

The man begins to make tea. Sounds: the metallic clicks and grating from the animal cage (almost metronomic), the creaking of the bed at every movement he makes, the whistle of the teakettle. Absolute silence outside.

—He's walking among the bodies. He has a ring on each hand. One has a question mark on it, the other has an x. Sharp edges, like razors. He's branding the wounded and dead. Whenever anyone argues with him he immediately pushes the x into their forehead. Or their cheeks.

The man is pouring tea at the table. The table and chairs, the cups are steel, the same color as the cage.

—The farmers are standing around the rice paddies. They're throwing firecrackers when the others come too close . . .

—Ready dear.

—There's a sniper on top of the Eiffel Tower . . .

—Come dear.

—Indians are coming down the canals in canoes. They have crossbows. And beards. And steel helmets with horns on them . . .

The woman turns suddenly, goes to the table, sits. *Long pause.* The man and the woman drink their tea. *Long pause.* The sounds from cage and bed continue; also, the teakettle is still whistling. (It continues to whistle for the duration of the play.) Spoons clink, mouths slurp, the woman speaks.

—Where are the children dear? Have you seen them lately? There are ten . . . no, eleven . . . of them.

—What? I think they went out. To play. Are there really that many now?

—What? I think so. Yes, at least eleven. When did they leave?

—What? I don't know. A few days ago I think.

Pause.

—*You* haven't been going out. To work I mean.

The woman stares across the table at the man.

—What was it you used to do?

—I was a physicist.

—But what did you *do*?

The man frowns in concentration; then smiles.

—Oh, you know. Entropy, information theory, stuff like that . . . I think.

The woman sips tea, stares into the cup.

—We're out of tea again.

—Mmmm. They dumped it all in the harbor.

—Sassafras.

—Mmmm. It's growing in the closet.

—Which one?

—Well, all of them as a matter of fact.

—The roach spray didn't work.

(He stares into his teacup.)

There is a crash, as of glass shattering, and a heavy object strikes the floor. The man leaps to his feet. The woman drops her cup, speaks.

—Mind the glass. It shattered the window, you might get a nasty cut.

—I'm not going near it. It might be a bomb.

—Don't be silly, it's a brick. Not a bomb. And there's a message wrapped around it.

—It could still be a bomb.

—But it's not even ticking or anything, it's perfectly quiet.

—So much the worse. I regard that as highly suspicious.

—It's a brick.

—But it has words on it. You have to admit it has words on it.

—Of course. A message would have words, wouldn't it.

The man pauses, considering.

—Not necessarily . . . What language?

—English.

—*See!* I told you.

They sit to their tea again. The brick remains on the floor, its message and presence ignored. The teakettle continues to whistle; the cage to give forth its clicks and rasps; the bed to creak at every movement the man makes. The woman begins to read from a newspaper. The man glances at the wall from time to time, nervously. They carry on with their afternoon tea. Finally the woman speaks, without looking up from the paper.

—Why don't you go look out dear. You look upset, that would help.

—No. No I was . . . just . . . wondering.

To the other sounds is added, now, the rustling of paper. After a while the woman says, idly,

—Someone just applied to Lloyd's to insure the human race.

—Incredible!

—Hmmm.

—They're still putting out the papers.

—Hmmm.

—We don't subscribe to one you know.

—What?

—Where did you get it?

—What.

—The paper, where did you get it?

—O. It was on the floor, by the front door. Someone had shoved it under the door, I suppose.

—When?

Pause.

—I don't know. I just noticed it today, this morning, it could have been longer.

The woman pages through the paper:

—There's no date on it, anywhere.

—Of course not. There wouldn't be, would there. How would they know.

The man suddenly gets up and walks to the wall. As he looks out, the sounds stop. The bed (which went into a frenzy when he stood), the teakettle. *Then* the sounds from the cage—he notices and turns. Walks toward the cage. Stands staring down.

—It died. You flushed it down the lav. Last week. Or the week before . . .

The man goes back to the wall. Motionless there, he assumes the position the woman held at the play's beginning. Now we can hear the sounds outside. Bombs, shouts, guns.

A scream.

SYPHILIS: A SYNOPSIS

The global outbreak of syphilis and gonorrhea spawned by
World War II came as no surprise to the medical world.

I've had syphilis in London, in Paris, in Timbuktu, in Istanbul, on
the road, in Hong Kong (it fit perfectly), in Delhis old and New. I've
had syphilis in Warsaw, in Cracow, in Berlin (twice), in Juarez, in
Rio, in Liverpool, in absentia. The most interesting experience I've
had with syphilis was in Borneo. There, it takes the form of living
snakes, which drop onto you from the trees. The worst period is
between two and six in the afternoon, especially during the rainy
season (March to December). No one escapes. Several tribes consider it a sacred disease, proof of enduring ancestral spirits; for
others it is a rite of passage, with coming of age marked from its
first inception.

In 1530 an Italian pathologist, Hieronymus Fracastorius,
wrote a poem entitled "Syphilis Sive Morbus Gallicus,"
which described the plight of a mythical shepherd lad
named Syphilus afflicted with the French disease as punishment for cursing the gods. The poem recognized the
venereal nature of the infection and was a compendium
of knowledge of the time regarding the disease.

It is common fact that Adolf Hitler had syphilis. So badly was his
vision impaired that it became necessary to construct a special typewriter with an inch-high typeface; and from this typewriter came
his later speeches, noted for their brevity and compression. Thus
is syphilis a primary influence on the course of world events. One
authority in fact states that the Great War was fought "to make the
world safe for syphilis."

Contracting syphilis, then, affords one a considerable historical perspective, meanwhile serving to make one feel ever more intensely a part of his world.

Among other famous syphilitics are Martin Luther, J.S. Bach, Voltaire, Thomas Aquinas, John Alden, Diogenes, and Pocahontas.

Of the literature dealing with syphilis, *Pinocchio* is, with its obvious symbolism, the best known.

> The Colombian school believes that syphilitic infection was endemic in Hispaniola (Haiti) and was subsequently contracted and carried to Europe by Columbus' crew when they returned to Spain following his second voyage.

I have myself known, some of them close friends, forty-seven syphilitics; I met the latest just this afternoon at the Coolidge Corner Café; others, I have wondered about. (Bob, Tom, Mark, Mike.) Last month a friend and I were walking down or perhaps up Forty-Second Street. My friend nodded toward an old man with no nose who stood dispensing Scientology bulletins on the corner outside one of several blood banks (*Immediate Payment*). "Syphilis," my friend said. A twelve-year-old Puerto Rican came up behind us, unwrapping a new necklace from lavender tissue the gift shop had set it among. "Crabs," he said.

It was in Kansas City that I had this story from a young man met by chance at the out-patient Coke machine:

"So I got this call one day, see. It's summer, and this old biology teacher of mine's calling up to take me to a movie because I was his best student. He's leaving, got a new job. It's with the Health Department and he's going to be working with VD. I'm about fourteen, see. Then later I hear he's been dismissed and I say guess what for—yeah, he was passing out free samples."

Syphilitics are often of such humorous turn of mind.

There is the case of Prince Lentille, who upon learning that he had contracted syphilis, caused every courtesan of the Royal Family to be killed and interred *dans les jardins de palais*. This is the first record of syphilitic dandelions.

The first documented outbreak of syphilis, or "the great pox," followed the siege of Naples by the French in 1494, giving rise to the now discounted legend that Columbus' men had brought the disease back from the New World.

Jane?
Gail?

It is obvious that neither theory of the origin of syphilis is entirely satisfactory.

Having suffered for some time from painful boils and difficult urination, a poet went finally to his physician.

You have contracted syphilis, the physician, a writer himself but only of prose, said following a brief examination. Examination consisted of asking the poet to drop his pants. Treatment involved asking the poet to drop his pants *and turn around*.

Not consumption? the poet asked sadly.

Keep trying! the physician said, plunging the needle in deep. He thought of his half-completed novel, waiting at home.

In some cases syphilis is accompanied by a condition known as penicillin shock.

"He who knows syphilis, knows medicine."
(Sir William Osler)

How to Get the Most Out of Your Syphilis
Syphilis Without Fear
The Syphilitic Cookbook
Joysores!
Le Mal anglais
VD: Home Cures
General Paresis and Private Parts

• • •

So they gave him the little book with the awful pictures and he promised to read it all. US Government Printing Office. Public Health Service Publication No. 1660. Rubber-stamped on flyleaf and title page:

Compliments of
New York City Dept. of Health
Bureau of Venereal Disease Control
LE 2-4280

That's as far as he gets. Immediately he calls a printer to have a tiny rubber stamp of his own made: Compliments of _____.

Lots of red ink.

From syphilis we learn that *sex is dangerous.*

Syphilis is often shared by husband and wife, much as they share the evening Globe, Johnson's shampoo, their paychecks, a bed, one of his T-shirts, the last scoop of ice cream.

It will be found that syphilis, though most generally introduced outside the marriage parameter, often functions to bring the family unit closer together.

In a recent poll, asked who had syphilis, twenty-six out of thirty preschoolers raised their hands.

While in the dank jungles of the Orient new strains develop, breed profusely, and prosper.

"That most democratic of diseases . . ."

And there is syphilis in Salt Lake City, like clouds. Syphilis storms the ramparts at San Antonio. Syphilis floats raft-like and silently on the river toward Memphis. There is syphilis in Des Moines, there is syphilis in Grand Rapids, there is syphilis in San Jose, syphilis in Forts Worth and Lauderdale. There is syphilis in Oxford, Nice, Toledo. There is no syphilis in Boston.

I've always wanted to go to Boston.

ONLY THE WORDS ARE DIFFERENT

1
Pulse

I just looked up and a man fell by my window with his arms waving. (Earlier, my thumb was engaged in moving across the paper like a chicken drumstick. Scratching, scratching.) He seems to have been in a great hurry, and possibly there was something he wanted to tell me. This may, I realize, have something to do with the scaffolding that grew outside my window during the night; it's out there now, as I write, a wood and steel doily of piping, ladders, planks and pant legs;

> the sky shows through
> in squares of blue.

I go to the window and there is a crowd below me, a red truck with two white attendants. The man is lying strangely on the pavement; perhaps he is very tired. Pigeons tiptoe down his legs and arms. Snails would be better, but snails are not in season—only strawberries. His mouth is full of strawberries. The red juice dribbles out of his mouth and streams along the pavement.

I wonder what it was that he wanted to tell me? Probably that he loved me.

2

Schlupp-thunkk. Schlupp-thunkk. The wipers mimic a heart. Beating.

Postmortems of parties dead and cold now, passing home in a bouncing car. You here beside me, warm with drinking, soft with sleep in your pumpkin dress that skis off one shoulder and slides along your leg. The child in your lap. Shapeless in her bundle of flannel.

—like it'll snow forever. And our Fiat crunches through the crust of that snow. The motor, in third, hums and whirrs. Thinking of our Ford gathering snow on the salvage yard. In the back seat now there are the remains of two pheasants and a bottle of brandy. The brandy rolls and clatters against the oven pan, rolls in its nest of birds' bones and greasy dressing. Snow stipples the flat gray air, slurs the streets. I smoke the last cigarette and watch for ice. Guilt in small actions, always. The heater growls.

Who was that girl?

I pass the cigarette to you, you drag once and hand it back. The tip is wet now. Of course.

The sexy one. You consider her, try to remember other qualities she may have had. Long hair, boots. The one who kept drinking the brandy.

I shrug. Undergrad, I think. Light from an oncoming car catches in my eyes, trapped under the ridges, supraorbital—as you say, like Pueblo cliffs, a moderately effete baboon. (And you . . . you have sat on those ledges and watched a world, the world in front, the world behind them . . . lived on the edge, looking.)

Painter?

That's the guy she was with. Workshop, I think. Supposed to be very good. She has a novel coming out next year, from Harper.

In your class?

Too obvious, dear. The brandy, or real annoyance? I shift into second to take a curve. The wipers are tossing snow away from the windshield. We are tossing away time. To buy our way home.

No. Not many of the writers are interested in Pope, they mostly go for modern lit. I've told you all that before.

The baby has crapped in its sleep and the smell fills the car. You reach for the cigarette, draw, encounter filter and throw it out, leaving the window a little open. You twist and rummage through your pockets; skirt, sweater, coat. I thought I had a pack of Salems somewhere . . .

We smoked them.

So: that sideways glance. A measured reprehension. A truck comes toward us, puffing chimney and cab outlined in small red lights. A huge interstate rig. We're out of the city, coming onto open road. I shift to fourth and see your face in the truck's lights. How many times, these five years, this same moment? The Fiat takes the curve and starts up a hill, dropping speed. Touching the shift, I almost touch your knee but you pull away. The road drops steadily into the darkness, the vacuum, behind us. The lights spread out in front of us, a dull flash-lightning inside the fog, that goes on and on.

Look! but we've passed it, whatever it was.

What . . .

A Styrofoam snowman. Someone has a goddamn Styrofoam snowman in their yard . . .

O *shit!* A Styrofoam snowman.

If another truck, even a car, came by, I might see you crying. But nothing else passes, we're alone on the road. I can only hear the sound of your breath in the dark. Finally you lean forward and shut off the heater.

How much further?

A few miles.

O.

3

Have you ever noticed how books accumulate around you? Like clouds. You don't remember putting them there, or buying them (and if you had bought them, you'd have put them on the coffee table, or a shelf, or perhaps beside the bed). And they couldn't have come through the mail slot; it's too small. The post office doesn't deliver. You never enter it: the Draft Board is just upstairs. But they go on accumulating, even now that you know, like clouds.

Then one day there appears on your desk—a surprise beside your morning coffee—this memo advocating the extinction of poems (though a few would be maintained in cages, well-fed and cared for, for the children to see; to which they might toss an occasional left-over letter, partly eaten or melted to a shapeless mess in their warm hands; perhaps an occasional colon or dash; an adjective, apostrophe). You quickly add your name—recalling it, letter by letter, as you write—to the already formidable list. This, it occurs to you now, is a petition. You pick it up and the first page comes apart in your hands like a newspaper. It begins to unfold, a very long list indeed. You follow the names through the study, library, den, kitchen, living room, dining room, up three flights of stairs to the bedroom. You jump out the window and run, as though you are (in October) flying a kite, and still the petition comes open, unfolds, like panels of toilet paper folded front to back, back to front, front to back. Each is stamped in blue *Property of the British Government* and you realize now that this was stolen from the Tate, more precisely from one of the toilet booths on the bottom floor by the cafeteria, behind the Trova and would-be Michelangelo virgin.

You run, you run, you're out of breath. Finally, in New Jersey, you reach the end of the list. It began with the names of several well-known artists (painters, sculptors, ceramists, filmmakers, mixed mediaists) and ends with the signature of the local cub reporter. The only names missing are those of the poets themselves—though a few of them, too, have signed. Under pressure, one presumes. Of their wives, publishers, bankers, typewriters, drugs, "humor." All the way back across mitred New Jersey, New York and Pennsylvania, you search for your name but are unable to find it, even in Philadelphia. But you *have* considered removing it and this, like the poetry itself, is a noble gesture. You are sure of that, at least . . .

Over dinner I explain all this to you, my wife, and your new friend Harrison. It apparently means little to you, but Harrison feigns interest quite well. And I like him. I feel myself attracted to this strange, quiet man. But let me warn you, Darling: *his name was not on that list!*

4
Story

They are in love. They go to the beach at Brighton and she is disappointed, there are only rocks, where is the sand. The Camden Town

Zoo. Shopping together at Heal's. The East and West for curry, West-bourne Grove (Notting Hill). Baby elephant. Theatre closed—seats outside for sale, want them, can't find anyone to ask. They return to Portobello Road and, stomachs rumbling from the Madras (this, like the sound of wind in the pastiche-Corbusier elephant house), make love. She wants "your child." Sadly watching him roll the rubber down over his penis, thinks of discarded peacock feathers lying on ground at zoo, they climax (him 3, her 2). Nothing is ever said. He returns with her to America (on the boat, his birthday, she has him lean his arms against the upper bunk and masturbates him, slowly). They take a flat just outside New York. Strain of isolation, his disori-entation, intimations of an affair apart from her. Their love, always silent, is now proclaimed in words. The words distort, fictionalize, lead them each into false emotion; they are farther apart with each day, each word. She still wants his child. He finally leaves in the middle of the night, after a (rationalized) argument—the words—over sex. Three days later she receives a small package. No name, no return address, postmark Grand Central Station. She opens the package, which is beautifully gift-wrapped, and takes out what is inside. Holds it up to the light of the kitchen window. A condom, the nipple filled with semen, knot tied just above it. Title: *Love Letter*.

5

Molly keeps a cockroach. It lives in a cage made of Japanese match-sticks, the size of a child's shoebox, floor covered with a jiggerful of sawdust. It lives on charcoal which it extracts from cigarette filters dropped into its cage by Molly and her lovers, rolling the residue of paper into tiny neat balls to store in one corner of the cage. When Molly mates, it climbs up the side, crawls upside-down halfway out across the top, then drops down into the litter and starts up the side again—faster and faster, again and again. Finally it falls onto its back and lies there in the sawdust, exhausted, moving its legs slowly, like eyelashes.

Afterwards Molly stands by the cage telling us, The roach is a dead end, it hasn't changed in a handful of thousands of years.

Later the roach will ascend to the light fixture and cry there for the crumbling dry bodies of flies. When Molly climbs on a chair to bring it down, it will stare at her with its one cold black eye, it will wave one leg frantically in her face. *J'accuse, J'accuse.*

The mayor has declared war on roaches, believing common cause will bring us together; restore esprit, order. Contraceptives have been burned in bonfires on Town Hall Square, people queue outside the compulsory strip shows, the city's water supply is pumped full of aphrodisiacs—and still, it's not enough. No one cares. No one, frankly, gives a damn. Anomie and entropy. The birthrate still declines, the city collapses into itself. Stronger measures are required, the Mayor declares from the top of the Town Hall steps (the sun on his skull; the smell of burnt rubber, burning plastic), We *must* act *now!*

Badges came last night, press-gang firemen, to bear Molly's roach away to its execution. She locked the door and shoved things against it—bureaus, bookshelves, the stove—and when they finally broke through, attacked them with shish kebob skewers. She blinded three, ruined another's hand, neatly burst the balloon-like testicles of the last. Holding her, kicking, screaming, against the wall (halls filled with inquisitive Citizens), they took the cage-cover off and discovered that she had (predictably, perhaps) killed the roach herself—with a gold stickpin left behind by one of her lovers—to keep them from getting it.

Molly, "The stars and the rivers and waves call you back."

And the Citizens, when they return to their flats from gaping and gasping in the hall—what is it that they do? There, in that abject privacy. Contained by those colorful walls.

EUROPEAN EXPERIENCE

It's happened again, I'm in bed with a stranger. Don't know her name. If I want to remember the curve of the bottom of her breasts, the way they rest on her ribs or rise to her shoulder, I'll have to reach out and touch them. Do I know her? She has a name, an address (which she refuses to give me), three telephone numbers at which I might reach her. Along with the last she has given me a chart showing the time of day I'm most likely to find her at each number. She has long hair. She is wearing a tight violet dress. Her eyes are green.

Also: I am being pursued. I saw the frost of his breath on the glass just a moment ago. Her lover, husband, father, friend? How am I to know? Each time I try to confront him, he flees. Last week in the press of crowds at Fourteenth Street he took the only way open to him and was crushed to death in the doors of one of the uptown trains. His last words were I kept my promise, Tell them. My suit is still stained with his blood. And for a moment I envied the dead man: he kept his promise, I must live up to mine. The next morning there was a certain wariness to his movements.

She has small breasts. When she lies down they hardly exist. Her hips are wide, thighs full, the whole lower half of her body out of proportion to the upper—breasts, slender torso, fragile arms. She is nude in the photograph, I can't remember what clothes she wore that day.

Someone has written a collection of short stories and published them under my name; they have even put my photograph on the back cover. I received a copy in the morning post. Anonymous, no return address, postmarked *Grnd Cntrl Stn*. The stories reveal the most intense and intimate movements of my life. My attorney is investigating the possibility of a lawsuit against the publisher but, as the work was copyrighted in my own name, there seems little we can do. The publisher expressed to my attorney his admiration for the book and desire to meet the author, relaying an invitation to a party at his home last night. Where I met this woman.

He follows me everywhere. Perhaps I am looking for associations where there are none. Perhaps he is nothing more than a hired assassin. Plotting my rotation around the events of the day. Then, certain, he will strike.

She was standing in a group and said You're here, You finally came, and took my arm. She was in the park by the lion-pawed fountain where we watched pigeons dive for pennies then silently walked away together. We were afraid of words, I think. It was a clear blue day, the water silver. It would never rain again. She was in the library. We had requested the same book and sat side by side at one of the long tables all alone in the vast Special Collections room. She was working at a restaurant, to show me the way to the table where we never arrived. She was beside me on the plane from London. She was sitting on the fire escape, crying softly, and I opened the window.

They are moving the city again and I am occasionally lost somewhere between her place and mine. It was at one of those times, coming up out of the subway into what I thought to be midtown Manhattan and finding myself in the open space of Queens, that I first approached my pursuer. He turned and threw himself onto the back of a truck just then pulling away, carrying off the skating rink from Rockefeller Plaza.

Her hair seems a different length and color each time I see her. Her neck a perfect curve, wing of a sparrow. Her eyes are astonished. They move slowly, as though through room after room after room.

Ice crashes off the roof and onto the ground outside. There are pigeons frozen alive inside it. She is gone. He has taken the photograph. He has gone away himself. And I am sitting here saying _____. Her name. And it all makes sense.

It does, it does.

I am waiting for a train to take me a little farther away. Here at Paddington Station. Out of the taxi with my single bag. Ducking. Halfcrown tip, smile, Ta. Now I'm larger, on the pavement walking away from the cab. Before that was a coach from Brighton, whatever I was doing in Brighton, and an 82 bus. Now I'm smaller, inside the vaulted station. And I'd like a ticket please. Certainly your destination sir. Anywhere. *Ailleurs.* I see and would that be return fare sir. No. I see sir that there is a departure from Gate D at eight o five that would be just about now sir the train arrives I forget where he said or when if that would be satisfactory sir. My hand pushes money through the grate. Stamp rubber ink. Have a pleasant journey then sir. Enjoy. Now down through Gate D and onto a coach and in to tea to look out at the backs of all these houses with gardens and gates and clotheslines wondering do I have my passport. Vowing to be more careful what I say.

I am French, born in a large wood house off the rue de Tournon in the sixth arrondissement, of a Polish mother who died, passing her frail substance on to me, as I came into being, and of a father who as he said belonged too much to France to remain there overlong. He read to me, peering over the slats of my *petit berceau*, Cendrars's "Prose du Transsibérien et de la petite Jeanne de France" and "Les Pâques à New York," and when I was six it was to New York that, bundled up, with my French *abécédaires* and my *grammaires anglaises*, I was sent *pour faire de l'éducation*. To that place that could never exist, that was something created only for Cendrars's poems, surely. That about to acquire a history, like myself, possessed already its ruins.

Do you still sit daily on the beach with your book and glass of green tea. That strange beach with rocks instead of sand. The people around you like rocks themselves, steaming faintly in the sun. Where I told you one day Your ears are like shells and you turned back to me in the sun and your copper sweater and smiled. Then looked in the water and it carried your face away. Do you still believe, you said it once, that I'm forever returning? And when you are lonely, when narrow room and beach overcome you, do you still go down to watch the London trains arrive?

I am English. Turning over my passport at the embassy. We trust you've given this matter serious consideration young man. Yes, yes I have. And your wish is to carry on. Yes. Well then. You should be receiving the new passport within the fortnight. Through the he pauses here other he pauses again embassy of course. Which should I suppose be requiring new photographs. Yes sir I'm off to that now the little shop just up the way on Oxford. That would be the one across from Heals. Yes sir. Splendid. Best of luck young man. Enjoy.

He won't be coming round anymore, you understand. You can put your favorite records back on the shelf with the rest. You can stop rolling new paper into the typewriter every day. You can put away the French grammars, the Polish dictionaries, that clochard of a thesaurus, even those wretched Cézanne reproductions. He hated them too.

I am in hospital in Poland dying. They have scraped out the inside of my chest like seeds from a melon till there's nothing more to scrape out but *moi-même*. Soon my heart will relocate to Berlin, my lungs learn Japanese, my eyes look out on Brazilian rainforests. Three times a day doctors gather at the foot of my bed and talk quietly among themselves. I lie here reading Bergson. Duration: the official biography. I know they are bargaining for the many pumps pedals and organs of my body. *Wypusc mu flaki.* I am twenty-four. Led to slaughter, I almost survived.

Down stairs. Black cab waiting there in snow. Gray sky above.

I'm an American. Your passport sir. Thank you. Welcome to New York. Sky and buildings locked irrevocably together, profiles of a single face. No beach here. But against the pale sky, just over there, she weeps too, this lady who, like myself, came all the way from France, home.

The car died again today.

Each morning the grocer leaves a pound of coffee and a carton of cigarettes outside the door for me. Mail is delivered with the morning papers. Today none were there. And there is nothing on the radio.

Or perhaps, to be precise, it died last night. In the dark and cold and snow. In bright sun I gently pried apart its hood, cleaned the plugs and checked they sat firmly in place. Dried out the carburetor and blew into the fuel pump, opened the feed a bit wider. Scraped the battery terminals and choked it manually. It wouldn't come around.

Nothing on the phone but recorded messages. Then "Let It Bleed," playing over and over.

K came. As always, punctually, at ten, with breakfast in a paper bag. The perfect curve of her bottom like an inverted heart. Sitting on the bed she tells me how much of herself she leaves behind in these rooms.

Why do you keep coming here, I ask her.

I say: A whale's penis even in repose is taller than I am.

But what else could I do?

She holds one hand in the air and, with it, the other; as though some element in this action—connection, superimposition, the reaching itself—explains everything.

D will be expecting me she says, looking at her watch, I must be off, I really must.

Later now. Darker. I have moved away from the window. K, nude, is painting them black. One breast is set lower on her chest than the other and a bit to the side, nearer her arm. The nipple of that one is inverted, the other three-fourths of an inch long. D, she tells me, has strong fingers.

They came for the car, dragging it away across fields of broken cornstalks through snow. It left a thin trail of oil behind.

Trying to start a fire, I drop the last match just as a snow-laden branch crashes to the ground outside and look up at her. Why do you keep coming back here. The radio begins to speak again of the weather, how it will change.

The pills. A white one, a green one, a red one. They are lined up as always on the bedside table. Light nudges at them, at the table they are on, and retreats to the room's corners.

She is wearing gray slacks tonight, of a thick material that follows the taper of her legs down to fit close about the ankle. Where there are white socks, tops turned down, and loafers. She is smoking. Her breasts move inside cashmere as she inhales.

Other times she would dress in black and prowl about the house in pitch darkness, changing the furniture inside rooms, and he couldn't see her. He would hear the sound of her breath in the dark, the rasp of wooden legs. Once, lying beside him in bed, she told him of her plan to have a peacock tail tattooed in full color on her bottom. Or she might just turn up sometime, and maybe she'd been gone for days, with her pubic hair shaved down till just initials remained. Maybe they would be his and maybe they wouldn't.

Artaud at his last reading in Paris. He'd been locked away in asylums for nine years, all the Paris elite came. And every few minutes he'd stop and look out at the audience, out at Gide and Breton and Jean Paulhan and Camus and Pichette and his friend Adamov and the others. And he would try to explain, When you come round you simply cannot find yourself again. Life itself has been permanently debased, and a portion of original goodness and joy lost forever. He would say, I have agreed once and for all to give in to my own inferiority. Then he would stop and look around at all the lined faces. Putting myself in your place I can see how completely uninteresting everything that I am saying must seem. What can I do to be completely sincere.

She is sitting up in bed as he tells her this. Smallness of her body in the tall window now, framed there as in a painting. Motel sign a smear of red on the glass. A single tear like a glacier courses down her face, which she turns away.

She would come back with her body bruised and torn. No explanation, I am doing what I must. What else could I do.

Living now in this old house in Pennsylvania. Peirce's house, of much the same vintage, just down the road. A plaque out front gives the official biography in four sentences. Peirce who himself put it in three: Actuality is something brute. There is no reason in it. I instance putting your shoulder against a door and trying to force it open against an unseen, silent, and unknown resistance.

So let me tell you how it will be. One night you will be lying alone in bed. You will hear sounds downstairs. You will hear feet coming slowly up the stairs. You will hear them pause at the door. You will hear the doorknob turning. You will hear the door open. You will hear the footsteps again, on the rug now. You will be lying alone in bed. You will never see his face. You will never know his name.

MY FRIEND ZARATHUSTRA

My friend Zarathustra has stolen my wife.

Yes—I mean what I say, and you must listen; must hear what's not said if you're to understand properly what is said. For, as with him, silence is to me an instinct.

So (I repeat) Zarathustra—carrier of the ashes of the old to the mountains in order to prepare a new beginning, spokesman for the inseparability of creation and destruction, teacher of the eternal recurrence—this same Zarathustra has stolen my wife.

The bastard.

I try to recall, now, when it might have begun between them; at which point, perhaps, she first reached out to touch the hand he offered, but memory fails—I must have been working too hard at the book to take notice. I suppose she may have loved him from the first. That those months of close friendship in the huge house on the hill overgrown with vines—the fires at night as we read together, the fourteen rooms, the quiet, hollow Sundays—concealed all along the slow slide of this fact, and others, beneath me. As I worked in my room on the top floor above the trees. Sometimes when I wake now alone in early morning hours, I imagine there were moments when I felt, dully, never perceiving the truth, that some intangible thing was slipping from me; felt some pale remain of sadness inside, irretrievable. If so, these moments were few, and quickly passed.

(There were times he was happy; he remembers. Now he stands at the window, looking down on the town. Neons are coming on, like exclamation marks for something the darkness is trying to say; they show red on the glass. In the distance, radio towers rise against the sky. Fragments accumulate on his desk. He is aware of the space between things. He holds broken facts in his hands.)

Her work grew ever better, the colors bold and the rapid strokes finding relief in sudden, unexpected islands of close detail, ever more explicit, the content increasingly erotic—a body in gray fleshtones with three heads turned each to the others, the lips livid, against a background of alizarins and ochre; my own became increasingly subtle and sparse, moving toward silence. It occurred to none of us, I think, to wonder for so much as a moment whether things outside proceeded along the course which had brought us, or driven us, there; to that sole, solitary refuge.

The hills spread about me now as I write, looking down on the tops of trees. A light fog resides forever inside them. The dampness of it enters the open window of my bedroom each morning, a clean, fresh smell appropriate to new beginnings. The sunrise is splendid, breaking in rainbows through the mist and drifting, light dew; most nights the Northern lights fan out and fill the sky, as though beautiful cities were burning far away. There is no life anywhere in these trees. Where birds once sang and young deer broke the crust of new-fallen snow.

My work—what can I say of it? I fear I am now past all ambition; that volition, like hope, has died within me and nothing will issue again from that still center. (There would be such comfort in despair.) Times were, a single image, a phrase, would imbue page upon page with life; stories would spring full-blown from the chance word of a friend, the pattern of light through leaves at the window, the eager edge of a razor. Now lifeless pages of notes and scattered scenes accumulate on my table like slices of cheese on a platter: these weak attempts to retrieve my life. This might, I suppose, be expected, a function of the events outside, an equivalent decay.

—Tonight J wants to play for us the piano. He sits on the bench beside her, his face in his hands, weeping. B's fingers form broad X's in the moisture on the tabletop. It is Chopin, she says. The keyboard is roughly sketched out with a carpenter's pencil at one end of the table; there are no halftones. And so we wait.

—This morning we found him in the tub, the drain closed, his own blood all around him; in aspic. His eyes stared up and forward at the tiles on which J has painted a cluster of grapes, and on them, a roach. One of the girls is pregnant. Bits and shreds of half-digested food cling to the sink's sides each morning.

—*Force of circumstances driving the protagonists to the commission of a dreadful act . . .*

(He is standing at the window. It is open, and he speaks words to it. They scatter on the darkness, random as facts, unforgiving. He has done this before. He will do this again. He is free.)

I remember the last night. We had just made love and she stood at the window, her stomach bulging slightly now and her breasts full, the old stretch-marks lost. The motel sign was red on the glass; darkness entered through the window. And she said, Jim. Jim . . . we're leaving. When she turned to me, light from the hall glinted on tears in her eyes that, now, would never fall. I'm sorry. After a moment I stood and nodded, then came up here and began to write down everything I remembered about her. At dawn I found I could write no more, and I realized she was gone.

(He is tall, large, with deep blue eyes and heavy ridges above them, like shelves for dark things that might fall out of the sky. He listens to his own voice ringing in the corridors of night. He smiles. It is almost over now.)

It is 3 A.M., a cool night wrapped in clouds, and again unable to sleep, I take down a book. It is a foreign edition and with a small silver knife I must cut the pages free as I read:

We are to recognize how all that comes into being must be ready for a sorrowful end; we are forced to look into the terrors of the individual existence—yet we are not to become rigid with fear: a metaphysical comfort tears us momentarily from the bustle of the changing figures. We are really for a brief moment—

But wait. There are sounds outside now. Voices milling about, feet. Voices. Together.

I go to the window. There are fires. The villagers have come at last.

DELTA FLIGHT 281

As I leave my apartment on the way to see you, I hear the sound of heavy artillery in the distance. Two short bursts, a barrage, then silence. Far away, an aura about the buildings on the farthest horizon of the city, I see the flames still burning. Where the day went down.

Madam: We regret to inform you that at 11:31 P.M. last Thursday, the fourth of February, while crossing St. Charles Avenue, your husband was struck in the head by a passing idea. As far as we can ascertain, this idea had flown out the window of a late-model Chevrolet just then turning into Fern Street. Death was instantaneous; we are certain that your husband experienced no pain whatsoever and passed peacefully and at peace from this world to a better; we trust this will be of some consolation. Meanwhile, please accept our most sincere sympathies. Bureau of Ideas, New Orleans, Louisiana (Orleans Parish).

Mid-flight, with only twelve blocks remaining, the stewardess announces there is no more crabmeat for the canapés. Citizens (first class cabin only) in uproar. Shouts and threats, a few knives, broken two-ounce bottles of bourbon, Scotch, gin. I calmly suggest that we draw lots: We will pass out pieces of paper, on one of them will be a black spot, whoever gets the black spot will be slaughtered to replenish the supplies. My suggestion meets with approval all around.

Looking down on rooftops as we descend, I have the vague notion to write a novel, something which has never before occurred to me. Halfway through my third canapé the stewardess comes down the aisle with a gun in one hand, a phone in the other, and plugs the phone into the console beside me:

"Hey there, Hector my boy. How's it going? Just wanted to let you know we sold out the second printing. Great book, Hector baby, great! We're looking forward to the next one up here at Halvah House, let me tell you that! Well, be seeing you then, my boy."

As the NO SMOKING light goes on, the stewardess returns with a sheaf of telegrams: the reviews of my second book, which my new publisher has wired me.

At the airport I push my way through the women, reporters, and literary hangers-on, decline offers to teach, and look for a cab. I finally find one, reasonably priced—a '68 Ford, $750—on the second lot I try. Driving through roadblocks and toppling camera dollies, with flashing lights behind me in the mirror, I head straight for your apartment. Make a good deal for the cab with one of the guys hanging around the corner newsstand.

I climb the ladder to your apartment, breaking each rung behind me so they can't follow. Throw my clothes down to them as I ascend.

I knock on your door and quickly step aside. *C-C-C-Cow.* Four bullets smash through the wood, stuttering.

Don't shoot again.

It's me.

THE FIRST FEW KINDS OF TRUTH

Five men are watching my wife walk down Rosedale.

One with a belly, one with an eye, one with an arm. The other two with legs.

(Look, it's a great idea, dynamite! We're putting on the play, see, I mean everything just like it was before, the way we've been doing it, but all through it these stagehands are carrying on parts of a body, you know, a foot, then a leg, a spare arm or two and so on, and they're putting them all together in the background, right against the drop, and then by the time the play's over, dig this, they've built a man back there. Maybe they plug in the eyes on the last line. And this guy they've put together, *he's* the one who does the curtain call. It'll knock 'em out, man. Have 'em up on the goddamn chairs clapping and shouting. The critics'll go wild, man, we'll get reviews like you've never *seen*.)

Five men are watching

My wife

Is walking down Rosedale to shop for food and pick up

(For a moment, minutes, she becomes a part of those men. For a longer time, their attention defines her. Does she notice. Does she know.)

Her mail.

J. Thank you for the check. Sadly, it did not make the wolves go away—they are still out there, rattling all their keys and trying to pick the lock—but at least the goddamned bird has stopped saying "Nevermore, Nevermore," over and over again. Now it just sits there and says, "Well, maybe. But I doubt it." If you can't send more money can you send a new razorblade. I can't afford to buy one and all mine are dull—I've read that it hurts, that way. Love. J.

Five men are watching my wife walk down Rosedale. Her hips, which are large, sway slightly from side to side. Her leg swings out, forward, in, in a tiny arc; then the other. They end in small, perfect feet. Like the top of her body, also small, with breasts you can cup in two bent fingers. Under that white shirt. The letter is tucked into the hip pocket of her jeans now.

This is a photograph

It was sent to me anonymously this morning

But upon closer inspection is not really a photograph. Or not a "real" photograph. If I can put those two words together? Someone has used light, and only a laser could provide such tight focus, to create this "photograph" on a blank plate, "drawing" on the photographic plate with the light, just as one applies pen to paper. The depiction is perfect. The representation almost flawless. The men are there, watching, solid. Only a slight blurring around my wife's body.

Why is it, she thinks (with the five men watching), that the period just *past* in your life is always that which seems, *now*, most satisfactory? You made yourself go away from it, and it from you; yet now it seems to contain all the best moments of your life, all the times you were happy—and against all good sense, knowledge, memory. It assumes the proportion of an ideal now and, while it happened, was hell, of a kind. Surely it's not just the immediacy of the experience; an accumulation of information which hasn't become truly "past" but is in the process of doing so, and you *feel* that process, the sorting and sifting, on some preconscious level. Or the psychosomatic ability to retain knowledge of pain only in the abstract (fully processed information). Or even the simple disorientation of always beginning again. When the difficulties seem for weeks, months, overwhelming, and the mind flees the present, goes back in abreaction to a time when things were at least a bit more settled, ordered in some *implicit* way however powerful the upsets, the arguments, the problems.

No, she thinks with the five men watching, it's more than that; those are only parts; there's more to it. But I don't know what. With the five men watching she remembers each dislocation, each move—each new home or apartment, with or without her husband, like a set of steps, nine so far, with nothing at the top. How each time, each place, for months it seemed that the time and place *before* was the best. And then the desperate letters, the phone calls at three in the morning, the promises spoken, forgotten, never meant. Because neither could change that much. Until the new days at last resolved, as they always did, into the monotony and vague, petty dissatisfactions which are *now*, the present. One is "happy" only, she decides, in retrospect. Recalls her husband once saying that his major talent as a writer lay in creating instant nostalgia. (But why does everything finally have to wind up as words.)

Five men are watching my wife walk down Rosedale. She notices one with a mouth. The mouth smiles, opens the rest of the way and says Hi. She thinks of last night, the theater and afterwards, how gentle he was; the book he gave her. It is late afternoon. Perhaps she should write her husband a letter tonight. She just read a story of his in a magazine. It was about her.

Five men. It rained during the night and worms have crawled out onto the sidewalk, are lying there dead. She looks down to avoid stepping on them. She is barefoot and has startling blue eyes, carefully highlighted with mascara and blue eyeshadow, and a fine line of green on the upper lid. The soles of her feet are hard and can never be fully clean. She has a momentary fantasy of a single enclosed room in absolutely *perfect* ecological balance; bugs, spiders, snails, mice, cats, birds, green plants. Lots of plants. She grows avocados. She has just written a syndicated newspaper column, illustrations and all, to tell *other* women how to grow avocados.

(The technique. We pitch camp on opposite sides of the marital river and in the best Roman tradition burn as many fires as possible, to try and show the other side we have more troops, more strength, than we actually do.)

She has stepped on one of the dead worms after all. With the five men watching she swings off the sidewalk and wipes her foot on the grass (*never forget the way that felt*), thinking of the collage she's just finished. The top is a photo of a crocodile partially submerged in green water, a black line bisecting the whole and the animal's evil black eyes just barely showing above the water's surface. Below that, she has cut out the second paragraph of the response to her application for a teaching position in studio art and drawn a black border around it. "Since you mentioned your acquaintance with Professor Lynn Jones and are living in Dallas, I feel I should tell you the tragic news that he died December second here in New

Orleans at his residence of suicide. We are all still quite shaken by the loss of a colleague we admired so much." Her only thought upon receiving the letter was, He's the first of us, our friends, to go the way I'm sure so many will. Now with the men watching she thinks again, The first of many.

She stands with her classic profile turned toward them just inside the window of a Winn-Dixie, waiting for the machine to deliver Top Value Stamps, her hair long again now. (It was short, shingled, in the photograph.) Pays the eight dollars thirteen cents. Picks up the bag of alligator pears, mushrooms, milk, ground meat and eggs.

Five men are watching my wife walk down Rosedale.

There is a worm in her belly, planted there last night.

There is a rose in her teeth.

She is crossing the street.

She is trying to sing.

It is five o'clock.

(Applause.)

SECOND THOUGHTS

I was wakened by a polite, quiet coughing in the front room. I crawled across the Murphy bed, pushed the door open and looked out. On the sofa sat a small, pale man. His legs were crossed and he stared silently out, watching as boats pulled themselves slowly down the river calling to one another through the fog. Lights entered by the same window. They flared in dark eyes, turned to shadow, dropped onto a white shirt. His hair was a startling black, cheekbones high, face narrow as a plank.

He turned his head slowly toward me. "What can I do to make you believe that I'm wholly sincere?" he said. It was then that I recognized him: this was Artaud.

I got out of bed, without speaking went to the desk for a pen and paper, put them before him.

"You don't know what it's like," he said. "You come out of it and you can't find yourself. Something is irretrievably lost."

Unthinkingly he began to draw on the paper, sketchy gray lines tumbling into patches of black scribble. Faces of those he knew, perhaps, devil masks, plugs of matter pulled from deep within the world's core.

I nodded and moved to switch on a small electric lamp beside him. He pulled himself up straight in the chair, alarmed. I stepped back. Another boat came into view in the window.

"'Very little is needed to destroy a man; he needs only the conviction that his work is useless,'" I said.

Outside, a car stopped in the street opposite and its headlights went off. There was the sound of doors closing, laughter, a young man and woman. Artaud listened intently, and only when their voices vanished into the house did he turn back, to stare down at the paper on his lap. Everything he had, everything he was, strained now toward the external world that lay outside himself, I felt: strained, and fell short.

On my way back to the bedroom I turned on the radio. Softly, so neighbors would not be bothered. Porter Waggoner was singing about "The Cold Hard Facts of Life." My visitor turned his head toward the radio and the light from outside hung on the bones of his face, making his cheeks look cavernous, hollow, reminding me of Yeats: "and took a mess of shadows for its meat."

Anne was four days gone. Slow glide along the ridge of mountain rimming our city at six in the morning, spilling over into America. When she told me she was leaving, I quoted Cavafy. Don't hope for new worlds or new seas, I told her. The way your life is ruined here in this small corner is the way it's ruined everywhere.

As I drifted back into sleep I realized another voice had joined that of my first visitor.

"Volition," said one.

"Guilt," said the other.

Antonin Artaud and Claude Eatherly were discussing the problem of conscience.

UNDER CONSTRUCTION

They stood together there in the center of the room. The man rubbed thumb against fingers, feeling the grit of dust and refuse he'd bent to lift from the floor. Turning on one foot, the woman reached to brush the wall with her hands, then brought them to her face. There were smears of grayish white on the palms, from the paint.

"It's lovely," she said.

"One of a kind," the real estate agent, a Mr. Means, told them.

"But rather dear," the man said.

"You *could* look at it that way, I suppose. Have you been looking long? Seen what's out there? I'm assuming this is your first unit together." There was a gleam in his eyes. Surgically implanted, the man had heard. He had no idea if it were true. You were always hearing these things.

The woman nodded.

"And not just everyone can appreciate character like this. An exact reproduction, you know. Here," he said, "let me show you."

Taking the two short strides needed to reach the room's far side, he pulled back what appeared to be paneling on the wall but was in fact a curtain. Man and woman alike drew startled breaths.

A window!

"Fine touch, isn't it? From an artisan upstate. Best there is. They say he worked for years just to get the staining right. Glass looks like it's been up there ten, twenty years."

Down in the street, not in the street actually, but next to it, in a long, broad alley, workmen were erecting a wall. A dozen or more stood on line, passing rough-cut blocks of stone from hand to hand. The last man in line set a stone in place atop the wall. Then he moved to the rear of the line to wait his turn as the others shifted forward.

On the way here the man and woman had come across a construction crew lined up alongside streetcar tracks. The tracks went for several blocks and ended as abruptly as they'd begun. There were no indications of further construction, or of a streetcar.

"I'm also assuming," Mr. Means said, "that this would be short term."

The woman looked first at the man, then toward the floor when he said, "Of course."

"Different rates, you see. Long term, now that, you ever want to consider it, sometime in the future maybe, that one has teeth. But short term, like I brought out to you on the wire, on that I can give you a sweet deal. *Good* numbers. Wouldn't even have to run them by my handler." He smiled. "Just so you know. Now you take your time, look around all you want, get the feel of the place. I'll just stand over here, out of your way."

So saying, he took up position by the outside door. If someone came in, they might hang a coat on him without thinking. If anyone else could have got in here.

He owed this to her, owed it to himself, the man was thinking. If life couldn't have some specialness to it, something at the center that really mattered, how could it matter at all? He'd watched all his parents and all those around him, all his life, go on and on and without. Same schedule, same events, same thoughts and feelings day after day. A gray blur, like the air above. Until finally the blur seeped into you as well, and settled there.

"We'll take it," the man said.

"Oh, darling!"

Mr. Means nodded. "I hoped you'd realize how right it is for the two of you. Saw that right away, myself." A recorder appeared. He held it half at arm's length, peering. Fingers moved on the eye. "Short term at—"

"Long term," the man said.

The woman turned her head sharply to him.

"Long term," Mr. Means said without missing a beat. "Of course. Now for that, like I brought out to you, I have to go by the book, get approval from my handler." Light touch on the eye here, little more than a brush, longer one there. Then the smile: "Course, I never was much one for the books."

Finished, Mr. Means thumbed the recorder to display mode.

The man looked it over and entered his code as Mr. Means glanced discreetly away.

"Welcome home," Mr. Means said, and went out the door.

When the man turned back, his wife (he'd have to start thinking of her that way now, he reminded himself) was gone. From the bathroom, that marvelous bathroom with crumbling plaster walls, broken tiles and rust stains, he heard the toilet flush. Mr. Means had shown them how the toilet used actual water, two gallons that got filtered, purified and recirculated again and again. There was a second flush as her clothes blew down into the vats for recycling. It sounded as though someone had held down adjacent keys on an accordion and tugged hard.

She came out after a moment and lay on the bed. Neither of them had thought to bring along new clothes; he'd have to go out later to purchase some. It had all happened so fast. But they'd heard about the apartment and rushed right over to see it. Now he'd signed away the equivalent of a full year's labor, enough to provide housing in the commons for the next ten.

Her dark hair lay long and loose on sheets that looked almost like cotton. When he sat beside her, one of the bed's bottom legs collapsed. The man and woman lurched together as though troughing a wave, and when they did, the other legs gave way as well. The man and woman laughed. With something that sounded very much like real joy.

"It's everything I could have imagined, darling," she said at length. "Everything. Oh, thank you!"

Maybe the old ways, some of them, *were* better, he told himself. Maybe we feel the way we do because we've lost all sense of tradition, all continuity. Maybe it's time for us to get some of that, what we can of it, back.

Periodically he woke to dial coffee or gruel from a console in the wall alongside the bed designed to look like an old radio. Once, he started from a dream of seas and dark skies and something coming toward him over the water.

He rose that time and stood by the window. Light had started up again by then. It swelled against the buildings, began enveloping them. Below in the alleyway he could see one of the workers peering over the top of the wall from within as the final bricks were set in place.

Later, when light had given way, had let go its hold again on buildings and sky, he lay awake still as she slept beside him. Cockroaches came out of the walls, following paths of inlaid wires, the same paths each time they appeared. Their eyes seemed to him to glow dully in the dark. He wondered if she knew they were mechanical.

ATTITUDE OF THE EARTH TOWARD OTHER BODIES

Because she is gone.

Each morning, still, he rises at five and puts on coffee. For an hour he studies—languages, usually—then takes the wireless terminal into the kitchen and with breakfast (grapefruit, one piece of wheat toast, a single scrambled egg or bowl of oatmeal) reviews new aspects of the project. All these are habits acquired in college and never given up. He showers then, dresses, and stands for a moment at the door, his apartment still and quiet as the sky.

He arrives, as always, before the others. "Good morning, Doctor," the guard says to him. He inserts his card into the slot, places his palm briefly against the glass plate. He goes through the door and repeats the clearance routine at another door, then down a long, narrow corridor. Here he says simply, "Good morning, Margaret."

"Good morning, John." The door opens for him. "I hope you slept well."

"Not very."

"Then I am sorry, John." A polite pause. "Where will we start this morning?"

"Program Aussie for a sweep of sector A-456/F, I think. Logarithm tables, continuous transmission."

"Duration?"

"Until redirected. And at whatever power levels we've been using in that sector."

All is quiet for a moment until Margaret says, "It is done. Transmission is beginning. You wish Granada to continue broadcasting geometrical theorems?"

"Yes, though maybe we could boost levels a little. Paris is still

sending out the Brandenburgs. Leave her on that. But let's switch
Nevsky over to something new."

After a moment Margaret says, "Yes?"

"I don't know—poetry, maybe."

"What poetry did you have in mind, John?"

"Milton maybe? Or Shakespeare, Dante—Pushkin?"

"Might I suggest Rilke?"

"Yes, Rilke by all means. The *Elegies*. Of course."

Margaret's voice fills the room:

> *Who, if I cried, would hear me among the angelic*
> *orders? And even if one of them suddenly*
> *pressed me against his heart, I should fade in the*
> *strength of his stronger existence.*

And he thinks how cruel it is now, though often before it had
filled his days with joy, that Margaret should have *her* voice.

"Leave all the others on current transmissions."

"Yes, John. Will there be something else?"

"Anything unusual incoming?"

"Some interesting variable emissions from Dresden's sector. A
possible new black hole in Paris's."

"You've notified astronomy, of course."

"Yes."

"Okay, just run off some copy for me and I'll have a look. The
rest of the morning's your own."

Printers begin spitting out sheets dense with numbers and
symbols.

"You'll call me, John, if there's anything else?"

"Certainly, Margaret. Thank you."

"It is my pleasure, John. *Au revoir.*"

And he is alone in the lab, without even her voice now. He looks
up through hanging plants and the skylight to a bright day with no
cloud in sight. There should be rain, he thinks, torrents of rain: *il
pleure dans mon coeur comme il pleut dans la ville.* Then he bends
over the printed sheets, peering into them as one looks into a friend's
face and knows instantly, without analysis, that friend's thoughts and

mood, entering into them as one exists in one's language, beyond particulates or grammar. The emissions from C-389/G-B were indeed most interesting, but (alas) still random.

Random as two people coming together in a sea of others. Random as the chances (they were, after all, so different) they'd fall in love.

She was a musician, working as a secretary to try and make ends meet. For two hours each day after work she practiced oboe. Most of the remaining time she bicycled or read, usually in the bathtub or curled up against the bed's headboard with a glass of wine close to hand. She had a mane of thick brown hair, a narrow waist, and worked at her desk in shirtsleeves, arms alarmingly soft and bare. From her first day she'd always smiled at him.

He watched her for a time, aware of her presence halfway across the building even as he worked, and finally began speaking to her, mostly in the stairwells or halls at first, a couple of times in the lunch line. Then they started coming across one another more often. One day she asked if he'd had lunch yet (he had) and the next day they went together. On the stairs he asked her to dinner. She sat cross-legged in the car with her feet tucked under and slid her hand, at the restaurant, up inside and around his arm. That night, Sunday, he could not sleep and went to the lab at three in the morning. Monday night she went back with him to his apartment. It was her birthday. Neither of them was at work on Tuesday.

They were both so wary, so afraid of being hurt, and yet they seemed unable to stop themselves, to control, whatever its source, the attraction they felt. Verbally, they circled one another like dancers: But what if it happened that . . . I couldn't stand it if . . . I don't want any more surprises. They were two moons circling that central attraction, trying desperately not to collide, knowing they would. Once Margaret spoke to him four times before he surfaced from his thoughts of her to respond. Later there would be an interfering sister, not a villainess, nothing is that simple, that easy, just a sister concerned, a sister afraid things were going too fast, suspicious (as well she might be) of his intentions. But none of it mattered.

Her name was Kim. She'd been through two awful marriages and much abused by the men in her life; she had difficulty believing that a man could be kind to her, could be giving, could truly care. She did not recognize that there was anything within her a man would be drawn to. She kept asking him, Why me? And he truly did not know. Perhaps her sister was right; perhaps he only wanted her, wanted her youth, her beauty, her obeisance.

Perhaps he was just afraid to be alone any longer under this sky pressing down on him.

And so he said, I will not lie to you. I want to be with you. If the time comes that I want to back away, I will tell you so.

You don't want to?

No. No, I don't. You must know that.

I thought you did, maybe. I was afraid.

He runs his hand up her spine, along the soft line of her arm. She leans her head against his chest. *To be so wanted.*

You should be getting home, he says.

Yes.

But they do not move. Car lights wash over them, the guard's flashlight washes over them, they are flooded in moonlight. And still she holds him close against her. From the heave of her chest he realizes she is crying. He asks if she is all right. Yes, she says, I'm fine, but this will all change, you know. It has to, she says. Someday we won't have it anymore. He looks down at the pale coarse skin of her hands and knows he has come too far now ever to be safe again.

He stands at the door of his apartment as though he'd just entered, trying to imagine how another, seeing this for the first time, how *she*, would perceive it. It has character, of course; it's a bit out of the ordinary. And comfortable, like the corduroy coat he wears most days. In fact the apartment is a fairly precise graph of his inmost life. His solitude, his passion for knowledge, the kenning of order and intuition so important to his work—all are there; there in the orderly stacks of books where Chomsky is sandwiched by Tolstoy and Tom Paine, in the bathroom where the medicine cabinet is stuffed with index cards, in the kitchen where he keeps most of the computer and electronic equipment, even in the series of small rugs thrown about seemingly at random over the carpets.

He decides that he would like the person who lived here. He would trust this person, somehow.

Listen to this, she tells him one night as they sit side by side reading, hands locking from time to time and (from time to time) reaching for wineglasses. It is by Flaubert, she says, then reads it aloud: *Human language is like a cracked kettle on which we beat out tunes for bears to dance to, when all the time we are longing to move the stars to pity.*

"That is for us, John," she says. "That was written for us, for the two of us alone."

He moves a hand toward her face and she bows her head to touch it. From far off they hear sirens, the sounds of traffic and slamming doors, the whine of wind, a babble of unintelligible voices.

Everything depends upon our interpretation of the noise surrounding us and the silence at our centers.

By the late-middle twentieth century (and he found this as beautiful as a kite looping into May sky, as the order in a closed system of numbers or the sudden flight of birds) science had advanced sufficiently that it ceased being merely descriptive—that is, narrative—and became almost lyrical. There is, after all, not much distance between William James's insight that reality is relative and multiple, that the human mind (and therefore the world) is a fluid shimmering of consciousness, and Schrodinger's cat. Science had become Wallace Stevens's blue guitar, a fecund reservoir of our attempts to understand, to contrive order. Trying to explain the world to me, Camus wrote, you are reduced to poetry. Perhaps he was right.

Language was at the base of both, of course, of everything finally, the limits of our language the limits of our world. And Chomsky believed that all the world's languages shared certain abstract rules and principles, not because these were implicit, particularly rational, or historical, but because they had been programmed into human minds by the information carried in DNA. He hoped in studying the most formal of these universals, rules and how those rules determine the structure of sentences—in short, basic grammar—to map the mind's self-limits. For grammar is a highly sophisticated information system, admitting messages, screening out noise.

Every day he sat surrounded by noise, tape upon tape of noise,

noise turned into simple, fluctuating graphs on the screens about him, noise as rows of binary figures on huge sheets of spindled paper, noise analyzed for him in several ways (only some of which he understood) by Margaret, searching for a single incontrovertible instance of *grammar*, for algorithms that would (he knew) leap from the noise surrounding them.

What he did not know, was what he would do when that happened; he had no doubt that it would. His life would in many ways be over then, his great work, the work for which he'd programmed himself so long, done—done at age thirty-six, or forty-nine, or fifty-three. He could spend his remaining years studying languages, he supposed. Or music.

He brought the brandy glass close to him and looked at the world upside-down within it, a tree, a black car, the house across the street. Remembered how on their first night together they had shared a glass of brandy and in the morning, after she was gone, he stood staring at traces of her lipstick on the glass's rim. How she'd left a note saying she couldn't talk to him now or she wouldn't be able to do it, then had phoned, and finally met him, because he had to understand, goddamn it, he just *had* to understand.

In quantum theory nothing is real unless it is observed. Or as Einstein held, It is the theory which decides what we can observe.

And so he watches her walk away from him into a stream of people sweeping toward the subway entrance. And in the morning he returns to Margaret, to his graphs, his paper, his noise.

But now, in a circle of light and the ever-present, distant din that is the city's pulse, he reads about the male spadefoot toad. For a year or more it waits buried beneath the parched surface of the Arizona desert, and when the rainstorm the toad awaits at last arrives, plunges into daylight, racing to the nearest pool of water and sending out frantic calls to females. If it does not mate on the first night, it may never mate at all; by morning the water will be dwindling, and the toad's life with it.

Because he wanted, just one more time, to be in love.

Gradually he realizes that he is awake. A sense of loss in the dreamworld receding from him; the brightness of the moon in his window; a murmur of wind. The phone rings again. His mouth is painfully dry. He tastes far back in his throat last night's Scotch.

"John? I rang earlier, just once, to allow you to awake a bit more naturally . . . Are you there?"

Her voice, as though continuing the dream.

He grunts.

"Barleycorn again, John? Are you all right?"

He grunts a second time.

"There is incoming you will want to see, now. Emissions from a new sector. They are diverse, unaccountable, and do not appear random."

He is instantly alert.

"Thank you, Margaret. I'll be right in. Please notify Security I'm on my way."

"I've already done so."

He glances at the clock beside him (2:59 A.M.) and downs a quart of orange juice while dressing and washing up. He glances in the mirror on his way out and sees a rumpled youngish man with round glasses and serious, down-turned mouth, hunched over as though always in a hurry, as though bent about some central pain deep within him or slowly closing in upon him. This fleeting image stays with him.

The night is clear, each star bright and perfect as a new idea. There is no traffic, no one else about. He is alone in the world. And for the nine minutes it takes him to reach the lab he is a part of the earth, and yet escapes its pull, its final possession, to enter into sky, as only the night walker, sheathed in solitude, ever does—something like Rilke's *angels*, he imagines, though transitory. He thinks of Goethe's "emptiness above us," of the first poem he can remember ever reading, Walter de la Mare's "The Listener."

A guard stands just inside the outer doors and unlocks them for him. He feeds his card into the terminal, places his palm against the glass: actions he no longer thinks about. Then through another door, past the second terminal, into the corridor. Hall lights come on as he advances, are shut off behind him.

"Thank you, Margaret."

"You are welcome. I hope that I've not disturbed you unnecessarily. Copy is on your desk. I will wait."

He goes into the lab and stands for a while at the window, looking out at the light-choked horizons of the city, at the dark above riddled with stars. Finally, knowing he is only delaying, he goes to the desk and looks closely at several of the thickly printed sheets. He senses that Margaret is about to speak.

"No," he says. "It is nothing. I thought, for a moment . . . But no."

"Then I am sorry, John."

"It's all right. My dreams were not good ones. I'd as soon be awake."

"That is not what I meant."

"I understand. Goodnight, Margaret."

Then, later, dawn not yet rosy-fingered but definitely poking about in the sky: "Margaret?"

"Yes, John."

"I want an override accessing me to all transmissions."

"There is no facility for such access."

"But it can be done?"

He sits watching incoming noise waver and change on the screens about him until (and it is by then full dawn) Margaret says, "It is done."

"Thank you."

"Is there anything else?"

"No, not now."

"I will wait, then."

"Margaret . . ."

After a moment: "Yes?"

"Nothing . . . I will talk to you later."

"I will wait."

He rolls his chair toward the console. For a long time he sits there motionless, considering, sorting through phrase after phrase, seeking the precise algorithms, the barest grammar, of his pain. Light blossoms about him like a wound.

With two fingers he types out *I loved her, and she is gone*, then a transmission code and Enter/Commit.

He waits. Day marches on outside, noise builds. A telephone rings somewhere. Graphs quiver and shimmer about him. Soon there will be an answer. Soon he will hear the click of printers starting up and his work will be done.

INTIMATIONS

Sometimes the child, who has no name, bangs the tin can (for water) along the bars of its cage.

She has not been in the room, near the room, for months now.

Each morning before he goes to work he snaps on the leash and takes it for a walk. Raising a leg, it waters fireplugs, trees, automobile tires.

In some ways the child is very bright.

Though he tried, at first, they do not talk of the child anymore.

He feeds it at five each day in the little bowl with the Disney characters on it, table scraps and rich red meat. It hunkers in the corner of the cage, the far corner (to which it always carries the bowl), and shoves the food into its mouth with tiny hands. This lasts two minutes.

Its hands are dexterous.

Sometimes at night he goes in and talks to it. Business, that is what he knows, that is what he speaks of. The events of his day, the latest Dow-Jones, the new management position in the Midwest.

It lies on its side on the floor of the cage, looking out at him with wide, uncomprehending eyes.

But there is a spark of intelligence deep within them.

His own IQ has tested out at, variously, 121, 136, and 156; he does not know hers, but it must be high. (Often, he suspects she is more intelligent than he.) She has an MFA. They have built a studio onto the house. She spends most of her time there. It has a daybed.

He wonders at these times if the child knows who he is. Why he is there.

He suspects it does.

One night it reached out to him as he talked. Its hand struck the bars of the cage. It made sounds.

I—no longer can I accept the burden (I had thought it freedom) of an impersonal "he"—stand in the park at Twelfth Street and Forest

Lane. While around me on this Monday morning range children retarding their journey to school and young girls (or so they seem) with bright cheeks pushing prams.

The air is clear and fresh, some freak of wind or a shift in direction having borne away our accustomed weekend smog. Sunlight rests almost palpably on every surface.

And the child paces the leash. No longer does it pull against it, run to the end, or ferry side to side; this has not happened for some time now.

I stop, and the child stops.

Above our heads in a willow tree (I know this because the bronze plaque on the trunk names it), an adult bird (male? female?) injects half-digested worms (insects?) into the gaping beaks of fledglings. Far off to the right, a plane appears to be plummeting through the blaze of morning and into the river.

I whistle softly and the child turns from its study of the dragonfly buzzing its face. Eyes like spots of tarnish move to my own.

I walk forward and unsnap the leash, coiling it about my wrist. I suppose I wonder (I must) if I know what I am doing. Or why.

(The eyes descend momentarily, return to mine.)

And I walk away from this.

Glancing back at the end of the walk strip (yes, Lot; yes, Orpheus—see: even now I try to distance the real event with allusion, dead things) to find the child trailing behind me.

I lift my arms. Wave them wildly; stamp my feet on the pavement. The child skitters away a few steps and ranges back.

And so—save me, that it should come to this; that I should have to confess it—I raised a foot upon which at that moment resided an Italian slipper of softest glove leather, and directed it toward the child's small, strange body. It struck him in the ribs; he fell.

Again and again I struck out at him and still he made no move. Six times. Until, on seven, his hand clawed at the grass beneath him. Eight, nine, he was to his knees, ten, his feet, running, eleven, going, gone.

Far horizons released the last captive strands of day.

And as he ran into it, I saw that he limped.

• • •

Into the room where I've never been, I move carefully. To see will these objects, forms accept me.

Light falls through orange glass and lays the head of a Renaissance lady dimly on the covers and green cushions of the daybed before me. In the corner beyond, stacks of newspapers and journals ascend, Babel-like, toward the ceiling. A huge ashtray supports a single smoldering cigarette.

On an easel by the window is a painting in progress. The background of park, grass, swings is well defined, the closer slide less so. On the slide a formless something courses toward the ground.

She is standing by the painting and, with but a brief glance at my face, passes beside me and into the hall. We do not speak. I follow.

Even before the door to his room, words do not pass between us, though perhaps at this point I nod once and quietly (I do not remember).

Silently, she swings the door out, steps inside, shuts it.

Now she sits in the far corner of the cage, looking out at me.

I think there is a smile on her face and as her hand moves toward the tin can, I realize she is thirsty.

THE INVASION OF DALLAS

There are 129,596 traffic signs in the city.

There are also other signs.

Most are gentle things: DRIVE FRIENDLY, STOP, YIELD.

But some are deadly.

Man is a social animal?

So the first reports stated, and so, on the surface, it seems. They travel in pairs, aggregate in groups.

But each (it cannot help realize, though it does not yet understand) is forever locked within its own skull.

THE LONELINESS.

As a man enters the body of a strange woman the first time, so the alien enters this new social order.

In its spaceship that looks like a '73 Datsun pickup, the alien explores the city. The cloverleaves, the freeways, the baskets that scoop up quarters. The traffic signs.

Later it explores a woman's body in much the same way. Here, too, it discovers, and in what led to this, there are traffic signs.

The language, it understands. But this other semantics, it does not, cannot.

It can see no difference, for instance, between the sprawling proud city and this woman's body.

The woman is driving down Turtle Creek Blvd. to a bar called The Stoneleigh P.

It is a Friday night.

The woman tells the alien about the three parties she is attending the next night, with whom it does not know.

This awakens in it, strange feelings it has not experienced before.

Sitting in The Stoneleigh P, it looks around, as the woman talks, at all the different—different!—faces, bodies, gestures. The semantics of a disorder which carries within it an implicit order it cannot conceive.

It wonders if it has come too late, if the city has been already infiltrated, if some of these others are not actually, like itself, aliens.

Three weeks have passed.

The concept of self-regeneration preoccupies the alien. It can grow a new hand, leg, organ. A thing it shares, or so it thinks, with certain lower species here.

For the first time it occurs to it that there may exist, deeper things which can*not* be replaced.

Where is it? What is it doing here?

The gratuitous semaphores which mean so much, the lineaments and cross-hatching of this new reality.

It fills notebooks.

It is to survey this city; the books contain notes on anthropology, psychology, sociology, defense.

There are other things it is supposed to do as well. (Increasingly, the notes concern the woman.)

THE LONELINESS.

The woman.

It chose her house at random, as it chose its features, build. Knocked on the woman's back door.

Jim, she said. We weren't expecting you this early.

The woman believes the alien is her divorced husband. "He" will stay with her over Christmas, on the couch in the den (male humans pick her up at the front door); after that, she finds "him" an apartment a few blocks away, to which she never comes.

The alien moves in, parking the spaceship on the street outside.

At times the woman will hug "him" (as though she does not want to let go) and kiss "him" on the cheek, say, I enjoy being with you.

One night it is sitting alone in the apartment, drinking and working at its notes.

The phone rings.

Can you keep the child Saturday night, the woman says. There's a party I want to go to.

The alien pauses.

Sure, it says.

What were you thinking.

Things, it says.

Better left unsaid, the woman says.

Two minutes later, she calls back,

Listen. You don't mind my going out do you, you don't think it's wrong.

No of course not.

I mean I don't want to feel guilty. I don't want to be disappointed. Or you either. You don't expect to have a relationship with me do you. I have a lot of people I go out with.

It is becoming more confused each day. Sex, it cannot conceive; no such thing exists on its world. Yet it knows, both from research and observation, that sex is, on *this* world, a primary motive force, that sex, the potential of it, floats like a fog about every human action. Or so it seems, as the alien tries to comprehend.

And these strange new feelings within? When it is with the woman, talking to the woman, away from the woman. What are they?

And how to interpret the woman's ambivalence. The contradictions, the crossfire, of her actions, words.

It does not understand.

It is not aware that the human form it has taken, from the time it approached the woman, is gathering itself into it.

It does not realize the simple, overwhelming *power* of this form.

Not strength. Power.

It finds alcohol (nothing like this exists on its world) an interesting, alluring experience.

It sits alone at night in its apartment and drinks.

It ponders the relationship of this activity with that of sex and of another human thing it cannot understand, death.

There are definite, definitive connections.

It understands that alcohol is an open door, a means of escape.

It does *not* understand what it is trying to escape from.

Its true self.

Its human form.

Another time, the alien returns the child and a male human is at the woman's house. The male human has wanted to meet "him" for some time. (The woman's husband is a writer; the male human wants to be.)

The alien and the male human talk. The woman asks the alien to stay for dinner. The alien and the male human talk further.

It becomes obvious that the male human is spending the night.

A half-gallon of wine disappears.

The alien leaves at ten.

It awakes in the night from a dream of the woman (this, dreaming, is, again, something it knows nothing of) and its appendage is spurting thick white fluid against the bedsheets.

Perhaps this is when it begins to understand.

The alien writes in one of the notebooks,

The woman's hips are broad, inviting; the torso above, fragile, delicate; the legs muscular, substantial.

She calls.

(Patter.)

The alien says, We need to talk.

About what.

You and me.

I told you that several days ago.

The alien invites her to go with it to a nearby city. (She has said she would like to go there.) It says, We can go together. You do what you want, see your friends, I do what I'm going there for.

(Patter.)

What, she says. You're suddenly subdued.

It hates telephones. And words are so inadequate, yet all these people have.

Okay, she says. We could drive down together, it would be fun. (Patter.)

Any time you want, then. Tonight, tomorrow. But what do we have to talk about.

You said last night we needed to talk.

I just don't want to feel guilty. I know what you want, what I'm going to do.

And that, the alien supposes, ends it. What to talk about indeed.

It does not understand this woman, the confusion.

Is it hers.

Its.

Jagged ruins of semantics rise into afternoon sky.

The alien sits looking at the dead phone, attempting to analyze the "emotions" it now experiences. A semantics in their own right.

But: something more.

A woman flees Neiman Marcus screaming.

A monster! There's a monster in there!

And so (though I escape) I am discovered.

And so the missiles are swung toward my world, missiles that will strike soon. Computers consulted (logic), steel making its way through void (poetry). Buttons pushed. And even in this, semantics of sexuality.

The woman is twelve blocks away.

My world is (or will be—what difference can it make?) in ruins.

Dead.

THE LONELINESS.

DRIVING

The signs began a few light years out:

YOU ARE APPROACHING THE END OF THE UNIVERSE
DRIVE CAREFULLY
LAST CHANCE FOR GAS FOOD PHONE LODGING
CURB YOUR DOG

I had a Harry Partch sonata on the player, I remember, and it seemed to be slowing appreciably as I approached, but with Partch it's hard to tell. Then I came around a sharp corner and saw what looked like a dirty shower curtain hanging there in the air, obliterating everything behind.

As I drove through, I saw other signs:

YOU ARE LEAVING THE UNIVERSE
WE HOPE THAT YOUR STAY HAS BEEN A PLEASANT ONE
AND THAT YOU WILL VISIT US
AGAIN SOMETIME

Just below that was a smaller sign:

DO NOT LITTER

There was a slight tingle, a *frisson*, as I passed through, nothing more. The sun shone brightly. I pulled to the side of the road for a moment and sat with the engine idling. Fields of tract houses stretched away from the road on either side, each with a small cedar fence, bank of lime-green steel garbage cans, and rusted-out VW. There was no sign anywhere of shops, restaurants, filling stations. I began to wish I'd paid more notice to the last chance signs; my fuel gauge was pegging pretty close to *E*.

As I sat there a truck pulled up alongside me. It was ancient. The bumpers, fenders and door were made of sheets of galvanized metal welded together at odd angles and then to the truck's body with no effort to camouflage the seams, which looked like raggedly healed knife wounds.

"Reckon you might be needing gas." An old man canted toward me in the truck's cab as though against a heavy wind, his left hand still hanging on to the wheel, his chin barely reaching above the truck's window. His beard appeared to be crusted solid with tobacco and food drippings.

I nodded.

"Thought so."

I waited, but that seemed to be all he had to say. I shut the engine off. Then after a while he said, "People don't take much to driving 'round these parts," and cackled with sudden laughter. Before I could reply he was climbing down out of his truck. He walked around to the back and stood there squinting into the distance. "Reckon it'll be along any time now," he said. Then he walked to the front of the truck and did the same thing. I noticed that he limped badly, favoring his right leg, on which he wore a cowboy boot. The other foot was in an old-fashioned, high-topped tennis shoe, a piece of twine tied around it near the toe.

"Excuse me," I said, "but you did mention gas."

He looked at me closely. "Things take time and time takes things." He looked away.

Just then a far corner of the community detached itself and began rolling toward us. As it came closer I saw that it was a fully equipped service station. In the center of an expanse of cement, in a small hut like a tollbooth, sat the attendant. When it pulled up before us, I started the engine and drove onto the lot, stopping by one of the pumps. I sat there.

"Self serve," the old man said. And as I got out and began filling the tank, he went over to the hut. The attendant broke a piece of gum in two and passed one half through the tiny front window. They talked together in low tones, gesturing vaguely toward the community, their voices occasionally rolling into soft laughter.

"No charge, son," the attendant said when I approached. He had a well-trained handlebar moustache and full, red lips. "Where you headed?"

"Just driving, I guess."

"Right. Driving." He nodded a couple of times, solemnly. "You drive careful now. Don't be getting in a hurry. Things take time and time takes things."

I thanked both him and the old man and pulled out of the station. In the rearview mirror I watched the station start its glide back toward the houses, then passed around a curve.

The road was absolutely level. Its wide shoulders quickly tapered to a narrow band of bare ground at either side, and beyond that there were only two seas of grass and, far off, twin gray horizons that grass spilled into.

I had just settled back into the seat for a long, relaxed drive and was spinning the radio dial to find some music (nothing but static) when I came over a hill and braked to a stop: with no warning, the road abruptly ended. I got out and stood on a small gray island in the middle of a green sea. No sign of other roads. The grass seemed uniformly six inches tall. There was a slight, unhurried wind.

After a while I turned and drove back toward the town. I was certain (but I may be wrong) that it took me far longer to return. I circled the town four times without finding any way to enter, or any sign of the service station, and finally pulled over and stopped the engine. Sooner or later . . .

I came awake with a start and realized that the old man had pulled his truck up behind me and was standing by my window. Though the sun was in the same place it had been before, I felt rested.

"You all right, young man?"

"Fine, thanks." I gestured back the way I'd come. "The road ends up there."

"Sure does. Don't need a road. No one ever goes that way."

"I did."

"Well, you tried, anyhow." He glanced off into the distance. "I expect you been trying to find a way into town, too."

I nodded.

"Town's closed. Can't nobody get in. Like to keep to themselves, those folks."

"But you—"

"Closed to me too. Old Zed at the gas station, he just keeps me up on the gossip sometimes."

"But if you don't live there, what are you doing here?"

He peered closely at me. "Why, I drive, son. Same as you do."

He walked back and got in his truck, then pulled up beside me and leaned over, just as he had the first time I saw him.

"Reckon you might try going that way," he said, nodding toward one of the narrow roads to the right. "That would be a good way to start."

"Start where?" I said.

"Driving, son. Just driving, that's all." He lifted a hand. "Be seeing you."

And I knew that he would.

I drove down the road he'd pointed out and after a while came across a hitchhiker, a small wiry fellow wearing a *yarmulke*. He got in, nodding thanks, and sat beside me quietly for some time. The road began to widen.

"Been here long?"

I shook my head. "You?"

"Forever." He looked out over the expanse of bright green grass. "How shall a man find his way?"

Beats me. I shrugged and turned on the radio. Clarinets and rippling dulcimers: *klezmer* music.

"That's good," he said. "Leave it on."

The road stretched out before us to the horizon, pulling us on. We picked up speed. Far off I thought I could make out boulders, clouds.

NEED

He wasn't sure exactly when he had first noticed the child, but several miles outside Milford, glancing up at the rearview mirror, he saw her there in the backseat and realized that she had been there, an unremarked presence, for some time. Yet he is certain they had no child along when they checked into the Fountain Bay last night. He tries to remember pulling out of the parking lot this morning, looking in the mirror as he would always do. He thinks maybe she was there then. But he's still not sure.

The girl is reading a hardbound book with a green cover. There seem to be (in the mirror it's difficult to tell) dancing bears on the cover, a family of them perhaps.

"Good book?" he says after a while.

"It's okay, Dad."

"What's it about?"

"I told you yesterday. A daughter who vanishes without a trace."

"Do they find her?"

"I don't know. I haven't finished it yet, silly."

"I bet they do."

Beside him Rosemary's needles continue their minute orbits around one another. Whatever she is knitting now is green also.

"Always reading, that one," she says.

"You want to stop for breakfast yet?"

"Not unless you do."

"Well, let's go on another hour or so, then."

"Fine. We could stop at that truck stop just this side of Helena where we stopped last year."

"Sounds good. I'd forgotten about it."

Beneath bare trees the grass remains green. There are scattered small pools shallow as mirrors from last night's rain. From the radio come strains of a waltz.

Once, waking from nightmares of loneliness (he no longer knew how long it had been, or cared), he found Rosemary beside him, as though she had always been there.

They pass through a crossroads with a crumbling onetime gas station (tin soft drink signs still cling to its sides), Mac's Home Cooking 24 Hrs., a small wood church set up on pylons, a feed store. There is a mile or so of fence then, thick posts with single boards nailed obliquely between them, like mirror-image Ns.

The girl puts her book down for a while and sleeps, curled into one corner of the seat. Rosemary pulls out an entire row and starts it again. He can hear the needles faintly clacking together.

They stop at a Union 76 for breakfast not too long after. The girl (Rosemary has started calling her Cynthia) does not want anything.

"Never eats anything, that one," Rosemary says.

There is not much traffic, and early in the afternoon a fleet of bright-colored balloons passes over. Behind them clouds gather as though towed into place by the balloons. At one point they follow a truck piled with sugarcane for several miles. Then they drive through a pounding rain back into sunlight. When they stop again to eat (and again Cynthia wants nothing) it is almost dark; the moon is like a round hole punched through the darkness.

They leave and drive into that darkness. There is more traffic now, as they near the city. He spins the dial between classical, country, jazz and rock, unable to decide. Billboards at the side of the road advertise topless bars, car dealers, restaurants and motels, Jesus, museums, snake farms. Cynthia wakes and asks, "Are we almost there, Dad?"

"Almost, honey," he says.

Beside him Rosemary winds in her yarn, tucks the needles away. "Try this on, Cyn," she says. He watches in the rearview mirror as his daughter pulls on the green sweater that fits her perfectly. For the first time he realizes that it is cold.

The traffic gets heavier. It comes from far away, tiny points of light like ideas. Then they come closer, and as they come, cars and trucks take shape around them.

OLD TIMES

The man in front of you in line says, "I don't suppose you could tell me if a crash is scheduled?"

You turn to shrug apologetically, impotently, at those behind you in line. Some harsh faces there. You quickly turn back.

He's thirtyish, well dressed in a middle-America sort of way, crumply brown slacks and sport coat, crisp white shirt with yellow knit tie, hair a close-clipped tangle of curls. There's a newspaper folded in one side coat pocket. An oversize flight bag lies crumpled on its side like a discarded boot beside him.

Smiling, the ticket clerk looks up at him and says, "You know I can't give out that information. Sorry, Paul." It's quite a smile, something she has a talent for.

New statistics scroll onto the board above her head.

FLIGHT INTERRUPTIONS DOWN BY 28%
FATALITIES TO DATE THIS MONTH . . . 923
LOWEST FARES—ALL FOR YOU

He glances briefly about, aware at last of the growing unrest here behind him.

"Hey, it's *me*, Gladys. The guy who taught you how to overbook, take double breaks—all the important stuff."

Her smile never wavers.

"I remember you, Paul."

"We used to be like *that*."

"Before you went to a competitor."

"Gladys. Western offered me almost twice the money, better hours, perks. What else could I do? What would *you* have done?"

Above her head, with the rest of the board remaining the same, FATALITIES shifts unremarked to 1180.

"Anyone understands, it has to be you. I'd have been right here punching buttons the rest of my life. With Western at least I had a chance—thought I had, anyway."

"It didn't work out for you, then."

"No. No, I'm sorry to say it didn't, not this time. But I'm on my way to an interview in Chicago, and this one, I've got a good feeling about."

She hands the envelope, tickets tucked safely away inside, boarding pass stapled to the outside, across the counter.

"Thank you for flying Allied," she says. "Next, please."

The man turns fleetingly and smiles at you, at this potential mob back there. Rip his heart out. So hard to get a break in this world. He turns back.

"Gladys," he says, "please. I haven't worked in almost a year. Now—finally—I have an interview. And I have a chance. But I need your help. For the old times?"

She looks at him, then down at her VDT. Walks fingers over her keyboard as FATALITIES blinks away at 1180. She looks over the rabbit she's pulled out of this electronic hat.

"You're confirmed straight through to Chicago, Mr. Paulson."

Thanking her, he reaches for her hand but she doesn't extend it. His own hovers there by the stack of luggage labels and credit card applications. Finally he withdraws it.

"I won't forget this," he says. "I owe you, Gladys."

He shrugs into his oversize shoulder bag and starts off toward the gate. There is a milling already at its mouth. We could all still make it.

"Friend of yours?" the ticket agent next to Gladys says.

"Sort of. Paul trained me. I had a crush on him like you wouldn't believe but he never so much as noticed me. I cried for weeks."

"Before that competitor got him."

"Yeah." She laughs. "The competitor. A blonde. Of course, we were all a lot younger then."

"Some things stay with you."

"Some things do."

She turns back and says, "Can I help you, sir?"

You hold out your ticket, but for a moment she goes on staring into space, a tight smile on her lips, and doesn't reach for it. You wonder if you really want to go to Chicago today.

BECOMING

Following many tests and much consultation among themselves, the doctors inform me that, slowly, inexorably, my body is turning to stone. Sheaves of computer printouts clutched in their hands, they show me X-rays, tracing of various internal pressures and electrical measurements, thick plastic sheets of CAT-scan records with multiple images of brain, liver, digestive system, heart. They tell me they can pinpoint where it began: *here* (a gentle finger taps at one of these icons of self), but cannot say why. It is, at any rate, progressive. And though they can't be certain, of course, since no one to the best or their knowledge has seen this before, the prognosis seems poor. They do not know how long the process will take. But we—myself, my family, friends—must not despair. There has been already much discussion among top specialists as to appropriate treatment regimens. The process could even reverse itself. This sometimes happens. And there is always hope from new research. They do not explain why anyone should be engaged in research on an illness, a condition, never before seen.

Because there is nothing else to be done, I am released from the hospital. In a lime-green glassy cage of an office a young lady all in white, pleated skirt, sleeveless T-shirt, white shadow on her eyes, guides me through what we still call paperwork, though of course no paper is involved. (Now even I am using the words *of course* reflexively. I've contracted this from the doctors.) In parting, the young lady passes me an appointment card. Several weeks' worth of follow-up visits are listed. White-sheathed lips smile and say good-bye, Dr. Bloom.

The doctors' conglomerate offices occupy a fashionably antique building, rambling and oddly shapeless, perhaps once a railway station or post office. In its cavernous lobby, near the outermost of half a dozen noodle stands and yogurt bars, there's even a callbooth, the first I can remember having seen in years. It appears still to be functional.

I punch in my PIC and stand for several moments before the screen as it prompts me, blinking:

PLEASE ENTER LINECODE

In a corner of the lobby, two steel doors like huge leaves open upward, outward, and sink to the floor. Two men and a barge loaded with boxes ascend operatically from the canals below. A part of my mind registers that barge and boxes alike are of the so-called organic alloy, banana byproducts and recycled plastic, of which increasingly everything in our world, clothing, containers, furniture, seems constructed.

PLEASE ENTER LINECODE OR CANCEL REQUEST

No one knew I was coming here. I have no idea who I might want to call, or what their linecode would be, if indeed they had one. Even less, what I would say, should I actually manage to place a call and have it answered.

IF YOU WISH TO REINSTITUTE, PLEASE ENTER PIC NOW

Three blips, and the screen washes. A blue-green photo of fields and misted mountains constructs itself slowly, piecemeal, in the prompt's place. Years of this image have burned away part of the screen; the highest mountaintop and a portion of cloud beyond it fail to materialize.

Leaving the building, I walk along the river. Business complexes like Colony South may be our closest equivalent to feudal land. For thousands of years humankind built, first its villages, then its ports and cities, alongside water. Now, *ex nihilo*, we create bodies of water wherever we erect our buildings, rivers and lakes, and lagoons that have no name. Colony South's office buildings, upscale restaurants, health clubs and luxury apartments sit along miles of serpentine river and canals whose banks are paved with tile and stone. Couples sit on scroll-like benches at waterside or stroll beneath the low stone arches of bridges and walkovers. Boats of every sort, flat ferries, maintenance and security outboards, rentable two-man paddlewheelers and canoes, make their way along the river and canals in the shadows of the buildings.

When I tire at last of walking, I take to one of the ferries. There's a pilot with throttle and joystick seated in front, a helmsman with wheel at back, a row of seats along either side. Half the seats are occupied. Across from me sit a young man and woman. They are ten years old perhaps. Both go on staring straight ahead as the books in their laps speak to one another.

There was a spider who more than anything in the world wanted to see London, about which he'd heard so much.

Yes, and one day, saying to himself, Why not, I may never have this chance again, he stowed away on a milk wagon.

Alfred his name was. It had been his father's name, too.

Soon, before he knew it, he was far, far away from everything he knew.

But he was not afraid.

Oh, no. And years later, he would remember the man who helped him.

Pigeons strut and peck on the paved banks, and squirrels chatter in trees overhead. The water's an astonishingly deep blue, the sky above not blue at all but instead a kind of whitish-gray, shot through with contrails, banners of industrial waste, clouds that seem never to change or move.

At river's edge, outside Hotel Evropa, I catch a cab. The driver doesn't know my part of the city, and I have to direct him onto the loop, to exit just inside the third beltway, and crosstown. Something gamelan-like, like programmed wind chimes, plays loudly on his tape machine. He turns the volume down.

"You have lived here long?"

All my life, I tell him, yes.

"It is for me two years now. A fine city." He looks about. "Fine. At first, just as I did in," and he names a country I make no sense of. "I piloted boats. Now I pilot this fine car. This is better."

Half a mile from my building we pull up, immobile, as a parade of Watchmen in full regalia, tunics, boots and berets, all black, goes by. My driver with a deep sigh at last shuts off his engine. Fast behind the Watch comes the usual second line of street folk, stray kids, vandals and petty criminals.

The computer says how good it is to have me back as I enter.

38 CALLS

Then:

26 COMPUTER-GENERATED

ELIMINATE?

TALLY?

"Eliminate."

9 AWAIT TRIAGE

TALLY?

"Please."

3 PERSONAL

4 PROFESSIONAL

2 UNCERTAIN

RUN?

"Hold."

I make a cup of maté at the corner sink. The cup is one I picked up in Mexico on a field trip years ago. Grad school? Must have been. Fired ceramic, but utterly hollow in the centimeter-and-a-half between outer and inner walls. The cup weighs less than plastic and feels as fragile as an eggshell. It's outlasted aluminum cookpots, jeans, four notebook computers, and every relationship I've had.

I bring my cup and maté back across the room. There are three others, but the only chair I ever sit in is the one by the console. Across from it (the room is narrow) stands a low bookcase. Books are stacked rather than placed, on their sides in double rows. Still, I know where each one is.

"Go."

RUNNING . . .

A voice I don't recognize starts up.

"I apologize for calling you at home Dr. Bloom, but . . ."

A student, then. Unable to make class this week, she tells me, though she fails to say what class, because of family illness. Marcie Desai. So it would be the graduate seminar, late Greek history.

I try to match a face to the voice and name, at first come up only with something vague around the eyes, a perpetually unfocused look. Then Marcie Desai's face reconstructs itself in my memory. Green eyes, with hazel flecks. Hair she almost certainly once spent hours each day trying to tame and now simply cuts short. A bright student, very bright. Hard, sure edge to her speech, what she says, the way she says it; and at the same time this subtext of deference in her gestures, motion. Accustomed not so much to being turned away as, instinctively, self-protectively, to turning away herself, everything in her life, major decisions to simple daily tasks, only degrees of departure.

END MESSAGE

FILE? DELETE?

"Delete."

CONTINUE?

"Please."

RUNNING . . .

The next two messages arrived online. In the screen's upper left corner an icon appears, a running stick-man, as the first message scrolls up.

RECEIVED YOURS ON THE 14TH, SORRY, 18TH (MUST REMEMBER TO LOOK AT THE CALENDAR PERIODICALLY), RE CONTEMPORARY (CONTEMP(T)?) MARXIST INTERPRETA-TIONS OF THE GREEK CITY-STATE. CERTAINLY THE ENTIRE GROANING, CLANKING MECHANISM OF THAT MARVELOUS

ATHENIAN FREEDOM, ITS DEMOCRATIC TOLERANCE, SOCIAL WELFARE AND CIVIC ACHIEVEMENT, THE ACCOMPLISHMENTS OF ITS PHILOSOPHY AND ARTS, WERE MADE POSSIBLE ONLY BY SLAVERY AND THE SO-CALLED NAVAL FUNDS, I.E., EXTRACTION OF PROTECTION MONEY (LEST BIG BAD BEAR PERSIA GOBBLE THEM UP) FROM OTHER GREEK STATES. NO ARGUMENT THERE. BUT I WONDER IF FINALLY THIS ISN'T JUST ANOTHER FACE FOR OUR OWN OLDEST BUGBEAR, WHAT WE HAVE TO CONTINUALLY REMIND NOT ONLY OUR OWN STUDENTS OF, BUT ALSO OURSELVES, CARLYLE'S SIMPLE TRUTH: THAT MOST HISTORY DESCRIBES NOT HOW LIFE WAS LIVED, BUT HOW IT WAS INTERRUPTED—BY INVASION, WARFARE, PLAGUE OR FAMINE, RIOT, DISEASE, STRIFE. DURING ALL OF WHICH, NONETHELESS, CROPS WENT ON BEING RAISED, HOMES, SMOKEHOUSES, AND OUTHOUSES GOT BUILT, MARRIAGES WERE ENTERED INTO, HUSBANDS AND FATHERS AND CHILDREN DISAPPEARED, FURNITURE WAS PASSED DOWN, BAD BOOKS WRITTEN.

I read this as the larger part of my mind still thinks of Marcie Desai. The set of her features, the softness of her eyes. Memory itself (I think) is a kind of stone. Nudging into place the moments and monuments, the interruptions and departures, that become our lives.

How despairingly Romans sought the secret, that simple, easy grace of Greek statuary. A kind of pure thought coaxed from stone. Stone tha, like the earth itself, bears weight: stone that *is* earth, *of* earth, ejected from earth yet still weighty with it. Stone we pile above our graves, stone from which we learn to construct fences, stone we come to write upon.

". . . I was so afraid then," I hear.

We're down to the last of the messages.

"Stop."

The stick-man icon stands still, blinking.

MESSAGE 7 REPEAT? DELETE?

"Repeat please."

"John? There's no reason you should remember me. I'm sure you don't, and I don't even know why I'm calling you now, or why you've come to mind after all these years. Jean? Jean Patrick? We had Dr. Davis's medieval history course together our first year at Tulane. I was so afraid then. Twelve years in a Catholic girl's school, then that. It was like falling out of a boat and watching the boat pull away. I kept writing down everything Dr. Davis had said in class and getting C's. You asked me out for coffee after class one day, and it got to be a regular thing. You were someone I could talk to. Look, this is ridiculous, I feel like an idiot of some sort, calling you after, what, almost thirty years? But if by some weird chance you do remember me, or if you'd just like to talk for a while, give me a call, okay? Bye!"

Her linecode and PIC come up onscreen.

> END MESSAGES
> FILE?
> DELETE?

"File last voice message. New folder: *Jean*. Print out online re Greek city-states. Delete others."

> CREATING FOLDER JEAN . . .
> DONE
> PRINTOUT GREEK CITY-STATE SEARCH IN PROGRESS
> PRINTING . . .
> CONFIRM DELETE?

"Confirmed."

> WORKING . . .

One of the first messages was from Laura. We've been seeing one another for almost a year now, quiet, rather stylized evenings for the most part, dinners out, theater and concerts, playing the pair among her peers or my own. Undoubtedly, at some level we care for one another. But once alone we have little to say; are careful, in a tiptoeing sort of way, it seems, to avoid much actual conversation.

I brew another cup of maté and, returning to the chair, place a call to Laura. I tell her computer what has happened: my pain and growing dysfunction, today's visit to the doctors, their diagnosis.

I'll be away from the apartment, I say, and will call back later.

Sipping, I gaze out my window. The sky has settled through deepening layers of gray to the color of ripe plums. Odd patches, catching the city's lights, glow like dull neon.

I place a call to Jean and say that yes of course I remember her (I don't) and that yes I'd love to see her (would I?). Maybe we could have lunch together. I'm free most days. Whatever is convenient for her.

I look up again then, into the crosshatch of branches moving gently, their fingers reading the braille of cloud, wind, dark sky.

From far away, in that other world, the computer tells me I have a call.

As I watch, the branches slow.

As I watch, they stop.

THREE STORIES

Afterwards

You were still alive then, and it was harder. It's not easy now, but I know the memories I have are all I *will* have.

I'd moved into a new apartment and, mornings, stood looking into the mirror over the rim of my tea cup, wondering if my sad eyes (you always called them that) had grown sadder. I ran in a nearby park twice a day, filled the other hours as best I could. I walked a lot. There wasn't much room in my head for anything but you and trying to understand why you were gone.

I still don't know if that last time was a mistake, if things might not have been better except for that. I play it over and over in my head, the way I replay so much of our life together, and I can never decide. It's all such a meld of good things and bad.

You'd been gone three weeks, and called to say you'd like to see me that Monday, that we had a lot to talk over. I picked you up at 12:30. Within the hour we were in bed at the old apartment, sun pushing in through blinds, hubbub of quarrels and children all about us.

Afterwards you dozed and, waking, rolled against me, the warmth of your skin, its weight, so familiar. Country music on the radio: your music.

"I really did want to kill myself," you said. "When I woke up still alive, I was furious."

"But why?" I said after a time.

"Don't ask hard questions." You rolled away for a pull of beer, Molson's Golden, and came back. Your hand lay on my leg like a promise. "One time in ICU, when I was on the ventilator, I came to briefly and someone was rubbing me between the legs." You took your hand away. "Like this," you said as I watched. We made love again then, and you slept. I got up for a beer and sat watching. For most of our last month together, after you came back from the hos- pital, you had slept. I sat for hours watching the long slope of your back, your unguarded breast, half-closed eyes. So many memories crowded into my mind. I felt so much for you then, such tenderness and sorrow.

In the car going back you told me that you couldn't go on hurting me and thought it would be easier this way. I watched you in yellow top and shorts walk away from me, the last time I saw you.

There was so much I should have said, so much I wanted to say. Some of it, a little, I put in the letters; one day I wrote you eight of them. Some of it I can never say, because it's unsayable. All the important things are, Wittgenstein tells us.

This was months ago, of course.

Gradually it became my apartment, this shell I'd moved into. I set routines that got me through the day. I sat in bars and restaurants and talked to strangers. I settled into work on a new book, one I'd begun when we were first together, sitting at the window downstairs and writing a page or so as you soaked in your bath, putting it away when you came back down to join me.

This morning at four I finished the book, drank half a bottle of gin, and slept. Around eleven I was heading toward the park to run when the apartment manager came to the office door and called out. I have a message for you, she said, handing me a small slip of yellow paper. I'm sorry, she said. She closed the door.

The paper told me you had died that morning in the emergency room at John Peter Smith. I still don't know who called.

I tucked the paper into my shorts, walked on to the park, and ran—ran with tears rolling on my face, sweat pouring from my body. When I got back, the ink had bled off the paper and there wasn't anything left of you. The apartment was small, and mine. I had a life, also small now, to go on with, whatever didn't happen in it.

Running Away

At the police station downtown the restroom on the third floor is locked because drunks and the homeless come in off the streets at night and sleep there. The officer who gives him the key tells him this with a smug assumption of accord. The building is old and shabby, with paint flaking from every wall, stairs worn dangerously swayback, great automobile-like dents in the filing cabinets.

Returning the key to the desk he sees her in a small room just beyond, sitting behind another girl who stares out into the squad-room drooling onto her AC/DC T-shirt. She, the runaway, is looking at the wall; her shoulders are hunched.

It's two o'clock in the morning and they've come to retrieve a daughter. Grounded for two weeks, she left a dramatic note and ran away. It was a scale-model runaway, to the dimensions of her life: six blocks to the mall and a phone call to a friend whose mother picked her up. There she was found by police, handcuffed and brought downtown. With her are the girl who drools and stares with doll's eyes, an 11-year-old prostitute, another runaway, a teenager who attacked her teacher with a razor.

The mother is hysterical and self-accusing, the father with-drawn. Institutions like this are nothing new to him, nor are the streets; he has survived both; he wants this only to be over. They answer questions, sign documents. The officer who picked her up talks to them for a moment and says they have a nice girl there, he hopes this will help them get things straightened out and if there's anything he can do to help just let him know. The girl is brought out. She does not look at them. She is told to check the contents of her purse and sign a release. An officer has a few final words with her. She says nothing.

They all walk, together for the last time, outside. Street-cleaning trucks are about, lobbing great tides of water onto the sidewalk and curbs. He watches the water break around his shoes. He unlocks and holds the door for each of them, starts the car, turns on the radio: Bartok. "Not *that* stuff again," his daughter says. He turns it off. The jagged city landscape heaves up over the car's hood as he tries to find his way through a labyrinth of one-way streets that keep delivering them back to the central city. He passes one newsstand four times. Then at last finds access to an interstate heading south.

In the backseat their daughter falls asleep. His wife looks steadily ahead into oncoming lights. He turns the radio on low, something large, shapeless, romantic. They pass the state hospital, a mile-long junkyard, the airport, and turn onto the narrow road that will take them home. Stores at roadside, closed many hours ago, are brightly lit. There is little traffic.

He is thinking about the time he sent flowers to her at the office, roses, simply because she'd told him she had always hoped someone might do that someday. Friends, she said years later, had told her that she just *had* to hold on to him. One morning, turning to him in bed, she said that all she'd ever wanted was someone she could love, someone who would love her. In New Orleans they drank café au lait outdoors and watched pigeons strut along the sidewalk. In San Antonio, drove among hills wondering where the city was. In his lunches sometimes he found her notes: *I'll miss you.*

But at the same time he realizes that something has shifted terminally in his mind, that despite these memories he is now looking ahead rather than behind. It is not what he wants, but it's what he has, what they all have.

A Brahms symphony comes on.

"Listen," he says. "When I was young, this was my favorite piece of music in the whole world," and he leans forward to turn up the volume.

"You'll disturb her," his wife says.

The lights of cars and passing billboards give to the drive their own pulsing, staccato rhythm, one in counterpoint to the Brahms he can barely hear.

"Have you ever been happy?" he asks after a while.

"Of course I have," she answers. "What a question."

Lights from an oncoming car blind him for a moment and instinctively he swerves to the right, then back. Soon they will be home.

Resurrection

Sheila killed a man today. Inadvertently, of course; nonetheless, there he is, dead in the pages of a major newspaper.

The call came at 6 A.M. Her editor gets up before dawn every day—opens his garage door to let the sun out, as she once put it—and cannot remember that others don't. Could she come in, he wanted to know, and write a retraction?

On a *Friday*? Sheila said. In the middle of the night?

The man's not dead, Miss Taylor. We've had calls from family, from friends, from his third-grade teacher. Finally he called, himself, to say that he was feeling much better now.

Give me an hour.

We need copy by eight.

She hung up and lay turned away from me, toward the window. Ice on the roof let go and sledded along it to crash onto the patio.

Problem? I asked.

Someone came back to life.

I thought at first, from her sadness, her distance, that she meant an old lover, but she turned and told me. How in a column she had mentioned this man, a painter once and briefly fashionable whom everyone, including the paper's arts editor and omniscient film critic, assured her was dead.

I didn't even write about him. You couldn't. There's not that much there, only what he might have been.

You're going to the office, then?

An hour. Less. Wait for me here?

As she showered and dressed, I stood in the kitchen grinding coffee, putting on water to boil, buttering toast. Outside, a squirrel threw itself between trees, and when it landed, falling in a slow arc through most of the visible sky, I found that I had been holding my breath. I thought of my own life.

Sheila was gone (sliding at that moment, though I didn't know it, over packed ice, a curb, a precipice) when I opened the front door to take out trash and discovered a man standing there.

No bell, he said. I knocked.

The front of the house stays shut off. Friends know to come around to the back. Others go away. Can I help you?

I was looking for Miss Taylor.

I'm afraid she's at the office.

Office, he said. Of course. As though I'd told him she was week-ending on Mars.

I lowered the trash bags, supple and sleek as skin, but cold, to the step.

Can *I* help you?

He looked briefly at the bag, at my hands. You are?

Always a good question. I said: Jim.

He nodded. She writes about you.

Sometimes.

And I, he said, holding out a hand, am the late George Kelley. I am feeling ever so much better, he said. Neither of us laughed. He turned and sat on the top step, looking off into trees, a scatter of ice and snow on the ground beneath them.

I sat beside him. Copies of the *Star-Telegram* and *New York Times* lay in their white bags in the driveway. A dim pulse of music, Vivaldi or Telemann, came from deep within the house.

I read her column, he said. Have for years now. Never can figure quite how she pulls it off. You think she's going one way, then all of a sudden you're somewhere else. Memories and feelings you'd all but forgotten, ways of holding onto the world that you'd thought long since unraveled.

Perhaps you could give her a message for me, he added after a while. We sat together watching as a covey of blackbirds swept from tree to tree down the block. A truck piled high with brush and sod crept by.

Tell her thank you for mentioning me, he said. Will you tell her that for me?

I'll tell her.

And perhaps you'd give her this as well, he said, drawing a roll of canvas tied with strings like old maps from beneath his coat.

Well, he said, standing. I'll take those down for you on my way if you like.

We thanked one another and walked off with our small burdens, George Kelley down the hill and out of sight again around the street's slow curve, myself back into Sheila's house where, coiled in the answering machine, a call from the hospital waited.

THE WESTERN CAMPAIGN

Plans continue on schedule. Today I defecated in the executive urinals, then excused myself from the office early, pleading illness, in time to pour whalebone oil into the VPs' crankcases. Their cars will go twenty, thirty miles, everything in order, before the engines fuse solid. Tomorrow I'll introduce ground bamboo into the cafeteria executive coffee urns.

This morning Zed called me into his office. You've not been with us long, have you, D, he said, British accent pushing words against one another oddly and clipping corners from the edges of things. The wall behind him was glass; he nodded amidst blue sky. Fish the size of his head were painted on the glass. But your work has been, a word I use neither lightly nor often, exceptional. I feel you should know that rather soon Morgan's will have an executive position available. Not something you're at liberty to repeat, of course. But I do suspect you're the man to fill that post.

This could mean the ruin of all my plans. See them gang aft agley, again. I'll have to take care, draw attention away from myself, cut a few false steps. It's all a dance. I spent the afternoon arranging rendezvous with several of the firm's secretaries on Zed's behalf, at the uptown bar where I knew he was to meet his wife after work.

J's waiting for me at the apartment on Charleston, wearing white jeans and a T-shirt the color of morning sky, seated on the low cement wall. Flowers tremble in the breeze behind her. Bushes intricately intertwined with honeysuckle. As I come up the walk, she stands.

"I hope you don't mind."

Shake your head no and step back at the door to let her enter.

Transition's been imperfect. Fragments remain of a previous life. This has never happened before. Should not have happened at all. Then why has it.

Just inside, she stops. Nothing familiar. The slate's been wiped clean, it's a different world in here.

She turns. I think how much I lose, going through these doors.

"You look good . . ." She lifts her hand palm up, propping the sentence open. Like a door.

"Demetrius," I say.

She nods. "Demetrius." On her voice I hear in that name whole lifetimes of foreign ships easing into harbor, men who've left behind land and its stable ways, women abandoned. I hear dark bars along a hundred waterfronts.

"It suits you somehow."

She says this, then tosses white hair over one shoulder and leans forward, wrapping arms about herself. The arms are long and deeply tanned, with slender straight fingers. She looks like a Greek statue someone has bronzed. Once so pale and white that new sheets looked dingy, gray, beneath her.

You remember those fingers lost in studio clay. From them (fingers, clay) issued bowls, pots, mugs and cups at once misshapen and of a strangely pure form. Containers all, all of them useful. New things in the world.

She steps close and takes my hand. Late sunlight lies on this brown rug like a discarded newspaper. Minutes drop off the edge of the world. Stand there watching.

I think how people say "there's history between us," and how history is never what happens. History is backwards invention, envelopes where, serving as your own travel agent, you tuck away airline tickets, hotel reservations, discount coupons and car rentals (and, always, your own invoice as agent) for your trip to Now.

"Once I loved a man named Marek."

"Yes," I say. "You did."

"He has a new life now. One with no place for me. I'd be a non sequitur, an anachronism. Like Senators wearing wristwatches in gladiator movies."

Glancing toward the window outside which, predictably (some things do still hold), another day goes down in flames, she takes my hand in hers and places them together on her stomach. She's become, herself, a kind of envelope.

After a moment I pull away my hand and go to the dresser. There under shirts fresh in paper bands from the laundry, burrowed in like field mice beneath underclothes and socks, are bundles of new bills. Fifties, hundreds. I scoop them out and give them to her. See her then to the door.

All this closed oak facing me down.

When parents died and money came to me I had no idea what to do with it. I'd been at poverty's door all my life. All I could think to do was turn it back on itself. I began chipping away at capitalist America.

Here's what happens then.

From the window Demetrius watches J climb into a cab in the street below. The cab is brown and white, owner's name stenciled on the fender but unreadable from up there. The cab's hire light goes off, it pulls into traffic. Two Gray Line tour buses fall in behind.

Demetrius closes the blinds. Demetrius who after tonight will not exist. Who even now begins to fade away.

Traffic sounds in darkness break and surge over him, like the sound of the sea far away, like all those other lives.

Now turn on the radio. Where friendly voices wait.

OCTOBERS

He watches her walk toward him. There is a long, low hill and she comes down it smiling. It does not occur to him to go and meet her. Her hair is pulled back in a bun, as she said it would be, and she wears steel-rimmed glasses tinted light blue, silver hoop earrings, sandals. "Leona," he says.

(They will walk for hours among manor-like old homes on Swiss Avenue. Runners roll by them, darting and mutable as their own conversation. Over some lawns float pale globes of light. Then with no memory of transition they find themselves abreast a span of cheap apartments and sway-backed bungalows and start back.)

They stop at a cafeteria to eat. She speaks of her time in Cuba, Peru and India. Can capitalist society survive, can it change itself from within. He has assumed for many years that America is merely stilting over ruins. She has advanced degrees yet pursues no career, working instead in temporary positions because she wants no stake in this society.

They speak of Eastern philosophy, Merton, Max Picard, Thoreau. Of one another's childhoods, families, marriages, fears. He talks, as he did so often in those days, of Marx, never suspecting how soon what he spoke would leap from his books, from his thoughts. There are islands of terrorism during the Republican Convention that year, riots in a few inner cities, university protest marches: American business as usual.

(She will walk among civilian patrols and endless fires, remembering his ready laugh, his sad brown eyes. She produces her papers on request and tells where she is going, where she lives, where employed. Says that yes, she knows she should not be on the streets after curfew.)

They walk past her house and she tells him of others who live there. It is fine, she says, except for cockroaches. The others, all women, are much older than she. They are teachers, secretaries, receptionists. The house is a modest, declining version of those on Swiss Avenue. Seven people live here, each with her own small room, her own unaccomplished biography.

(At two he will wake her to say the cell's been infiltrated, four of them taken, the rest in flight. He won't be around for a while, he tells her. The following morning, taken to the police station and questioned by a man in casual military dress, she knows nothing.)

Buses throw themselves past, dragging cars in their wake. There are no runners here, only occasional beer drinkers on front porches or car hoods. There is so much to say; they want to know everything about one another. The moon crawls in and out of clouds like an insect bumping its way over driveway gravel.

(At last she will admit he is not going to return. She walks near his apartment each day, hoping to find old friends with some word of him, even rumor, but she sees only strangers. She awaits the sporadic postmen. He can't write, of course. But there might be a page of Thoreau, a quote from Hesse in neat calligraphy, an Eliot poem.)

Hours later they stop for coffee at an all-night café. Her fingers slim as she lifts the cup. And parting, she offers her hand; days later he recalls the exact warmth and pressure of it. There is no answer at the phone number she gives him. He waits. Days go by: soldiers, kites. She calls. She tells him she is involved with someone already, that she can't see him anymore. He says he understands. There is a long pause. She says, Today's a good day for a change.

(It will be over quickly at first, then more slowly as one by one in ensuing months, islands of resistance are overcome. Party leaders find themselves looking out at shattered buildings with amazement, faced with a rapid shift from rhetoric to real action: to governing this country *bouleversé*.)

The first day they're together twelve hours and the following afternoon together another way on soiled sheets in his basement apartment beneath a map of Russia in Cyrillic, tiers of books on brick-and-board shelves, a bust of Wagner with one ear missing. At first she talks softly, then falls silent. Her eyes close and, just as her body arches upward, spring open again as though something has leapt from them into his own. A jolt runs along his spine into his hips and forward, outward, closing the circuit. "Leona," he says.

(Years later, dying in another strange and torn land, he will say again, "Leona." He remembers for a moment how her eyes sprang open that day. His own eyes close.)

Afterwards they make tea and she sits cross-legged on his mattress cradling the cup with its broken handle in both hands. She's unwound her hair and pulled it forward over her shoulders; it flows into, joins, the other, darker hair at the base of her belly. Cézanne-like, she has become a series of interlocking triangles: pubis, body, and splayed knees, cupped hands and elbows—even her face clipped to such angularity by fading light. The world is geometry, he thinks. The world, he says, is geometry, weather and misunderstanding: a few solid shapes repeating themselves over and over in the gray fog of a thousand formless things and thoughts, light forever fading.

(The revolution will last, will endure, three years. Then like an overturned beetle, legs flailing, the old society rights itself and goes about its business. Party leaders are taken into Washington bureaucracies, deposited behind computer-cluttered desks with secretaries who soon grow weary of filing nails and forms and, with little else to do, become surly. Committee reports roll off computers and race over telephone lines to congressmen and "interested parties." The only true revolution is absorption, this purest form of dialectic.)

He has another forceful memory of her, one he'll extract again and again in that strange, torn land that leans down over his death. Waking, he finds himself alone in bed. She is at the window; he watches her long hair and half-turned face against the orange glow. There are fires everywhere, she says. Everything is burning. The past is almost gone, I think. She turns fully to him, a tear pulling at one cheek, one eye. What else do we have, Mark, what else but the past? Unseen fires turn the tear into a small sun there below her blue glasses, beside the silver earring.

(She will come each day to the beach. Only here can she be alone, without history, weightless. For the past consoles; it is history that bears things away. Behind her, fires still leap and churn against the sky. Fire details rarely respond anymore. The beach around her is littered with decomposing bodies of birds, fish, young people. She watches the sea hurl itself endlessly onto that beach and feels new life falling into place about her somehow despite it all, all these new lives taking shape now, breaking on the broken beaches of the old, endlessly.)

UPSTREAM

I went through the curtain at 2:42.

And found myself standing at a slant in a doorway. Strange how one seems always to arrive in doorways of a sort: foyers, anterooms, hallways—always a sill. I encountered, as ever, that moment of odd disorientation, the sudden light an assault, volumes and sheer mass of the room threatening, yet the whole awash in blurs of gray, indecisive, ill-defined, as though eyes and mind for a moment had mutinied, refusing to focus. The scene, as it does so often, seemed familiar.

A woman sat wearing a T-shirt and overalls hacked roughly off above the knee to form shorts, hair pinned loosely, with two visible pins, atop her head, something of an architectural marvel. One waited for the word or stray gust of wind that would bring it tumbling down. Over her shoulder, on a computer screen set into the wall by the desk, multiple cursors and cues blinked, another face beside her own. She looked up as I appeared, requiring a moment, herself, to focus, wondering, no doubt, how long I might have been there and where I might have come from, though no alarm showed in her face. She had survived the worst America could do to one of its own, and was far past alarm.

She sat over a notebook, pen and hand remaining poised there as she looked up. Images (recalled? imagined?) trailed momentarily through my mind—then were gone.

"You cannot write that," I said to her.

"Sorry?"

"You are working on your memoirs of the conversion."

She nodded. No surprise that I should suppose this. For years now publishers, first one, then another, had been issuing announcements of the memoirs' imminent appearance.

"They will change the world," I told her.

For a moment she went on watching me. Then she capped the

pen, an actual fountain pen from the look of it, laid it against the page upon which she had been writing, and closed the notebook.

"Well. That's precisely what we all want, of course. Every writer, every artist with his cache of pitiful paintings, his handful of understanding scattered about like chicken feed. But how rare it is for us to know that our work has had any effect at all."

"The changes will not be good ones."

"I see." And now she smiled. "Among the many things one might wonder, of course, are for whom the changes will not be good, just why you should lay claim to this peremptory knowledge, and why, possessing it, you would choose to bring the coals of this knowledge to Newcastle.

"Never mind," she said at my obvious confusion over the idiom. But her dismissal, despite all my language coaching, was every bit as indecipherable as the original phrase. (*Coals to Newcastle? Never mind?*) She saw that too, and laughed; then with two fingers forked errant hair away from her face. Again those trailing, memory-like images.

"Leaps of faith are not much in currency these days."

"Were they ever?"

She rose and stepped around the desk to stand before me. We were much of a size, I found.

"Among some, they were. That was what fueled us, what kept us going. What else could?" She leaned close to me, wrinkling her nose. "And if I'm not mistaken, I smell it on you now as well—that stink of belief. I know it well. It smells like self-importance, only sharper."

I shook my head. "It's you who are important. I am nothing . . . history's tool."

She laughed. "But how, my serious young man, how are any of us—ever—anything more?"

Taking my arm, she guided me to the window. I felt the heat of her body behind me as we stood looking out. When at last she spoke, her breath came against me in a tide at the same moment, and as affectingly, as did her voice.

"For hundreds upon hundreds of years we believed in progress. Believed in that, and not much else. We bowed down to progress, suffered and killed in its name, destroyed cities and whole civilizations to make room for it, fed our children into its maw.

"There below is what came of our belief. The world's great city, where I live. Where, in a sense, we all live now. For we found that progress forever eluded us. We couldn't create, we could only edit, endlessly rewriting, moving paragraphs of our history from here to there, cutting, pasting. Looping back to redo the same few scenes again and yet again, never getting them right but restlessly moving on anyway, only to be drawn back once more. Whatever we did, however we reorganized it, the text remained the same."

"There was a time you thought differently."

"Exactly my point. There was a time I had to." She turned back to me. "People down there in the great city are eating rats, pigeons. Those are the lucky ones. Their fondest hope is that someday bread, even stone-ground mustard, will be provided."

"*The exhaustion of resources, the exhaustion of the frontier, straggles down inevitably to an exhaustion of hope. Sea's edge, so long a wonder and a transport, becomes a kind of wall, a closure. Our cities no longer reflect, but contain, us.*"

"Empty rhetoric."

"Rhetoric, yes. But hardly empty. That is what you were about to write." I picked up the notebook and opened it. "How long this morning had you sat there casting for words, knowing the old ones had been too much and too long used, that they were failing you again and always would? How long, before you found the phrase—" Here I read. "*—The exhaustion of resources* unfurling out of your pen, pulling your mind and the rest along?"

At the door, a disturbance. First a knock, then his shy entrance, this four-year-old working so hard at being all grown up. "Mother I'm sorry, but I'm hungry."

"Of course you are, dear. You go on out to the kitchen. I'll be right there. We'll have breakfast together, shall we?"

"Hello, sir," the boy said to me. "I do apologize for disturbing you."

"You needn't apologize. It is I who intrudes."

Stepping towards me, he offered his hand, so absurdly small and proper. "I don't believe we've met. My name is Edouard. You are a friend of my mother? A colleague, perhaps?"

"A pleasure to meet you, Edouard. I—"

"Edouard, perhaps you might go ahead and get the kettle started," his mother said.

"Yes, ma'am. Good-bye, sir. Take care."

"Thank you, Edouard." Then, when he was gone: "A fine child."

"Yes," she said after a moment. "Yes, he is, isn't he?"

When I made to return the notebook to her desk, she shook her head. "It's yours," she said. "Keep it. I believe you're right. I'll make a—I should say another—fresh start."

I removed the fountain pen and handed it to her. Our fingers touched.

"Yes," she said. "Thank you. Continuity is important."

And with that, my assignment was done. I turned to pass back through the doorway. She may have stepped up to it to watch me, I believe, as I left. If so, she would have seen nothing: in an instant, I was gone.

In that instant I shot, as from a catapult, back towards my own time.

Nowadays the changes come so fast that we have no way of knowing what, of the images that move through our minds, may be memory, what mere shadow, imagining, dream. The myriad ghosts of our lives, lives that were, trail back in tatters, more tenuous with each moment, each remembering, and are lost. Long before I departed on this assignment, banks of computers cast and spun, weaving this newest, waiting world's probable face; they cast and spin still. Patterns appear beneath the loom's restless shuttle. But we can never really know to what sort of world we will be returning, never. This requires a massive act of faith—like my mother's.

I went through the curtain at 3:01.

I SAW ROBERT JOHNSON

Let me explain.

I'm an insomniac, you see. Not the kind that has trouble getting to sleep, because three minutes after my head's down, I'm out, but the kind that has trouble staying so: at two or half-past three I'm up and wide-eyed, prowling around the efficiency like a werewolf.

So it was particularly surprising to wake this morning and discover that it was already light outside—that I had slept the night through for the first time in many years. I lay listening to birds sing, the slam of doors across the street, a weather report from my neighbor's radio.

I turned on my side and something leaf-light fell onto my lower lip. I touched it with a finger and the finger came away with a brownish smudge. I rubbed a palm against my cheek and that too was reddish-brown. It was blood, old blood. I swung out of bed then and stood in front of the mirror on the closet door nearby. My entire face was covered with it. Like the facials women get, like make-up base, like warpaint or a mask. There were spatters elsewhere, on my chest, legs and feet, but mostly it was on my face. And a long line tracing the descent of breastbone to pudenda. My hands, apparently, had been washed clean.

Perhaps a few words concerning where I live now, and how I came to be here.

My wife, tolerant, compassionate being that she was, had finally told me to get it together or get out, and so I had, taking a garage apartment within walking distance of both my old house (for tradition's sake) and the university (which had an outstanding collection of old blues records). Across the street is a daycare center, and each morning I sit by the window watching shapely young women deliver their children, opera glasses which have known the soaring Valkyries and shared Carmen's pitiable death now focused on bouncing bosoms, long legs in high heels, waggling buttocks. At a distance, every woman is erotic.

So many people fear being alone. But if you cannot be alone, you cannot know who you are. Listen: this culture conspires to make such essential solitude impossible. Perhaps it fears the individual; certainly the individual has reason to fear *it*.

This place is a dump, one in which the blues records checked out from the school's library seem quite at home. Turning off the lights at night I can hear the roaches begin their peregrinations. Dragging their spurred feet across Bessie Smith's "Empty Bed Blues," or mounting the minute summits of Lonnie Johnson's "Careless Love." I have cleaned and cleaned without result. The odor of mildew and carbon monoxide clings to every corner and crevice; spiders and crane flies perch like dull thoughts on the walls.

There were on my body no cuts, no wounds to explain all this blood. And I had no memory of the night, only a vague remembrance of dreaming: trees with the face of my wife, grass mowed down that spoke in the voice of my daughter, a parliament of fowls done up in tight skirts and unbuttoned shirtwaists.

The women had begun dropping off children, and I stood at the window nude, my face blood-smeared, wondering what would happen if they should see me. But they did not. Always first the blonde with the pastel sweatsuits and tiny waist. Then the beautiful Latin girl with straight, crow-black hair almost to her knees, always in skirt and jacket. Then the one with impossibly long legs; the pony-tailed redhead who always looked so unhappy; the woman with short brown hair who was always still putting on makeup in the rearview mirror as she pulled away. I know them all, and could not step away from the window until the morning rituals were done. The prettiest of them all, though, a tiny Vietnamese woman, perfectly formed, did not come today.

I brewed a pot of tea and sat at the desk staring out into the yard and drinking tea slowly, cup after cup. The powerful winds of past days had at last blown themselves out and only a mild breeze remained of them. After a time I realized that the lizard I'd been watching run here and there was actually chasing birds; it would wait in the grass until birds settled, then dash toward them, rippling silver in the sunlight, until they flushed and flew away. The lizard did this again and again. I have no idea why.

I will not turn on the radio, I thought. There will be horrible news. There is always horrible news. A tractor-trailer has plunged from an embankment, crushing a bus filled with schoolchildren. A man without food for a week has killed and eaten his neighbor's dog. A woman and daughter living in a house nearby were killed during the night, cut to pieces in their beds. A young Vietnamese was found dead at her apartment early this morning by a friend, murdered. That sort of thing. I will sit here and drink tea, at ease with the world, and then I will call them.

But there was no answer, as you know.

I had not realized so much time had passed, but soon (or so it seemed) the women began picking up their children and I still sat as I had that morning. Watching through the opera glasses as the blond woman's buttocks and breasts swung freely under the turquoise fabric, I began suddenly to tremble. When they were all gone, I got up and put on some Ma Rainey, stood looking at myself again in the mirror. I tried to imagine what it was like to be black in the thirties, the rage and hatred you were always having to shove back down inside, shut away again and again, until it finally bubbled to the surface in the blues. In the terrible ache that's become all I can feel now. I put on some Son House, remembering the blond woman moving underneath her clothes, a rhythm like the earth's itself, like the rise and fall of Son House's moan, like a lizard in the grass. I played the records one after another, some of them twice, and by then it was dark. The drapes closed over my face in the glass, watching.

I drew a hot bath and lay in it for a long time, adding hot water now and again by turning the tap on with my toes. Then I splashed water onto my face and the blood began to come away, swirling out into the water like rust. Yes, *rust*. I sat in the tub and watched it spin off into the drain.

After that I stood staring at the closed drapes. Behind them I could see all those women moving around still, their breasts and hands brushing against the back of the drapes. I could see gin-soaked Bessie Smith bleeding to death on a Mississippi highway. I saw Robert Johnson huddled in a corner, his back to me, singing about his hellhound.

OTHERS

The best part was when he got a new letter, walking back from the mailbox with it, reading it over and over, the possibilities that crowded in on him then. A few were so very powerful, so redolent of potential, that he never answered them. Sometimes he would put a letter, unopened, on his desk and force himself to wait an hour, even two, before reading it. Then he would read each line many times before going to the next. All during the day he'd be pulling out one or another of them, savoring their individual flavors, trying (though never successfully) to capture those first magic moments.

This was all he used the desk for now. Ever since he could remember, he had wanted to be a writer. And with his wife's sudden death (a stroke at age thirty-four, then pneumonia) he had quit his job and set himself up as a novelist, living off the insurance money. The first novel had been about her and was titled *Julia*, her name; it went unpublished. There came then a string of books: mysteries, science fiction, teen romances, pornography, each completed in precisely thirty days. A few were published, each by a different house, and his royalty statements showed him owing more than the money advanced him. He attended college for a time, taking mainly philosophy courses; made a stab at learning Spanish; worked briefly in a bookstore catering to collectors.

He discovered *The Pen* two years after Julia died, about the time he was writing his last book, a serious novel about a man who moves into a new apartment and gradually discovers (or becomes convinced) that his predecessor was an agent of some sort, a man more of shadow than substance whose whole identity was assumed, manufactured—then abandoned for another again and again, endlessly.

The Pen was a biweekly "alternative" newspaper devoted chiefly to the arts and left-wing journalism. But each issue contained five or six pages of classified advertisements grouped under such headings

as Women Seek Men, Men Seek Women, Gay, Miscellaneous. He
became an instant convert; subscribed, but haunted newsstands for
early copies; responded to every plausible ad with lengthy letters in
perfect handwriting. Certain things led him to discount automatically any advertisement: undue emphasis on appearance or wealth,
statistics (age, measurements, weight, salary, height), puns, any
reference to a 10, the words "sensitive," "gentle," and "professional,"
use of song titles, undue length, poor grammar. There still remained,
however, a large number, and he answered them all.

Each morning he sat down with his second cup of coffee and
again read through recent arrivals.

> Dear John,
> Thank you for answering my ad. I'm "Farmer's Daughter,"
> all alone out here. I was glad to hear about your childhood
> on the farm in Iowa, how much that's meant to you. If you'd
> like, maybe we could get together over a homecooked meal
> some night and I could show you the place.

Not too many more possibilities to explore there; it was pretty
obvious. He put that one in the dead file.

> Carl,
> Yes, it *is* a lonely world and we *should do* everything we can
> to help one another—*must*. I hope very much that when you
> return to "the States" from Central America, you will write
> me. As I told you in the last letter, I am overweight and not
> very pretty, I think, but under the right man's hand I could
> be anything he wished.

Often after the third or fourth letter he would call, not uncommonly talking two or three hours, but then, after that, would not
write again. He changed his post office box frequently. All we truly
want, and can never have (he had decided some time ago), is to
know another person, to bridge this awful solitude we're locked
into. Power, influence, knowledge of every arcane, recondite sort,
our impulses to art, sex—all were merely analogs, pale reflections

of that simple basic, unfulfillable drive. Instinctively he knew that with his letters he approached as close as one really ever could to other people. And certainly he knew that the rest would be messy: awkward pauses, inferred obligations, misunderstandings, rejection.

David,
It sounds as though a single dip in your lake might wash off all the dirt of previous relationships.

Carlos,
I just want someone to hold me sometimes. I am a career woman with three degrees, own my own business, play aggressive racquetball.

Hi Jonathan!
I'm "41, Mensa member." Want to push some pawns? QP—QP4!

Once he'd gone so far (she had a lovely voice, and her interests overlay his own exactly) as to arrange a meeting. From afar he had watched her arrive, look about, seat herself and order tea, read for a while and finally depart. He was terrified the whole time. She did not seem unduly surprised or upset. He watched men's eyes following her out the door.

Dear Elizabeth,
I have read your ad with great interest, noting in particular your love of cats and Bach. As it happens, at the time I first came across your ad I was sitting on the patio, my own Siamese curled in my lap and the initial strains of the Air for G-string drifting out from the house into the gathering twilight—surely an omen, if one could believe such things.
    This is all so new to me, I don't know what to write, what you expect to hear. I am in my late thirties, a widower, not bad looking but no prize either. I suppose that my strong points are kindness, caring, concern. I can recite the whole

of Chaucer in middle English and tell *Beowulf* from Grendel's point of view.

Debra,
Since you ask, my favorite movie is the first *Robin Hood*, because it has that scene where someone (a beautiful girl?) says, You speak treason! And Robin responds: Fluently.

Judith,
I'm sorry, but I am not *allowed* to tell you about what I do for a living; I can only say that it is boring, repetitive, often difficult. Many days I feel that I no longer belong to the human race. Of course I am quite well paid.

Around noon he always broke off for a while, brewed another pot of coffee, had a light lunch of cheese and fruit or soup if some was left over from the previous evening. He would browse randomly among favorite books, stories and poems: *Heart of Darkness*, Gerard Manley Hopkins, later Yeats, *Moby-Dick*, most of Hawthorne, "Entropy," Robbe-Grillet. Frequently he thought of the fascination for masks in Greek tragedy, romantic and gothic fiction, Durrell's *Alexandria Quartet*.

Dear Sammi,
Like you I am tired of games, tired of bodies that won't quit and minds that have to be jumpstarted.

June,
It is evening. Frogs on the pond not far away do Hoagy Carmichael songs you've never heard. From my garden seat all I can see are trees, grass, sky. All about me there is a low whisper.

And others declaiming the nonimportance of money, the supremacy of art, how hard it was to meet people and how hard they were once met. Only in these letters could he, did he, truly live.

One in particular, however, bothered him. It was so adaptive, so labile, like the letters he himself composed so carefully on the pegs of others' dreams. He thought of the famous Marx Brothers mirror routine, Harpo (or was it Chico?) suspecting that the doorway was not in truth a mirror but unable to prove it, the "reflection's" movements never deviating from, or lagging behind, his own. Perhaps this letter was from a female counterpart. Perhaps there were many like himself, living submerged in this system of correspondence like deep sea animals, never coming up for air.

At five or so he would put the letters aside and have dinner on the patio, generally soup and fruit or a simple stew followed with bread (which he baked himself) and cheese. But this time he had brought with him her latest letter.

> Dear John,
> I am so comfortable writing to you, as though we've been friends a long time. Truly, I wonder if you are not the one I've waited for all these lonely years. We have so very much in common - more than you realize. Please write again soon or call me. I am waiting.

He finished his meal and sat watching a squirrel leap from tree to tree. Wind ferried in a smell of dust and the sun rolled across moving clouds. He thought of the bouncing ball over song lyrics in "short subjects" that once accompanied all movies. Nothing like that now. Nothing but ads now, ads and future attractions. Sex, violence, power, war, wealth.

After a time he stood and walked to the edge of the patio, looking out into the thick growth of oak, ivy, kudzu, honeysuckle. He knew that he would write to her again. He knew that he would call then, and just how her voice would sound. He knew that he would talk and talk—talk for an hour, two, three if she would listen—trying to hold off the inevitable moment there was no more to say: the moment the phone fell back into its cradle, taking her away from him forever

BLUE LAB

Some years ago I lived next to a madman about whom I knew only that he was involved in "basic research—behavior and learning." This research had to be done every day. A few minutes past seven each evening, a half-hour or so after the joggers limped back in, I would watch as he walked into view beneath the trees with two six-packs of beer stacked into a brown bag under his arm, checked the rusty, scaling mailbox by the street, and started up the gravel drive to the cottage just behind my own.

They were of course not cottages, but garages. *Bungalow*, the advertisement said, his bungalow comprising the whole floorspace, one-half of my own (there was a thin wall) yet garage. I had made mine livable, covering the worst stains with throw rugs, scouring all available surfaces three times, covering cracks in the walls (not so much cracks as chasms) with duct tape. I don't know what he had done with his.

It was in fact from him that I rented the place; he had shown it for the owner, and that was when I heard about the "basic research," shuffled in among a generous ten or twelve other words. Then he took my check, gave me the key, and I neither heard nor saw anything more of him for a month or more. Gradually, though, as I became convinced that my marriage was indeed over, I started settling back into regular work habits, and so each day (I never saw him at any other time) caught sight of him returning from work. The first and second times, I was at the typewriter. The third, I was stuffing newspapers into the yawning space between air conditioner and window. I had a roll of duct tape around my wrist like a bracelet.

"Little windy for you?" he said.

"No, no, I like a good breeze. It's the sound—that unending whistle. D is so bright and depressing . . ."

He stood there a moment, and when he said no more, I got back to work.

"Girl lived there before never did anything. Don't even think she was ever there, or much."

Then he went on past, shouted hello to the dog next door, and vanished into his bungalow.

That night it was windy, and waking in the early morning without knowing why, I slowly became aware of a persistent, variable singing in the air around me. Cut off from its customary passage, the wind had found its way into the house's many other cracks and crannies, often under some pressure, giving forth a many-toned moan that rose and fell with the bank of the wind; as in Gregorian chants, the harmonies were ever shifting. I fell asleep again shortly before dawn, the memory of that late-night concert spilling imperceptibly into the cries of the birds which woke me.

It was several days before I again saw my neighbor. Occasionally, always late at night, I would hear his radio on full-volume for a time, then silence. During the day I listened to his phone ring. In truth I had ceased to pay much attention, for a new book had begun taking shape and as always, I was half in that world, half out of this one. I watched birds coming to the feeder I'd put outside my window with no more recognition of their separateness than I had for my own fingers on the typewriter; both were simply random patterns shimmering and shifting around the stone of my concentration.

When I am at work, walking is my great problem solver, and four weeks or so into the book, about halfway through the first draft, I was out most of an afternoon trying to find a way to make one of the characters do what I needed him to do. The story was nothing terribly original in scope—I'd often before ransomed my life by turning it to fiction—but this time, I suppose, I lacked the necessary distance, and the story kept hauling itself, against my will, back from the fictional characters and episodes I'd intended, to what actually went on between Judith and myself.

Suddenly rain exploded from the sky, and I took refuge in a nearby café. On one of the orange seats (the others were green and purple) my neighbor sat with what looked like a porkchop between two slices of bread.

"Mind if I join you?"

He nodded his head toward me slightly and continued eating

his sandwich, biting, swallowing, biting, swallowing. By the time I'd got seated the sandwich was gone and he was starting in on a huge glass of iced tea.

"This part of your routine?" I asked, and again he nodded.

"Ever' day for two years, never missed one." He threw back the tea like someone might a shot glass. "Good food."

I wondered how he knew.

I asked the waitress for a cup of coffee and when he got up to leave said, "Keep me company?"

He looked as if he thought that was a strange request but settled back onto the stool.

"Have anything?"

"Already ate."

"Tell me about your work at the university," I said after several moments' silence.

"Not work—research."

"Research, then. What's it all about?"

He looked at me for some time, then turned away and began speaking.

"You ever wonder if a man can change? I mean change completely, like you take a crazy man and make him a bank president. Or you take a murderer maybe, someone who's done terrible things in his life, and you turn him into someone who doesn't remember all those things."

"Sure. Everybody must wonder about that, especially with the news these days."

An elderly couple came in and sat at the table behind us. *Usual?* the waitress asked them. They held hands as they waited.

"You think that's possible?"

"I don't know," I told him. "There's been a lot of debate about that, from Aristotle and Plato, Buddha and Gandhi, on up to people like Skinner. But I wonder if the individual's essential nature isn't formed at birth and in the years just after. I wonder if you can ever really do more than change it superficially."

He sat nodding. "Maybe," he said when I was done. "Maybe not."

Outside, the rain had ended as it began, suddenly, and the couple, my neighbor and I all lined up at the register to pay.

"Is that what your research is all about, then?" I said as we stepped out of the smell of stale grease into fresh air. A taxi slowed. I waved it on.

"Something like that. Just animals, rats and monkeys and so on so far, but it's almost time for a man now. Almost. In the blue lab."

He thanked me for buying his dinner and said the next time was on him, but there was no next time.

That night I had a dream, though it seemed no dream then, that someone was in the room with me muttering on and on about evil and redemption. Still I can close my eyes and see behind them a face become mask: rigid, horrible, unyielding. I rose the next morning and, with that image as springboard, completed the new book in a week-long orgy of naps and marathon sessions at the desk, afterwards dropping the manuscript into the post to my agent and myself into a case of gin and a month of sleeping and drinking broken only by random daily liaisons with women picked up at the movies, library, or A&P. Dimly I registered daily accounts of some guy in downtown Dayton attacking couples, always couples, and his eventual apprehension. In my fatigued, still-firing brain these stories mixed inextricably with worsening situations in the Middle East and South America, with planes shot down over questionably foreign airspace, with the CIA's latest *coup*.

Probably I'd remember none of this if I had not, some months later, again run across my one-time neighbor.

After that evening I had not seen him, and a few weeks later our landlord drove in from north Cleveland (for the first time in how long, I wondered) to check his apartment. About 10 P.M. he knocked at my door and when I opened it stepped in, looking about.

"Wilson," he said. "I own this place."

"You want it back, or what?"

"No. No, of course not, Mr. —?"

"Booth."

"Mr. Booth. But I haven't heard from Jefferson for a long time and I was wondering if you had any idea where he might have gone, or what was going on."

"Jefferson?"

He hooked a thumb to the rear. "Back there. The other bungalow. Guy that rented it out to you."

"Oh." I told him I hadn't seen my neighbor since the night at the café.

"Right. Then I guess we can assume he's split, no? Hey. You mind showing the place for me?"

"You're not gonna clean it up or anything?"

"Hell, man, why bother?" He looked quickly about. "No offense."

"Right," I said. "You check with the university?"

"About what?"

"Jefferson."

"Why would I do that?"

"Well, you know. His research and all that."

"We're not talking about the same person."

I shrugged. A twenty-three-year-old blonde from the liquor store around the corner was scheduled to show up soon, I hoped with samples; why encourage this joker?

"Sure," I said. "I'll show the place."

He handed me a key and a handful of papers. Later I looked at the papers. Rental agreement, references, lists of things the apartment supposedly had (62 percent, I figured, were actually there).

"Call me if there's a problem. Otherwise just send the check and this stuff on through."

"Right."

A young woman moved in a month or two later—an ecologist, she said, though what an ecologist would be doing in Dayton I can't imagine. Anyhow she had a pretty voice, nice long hair, and she jogged. I started getting up early again and keeping the drapes open later at night. Eventually the book was published, not by my old publisher but by a new one, and it did okay. Not too long after, I'd moved back in with Judith, and that did okay too, for a while. Some nights we'd read passages from the book to one another, alternately howling with laughter and moved beyond all expectation or reason. Then one afternoon I was hurrying between stores in a shopping mall when a well-dressed young man stepped into my way.

"Excuse me," he said.

I reached out to help him back to his feet. He smiled and took my hand.

"It's you!" I said, and he looked at me, not understanding. "The bungalows."

He wore a blue blazer and gray slacks, maroon wool tie. A paper badge sheathed in plastic was pinned to his lapel.

"Your research project must have paid off, I guess."

"Research? Project?" You could almost see gears spinning, failing to catch.

"On changing human nature," I said.

"Human nature. Changing. Of course—you're Booth. How have you been? I'm sorry, I should have recognized you, but . . ." He waved a diffident hand. "How are the roaches?"

"Still quite healthy, the little buggers. Fruitful and multiplying."

"It's all about family."

"Exactly. And you?"

"I can't complain."

I pointed at the nametag.

"What's this, you gave up psychology?"

"Gave up . . . ?" He looked around as though someone might walk up and explain. When no one did, he looked back at me and said, "I'm afraid you misunderstood. I thought you knew: I was not one of the scientists, I was the experiment."

He said good-bye, that it was grand to see me again (yes: grand), and stepped off into the crowd. A yard or so away he suddenly turned and said, "Come see me at the store," tapping a finger against the nametag, his own name beneath that of one of the major department stores. Then he was gone.

Many years have passed. The book is something of a classic now, I guess, taught in many literature courses and continuously in print in numerous editions. I am alone again, having weathered the spring and sudden winter of yet another marriage, living in a remodeled carriage house across the street from (of all things) a monastery. Here a stream of polite, neatly-dressed young men comes to my door asking for the former tenant, Teresa.

OBLATIONS

The first of the lesions (as he'd come to think of them) had appeared three weeks ago after he and Anne quarreled over a dinner engagement. He had drawn back a fist to strike her and, astonished at what he was about to do, almost fainted. Showering that night, he had found it on his thigh, a red excrescence the size of a pinhead, itching slightly.

He'd thought it nothing, a pimple or infected follicle perhaps. Then, listening to a report on Salvador over National Public Radio a few days later on the way to work, he had pulled off to the side of the road to watch another form on the inside of his wrist. There was a pressure, a warmth—then the lesion's appearance, like a tiny volcano.

That day at work Samuelson, a one-time champion salesman now gone to booze and bosses' girls in motel rooms, was finally fired, and as he sat in the coffee shop across the street at 9:56, Morgan felt the twitch, the quick spasm, as another lesion sprang up, this one just above his ribcage where the shirt rubbed whenever he changed position.

For several days then, there were no more. Perhaps, he began to think, it was over. From the office he called and told Anne to get a sitter and be ready for dinner and a night of dancing. "On a Tuesday? At our age?" she'd asked, laughing.

Not long after, Morgan heard someone say "Busy?" and looked up to see McDowell in the doorway, ducking his head slightly to fit.

"Beaverish. How's the family?"

"I don't know." McDowell had sprawled into the so-called client's chair, and when Morgan glanced up sharply, added, "I'm alone now, Bill."

"You? That's hard to believe, Sean."

"Hard for you, harder for me."

"How long? What the hell happened?"

"Six months. I woke up one morning and everybody was gone. A week's supply of clean clothes was folded and laid out by the washer. Alice had left a note beside them, weighed down by the iron. Said she needed more space for herself, and time. She didn't mention it, but apparently she needed money as well: she cleaned out the checking account."

"How much do you need, Sean?"

"I wasn't meaning that." He shifted in the chair. No one had ever built a chair he was comfortable in, and he sat in all of them as though half-expecting them to collapse under his broad, 6'6" frame. "But thanks. Tell you what I do need, though, Bill. That house gets awful lonely, going back there every night, sitting just waiting until bedtime. What I was wondering was, if you'd maybe want to go out after work and have a few drinks. You know, just talk awhile, then grab a couple of steaks."

"Love to. But hey, it's gonna have to be tomorrow, okay? Already told Anne we were going out."

McDowell stood. "Sure, Bill. Great. See you tomorrow, then. Looking forward to it." Going out the door, he ducked his head and pulled his elbows in close to his sides. His suit was badly rumpled.

They had pasta and veal at Arthur's, a rare extravagance, with brandy and espresso afterwards. They were at the Blue Wave then until almost two, but found the band so outstanding they wound up listening more than dancing. And talking. After twelve years of marriage, Morgan still could not wait to see her at night and tell her everything that had happened during the day; he could not hear enough about her childhood or college years before he knew her, about books she loved, people she remembered.

It was near dawn when they fell asleep, spent, against one another, and not much more than an hour later the radio began playing, very softly, Mahler's Second. He slipped out of bed without waking her, showered in the kids' bath (they'd sleep through anything), shaved in the car on the way to work. At 10:23 Anne called to tell him good morning. McDowell did not come in. At 12:41 they found him hanging from the doorframe in the basement game room of his house, an overturned chair nearby. A carefully penned will lay on the pool table beside him, leaving everything to Alice.

The room had been built especially large, probably the only room he ever felt comfortable in.

Seated at the desk as the office manager, Raleigh, told him this, Morgan felt new lesions erupt on his chest: that now-familiar pressure, the dimpling, appearance.

Raleigh gone, Morgan walked out into the general office and poured coffee into a plastic cup. Then he went back into his own office and stood at the window looking down, holding the cup in one hand. So many people he would meet, love, struggle with; so much sadness and pain. And standing there he could feel them, feel them all, tiny points of pressure beneath the skin, waiting to be born.

MEN'S CLUB

No one remembers now whose idea it was, perhaps it came to all of them at the same time, they all saw her every day, and when they go down into the old room, or just one of them goes, into that room with sweating walls and the stench of butane where the girl lies in her chains, those sharp, darting eyes of hers and the smell of her too, a mix of fear, endless rut and blood, the smell of the dirt floor in her too, and she stands and waits, smiling, always smiling, never drawing away whatever they do, whatever one of them does, they realize they have forgotten the name she certainly must once have had.

The men are much kinder to their wives and daughters now. At their work they prosper. Meeting by chance on the stairs they will relate high profits, a new position, political aspirations, mergers, though always as they approach the end of the stairs they fall, as though by common, though unspoken agreement, silent.

No one has missed the idiot girl, or inquired after her. Of course, there was only the old man who'd taken care of her, at one time he had run the mill and had remained living there, wheel and building rotting out from under, and with him dead no one else was likely to concern himself, concern herself, with the poor creature.

It does not occur to them to wonder what she feels, if she feels, she is smiling, always smiling, and cries only when, whatever they do to her, whatever one of them does, they leave. Perhaps she is sixteen, certainly no more than that, with large breasts gone puffy with rough use and covered with scars from the nicks of teeth and nails. Her ribs protrude under those breasts, making them appear even larger, and her skin is a waxy yellow. Several of the ribs have been broken, many of the teeth now are gone, and the bush between her legs is mostly worn away or has been pulled out, piece by piece, by probing fingers.

For a long time, at first, the little room was in almost continual use. One of them had set up a cask of wine and plastic cups on a table just at the base of the stairs by the door, and here they would, upon arriving and discovering the room already in use, wait their turn. Some brought books, magazines or work from the office in monogrammed attachés, for conversation, even upon those occasions when several waited together, was never undertaken. Each sat somewhat turned away from the others, wrapped in his own work, his own waiting, own wants. Through a narrow window at ground level, at every time of day, it seemed, a light as opaque and unsavory as dishwater poured down on them.

Gradually fewer of them will be found in the outside room, and at increasing intervals; the cask will be again drained and this time go unreplaced. The flood become river, stream, brook, pond, draught. Finally the girl lies alone in her chains, waiting.

It is the wives and daughters, of course, who will bear the burden of their abjuration.

Perhaps the girl (whose name, I will tell you now, is Barbara) somehow will remain alive down there. Perhaps at every creak of the ancient, empty house above her, she looks to the door and stands (as long as she *can* stand) expectantly, smiling, always smiling. Perhaps on the wind at night she hears the names of her nameless lovers, saying them over and over, remembering them, in her tongueless mouth.

ALLOWING THE LION

It was in early April, on a day whose radiant weather they remember well, that the monster came to live with them. Its manners were excellent. It would not hear of discomforting them further, for surely its mere presence in their home was imposition enough, it said, and declined their offer of the second bedroom, bedding down instead in a corner of the living room and attending (whatever those were) to its own needs. It did eat with them, however, each time leaving at its place, despite continued protestations, a five-dollar bill.

At first they turned away, but then found themselves drawn back and would sit watching the monster's vast head and its hands that manipulated so adroitly and with such casual grace the various spoons, forks and knives. It had a particular fondness for soups and fresh-baked bread, and was adamantly vegetarian. Some evenings it would tell them amazing stories of its own far land.

For many years they, Kathryn and Karl, had slept in separate rooms. Some weeks after the monster's arrival they moved all their things into the smaller of the two bedrooms, telling themselves that the monster might after all wish to use the other. At night, as they watched the monster eat and upon occasion heard its stories (for it disliked, it said, though in fact, without its monopolizing the conversation, there was none), he began to notice that she was looking across the table at him in an old, barely remembered way, and he himself felt stirrings long forgotten. Standing, he would contract the muscles of his stomach, jam a hand into one pocket, lean backwards against his bending spine. She would worry at her hair, take time each morning selecting her clothes and often change them, breathe through the words she said to him.

At the end of the first year the monster spent with them, she awoke one morning to find him sleeping beside her in the narrow bed. Some weeks or months later she awoke to the same surprise, and with his hand, moreover, at her breast. This was repeated many times, neither of them speaking of it, and then came the night that, just after retiring, she heard his feet on the floor, crossing to her, and the wind of the covers lifting, the warm hardness of him behind her, then inside her.

The next morning they looked everywhere for the monster, for their guest, but it was not to be found. There remained only the faint scent of its perfume in the living room, a few torn rags in the room's corner, the memory of its eloquently trilled Rs.

IMPOSSIBLE THINGS
BEFORE BREAKFAST

Each morning my cat Ahab returns from nightly wanderings to tell me all he has seen. It does not go well, Ahab says. Plague and pestilence have followed close upon the heels of initial destruction. Ahab has seen groups of men and packs of dogs fighting over abandoned bodies. Near the center of what was once town these bodies are piled high within a compound of barbed wire, and are burned daily.

For some time I believed that Ahab made up these stories to amuse me, aware of how bored I grew with his daily reports; I am still not completely certain. Details change from day to day, waver as though windblown, but his descriptive powers are so profound that surely he *has* to have seen what he recounts; surely he cannot be *that* creative.

After he has gone and Motherdear brings breakfast and bath, I lie here thinking what it was like before. I am supposed to study during this time, but I cannot imagine why. What could I possibly do with knowledge? And in the world Ahab brings me, what use could study ever be—or anything else?

Actually, I remember very little from before. I imagine that I can feel myself pulling against a swing's ropes and lifting my feet to see blue squares of sky approaching, receding, returning. I think I may recall sometimes the feel of sunlight and wind on bare legs, on my face, the sound of words blossoming in my mouth, Father's hand on mine.

All this was in a different world, of course. And as with Ahab's tales, I may be conjuring it all up, spinning these stories on memory's loom with thin air in place of flax.

Flax was in my vocabulary lesson yesterday.

I am almost fourteen. Motherdear brings me books from the library about fourteen-year-olds who spend all week worrying over who'll ask them to the Saturday dance and whether Sally or Billy still likes them. After dinner Motherdear turns me onto my side and the TV to a sitcom. As soon as she is gone I use my chin to switch to evening news. Central America simmers on the back burners while, pushed to the front, the Middle East boils over. Soviets and the CIA take turns overrunning smaller, neighboring nations. There's no one alive who can understand why there has to be so much hatred and pain in the world. Perhaps there's really no one alive even to try anymore. But again, as with Ahab's stories and my memories, I've no way of knowing what, if any, of all this is true. Is the human race's hatred, greed and fear about to bring it to wipe itself off the face of the earth like a spreading spill, and everything else with it? Maybe that is what should, must, happen. But all this, this news, could be, like the sitcoms, just another form of entertainment, only something to distract us, something to divert attention from private, unbearable despair.

Sometimes at night, after Motherdear retires, I am able to switch the TV back on and watch the adult-entertainment channel. It's about then also that Ahab wakes from his daylong nappings, dark pearls on a string. He always comes to see me before leaving, peering curiously at what takes place on the screen, much as I watch the news, I think, then vaulting onto the sill by the open window (open always for fresh air) and, muscles bunching under his sleek coat, into the night.

Days ago when Ahab returned there was a cricket in the room and I'd been unable to sleep for many hours, its chirring like an electric current in the darkness. Ahab listened for a moment and went directly to where the cricket hid in a corner beneath the bureau, but somehow understood that I did not wish it harmed. Emerging from beneath the bureau he brought it to show me (black as himself, and just as alive), then dropped it onto the grass outside the window. He told me of bodies burst open like melons, of others wearing black coverings of ants and carrion birds.

Breakfast has been only oatmeal or other cereal with dried fruit added for weeks now, sometimes with watery milk, once with even a small cup of cocoa. It is all there is, Motherdear says, and it is good for you. I eat what I can of it. The skin of Motherdear's arms has turned hard and transparent; they are two yellow candles, hands flicking about at their ends like pale flames. I have noticed that she has difficulty lifting even a part of me from the bed as she straightens it and bathes me each morning now. Every day she comes to my room a little later.

Sometimes I imagine that I remember (though of course I could not possibly do so) the afternoon this world began ending. Maybe it's just another story Ahab has told me. I hear the doctor outside telling Motherdear (though she wasn't then, not yet, Motherdear) that "the most we can hope for's a quad." "A what?" she says. "A quadriplegic." Then a brief pause. "That's my daughter, young man," Motherdear says. "That's my ten-year-old daughter in there." I see Billy Devin, the one who dared me to jump, huddled into a corner by shelves. He must have been one of the first to die.

And that was the end of before. For a time, friends came to visit, even Billy and some of the teachers, but no one comes anymore. Even Motherdear doesn't want to come.

How can people so uncaring, so taken with their own needs, with their tiny plots and lives, people inured or oblivious to others' pain and terrible loneliness, possibly expect to survive?

Ahab comes late this morning: Motherdear is already here. "Ahab?" she says. "A cat? But you *have* no cat, dear. We had to get rid of the cat, surely you remember. The doctors insisted."

Very well. But Motherdear will not be back tomorrow.

And soon there will be none other than Ahab and myself, no one but us to begin the new world. In the mornings he will bring me food and news (insects, at least, will survive, they say) and in the long nights lie beside me, his cruel, soft paw against my quickening thigh.

POTATO TREE

"We've found the problem," Dr. Morgan told me.

After a moment I said, "Yes?"

"Basically," he said, "you're crazy as batshit."

He was right, of course, but at ninety dollars an hour I had expected more. I waited. That seemed to be it.

"I see. Well. Is there anything you can do?"

"Oh, yes, a number of things. There are several quite interesting drugs on the market. Years of psychiatry—that might be fun. Shock, megavitamin therapy, behavioral training. Probably a lot of others. I'd have to look it all up."

He swiveled his chair to watch a traffic helicopter swing by outside the window. From his new position he said, "Of course, none of them will help any. You're crazy as batshit and basically you're just going to have to live with it, accept it. Here, I wrote it down for you."

He swiveled back and handed me an index card upon which was printed in large block letters: *C A B S*. Below, in a painstaking tiny script, were an asterisk and the words *crazy as batshit*.

"It shouldn't really be any great bother. I mean, you'll be able to keep on going to dentists, reading cereal boxes, having regular bowel movements, humming old songs—all the important stuff. Just a little bit of an interpretive dysfunction, that's all. You just won't ever know if things are as they seem to you; they could be *quite* different."

He wet a finger and wiped at a smudge on the desktop.

"I, for instance, could well be a wig-maker. A canoeist. We may at this moment be the sole attendants of a missile silo in Kansas. Do you play bridge?"

"No."

"Good. Hate that damned game."

He swiveled again to look out the window.

"Is there anything else you can tell me?" I said after a while. "Any advice, recommendations?"

"Only this," he said. "Go with it, ride it. Enjoy it." He turned back to me. "Most of us live in a much duller world than yours, you know." There was something very like envy in the poor man's voice.

"Thank you, Doctor," I said, rising from my chair and looking for the last time at his wall of diplomas. "You've been a great help."

"It's nothing." He removed his glasses, breathed against them, fumbled in pockets for a handkerchief. "Give me a call now and again to let me know how you're getting along." He looked back at the smudge through clean glasses.

"I'll do that."

I walked a few steps to the door. There was no knob, only a hand protruding from the wood which clasped my own in a handshake. I pulled against it, opening the door.

"Don't forget your diagnosis," the doctor said behind me. I turned. The index card dropped to the floor and scuttled toward me.

The world looked not at all different, unchanged by my illness as it had been by my former health, in short, uncaring. The first elevator was full—all of them wearing the doctor's face, perhaps patients of his—and I waited. Eventually I made it down to the plaza and sat on one of the benches under a potato tree. Some of the hospital patients were having a wheelchair race on the grounds, pursued by grim-faced, limping nurses.

"May I join you for just a moment?"

I looked up into a face of great and radiant beauty, though pale. She collapsed onto the bench beside me.

"Are you all right?"

"Fine. Just give me a moment, I'll be okay. Please."

I spent the moment looking at the oxblood gleam of her boots, at the tug and thrust of sweater, into the depths of her gray eyes. Never had I felt more alone; loneliness entered me like a bullet.

"Well. I proved they were wrong, at least," she said.

"I'm sorry?"

"The doctors . . . Listen, forgive me. I don't want to inflict you with my troubles. You must have plenty of your own."

"Not really. I'm crazy, you see: nothing can touch me."

I took out the index card and showed it to her. A potato fell to the ground at our feet. The index card leapt onto it and began to feed.

"How wonderful, to have an *interesting* disease. All I have's cancer."

"What kind?"

"The worst kind, of course, but it's still pretty dull."

I put out my hand and she held it, just as the door had earlier. We sat together looking out over the grounds as a light snow began to fall. Beside us the potato tree thrust into the sky as though *it* were a hand intent upon tearing out that white down, intent upon opening it. The patients had turned on their nurses and were chasing them about the grounds, laughing joyously as they crunched bones with the wheelchairs. Children sat watching.

"How long do you have?" I said finally.

"Not long. They said I wouldn't even get out of the building, it was so bad."

"*How* long?"

She looked at her watch.

"Ten minutes," she said, floating into my arms.

FINGER AND FLAME

So she left and he was dead for a while and then, very slowly, he was alive again.

At the studio everything turned into her: expressionist landscapes, still-life, abstract. Then he met Flame.

She was wearing a green T-shirt and green shorts. She had a small shopping basket full of avocados. Beneath the T-shirt her breasts were themselves like avocadoes. She had long hair tied at the back, a shy smile, worried eyes.

I am in love, he said to himself, and to her: Will you have coffee with me?

No, she said. Then, catching the disappointment in his face: I don't drink coffee, I meant to say. But tea would be nice. There's a shop I like not far away.

Vaguely oriental music, scented candles, woodgrain plastic chairs, two other people. She stowed the avocadoes behind her, against the wall, and settled back. They ordered tea and a tray of sweetcakes.

I'm Flame, she said.

Finger.

Is this place okay?

It's fine. I like it. I'm not into crowds.

I don't know you, do I? I mean, I didn't meet you at a party of anything like that.

No.

Well, I wasn't sure. I get pretty wasted sometimes. People'll come up to me and talk like we're friends and I don't know them from water. You'd be surprised.

Will you come home with me, Flame?

Wow. She touched her left breast with her right hand, gently. Can we have our tea and stuff first, you think?

Not really home—the studio. I do have an apartment, but I haven't been there in weeks.

It's close? The studio?

A couple of blocks. An old gas station I bid for and refurbished. No one else wanted it.

You married or anything?

Nothing.

And you're, what, an artist?

Yes.

Like a painter?

Mainly.

Wow. Right hand to left breast again, less gently. Here's the goods. I'll pour. Cream?

Please.

You paint strange stuff?

Sometimes.

Who's your favorite artist?

Matisse, most days. Sometimes Rothko. What do *you* do, Flame?

Lots of things.

In the realm of awkward beginnings, it was right up there. But all told, there was, too, a kind of grace.

One of the things I do best, she went on, is make other people happy. Are *you* happy, Finger?

On his studio daybed that night she opened her legs and urged his head into place between them. Tension gathered in trembling limbs as her hips strained against him and she said, Please, Please. And finally O my God, as she came.

And Flame, that simply, was his life.

Everything he did, everything he thought, was for her, to redeem her sorrow, to protect her, to make her less unhappy, to give her fear and sadness a voice, to keep her.

She moved in the next day. He'd never felt this way about anyone else, never would again. (He was right about that.) They began slowly to map one another's contours, the coastlines they'd have to drift along, their overlapping catalogs of need, of debility.

She told him how as a child she'd put the frogs she caught in cardboard boxes, carefully drawing in furniture and doorways, and find them dead there the next morning.

He told her about the first time he heard Mahler.

She told him about her first husband at age sixteen, the way she fled her parents' house and sister, how strong his hands were and how tender some nights, that first year.

He told her about Pam in London. How they'd work together for hours at opposite ends of the studio and fall together finally, exhausted, unable to continue work, on the raw wood floor spattered with paint, and afterwards sleep there. Have tea together in the morning and both go back home.

Then she left me, Finger told Flame. Just didn't show up one day and wouldn't answer when I called. That's what women do, Flame. They leave me.

I'm different, she said. None of the others loved you the way I do.

Long after she was asleep he lay watching the ceiling. Lights slid across it. A spider crossed it obliquely, reminding him of geometrical theorems. They'd been together six weeks.

Flame, he said, very quietly, then louder: Flame. She lay on her stomach. He put his hand on the back of her leg. He loved her so much. Flame, he said. I want to tell you something.

Hmmm.

She turned toward him, threw an arm and leg across him. Grazed back into her dreams.

Something I've never told anyone, he said. There's this trick I can do.

On the nightstand her cigarettes moved closer to her, and one nudged out of the pack. Her mauve Bic lighter came alive with flame.

It doesn't amount to much, he said. One of those things you have inside you, like good manners, or grammar, that the world doesn't care about. No one else knows.

She slept on. And, eventually, he too (keeping watch for the spider, thinking of right and isosceles triangles, recalling their first days together, her body in moonlight) slept.

At the studio that morning he stretched a new canvas and fell to painting with an abandon, an *otherness*, he'd not known for a long time. By twelve he had a finished work, something wholly unlike anything he'd done before, undeniably important and powerful. Such *feeling* to it, so much fear, and strength.

It was all intuition. And that intuition spilled over: he returned home half-expecting what he found there.

Hi, she said. She was sitting on the bed with grocery bags beside her. The bags were full of her things. He could feel the spaces left behind, the hollows in drawers and closet. I was wrong, Finger, she said: I'm not different. I wanted to be, but I'm just like the others. I'm sorry.

Why, he said.

I don't know.

Okay.

So, sudden and swift and light as that, there was no Flame.

He stood looking at the door for a long time. Then he walked through the apartment again and again, looking (he supposed) for scraps and tatters, for something as substantial as his memories, his pain. Against the back wall of the closet he found her pink tennis shoes—all that was left of her. He stood for a long time watching them. Very slowly, first the left one, then the right, they began walking toward him.

WALLS OF AFFECTION

Setting his drink on the table, he caught the barest flash of motion in the corner of his eye and looked instinctively away from his book. *Ignore it*, he thought, but a moment later was looking back. It came slowly around the curve of the glass then and through a hole in one of the ice cubes, a sky-blue fish the size of a pea.

The first time this happened, three weeks back, he'd been in a restaurant, their favorite, with Paula, trying yet again to work things out. Past months had not gone well, replete with week-long quarrels, shuddering silences, withholdings. Finally she had moved into a separate apartment close by. Before, there had always been tacit agreement to go on, and gentle conciliations that lasted hours, days, even weeks. This time they both sensed there would be no such thing, and after half an hour of dodging conversation, Paula told him (surprised, herself, to be saying it: she had not intended to) that it was over.

He'd looked dramatically into the depths of his drink and said, "I don't believe it."

"I'm sorry, Stan. It isn't what I wanted either."

"There's a tadpole in my martini," he went on, then looked up. "Did you get one, too? Maybe they're out of olives?"

"This isn't funny, Stan. You have to be serious about some things."

In response he put the glass on the table between them and together they watched the small blue fish submerged in clear depths, swimming in slow circles.

"It's beautiful," his wife said.

He had himself been half-submerged in a new book, a comic novel about a man who falls in love every Monday and is inevitably alone again by Thursday, and to forestall the pain of Paula's absence he dove ever deeper, finishing the book in just over two weeks. He had a drink with his agent to deliver the manuscript and found another fish. He didn't mention it to Carl and left the drink untouched, ordering coffee instead.

Now, at ten at night, he was reading *Candide*, something he did every few months, and watching a small blue fish come 'round and 'round again in the glass beside him.

He thought of carousel music; of moons circling planets, day and night caught in that looping; of seasons and years cradled in the swing of worlds 'round stars. And because Paula was gone, because he was thinking far too much, remembering too much, because even Voltaire could not bear him away, and because a small blue fish circled endlessly in the glass alongside, he felt walls closing in on him.

They had lived together what seemed a long time here. Nothing failed to bear her impression. Even the mirrors remembered her: her body stepping before them wet from showers, face leaning close in the mornings for makeup. Their bed recalled her form and drew him toward it. Pillows and sheets still smelled of her.

At twelve he threw a sport coat over sweatshirt and jeans and walked two blocks to Bennigan's. Loud characterless music and lots of smoke, dreams on sleeves, and hope smoldering down toward early, lonely hours. He took a seat at the bar, ordered beer, smiled at the woman on the barstool beside him. She was thirtyish, blond, knee wrapped over knee with a quiet show of thigh.

She was having Black Russians. He bought her one. She was smoking. He lit her cigarette with bar matches.

Her name was Linda; she taught history in high school. A month ago her boyfriend failed to come home one night after work and a couple of days later phoned to say he needed time, he couldn't make the commitments she wanted just now. She didn't know what to do. She loved him so much. She tried just to go on. There were awkward, agonizing phone calls they both regretted. Nights he'd come over and leave after they'd made love. Nights like this one and three before, when he didn't come, or call, at all.

"I've forgotten how to be alone," she said. "It scares me."

"You don't have to be."

"I just want someone who cares. Even if it's just for an hour, just for the night. I can't be this alone anymore."

"I understand."

And after he told her something of his own story she said, "I think you do."

At his apartment, ghosts of Paula whispered, and *her* form gave way in the mirror to Linda's. He reached across her body and switched the radio from country to classical. Lay with his head cradled on her shoulder, hand gently at her waist.

After a while in blundering dark he said, "Thank you," and she said, "Thank *you*."

He got up and brought wine, glasses, from the tiny kitchen. A bottle long held in reserve.

She sat in his bed with the sheet at her waist and reached toward him, breast swinging freely. He poured wine as dawn was starting up outside. They held their glasses together in a toast. Within them, small blue fish swam toward one another, swam toward the glass walls of their ever-separate worlds.

CHANGES

"You will not find me. Get this sad
certainty firmly into your head."
—Jean Cocteau

I should like very much to begin this account by writing "When I was a child," then go on to catalogue the discoveries and anxieties of, say, an average childhood in Brighton, or Hoave. This has forever seemed to me the most honest, the most direct mode of autobiographical narration; even Master Copperfield could do no better. Furthermore, it would seem that after sixty-some years I should be entitled to so small a favor. But the truth is, of course, that I never *was* a child: I was born when I was twenty years old and I was walking across the university campus at the time.

Curiously, the arrival of consciousness was some delayed, and I reeled for several minutes beneath the sudden impact of simple, pure perception: color and motion. I am told that I dropped to my knees then fell prostrate into a nearby flowerbed, and that my eyes closed. It is generally agreed that I assumed the classic fetal position, though none of the witnesses can be certain on this point. At any rate, a student strolling back into his rooms from a class in elementary calculus was the first to come upon me. By his own testimony he stood for a moment indecisively, then walked over to ask if he might be of some assistance. It was at this very moment that consciousness beset me, and I began to wail.

The university professors were quick to take me in. Together they fed and clothed me, saw to my every need. During days their wives would fondle me and push me in oversize prams through the park. Articles concerning my education and development appeared in every leading learned journal. Educators, psychologists and sociologists made hegiras from all about this world I was gradually coming to know, till at last it was impossible for me to leave the guarded campus grounds; such was my fame. I was given a room at the university. Domestic servants were also provided, and a call to the Board of Regents on my private phone would, at any late hour, produce whatever—anything—I might desire. As my education continued.

At the age of four I destroyed the chemical laboratory and burned the phys ed building to the ground. At five I killed the Dean of Arts and Sciences and successfully breached three out of the four women's dormitories.

But I can recite *The Canterbury Tales* in the original, complete with variants, and the same with all Shakespeare. I can conjugate Latin verbs without conscious thought while working the *London Times* crossword. I can even tell you where a staff vacancy exists in seventeenth century drama, and the manner in which Mrs. Bonfiglioni passes her time while the good professor is leading undergraduates down some tricky path of *The Faerie Queene.*

In America I became an artist and took a studio on Eighth Street. Commissioned to provide for the Audubon Society a statue to be set in cement outside their national offices, I conceived a project in which the statue of a robin, ten feet high, would be composed of a substance impervious to weather and general attrition, but highly sensitive to the droppings of our city's pigeons: as the pigeons frolicked on and about the statue, decorating it again and again with their droppings, the statue would slowly deteriorate, a kind of living, ever-changing sculpture. Put in place, it was an instant success, and a continual source of temptation for the community's youngsters.

For a time I was supported by women. One would feed me each night; another would replace buttons on my clothes; yet another would crouch beside me at the championship marble tournaments, cheering. I attempted to express my gratitude, feebly, with flowers and lines of verse, typing up three copies of each poem and dedicating one to each of the kind, glad ladies. (It was the least I could do.) To one, on her birthday, I sent a dozen yellow roses. The roses wilted in three days, then I replaced, while she was away from the house, a single flower; it stood among the others, a lonely, bright exemplum of hope. And for more than a month I secretly replaced this rose again and again, while she marveled and brought friends around to see it, this amazing reminder.

I arrived in Buffalo without money, family, or friends. The only jobs available were doughnut cooking, computer programming, and bounty hunting, and, with adults bringing in so little a head, I turned my attention to wayward young folk, bagging thirty-three before I took my just rewards and departed with those rewards to Canada where I applied for a position executing draft dodgers for the United States government.

Shortly after my misadventures in Yucatan I got a job at the New Orleans morgue, filing dead letters and performing the occasional autopsy. Working alongside me were Zipporah Grosche, who had the largest collection of perfumed letters in existence, and Clarence Culbreath, whose belts came in form-fitting plastic cases and who had worked the past summer on the road gangs in order to buy his mother, who was thought to be blind, a color TV. There was also a cute little thing in a miniskirt whose name was, I believe, Edward. While working at the morgue I surpassed all previous records by resurrecting three hundred and eighteen letters. At the time I was wearing my hair long, the sides brushed back over my ears and the top flopped over like an omelet. It was very difficult work—grueling, as they say—and each night in the solitude of my own room I wept for the poor lost things which were in my care, but without it I could never have made a successful career in politics. I saw trouble brewing when I grew so popular that 74.8 percent of the letters reaching my office were addressed to me personally. A scant few months after this began, I was dismissed by the authorities and made my way to Salt Lake City where I began voice lessons.

At about this time there developed a sort of game which I played every morning. Getting out of bed, with eyes still closed I tried to decide, by touch alone, where I was: then, should I find myself in my own apartment, I would try to decide, again by touch, who the woman with me might be. If I failed at this I would ask her name, but never remained long enough to hear the answer—for immediately upon speaking I would dive from the room and flee with whatever clothing happened to hand. For some time then, I would walk in Central Park—wearing perhaps an overcoat or a skirt—until I summoned courage to call my landlady. Good Mrs. Deal would put a drinking glass against the common wall and listen. When she announced that sound had ceased, after several phone calls on my part, I could generally return home safely.

I fell in love. (This was my religious period, just before I wrote my best-selling sci-fi novel *It Came from Out of Town*.) She was a *petite chose* and French major from Georgia, with rings on all her fingers and little happy smiles sitting in her eyes getting fat; her hair was drawn to one side, where, shouting for help, it cascaded back over one shoulder. We ate fried clams together at Howard Johnson's and visited the snake house at the St. Louis zoo, among other things. I was wearing my hair short and heavy workmen's boots. We both wore lederhosen, in which we hid matching copies of *The Prophet*, Scientology bulletins and leaflets proclaiming New York "A Summer Festival." I lost her to a wrangler down in Dallas on the way to Amarillo. She met him at McDonald's while I was washing out a few things at a nearby laundromat and I never saw her again, though for a month she telegraphed greetings every morning at five o'clock. (The delivery boy and I grew close; many mornings he stayed to breakfast with me, dissolving with his good cheer, the bright, hot pearl of hurt.) It is difficult, as she once remarked, to say no to the world champion bulldogger.

In the District of Columbia I was stricken with social conscience and, purchasing a wig and shaving my legs, marched with the women against the Washington Monument. After demanding that the monument be sheathed in a huge pink condom we moved on to Newport, Grand Rapids and San Francisco. By day I marched and by night I studied cosmetology in a beautician's school and sculpture in a college of continuing education, studies which several months later resulted in my being appointed hair-dresser to Mount Rushmore.

Once, having played for two seasons on a Boston pro football team, I experienced a nervous breakdown, grew unable to remember the

302 • JAMES SALLIS

plays, and was interned in a revolutionary new psychiatric hospital in Hartford, Conn., to which I was driven in the team's bus. It was unlike the hospitals I'd previously known in East Orange and West-chester. There was no occupational therapy, no baseball playing, not even the enjoyable bouts of bingo and square dancing with joyful schizophrenics in the name of recreation. Instead, the nurses wore overalls and attended small vegetable patches outside the dormito-ries where we slept in hammocks and dogtents pitched anew each night. The sole therapy was simple and direct: upon internment each patient was given a guitar and when he learned to play it, was discharged. Doctors roved the halls at night with cassette recorders, occasionally making trades.

Finally, in late 197—, I was apprehended and returned to Europe, where I settled back at the University and instituted a program of American Studies. These several months, bored with my classes, I have had much time to think over the events of the past, which thoughts have led to my setting down these incidents by way of notes for my memoirs; meanwhile I busy myself with trying out for amateur plays, serving as second on the rowing team and, having no taste for Spenser, with Mrs. Bonfiglioni.

She of the grand imagination and large thighs, O!

MIRANDA-ESCOBEDO

I'd been on beat patrol in the East Village for four days when I came across the motorbike accident.

"I want to go where the action is," I'd told the loot again and again, until he went ahead and put papers through, as much to shut me up as anything else. And I hadn't done bad, four Positives and ten Probables. Had to fight for a couple of those Probs.

I was walking down the street kind of slow, looking around me, thinking of all the years I'd wasted in Identification staring at loops, whirls, ridges, auras. But this, where I was now, this was whoosh, for sure.

The accident had taken place outside a bookstore. Copies of *The Exorcist* along with a dozen or so of the book's grandchildren were highlighted in the window. A youngish man on a motorbike had come flashing down the street and ploughed into the back of a '55 Chevy driven by an elderly schoolteacher. "I tried to get out of his way," she was telling the cops between sobs.

The young man was obviously gone. Both legs were bent back under at odd angles, his chest looked like a broke-open watermelon, and one eye had been torn out.

He was standing there looking down at his body.

I sniffed at his aura and said, "That's it, buddy, let's go."

At first he didn't hear me, or didn't seem to. They always take it hard. Give the new ones a few minutes, the manual says. And we've got trauma centers, of course, for those that need them.

It didn't take too long. He must have sensed me standing beside him. Anyway, he looked around, and I knew I didn't have to repeat what I'd said, or explain anything. He knew what I was doing there. They usually do.

"Now wait a minute, man," Fifteen said. "You ain't got nothing on me."

"No? Take a whiff of that aura." He couldn't, naturally. "Obviously damaged—and that's Probable Cause. We'll let ID take it from there, okay? You're coming with me."

I had a momentary vision of my prior colleagues down in ID receiving the request, signed by me, and marked, of course, Rush/Urgent, as all our requests were.

I got the bell jar out of my pocket and held it out toward him, but I kept the top on. Still, the little foil leaves trembled. That's when most of them, even the real hardrails, give up and pack it in.

I could see from the way he looked down briefly, then back up with a smile, that this guy wasn't gonna be the tag-along kind.

"Hey, now," Fifteen said. "Look, you just check, you'll see. Made the vig last week, full amount."

So he was in the game. Looking better every minute.

"What I'm saying is, you can't touch me, man."

"Like *hell* I can't," I said. That shook him.

He looked around nervously. But I was getting concerned, myself. This collar was taking too long and the others weren't usually far behind us.

Suddenly Fifteen looked up. The smile had changed. Something had changed it.

"You didn't read me my rights," Fifteen said.

So I looked and there he was, standing at the edge of the crowd wearing the usual white linen suit. Hogan. I'd been warned about him. The best around, and a poacher, have your collar out from under you before you knew it, and no one knew how. Guys back at the house said if this was a Western he'd be notching the grip of his gun.

I told Fifteen to stay right where he was and went over to the interloper.

"Egan," I said. "Fourteenth precinct."

"Hogan, eighty-seventh."

"Well, what do you think?"

He was looking at the bookstore window. "You read that?"

"What?"

"That book. You read it?"

"No. Meant to, but—you know how it is, with the job and all."

"Good book," he said. "The original. Those others . . ." He took out a handkerchief and blew his nose.

I waited till he was through and asked again.

"The aura's obviously damaged."

"Right," I said.

"But there's the matter of the Agreed."

"You know as well as I do," I said, "that it's not binding."

"Guidelines, a yardstick—right." He looked back at the suspect. I wondered if he had his ID people running a check. Or if he even bothered. "There's also the matter of your failure to read him his rights."

There, he had me. The collar'd probably get tossed for not following procedure.

"Look," he said. "We're short on space—not like your folk at all— so any other day I'd just pat you both on the back and he'd be yours."

I heard the shoe drop before it hit the floor.

"But the truth is," he said, "I haven't filled my quota for the week. And I'm up for promotion."

"Okay, okay. You got him."

He nodded, took out the bell jar, and walked over to no-longer-Fifteen. Held the jar out, took the top off. There was a quiet *pop*, and the foil leaves danced.

He walked past me on his way back up the street.

"What the hell," he said, "right?"

I finished the shift and the next day, after a sleepless night, put in for a transfer to Central Holding, a joint service. Just a lot of paperwork and PR, but regular hours, solid ground beneath my feet, and like Hogan the Poacher said: What the hell.

DOGS IN THE NIGHTTIME

Bob and Marge live in the house behind us, across the alley. They are incredibly in love and have been for fifteen years. Twenty minutes ago I heard gunfire from their house, a single, cracking shot, perhaps a .38.

Alice's eyes briefly lifted—other times I might not have noticed, but we'd just quarreled again and I was, as usual following these quarrels, especially sensitive to her moods—then returned to her magazine.

I sat staring at the word *missing* on page 84 of a Raymond Chandler novel for some time before I spoke.

"Did you hear something, Dear?"

"Hear something?" She watched me over the half-lens of her reading glasses.

"Yes. Just now."

"Such as?" Eyes moving back to the magazine. Its cover bore the legend How to *Tell If He Loves You: Five Questions You Can Ask.*

"I don't know, really. A slammed door? Backfire? A gunshot, maybe."

Her eyes quickly took in the cover of my book, went back to her own reading.

"I heard nothing, John, at least that I can recall."

"The curious incident of the dog in the nighttime . . ."

"Pardon?"

"Nothing, Dear. Just something from the Holmes' stories."

Alice put her magazine on the end table and asked if I'd like a nightcap.

"Perhaps you should get away from mysteries and detective stories for just a while," she said as I followed her into the kitchen. "They've become almost an obsession, you know. We could pick up some nice science fiction at the library. Historical novels, romances, biographies. Whatever."

"I guess so." She handed over a brandy and soda and I sipped at it. "But this is what I really like. I've tried to explain why, how the truth very gradually comes to light, piece by piece, through layers of misdirection and camouflage. Like a worm fighting its way to the surface after hard rain."

"Yes, John, I know." Hers was Irish coffee, and she blew once across it, glasses fogging. "But there comes a time one wonders." She folded the glasses and laid them on the counter by a spoon rest. Released from bondage, her eyes became astonishingly blue and reactive. She sipped at her coffee.

"Last Thursday, after we'd eaten at Scobbo's," she said. "A drunk had fallen asleep on the bus. You insisted that he'd been assassinated."

"Humor, Alice. I was feeling good, from the food, from the wine. It was our anniversary. I thought it would make you laugh."

"And all that talk about the teacher who disappeared at the high school. What do you think the kids make of all that? They have to repeat it, you know, all that talk about plots and conspiracies."

"I guess so, Dear. I understand, and I'll be careful what I say. Just don't make me read any romances—please."

We took our drinks back into the living room where I sat looking at the word *clues* (page 85) and remembering times I'd come home recently and found Alice and Marge huddled together over coffee in the kitchen, remembering their low voices and sudden, guarded looks. Once I'd asked if Bob and Marge could be having problems. The usual misunderstandings and squabbles, I guess, Alice said; those are inevitable.

We have closed our book and magazine and are about to go up to bed when the second shot sounds, slicing into the night's silence. For some reason Shawna's face comes to me—thirteen and Bob's delight, a quiet, gentle girl. Neither of us moves. Clearing my throat at last, I stand.

"I wouldn't go over there just now," Alice says.

I sink back into my seat. Outside there is a silence like stone.

WOLF

We had this arrangement. My wife lived six months of the year with her parents, the rest with me—I don't know why we didn't think of it earlier. The last I counted, she'd left me eighteen times. Another couple of times the folks came and (to use her word) removed her. They said I make her crazy, but *they* wanted to keep her a child. It's all really strange.

It was working out pretty well. I'm a freelance journalist, the kind others call a wolf, and in a bag by the door at all times I keep two suits, four shirts and ties, underwear, socks, toilet articles, notebook and pens; I can be on the trail of a story in minutes. But I could afford to turn down assignments when she was with me and double up when she wasn't. So we really had a lot more time together than most people do. It was great—movies every afternoon, hanging out by the pool when everybody else was at work, late-night strolls, breakfast at 3 A.M.

But slowly she began to hate me. I could see it deep inside her eyes as she lay across my chest in the mornings, a hard edge of self-interrogation. What would it be like without me; could she cope; how will she go about ridding herself of me—that sort of thing.

Then one day as we stood side by side in the kitchen preparing dinner (a corn soufflé, asparagus vinaigrette, pasta) she told me that she wasn't going back to her parents.

In a panic I tried calling her folks that night and got no answer. I tried again the next morning, that afternoon, and twice that night. Finally I phoned around and told everybody to get me some assignments, fast.

"Sounds like life or death," Harrison at the *Globe* said.

"For all I know, it may be."

"Even the best domestic arrangements can't last forever, friend, and you've been luckier than most."

I once knew a guy who had a big doormat that said GO AWAY.

Nicest guy you'd want to meet, do anything for you, but he just didn't like unexpected guests. Suddenly that's the way it was with my editors. Delighted to hear from me, they'd chat along for an hour or more about things coming up, but for now all trees and cupboards stayed bare. I began to think horrible thoughts like city desk, food editor, *political analyst*. (Such was my despair and terror.)

It was about this time that I realized all the movies we were watching in those long summer afternoons were mysteries: a Hitchcock festival, Bogart films at the museum, Charlie Chan on TV. Books by Hammett and Chandler littered the apartment. Since bizarre crimes were a kind of specialty—I had a knack for somehow getting inside the criminal's mind and more or less writing from in there—in my leisure time, generally, I steered away from such preoccupation. But now I found myself scanning the dailies for just such accounts.

COWED HUSBAND SERVES POODLE

TO WIFE IN STEW

MAN TIED TO CHAIR AND *FED* TO DEATH

THE LAMP TOLD ME TO DO IT, MURDERER SAYS

That sort of thing.

Life between us, except for that knowledge like a drowned body deep within her eyes, except for almost imperceptible pauses before she replied (as though she were drifting toward worlds farther from the sun, and colder), continued much as before. In mid-July we attended a retrospective of horror films from the past forty years, in early August an "atrocity exhibition" (photographs from Auschwitz altered to show the prisoners with wide smiles and contemporary three-piece suits) at a local gallery.

In slow, plodding fashion I'd begun gaining weight from the food we spent hours in the kitchen preparing each day and from inactivity, from the sheer inertia of our days together. Talking it over, and reading two or three books on the subject, we took to running several times a day in the park nearby, circling again and again the park's pate-like copse of trees and skirting narrow trails littered with family picnickers, scavenging dogs and benches

carved deep with old lovers' initials. My wife quite early exhib-
ited an altogether unsuspected natural gift for it, heaving out far
ahead—a yard, two yards, steadily farther and farther—as I fell,
huffing and lame, behind. Many nights she would go back out
alone, saying that she loved to run in moonlight. At first, pro
forma, she asked me to go along, but rather soon that civility (for
it was no more) ceased; and this became, in fact, my only time
apart from her, except in sleep.

Need I say that sleep was troubled? In one dream a man I knew,
but whose face I could not place, stood on the other side of a locked
door smearing the bloody entrails of a turtle against the glass, slowly
robbing me of light. In another a child's legs were gone from the
thighs down; only the bones protruded, and tennis shoes were laced
to the knobby ankle sockets.

There was, too, the eventual revelation that I had not worked in
almost eight months. Flurries of calls from editors had tapered off,
then subsided, as I refused assignment after assignment; I could
not now remember how long it had been since the phone rang. I
didn't know, but thought that I must surely be almost out of money.
I tried to recall what writing was like: bent over notebooks in cabs
or planes or the bathrooms of hotels; the world that came into your
head as you blindly strung together word after word and then, in
those words, ever growing, appeared there before you, part of *this*
world now. It was unimaginable. And yet for so many years this was
what I did, what I *was*: a channel, a voice, a mirror at once giving
back less, and more, than what entered it.

And if that was what I had been, what was I now?

Somber September slipped in through cracks beneath the door.
My wife's time away from me, her moonlight runs, lengthened even
as the days contracted. Our fare grew plainer, and we began foraging
(though perhaps this is only another dream) in the gardens and
basements of neighbors. Pounds fell away from her; she grew lean
and brown. We seldom spoke anymore. I lay alone shivering against
the night, watching my own breath rise in the air above me like a
ghostly, insubstantial penis.

And now it is November, strangely my birthday. In the kitchen
my wife prepares to eat. I can hear her but a wall away, padding

about on bare feet (for she has given up shoes and, largely, clothing) as she makes that keening, unforgettable hunger sound. I hear her at the door, dropping (or do I imagine this?) onto all fours. I only hope that I can finish this, my last story, before the story ends. That is all I ask of life now.

MEMORY

At two in the morning in the new house he lies awake staring past windows at the moon's blank face. Faintly he hears from across the hall, or imagines that he hears, the girls' breathing. The air conditioner cycles briefly on, as though routinely checking its own vital signs. Never an overtly imaginative man, nevertheless he imagines this pulse of air as a sudden vortex: envisions it spinning hungrily out into the world then abruptly recalled, gone, only the hunger left behind, perhaps. Faith remains fast asleep beside him following their nighttime litany of household costs, shopping plans, new redecoration. And how long has it been since they made love? He can't remember. Trying, he sees only her face: head thrown back, the narrow band of white that always shows at the bottom of closed eyes, her mouth straining open.

The way she looked the night Wayne died.

It was early morning then too, two or three, and he'd had to pound at the door for what seemed a terribly long time before she came down. Lights from the interstate caught in the picture window, slid across the front of the house, dropped onto her face. At last she raised a hand into the light as well, as though to push it away, saying, It's Wayne, isn't it, and he had nodded. Only later could he talk, only then was he able to tell her how the car had been found abandoned, Wayne's body a mile or so further into the woods. She hadn't said anything else, simply reached for him. Afterwards they drank dark chicory coffee out on the gallery and talked about Wayne's pension, funeral arrangements, what she would do, the girls, as the sun floated up out of the bayou like a huge bubble and cars began lining up on the highway for their long daily glides into the city.

Faith turns onto her left side, into moonlight, and the gown falls away from one large-nippled breast. His hand moves there, nests there, without thought, without volition, itself now entering moonlight. Soundly asleep, she backs into him and covers his hand with her own. How subtly, how imperceptibly, things change and are lost. He can remember nights of such tenderness that tears ballooned behind his eyes; recalls watching morning after morning break in the small sky of the window across her bare body, a riot of birdsong outside, the loamy, sharp smell of cypress and swamp mingling with their own there in that bed, that room.

No one had been too surprised when he and Faith took up together. They'd always been together a lot anyway, what with him and Wayne being so close, and it all just fell naturally into place. The mayor himself was best man. They'd used Wayne's insurance money to build the new house. The girls took to him quickly and within the year were calling him Daddy.

He hears a siren and wonders what Jimmie's up to out there, what might be going on. Maybe he should call in and check. Wayne used to do that. Kept a radio beside the bed. And slow nights when he couldn't sleep at all, sometimes he'd bring a bottle down to the station and sit sipping Jack Daniels till dawn, then have breakfast at Ti-Jean's and a quick shower and go on about his day's work, never the worse for wear, near as anyone could tell.

Wayne had been so happy when the girls were born. *My life finally means something*, he said. And spent his meager spare time making things for them—toy chests, walnut rocking horses, stilts— or remodeling the house, till it was like an idea that kept changing. Late one Saturday over a case of beer he and Wayne had put in a picture window he'd been talking about for months. Faith had a big meal waiting for them when they finished, everything from pot roast to homemade pickles and Karo pecan pie. Then he and Wayne stayed up most of the night drinking and went out for squirrel that morning. By then, Wayne had decided he didn't like the window where it was.

Lately whenever he looks at the older girl, at Mandy, he sees Wayne. Something in her face, hard and soft at the same time, or in those gray eyes. The way she lifts a hand to wave, barely moving it. He knows that Faith sees it too; he catches her sometimes, watching.

Mandy's twelve and remembers her father, even talks about doing police work herself when she grows up. June thinks of *him* as her father. The two girls are as different as sisters, as two children, could be. But they are forever polite, deferential; there's about them both a gentleness he knows all too well. And even in June now he sometimes encounters Wayne suddenly peering out at him.

With Faith, their apartness, it wasn't so much a forfeiture as it was a slow, cumulative exempting: a kind of forgetting, really. Days and nights fell away unquestioned, untried, until finally even desire, the possibility of it, seemed impossibly distant, and he found himself lying here beside her night after night in the company of memories.

The past (or so he tried to console himself) is all a man ever really owns anyway.

But he still loved her, still felt for her what he'd always felt. He was sure of that. That was almost all he was sure of.

There were reasons why it happened, of course—reasons upon reasons. Everything was so complicated. Whatever you did or didn't do, started four other things going. And so finally it had just seemed easier this way, to go along, get used to it, despite the longing, despite the ache and the hollows.

Whenever life takes with one hand, it gives with the other: he'd heard that all his life. But what could ever take Wayne's place in his own life, in Faith's, in the girls'? What could possibly ever replace the love he and Faith once had? And what could even begin to fill the space left behind, the hollow, now that it was gone, if it was?

He hears the siren again and almost immediately the phone rings. He reaches for it, hoping not to wake Faith; it's Mayor Broussard, who hates to disturb him this time of night. But he's just had a call from daughter Lizette, now working the radio desk on deep nights (a hopeless attempt to keep her out of strange beds and too-familiar bars), and it seems that Jimmie's got himself drunk and is driving his squad all over town with the siren and lights and occasionally the PA going.

"Doesn't sound much like Jimmie," he tells the mayor.

"That's exactly why I'm calling you, Al. It's woman trouble, Lizette tells me. Went home this morning and found his girl'd packed it all up and left, dishes, catbox, fly rod and all. Didn't even trouble to leave him a note."

"Funny he didn't say anything to me."

"You're like that boy's father, Al; I know that. But we both know what that kind of trouble can do to a man. He's a good boy, he doesn't mean anything by it. But you'd best get on out there and pull him down before I start getting citizen complaints and have to do something."

"I will, A.C. It's taken care of—and thanks."

There's a pause.

"I've backed you from the first, Al, you know that. Everything going all right?"

"Yes sir, it is."

"How's Faith?"

"Fine as ever."

"That's real good to hear. And those girls?"

"Prettier and smarter every day, A.C."

"And more and more like Wayne, I'd be willing to bet. Listen, you all have to come out here for dinner some night soon. It's been way too long."

"We'd like that."

"Good. Good, it's settled then. You give us a call."

"Right. And thanks again, A.C."

He hangs up the phone and listens for Jimmie's siren but doesn't hear it. So he steps out the French doors onto the gallery.

He can hear the guttural call of frogs deep in the swamp. Something, a bat, a pelican, flies against the moon, already gone when he glances up. This swamp itself is a kind of memory, he thinks, looking out at the ageless, ancient stand of cypress draped in Spanish moss: a deeper one than we'll ever know.

Wakened by the phone or by conversation, Faith has been to the bathroom. She comes back now and lies on the bed in a long cotton gown green like old copper. After a moment he lies beside her. Without thinking, without intention, he turns to her and puts a hand on her breast.

"I'd like to, Al," she tells him. "For a long time I've wanted to. I was afraid."

He moves onto her then, and into the old, familiar rhythms. Out in the streets somewhere, in *that* world, he hears the siren swing by again, Jimmie's voice a blur on the bullhorn. The telephone begins to ring, unattended, as Faith's hips rise to meet his own.

"I killed him," he tells her, feeling the shudder tear at those hips, "for you," feeling the vortex open beneath him, feeling the hollows fill, *the hunger, oblivion.*

JOYRIDE

We dump the bodies in a ravine outside town, have some drinks at a roadhouse, and buy sixpacks at a Circle K for the ride home. None of us knows the others' names.

We ride along silently for a while, sipping at beers and popping new ones, as dark comes down. There's country music, kind of loud, on the radio. Finally the driver reaches over and turns it down.

"When I was a kid, not more than nine or ten," he says, "there was this girl down the block I always played with. Donna was her name, Donna Sue. I don't remember who made it up, but we always played the same game. *Play-play*, we called it; *play-play number one*. She was a beautiful princess and I was her wicked uncle, and I had stolen her from her parents, kidnapped her. They'd never see her again, or she, them. And in the meantime she'd learn to love me instead."

He hands me an empty can and I trade him a full one for it.

"You think you can fall in love that young?" he says, then shrugs. "Oh who the fuck cares?" He takes a long swallow. "But I been most of my life trying to find again what I had that year, the excitement, the sense of controlling it all. Picking up women in bars or laundromats and pretending I'd kidnapped 'em. Even had a few I got to know real well who'd kinda go along with the gag. Never thought it would really happen, though." He holds up his can in a toast. A blade of light slashes through the car. "Best day of my life, gentlemen."

We come around a curve into a traffic jam, cars as far as you can see. He pulls us across three lanes, horns and brakes screaming close behind, up onto the shoulder, then down the embankment to a service road.

He pulls into a 7-Eleven. "Might as well stop for more beer, since we're here."

"What's all this?" he asks at the counter as we pay, nodding back toward the tie-up.

"Accident, they tell me. Say there's bodies all over the road up there a ways. Always say that, though. That'll be twelve ninety-three. Don't need no gas?"

"Not this time."

"Ain't sold no gas all day long. Just beer and cigarettes and a sandwich or two and them girlie magazines there. Here's your change, and I thank you. Drive careful, now."

Two teenage girls are hanging around the Coke machine outside. "You girls need a ride?" the driver asks.

They shake their heads, looking at one another. Both wear tight shorts and men's shirts tied at the waist.

"Anything else you *do* need?" Driver says.

The girls giggle at one another.

We climb back in the car, run the service road a few blocks and eventually get back on the interstate. We pop new, cold beers and sit watching lights stream by. Almost no traffic up here above the jam. A few cars going the other way, away from town.

"We were dirt poor," one of the guys in the back seat says after a while. "Lived in one room, first I remember. A garage apartment, I think; I remember trees, stairs. Friday nights my old man—I think he was my old man, anyway—would come home late and drunk. I'd get put in the bathroom, in the bathtub with my pillow and blankets and all. And out there I'd hear the old lady hollerin' and beggin' for him not to hurt her. He'd rape her's what he'd do. Have her right there on the floor, on the kitchen table. Wherever. Never touch her otherwise. Then later on he'd come in to take a piss and she'd still be out there cryin'. Hey, you guys think about getting something to eat?"

"*I* could do with something."

"Yeah, let's chow down."

"Sounds good."

Driver edges over into the right lane, scouting the roadside.

"I was, I don't know, twelve or thirteen maybe, when he left," the guy in the back seat goes on. "I always *was* sorry I didn't have a chance to get to know him. The old lady run off not long afterward. Some guy she met at church or something."

"Burgers, or what?" Driver asks.

"Mexican?"

"Whatever."

"Lotsa help," Driver says.

We wind up at Denny's. Half a chicken; Mexican plate; soup and salad; coffee and pie. A cop at the counter is asking questions about the bearded young man and scantily clad girl at one corner booth. He drinks five cups of coffee, heavy cream, before his radio goes off. Possible homicide, Main and Tenth.

"Death," I tell them. "It always fascinated me. At age eleven I killed my first bird, and wept for hours. The next day I killed a squirrel, a week later a deer. I began reading poetry about the same time, Donne and all the others. Pavese: *Death will come, and will have your eyes.* I wanted no other lover."

I look about, at their unknown faces, and know they understand. Amazing, that we've found one another as we have. That we've been able to help birth one another's dreams. I pay, and we again mount the car. Hang on, Driver says. He tears past stop signs onto the interstate. Red moon in the sky. Billboards advertising condominiums, topless clubs, social services, Jesus, abortion, groceries.

"There's a story we haven't heard still," I say.

The other guy in the back seat lifts his head. He has longish hair, a trim moustache, fair skin. Trusting eyes.

"Nothing like what *you* guys have, I'm afraid," he says. "No great obsession or the like. Just a premonition, a vision I've carried with me from earliest childhood. The reason all your faces were familiar when we first met."

The rest comes in a rush, like ants from a damaged hill.

"Four men in a car, two bodies left well behind. Three of the men have lived their dreams, fulfilled their lifelong fantasies, today. The other is about to."

He drains his can and rolls its coolness along his forehead.

"The car is coming into a sharp curve. A limousine pulls alongside, then suddenly in front. Control is lost. No one survives."

I feel Driver haul us hard to the right and look around, ahead, in time to see the car pull into our lane. It's a long limo, blue as the sky, our sudden horizon.

PURE REASON

There is such gentleness, such ease, in death: with a long sigh the world slips away.

In one of his letters Chandler describes the perfect death scene. A man, dying, has fallen onto his desk and far across it sees a paperclip. He seizes upon this. His hand reaches for it. It is all he knows, all that remains for him of the world, this single object, and his reaching for it.

I am writing this where I live, in a bone-white room in Fort Worth, Texas. Half an hour ago, hiding herself away again in jean skirt and long green sweater, Linda departed, moving back into her widowhood, into the loneliness that defines her, and her house full of things.

It's a warm night, and for a time I stood on the narrow balcony with a pear gone perhaps a bit ripe at the corner of a kitchen cabinet, and with a small knife. The epicene white flesh of magnolias hung before me. I heard the couple next door quarreling.

Linda is a teacher, a geologist. Our conversations, when once upon a time we had them, encompassed the far reach of earth's history: seas becoming desert, fish swimming into the heart of stone. Now when she comes we drink, listen to music, maybe ask one another how life goes, and go to bed. Once she was bewildered by my bare mattress, battered leather chair, stack of odd-sized boxes against one wall, all of it bought for forty dollars at Thrift Town; now she accepts all this. It hardly matters by what we are surrounded, only that we are. Linda knows that silence is the greatest lesson the ages have for us. And this is the rock I've swum into, where you will find me someday.

When this began, I lived in motels, sometimes for two days or a week, often for a month, for several. There was a certain coherence to life then, a constancy of line: the same furniture and TV, tiled bathroom, white towels, view. I could have been (and imagined myself) anywhere in the United States, in any major city. A businessman, perhaps, or a journalist courting discarded truths. A fugitive on the run. I ate in whatever restaurants or fast-food chains had attached themselves like pilot fish to the motel, carting orders back to the room where sacks and containers nightly overfilled plastic trash cans sleeved with white. I packed the sink with ice and cans of beer from 7-Elevens. And woke at two or three each morning with the TV on (acquiring a sudden, terrible presence) and traffic spinning by relentlessly outside.

I had grown certain that I was not human, you see. This knowledge came to me, suddenly and without overture as such knowledge often does, some ten months after my wife's departure, as I sat one morning listening to Robert Johnson's "Stones in My Passway" blend with birdsongs from the open windows. Those windows, the quality of light there, were the reason I'd taken the apartment. Previously I had lived in cave-like quarters in nearby Arlington with a single window in one room and, in the other, a slit like a ship's gunport near the top of a wall. When I'd come to look at the apartment on Taylor just off Camp Bowie, it had just been repainted; everything was white, every window uncovered, morning light everywhere. On the second floor and set among trees, there was much of the treehouse about it, and I took it at once.

My third attempt at intimacy had ended that night with neither of us certain, after hours of earnest talk, just which had severed the Baptist's head. Though I had come to care for the women involved— one of them, at least, a great deal—none of these attempts had endured more than a month or two. I recognized certain patterns in my courting of these women, of course. Who could embrace so violent a need yoked at the same time to such apartness? Monday's roses and wrenching, confessional letters were abridged by a week's silence as I failed to call or to acknowledge her calls, calls that I would listen to again and again on the machine's brief tape, not knowing what I wanted, or rather, wanting the two conflicting things at once, perhaps.

Light was just starting up outside, and I turned my head toward the window where plants lined the sill. I thought: *What sort of creature am I?*

With that thought, that realization, many things fell into place. My solitude and yearnings became clear to me. Of course I had to be alone; there was no other way. I understood so much. I *knew*, knew as only the true outsider can know. I had said goodbye to all that, to the pain and pettiness of it, to newspapers and dentists and daily appointments, and was exempt.

A little past ten the mailbox rattled at the bottom of the stairs and I went down them. The mailman folded himself back into his car. I had been listening to Messiaen's *Quartet for the End of Time*, the second movement, "Vocalise, pour l'Ange qui annonce la fin du temps," an angel who must be much like Rilke's angels, I think. I sat on the porch then in a still, bright morning watching paired runners, a group of young women in spandex walking briskly together, heads swiveling one to another, an elderly black man sorting through trash at curbside, his lightweight aluminum cart propped alongside, this landscape in which I did not belong, to which I was alien, and knew what I must do.

Something about her, a certain guarded, vulnerable look about the eyes, through which she peered, the curve of her calf just as it vanished beneath her shorts, caught my attention, and I followed her to the laundromat. Not so much that I sought her out as that she was presented to me. So often life is like this. The idea of a yellow bicycle, a blue guitar, occurs to you one morning, and suddenly there are blue guitars and yellow bicycles everywhere.

At McDonald's she had eaten a McDLT and fries. She ate in small, precise bites, a magazine folded back on the table's tiny plateau. I'd scarcely begun my coffee but when she stood to leave, left it there on the table by the window. At two in the afternoon we were the only ones there. Traffic swept by just outside, on its way to downtown Fort Worth, art galleries, the riverside park, Omni Theater.

Her clothes were in a faded pink pillowcase. I took a seat near a bank of chugging washers as though they were mine and opened a paperback I generally carried in a back pocket, some harmless mystery, probably British, long since read and forgotten: protective coloration. Two small children pushed plastic laundry baskets into one another, bouncing back and laughing gleefully when they collided. Their mother sat suspended in the murky pages of a paper-back romance so shopworn that pages occasionally fell away as she finished, and turned, them. A young Latin in muscle shirt and white shorts stood by a window staring out blankly, pursuing, or pursued by, memories, demons, the usual limping dreams.

The clothes all seemed to be hers. Two bright summer dresses, a pair of fraying black jeans, dark T-shirts, and an oversize chambray workshirt, unmatched pastel washcloths and towels. Only the underclothes stood out: two sets bedecked with gingerbread-like lace, one pale pink, one light green, the rest workaday cotton, bras white and nondescript (at least one with safety pin attached), pants mostly blue and thinned by many washings. She used Fresh Start and added a sheet of Bounce when dryer time came, smelling it briefly before dropping it in.

By then I'd contrived to start conversation with her, crossing her aisle again and again on mock errands and managing to become a little more visible each time in a time-lapse version of people meeting week after week in some public place and finally introducing themselves. On the last swing by, having called my answering machine and listened to its *Yes*, then silence, then a dial tone, I spoke.

"Hottest part of the day."

"What?" Her eyes met mine directly for the first time, though I knew she had been increasingly aware of my presence, touching her hair and tugging at clothes, glancing at me then quickly away when I passed. "Oh. I don't mind. Less crowded, anyway."

"There's that."

She tugged the underclothes toward her, unconsciously, I think, tucking them under a towel. Her eyes kept wandering away, to the windows, game and vending machines, other patrons, and back to my own. Yeats was right: the dancer *is* the dance, or becomes it. Her arm was bare, the gentle swell of her biceps and bare armpit pulling at something deep within me, something long undisturbed which surfaced now as an almost unbearable ache.

"You live around here?"

"Why?" She had begun stacking folded clothes back inside the pillowcase.

"Noticed you were walking, that's all. Hot day. Especially in here. Thought maybe a cool drink might help, if you'd like. My dime."

Her face told me she'd already decided.

"Okay, sounds good. There's a little restaurant a few streets over—"

"The Como Café."

"You know it?"

"Saw it on the way here."

"That be all right?"

"Great."

"Best coffee in town."

She took it iced, with milk floated on top, not stirred.

The cook and waitress sat at a table in back, sharing a beer and crossword puzzle. Sounds drifted in from the self-service car wash across the parking lot and narrow street. I leaned back in the booth and, with only minor prodding, providing the faintest vacuum, found out about Tracy Harrings.

Born in the late sixties, she came of a family which had somehow detached itself from the fifties and floated, for the most part undisturbed, into the present. She opened her mouth and cheerleaders fell out. Bobby sox, breakfast cereals, the daring of a double-date for a show and Coke. It was a kind of innocence you don't see anymore, deluged as we are by media, assaulted by information at every turn, with the weight of the world settling on every one of our shoulders.

She had to know these things, of course; but distracted by life, by simple pleasures and expectations, she failed to acknowledge them: they existed outside herself.

I told her about Nabokov getting the idea for *Lolita* from a news story about an ape who, given crayon and paper to communicate, drew over and over only the bars of its cage.

I don't understand, she said.

There was a brother in law school somewhere, a father dead of multiple strokes at age forty-nine after almost thirty years of selling aluminum doors, sports gear, and police equipment, an endlessly grieving mother.

Tracy worked for an optometrist (I have to wear a lab coat and plain-glass glasses Dr. Vietch made for me, she said) and went to school part-time at the community college—just, you know, taking courses. She lived alone.

For fun? Well, she liked to swim a lot. And horror movies. Not the gory ones they put out these days, but old ones, where you hardly ever *saw* anything, really, where it was all atmosphere and suggestion, something always just out of sight, offscreen, about to happen.

Self-knowledge, I said.

What?

The real horror of life is not that people do terrible, evil things; it's our capacity to persuade ourselves, whatever we do, however terrible those things are, that we're right. That somehow we're actually doing good. In classic horror movies, that self-delusion collapses. It's evil he's doing, and can't help himself. He knows that he is becoming unhuman, becoming *other*. And he's powerless to help that, too.

I guess, she said.

She'd been kind of patting at the pillowcase of laundry on the seat beside her and now said: Guess I better be going.

I could go with you.

Her eyes met mine and held. In her face, as it opened to me, I saw something of my own, something of the face I once had, something pure and human. In that moment she was exquisitely beautiful.

I told her that just before I killed her.

The cook and waitress sat still sharing a beer, maybe the same one. An older couple occupied a back booth; when their meal came, they held hands and prayed.

He was waiting for me, in the booth Tracy and I had sat in, just as I knew he would be, his clothing little more than rags, his brimless, battered hat on the seat beside him.

"*Dobroy den*," he said. "I have taken the liberty of ordering tea for you. *Po-russkie*, of course."

Hot tea, steaming, in a glass. One stirs in marmalade, or holds a sugar cube in one's teeth as one drinks.

"*Spaceba*."

After a moment I said: "He had plunged so far within himself, into so complete an isolation, that he feared meeting anyone at all."

"Yes."

"Yet something now suddenly begins to draw him to people. Something new is taking place within him, and with this goes a kind of craving for people. After such melancholy and gloomy excitement he is so weary that he wants to take breath in some other world, he must."

"Yes. You do understand. You take to yourself the victim's own terrible suffering."

"And feel a great common humanity swelling within. Just as you thought."

"As *we* thought, yes."

We sat together drinking tea. I sensed love flowing in warm, easy currents between the man and woman now conversing quietly over a second cup of coffee; felt the mute, accustomed comradeship of cook and waitress at their table. Water from the car wash cleansed and began everything anew. The sun outside was a hand, a heart, opening.

"*Dasvedanya*," I said when Raskolnikov stood to leave, then "*Au revoir*," knowing we would meet again.

HAZARDS OF AUTOBIOGRAPHY

1

I was sitting quietly in a small café off the Champs-Elysées. From time to time a cricket would chirrup *pickup*, *pickup*, *pickup*, and groups of people would walk by the café singing. I was out of cigarettes, patience and sorts. Michele in the dark of that very night had gone off to Switzerland with the owner of a German brewery. She informed me of this in a note written with lipstick on our bathroom mirror. My skis were also missing.

A young man at the next table watches a girl who has just come in and now is being greeted by several of the customers.

Who's she, he asks his companion.

They call her Crow Jane. Supposedly she has some rare blood disease. Written up in all the journals, they say.

Fame. He peers at the cocoon of smoke enshrouding his friend. What are you writing.

A poem.

Looks more like a letter.

No, it's a poem. I'll break up the lines later. When I have more time.

O.

It's content that matters. You know that. Voice. Style. Approach.

O.

You could say that everything we write is a letter, in a manner of speaking.

At another table:

See, I come back to the house at night and I try to read what he's written during the day. He leaves it behind there on the desk. And it's getting stranger all the time; almost impossible to follow. I think he may be forgetting English again.

What do you mean.

Well it happened once before. Last year. We had to start all over again. Wawa, tee-tee and so on. Christ he's thirty years old. And yesterday he wrote the immigration bureau, applying for an extension of my visa, don't you think that's strange.

Quite the contrary. Seems eminently reasonable to me.

But I'm French.

Yes. You do have a point there. Still, one can't be too cautious. Sticklers for detail, these French.

I have to admit he did some of his best writing back then.

At another table a man just dropped a bottle of pills. They rattled like maracas as they struck the floor and rolled. The man is becoming a deep and rather lovely shade of blue, weakly waving his arm in the air to summon the waiter. His fingers filled with gold wedding bands.

But the waiter has stopped at a table closer to me. He shrugs his shoulders in my direction and says to the man and woman seated there, He's listening you know.

I picked up my book and left.

2

I had just returned from adventures in London and New York, Bretagne and Lodz. My beard was long, corners of my moustache caught in corners of my mouth, my hair bore burrs and briars from Camden Town, Notting Hill, Park Avenue and the Lower East Side. These included one particularly fine example, like a perfect sphere of gold coral, or the ball of a mace, from Meshed.

Now the nose of the plane dips once, gently, and I touch (my hand on the window) the edge of America.

I wore embroidered silk. My left hand was adorned with rings, bracelets, the watch you gave me, the right bare save for a childhood scar that crosses my fingers diagonally through the knuckles, a healed knife wound. I hold my hand out before me and the blood fills my palm for hours.

Guilt expires, even as air congeals away from the mouths of the jets.

But I returned. To you. Offered my passport to the man at the lectern there. *For* you. He was reluctant; at last took it. It came apart like a newspaper in his hands. You're traveling alone?

Yes sir.

Have you visited Pennsylvania before?

Yes.

And New Jersey? You'll have to pass through there you see.

Yes. Yes I know.

How much money do you have on you sir? And I search silk pockets. Assorted quarters, dimes, pennies of two sizes, a Churchill crown, a florin, francs, złoty (several of these), one of the new ten-pence pieces. Geometrical coins, coins without centers, coins with empty crosses for centers, milled, unmilled. They collect on the counter before him. With the side of his hand he slides them into a scoop and from there into a kind of plastic ant farm. Numbers accumulate beneath a red needle. Telephones ring. Lights flicker and dim.

I receive a handful of suspicious-looking currency, invitations to contribute to charities or to subscribe at fantastic one-time-only rates to magazines and join various societies, tax forms, overdue bills. Home at last.

And the purpose of your visit sir?

When I fail to answer he says, I have to put something down you see.

Would it be possible for me to get back to you on that? I ask. Because this is today who I am: the man who gets back, the man who returns.

No problem. Absolutely, he says. Take this along with you, fill it out at your convenience. Drop it in any mailbox.

He hands me an envelope. Good luck sir.

With?

He waves his hand toward the doors. America is out there. A wilderness.

We can't be much help after this, I'm afraid. You've been away a long time sir. Things have changed.

O.

And an escalator bears me lumpily toward the top floors.

You are there, above, behind the glass. With fishnet stockings and a dress of green sequins. I have nothing to declare. The remains of London, the beautiful white ruins of America. And now through escalators, electric doors, walkways, hallways and people we rush forward together, our mouths opening round like those of fish, and we try, we clutch and move our hands slowly in the suddenly stale air, to embrace.

Behind glass the others applaud.

3

This day it's bright and with streamers. Big machines go over our heads. And bundles up ramps on backs. These men like barrels with beer on their breath. A Rolls at the end of the pier with bankers in gray. How long does it take them to get that look about them, they all have it. While clouds roll like seals at play. Sun and blue clouds, a solitary gull.

Some of them wonder who I might be. I watch as faces find mine, watch as thoughts flare behind eyes and eyes move on. Like myself: the man who moves on.

Four of them mount a makeshift platform, as for parades. Grand hurried speeches are made. Phrases are dropped like coins into slots of cameras and microphones. When the crowd parts, I'm there. I gave her that dress. Strange she should wear it now.

So, she says.

Wait for the cry of a tug to die off harbor. That man with a clipboard under his arm in clothes like mine nods. Knows who I am. Remembers.

So you're off again, I say.

I won't stop trying. I can't.

Even now that you're no longer a believer.

He believes.

Hold out the book and wait for her hand to find it. And her mouth to wonder if it's what it is.

You finished.

Yes. It's the only copy.

Light catches on the stone in her ring as she opens the book, runs her fingers over pages. As though she can soak up its substance by touch alone.

So much noise here, so many feet and faces. People climbing the ramps now smiling, flashbulbs and banners. It was quiet the day we left, no blue clouds like these. So long ago.

I didn't think you would come. Thank you, she says. And is gone.

Up here there is wind and my coat and the aloneness of harbors. Questions from the press, who have got on to me, that I ignore. As she goes up the ramp with the others, turning at the last moment. Sun and blue clouds in her glasses. Sun and blue clouds.

4

This morning when it has light and four men at the top of the hill there. Stand with rain running off their hats. Then descend, the container between them, bumping their legs. While clouds rumble gray bellies and people below look up expectantly. New-dug hole filling with water.

I can hear him from in here. He has found something to say after all. After much shuffling and scuttling about in his books, I should think. While his wife so patiently waited. Thank you for his wife. His voice sounds far off and soft. And while I am certain he says good things, he just goes on and on, like the rain.

Finally I rap at the bottom of the lid. Fine wood. Thank you for this wood. He leans close. Yes?

Father could I have one last look.

He swings up the lid and I open my eyes. Rain runs over them. Are there many here Father?

A few, he says. Not at all a bad turnout for so poor and rainy a day. I smell the brandy on his breath.

Thank you Father.

Rain strikes and slides over my eyes but I cannot feel it. I close them now. My last sight the onyx ring on his index finger as he eases the lid shut. For a time as he resumes I try to concentrate on what he says.

And finally this.

Father.

Yes my son. He leans close.

That's very nice. Thank you.

Yes my son.

But can't we just get on with it.

Yes my son.

Another sound replaces his voice now, a sound just as soft and distant and welcome, a sound like the rain. And that's the dirt coming down.

THE GOOD IN MEN

From my desk I see the red flag shaking itself like a fist in the air above our new capitol. I fear, in all truth, that the revolution is badly off course. "Bloody Boris" has taken to powdered wigs and robes, Manuel lies about all day in a bathtub in the council chambers, Hans has become a kind of manifesto machine, fueling himself with tarry black coffee for the day's writing. And I, of course, have withdrawn to this attic, these memoirs.

Most of the reporters are gone now. After the takeover and a few human-interest pieces, there was little here for them. One, a young drunk named Billy, remains. The revolution's never over, he says, until *after* the reporters leave.

Food is again in the city: potatoes, cabbage, some carrots. In order to have my time wholly free I have made up a huge pot of soup (for the water must be boiled anyway) and simply warm it when hungry.

In truth I am seldom hungry, or aware of hunger at any rate, for the work absorbs me utterly. I have just detailed the second month of the revolutionary congress when Jorge (may he now rest) fought so hard and long for Article Seven, and in writing of it I found all the voices, the clamor and excitement, the *faith*, returning to me. I do not know where that faith has gone; I cannot recall its passing. But it is with me only when I write, and when I stop, blinking out into this bright day and working my fingers to get blood back into them, it fades quickly.

But I find that increasingly (as now) my pen wanders from the history to memories of days before the revolution began gathering, and of the year we spent together. Do you recall the screen we built and handpainted during long summer days, and how we set it up before the fire all that winter in the huge living room; how we pretended we were in some tiny pauper's room? Till finally the paint cracked from the heat and started flaking away.

You should not have fled, Monetta. You did not understand what momentum our beliefs had—that for the first time a revolution would occur unoccasioned by actual hunger or grave social discord, but by simple desires to set things right, to create a moral order.

The revolutionary's goal must be to create a world in which he is superfluous. We seem in many ways, surrounded as we are by good men and virtuous action (and with thought toward the idle posturing of Boris and Manuel, the self-contained dynamo that is Hans), to have succeeded. In other ways, I have no doubt, we have failed.

In the final hours of Jorge's marathon filibuster and fast, he had to lean against the podium and hold on to it to remain standing, for of course if he no longer stood, the floor passed to another. Sweat had long ago soaked his clothes and he gave off a rancid, sour smell. For many hours he had recited from memory great portions of *El Cid*, Euripides, Plato, Santayana, Rousseau and Voltaire. Then he took a long breath (there was a hush of anticipation throughout the hall) and said: "In short, my friends—we must love one another or die." General applause broke out in the assembly. "Brilliant," one of the councilmen was heard to say. "Auden," Jorge responded, and took his seat.

Mixed with my memory of the smell of the bread we baked together is your own smell, and the scent of honeysuckle on the wind that last night we walked in the garden of what is now the capitol. You had knocked at my door (for I was then greatly occupied with the coming change) to tell me you were leaving. I hope so much that you are safe, that you've found a place there in the old world.

Soon, I think, I must return to the capitol, to our old home. Once we give ourselves over to history, history from that moment claims us entire. One day they will sing of you in the streets. How could it be possible for men who have been so important, men who have changed the world, to resume ordinary life as ordinary men, *however* they might try? I have been told that several days ago Hans looked up from his desk in tears, saying: "But I can think of nothing else to write!" Manuel has quit his tub for the hockey field. Boris comes daily to my room. Enemies of the state are abroad, he says. We must turn them out; we must "dress them in scarlet."

MORE LIGHT

I noticed him the minute he came out the door at Dillard's. Wearing jeans and a square-billed red cap, sweatshirt with a torn neck over a high-necked T-shirt: there was that look about him. He paced unhurriedly down one of the broad alleys between cars, puffing into his hands to warm them. I looked a few yards ahead to the well-dressed woman walking briskly to her car, wind whipping at the tails of her long coat. I turned and looked down the parking lot and there it was, maybe twenty yards off: a dusty brown truck, Toyota or Honda, white smoke pluming from its exhaust.

I snapped the lid back on the coffee I was drinking to stay warm and started my own engine. The radio came on to a news update. I turned it off.

It was mid-afternoon and the mall, this end of it anyway, away from the video games and food stalls, wasn't busy. Cars, trucks and vans, the occasional walker, straggled in and out. One elderly man with thick glasses sat in his ten-year-old Lincoln reading a paper. In the lane behind me a mother who didn't look much over fourteen herself bent over in pink stretch pants to haul out of the trunk a baby carriage that unfolded and unfolded again till it was almost as large as the car it came out of. Next they'll be putting TVs on the things. Halogen lamps, sound systems, a tiny Jacuzzi.

He kept blowing into his hands, pacing closer as she turned into the lane of cars and pulled out keys. He never looked up or around; his concentration was perfectly on her.

A silver Volvo.

She leaned in slightly to unlock it—and he was suddenly there.

I heard a crash as he struck the side of the car to draw her attention away, heard her scream "You son of a bitch, I saw you, you son of a bitch," and watched the two of them break like rabbits, he falling back into the long, continuous curve that had borne him close and now swept him away, she taking out in pursuit on low heels, holding her own at first (driven by adrenaline and rage), then losing ground.

"You son of a bitch," she said again, stopping.

Down the way, the dusty brown Toyota or Honda peeled out of its place.

And he ran.

He almost made it, too. He was a good runner. But he ran into something.

That was me.

His face flattened against the windshield by me, then slid down it. There was quite a bit of blood where his nose had been. I thought of those stuffed cats everyone used to have in their cars, hanging on for dear life to the inside of all those windshields. His red cap blew out across the lot.

The Toyota (I could tell that now), which had begun braking for the pickup, thought better of it and, with only the briefest of pauses, the instant it took a foot to swivel from brake to accelerator, heaved itself out of the parking area toward the perimeter road, gathering speed all the while, tailpipe bucking with the effort.

I let the binoculars fall back around my neck and scribbled the license number on a pad taped to the dash. I'd see the intended victim got it. The cops would be dropping by to chat with that driver. There wasn't much they could do, really, but it would give him something to think about. You never know what effect your actions might have, even the smallest ones.

I opened my door out over his legs, picked up the purse and handed it to her along with the license number. She took both but stood looking down at him there at our feet without saying anything. Whenever he breathed, there was a dull, far-off gurgling sound, and little gobbets of blood would belly up over the rim of his nostril.

By ones and twos a crowd was beginning to gather. Security would be along soon; someone would have gone in to get them.

The woman looked at me.

"I'm okay," she said.

I nodded.

In the rearview mirror I saw her take a sketchy half-step toward me until her foot hit his leg and stopped there. Others briefly watched me pull away and looked back to her, talking among themselves, couples mostly. Wind picked at their scarves, skirts and coattails.

I drove around to the other side of the mall, parked and went in for more coffee: mine was cold. The food court was packed with young people in outlandish leisure clothes and mall workers on dinner break in various interpretations of business dress. A few families sat in the center, near the escalators and fountain, several couples farther out in the overgrowth of chairs and tables. Sometimes I can almost remember what that was like, having someone there beside you, thinking it would be like that, could be like that, forever.

The elderly man had moved in from his car. A gray cardboard tray of tacos, each diapered in paper translucent with grease, and a waxed cup the size of a child's hat sat before him on a button-like table lost somewhere between yellow and tan. He had his paper folded in quarters the way city people on buses do, and I could make out partial headlines over the tops of irregular blocks of print.

MAN KILLS FOUR
MILITARY ACTION INCREASES IN
HOMELESS MULTIPLY

I looked away.

Then my coffee came and I went back out and sat in the car, holding the cup with both hands, breathing in that rich, earthy steam as it fogged up my glasses in a breath, a sudden tide, from the bottom up. All breath's like that, sudden and warm and alive—then just as suddenly gone.

The sun fell into a narrow pass between clouds and horizon and bathed everything in cold light.

I sat there thinking for a moment about Karyn, all the things I'd wanted to tell her, how I had never imagined there might not be time for them all. Our daughter would have been almost five now.

Traffic around the mall was beginning to pick up. Two police cars swung in off the interstate and headed toward the other side, by Dillard's.

Back when I was getting started in the business, I did layout for our Dillard's account. Then, when we found I had a knack for it, I shifted over to writing copy. I'll grant you there've been some problems in recent years, especially after Karyn. But you ask anyone in the business and he'll tell you: Charlie's a pro, he's *good*. I still remember how it was when I first realized I could take all these bits and pieces of things and move them around, take out a word here, open up space there, and suddenly it turned into something, it started making sense.

I guess that's what I'm still doing.

BUG

I usually check out all the postcards and ads in the morning while I'm making rounds and save the magazines for lunch. If I hurry I can take a couple hours then. I'm a regular reader of *Aviation Quarterly*, *American Scholar*, *Mother Earth News*, *Business Week* and several others. It's an education. And you'd be surprised the things people will put on postcards these days.

Of course you learn a lot about people by the kind of mail they get after you've been on a route a while. There's one old guy out there, Mr. Deal, who gets nothing but third class presort, but lots of that. I've seen him pull it out of the box as I head next door, carefully shuffling through the pile as though each was a precious letter. Then there's Mrs. Dootz, who's always waiting at the door for her plain-brown magazines from California the second Thursday every month. And Mr. Szerchevski's perfumed letters once or twice a week—I still don't know how he keeps his wife from finding them, or at least smelling them.

It's strange. You're not a part of the community, you're an outsider; yet in another way you *are* a part of it, intimately connected.

I had a postage due on 1123 Carpington. All I knew about the resident was that he didn't get much mail and always had his trash out every Tuesday and Friday right on the dot at nine. He put it out wrapped in old newspapers, neat little parcels tied with string, stacked between the sidewalk and street. I'd never seen him.

I knocked and after a minute or two the door opened. He was a young guy, not much older than me, which kind of surprised me. He was wearing old jeans and a brown sweater without a shirt under it, no shoes. His hair was cut short. He stood looking out at me like he was trying to see something a long way off, or was looking through water.

"I have a parcel for you, Mr. Johnson. There's—"

"My cat's dying," he said, and turned and walked back into the house, not closing the door. I stood there, then followed him. There were only two rooms to the house, a huge one in front broken into dining and living areas, with a stove and sink against the back wall, and a much smaller one behind. It was like one of the studies of perspective you see blocked out in art magazines, everything getting smaller as it gets farther away.

The cat was in the smaller room, in a wicker basket on an old wooden desk. The desk was in the center of the room and there were bookshelves made from boards and bricks and a couple of tall filing cabinets behind it. A weird painting hung on one sidewall, this huge shapeless face eating lots of tiny people, done all in grays and browns except for a tiny red heart on each of the little people. The other sidewall was taken up with stereo equipment and shelves— the steel kind you buy at Sears for storage—full of records. Music was playing, something very ordered and precise, maybe Mozart.

"Look, it's only twelve cents," I said. "If you don't have it on you right now, just drop it in the box tomorrow. No problem."

"What?" he said. Then: "No, no. Here, let me get it for you." He pulled open a drawer, rummaged in a cup or something there, came out with a dime and two pennies. He was still standing by the desk so I went over and took the money from him. I put the parcel down beside the wicker basket. "Well," I said. I don't know why I didn't go ahead and leave. But after another minute or two I said, "You a teacher?"

"Teacher?" he said. "Oh, the room. No, I write books."

"Hey, really. What kind?" I was trying to remember if I'd ever come across his name on anything.

"Detective stuff, mostly. Paperback originals. Mysteries, karate, avengers. They all come out under different names."

"And you make a living at it."

He smiled. "Most of time now. I didn't, not for a long time."

"How'd you get into that?"

"It just happened, really. I've never been much good around people, and I needed something, some way of making a living, that didn't require my being around them. I knew a man who wrote for a living back then, he turned out a lot of profile pieces for magazines, and I decided to try something like that. So I went downtown and bought a big stack of detective stories. I knew they were popular, though I'd never read any of them. I spent two days and two nights reading every one of those books and magazines, one after another. I spent the next four days and nights writing one. Then I sent it out and slept for almost a whole week. But that book sold. I rarely have to leave the house anymore." He looked across the desk at me. "I'm sorry. Would you like a chair?"

I shook my head. "Thanks, but I've still got most of my route to go." This stop was cutting into my lunchtime already.

"Please. A beer, maybe?"

"Well," I said. He brought a couple beers and a chair from the other room and we sat down together by the desk like two guys waiting for the banker to come back. He took the cat out of the basket and laid it on his lap. He went on telling me about his books. The cat was black and white, with long hair. It looked frail and weightless, almost birdlike, with a small head, narrow face, and round eyes filmed but open wide. Its nose and mouth were colorless; a thin line of spit ran from the side of its mouth onto the man's jeans. The way it was lying across his legs, it seemed to have no bones at all. It was having trouble breathing.

He didn't pet the cat but just laid his hand gently on its side, and as he went on talking about his books, how his editor always wanted more violence, more exotic settings, I was thinking that I'd never made a delivery to 1123 Carpington that looked like a book, a letter from a publishing house, or anything like that. In fact, I couldn't recall much of anything besides circulars and the usual bills and stuff. It occurred to me that the guy could be making all this up. He might *believe* it, but he still might be making it up. People do that. But then, for all I knew everything was handled at the other end: payments and everything sent to an agent, maybe; money deposited directly into his bank; whatever. How could you ever know what was true and what wasn't? There were so many explanations for everything.

I hadn't really been listening but realized he'd stopped talking a while back. When I looked up he was watching me.

"I called her Bug because when she was little she made a sound like one. She never did learn to meow. She wasn't ever healthy, never weighed anything, but she loved liver. I used to go out and get here those little cans." He looked down at the cat there on his lap. "Never realized before how small this house is." After a while he looked back up.

"It won't be long now," he said. "You probably need to get going. Your letters and all."

"They can wait," I told him. And we sat there, not talking anymore, just together, waiting ourselves.

MOMENTS OF
PERSONAL ADVENTURE

Propellorman does not want to marry Lucy.

But just now, plying his trade, he faces an expanse of dark glass and the light-studded world beyond.

"You have to understand," his host says, turning briefly to the window against which the city throws its bright self silently again and again. In soft light his hair gleams with health. His motions are graceful, almost athletic. "At age nineteen I had an idea, a single idea; it came to me as I rode the escalator to work one afternoon. Within three months that idea had become this company, myself its president and principal shareholder."

He holds his brandy up to the light. "You're certain you don't care for some?"

Propellorman shakes his head deferentially, smiles.

"The rest is largely silence, Mr. Porter. That single day, that one idea, has been my life. And the years since, only a waiting."

"For what, Mr. Mills?"

A smile as finely turned as French curves. "What do we *all* wait for, my friend? Salvation. An end to our pain and confusion, to our hungers. Some explanation for all this."

He places the snifter squarely on the blotter before him and leans, one inch, perhaps two, closer.

"I hope you'll not be too harsh with me in your article, Mr. Porter. I am not, generally, so melancholic an individual. My wife has just been admitted, for the sixth time in as many months, to a psychiatric hospital. I seem quite unable to help her in any real way, for all my resources. And should one be of an analytical turn of mind—a curse I indeed carry, though a quality of which my wife seems wholly innocent—then after a time one comes to reexamine values, to wonder if everything one has believed and lived might not in fact be false, fleeting, futile."

"I understand."

"Somehow I believe that you do. And I thank you once again for coming."

Propellorman leaves him there in that dark room and rides the elevator steadily down. It is brightly lit and smells of cigar smoke.

Near the entrance he comes across a bar and goes in. Eight or ten real wood tables, Doré prints on papered walls, Vivaldi. All his.

He never takes notes during an interview but afterwards scrambles for the nearest shelter to write down, as quickly as he can and often virtually verbatim, all that was said. It's a habit begun, like many others, in college, where he'd sit in the student union following American Positivism or Anthropology 402 and fill page after page of his notebooks (always, even then, yellow) with Peirce, Dewey, *Australopithecus*, Sapir-Whorf.

Sitting at the bar (the bartender doesn't even get off his stool behind it), he orders a beer and begins writing, two lines of precise script between each blue-ruled line. Orders a martini and writes more, some of it just as it will appear in the final piece, some only an associative word or phrase, rag-ends of description, brackets with nothing inside them.

Once he thought he might restore the world to readers with his language; now he knows that often he will only further obscure it. They will come to his words expecting him to say only what they already know, and even if he does not say it, that is nevertheless what they will hear, until finally the words will not bear even their own weight. But once, in an essay on living alone, he wrote one sentence of absolute truth, and it has haunted him since.

He is a man who has been much loved by women, and now, after many years of living apart from and alongside them, he loves two. Lucy is bright and childlike and cannot do enough for him, with him. In Valerie there is something fatally damaged, a wound deep at her center that sometimes surfaces in her eyes. With Lucy he knows the world is good; with Valerie he understands the tremendous, silent struggles that make it so.

Gradually he becomes aware of the woman sitting beside him, knows she has been there for some time.

"Welcome back," she says. "To the world."

"That obvious."

"Yes."

"Well." Propellorman looks around. There is danger everywhere, his archenemy a master of disguise. Nothing is what it seems. "Another drink?"

She nods, hair tumbling over the distal shoulder. "If you'll let me buy *you* one."

"Done."

Something, then, of Alphonse and Gaston, neither willing to accept the final drink till at last, mutually befuddled, they lose count of rounds and agree to call it even.

Her apartment is on the second floor above a florist's, a single rectangular room long enough that light coming in the windows at the far end tires halfway across the floor. Low screens, make-shift bookshelves and a scatter of bright rugs divide the room into ragged continents. Everything—walls, screens, shelves, floor—is painted white. There are no chairs. They sit on stacked mattresses by the windows drinking coffee, words rushing in to fill the space between them.

Poets console us, Apollinaire said, for the loose words that pile up on earth and unleash catastrophes. And so as the night deepens, they move closer, bailing words out onto the floor, hoping to stay afloat.

There is more coffee, then scrambled eggs, then a long-reserved bottle of wine.

"I have to tell you," she says beside him. "There was . . . an accident. Please."

He opens her shirt and follows the web of scars across her breasts (nipple torn from one) and down along her body onto her legs. In this lurid windowlight the scars seem to have a life, a luminous existence, of their own, and he finds himself responding as he had never known possible, with an urgency he could never have imagined, almost as though propelled by something outside himself, some terrible, irresistible force.

"Who did this to you?" he asks long afterwards through the darkness.

"I did," she tells him. And later: "Will I see you again?"

But he doesn't know, doesn't know anything now, and so he doesn't answer, letting the silence carry whatever message it will.

Later, back at his own apartment, he'll wake at three with a terrible thirst. For a long time he'll lie listening to feet on stairs outside, to the sweep of traffic. Finally then, he'll rise and walk uptown to Horse's studio with its smell of sour wax and manifold mirrors. Horse, the sculptor, there among his ravaged steel bodies, will know what to say, will surely explain it all to him.

BREAKFAST WITH RALPH

At breakfast Katie drops a piece of egg on the floor. One of the younger roaches catches it on the bounce and wheels off toward a closet. Buttered biscuit in one hand, coffee in the other, Mr. Dosey swivels in his chair and plants a foot (size 13, orange sneakers) in its way.

"Just a minute," he says. "Hold on there. How are we ever going to live on this earth in harmony as a single being, etcetera, etcetera—all that stuff in the Charter; you know it as well as I do—if you can't even mind your manners?"

"I'm sorry, sir," the cockroach says. "Might I please have this stray bit of egg?"

"Well of course you may, my young friend," Mr. Dosey says. "And how's the family, if I might ask?"

"*Well*, sir, I'm pleased to say. Except for Paulie, that is."

"Still sickly, is he?"

"Yes, sir."

"Sorry to hear it. But then, I suppose there's nothing for it but time."

"I suppose not, sir. That's what old Doc Branson says, at any rate."

Outside, Conestogas creak past on their way to a new world. Milkcarts take the corner on two wheels, bottles ringing together like chimes, rattling like scrap metal. A toothless old man hawks papers from the curb. AMELIA EARHART LANDS AT LA GUARDIA, one of the headlines reads.

"The boy really *is* sorry, sir," a new arrival says. "It's so difficult to bring them up right, these days. *You* try raising eighty-three children. And I'm a lawyer: successful, well-paid (by *our* standards, of course), secure. I don't know how others manage. My nephew, for instance. A mere nineteen kids and he still can't hack it. Makes you wonder what it's all coming to."

"O yes," Katie says. "At school we study the economics. It is good. Things go badly and will go worse."

Something of an *idiot savant*, Katie has problems with the four languages she speaks, all of them somehow sounding pretty much the same when she speaks them, relics of a weekend spent beside the short-wave radio at her uncle's. Neither is she very well coordinated. A second piece of egg drops to the floor. Everyone ignores it. Four of the roaches are working up a barbershop-quartet version of "My Old Kentucky Home."

"Free enterprise, this may not be the answer," Katie says, "the ultimate answer, I mean. Perhaps it is that we must, so to speak, think in different categories, no?"

And soon all are gathered around the table for a lively discussion of political means and ends. That the roaches are somewhat more conservative is almost certainly explained by their having (species-wise) been around so much longer. A kind of adaptive ultimate, they've not evolved physically in thousands of years on the principle that if something's not broken, don't fix it.

"The one I worry about most, though," the older roach says after a while, "is Gary George. Fancies himself a poet. Always scribbling on napkins and things. Free bus rides for poets in Guatemala, of course, but what *else* is there?"

"Alcoholism, suicide, despair," Mr. Dosey's wife, the children's mother, Dee, says. "Random sex with writing students. Strange enthusiasms for suspect literatures. Terrible mood swings. Resentment. Fury. Silence."

"Really?" Mr. Dosey says.

"All that?" the roach (whose name, he later explains, is Ralph) says.

"And more." Dee gets up and pours more coffee for all.

"Plato banished poets from his republic," Paulie says.

"In the old days, Presidents Nixon and Reagan required the CIA to maintain lists of practicing poets alongside those of potential and manifest subversives. Youngish men in gray suits and short haircuts regularly attended poetry readings. Sometimes they were the only ones there."

This again from Dee, who goes on to recite, proud that she does not sing-song it, "The Raven." Then "The Bells" and a pound or two of Edna St. Vincent Millay. "I shall die but / that is all that I shall do for death," "Life must go on; / I forget just why," Wine from these grapes, etcetera.

"I had no idea you loved poetry so," Mr. Dosey says to his wife.

"As a child I spent a great deal of time alone," Dee says. "I dreamed. I wondered. Words, for me, were new worlds. By nine or so most nights my parents had passed out in their bedroom; they drank. The younger kids were all asleep. For an hour or two I would own the whole world."

"*We'll* someday own the world, my father says." One of the youngest of the roaches. "We must only be patient."

"That may well be the case—"

"The world is the case, according to Wittgenstein," Katie says.

"And I hope you'll be kinder to it, less apart from it, than my own kind has been."

"Aren't we all morbid for such a beautiful early morning," Dee says.

"Gotta be a pony here somewhere," one child says, and the others laugh, knowing Dee so well.

"I thought after breakfast we'd have a nice stroll down to the museum," Dee goes on. "Perhaps on our way back we might stop off at the library. You *will* come along, won't you?" she says to the roaches.

"Well, of course I'd have to ask my wife—"

"Please, Daddy, please, can't we?"

"—but yes, I believe we'd like that. And you'll take tea with us afterwards, of course."

"Of course," Dee says.

"'Civilization is two men sitting over tea as the world falls apart,'" Katie says.

"Not two men," Mr. Dosey corrects her. "Man and roach together. It makes a difference."

Outside, unaccountably, Conestogas begin circling the house. Milk bottles crash against its sides. Wind ferries in the war cries of Indians, aberrant children, or enraged economists.

"It's a strange world, my friend," Mr. Dosey says.

"And a tasty one," Ralph answers, finishing off the eggs.

ANSLEY'S DEMONS

Somehow, instinctively, he knew not to open his eyes, knew that it would end if he did. The touch of those lips lightly and so familiar against his own—and when, again instinctively, he reached up and around, his hand remembered the long curve of her back. For it *was* her: he did not question that.

And somehow she moved within him as well as upon him. Though he felt nothing beneath it, though he did not will this, one hand, then the other, rose into air above him and cupped themselves where breasts would be.

"Ansley," he said.

Outside his window a tide-like wind tugged momentarily at the edge of the house. Across the room close to the floor, a light breeze scuttled, lifting a page of the newspaper lying there, briefly disturbing the leaves of a plant she'd given him on a birthday—hers, not his.

Shhhh, the wind told him.

That was a Monday, and she was gone almost as soon as he realized she was there with him. Tears spilled down the side of his face onto ears and pillow, and his penis throbbed, half-erect, above him. For a moment then, wind howled, and it was like the howling of his own bereft soul.

She returned on Thursday, but left almost as soon. He lay for a long time afterward watching lights from cars outside fall across the ceiling; lay probing at his memories as one unpacks luggage, small and much-used things on top and in odd corners, more substantial belongings farther down; then turned and found her again in his sleep.

Sunday she stayed, even afterward, as he settled back breathless and limp onto the bedding. He stretched out his arm, and memory, or the moment, was so strong that he imagined he almost felt her shoulder in the palm of his hand.

"How . . . ?" he said.

There was no wind. Or only the small one of her breath in his ear where she lay against him.

That December, it was unseasonably, impossibly warm, closer to Mississippi Delta autumns than to any Massachusetts winter he'd ever known. Even the birds seemed confused. They'd wheel off into a morning sky in great sweeping waves and disappear, then late the same day be back, chittering and thrashing about, in their accustomed trees.

Those same mornings he fell into the habit of passing his time at a park across town, an oblong block of half-hearted shrubs and bright yellow benches perched at city's edge over a twin abyss of suburb and barrio. He'd sit there watching children dash toward school, their parents plummet to the shopping malls and office complexes where they worked, and he'd think about ambition: what was it like to have it? A phrase he'd picked up somewhere in his reading, *wandering to find direction*, rolled about in his head like a barrel broken loose in the ship's hold. But he didn't want direction. If anyone had asked (though no one did, of course), he would have answered that he didn't want anything.

A woman of twenty or so with long black hair and round glasses, black sweater, yellow tennis shoes, was there some days, and gradually they began to nod, to acknowledge one another. Usually she carried a book, other times a bag filled with papers and composition books. Like himself, she was always alone.

The birds had a fondness for cheese popcorn, and often he stopped at a party-goods store on the way to the park to buy a bag. One morning he looked up from the cluster at his feet (sparrows, wrens, lackluster blue-green pigeons shunning a single albino one) to see her on the opposite bench. Her head came up from her book just then, too, and she smiled. After a moment he walked over and sat beside her. Most of the flock of birds followed.

"Want to help feed them?" He held out the bag.

"Well, actually," she said, "I keep coming here hoping they might feed me."

"And have they?"

She closed the book on one finger and held it against her leg.

"We don't always know right away. Other things, we *do* know, from the first."

He reached over and pivoted the book: *The Surrealist Moment.* "You're an artist?"

"Art historian. Final refuge for those who love it and can't do it. I tried. Perspective might as well have been Greek, colors swam away from me. But all my life, ever since I can remember, I loved history, too. I read history textbooks the way other kids did comics, starting when I was only nine or ten. I think at one time I may have known everything there was to know about the antebellum South. Then I discovered Matisse, Bonnard, Delvaux . . ."

"And you teach—I've seen you with papers."

She nodded. "Art appreciation at the community college. Part-time and substitute at the university. That's the best I could find. Oh, and I do occasional reviews for the *Telegram.*"

"I may have seen your name, then."

"If so, you'd probably remember it. I never, ever, felt like an Ann, or a Barbara, which were the names my parents gave me. So when I went off to school, I made up a name I *did* like, and had everyone call me that. I've been Ansley ever since. Ansley Devereaux."

"French?"

"Cajun, yes. From a little town nearer Baton Rouge than any other place you've ever heard of, where half the store signs were in English, half in French, and all were misspelled."

"You're a long way from home, Ansley."

"Aren't we all."

"Yeah. Yeah, I guess we are."

He scattered the rest of the popcorn and watched the birds scatter with it. They came back to his feet and waited, then, one by one, flew away.

"Would you like to get some coffee?" he asked.

"That would be good." She put the book away and slipped her arm though the purse's shoulder strap. "But what I'd really like is to spend the afternoon with you."

A bird dropped from one of the trees, shot by just over their heads and wheeled away again, pursued by another. Ansley looked down at the caterpillar the bird had dropped in her lap. It moved tentatively, just the front of it, exploring this new, sudden environment.

"See?" she said.

That there was great evil in the world, evil requiring only the smallest sliphole, an opening, he had never doubted; in their second year together, a piece of that evil detached itself and walked beside them.

After a flurry of short-term jobs, he'd gone to work for the paper, floating steadily upwards from writing bridal news to handling department rewrites to doing layout for the lifestyles section. She had helped at first, on that, but both soon realized that he had the greater knack for it; had, in fact, something of a gift.

About April she began a long siege of illness: initially nausea and cramps which they thought (with a strange mixture of alarm and elation) meant she was pregnant; then a series of colds and respiratory infections leading to hospitalization for pneumonia; and above it all, hovering there, an inexorable weakness, her ever-increasing sense of malaise, helplessness, surrender.

Then just as suddenly and fiercely as they had begun, the symptoms subsided—only to return six weeks later.

Again the hospital, where, after days of blood tests, special procedures in closet-sized rooms, a storm of lengthy, incomprehensible explanations and acronyms (CT, ABG, MRI), they had a name for the evil that had attached itself to them.

Lupus.

She woke that night near dawn. He felt her presence and turned from the window where he sat watching cars climb across the city's concrete horizons. They were on the eighth floor of a building called Hope Memorial.

"How do you feel?"

"Not so good. You get any sleep?"

"A little."

"I told you you should go on home."

"Home is wherever you are."

"You know," she said, "you've always had a habit of saying the right thing, even when you made a fool of yourself."

"But one of my endearing traits."

"Oh yeah? You got a list of the others?"

"I'll get back to you."

"Right."

He walked over and sat beside her on the narrow bed, took her hand in his. In coming months, siege after siege, hospitalization after hospitalization, he would watch flesh fade from that hand as he held it, watch it withdraw imperceptibly until the hand was little more than a glove of parchment draped over bone.

She turned toward him and the gown fell away from her breast. He resisted an impulse to put his other hand there. Dawn pried at the horizon. Time has the best gig going, he thought: it passes so successfully, whatever goes on in our lives.

"I always knew something was wrong," she said, "even as a child. I never spoke about it, I was afraid that somehow the words might make it more real, I guess, but I knew. I was different."

In coming months they would speak of many things they had not before, and most they had. Ice, then birds attempting a nest, appeared in the windows of rooms they occupied. Toward the end, too weak perhaps, her failing energies focused on passage (or on holding it off from her), she spoke hardly at all.

Near another dawn, he woke to his name on her breath, uncertain in that still, blue room whether she had actually spoken or he had imagined it. Her breath was the barest pulse and all light was gone behind her eyes, but as he leaned above her, his name formed again on her lips and balanced on a brief column of air.

"This is forever," she told him then. "I hope you know that."

All that is best of dark and light, he'd think often in the following months. Then, inevitably: Fuck you, Byron, and the simpering romantic horse you rode in on. For the territory in which he found himself could be understood (if at all) only by a Poe, a Baudelaire.

She came to him that first time—somehow, instinctively, he knew not to open his eyes, knew that it would end if he did, knew it was her—almost six months afterward, when grief had shrunk to a hot black pearl deep inside and, it seemed, might pass.

She came that Monday, then Thursday, Sunday, another Monday.

Then, for a week or more, every night—and, as suddenly, was gone. He waited, tumescent at the merest hush of wind, thinking each moment that the creak and sway of wires outside his window in the wind might become more.

His grief, his loss, had seemed unendurable, and then, with her second departure, *was*.

Eventually friends came to the apartment and found him there, all but speechless, in a litter of fast-food cartons, discarded clothing, and offal. They took him to Hope Memorial where one hour a day of group therapy and sixteen hours a day of vintage TV pulled him back into focus.

His pain, he thought then, was a river gone underground.

But time blunts even the sharpest teeth. Slowly, the days he navigated by forms, going about them woodenly and at some distance—rising at six, ceremonial shower, conventional breakfast, hard, steady work, good dinner—began to take on substance, and feelings filtered in through the curtains. At dinner one night with the friends who had helped him, an hour or so into the meal, he suddenly realized that he had become again participant and not observer; that for some time now he had been enjoying himself. It was a revelation.

Anne, he met a few nights later, she leaving La Madeleine, he entering, their coats brushing against one another, leather on leather, among close-set tables. Whenever there's a collision, even with no damage done, you're supposed to exchange numbers, he told her. And called her the next day for lunch (which she couldn't make) then for dinner (which she could, barely, in the space before a scheduled concert with friends at which she never arrived).

Conversation embraced childhoods, work, the dew, popcorn and carrots, the inexhaustible process by which we become our parents.

They had coffee at a downtown diner at one in the morning, sandwiches at a highway truck stop at six. Leaden, indigestible doughnuts and more coffee at ten.

After that, they began spending all their free time together, each day retracing those same improvised routes to the interior, to the heart of their new content and continent.

Things moved slowly through hour-long back rubs, languorous

walks taking in most of the city, encyclopedias of talk. She had been "mostly alone" for two years or more, they were so different after all, she was afraid. What surprised *him*, what astonished him one Tuesday morning when it tumbled into his head, something he'd known for some time, known from the first and never acknowledged, was that he was *not* afraid.

Sometimes that old despair licked at him in odd moments and sent chills stamping up his spine; he saw himself again in that solitary room, surrounded by sacks of half-eaten food and his own waste. But more often he looked away from that—to mornings and years where he and Anne sat together over coffee and Sunday papers at La Madeleine, where they walked along the gentle curve of a river as evening shelled the sky, or sat side by side in a circle of light with wind and the dark amoan outside.

He rarely thought of Ansley now, until one night he looked up and, for a moment, saw her face there above him. But then it was Anne's again, framed in a fall of red hair, familiar, endearing, constant.

Afterward he tried, in his mind, to bring back that face, and could not. One eye, a foothill of cheek and lip, would come into focus, then (when he moved on to retrieve some other portion) blur, dissolve, flow away. His mind lunged back into their time together, his and Ansley's—that slow, early awakening, the easy accommodations as they grew to know one another and respond at levels words could not penetrate, the twilight thickening between them in all those faceless rooms—then, with a massive thrust of will, he shut that door forever.

Memory, he thought, is a demon, promising to bring us respite and ease for what we have lost even as it carries away in its stumpy arms what little we have held on to.

That night she, Anne, tells him: I've thought about you all day. I've had this feeling, this sense, that something is wrong.

The question trembles between them and expires. They've lit a candle, and its pale light washes erratically over them and into the room's corners.

Briefly her face moves down to him, then back into the darkness above, where she arches her back and begins to move, very slowly and without words, at levels words cannot penetrate, upon him.

Somehow, instinctively, he knows they are not alone. And though he does not move, something moves within him. He watches as, without volition, his hands rise, not to her breasts, Anne's, but to her neck, where they whiten. He watches her face there, like a flower's, the surprise, the growing shock and struggle, the sudden stillness. And on his lips in that speechless room he finds the word *forever*.

ECHO

The door swings shut and locks. Light comes from a caged bulb overhead; it is dim. The walls are gray.

"Hello, Lauris."

After a long pause: "Say hello, Lauris."

The young man's eyes flicker to the doctor, back to you. Fear is running down the inside of them like rain on a window. He wraps his arms around himself and pushes back against the wall. He is very thin. His eyes slide to the corners of the room and back. There is danger everywhere.

The doctor steps forward, closer to him.

"Lauris. What is today's date?"

"The fourteenth."

"Of?"

"May."

"Do you know where you are? Where are you?"

"In . . . hospital. A hospital."

"What kind of hospital, Lauris?"

". . . A mental hospital."

"Do you know why you're here?"

"Yes."

"And who I am?"

"Yes, sir."

The doctor pauses and glances at you. He walks across the tile floor and puts his hand on the young man's shoulder. The young man looks down at it as though this is the first time he has ever seen a hand; he is trying to imagine its use.

"Lauris, can you tell me what this means? 'People in glass houses shouldn't throw stones.'"

He looks up into the doctor's face. "Yes, sir: 'Let he who is . . . without sin . . . cast the first stone.'"

"Very good." The doctor pats the young man's shoulder and

moves back across the room. "I think he'll talk to you now. Will you talk to Mr. Vandiver, Lauris?"

"Yes, sir . . . I'll try."

"Call me Bill, Lauris," you say.

"Yes, sir."

Outside, the sun is just now pushing up above the trees. It would be best in the morning, the doctor had said when you called for the interview; they're all more responsive, more in control, in the morning. A group of patients crosses a patch of grass outside the window, an attendant at each end of the line. The one in front has a volleyball under his arm. All of them have their heads down.

"Do you know why I'm here, Lauris?"

Several moments pass, and the patients are out of sight now.

"I want to write about you. About people like you. So that other people can understand."

He is still silent; you look to the doctor for assistance. He smiles.

"Sometimes Lauris doesn't want to talk. Lauris, talk to Mr. Vandiver. It's important."

"I . . . the room . . ."

"You have to ignore those feelings, Lauris; I've told you that. You have to learn to live with them, function despite them. Would you feel better if Tom were here?" Turning to face you. "Tom is one of the attendants, the person Lauris is most responsive to."

"Doctor, I—" He shakes his head violently. "I'll try. I . . . will." He rubs his eyes with the back of his hand; there are jagged scars across the wrist. ("He came to us after his third attempt at suicide. I think you'll find him satisfactory for the interview: he's more in touch than the others. But then, he's still quite young.") He stares at his hand and says, "My hand doesn't know what to do."

"Don't talk that way, Lauris."

"But you're both watching it."

"No, Lauris."

He puts his hand in his lap and covers it with the other. He stares at the floor. "I know, Doctor Ball," he says. "I know you're not."

"Lauris?"

"Yes, sir?"

"I've asked the doctor to let me talk to you so that I can tell people your story. So that they can understand what it's like."

He looks up at you. His eyes are empty now, dull as old pennies.

"You don't believe that, do you? You don't believe anyone can know what it's like. And maybe you're right. But we can *try* to know, we can *try* to understand. You can help us."

He turns to look out the window and in that instant, goes away from you. ("He'll be relatively clear when you see him, though he'll seem distracted, inattentive. Try to remember that he's not always like that; those are his good times. Others, he is totally out of control, barely conscious of what he does. And he knows what's happening to him. He can feel himself being pulled to the edge, losing control. He's terrified—all the time. Whatever he does, he's working through that terror. It's like a fog all around him.")

The doctor, finally: "Lauris?"

"Yes, sir?" He still has not turned his head. As though watching something beyond the window, but nothing is there.

"Mr. Vandiver wants you to tell him how it feels."

"It feels . . . like I'm dying. Being crushed. All the time." He looks up at the doctor as though he should know this. He tilts his head, listening. "I'm not supposed to talk to him."

"Why?"

"Because . . . he doesn't understand. They say he'll hurt me."

"*You* say, Lauris. You know I won't let him hurt you, I won't let anyone hurt you. But you must talk to him."

The doctor looks at you and you say, "When did you first realize you had this, Lauris?"

His eyes move about the room, searching for support, relief.

"Ever since . . . since I can remember. I remember being a kid, a little kid, and . . . afraid, I guess, just afraid. I didn't know what it was. I'd . . . scream. I scream sometimes now, I think."

"I see. When did you first know it for what it is?"

He shakes his head again, tentatively. His mouth moves several times, shaping words, before he speaks.

"I was . . . eight or nine. My teachers saw . . . something different, about me, they said. Doctors asked me stuff, did stuff. Then they . . . explained it to me."

"And you were twelve when you were sent to a hospital for the first time?"

"Yes . . . yes, sir. My parents . . . sent me."

"And this is your tenth commitment."

"I live here now."

The doctor frowns and clears his throat. Lauris is moving his eyes slowly across the floor, as though counting individual tiles. You think of him now, for the first time, as a boy.

"Lauris, are you receiving?" the doctor asks.

The boy faintly nods.

"I thought so." The doctor turns to you. "He seems to be peaking again. He spent much of the last week in seclusion; it shouldn't be happening again so soon."

"Perhaps the stress of the interview—"

The doctor crosses the room and moves his hand across the space directly before the boy's eyes. There is no response.

"It's no use now, Mr. Vandiver. He's out of touch again. I'm afraid we'll have to terminate the interview."

"'Receiving,' you said. He was actually reading my thoughts?"

The doctor purses his mouth and frowns again. "Not thoughts, Mr. Vandiver—feelings. I was under the impression that you understood that. Feelings, you see, are illogical, confused, destructive. Right now he's picking up on several hundred people. He's taking all that on himself, with no way to get rid of it or shut it off. And you see the result."

"It's not quite the way we thought it would be, is it?" you say. The boy is shaking, his entire body, as though he's being pulled in many directions at once. Which, you suppose, is the truth of the thing. "How many are there like him?"

"In our facility, twenty-three."

"And what will become of him now?"

"He'll be put in a padded room, and in restraint should he become violent; we can't allow him to injure himself. Perhaps he'll come back to us, perhaps not; we never know. He'll be given injections—often the drugs help psychotics think more clearly—and, if all else fails, electroshock."

"I didn't think anyone used electroshock anymore."

"What would you have us do? We feel we have to try everything, whatever might help. Our approach here is reality oriented. We—"

He stops because the boy has stood and walked closer to you. For a moment his eyes go bright. He says, "Will you come again to see me, Mr. Vandiver?" And now the eyes blank out again. Blue and still.

"I'm afraid I must insist we leave; he could become violent at any moment."

So hard to believe those lost eyes violent. But you turn and move toward the door, and for the first time something flickers behind the doctor's professional mien.

"Don't let it get to you, what he just said. It takes some getting used to. He's a good kid; everyone likes him." He moves his hands for a moment, reaching for words, and says again, as though he can think of nothing else, "It takes some getting used to."

Now the door closes behind you, and something else closes within you. The hall is brightly lit; you blink in the sudden light. The hall is empty.

"Then there's nothing anyone can do."

"Nothing *more*, Mr. Vandiver."

Inside, you hear a scream.

NOTES

1. It can hardly escape the reader's notice that the first and concluding words of the story are *nothing*, the former in a peripheral character's dialog ("'Nothing wrong with that'"), the latter in the text of the story itself ("That night by the moon's pale light he dreamed of nothing at all, nothing").

2. Here we encounter one of the first variants: "this" or "his"? The source text reprinted here is from *Anvil & Stirrup*, a small-circulation quarterly; between that and our best fair copy, an early draft on yellow "second" paper from the author's files, a number of variants exist, perhaps resulting from editorial changes, possibly from subsequent authorial revision.

3. The author had at this point just met Roz (Rosyln Robyns), the woman who was to become his companion for the rest of his life.

4. From his story "Wasp Pounding Stone Onto Tunnel With Tool": "Their life together was a landscape, Barbizon by way of Wyatt. From on high you'd look down on something very much like Appalachia: hills unfolding into sudden groves, long-forgotten pools of still water, these soundless footfalls of history."

5. *Shirt.* Variant: an *r* appears in the A&S text that does not exist on the second sheets. Author's correction or editorial addition?

6. "Miracles happen in the corners of lives," the author was fond of quoting in these days. (Conversation with Eric Stall.)

7. "Waiting for the Echo" begins: "Tuesday night, early morning actually, 4:15, darkness rolling over to show its dull silver underbelly, Jan dreams that he is a corpse."

8. In his copy of John Banville's *The Newton Letter* the author underscored this passage concerning "tradesmen, the sellers and the makers of things": "They would seem to have something to tell me; not of their trades, nor even of how they conduct their lives; nothing, I believe, in words. They are, if you will understand it, themselves the things they might tell."

9. The author's phonetic spelling here prepares for the outrageous pun—*Dja startchur own shurts* ("Do you starch your own shirts?") is heard as "Did you start your own church?"—that precipitates a page of truly strange dialog and provides the story's plot.

10. "Destined as we are by fate and our own disabilities to be wrong, we might at least contrive to be wildly, brashly, definitively wrong. That's the full measure of grace given us." *Life: A Fair Copy*.

11. *Civilisation, elegance and terror*—to invoke once again the encomium employed by University of Nebraska Press on its first slim volume of the author's stories and carried down, such that it has become with title and author's name a kind of single parcel, from edition to edition.

12. At this point in the draft a single oblique line scores across the following paragraph: "Perhaps our lives consist not so much of what happens in them as of the explanations and connections we make." In the margin is penned: "The same is true of deletions."

AN ASCENT OF THE MOON

His longest relationship, it began over two years ago.

There had been a youthful marriage at age nineteen, a union which wandered about, in and out of various apartments and abandonments, like a movie heroine searching some castle's cavernous hallways and chambers for an outside doorway. But with all that coming and going, the marriage had been patchy and disjunctive at best, and anyway was more than twenty years past.

There followed a six-year affair (using words loosely, which, tacitly, they always insisted upon) with a woman who worked as an agricultural advisor in Africa and returned to Dallas two or three times a year on what were essentially layovers.

In December two years ago he had come across the apartment during an evening walk in the university area. He didn't know why he took notice of the to-let sign, but stood there only a moment, glancing about him at the two-story houses, each distinct in overall form but identical in detail, doorways and material, before mounting the stoop to inquire. He was shown the room by a youngish woman whose already-pale skin was blanched in patches as though randomly daubed with bleach. She wore a denim wraparound skirt and a man's blue oxford dress shirt falling well below her knees and extending so far beyond her hands that it gave her a vaguely simian look.

The apartment consisted of two rooms tenuously connected by a shoulder-wide hallway which without at all changing its nature suddenly turned downward to become a stairway. Rooms and hallway together comprised a false half-story, unperceived from outside the house, carved from attic and second-floor space.

One room was afterthought (or afterbirth, as he first thought upon seeing it), a windowless parallelogram too narrow save at the far end to be of much use.

The other, running the house's full length, was less than three yards deep, and along the side, opposite the doorway, ranged a motley of windows of every conceivable form and size—picked up at a bargain, or as surplus, perhaps. Even at this time of late evening, his favorite, neither quite dark nor yet quite light, but something forever in between, something unnamable, unknowable, the room was rich with light. Two ancient trees dipped in from either side and at a distance obscured all but one of the windows. Through this, he saw an expanse of the house opposite: two oversize windows and within them a bedroom, dimly lit, predominantly pink and white.

He moved in a week later, heaving his few possessions up the narrow stairs on his back like a snail. Long ago he had vowed to own nothing that could not be broken down easily for transport or abandoned without regret. In just over an hour furnishings were reassembled, housewares set up and out, clothing, toiletries, books and tapes put away.

That first evening, relocation accomplished, he stood drinking coffee and looking through the chink in the trees. The drapes over there were closed. Once he thought he saw someone moving around behind them, touching gently at their backs, but decided it was only his imagination—or the wind, perhaps.

The drapes remained closed, and he had come to believe the house unoccupied (it was, after all, a neighborhood of students and young families quick to move on) when one evening after his bath, standing as yet undressed near the windows, he looked up and saw the drapes open. A woman of his age or perhaps a bit older stood there, to all appearances watching him through the trees. Slowly her hand reached toward the window. The drapes closed.

The following evening, at the same time, he emerged from his bath and immediately looked up to see the drapes once again open. Tonight, however, the room was unlit, and in the half-dark he could make out only the shape of her, see enough to confirm only that she was again there, again watching.

It continued this way for some time. He would emerge from his bath, at first wearing a robe, later without, and find her there in the window, waiting. They would stand watching as darkness fell. She would reach out and close the drapes.

His days began to gather around these encounters. Whatever

those days held (and in truth they held little: students and classes had long since lost any appeal they once may have had), he was at the apartment each evening. The pretense of a shower soon passed. He simply stood by the window and removed his clothes.

Then one evening as he stood there peering across, trying to make out some detail, any detail, in the window opposite, her room suddenly filled with light. He saw her clearly, all but her face, which remained in shadow. She held out her hand, touched softly with its back at the back of the window, and began to remove her own clothes. Only when they were gone (and they went ever so slowly) did she reach out again, to close the drapes. Pulling his blinds closed, he found that he was shaking.

Thereafter, opening his blinds at the proper time, he would see her drapes also opening. Some evenings she would be in nothing but a terry housecoat, others in long skirt and sweater or jeans, once in a formal gown many years out of fashion.

One day then, leaving for a late-afternoon class in first-year Greek, he stepped onto the sidewalk to find a woman standing there before the house opposite, speaking with the postman. Briefly their eyes met, though neither gave any sign of recognition.

That night he waited at the window, looking across at a dark, shrouded window. He believed that he had lost her and did not think he could go on without her. No: he knew that he could not.

For three nights he stood waiting, nibbled at by imagination, sorrow, devastating loss. And when, on the fourth, he opened his blinds and saw drapes parting there in that far window, blood careened wildly inside him and he put his hand on the windowsill to steady himself. Her own hand moved between her legs. Her body twitched and swayed at the end of it. Her eyes never left him.

That night it rained, and afterwards a brilliant yellow moon rose into the sky. For hours he walked gleaming streets. Primitives have always afforded the moon great powers, he thought. Romance, mystery, madness, passion. And any hospital or emergency service will tell you how a full moon calls forth new birth, domestic violence, wave after wave of bodies violated by knives, guns, collisions.

In such a world, he thought, how rare, how very pure and inviolable, was a love like his own.

AUTUMN LEAVES

The call I never expected would actually come came at 4:32 one Tuesday morning. I hung up and went to the closet for my bag. It had been in there, packed, for well over six years. Karyn sat propped in bed watching, eyes huge. She knew what this meant, and not to ask more. "I'll call when I can," I said. After a moment, the space between us growing ever larger all the while, she nodded. Half an hour later I was in a military helicopter thwacking its way out of the city over rivers and inlets and down the coastline. There were four of us aboard. The pilot had a scrubbed, pink, midwestern look about him. You could have impaled olives on his brush cut.

"So you're one of the doctors."

I wasn't, I was a nurse with some very special training who with the phone's first ring had gone from being one among thousands of faceless health-care workers—in my case, taking care of terminal cancer patients, children mostly—to Authority. But those who trained us down in Virginia taught us that people were happier thinking what they wanted to think and it was to our advantage to let them do so, so I nodded.

Outside Washington we joined a dozen or so others and enplaned for the long haul. Boxed chicken lunches and sacks of little bottles of booze were passed around. Cans of beer in a full-size refrigerator and fresh-brewed coffee in an urn half as large waited our beck and call, we were told. A few had brought books: *Forensics for the General Practitioner*, *Getting Along with Heart Disease*, a Tom Clancy thriller, a novel whose bright white teeth and drops of blood looked as though they might slide off the slick cover into the reader's lap at any moment. The rest of us sat staring into space, minds as full as expressions were empty. I found some back corner of my brain providing words for the music playing quietly over the sound system.

Since you went away, the days grow long . . .

Our training was as specific as it was thorough. Four, five doctors in the whole country might be able to identify, say, bubonic plague if they saw it. But every last one of us would immediately recognize signs and symptoms of anthrax, smallpox, typhoid, Ebola and half a dozen others. Incubation times, vectors, previous outbreaks or occurrences, possible vaccines and treatments were engraved in the very folds of our brains. We came on the scene, it got handed over to us, baby, bathwater and all. Local police and officials, medical personnel, military—everyone deferred.

I'd been in New Orleans a couple of times before, once back around century's end with Karyn for the Jazz Festival, once during training. The country's sole remaining leprosarium was in Louisiana, and instructors brought us down to see things firsthand. The city had always looked ancient, blasted, and at first there seemed little difference: abandoned, half-gutted buildings, heaps of trash, mattresses and dead animals at curbside. Then you realized almost no one was on the streets.

Military trucks carted us in from the city's outskirts along water's edge to Camp Alpha. Off to each side all the way, close by and in the middle distance, black smoke rose from fires. The few civilian vehicles we encountered pulled off the road to let us pass. The city had become a patchwork of camps, this the largest of them, acre upon acre of tents, lean-tos and sheds running over the low wall right up to Lake Ponchartrain and back onto what had long been the city's dearest real estate. Officials had set up HQ in a house designed by Frank Lloyd Wright. It was bone white, a thing of curves, and looked like a huge ship, complete with foredeck, gone aground among trees. Autodidact James K. Feibleman, a millionaire without formal training or degree who'd become head of Tulane's philosophy department, had lived here, as had writer wife Shirley Ann Grau and writer son Peter. Tulane's campus, meanwhile, along with that of Loyola and adjoining Audubon Park with its hundred-year-old water oaks, had become another sprawling tent city.

Briefing took place in what was once the kitchen of Feibleman's home. Dozens of folding chairs had butts holding them down. The rest of us spilled out, sitting, standing, propped against walls, through sliding doors onto the patio as Dr. Fachid Ramadan, all four feet six of him, bustled to the room's front, by the monolith of the refrigerator's stainless-steel door.

"We do not know what it is," he said without preamble, eyes large as globes behind thick eyeglasses, "though of course we are hoping all of you will be able to help us with this." His phrases had an intrinsic rhythm to them, a quiet rise and fall, as though he were reading poetry. "This could scarcely be more confusing, more difficult to get a handle on. Yes—as I know many of you are about to ask—at this point we *are* assuming a seeding. Undifferentiated flulike symptoms at first. Slow gather, sudden crash. By the time you admit that you and loved ones are sick, it is too late." He went on to detail our small fund of actual information, providing a long, intricate list of possible signs and symptoms, a checklist of similarities and divergence from disease processes with which we were all familiar. Poorly spelled and unchecked in the rush, copies of the lists floated onto a projector screen behind him as he spoke.

I held up my hand:

"Vectors?"

"We do not know. Not airborne—we are fairly certain of this. Direct contact, bodily fluids. Insects have yet to be ruled out. A handful of cases may be traceable to rodents. Squirrels, nutria."

"Staff?" I asked.

"None yet. But we barely have our feet in the door. I was on site in Malaysia, was fetched by Air Force officials and flown here. This was forty-six hours ago. I have been a stranger to pillows since. We have no idea what the incubation period might be."

First rule: Expect the worst.

And we did—though ultimately expectation and imagination proved as unequal to the challenge as did our knowledge.

Having gone through the program together and been for the duration propinquous friends, despite a dozen or so dinners and wine-soft evenings in the mix, Sara Freedman and I had little reason ever to anticipate seeing one another again. Now we walked along the river's slow curve carrying kebobs bought from street vendors where Café du Monde used to be and a bottle of Chilean Merlot. Carrying lots of things. And talking with a freedom and absolute lack of self-consciousness I thought left behind forever, shed skin of adolescence, telling one another secrets, fears.

"Not a good idea under the circumstances," I remarked when Sara dangled feet, sandals and all, in the water. But when she pointed out that every day we were smack among the actual as opposed to the theoretical, I relented, feeling foolish.

"This river used to be filled with boats," I said. "Coming in from the Gulf, heading up to Natchez and Memphis and St. Louis. For three hundred years."

No boats now. Only trash, dead fish, bloated human bodies. They floated, careened spinning from bank to bank, lazily, as though in a dream.

"Things change."

"I don't think the word *change* covers what's happening now."

"Maybe nothing does."

It was fall—have I mentioned that? Leaves gone crimson and gold on the trees even this far south. I hungered for New England autumns, feet shuffling through layers of ankle-deep leaves. Our bodies have those same changes as voids within them, waiting.

"I've thought of you, you know," Sara said. "Often, and fondly."

I passed her a kebob. A chunk of cucumber. Levered out the cork and poured wine into plastic cups. We sat without speaking. At water's edge, a line of ants methodically dismembered a sphinx moth's body and carried it off. Two others, one pushing, one pulling, steadily moved along a chunk of celery easily twenty times their size. Stew for dinner?

Maybe it was their time now.

We'd lost a dozen or more the night before. Toward dawn I was awakened by one of the nurses, knowing as I opened my eyes that it wasn't yet daylight, knowing little else. I'd been asleep just under two hours, she told me, and she was sorry, but the boy was having trouble breathing. The boy was nineteen. We'd watched other members of his department go down one by one, till he was the only one remaining, de facto sheriff. Terror in his eyes. Just past dawn, the terror passed as he joined the others.

Later that night, both sleepless, Sara and I wandered at the same time into the kitchen. Without speaking she turned and leaned across the counter. I pulled down her shorts just far enough, ground into her soundlessly from behind as she watched our single shadow on the wall, but could not stay hard. Around us everywhere the cries and moans of those in our care.

Two months later I'd fly out by copter, hauled above and across the dead city by the machine's brute force, New Orleans now like nothing so much as the still, crumbling husk of an insect. I'd remember how, as I came here on the plane, "Autumn Leaves" was playing: *Since you went away* . . . In memory, in the weeks I had left, Sara's face would look up at me again and again as she struggled for breath, and again and again I'd place a hand on hers. I never called Karyn. She was gone by the time I got back. Gone like Sara.

That morning in the copter I would remember an old song by Woodie Guthrie, something I'd not thought of in twenty years. Field workers had been brought in from Mexico and, their job done, put on a plane to be sent back. But the plane caught fire over Los Gatos Canyon.

> *Who are these friends who are falling like dry leaves?*
> *The radio says they're just deportees.*

We're all itinerants, shipped in, trucked away once the work's done. Dry leaves. Autumn leaves. Everything leaves. Everything leaves, everything changes. Treasure the margins while they last, treasure everything that sinks into the blur, treasure it all.

Treasure it all.

DAWN OVER DOLDRUMS

Sitting for coffee, he glances back briefly at the doorway with its improvised deadbolt, chain, deadfall bar. She thinks how the sound of unfastenings has replaced a cock's crow as harbinger of morning for them here, and wonders what Keats might have done with that. She thinks of the boundless symbolism in everything, how the simplest objects and actions are replete with meaning, with resonance: hasp embracing flange, the bar's leap of faith into concavity. Everything connects. Once a poet's wife and ruined by it, she puts coffee down and leans into him, arm resting across, pressing on, his shoulder, as her hand lightly grazes his chest.

"How did you sleep?"

"Fairly well," she tells him. "The first part, anyway."

"I was restless?"

She nods. Remembers an old poem of David's: *All night the beast beat about its room as I lay forgetting you.* As usual, David had thought he was writing fantasy—what he lived—and would never know how right he was, how prophetic, all those years ago.

Everything connects.

Now this man's hand still shakes, and she reaches out to steady it. What they drink is a distillate from one of the mancuspia's holding-glands, not coffee at all; but as with many things here, they have kept the familiar words.

"Sorry," he says. Never apologizing for what happens at night (this silence, tacitly, is understood), but, in effect, for needing her, for this small weakness.

You're simply *away*, he told her once, early on, when some of the others were still with them. Then you come back: walk into an apartment that looks just like your own but where someone else lives. You don't know what has changed, and there's nothing you can take for granted. Your body fails to do what you expect. You watch your own hand reach out into the world without your willing it.

She gets up and pours more coffee. His hand is steadier now. "Hungry?"

"Can we wait?"

"Of course."

She moves closer to him, against him, and his arm goes up over her head (she ducks, readjusts) and behind, to her shoulder. One breast nudges at his palm. She moves until that hand is filled.

Deep in the evening, shortly after the bolts and locks have fallen, winds begin to gather on the far horizon and blow in across the dry swampland she's taken to calling the Doldrums. It's a silent wind, seen in gentle displacements of grass, felt (but only at its peak) against the face, and for her this wind has become the voice of the mancuspia.

One morning long ago she had looked up the word *keening*, simply because the mancuspia's brimful, silent faces brought that word to mind. The computer told her: A lamentation for the dead uttered in a loud wailing voice, or sometimes in a wordless cry. Yes.

They'd known something of the mancuspia's adaptive gifts from initial reports, of course. The animals could live on almost anything, or (more to the point of what this world offered) on virtually nothing. Only when supplies were exhausted and early survivors scrabbled for basics did they begin noticing what a true wonder the mancuspia was. For if the mancuspia could live on virtually nothing, they discovered, another species could live off the mancuspia.

The mancuspia had come among them during their first days here, appearing outside the squat-huts one afternoon without fanfare or prologue. After first fearing then largely ignoring them, the team tried to domesticate them, taking one of the knobby, shapeless animals into the huts where it promptly died, as though to tell them: I will not be kept. More from curiosity and boredom than any other motive, Marc Gavruski, the team biologist and medic, dissected the creature—an autopsy, they eventually took to calling it. And what he discovered was a machine of exquisite precision. From the rubble and scant, equivocal vegetation of this place, from sunlight and that silent wind and whispers far beyond hearing in the twists and turns of its genetic makeup, the mancuspia urged forth the very basics of life, nutrients, water, essential minerals, all of which it stored away in glands easily accessible.

Since that time, they have not seen a mancuspia die. Of course, the individuals are indistinguishable one from another, and they assume (since numbers are constant) that periodically one of the animals must wander off to its end to be replaced by another, though they have never witnessed young or any evidence of same.

She must know more about the mancuspia than anyone else, she supposes; must know them better. The work of caring for them, initially shared with others—and now almost the only work remaining—fell to her by degrees, at first because she enjoyed its variance from her mapping and geographical duties and because the mancuspia readily accepted her presence, then because, increasingly, there was no one else to become involved in such quotidian concerns. Now Eric spends his days hoarded scrivener-like among the indecipherable artifacts of a long-defunct alien culture. And as the group's number declined, as their reliance on the mancuspia redoubled, there seemed always to be more work. The mancuspia would no longer graze; soil and vegetation perforce were brought to them. Their exiguous waste products (since almost everything was somehow used, converted) had to be carried off.

Because it is mindless work, though, it is welcome. And maybe, just maybe (she thinks), there is some extreme, innate truth to woman as nurturer, tenuous threads tacking them still to the race's long traditions and history, echoes of whispers in the bright, cluttered spirals of their genes.

Deep in the evening she sits looking out over the Doldrums and feels the wind against her face like a lover's hand. Hears behind her the rattle and drumming of locks, bolts, chains, doors.

They found Diane one afternoon in the galley, laid out on a long stainless-steel table as though for possible reassembly. Someone— Nyugen, possibly—had gone in to fetch tea and cakes and come back out blanched, gesturing, unable to speak. They were halfway into their fifth month on the world they'd begun calling Catarrh.

Most of her midsection was gone, torn away, scooped out and tossed in gobbets against walls and floor. Her own hand had been forced, up to the wrist, into her mouth, tearing it at both corners into a clown's mouth, rupturing the mandible so that it hung down like a necklace. The fingers of the other hand were neatly severed and laid out in an asterisk at the table's bottom left corner. Bowels, ravelled out like yarn, were a heavy, glistening mound on the floor nearby. An eyeball peered from what remained of her vagina.

They had not known what to do with the body, finally tucking it in a sealed bag meant for geological specimens and depositing it on a rock ledge outside the huts. None of them could bring him- or herself (though this was protocol) to commit Diane's body to the Deconstructor. In all of them, perhaps, lay some vague notion of taking her body home, back to its own planet, for burial.

After a while there was quite a stack of bags on that ledge.

One day (for those, days, had become as indistinguishable as the mancuspia) Evelyn took the Mini out, scooped up the bags in its jaws and hauled them away, out of sight.

A week or so later, she went after them and brought them back.

More than anything else, he had to *understand*.

To understand this world, at first: sitting before the computer sifting in blocks of seemingly unrelated information, driving head-long (he hoped) for syncretism—much as, ten years old, he had built, on his first computer, a working model of the solar system.

He tried to understand what was happening to them here, log-ging each drift of personality, each storm or withdrawal in those early days, plotting these against every imaginable variable: weather conditions (though there scarcely *was* weather), changing diet and metabolism, declensions of the planet itself, a bevy of biological and psychological tests. What he derived was as intricate, compel-ling and ultimately useless as that childhood solar-system model.

Anything was bearable, if only it was understood. But he could not understand a world; and, finally, he could not understand any-thing of what was happening to them here. None of them could.

So, finally, he came to the Boroch.

They were a race, or species, long extinct, and so little of them remained that surely in short order (he thought) he would know all about the Boroch there was to know. And perhaps, now, he did.

Of a material nature, aside from a handful of scattered small artifacts, there wasn't much. Some concave objects of an extremely hard substance which absorbed all light, ranging in size from that of the ball of a man's thumb to roughly that of a newborn's skull. (Bowls? Or containers of another sort, perhaps. Body decorations. Religious vestments or utensils. Or for that matter—just as easily—a set of measuring spoons.) A few narrow, vertical slabs resembling nothing so much as the gravestones one sees in history books, each of these inscribed with what might be language—or simply attritions of time and weather.

And that was pretty much it. No libraries, no great government repositories, record-houses or munitions dumps, no museums. No buildings at all, in fact, save one. If, indeed, it *was* one. For it might as easily be (and this had become maddening for him) some inscrutable monument or artwork; a train station, vending machine, aquarium.

Five sides, irregular yet still somehow fitting together in a welter of bends and all but imperceptible curves, the whole of the structure perhaps eight feet at its greatest height, five at its lowest, and ten or twelve feet in circumference. It was mostly the color of the drab, surrounding ground itself, save midday when, for a brief moment, light angled down, caught in it somehow and, pale yellow, spread across its surface, gone then as abruptly as it came. No discernible doors or other egress. But set in each side (each of them at a different level) were semi-transparent sections, at times virtually opaque, other times limpid as pool water.

Windows of a sort? Screens?

Periodically mancuspia came to the structure, sat by it unmoving for a few moments or as long as a day, then went on about whatever business they might have, to all appearances wholly unaffected by their tryst.

Early on, he and Evelyn spent much of their free time observing the mancuspia at this sentry. Drawing close, they would themselves peer by the hour into those watery sections and occasionally see, or believe they saw, vague motions, like movement sensed just outside sight's orbit yet never there when the eye turns to it.

In a notebook whose cover is ringed with layers of overlapping blurred rings, memories of half-drunk cups of coffee in a riot of Venn diagrams, he has copied out, among sketches of artifacts, half-remembered fragments of conversation, and markers for the dead (*Jules Yasner; 5-28?*), something from a book he'd read in the drawl of their first weeks when each day, each hour, stretched endlessly to the horizon. Imbedded in a discussion of some French writer he'd never read, or indeed, so much as heard of—in a book like many another, taken up utterly at random—the passage meant little to him at the time, but later, unaccountably, drew him back.

> *Rarely do the monuments erected by a culture in its aspirations to eternity betray the forces that propel individuals toward destruction as the affirmative willingness to lose things, meaning, and even self.*

He was remembering that passage when one night, as they stood by the structure, he suddenly said, without thought: "It was suicide."

And knew he was right.

"Racial suicide. The Boroch simply chose, at last, not to go on. I don't know how I know that, I have nothing to support it—but I know."

"And the mancuspia?"

He paused.

"The mancuspia . . . have been waiting."

There were five of them. Five of the fourteen who came.

"We should call it the Doldrums," Eric said, looking out across the dry swampland. Of late they'd taken to renaming things. "The land where nothing continues to happen."

"Enough is happening in here to fill a dozen lands," O'Carolan said. "What does Control say now?"

"What does Control always say?" Solomon stood beside Eric, also looking out. "Run some tests, set up new safety standards, keep us informed, we'll get back to you."

"If this goes on . . ."

"And we have no reason to believe it will do otherwise."

". . . there won't be any *you* to get back to."

They were all silent a moment.

"It can't be a virus, then."

"Nothing we can detect, at least."

"Or any physical mutation."

"And why only the men?"

"We're a bit closer to beasts to begin with, no?"

"There *are* genetic differences, whether or not it's polite to say so, dear."

It was the last of their strategy conferences, brainstorming sessions which had become, in their futility and repetitiveness, little more than ritual.

Lin Fu brought green tea for them all in the tiny enameled cups he'd packed so carefully among his personal belongings. They had been his grandfather's and father's before him.

"Ceremony is important at such times," Lin Fu said in his quiet voice.

"Especially when there's not a thing else."

That night O'Carolan was killed, and they would hear his brash, bold voice no more.

Some weeks later, Lin Fu. They found him among his shattered cups.

Then Solomon.

Until there were only the two of them.

"What are you doing?" she had asked Eric the afternoon of the day she found Solomon. He stood by one of the storeroom doors, beside him a cart scattered with small tools, chains, metal fixtures.

"Making my bed," he told her.

She remembers a story by Gogol, how the texture of the protagonist's world begins to unravel. One morning on the street he observes two dogs conversing quite civilly; before long he's come to believe he's the King of Spain and dates his journal entries "April 43rd, 2000" or "86th Martober, between day and night."

Poetry is nothing, David had always said, if it's not possibility.

(The possibility of fantasies at once crueler than truth and more comforting. Of words becoming action; action, words. Of other, distant, forfeited lives.)

On this world where, employed for their comforting familiarity, gently humorous and wayward as orphans, words seldom mean what they say—Catarrh, Deconstructor, the Doldrums—she does not know any more what is real, or greatly care. That wind at night is real; it must be. The heave and metallic leaf-rattle of lock and chain, that piercing aloneness, the sadness in his eyes (or in her own, perceiving it) come morning. Though she knows, she grants, she allows, she accepts, that date and time, day or night, have little meaning now.

She is not altogether surprised then when, one night in the crowded hours before dawn, she looks up to see him there. Not *him*, really, but what he becomes, something she has never before seen. Behind him, locks lie open and unavailing. Has he sprung them? Or has she somehow forgotten, neglected, to fasten them securely?

"I love you, Eric," she says.

He starts toward her. Not *him*, she reminds herself; that is not Eric, cannot be Eric, behind those eyes. And for a moment she thinks she sees, she almost sees, the mancuspia's pale forms there between them in the near dark. They stand unmoving, as before the Boroch's structure.

A blink, and they are gone.

Another blink and Eric staggers, comes to a stop, folds slowly, head onto chest, chest onto knees, knees down, onto the floor.

"You didn't lock the storeroom," he said hours later.

She poured coffee, or whatever it really was, for them both.

"I don't know," she said. "I've sat here wondering, waiting for you to surface. I *thought* I had locked it. But it's possible, at some level, that I left things open intentionally. That I wanted you to escape, or—"

"It doesn't matter."

"The *or* matters."

"No. It doesn't."

He reached across the table and put his hand atop hers.

"The mancuspia will not let us die, Evelyn. I understand that now."

He smiled.

"They and the Boroch must have lived in a near-perfect symbiosis. The Boroch had no factories, no food-processing plants, no centers of government because they had no use for them; the mancuspia provided everything they needed. And when the Boroch decided, collectively, to end, the mancuspia chose *not* to. We're their answer, their means for going on. All along we thought we were using the mancuspia—and they've been using us."

"But what of all that's happened here?"

"It had nothing to do with the mancuspia. For all they knew, that was the way we had always lived. But now they know it's not. They stopped me last night. They won't let it happen again. We're too important to them, they've waited too long."

After a while she said, "More coffee?" and he nodded. It was fully light outside, and they sat in the squat-hut looking out at the stack of bags on the ledge, sinking into history and memory, getting ready, like the mancuspia before them, to go on.

POWERS OF FLIGHT

As he steps away from the shop door, he begins to rise into air, his feet at first scuffing at pavement, then he is above it, clear, floating now over the heads of fireplugs, children, streetlamps, feeling the ground, with something like a long sigh, give up its claim. There is a light breeze and he drifts gently toward the shipyard, the strip of crab houses, checkerboards of docked pleasure boats. Faces turn up to him. I am falling, he thinks, upwards; I am falling into freedom.

"Maybe it's just," Sheila says, "not meant to be." She peers up from a column of figures atop which she has been picturing a diminutive man reposing nude, looking out at her. "Maybe I'll just never be loved, never find the right man out there."

"You could have mine," Jeffrey says. "If I *had* one, that is."

"You and Brian aren't together anymore?"

"Barbells to Beethoven, all gone. Empty room in the flat, black hole for a heart."

"I'm so sorry, Jeff."

"That's what *he* said—right before he hooked our CD player with a little finger and hauled it out to Larry's VW."

"Perhaps you're right, dear," Sheila's father says, turning from the window where he's just watched her latest young man (Blair, he thinks; they all have these odd names nowadays) float away in a wash of pigeons and seagulls. "Or perhaps," because he knows how much this means to her, "it's just that you've been trying too hard. You should concentrate on your career. Watched pots and all that, you know."

"But I haven't been trying at all Papa. If there's anything I *don't* want, it's all this pain, this having to be around someone all the time, always wondering how *he* feels, what will become of the two of us. Having my life torn up all the time like a road under repair. I hid in my apartment for five months once, remember? Came to work, went home, locked the door. Then one day it was so gorgeous that I thought, I'll just hurry this trash out to the dumpster, no harm in that. So standing there with cans and paper towels falling out of tears in the plastic bags, and a week or more of old newspapers skewing out from under my arms, I met Stephen."

Whom Mr. Taylor had last seen, he was fairly sure, outside the fifteenth floor of Campbell Center, tiny multiple images of him reflected in the building's mirrored surfaces as he rose into a blinding dazzle of sunlight.

"Where'd you have lunch?" he had asked Sheila when she returned to the shop.

"Le Chardonnay."

"The one in Campbell Center?"

"I don't think there *is* another one."

"Eat alone?"

"Well . . ."

Stephen was followed close on the heels by Claude, then by David, Seth, Ramon. Mr. Taylor began to look up at the sky with dread. He took new interest in reports from traffic helicopters.

His own wife, Sheila's mother, vanished early one March. Snow crept toward them through weeks of sun-drenched weather and finally sprang, and when it was gone (though podlike shells of it hung on for days in dark places), so was Elizabeth. After that, life for Mr. Taylor became largely people and things taken from him. He sometimes feels that Sheila is all he really has left: what his life has come down to.

"Papa, I'll always be here to take care of you, just as Momma asked," Sheila would say as a child. She doesn't say that anymore. And when he goes for dinner to her tiny apartment, she listens again to the stories she's heard so often before and tells him hers (many of them, though he doesn't know this, invented), but her eyes reach out toward the city and its lights, the dwelling darkness, sequestered horizons. This is something they never speak of.

She and Jeffrey, however, often speak of such things. The heart opens like a flower, one will say, and the other continue: and closes again like a damaged fist.

So it is that Jeffrey knows something Mr. Taylor does not. For several weeks now, Sheila has been deeply involved, not with one man, but two. The first, Blaine, whom she met standing in line at her bank, this afternoon has floated off into the sky like a child's balloon. The second's name—he runs a specialty bike shop in one of the northside malls and lives in a garage apartment choked with art deco—is Ian.

"I love him so much, Jeffrey," Sheila says now. "Ian, I mean. There's almost a . . . a physical *pain* to it, I love him so much."

At which point Jeffrey begins to look rather more interested in what she is saying.

"But poor Blaine. He knows there's someone else, despite all I said. You could tell it from his eyes, from the way he almost touched me, then at the last moment drew back. Do you think I'll ever see him again, Jeffrey?"

"Hard to say," Jeffrey, who has watched from another window the spurned lover's ascent, says. "Sometimes it is possible, *enfin*, to become friends again."

"Oh, Jeff, I hope so."

There's a fall of customers then, and for almost an hour the three of them are diverted from the narrow streets of their own lives onto the boulevards of commerce.

"*Well*," Mr. Taylor says when the customers are gone. "That seems *quite* enough for one day's work. I vote we shut it down and have a few drinks together by way of celebration. Seconds?"

Jeffrey raises one arm, looking at his watch on the other. Two-fifty. He wonders what Brian's doing. And what *he'll* do for the rest of the day, leaving this early.

"Oh, Papa, how wonderful!"

They decide on Schopenhauer's and gather their various coats and jackets, hats, parcels, bags. With two fingers Jeffrey forklifts a thatch of hair half an inch to the right to cover an isthmus of bald scalp.

They walk out into an afternoon of empty streets and wind. Coming toward them on the opposite sidewalk, muffler blowing out like twin exhausts, is a man whom Jeffrey knows, instantly, must be Ian. He is dressed in a gray corduroy suit and brown wool porkpie hat and, seeing them emerge from the shop, starts walking faster.

"So this is where you hide." He reaches for the hand she tucks quickly away in a pocket.

"Papa," Sheila says. "Papa, this is Ian Whatley."

"Whatley," her father says.

"Mr. Taylor. I am pleased." He offers the forsaken hand, which is this time, somewhat hesitantly, accepted.

"And Jeffrey."

They also shake hands.

"We've been, sort of, seeing one another, Papa."

"Seeing one another," Mr. Taylor says.

"Quite a lot, actually, Papa."

"I love your daughter, sir. I did want to come and tell you that."

Sheila turns from her father to look at Ian and sees that he has grown taller: she must now, as never before, look up at him. She turns back, then back again to Ian, beginning to understand in some instinctive way that needs no words.

Wind comes up strongly just then, like waves heaving up against a ship, and very quietly Sheila says, "I'm sorry, Papa," as he begins to rise, slowly at first, then ever faster, into the sky. Leaning out ahead of the wind with feet trailing behind, almost reclining, he moves out of sight through the downtown skyline.

"I love you too," she tells Ian as her father joins the horizon.

STEPPING AWAY
FROM THE STONE

He left her there on the litter by her parent's trunk, knowing she'd need to be alone now.

He went out into the other room and sat by the open door sipping at the pod of warm pulp she'd set out for him before. It was dark outside, gray turning relentlessly over inside itself, almost morning. In the open square just beyond the door a tree moved several steps to the right, into a patch of dull light, and resettled itself with something like a sigh sounding in its leaves. The leaves were perfectly rectangular, curling toward midline and tip like a tongue.

Much of his life, he knew, would be spent contemplating what had just taken place. But for now, newly set adrift on his future, he took refuge in the past, in his own memories and those of his parents.

A limitless white ceiling, the only world he yet had. The voices that came to him there, like a rain one heard—voices that came to him still sometimes, unbidden.

A crimson, restless sea.

Fields of migrating grain.

The husk of his parent's body just before he returned it to the trees.

The tree moved again, to the left this time, and settled back. He thought how so much of their lives, fiber for clothing, materials for shelter, medicines, even basic sustenance, came from the trees.

Then she emerged from the back room.

They sat together in the doorway, soles of their feet pressed against one another. He passed the pod and she drank. Pulp, from the tree.

The world looks no different, she signed.

No.

But it is. I thank you for your choice, for my freedom.

He signed that it was of no import and passed the pod to her again. Lowering her head, she drank. Lifting the pod, he drank. Light pushed gently at the backside of gray beyond the door. The tree shifted again, into whatever tatters remained of darkness.

She drank off the last of the liquor, gathering final shreds of pulp onto her smaller thumb and offering it to him.

There is more, she signed. He assented, and she went to draw another podful from the gourd as, waiting, he witnessed morning's arrival. Slow eddies gave way to pools of silver above the trees; then, riding from its center, there was sudden light. Around them the low, wordless moan of the trees.

And with the morning, morning's chill.

She closed the door and sat beside him again, soles of her feet against his. He watched her across this chasm, you could bridge it with an outreached hand but no one ever would, her lidless eyes, pale blue skin.

Passing the pod from hand to hand, they drank. Unseen light went on growing outside, reclaiming its world. A general sense of increment, augmentation. A growing sense of loss.

These walls, he signed. That shut us away?

He sat watching one. Pale white like the pith of plants rising from still water, like every wall he had ever seen.

There could be openings, he signed. Eyes in the walls. Out of those eyes we would continue as part of the world, never again be shut away from it. Those eyes would be formed of some material one could see through.

But there is nothing like that, she signed, nothing one can see through.

He assented. Then stood to sign:

There is a stone, a tree. Man waits. In due time, he steps away from the stone.

Woman waits too, she signed. In due time, she steps away from the tree.

He took from her the bundle she offered. Tied with a single white ribbon, it was almost weightless.

Nothing left but the world now, he thought as he went out the door. All this light. All this future he carried with him. The new memories he would have.

Flagging a barge nestwards, he sat on narrow branches among others rushing to or from. At length as they watched, dark began to gather, coming not from the sky, not as descent, but pooling up from the ground like oil: tree and stone united.

Nested, he pulled loose the ribbon tie about the bundle she'd given him. Light as thistledown it unscrolled, barely there at all, floor visible beneath as through water.

Some material one could see through.

Her face fell lightly, transparently, almost weightless, against his hand. Vacant eye slots looking up.

As dark fell then, lifting this precious skin to his lips, he began to eat, began to remember.

ROOFS AND FORGIVENESS IN THE EARLY DAWN

They started early tonight. Susan and I sat listening to their legs dragging across the roof and shutters, the soft snicker of their calls, the occasional brief whirr of wings. At their size, the wings aren't of much use—best they do is provide a kind of controlled fall.

Susan got up, went to the window to peer out between slats of the shutter, at the roof directly across from ours. Broken bottles baked into tar, part of what appeared to be a toaster with power cord trailing out like a tail behind, a few sacks and plastic bags of trash. One of them was dead over there, on its back. No, not dead, dying. Its legs twitched as I watched. Two others were eating it.

"They're really rather beautiful, you know. In their way."

I shrugged. Susan sees things the rest of us don't, or sees them in ways we can't. This is what makes her what she is. Against the wall opposite the window is her latest painting. Struck by morning light, half in sun, half in twilight, a sort of hive looking (inasmuch as it resembles anything at all familiar) like the communities of Anasazi cliff dwellers. Above the hive one of them hangs in midair. "They can't fly like that, of course," Susan said when I first saw it.

There can't be much food left for them here, after all these years. While we go on living off the bounty of our ancestors, cans of Spam, peas, Spaghetti-O's, tomato soup, Pepsi, corned beef hash, asparagus, sardines, potted meat, green beans.

She turned back to me. Must be a full moon out there. Light fell in a soft lash across her breasts. Her soft breasts. But they're not, really. Small and hard, rather. Dried-up, used-up, like the rest of our world. Always desirable, though. Each night she stands at the window like this for hours before we go to bed. Yet another thing I try not to think about. What it means, how so much is different. How it all has changed.

Soon Susan was asleep. I turned on the radio, spun back and forth across the dial till I found something. You never knew. A few stations were still around and broadcast when they could. Some nights even the static was comforting.

Good morning, all you. Dark here, don't we know—but always morning somewhere. You're listening to The Voice of the People, Free Radio 102 point 4. What you've just heard was Shen O-Wah reading from her new book, Slide It In.

My God, I thought, someone is still publishing books. Susan drifted toward the surface in her sleep. She turned and moved closer to me, said (roughly) *Mmgh.* I was on my right side. Her arm came across my chest, hand hanging into space. I took it in my own and drew it to me. We were one.

Reports are just in from our watchers. Heaviest activity tonight is in the southwest part of the city,

Our part.

from riverside up to the old Beltway. That's the current hot zone. Stay tuned for updates. We'll be with you all night here. Who can sleep, after all?

Susan could, for one. There was some kind of switch in her head. She threw it and the cogs disengaged, she slowed and stopped. By contrast I felt I never slept at all and spent the night with my mind whirring about snatches of songs and thought, never quite getting purchase. I did sleep, though, I must have, because from time to time I'd rouse with tatters of dreams drifting up, there for a second or two, almost graspable, before they trailed off and were gone.

Lot of us around the station have been listening to Ornette Coleman these past weeks. Here's one of the tunes where Coleman and his crew broke through for the first time. To us, this sounds like the world we live in.

He was right, it did. So would Ravel's *La Valse.* The difference was that in *La Valse* we started out on solid ground, witnessed the unwinding, the unraveling into chaos. With Coleman, chaos was already there, waiting like slippers and robe, a comfortable pair of jeans.

I heard the whirr of wings, moments later the thump of one of them hitting the shutters outside. The six-inch spurs of its legs ground against wood, a sound like a wire brush, as it groped for footholds.

Susan, I realized, was awake.

"You remember when we thought they might just go away? We'd get up one day and they'd be gone, gone as suddenly as they appeared."

I did. We're a hopeful species. And things went well for us for a long time. Longer than we had any right to expect.

Sorry to break in. Ornette does grab on and hold, doesn't he? But new information's just come in. Our watchers tell us that activity seems to be shifting heavily toward the northeast. We don't know why. But we never do, do we?

Susan got up, went to the window. She put her hand on the glass, opposite one of its feet. At length then, she turned back to me. Light fell in a slant across her thighs.

"Do you remember birds, Jean-Luc?"

I nodded.

"I can—just barely." And such sadness in her eyes. "It's their world now."

What could I say? What could Ornette say, other than to honk away on his plastic horn? Then a scrambling rasp as our latest visitor dropped off the window, trusting itself to the grace of those lamentable wings.

"It's their world and they know it," Susan said.

It was highly unlikely, of course, that they knew anything at all, but I didn't point this out. With them all was hunger and instinct. We humans have always valued our precious intelligence far more than it deserves. My brother told me that just before he went home to dive off his fourteenth-floor balcony, almost ten years ago now. Two or three years after they began showing up.

Outside, the sky had begun to lighten. Those who hadn't already moved on across the city would be heading back now to wherever it is they go.

I looked at Susan and had a vision of her throwing back the shutters, leaning into the window. I saw her legs slide across the sill, heard the soft snicker of its call, the whirr of wings, as she fell into the arms of the future. I took her, before that happened, into my own.

DEAR FLOODS OF HER HAIR

Muriel left me, left us, I should say, on Monday. The tap in the kitchen sink sprang a leak, spewing a mist of cold water onto sheets I spread on the floor, and a hummingbird, furious that she'd forgotten to refill its feeder just outside, beat at the window again and again. By the time friends, family and mourners began arriving, Thursday around noon, preparations were almost complete.

First thing I did was draw up a schedule. Muriel would have been proud of me, I thought as I sat at the kitchen table with pen and a pad of her notepaper, water from the spewing tap slowly soaking into the corduroy slippers she'd given me last Christmas. Here I'd always been the improviser, treading water, swimming reflexively for whatever shore showed itself, while Muriel weighed out options like an assayer, made lists and kept files, saw that laundry got done *before* the last sock fell, shoehorned order into our lives. And now it was all up to me.

Somewhere between sixteen and twenty on my list, the hummingbird gave up its strafing runs and simply hovered an inch from the glass, glaring in at me. They could be remarkably aggressive. Seventeen species of them where we lived. Anna's hummers, Costa's, and black-chinned around all year, Rufous, calliope and the rest migrating in from Mexico or various mountain ranges. In that way birds have, males are the colorful ones, mating rituals often spectacular. Some will dive ninety feet straight up, making sure sunlight strikes them in such a way that their metallic colors flare dramatically for females watching from below. These females are dull so as to be inconspicuous on nests the size of walnuts.

Muriel loved this place of cactus and endless sky, mountains looming like the world's own jagged edge, loved the cholla, prickly pear, palo verde, geckos with feet spurred into the back of our window screens at night.

Most of all, though, she loved hummingbirds. Even drew a tiny, stylized hummer for stationery, envelopes, and cards and had it silkscreened onto the sweatshirts she often wore as she sat in front of the computer, daily attending to details of the business (cottage industries, they used to call them) that kept us comfortable here.

That same hummer hovered silently in the upper left corner of the notepad as I inscribed *24*.

I gave it a pointed beard and round glasses.

Favorite bird. Hummingbird. Favorite music. *Wozzeck*, Arvo Pärt's *Litany*. Favorite color. Emerald green. Favorite poem.

Memories of my father were also in mind, of course. The one who taught me. I was ten years old when it began, sitting on the floor in a safe corner with knees drawn up reading H.G. Wells, a favorite still. Suddenly I felt *watched*, and when I glanced up, Father's eyes were on me. Good book? he asked. At that point I couldn't imagine a bad one. Just that some were better than others. I lit the next one off the smoldering butt of the last. They all are, I told him. No, he said. A lot of them just make up things.

Mrs. Abneg spoke then. Charles, he's too young, she said. Father looked at her. No. He's ready. Earlier than most, I agree, but this is *our* son. He's not like the rest. Mrs. Abneg ducked her head. The female must be dull so as to be inconspicuous on the nest.

And so I was allowed for the first time into my father's basement workshop. I could barely see over the tops of the sinks, benches, the tilted stainless-steel table with its runnels and drains. Shelves filled with magical jars and pegboards hung with marvelous tools loomed above like promises I would someday keep.

That first session went on for perhaps an hour. I understood little of what my father said then, though whenever he asked was something or another clear I always nodded dutifully yes. Knowledge is a kind of osmosis. And soon enough, of course, our time together in the basement workroom fulfilled itself. Others found themselves shut out. For a time I wondered what Mrs. Abneg or my younger brother might be doing there up above, but not for long. Procedures and practicums, the rigors of my apprenticeship, soon occupied my full attention and all free time. I had far too much to do to squander myself on idle thoughts.

Just as now, I thought.

I set to work.

As I worked, I sang *Wozzeck*.

Drudgery goes best when attention's directed elsewhere— not that pain and loss don't nibble away at us then. Stopping only to feed or rest myself when I could go on no longer, shedding gloves like old skin, I performed as my father taught me. Handsaws, augers and tongs, tools for which there were no names, came into use. I tipped fluids from bright-colored decanters, changed gloves, went on.

Wozzeck was the piece Muriel and I had decided on; with tutorials twice a week and daily practice, I'd got it down as well as might be expected. Not a professional job, certainly, but competent. I sang the parts in rotation, altering pitch and range as required, hearing my own transformed voice roll back from the cellar's recesses.

I'd never really understood painting, poetry, old music, things like that—opera least of all. Whatever I couldn't weigh, quantify, plot on a chart, I had to wonder if it existed at all. I knew how important all this was to Muriel, of course. I'd sit beside her through that aria she loved from *Turandot*, "Nessun dorma," or the second movement of Mozart's Clarinet Quintet, watching tears course down her face. I'd see her put down a book and for a moment there'd be this blank look, this stillness, as though she were lost between worlds: deciding.

Often Muriel and I would discuss how we'd come together, the chance and circumspectness of it, other times the many ways in which, jigsaw-like, our curves and turnings had become a whole. Then, teasing relentlessly, she would argue that, as an anthropologist, I was not truly a scientist. But I was. And who more alert to the place of ritual in lives?

My father trained me well. I had not expected ever to bring my skills into practice so soon, of course. How could we have known? Officers had one day appeared at the door just past noon. One was young, perhaps twenty, undergrowth of beard, single discrete earring, the other middle-aged, hair folded over to cover balding scalp. I was twelve. Answered the door wearing shorts and a T-shirt that read *Stress? What Stress?!* Mr. Abneg? the officers addressed me so I knew. The older one confirmed it: Father was gone, he'd stepped unaware into one of the city's many perilous sinkholes. And so Mrs.

Abneg became my responsibility. I had taken care of her, just as Father taught me. Fine workmanship. He would have been proud. And now, Muriel.

The skull must be boiled (Father taught, all those years ago) until it becomes smooth as stone, then reattached.

This I accomplished with a battery-driven drill and eighteen silver pins from the cloisonned box my father passed on to me, his father's before him. Singing Berg the whole while. I'd learned *all* my lessons well.

Legs must fall just so on the chair.

One arm at rest. The other upraised. Each finger arranged according to intricate plan.

Exacting, demanding work.

Fine music, though.

By Thursday Muriel looked more beautiful than ever before— I know this is hard to believe. That afternoon I lifted the wig from its case and placed it on her. Draped the blue veil across the preserved flesh of her chest.

(I, too, can be practical, my dear, see? I can make plans, follow through, take charge. Do what needs be done. And finally have become an artist of sorts in my own right, I suppose.)

The doorbell rang.

Thank you all for coming.

Glasses clink. Steaming cups are raised. There is enough food here to feed the city's teeming poor. I circulate among our guests, Uncle Van, Mrs. Abneg's sister, cousins and nephews, close friends. Some, I can no longer speak to, of course. To others I present small boxes wrapped in bright paper: a toenail or fingernail perhaps, sliver of bone, divot of pickled flesh.

Yes. She looks beautiful, doesn't she?

Outside, whispering, night arrives. No whispers in here, as family, friends, and mourners move from lit space to lit space. They manipulate Muriel's limbs into various symbolic patterns. Group about her. Pictures are taken.

It's time, Muriel's brother says, stepping beside me.

And *I* say, Please—as instantly the room falls quiet.

I want to tell you all how much I love her.

I want to tell you we'll be happy now. Together. Everything is in place.

I want to tell you how much we will miss you all.

Listen . . .

One day you'll walk out, a day like any other, to fetch laundry, pick up coffee at the store, drop off mail. You'll take the same route you always do, turn corners as familiar to you as the back of your hand, thinking of nothing in particular. And that's when it will happen. The beauty of this world will fall upon you, push the very words and breath from your lungs. Suddenly, irrevocably, the beauty of this world will break your heart; and lifting hand to face, you will find tears there.

Those tears will be the same as mine, now.

VOCALITIES

Tonight well, tonight there won't be any music. I'm sorry. I know a lot of you are just getting in from work, looking forward to a few hours of fine old jazz, the real thing, and where else are you going to hear that on the radio these days, before going to bed. The rest of you don't or can't sleep much anymore, you're the ones who keep watch while others do. And maybe you've come to rely on me in some small way, my voice and this music out here, staying with you, making the world seem a little less, what's the word I'm looking for, impersonal.

I mean, some of us have gotten to know each other, haven't we? You call up to request Sarah Vaughan, Joe Williams, Lady Day, we talk a while. And the next time you call, likely as not I'll know your voice, remember what music you like best.

I don't mind telling you, that's helped me get through a few bad nights. You too, I hope. Part of what all this, a show like this, is about. Not to mention the music itself.

But tonight's different. I'm sorry.

Without music, life would be a mistake. Nietzsche said that.

I guess maybe that could mean tonight's a mistake?

They say Mozart had music coming to him all the time—while dining with friends, pulling down Costanza's corset, shooting billiards, drinking wine—the music went on through it all, through everything, sounding perfectly in his head. Like a door that was always open, with this wind of music blowing through from somewhere else. All he had to do whenever he wanted to was stop, sit down, write out what he heard.

Remember Murray Abraham playing Salieri in the movie they made about Mozart, *Amadeus*? They're rolling Salieri through the halls of the insane asylum there at the end. "I absolve you. I absolve you all."

Most of you know, I've been doing this show a long time now, ten to three every night, seven days a week. I get home about four, I'm still wired, it's going to be hours before I can even think about getting to sleep. Martha (that's my wife?) she's been in bed since a little after I left, and she'll be getting up for work about the time I'm going down. I used to spend the time watching old movies. *Citizen Kane*, *The Big Clock*, *Casablanca*. Then a few years into it, I figured I'd seen all the good ones, most of them several times. Did I mention *Philadelphia Story*? They don't make many good ones anymore, a few. And movies, even the really good ones, aren't like music. Movies wear out on you.

None of you know Martha, of course, and she never listens to the show, so she doesn't know anything at all about you. Sometimes lately it feels like I'm living two separate lives. Like those stories you hear, some guy had a family in Detroit, another one in San Diego, owned two homes, had kids, and neither life had anything to do with the other. So I have this one life, where I sit here playing music or talking to you, with most of the city shut down around us. And then there's this other one, where I eat meals, take Martha out for Italian when I can, pay bills and worry about them, cut the legs off old jeans to make shorts, pull up bedspreads at the top and tuck them in at the bottom. And neither life has anything at all to do with the other.

Any of you remember that story by Hemingway, "A Clean Well-Lit Place," something like that? I read it back in high school. My father who art in nada, hallowed be thy nada, and so on. I was fifteen, sixteen, I thought that said it all. I don't know. Maybe in a way it does. I guess Hemingway must have thought so when he pulled his favorite shotgun down off the wall and stuck it in his mouth to kiss it goodbye.

Kind of scary how much of my life I've spent right here in this chair, when I think about it. Some of the most important parts, anyway, parts I remember best. You think on it long enough, everything comes down to parts. Of course, I'm just a voice to You Out There. None of you have any idea what it looks like in here, where the voice comes from. Where it lives. Okay. It's well-lit—for a circle about three feet all around me anyway. Clean, well, that's another thing.

Kind of a *non*place, now that I think about it, somehow exempt from the world. Floats like a lily pad, always the same, while under-neath, everything else goes on changing.

I've got two big steel desks, big enough you could park cars on them, pushed up together to make an L. Equipment's on one of the desks and pretty well covers it, turntables, CD players, mike and all that. Other one has the log, a ledger where I have to write down what goes on, what music I play, the times. Most people don't know we have to keep records like that. Second desk's also got what folks in the business call the trades, *Billboard* and so on, on it, and a stack of memos from station managers that I've been watching grow all these years, has to be six, seven inches high by now. Which is about how many station managers we've had in the same period, six or seven.

The chair, the very same chair all these years, all of us taking turns in it, is green plastic, with padding torn away at the arms and worn away at the back and bursts of thick cotton stuffing like fusilli hanging from the seat. It's on rollers that work part-time. It's our history.

There's nobody else here, never is. Not like on TV where the talk-show host and his producer or engineer are always signaling to each other like a couple of fools through the glass. There's an engineer all right, but he's in a separate building, a Quonset hut kind of thing out by the interstate, with a broadcast tower that looks like a skinny oil derrick above it and a Denny's next door.

So I'm all alone here.

Except for you, of course.

Martha never did understand fine music. Couldn't see the point somehow. It just goes on and *on*, doesn't it? she'd say when I put on Brahms or Mahler. And jazz made her nervous. Said she could never tell where it was going. Which is kind of the point, of course. But sometimes you see it's just not going to do you any good to go on talking, and you give up.

Look, here's something else: there aren't going to be any PSAs—that's public service announcements—any giveaway tickets or news updates off the wire tonight, either. Who knows, maybe we should even have a few minutes of silence later on. One of the big prob-lems these days is how small the world's become. We've stuffed it full of things—information, facts, theories, buildings, people, cars.

And now we think *everything* has to be filled, every moment, every newspaper or magazine, every moment of free time, every broadcast hour, every conversation. Till it's all so full there's no room left in the world for mystery anymore . . .

. . . No, that wasn't the moment of silence I mentioned earlier. I had a phone call, something I had to take care of. Ordinarily, of course, I'd have been playing music while I talked, some Bessie Smith, maybe the Mound City Blue Blowers. But tonight's different.

Some of *you* may be trying to call, too. So I need to save you the trouble, tell you the phone's not working anymore. Lot of things stop working after a while.

I'm standing at the window now looking out, with the headset on, so you can still hear me. Nothing but darkness out there. I'm standing in darkness, too. Desks and the circle of light back there like a campfire, or a city, I've walked away from. Stars overhead. Tiny points of light all but lost in the sky, that people keep trying to make sense of.

Most things you *can't* make sense of, it's that simple.

Back when we first got together, I spent hours playing sides for Martha, telling her about New Orleans, the Chicago sound, bebop, Bill Evans. I'd turn down the volume on Mozart arias to hum themes before they emerged. If the human voice isn't in it somewhere, I told her, it's not music . . .

. . . Now here we all are, on the night watch again. Walking the deck at midnight. You know what I sometimes think? That the only reason we're here is to keep watch while others sleep, make sure the world doesn't change too much on them.

I'm not sure what just happened. The lights went off. Black as the inside of a black box in here. Power failure of some kind, I assume—though I still see streetlights burning outside, half a mile or so away up the hill, where the houses start.

I can't see enough to tell, but probably the emergency generator's already kicked in. If it hasn't, then it will any minute now. So I'll just keep talking. Some of you could be in darkness too. Maybe my voice is all you have to hold on to. And if we can't help one another at times like this, what good's any of the rest of it?

But I've thought some more about it, and I'm going to have to go back on what I told you earlier. There *will* be music tonight after all, while we wait for them to get the power back on, wait for whatever broke to get fixed.

I've cued it up already, working by touch in the darkness.

I'm going to play Mozart's *Requiem* for you. Because it's great music, sure. Some of the finest ever written. But also because it's what I played for Martha after dinner tonight, before I came to the studio.

She loved it.

UKULELE AND THE WORLD'S PAIN

Sure, I killed the son of a bitch. I mean, what right did he think he had, bursting out in laughter like that when I took Miss Shelley out of her case? I'm a professional, too. I was getting scale just like him. I've paid my union dues and a lot more dues besides.

It was a good date. Sonny Martin had made a name for himself in country music, and now he was doing what he'd been talking about doing for years, he was cutting a jazz album. I'd played on a couple of Martin sessions before. He liked the freshness of the sound, I guess. And he knew that jazz was my first love, too. One time during a session break, I remember, I think this was on his album *Longneck Love*, we started goofing on "Don't Get Around Much Anymore," just the two of us, and before we knew, everybody else had picked his instrument back up and was playing along.

Playing music's not about making sounds, you know, it's about listening. Everything unfolds out of the first note, that first attack.

Sonny always reminded me a lot of the great George Barnes, just this plain, balding, fat guy with a Barcalounger and two or three cheap suits at home doing his job, only his job happened to be, instead of working as an auto mechanic or Sears salesman, recording country hits. Or in this case, playing great jazz and backup. You half-expected a cigar stump to be sticking out of his mouth there above the Gibson.

By contrast, the guy who thought Miss Shelley was so funny was a real Bubba type with stringy hair, glasses that kept sliding down his nose and getting pushed back up, and run-over white shoes with plastic buckles most of the gold paint had come off of. He played a fair guitar, but you know what? That's not enough. Besides him, there was a drummer who looked vaguely familiar and couldn't have been more than nineteen, the great, loose Morty Epstein on bass, and a pianist who gave the impression of spending more time in concert halls than with the likes of us.

We slammed around on a twelve-bar shuffle just to start the thing running and get acquainted, and that went well, with the guitar sliding in these little pulls, bends and stumbling, broken runs way up high—Sonny's guitar was so solid Bubba could float. But toward the end he left off that and, staying high, started strumming on just two or three strings, looking over at me.

Sonny called "Sweet Georgia Brown" and we worked it through a time or two by ear, kind of clanging and clunking along, then Sonny had the guitar player scribble out some quick charts. I got mine and we started running it and a line or two in, looking ahead, I can see it's wrong. So I just played right on past it, grinning at the guitar player the whole time. As we started winding down, Sonny nodded me in for a solo. I took a chorus and it was pretty hot and he signaled for another and that one was steaming, and then we all took off again. I looked over and the piano man's staring at me, shaking his head, fingers going on about their business there below. Looks like he just ate a cat.

Next we worked up a head version of a slow, ballady blues, then put some time in on jamming "Take the A Train" and "Lulu's Back in Town." Again Bubba threw some charts together and again mine was wrong—wildly wrong this time. He did everything but hop keys on me. I don't know, maybe his mother was frightened by some Hawaiian when he was in there in the womb growing that greasy hair and trying on those white shoes.

That's where Miss Shelley and her kin came from—you all know that. But you probably don't know much more. That it emerged around 1877, most likely as a derivative of a four-string folk guitar, the *machada* or *machete*, introduced to the islands by the Portuguese. Or how it hitched a ride back to the US with returning sailors and soldiers. Martin started selling them in 1916; Gibson, Regal, Vega, Harmony and Kay all offered standard to premium models alongside their guitars, banjos and mandolins; National manufactured resonator ukes. Briefly, banjo ukuleles came into favor. Other variations include the somewhat larger taropatch, an eight-string uke of paired strings, and the tiple, whose two outer courses of steel strings are doubled, with an additional third string added to the two inner courses and tuned an octave lower. Mario Maccaferri, the man who designed the great Django Reinhardt's guitar, after losing half a million or so with plastic guitars no one would buy, recouped with sale of some nine million plastic ukes. And the players! The ever-amazing Roy Smeck. Cliff Edwards, known as Ukulele Ike. Or Lyle Ritz. Trained on violin, he was a top studio bass player in the sixties and seventies and turned out three astonishing albums of straightahead jazz ukulele.

We worked through what we had again, then broke for lunch. Morty and I grabbed hot dogs at the taco stand by the park across the street and sat on a bench catching up. The fountain was clogged with food wrappers, leaves and cigarette butts as usual. Kids in swings were shoved screaming toward the sky. Old men sat on benches tossing stale bread at pigeons. Morty's son had just started college all the way up in Iowa, he told me, studying physical chemistry, whatever that was. Better be looking for more gigs, I said. He shook his head. Don't I know it, he said. Don't I know it. I told Morty I had a quick errand that couldn't wait, I'd see him inside.

Well, we got back from lunch break, as you know, everybody but the guitar player, and after we wait a while and drink up a pot of coffee Sonny says: Anybody see Walt out there? But none of us know him, of course, and who'd want to look at that greasy hair while he was eating?

So we—Sonny, I should say—finally called the session off, shut it down. And I do regret that. Some fine music was *this close* to being cut.

Can I tell you one thing before we go?

There's this story about Eric Dolphy. He's called in to overdub on a session. Brings all his instruments along. He listens to the tape and what he does is he adds this single note, on bass clarinet, right at the end. That's it. He collects scale for the session, puts his horn back in the case, and goes home. But what he did there, what that one note was, was Dolphy finding his holy moment, you know? That's what we're all looking for, what we go on looking for, that single holy moment, all our lives.

DRIVE

Much later, as he sat with his back against an inside wall of a Motel 6 just north of Phoenix, watching the pool of blood lap toward him, Driver would wonder whether he had made a terrible mistake. Later still, of course, there'd be no doubt. But for now Driver is, as they say, in the moment. And the moment includes this blood lapping toward him, the pressure of dawn's late light at windows and door, traffic sounds from the interstate nearby, the sound of someone weeping in the next room.

The blood was coming from the woman, the one who called herself Blanche and claimed to be from New Orleans even when everything about her except the put-on accent screamed East Coast—Bensonhurst, maybe, or some other far reach of Brooklyn. Blanche's shoulders lay across the bathroom door's threshold. Not much of her head left in there: he knew that.

Their room was 212, second floor, foundation and floors close enough to plumb that the pool of blood advanced slowly, tracing the contour of her body just as he had, moving toward him like an accusing finger. His arm hurt like a son of a bitch. This was the other thing he knew: it would be hurting a hell of a lot more soon.

Driver realized then that he was holding his breath. Listening for sirens, for the sound of people gathering on stairways or down in the parking lot, for the scramble of feet beyond the door as others arrived and stood there, waiting, poised. If there were others.

Once again Driver's eyes swept the room. Near the half-open front door a body lay, that of a skinny, tallish man, possibly an albino. Oddly, not much blood there. Maybe it was only waiting. Maybe when they lifted him, turned him, it would all come pouring out at once. But for now, only the dull flash of neon and headlights off pale skin.

The second body was in the bathroom, lodged securely in the window from outside. That's where Driver had found him, unable to move forward or back. This one had carried a shotgun. Blood from his neck had gathered in the sink below, a thick pudding. Driver used a straight razor when he shaved. It had been his father's. Whenever he moved into a new room, he set out his things first. The razor had been there by the sink, lined up with toothbrush and comb.

Just the two so far. From the first, the guy jammed in the window, he'd taken the shotgun that felled the second. It was a Remington 870, barrel cut down to the length of the magazine, fifteen inches maybe. He knew that from a *Mad Max* rip-off he'd worked on. Driver paid attention.

Now he waited. Listening. For the sound of feet, sirens, slammed doors.

What he heard was the drip of the tub's faucet in the bathroom. Then something else as well. Something scratching, scrabbling . . .

Some time passed before he realized it was his own arm jumping involuntarily, knuckles rapping on the floor, fingers scratching and thumping as the hand contracted.

Then the sounds stopped. No feeling at all left in the arm, no movement. It hung there, apart from him, unconnected, like an abandoned shoe. Driver willed it to move. Nothing happened.

Worry about that later.

He looked back at the open door. Maybe that's it, Driver thought. Maybe no one else is coming, maybe it's over. Maybe, for now, three bodies are enough.

Up to the time Driver got his growth about age twelve, he was small for his age, an attribute of which his father made full use. The boy could fit easily through small openings, bathroom windows, pet doors and so on, making him a considerable helpmate at his father's trade, which happened to be burglary. When he did get his growth he got it all at once, shooting up from just below four feet to six-two almost overnight, it seemed. He'd been something of a stranger to and in his body ever since. When he walks, his arms flail about and he shambles. If he tries to run, often as not he'll trip and fall over. One thing he can do, though, is drive. And he drives like a son of a bitch.

Once he'd got his growth, his father had little use for him. His father had had little use for his mother for a lot longer. So Driver wasn't surprised when one night at the dinner table she went after his old man with butcher and bread knives, one in each fist like a ninja in a red-checked apron. She had one ear off and a wide red mouth drawn in his throat before he could set his coffee cup down. Driver watched, then went on eating his sandwich: Spam and mint jelly on toast. That was about the extent of his mother's cooking.

He'd always marveled at the force of this docile, silent woman's attack—as though her entire life had gathered toward that single, sudden bolt of action. She was never good for much else afterwards. Driver did what he could. But eventually the state came in and prised her from the crusted filth of an overstuffed chair complete with antimacassar. Driver they packed off to foster parents who right up till the day he left registered surprise whenever he came through the front door or emerged from the tiny attic room where he lived like a wren.

A few days before his sixteenth birthday, Driver came down the stairs from that attic room with all his possessions in a duffel bag and the spare key to the Ford Galaxie. His foster father was at work, his foster mother off conducting classes at Vacation Bible School where, two or three years back, before he stopped going, Driver won the prize for memorizing the most scripture. It was mid-summer, unbearably hot up in his room, not much better down here in the kitchen, and drops of sweat fell onto the note as he wrote it.

I'm sorry about the car, but I have to have wheels.
I haven't taken anything else. Thank you for taking
me in, for everything you've done. I mean that.

Throwing the duffel bag over the seat, he backed out of the garage, pulled up by the stop sign at the end of the street, and made a hard left to California.

They met at a low-rent bar between Sunset and Hollywood, east of Highland. Uniformed Catholic schoolgirls waited for buses across from a lace, leather and lingerie store and shoe shops full of spike heels size fifteen and up. He knew the guy right away when he stepped through the door. Pressed chinos, T-shirt, sport coat with sleeves pushed up. De rigueur gold wristwatch. Copse of rings at finger and ear. Soft jazz spread from the jukebox, a piano trio, possibly a quartet, something rhythmically slippery, you couldn't quite get a hold on it.

He grabbed a neat whiskey, Driver stayed with what he had, and they went to a table near the back. Driver dropped the shot glass of vodka, like a depth bomb, into his beer.

"What I hear is, you're the best."

"I am."

"Other thing I hear is you can be hard to work with."

"Not if we understand one another."

"What's to understand? I run the team, I call all the shots. Either you sign on to the team or you don't."

"Okay. Then I don't."

Guy threw back what remained of his whiskey and went to the bar for a new round.

"Care to tell me why?" he asked, setting down a new beer and shot.

"I drive. That's *all* I do. I don't sit in while you're planning it or running it down. I don't take part, I don't know anyone, I don't carry weapons. I just drive."

"Attitude like that has to cut down something fierce on offers."

"It's not attitude—it's principle. And I turn down more work than I take."

"This one's sweet."

Briefly, he told Driver about the score. One of those rich communities north of Phoenix, seven-hour drive, acre upon acre of half-a-mill homes like rabbit warrens, crowding out the desert's cactus. Then, writing something on a piece of paper, he pushed it across the table with two fingers. Driver remembered car salesmen doing that. People were so goddamned stupid. Who with any kind of pride, any sense of self, would go along with that? What kind of fool would even put up with it?

"This is a joke, right?" Driver said.

"You don't want to participate, don't want a cut, there it is. Fee for service. Keep it simple."

Driver stood. "Sorry to have wasted your time."

"Add a zero to it," he said.

"Add three."

"No one's that good."

Driver shrugged. "Plenty of drivers out there. Take your pick."

"I think I have." He held up his empty glass. "Four on the team, we split five ways. Two shares for me, one for each of the rest of you. Done?"

Driver nodded.

Just as the alto sax jumped on the tune's tailgate for a long, slow ride.

He wasn't supposed to have the money. He wasn't supposed to be a part of it at all. And he ought to be back at work doing double-eights and turnarounds. Jimmie, his agent, probably had a stack of calls for him. Not to mention the shoot he was supposed to be working on. The sequences didn't make much sense to him, but they rarely did. He never saw scripts; suspected the sequences wouldn't make a lot more sense to the audience. But they had flash aplenty. Meanwhile all he had to do was show up, hit the mark, do the trick. "Deliver the goods," as Jimmie put it. And he always did.

That Italian guy with all the forehead creases and warts was on the shoot, starring. Driver didn't go to movies and could never remember his name, but he'd worked with him a couple of times before. Always brought his coffee maker with him, slammed espressos the whole day like cough drops. Sometimes his mother showed up and got escorted around like she was queen.

So here he was.

The score'd been set for nine that morning, just after opening. Seemed ages ago now. Four in the crew. Cook who'd put it together. New muscle up from Houston by the name of Strong. The girl, Blanche. Him driving, of course. They'd pulled out of LA at midnight. Blanche would grab everyone's attention while Cook and Strong moved in.

Driver'd been out three days before to get a car. He always picked his own car. The cars weren't stolen, which was the first mistake people made, pros and amateurs alike. Instead, he bought them off

410 • JAMES SALLIS

small lots. You looked for something bland, something that would fade into the background. But you also wanted a ride that could get up on its rear wheels and paw air if you needed it to. Himself, he had a preference for older Buicks, mid-range, some shade of brown or gray, but he wasn't locked in. This time what he found was a ten-year-old Dodge. You could run this thing into the side of a tank and not dent it. Drop anvils on it, they'd bounce off. But when he turned the motor over, it was like this honey was just clearing its throat, getting ready to talk.

"Got a back seat for it?" he asked the salesman who'd gone along on the test drive. You didn't have to push the car, just run it through its paces. See how it cornered, if its center stayed put when you accelerated, slowed, cut in or out. Most of all, listen. There was a little too much play in the transmission for his taste. Clutch needed to come up some. And it pulled to the right. But otherwise it was about as perfect as he had any right to expect. Back at the lot, he crawled underneath to be sure the carriage was straight, axles and ties in good shape. Then asked about the back seat.

"We can find one."

He paid the man cash and drove it off the lot to one of several garages he used. They'd give it the works, new tires, oil and lube, new belts and hoses, a tune-up, then store it, where it would be out of sight till he picked it up for the job.

Next day, his call was at 6 A.M., which in Hollywoodese translated to show up around eight, nine. Guy working second unit held out for a quick take (why wouldn't he, that's what he got paid for) but Driver insisted on a trial run. Buggy they gave him was a white-over-aqua '58 Chevy. Looked cherry, but it drove like a goddamned mango. First run, he missed the last mark by half a yard. Good enough, the second-unit guy said. Not for me, Driver told him. Man, second-unit came back, this is what? two minutes of a film that lasts almost two hours? That rocked! Plenty of drivers out there, Driver told him. Call the union.

Second run went like a song. Driver gave himself a little more time to get up to speed, hit the ramp to go up on two wheels as he sailed through the alley, came back down onto four and into a moonshiner's reverse to face the way he'd come. The ramp would be erased in editing, and the alley would look a lot longer than it was.

The crew applauded.

He had one other scene blocked for the day, a simple run against traffic down an interstate. By the time the crew finished setting up, always the hardest part, it was almost one. Driver nailed it on the first run. Two-twenty-three, and the rest of the day belonged to him.

He caught a double-header of Mexican movies out on Pico, downed a couple of slow beers at a bar nearby making polite conversation with the guy on the next stool, then had dinner at the Salvadoran restaurant up the street from his crib, rice cooked with shrimp and chicken, fat tortillas with that great bean dip they do, sliced cucumbers and tomatoes.

By then he'd killed most of the evening, which is pretty much what he did when he wasn't working one job or the other. But even after a bath and half a glass of scotch he couldn't get to sleep. Should have paid attention then. Life sends us messages all the time, then sits laughing over how we're not gonna be able to figure them out.

So at 3 A.M. he's looking out the window at the loading dock across the street wondering if the crew over there, hauling stuff out of the warehouse and tucking it away in various trucks, is legal. Probably not. No further activity on the dock, no job boss, a certain furtiveness. Maybe he should heat things up, call the police, watch while it got more interesting. But he doesn't.

Around five, he pulled on jeans and an old sweatshirt and went out for breakfast at the Greek's.

Things start going wrong on a job, sometimes it starts so subtly you don't see it at first. Other times, it's all dominoes and fireworks.

This was somewhere in between.

Sitting in the Dodge pretending to read a newspaper, Driver watched the others enter. There'd been a small line waiting outside the door, five or six people. He could see them all through the blinds. Blanche chatting with the security guard just inside the door. Other two looking around, at the point of putting guns in the mix. Everyone still smiling, for now.

Driver also watched:

An old man sitting on the low brick wall across from the storefront, knees stuck up like a grasshopper's, struggling to get his breath;

Two kids, twelve or so, skateboarding down the sidewalk opposite;

The usual pack of suit-and-dress people heading for work clutching briefcases and shoulder bags, looking tired already;

An attractive, well-dressed woman perhaps forty years old walking a boxer from both sides of whose mouth strings of gluey saliva hung;

A muscular Latino offloading crates of vegetables from his double-parked pickup to a Middle Eastern restaurant down the block;

A Chevy in the narrow alley three storefronts down.

That one brought him up short. It was like looking in a mirror. Car sitting there, driver inside, eyes moving right to left, up, down. Didn't fit the scene at all. Absolutely no reason for that car to be where it was.

Then sudden motion inside caught his attention—everything happened fast, much of it he'd put together later—and Driver saw the backup guy, Strong, turn toward Blanche, lips moving. Watched him go down as she drew and fired before hitting the floor as though she'd been shot herself. Cook, the guy who'd put it all together, had begun firing in her direction.

He was still thinking *What the fuck?* when Blanche came barreling out with the bag of money and threw it onto the new back seat.

Drive!

Drive he did, pulling out in a brake-accelerator skid between a Fed Ex truck and a Volvo with a couple dozen dolls on the shelf by the rear windshield and a license plate that read EARTHSHIP2, not at all surprised to find the Chevy wheeling in behind him as he watched Earthship2 crash-land into the sidewalk bins of a secondhand book-and-records store.

Air would be thin there for Earthship2, the new world's natives hostile.

The Chevy stayed with them for a long time—the guy was that good—as Blanche sat beside him hauling money by the handful out of the gym bag, shaking her head and going, *Shit! Shit!*

The suburbs saved them, just as they saved so many others from the city's awful influence. Finding his way to the subdivision he had scouted earlier, Driver barreled onto a quiet residential street, tapping the brakes once, again, then again, so that by the time he reached the speed trap he was cruising a steady twenty-five. Not knowing the area and not wanting to lose them, the Chevy had come charging in. Driver watched in the rearview mirror as local cops pulled it over. Squad pulled up at an angle behind, motorcycle mountie in front. Guys would be telling this story back at the station for weeks.

"Shit," Blanche said beside him. "Lot more money here than there ought to be. Has to be close to a quarter of a million. Shit!"

"I'm gonna run across and grab something to eat," Blanche said. "I saw a Pizza Hut over there and I'm starved. Sausage and extra cheese okay?"

"Sure," he said, standing near the door, by one of those picture windows on aluminum tracks that all motels seems to have. The lower left corner had sprung out of the frame and he could feel warm air from outside pouring in. They were in a second-floor room facing front, with only the balcony, stairway and twenty yards or so of parking lot between them and the interstate. The motel itself had three separate exits. One ramp onto the interstate was off the intersection beyond the parking lot. Another was just up the street.

Had to be Blanche, of course. No other way the Chevy was down there in the parking lot.

She'd taken a brush out of her purse and started into the bathroom.

He heard her say "What—"

Then the dull boom of the shotgun.

Driver went in around Blanche's body, saw the man in the window, then slipped in blood and slammed into the shower stall, shattering the glass door and ripping his arm open. The man still struggled to free himself. But now he was lifting the gun again and swinging it toward Driver, who, without thinking, picked up a piece of the jagged glass and threw. It hit the man full on in the forehead.

Pink flesh flowered there, blood poured into the man's eyes, and he dropped the shotgun. Driver saw the razor by the sink. He used it.

The other one was doing his best to kick the door in. That's what Driver had been hearing all along without realizing what it was, that dull drumming sound. He broke through just as Driver came back into the room—just in time for the shotgun's second load. Thing was maybe twenty inches long and it kicked like a son of a bitch, doing more damage to his arm. Driver could see flesh and muscle and bone in there.

Not that he was complaining, mind you.

From inside he heard the bleating of a terminally wounded saxophone. Doc had ideas about music that were different from most people's.

"Been a while," Driver said when the door opened to a nose like a bloated mushroom, poached eyes.

Doc stood there blankly. The sax went on bleating behind him. He glanced back that way, and for a moment Driver thought he might yell over his shoulder for it to shut up.

"No one plays like that anymore," Doc said with a sigh.

He looked down then, for what seemed a long time. "You're dripping on my welcome mat."

"You don't have a welcome mat."

"Used to. Then people somehow started getting the notion I meant it . . . You're selling blood, I don't need any."

"*I* will, if you don't let me in."

Doc backed off, gap in the door widening. Man had been living in a garage when he and Driver first met, more years ago than either of them wanted to think about. Here he was, still living in a garage. Bigger one, though; Driver'd give him that. Doc had spent half a lifetime dispensing marginal drugs to the Hollywood crowd before he got shut down. Had a mansion up in the Hills, people said, so many rooms no one ever knew who was living there. People would wander up a stairwell during a party and not show up again for days.

"Have a taste?" Doc asked, pouring from a half-gallon urn of drugstore-brand bourbon.

"Why not?" If things went the way he hoped, he'd need it. If not, he'd need it even more. "Cheers," he said. Doc had all but filled a glass so bleary it might have been smeared with dirty Vaseline.

"That arm doesn't look so good."

"You think?"

"You want, I could have a look at it."

"You sure?"

"Please," he said. "Let me help. Let me be of use to someone again, just this once."

He scurried about gathering things. Driver watched closely. Some of the things he gathered were a little scary.

"Can't tell you how much I miss it," Doc said. "Medicine was the great love of my life. Never had another woman, never needed one. Been a while, though, like you say. Sure hope I remember how."

Rotted teeth broke into a smile.

"Relax, young man," he said, pushing Driver into a chair and swiveling a cheap desk lamp toward him. "Just having my fun. Just kidding." The bulb flickered, failed, came back when Doc thumped it. Taking a healthy swig himself, he handed Driver the half-gallon of bourbon.

"Have a few more hits off this, boy. Chances are you'll need them. Maybe we both will, before this is over. You ready?"

Nothing in the car to lead him anywhere. He'd have been surprised if there were. Clean as a parched bone.

He had no way of running down the registration. Even if he had, it would almost certainly turn out to be faked.

Okay.

When the heavyweights didn't come back, whoever had sent them, whatever heads and bosses were up there above the whole thing, they'd would start looking for the car. Driver figured the best thing he could do was move the Chevy, stow it where it would be hard but not *too* hard to find, hang out and wait.

So for two days, arm aching like a son of a bitch every moment of every minute of every hour, imaginary knives slitting it from shoulder to wrist again and again, Driver sat across from the mall where he'd parked the Chevy. He forced himself to use the arm, even for the chi-chi coffee he bought, $3.68 a cup, at the open stand just inside the mall's east entrance. This was in Scottsdale, back toward

Phoenix proper, a high-end suburb where each community had its own walls, and where stores in malls tended toward a Neiman-Marcus/Williams-Sonoma axis. Sort of place a vintage car like the Chevy wouldn't seem out of place. But Driver'd parked it on the lot's outer edge in the sketchy shade of a couple of paloverdes to make it easier to spot.

Not that it much mattered at this point, but he kept running things down in his head.

Cook had set them all up, of course. Driver'd seen Strong, go down—for good, to every appearance. Maybe Strong had been part of the set-up, maybe just a pawn in Cook's game. Blanche he wasn't sure about. She could have been in from the first, but it didn't feel that way. Maybe she was only looking out for herself, keeping options open, trying to find her way out of the corner she and Driver had been shoved into. Far as he knew, Cook was still a player. No way Cook had the weight or stones for those guys in the Chevy, though. So he had to be fronting.

Making the question: Who was likely to show?

Any minute a car could pull up with goombahs inside.

Or maybe, just maybe, the bosses would insist, the way it sometimes worked, that Cook clean up after himself.

Nine-forty A.M. on the third day, every breeze in the state gone severely south and blacktop already blistering, arm hanging off his shoulder like a hot anvil, Driver thought: *Okay then, Plan B*. He watched Cook in a Crown Vic circle twice on the outer ring and pull into the lot just past the Chevy. Watched him get out, look around, amble toward the parked car, key in hand. Cook opened the driver's side, slid in. Soon he emerged, went around back and popped the trunk, leaned in.

Then, suddenly, he straightened and started to turn.

Driver was there.

"Shotgun's not much good anymore," he said. "Blanche isn't, either. But I thought a few props might help you remember what went down, what you're responsible for."

He had Cook in a choke hold he'd picked up on breaks from a stunt man he worked with on a Jackie Chan movie.

"Hey, relax. Guy I learned this from told me the hold's absolutely safe on a short-term basis," he said. "After four minutes, the brain starts shutting down, but up till then—"

Loosening his hold, he let Cook drop to the ground. Cook's tongue was extended and he wasn't breathing. A certain blueness to the skin. Tiny stars of burst blood vessels about the face.

"Always a chance I didn't get it quite right, of course. And it has been a while."

Driver took Cook's wallet, nothing much of use or note there, then went to the Crown Vic to toss that. A clutch of gas-station receipts jammed into the glove compartment, all of them from the downtown area, Seventh Street, McDowell, Central. Four or five pages of scrawled directions to various spots in and around Phoenix, mostly unreadable. An Arizona roadmap. A sheaf of coupons bound together with a rubber band:

NINO'S PIZZA
(RESTAURANT IN BACK)
719 E. LYNWOOD
(480) 258-1433

From a phonebooth, Driver called the number on the coupons. The phone rang and rang—after all, it was still early. Whoever answered was adamant, as adamant as one could be in dodgy English, that Nino's was not open, that he would please have to call back after eleven.

"I could do that," Driver said, "but I don't think your boss will be happy waiting that long. Why don't you go tell him I've taken over for Cook."

Shortly a heavy, chesty voice came on.

"Nino." Probably couldn't spell it, but he pronounced it with authority.

"I have something of yours."

"Yeah, well, lots of people do. I got a lot of stuff. You have a name, too?"

"I do. Just as soon keep it."

"Whatever you say. I don't need no more names. What's this about Cook?"

"Wanted to let you know he's now keeping company with Strong and Blanche. Not to mention the goons you sent to a certain Motel 6."

Driver could hear the man breathing there at the end of the line.

"You some kind of fuckin' army?"

"I drive. That's what I do. All I do."

"Have to tell you, it's sounding like sometimes you might give a little extra value for the money, you know what I mean?"

"People make deals, they need to stick to them."

"That's what my old man always said. Been known to repeat it a few times myself."

"I haven't counted, but Blanche told me there was something like two hundred grand."

"And you're telling me this why?"

"It's your money. You say the word, it could be at your back door within the hour. But once it shows, we're even, right? That's the deal. You forget Cook, the goons. You forget all of it. No one steps up to me a week from now with your regards."

"Hey. I can live with that."

Six A.M., first light of dawn, like the world was stitching itself back together out there, recreating itself as he looked on. Blink, and the warehouse across the way was back. Blink again, the city loomed in the distance, like a ship coming into port. Half a dozen nervous birds skittered from ragged tree to ragged tree. Cars idled at curbside, took on human freight, pulled away.

Streets and highways filling.

Driver sat in his apartment sipping Scotch from the only glass he'd kept. The Scotch was Buchanan's, a mid-range blend. Not bad at all. Forties swing played on a cheap radio beside him. There was no phone, nothing of value, no furniture beside what came with the apartment. Clothes, razor, money and other essentials stayed in a duffel bag by the door.

A good car waited in the parking lot.

Sooner or later they'd come after him, of course, despite Nino's assurances. It was only a matter of time. Sooner or later Nino, money securely in hand, would get around to thinking how the bosses couldn't let this go—how they couldn't let it get out that hired help had brought them to heel.

Probably Nino had known that from the first. Driver, too.

So sky might fall, or ground rear up. If word failed to issue from Nino, bosses would send it down: Take care of this. Or it would rise from young enforcers looking to make themselves: I'll take care of this. One or the other.

Driver looked out on interstate, balcony, parking lot. Poured the last of the Buchanan's into his last glass. Guests soon, no doubt about it.

WHEN FIRE KNEW MY NAME

Cold, driving weather like this always brought them out.

It had been there in early morning, a presence, a threat, a promise, and by seven had honed itself to a cleaver-like edge on the strop of wind. From my window on the fifth floor I listened to the schlep-schlep-schlep of that edge on the strop and watched as day congealed and the blade began to slice away at the city.

They emerged on their canes and crutches, in wheelchairs, tottering on artificial and makeshift limbs or balanced like flat-bottomed urns on low carts, pulling themselves along with gloved hands. At these times there is an expression on their faces that's difficult to describe. Pain, yes—but within it, at the core, the thing that pain comes wrapped around, a kind of joyfulness, I think.

Others, those to whom the world belonged, walked with heads down, swaddled in scarves and layers of wool and heavy caps. But the survivors tore open their own shabby coats and raised faces to the sky, threw out their arms to embrace it all: this wind, this blade, this impossible city.

"Don't tell me. The fire brigade's out." Somehow or another, originating in the punch line of a joke, I'm sure, that had become our name for them. Sandra stood in the doorway arch whose frame evoked both Chinese calligraphy and *pi* with sheet and blanket wrapped about her, a human teepee. Her hair, so blond it was almost white, had begun growing back in. It poked out a quarter-inch or so all around and she was convinced she looked like a dandelion. "Shut the shockin' window before your nose falls off."

"Yeah, and I've only got *one* of those."

In college, as was the fad for a couple of years, she'd had an ear removed. Half the people in the city her age were walking around with newly grown ones, but that wasn't Sandra's style. She started something, she stayed with it.

"If I shut the window, it frosts over and I can't see out."

"What—they look different this time?"

But of course they never did. They were as generic and predictable as spring, as the run of our daily lives, the news and entertainment piped in to us, what we said to one another. I shut the window. Wind howled as though in complaint and shook the pane fiercely with both hands.

"Breakfast?"

"I'd planned on fishes, but we're fresh out of loaves."

"The cupboard was bare."

"In a word."

"Not even a bone."

"A few exoskeletons, but I don't think those count."

Sandra and wrappings sank into one of the chairs. "I was dreaming," she told me. "Standing on the street looking up at a billboard." With one hand she sketched its cadence, form and line breaks on air. "We're almost done / World finished soon / Thank you for your patience / B&D Construction.

"I'm standing there and I have this warm feeling in my stomach. I realize that for months, as cold winds blew in across bare plains to the east, I've been coming out each morning to admire new buildings that appear overnight, to be among the first to stroll new plazas, arcades, explore tiny parks. I'm tremendously proud of my city, what it's becoming.

"But there's also, it seems, a problem. When I return to my apartment, six brutally handsome young men in jeans, black T-shirts and low-slung tool belts are waiting in the hall outside. They have to tear out my floor, they say. Possibly the walls as well. They'll know once they get started. But will I be able to stay here while you work? I ask them. Sure, no problem, the foreman says. Long as you don't need a floor or walls."

Rising, Sandra walked into the kitchen area and, ever the child of Famine parents, came out with a half-loaf of bread fetched from one hiding spot or another. I drew hot water, crumbled in tea leaves, and we fell to.

We'd been together almost four years. I'd gone with friends to HOUSE OF th'OUGHT and wound up sitting beside her. The House was another of those intermittent hot spots thronged with patrons

for months when it opened, afterwards all but abandoned. Here
great books were read aloud, in shifts, by professional readers.
We were never able to agree on what was being read at the time. I
remembered *Tristram Shandy*; Sandra insisted that, by then, Burning
Cinder Person, the House's star reader and frequent subject of profiles in local papers during the House's brief heyday, was well into
the nineteenth century.

(*In halflight she turns, murmuring, and I trace the scars along her
back, by the shoulder blades. The sky splits open like a wound, and
birds cough the sun into morning.*)

"So what's on for today?" she asked.

"Have to deliver my Cowboy tapes to Epoch-Z."

Cowboy's a figure so legendary that many claim he never existed.
Supposedly he was the first of the great urban freedom fighters—
some say the last as well—and went down in the siege of the markets.
But street wisdom has it that Cowboy's still out there. He'd never
been photographed except—possibly—for less than sixty seconds of
blurry footage I'd caught years ago while filming deconstruction of
the Skystop Building. One of the news channels was putting together
a documentary on Cowboy. They'd learned of my tapes and offered
enough money to keep me afloat, us afloat, for a year.

"What, you can't just shoot it to them? You're going outside? To
someone's shockin' *office*?"

I shrugged. "They actually called up, on the phone. 'We may
be on the bitter sharp edge, but we're also a little old-fashioned
'round here,' they tell me, 'in our own way.' Before I know it, I'm in
a conference call with half a dozen vice presidents ranging in age
between eighteen and eighteen-and-a-half. 'We like our people to
have faces,' they tell me."

Jack London said to understand totalitarianism, picture a boot
heel stamping on a human face—forever. Big business is soft Italian-
leather loafers caressing that same face. However long and hard we
espouse bohemian, alternative, libertarian, contrary lifestyles, we
all live off big business, fleas on a dog. I tried to remember when
heads of major corporations had begun showing up for work in
pullovers and jeans. Revolution in America? Radical change? The
country's very genius is its capacity to absorb anything, absolutely

anything—to appropriate it, bear it on a flood into the mainstream, vitiate it.

"Anything I can pick up while I'm out?" I asked.

"Ginger would be good, for tonight's curry. Oh, and I guess some vegetables and rice. So there'll *be* a curry? Assuming I ever see you again."

"Think of it as an adventure," I said.

"Think of it as stupid," she said. "Not to mention the possibility of freezing nose, fingers and like wee appendages off."

"*Wee?* Did you say *wee?*" Reaching for a Scottish accent, which came out, inexplicably, Jamaican.

"Don't forget the ginger."

We say it together: "A Redemptionist never forgets."

There on the street away from river's edge, I encountered a more normal population—normal for this quarter of the city, that is. Fully half those out in the bite and slash hobbled along on feet with tendons fatally damaged by the police's standard interrogation technique: if they didn't like your answer, they stood on your foot and heaved you mightily backwards. Meanwhile uptown folk were paying clinics huge sums to have facial muscles injected with botulism. The bacteria paralyze the muscle and, in doing so, erase age lines. When these people talk, their eyebrows don't move but float cloudlike above their mouths, like dialog balloons in cartoons.

I began to penetrate the city's many folds and strata. I've always suspected it to be more laminate than veneer, thin sheets pressed close to form something of apparent substance, nothing, not even inferior materials, at its core.

At the corner of Market and Force, several hundred protestors converged in absolute silence on the plaza before City Hall. Riot police formed a human moat around the complex, beating sticks backhand against shields. The juxtaposition was uncanny. Protestors stood motionless looking across. Police beat at their shields. At some invisible cue the protestors withdrew as silently as they'd come.

At First and Desire, a small park had been set fire by the Children's Army. *We burn the bones they throw us*, a placard read. Children in red armbands stood alongside monitoring, making certain the fires did not spread. The fires were doing anything but, however. They were lowering, folding in upon themselves, benches turning to smolder. One of the children stepped forward into the park and gave a fingers-into-palm, come-to-me sign. *Incoming*, he shouted as half a dozen Molotov cocktails rained from windows of the high-rise project skirting the park.

Two blocks up, a crowd had gathered. They shouted encouragement, chanted, raised fists in the air. Leaning against the wall of a nearby credit union was a piece of cardboard cut from a heavy box and laboriously hand-lettered in cockeyed, backward-leaning block letters.

STREET FITING!

It was already over, though, the crowd dispersing, as I approached. One man lay broken and bleeding, body in the street, head on the curb as though on a pillow. I watched as his eyes went still. The other, the winner, wiped blood from *his* eyes and picked up the hat with the money. Then he walked to the sign, lifted it for a closer look, tucked it underarm. His now. Spoils.

The city I find when I come out into it, the one I'm a part of, is invisible to many. As though the city's gone belly up, as though this gray sky were an overturned stone. These are the forgotten people, the ones who don't matter, those ground down on the city's mill, used up, thrown beneath the wheels. Here there is neither history nor future, only a perpetual present tense of motion, hunger, need, and momentary ease, a fire that consumes and goes on consuming, through whose flickering silent tongues sometimes we glimpse the shape, the form, the suggestion, of another reality, another world. A better one? Different, at least. And different is enough.

"Cowboy!" I cried out.

He stood at a street corner, buckskin fringe blowing in the breeze, looking a little confused when I approached him. We were at the dangerous border between uptown and down. Age lines crouched like homesteaders, deep-set, at eyes and mouth. I took note of the missing ear.

"What's up?" I said. Like so many others, looking for guidance.

"What's ever up but more of the same? Just they practice new grimaces in the mirror is all, tell us more outrageous lies. *You* feel connected?"

No.

But had I ever?

"We have to keep changing. Dodging under, going over, scrambling. We can't let them get a hold, take us for granted."

"But you . . ."

Seeing the sudden sadness in his eyes, I understood. He was an icon. He couldn't change.

"Here's my ride," he said, stepping not into the city bus one would have thought he awaited but into an ancient VW bus. "Keep the faith?"

I watched him pull away.

Against the horizon the day still burned into life and burned steadily away, like alcohol, in a blue flame. No heat to any of it. What could a man do?

After a moment I snapped an ear plug off the tab and fit it in as I started walking again along the street, past crews of workers tearing up streets, crews of workers rebuilding them. You never know what you'll get, of course, that's part of the deal, but this was okay. *We'll Meet Again in Glory*. I watched my breath go out in plumes with each step.

Glory was the next town over.

GET ALONG HOME

It won't be long.

I nodded.

Sorry to take you away.

No problem. I told you I'd be here.

I always knew you would.

A nurse practitioner stepped into the room. As she did so, lighting came up perceptibly, brightening around our small island of bed, table, chair. Is there anything you need? she asked. Her signing was rapid, assured; until then I'd not been conscious of signing, only that we were speaking, speaking the way it seemed we'd always spoken. I'd slipped back into it so naturally, after all these years.

No, but thank you, Tish said. You're so kind.

And to me, once the nurse had withdrawn: There's so much I have to tell you, to ask you.

I nodded. A pigeon lit on the sill outside. Sad looking bird. It staggered on its way to the window, its beak bent back on itself when it pecked at the window. But a bird nonetheless. Most of the others were extinct. How long since I'd even seen one?

Have you been happy? she asked.

Yes.

And are you now?

Most days, I think.

You always had good answers, love.

The pigeon's eye was an orange jewel. It bobbed its head up and down, side to side in that curious stitch they have, trying to understand. Knew it should be wary, wasn't sure of just what.

Everything.

We never get very far from where we start, do we?

That said, her hand fell back exhausted onto the sheet. The word *breathless* came to me.

It's what they call in sports a broken-field run, I told her. They all know where you're headed, but there's that whole field between here and there. You keep moving, keep dodging. Everything's footwork, evasion, misdirection.

They?

The opposition. The visiting team.

She sat looking out at the pigeon.

I hate to ask this, but . . .

Seeing where her eyes went, I said: It's all right. I arranged her gown about her, helped her onto the bed pan. Flesh on hips and stomach had collapsed, folding in on itself like a tent being taken down. She seemed almost weightless. Breasts, too, hung limp and deflated. Our selves, our identities, are so linked to sexuality. When we no longer have that, in a sense I suppose we become something else.

Once I had wanted this woman so badly. And once this body, like my own, ached just to be wanted. Where do all those feelings go? Into some ozone layer, maybe, out of sight and mind. Forever building up, protecting us quietly.

She turned her face to the wall, eyes unblinking, as I cleaned her.

I brought this for you, I said afterwards.

She held up the clear disk, turning it side to side, watching me through it.

A game I designed. I worked on it a long time. The producers think it's a sure hit.

Her eyes said: Tell me about it.

A man is on his way home from work. Everything goes wrong. He doesn't have exact change, the subway founders, a trio of terrible musicians comes aboard his car. Finally he exits, and comes up into a part of the city he can't recognize at all. He begins walking. Nothing is familiar. He's surrounded by whores in red boots, guys without bottom halves who cruise the city on plywood rafts atop roller skates, twitchy teens stepping off curbs to meet cars and glancing up every four seconds to rooftops, lawyers who've set up offices on the street like lemonade stands, an Islamic Mormon shepherding his flock of wives down toward the harbor. The goal's to get him home.

I hope it does well for you.

Me too. I've a lot of time invested.

Years ago, she said after a moment, I knew a man who was going to be a painter.

Yes, I said. I knew him too.

She nodded, and her eyes went to the window. The pigeon was gone. Rectangle full of darkening sky.

Maybe you should rest now.

Okay.

There are some things I need to take care of. I'll be back later.

Smiling, she closed her eyes. I was almost to the door when I heard her knock on the bedside table, and turned.

"I thought this would be more interesting," she said, aloud. From such long disuse and from the damage done, her voice was a poor engine. She had to repeat what she'd said before I understood. Many years had passed since last I heard it, but the disappointment in her voice was something I knew well.

As I stepped into the hall, the nurse practitioner rose from a molded plastic chair. She held one of those heavily waxed packages of juice with a midget straw. Her name tag was a simple rectangle: Carson.

"Do you have any questions?"

I shook my head.

"You do understand, I hope: It wasn't a decision she made lightly."

"To die, you mean."

"We all die, Mr. Decker."

"Most of us for reason, though."

"She has reasons. Some of them we can understand, a lot we never will. Not that it matters."

"That sounds perilously close to mysticism, Ms. Carson."

"We don't much pretend to science here. We're more like . . . I don't know . . . wilderness guides, maybe. Helpmates."

She finished her drink and dropped the package into a reclamation bin. With some surprise I realized that we'd been speaking aloud. I had resurfaced, I was back in the world.

"She never could stand decisions being made for her. You know that better than anyone. And it explains a lot, for those of us who need explanations."

"One could look at it that way. Or as easily consider it little more than another expression of massive ego. Just another performance."

Like the time she'd crawled, naked and without language, out of the ice sculpture of a mammoth that artisans had spent eighteen hours carving. Or the way, years back, back when she spoke, she'd sit on stage and slit her skin with razors while reading aloud from the daily newspaper.

"It won't be long, Mr. Decker. You're leaving?"

I nodded.

"I'll call you, if you'd like."

I thanked her and gave her my number. Like the pigeon, I left. Soon I'd be extinct, too. We all would. Meanwhile the goal was to get me home. I had a good chance of making it.

BLUE YONDERS

I stood and watched as the dogs, our dogs, swept down the hill into battle, a thrilling sight however many times one has seen it. Their own, emerging from runnels and arroyos, appeared instantly to meet ours, as if somehow materialized from the ground itself. Soon the field was a mass of leaping, tumbling, snapping, tearing bodies. Some of the dogs went straight for the throat; others struck at haunches or flanks to maim and disable, to bring their opponents down quickly, then moved on. Wave after wave drove down from the trees, off the horizon cradled atop this hill. Rank after rank rose from the low ground to meet them. The dogs went about their work in absolute silence.

Eventually, as always it must be, it was over. Their general stood now on the hill across from mine. As I walked down into the valley, as I lifted my eyes, he lowered his. We nodded to one another.

Unlike the dogs, we, the people of my village, did not go silently about our business, but called out encouragement and direction to one another over their bodies, spoke quietly, commented, even laughed from time to time, as we cleared the field. Men hoisted the bodies chest-high and laid them out on carts and litters; women followed, scooping up severed limbs and entrails in wooden shovels; small children pulled travoises or carried water about to workers. The clearing took, as always it does, many hours, at the end of which we were in equal parts exhausted, exhilarated.

In the village, afterwards, there was feasting. Fresh meat grilled on skewers over slow fires of cypress and fig, fresh meat stewed with turnips and a variety of other roots in clay pots over those same fires, fresh meat chopped with purple and green peppers, wrapped in palm leaves and buried in the coals. Savory smoke rolled everywhere, eyes and mouths watered. Bal strummed the single string of his banjer as Ariana improvised songs celebrating our triumph, celebrating, too, each of the dogs that had given its life for us. At one point Bal, taken up with the song, strummed so fiercely that the string broke. As he set about preparing another, this being a process that required some time, Ariana continued a capella her praise of the dogs, of their courage and devotion: praise of the flesh that, having so ably and expertly defended us, now enriched us.

Later along still, when feasting and songs were over and only dregs of sweet-potato wine remained asludge in the bellies of the barrels, three young women sat cross-legged outside my tent, speaking in low whispers among themselves. Twelve to fourteen summers they had seen, perhaps a dozen such great wars. Baskets of fruit ripe like themselves sat beside these women, other baskets filled with stones polished round and smooth by the river, sacred mud still clinging to them. Taking a bite from each of the fruits, I set them in a line before the woman I'd chosen and circled her with stones. The others departed to return to their families, their parents, brothers; to await the next deliverance.

Her name, she told me, was Chai. Because she came from another village, it was a name I had not heard before, the *C* turning, almost before one heard it, into an *S* on her lips. She smiled then took in her breath quickly when I entered and broke her, and afterwards, in her sleep, spoke quietly to herself or perhaps to some dream companion, drawing up her knees like a child.

A short night it was, and the whole of it I lay there alongside Chai, my wife. Outside, the moon shone and rippled like a pool of white water. Toward dawn a plaintive wind blew up from the lowlands. In their corrals, in their sleep, the new dogs moaned and tossed restlessly about, hungry for glory.

CHRISTIAN

Sometimes he is there again, with the field burning around him, trees at the perimeter igniting one by one, flaring up like birthday candles. Sometimes it happens at night and he wakes in a pool of sweat. Sometimes he hears the pop-pop-pop of rifles in the distance set against the whoosh of trees igniting, sometimes it all takes place in silence. Sometimes, though not as often, it comes upon him by day.

The ceiling is so low that, legs spread and raised straight up, short as she is, her toenails scratch at it. Basically her home is a cardboard shipping case that's been stuccoed into some sort of permanence and place. Her toenails are long and slightly curved. He listens to this, listens to the scrape of the swayback bed against the wall as he pushes into her, hears the cry of hawkers in the street outside with their vegetables and rice, their bundles of lemongrass and herbs and seasoned rice tied with twine, their canvas bags of prawns and tiny crabs. She has not said a word the whole time, nor will she. She never does. Two infants stand on tiptoe in a crib made of green bamboo, watching, eyes white as boiled eggs.

He got to be known as Christian because once, upon completing an assignment, he stood for a moment with head down—as though in prayer, his backup, an ill-dressed, illiterate young man of twenty or so, thought.

   He was tired, nothing more, but the name stuck.

He's five and his father has taken him for ice cream. One of those late summer evenings that seem to go on forever. They sit outside, a low stone wall onto which Father has lifted him. City lights gleam behind. He can smell the sweet flowers at the base of the wall as insects bang into his ears and neck. I have spent my life leaving, his father says. A lifetime of giving things up. Leaving behind my class, my home, my country—my soul. Promise me you won't let the world to do to you what it has done to me. The boy has no idea what Father is talking about, of course. But dutifully he promises.

The bark and roar of fireworks began. In his sixth-floor apartment through a rift between buildings off Third Avenue Christian watched them: spinning wheels, nebulae, immense palm trees of red and blue and green that sprouted, grew huge in an instant, and expired. Earlier, pigeons had been lined up like putti in the crannies of buildings and peering down from cornices. Now they were gone.

He'd been in New York for most of a week, since June 29th, living in an apartment sublet through an ad in the New York Review of Books. Its owner wished to evade the worst of the New York summer and spend these months, instead, on a beach in Massachusetts. He could have provided references, of course, but the heft of his check (drawn to an account he'd never again use) proved reference enough.

He found himself quite close by Gramercy Park, that odd bit of city real estate reserved for local homeowners and hotel guests, all of whom are in possession of keys. Meanwhile, outside, the flotsam of the city, its driftwood, washes by. From time to time these can be seen with faces pressed to the bars and locked gates.

In Chinatown the stores were filled with takeouts for hell. The Chinese burn paper imitations of things from this life to send with the newly dead into the other, things they will have need of there. Hell notes—false paper money—had always been available. But now the shops held shelf upon shelf of paper shirts, cars, make-up kits, evening slippers, cutlery, keys, armchairs, luggage, tea sets. Since his last visit, paper computers, cell phones and CD players had appeared as well—even a palm pilot or two. Like us, the dead must keep track of their appointments.

Christian had an appointment of his own. He was looking for a man named Shelley, a man who in public life, as a Washington lobbyist, wielded tremendous invisible power and who, in personal life, was enamored of anything perceived to be on the cultural cutting edge. Christian had spent his nights on roundabout tours of the Village, SoHo, NoHo, Tribeca, Park Slope, Queens. He'd witnessed klezmer played by an orchestra of kazoos of every size, exhibitions of toast sculpture and lawn ornaments, a theatrical improvisation in which the title on the marquee was left blank to be filled in after the performance, plays delivered with actors' backs turned to the audience, a one-man show featuring an old tin washtub in which the ice sculpture of a half-submerged, bright-green alligator slowly melted. Then, out in Williamsburg, in the basement of a Unitarian church, an extraordinary dance recital.

The curtain opened on a group of androgynous dancers in blue-green light. They lay, at first, motionless on the floor, and when they began to move, it was slowly, so slowly that one couldn't be sure there'd been movement at all. Something troubling, alien, even repulsive about it. They writhed and rolled and reached about in ways that had nothing to do with being human. They had become primitive organisms, sea-creatures just beginning to explore their surround, groping blindly toward food, reproduction, spinal columns, dry land, cliff dwellings, cities. All this conducted in absolute silence.

Christian carried those forms away with him. In doorways as he walked to the subway stop, past the train's window at Bedford Avenue and at Fulton Street, in dark recesses of stations and in crèches passed once the train dove underground, those primordial creatures writhed still in their agony of becoming.

At Bergen they transferred. Just past Jay Street-Borough Hall, Christian moved onto the seat alongside Shelley.

He lives in Hoboken, New Jersey, but sometimes, remembering his father's stories, imagines himself in the old country, in a courtyard there. Smell of cabbage soup seeping down like a stain from upper floors, an old man seated in a kitchen chair outside one of the identical doors of the featureless block of apartments playing accordion. He's twelve. He waits out back by the trash bins. Soon enough she'll be along. She'll crouch low staring at him and after a while, still in a crouch, ease forward to the spillover about the bins, sniffing through it for food. For weeks he sat without moving against the far wall. Then began moving closer, inches each day. Eventually he got her to take a frankfurter (all he could raid from the refrigerator with some chance it might not be noticed) from his extended hand. She never came closer to him than that. She'd approach cautiously, take the food, and withdraw a yard or so to eat, watching him the whole time.

Sometimes other cats showed up there as well. They'd arch backs, turn sideways to make themselves appear larger, hiss, growl. But Gray wasn't like that. Half the size of most of them, scrawny and chronically undernourished, she never hesitated, never displayed. She simply, upon sight, rushed and tore into them. Most of her teeth were gone, probably from just such confrontations. But those other cats always fled.

Much of a year went by. He gained over a foot in height, a frosting of dark hair on his face, a voice he couldn't control. Gray gained weight; her coat began to look smooth and full. Then one day after school, as always, he went out to see her, carrying food he'd saved from his cafeteria lunch, and found something there by the bins that he didn't understand. He walked closer. It was an animal trap of some kind. And under its sharp jaws, in a pool of thick dark stuff, lay what looked like a rabbit foot.

He never saw Gray again. But he waited there for hours with his baseball bat until the trap's setter came to check. An older man from the apartments, who wore plaid pants and a yellow nylon shirt and kept licking his lips, and who smelled bad.

He'd tried on the good American life. It didn't fit.

The ideal world inside his parents' eighteen-inch TV had little to do with the real one he saw around him. Like a pinball he bounced from college to jungle back to college to advertising copywriter to teaching at a junior college. His country kept threatening war against largely TV-less countries. Its heroes turned from statesmen and creative artists to eighteen-year-old singers and movie actors of dubious talent.

Suddenly he had a wife, and this house in Dallas not far from Highland Park. Then one day as he left work on the way home he just kept driving. He'd called before he left; she was fixing meatloaf and mashed potatoes for dinner. Up around Plano, when the BMW ran out of gas, he got out and walked.

• • •

She was a liberal running for congress in proto-conservative Arizona and had the opposition running scared. She didn't think of herself as a liberal, far from it, but she had these peculiar notions, absolute equality, percentage taxation without breaks, open access to medical care, things like that, all of which made her suspect despite the fact that she'd served in the Air Force, a pilot no less, and been multiply decorated during the Gulf War. The good old boys who shepherded party and state just had no idea what to do with or about her. They ignored her as long as they could.

Way it works is, you get a message, usually by phone. You call back, they call back. Till finally there's a meeting somewhere and the job gets laid out.

Christian liked her from the first, as he watched from afar. The way she carried herself. Strands of gray that ran through her hair. The dark suit she wore that first time he saw her, almost like a man's, even to a kind of stylized necktie. He carried back the sound and sight of her laughter to his room at Motel 6. Next day he went to the library, the one downtown that looked like a ship under sail, and dug in.

"What the hell's this?" his runner asked three days later.

"Front money," Christian said.

"So—what? You're not fulfilling the contract?"

"Discretion's implicit. I'm discretioning."

"They won't like this."

Christian shrugged. His hand fell onto the runner's atop the table and gripped it hard.

"Take a message back for me. Tell them nothing happens to her."

"Just what the fuck's *your* problem?"

"Anything does—anything even starts to happen to her—first, I come after you. Then I take down the contractor. Then I go after the clients."

"You really think you can do that, man? There are too many of them."

"There always are."

Christian released his hand.

He put the runner down two weeks later, leaving him in the restroom of a $$$$ restaurant in Georgetown with credit cards fanned at his feet like a poker hand. The first contractor was found garroted on the butcher-block table in the house to the right of the congresswoman. It had been on the market for two months. A half-assembled rifle lay beside him. Days later, a body showed up in the pool of another house just down the street, at the intersection, rubber duck glued to the coarse hair and thick blood on its chest.

Downtown, looking over at the spire of Westward Ho!, once Phoenix's luxury hotel and bustling with celebrities, he sat as a herd of young children on a field trip broke around him, their adventure overseen by stale, sweet-smelling men in khaki slacks, print shirts and running shoes. The children all lugged backpacks. It would be a tough journey.

PPs, his father had called them. The privileged proletariat. Mottled pink cheeks, hair snipped to uniform height and perfect lines like their lawns, even the light in their eyes dialed down to a modest gleam. Nothing in the world, not giant rats nor pestilence nor the man stepping out of the alley with a broken bottle as you pass, was scarier than these folk.

Christian glanced at his watch. Almost one. The man he was looking for would be along shortly.

Long ago the Roseannes, Mariah Careys and George Bushes of this country had colonized imaginations, took them over entire. Hackneyed dreams have been driven like shrapnel into our beings and, lodged too close to vital organs, cannot be removed. Feudalism has been reinstated. The media live in the big house.

Two messengers had been sent after him so far, two that he knew of, the first a shooter intending a single, clean takedown off the roof of a midtown garage (he'd caught the glint of the rifle barrel in a car window), the second a couple of guys who stepped up to him out of an alley downtown and wanted, before doing their job, to make sure he understood how tough they were and who moments later lay in the alley's mouth, participles eternally adangle, grammar forever uncorrected.

• • •

Election night, Christian sat up late, sipping brandy and levering Vienna sausages from cans with thumb and forefinger, clicking back and forth from an old movie to poll results. His candidate (and he smiled, thinking how this was the way he thought of her, this man who had never and would never vote) won by a narrow margin.

He supposed he must have been very drunk by the time final results were in. Vaguely, the next morning, he remembered standing before a mirror in conversation.

I won't try to explain my actions, he said . . . This has nothing to do with redemption . . . After a lifetime, one good act, even that one equivocal, it can't make much difference . . . She's a decent, honest woman . . .

He remembered turning then from mirror to window, where rain ran down, bearing the world away.

Sometimes he is there again, with the field burning around him, trees at the perimeter igniting one by one, flaring up like birthday candles. Sometimes it happens at night and he wakes in a pool of sweat with the pop-pop-pop of rifles and the whoosh of trees still in his ears. Sometimes, though not as often, it comes upon him by day.

And this, too: One time, not far off, he steps from the cover of tall buildings into an open space, into sunlight, and looks up. There is no reason for the shadow he sees there before him. No tree or cloud, no tower, no plane. What I did, he thinks, was small, but good. He steps into the shadow and comes to a standstill there, smiling, waiting.

CONCERTO FOR VIOLENCE
AND ORCHESTRA

To the memory of Jean-Patrick Manchette

It is a beautiful fall day and he has driven nonstop, two days chewed down to the rind and the rind spit out, from New York. He should be tired, exhausted in fact, spent, but he isn't. Every few hours he stops for a meal, briefly trading the warm vinyl Volvo seat for one not unlike it in a string of Shoney's, Denny's and Union 76 truck stops. On the seat and the floorboard beside him are packets of water crackers, plugs of cheese, bottles of seltzer and depleted carry-out cups of coffee, wasabi peas. In the old world he drove away from, tips of leaves had gone crimson, bright yellow and orange, gold. Now he is coming into the desert outside Phoenix, the nearest thing he ever had to a home. Crisp morning air rushes into open windows. He passes an ostrich farm, impossibly canting stacks of huge stone-like primitive altars out among the low scrub and cholla, a burning car at roadside with no one nearby. On the radio a song he vaguely remembers from what he thinks of as Back Then plays. He is happy. Strangely, this has nothing to do with the fact that soon he will be dead or that within the past month he has killed four people.

Pryor was the one who told him about it. There were these small rooms behind the huge open basement area used for church dinners, summer Bible School, youth meetings, evenings of amateur entertainment where groups of teenagers blackened faces with burnt cork and donned peculiar hats for minstrel shows, nerdish young men in ill-fitting suits and top hats urged objects from thin air and underscored the tentativeness of it all by transforming silk handkerchiefs to doves, sponge balls to coins, and where the church's music director in his hairpiece trucked out again and again, relentlessly, his repertoire of pantomime skits: a man flying for the first time, a foreigner confronted for the first time by Jell-o, a child on his first fishing trip forced to bait his own hook. (Is there something intrinsically funny about firsts?)

In the ceiling of one of those rooms was a small framed section, like a doorway. You could drag the table beneath, Pryor said, place a chair on the table, reach up and push the inset away. Then you could climb up in there. And if you kept going, always up, along stairways and ladders and catwalks, in and out of cramped crawlspaces, eventually you'd arrive at the steeple, where few before had ever ventured. A great secret, Pryor intimated. The whole climb was probably the equivalent of three floors at the most. But to Quentin's eyes and imagination then, the climb seemed vast, illimitable, and he felt as though he might be ascending into a different, perhaps even a better, world.

It would not take much, after all. For it to be a better world.

Pushing the door out of its frame and pulling up from the chair, legs flailing, Quentin found himself in a low chamber much like a closet turned on its side. He couldn't stand erect, but the far end of the chamber was unenclosed, and he passed through into an open, vault-like space with a narrow walkway of bare boards nailed to beams. The nailheads were the size of dimes. Four yards or so further along, this walkway turned sharply right, fetching up rather soon at the base of a stairway steep and narrow as a ladder. The last few yards indeed *became* a ladder. Then he was there. Alone and far above the mundane, the ordinary, all those lives in their suits and cars and their cluttered houses with pot roasts cooking in ovens and laundry drying on lines out back. Quentin had seen *Around the World in Eighty Days* half a dozen times. This must be what it was like to go up in a balloon, float free, feel the ground surrender its claim on you. He was becoming David Niven.

Meanwhile he'd given no thought to Pryor, who seemed to have failed to follow, if indeed Pryor had begun at all.

Sunday School teacher Mr. Robert, however, had been giving them both thought. He'd only a quarter-hour past dismissed the boys, and now took note of their absence from services. So it was that, shortly after attaining his steeple, Quentin found himself being escorted down the aisle alongside Pryor and deposited in a front pew as Brother Douglas paused dramatically in his sermon, light fell like an accusing finger through stained-glass windows illustrating parables, and the entire congregation looked on.

He was caught that time, but never again.

The steeple became Quentin's special place. Just as other children spend hours and whole days of their lives sunk into books, board games or television, so Quentin spent his in the steeple, there by speaker horns that had taken the place of bells, sandwiches and a thermos of juice packed away in his school lunch box. Since of all things at his disposal his parents were least likely to miss one can of it among many, the sandwiches were generally Spam, which Quentin liked with mayonnaise and lots of pepper, sometimes sliced pickles. The bread was white, the juice that in name only, wholly innocent of fruit, rather some marvelous, alchemical compounding of concentrates, artificial flavors and Paracelsus knows what else.

Sometimes up there in the steeple Quentin would pull himself to the edge and lie prone, propping elbows at the correct angle and sighting along an imaginary rifle as Jenny Bulow, Doug Prather or the straggling Dowdy family climbed from cars and crossed the parking lot below.

Years later, half a world away and more than once, Quentin would find himself again in exactly that same position.

But this has nothing to do with his life now, he always insisted—to himself, for few others knew about it. That was another time, another place. Another person, you might as well say. Quentin came home from that undeclared war and its long aftermath an undeclared hero even to himself, and after much searching (*You have no college? You have to have college!*) took a job at Allied Beverage, where he still works. Where he worked until last month, at least. He hasn't been in, or called, and doubts they've held the position for him. It's not as though they'd have much difficulty finding someone to take up his slack: keep track of health-care benefits, paid time off, excused absences, time and attendance, IRAs. Holidays the company loaded employees up with discontinued lines, champagnes no one asked to the prom, odd bottled concoctions of such things as cranberry juice and vodka, lemonade and brandy, licorice-flavored liqueurs. After work they'd all be out in the parking lot stowing this stuff in trunks. It would follow them home, go about its unassuming existence on various shelves and in various cabinets till, months or years later, it got thrown out. The company made little more ado over throwing away its people.

He pushed. Recently there'd been rain, and enough water remained to bear the body away. But you couldn't see the water. It looked as though the body were sliding on its back, on its own momentum, along the canal. Further on, an oil slick broke into a sickly rainbow. Food wrappers, drink containers, condoms, beer cans and unidentifiable bits of clothing decorated the canal's edge. Down here one entered an elemental world, cement belly curved like a ship's hold, walls to either side as far as one could see. Jonah's whale, what Mars or the moon might look like, a landscape even more basic than that stretching for endless miles around the city. Out there, barren land and plants like something dredged from sea bottoms. He looked up. Air shimmered atop the canal's cement walls, half a dozen palm trees thrust shaggy heads into the sky. The body moved slowly away from him in absolute silence. Out a few yards, it hit deeper water, an imperceptible incline perhaps, and picked up speed, began to turn slowly round and round. Water had soaked into the fabric of the man's cheap blue suit and turned it purple. Blue dye spread out like a stain in the water beneath him. When he looked up again, two kids were there on the wall, peering over. Their eyes went back and forth from the body to him. He waved.

He'd picked up a new car nearby, in one of those suburbs with walls behind which the rich live so safely, at a mall there. Tempted by a Lexus, he settled on a Honda Accord. That's what this country does, of course, it holds out temptation after temptation, forever building appetites that can't be assuaged. He didn't know if the Crown Vic was on anyone's list yet, but over the past few days he'd pushed it pretty hard. Probably time to change mounts. He left it there by the Accord. The whole exchange took perhaps five minutes.

For that matter, he had no reason to believe anyone might be on him, but one didn't take chances. Never move in straight lines.

He drove out of town, out into the desert, everything earth-colored so that it was difficult to say where city ended, desert began. But after a time, the walls, walls around individual houses, walls around whole communities, petered away. Lemon trees were in bloom, filling the air with their sweet sting. Bursts of vivid oleander at roadside. Imperial cactus.

The Accord handled wonderfully, a pleasure to drive. He settled back and, looking about, started to come to some sense of the life its owner lived. A small life, circumscribed, routine. Scattering bits of rainbow, a crystal keychain swung from the rearview mirror. The compartment behind the gear shift held tapes of Willie Nelson, Johnny Mathis, Enya, Van Morrison. A much-thumbed copy of *Atlas Shrugged* on the floor. The owner had tossed empty water bottles behind his seat after screwing the tops back on, so that many of them had collapsed into themselves. There were a couple of bronchodilator inhalers in the glove compartment. Find yourself without one, tap the guy next to you and borrow his: everyone in the state carries them. Physicians used to send what were then called chest patients here for their health. They came, bringing their plants and their cars with them. Drive into Phoenix, the first thing you see's a brown film on the horizon. The city diverts water from all over to keep lawns and golf courses green, buys electric power at a premium to run the city's myriad air conditioners. Its children gulp for air.

On the rear floor there were two-hundred-dollar running shoes, in the backseat itself a sweatshirt and windbreaker from Land's End, a red baseball cap, a deflated soccer ball, a thick yellow towel. In the bin just fore of the gearshift he found the notice of a bank overdrawal that George Hassler (he knew the name from the registration) had crumpled and thrown there. Angrily?

America.

Was there any more alien a landscape than the one in which he found himself—this long, trailing exhaust of desert, mountains forever in the distance—anywhere? He drove across dry runnels marked Coyote Wash or Aqua Fria River, chugged in the new carapace past piles, pillars and Πs of stone to challenge Stonehenge or Carnac, past crass billboards, cement oases of gas stations, fast-food stalls and convenience stores chock full of sugary drinks, salty snacks, racks of sunglasses, souvenir T-shirts, Indian jewelry. Past those regal cactus.

They stood like sentinels, in an endless variety of configurations, on hillside and plain, some of them over forty feet. Most never made it through their first year of life. Those that did, grew slowly. A saguaro could take 150 years to reach full height; in another fifty years it died. Some would never develop arms, while others might have two or four or six all upraised like candelabras, or dozens of them twisted and pointing in all directions. No one knew why this happened. Shallow and close to the surface, root systems ran out as much as a hundred feet, allowing the plants rapidly to soak up even minimal rainfalls. As the cactus took on water, its accordion-like pleats expanded. Woodpeckers and other birds often made their way into it to nest. Some, particularly hawks and the cactus wren, preferred to nest at junctures of arm and trunk. Red-tailed hawks would build large platform nests there; they'd come back again and again, every year, till the pair stopped nesting altogether. Over a six-week period in May and June, brilliant flowers emerged atop mature cacti. These would bloom for twenty-four hours only, opening at night, closing forever against the heat of day.

Lizards were everywhere, and just as ancient. They scampered out from beneath tangles of cholla, crouched soaking up sun atop stones, skittered across the highway, minds clenched on memories of endless rain forests, green shade, green sunlight. Brains the size of BB shot enfolded dioramas, whole maps in stark detail, of worlds long gone, worlds long ago lost.

At a truck stop near Benson, Arizona, where the pie was excellent, a young man came up to say he'd seen him arrive in the Honda Accord. On one wall dinner plates with figures of wildlife hung among framed photographs of motorbikes and vintage automobiles; on the other, portraits of John Wayne, Elvis, Marilyn and James Dean. Out back, a crude hand-painted sign with the cameo of a Confederate soldier and the legend Rebel Cafe leaned against a crèche of discarded water heaters, stoves, sinks and minor appliances from which a rheumy-eyed dog peered out, as from an undersea grotto.

The young man wore an XXL purple-and-blue plaid shirt over

a red T-shirt gone dull maroon, and well-used black jeans a couple of inches too long. The back half or so of the leg bottoms had been trod to shreds. Quentin's first thought as the young man approached was that he wore a baseball cap in the currently fashionable front-to-back style. But now he saw it was a skullcap. Knit, like those he'd seen on Africans.

"Had the Accord long?"

Quentin looked up at the young man. For all the alarm his question set off, this was obviously no cop. No more challenge or anxiety in those eyes than in Quentin's own. He approved, too, of the way the young man held back, staying on his feet, not presuming. Quentin nodded to the young man to join him. A corner booth. Nondescript beige plastic covering, blue paint above. Carpentry tacks stood out like a line of small brass turtles crossing the horizon.

"Had one myself," the young man said. "Accord, just like yours. Got off from work one day, came out and it was gone. First time I ever talked to police face to face."

The waitress came to refill Quentin's coffee. He asked if the young man wanted anything. He shook his head.

"Same week, my apartment got broken into. Took the stereo, TV, small appliances, most of the clothes. Even hauled off a footlocker I'd had since college, filled with God knows what. I came home from a six-mile run, took one look around, and said fuck it. Knew at some level I'd been *wanting* this to happen. Clear the decks. Free me to start over."

Sipping his third cup of coffee, Quentin watched truckers as they bowed heads over eggs and ham, looking to be in prayer. From nearby booths drifted strains of pragmatic seductions, complaints about jobs and wives, political discussions. A hash of all the age-old songs.

In the car the young man fell asleep almost at once. He'd propped feet on his duffel bag; the world bucked up unseen, unfired upon, in the notch of his knees. Choppy piano music played on the local university station. Quentin hit Scan. Sound and world alike tilted all about him, falling away, rearranging itself. Rock, country, news, chatter. Stone, cactus, wildflowers, trailer park.

Awake now, Quentin's passenger said, "Where are we?"

"Pretty much where we were before. It's only been a couple of hours."

He thought about that.

"Damn."

Roadside, an elderly Latino sold cabbage, cucumbers and bags of peppers out of the bed of his truck, the cover of which unfolded and sat atop rough wood legs to form a tent. A younger woman (daughter? wife?) sat on the ground in the shade of the truck, reading.

"Where we going?" Quentin's passenger said.

"East."

Toward El Paso, one of America's great in-between cities. They ate in a truck stop on I-10 just outside Los Cruces, a place the size of a gymnasium smelling of onions, hot grease and diesel. Meat loaf was the daily special, with mashed potatoes and boiled cabbage on the side. Using his fork like a squeegee, Quentin's passenger scraped his plate clean, then caught up with a piece of bread what miniscule leavings remained.

Eschewing the interstate, Quentin took the long way in, the back road as locals say, Route 28, skirting fields of cotton, chilis, onions and alfalfa, tunneling through the 2.7-mile green, cool canopy of Stahman Farm's pecan orchards, up past San Miguel, La Mesa, Chambertino, La Union. The sun was settling into the cleft of the mountains to the left, throwing out its net of evening to reel the world in. As they pulled onto Mesa, parking lots outside shops and offices were emptying, streets filling with cars, street lights coming on.

"You can let me out up at that corner," Quentin's passenger said. "Appreciate the ride. Looks like a good place, El Paso. For a while." He leaned back into the window. "They're all good places for a while, right?"

Dinner became caldo and chicken mole at Casa Herado, the rest of the evening a movie on the cable channel at La Quinta off Mesa on Remcon Circle.

In the space between seat and door on passenger's side, Quentin found a well-worn wallet bound with rubber bands and containing a driver's license, social security card and two or three low-end charge cards for James Parker. Left behind, obviously, by his passenger. Had the young man stolen it, lifted it, liberated it? Much of the gypsy about him, no doubt about that. But mostly Quentin remembered the young man's remarks about becoming free, starting over.

By five in the morning, light in hot pursuit, Quentin was on Transmountain Road heading through Smuggler's Pass to Rim Road where, at one of the slumbering residential palaces there, he swapped the Honda for a Crown Vic. Some banker or real estate salesman would greet the morning with unaccustomed surprise. Quentin hoped the man liked his new car. His own smelt faintly of cigars, spilled milk and bourbon. Wires had hung below the dash even before those Quentin tugged out and touched together. But when he goosed the accelerator in query, the car shuddered and roared to let him know it was ready.

Years ago in Texas, Quentin had witnessed an execution. The whole lethal injection thing was new back then, and no one knew just how to proceed. Some sort of ritual seemed in order, though, so things were said by the warden, a grizzled, stoop-shouldered man looking twice his probable age, then by a tow-headed chaplain looking half his. It was difficult to find much to say. Casey Cortland had led a wholly unremarkable, all but invisible life before one warm Friday evening in the space of an hour killing his wife of twelve years, his ten-year-old son and eight-year-old daughter, and the lay minister of a local church. Cortland was brought in and strapped to a table. Beneath prison overalls, Quentin knew, he was diapered. Unlike the warden and chaplain, Cortland had no final words. When they injected the fatal drug, he seized: the IV line pulled out and went flying, dousing all those seated close by with toxic chemicals. State police took Quentin, who'd caught the spray directly in his eyes, to Parkland. Though basically unharmed, for several weeks he suffered blurred vision and headaches. Hours later on the prison parking lot Quentin reclaimed his Volvo, then I-30. Hour by hour, chunks of Texas broke off and fell away in his rearview mirror. That night he had the dream for the first time. In the dream, along with an estimated half-million other viewers he watched as Tiffany's father was eaten on camera, the midmorning show live, producers and cameramen too stunned to shut it all down. Tiffany used to have a pair of earrings with the bottom half of a man hanging out of a shark's mouth. That's not what it was like. It wasn't like anything Quentin or other viewers had ever seen. Tiffany's father's legs rolled back and forth, feet pointing north-northeast, north-northwest, as the tiger chewed and pawed and pulled back its head to tear away chunks. There were sounds. Screams at first, then not so many. Gristle sounds, bone sounds. Growls. Or was it purring? Panels of experts, rapidly assembled, offered explanations of what this event said about society's implicit violence. Then Tiffany herself was there, sobbing into the microphone held close to her face like a second, bulbous nose. Daddy only did it for her, she said. He did everything for her.

All that day off and on, Back Then as he now thought of it, Quentin had spent writing a letter he hoped might persuade Allied's insurance carriers to reconsider Sandy Buford's claim. Every two minutes the phone rang, people kept washing up from the passageway outside his cubicle, his boss broke in like a barge with queries re one or another file, the list of calls to return and calls to be made seemed as always to grow longer instead of shorter. Sandy had hurt his back on the job and now, following surgery, wasn't able to lift the poundage Allied's job description required. He was a good worker, with the company over fourteen years. But since the surgeon had released him and he couldn't meet the job's bottom line—even though Sandy's actual work from day to day didn't call for lifting—the insurance carrier had begun disallowing all claims, refusing payment to physicians, labs and physical therapists, and effectively blocking the company's efforts to reemploy him. Quentin's letter summarized the case in concise detail, explained why Allied believed the carrier's disallowment to be inappropriate and in error, and put forth a convincing argument (Quentin hoped) for reevaluation.

Pulling out of the parking lot at 6:18, just a little over an hour late leaving, on the spur of the moment Quentin decided to swing by Sandy Buford's and drop off a copy of the letter, let him know someone cared. Quentin had called to let Ellie know how late he was running; she was expecting him home. But this would only take a few minutes.

Buford's address bore him to a sea of duplexes and shabby apartment buildings at city's edge. Many of them looked like something giant children, given blocks and stucco, might erect. Discarded appliances formed victory gardens in side and back yards. Long-dead cars and trucks sat in driveways, ancient life forms partially reconstructed from remains.

Quentin waded through front yards that may well have seen conga lines of children dancing their parents' preference for Adlai Stevenson over Ike (when had people stopped caring that much?) and climbed a stairwell where the Rosenbergs' execution could have been a major topic of discussion. One expected the smell of cooking cabbage. These days the smell of Quarter Pounders, Whoppers, Pizza Hut and KFC were far more likely, maybe a bit of cumin or curry mixed in.

Buford's apartment was on the third floor. There was music playing inside, sounded like maybe a TV as well, but no one responded to Quentin's knocks. Finally he pushed a copy of the letter, tucked into an Allied Beverage pay envelope, beneath it. He was almost to the second landing when he heard four loud cracks, like limbs breaking. Instinctively he drew back against the wall as two young men burst from the apartment nearest the stairwell. Both wore nylon stockings over their faces. Quentin moved forward, peered over the banister just as one of them after pulling off his stocking glanced up.

That was the footprint he left.

Careful to give the two men ample time to exit, Quentin continued down the stairs. He was turning the corner onto Central in his Taurus when the first police cars came barreling down it.

A dozen blocks along, he began to wonder if those were the same headlights behind him. He turned onto Magnolia, abruptly into the parking lot at Cambridge Arms, pulled back out onto Elm. Still there. Same brilliance, same level, dipping a beat or so after he dipped, buoying up moments later. He pulled into a Sonic and ordered a drink. Drove on a half mile or more before pulling up at the curb and getting out, motor left idling, to buy the early edition of tomorrow's newspaper. No lights behind him when he took to the street. Whoever it had been, back there, following him, was gone. If there'd been anyone. Only his imagination, most likely.

He said nothing of this to Ellie, neither as they had a preprandial glass of wine before the fireplace, nor as she pulled plates of flank steak, mashed potatoes and brussels sprouts, foil covered, from the oven, nor as, afterwards, they sat before the lowering fire with coffee. He spoke, instead, of the minutiae of his day. Office politics, the latest barge of rumor and gossip making its way upriver, cylinders banging, his concern over Sandy Buford. She shared in turn the minutiae of *her* day, including a visit to Dr. Worrell.

Head against his shoulder, 12:37 when last he glanced at the clock bedside, Ellie fell fast asleep. Quentin himself was almost asleep when he heard the crash of a window downstairs.

The car hesitates, only a moment, though it must seem forever, there at the lip.

He's not sure of any of this, of course. Not sure if it really happened, how it happened, where or when. More than once he's thought it might be only something suggested to him by a therapist; something he's read or seen on the dayroom TV whose eye is as bleary and unfocused as those of its watchers; something that he's imagined, a dream breaking like a whale from the depths of that long sleep. Yet it keeps coming back—like that other dream of a man being eaten by a tiger on live TV. Again and again in his mind's eye he *sees* it. It's as real as the plastic furniture, coffee makers and floor polishers around him—realer than most things in this world he's begun reentering. But mind is only a screen, upon which anything may be projected.

Go on, then.

The car hesitates there at the lip.

With no warning a woman's nude body, pale as the moon, had stepped into his headlights on that barren stretch of road. Flying saucers might just as well have set down beside him.

He'd left Cave Creek half an hour past. No houses or much of anything else out here, no lights, headlights or other cars, this time of night at least, few signs of human life at all, just this vast scoop of dark sky above and, at the edge of his lights, vague huddled shapes of low scrub, creosote, cholla, prickly pear. Further off the road, tall saguaro with arms upraised—then the heavier darkness of sawtooth mountains.

Had he a destination in mind? Into Phoenix via some roundabout route to take dinner at a crowded restaurant perhaps, hopscotching over his isolation, his loneliness? Or, as he pushed ever deeper into the desert, did he mean to flee something else altogether, the dribble of headlights on gravel roads about him, high-riding headlights of trucks and SUVs behind, silhouettes of houses on hills half a mile away, himself?

His name was Parker.

He'd taken over a light-struck house with exposed beams and white shutters, leaving behind, at the apartment where he'd been staying, the pump of accordions through open windows, songs whose tag line always seemed to be *mi corazon*, afternoons filled with the sound of stationary racing motors from tanklike ancient Fords and Buicks being worked on in the parking lot. Coyotes at twilight walked three or four to the pack down the middle of streets. First night there, he'd sat watching a hawk fall from the sky to carry off a cat. The cat had come over to investigate this new person or say hello. It had leapt onto the halfwall facing his front door, ground to wall in that effortless, levitating way they have, here one moment, there the next. Then just as suddenly the hawk had appeared— swooping away with the cat into a sunset like silent bursting shells.

He remembered eating dinner, some pasta concoction he had only to pop into the microwave. Then he'd gone outside with a bottle of wine, watching day bleed away to its end, watching the hawk make off with the cat, watching as night parachuted grandly into the mountains. He'd gone in to watch part of a movie, then, bottle depleted, decided on a ride. In the car he found a tape of Indian flute music. Drove off, empty himself, into the desert's greater and somehow comforting emptiness.

Till the nude woman appeared before him.

Again: he has no idea how much of this is actual; how much remembered, suggested, imagined. Why, just returned from a turn-about trip to New York, and at that time of night, would he have driven off into the desert—driven anywhere, for that matter? What could have borne him off the highway onto that road, through fence breaks and boulders, up the bare mountainside, to its edge? What could the woman have been doing there, nude, in his headlights?

Seeing her, he swerves, instinctively left, away from the rim, but fetches up against a rise there and slides back, loose stone giving way at his rear when he hits his brakes.

The car rocks back.

In the moment before his windshield fills with dark sky and stars, he sees her there before the car, arms out like a bullfighter, breasts swaying. Braid of dark hair. In his rearview mirror, a canyon of the sort Cochise and his men might have used, subterranean rivers from which they'd suddenly rise into the white man's world to strike, into which they'd sink again without trace.

Though the car's motor has stalled, the tape plays on as the flutist begins to sing wordlessly behind the breath of his instrument, providing his own ghostly accompaniment. A lizard scampers across the windshield. Music, sky and lizard alike go with him over the edge and down—down for a long time.

His name, the name of the person to whom this happens, is Parker.

Without thought, he left her there.

Acting purely on instinct, he was halfway across the roof before anything like actual thought or volition came, before the webwork of choices began forming in his mind. Never let the opponent choose the ground. Withdraw, lure the opponent onto your own, or at least onto neutral ground. By then years of training and action had broken over him like a flood. Four days later, on a Monday, Quentin stood looking down at two bodies. These were the men he'd seen fleeing the apartment below Sandy Buford's. For a moment it was Ellie's body he saw there on the floor of that faceless motel room. He knew from newspaper accounts that the two of them had spent some time at the house once he'd fled. He tried not to think how long, tried not to imagine what had happened there.

Surprisingly, as in the old days, he bore them no direct ill will.

They were working men like himself, long riders, dogs let loose on the grounds.

Himself who, hearing the window crash downstairs, rolled from bed onto his feet and was edging out onto the roof even as footsteps sounded on the stairs. Then was up and over.

With small enough satisfaction he took their car, a mid-range Buick. A simple thing to pull wires out from beneath the dash, cross them. Somewhere in it he would find the map he needed, something about the car would guide him. He had that faith. Everyone left footprints.

Never blame the cannon. Find the hands that set elevation, loaded and primed it, lit the fuse. Find the mouth that gave the order.

They'd have to die, of course, those two. But that was only the beginning.

The world comes back by degrees. There are shapes, patterns of dark and light, motion that corresponds in some vague way to sounds arriving from out there. They knock at your door with luggage in hand, these sounds. While in here you have a great deal of time to think, to sink back into image and sensation in which language has no place. Again and again you see a sky strewn with stars, a lizard's form huge among them, a woman's pale body.

Constantly, it seems, you are aware of your breathing as an envelope that surrounds you, contains you.

For some reason flute music, itself a kind of breath, remains, tendrils of memory drifting through random moments of consciousness. Memory and present time have fused. Each moment's from a book. You page backward, forward, back again. All of it has the same import, same imprimatur.

Faces bend close above you. When you see them, they all look the same. You're fed bitter pastes of vegetables and meat. Someone pulls at your leg, rotates the ankle, pushes up on the ball of your foot to flex it. Two women talk overhead, about home and boyfriends and errant children, as they roll you side to side, wiping away excrement, changing sheets. One day you realize that you can feel the scratchiness, the warmth, of their washclothes.

The TV is left on all the time. At night (you know it's night because no one disturbs you then) the rise and fall of this voice proves strangely comforting. Worst is midmorning when everything goes shrill: voices of announcers and game-show hosts, the edgy canned laughter of sitcoms, commercials kicked into overdrive.

There are, too, endless interrogations. At first, even when you can't, even when it's all you can do to keep from drowning in the flood of words and you're wholly unable to respond, you try to answer. Further along, having answered much the same queries for daily generations of social workers, medical students and interns, you refuse to participate, silent now for quite a different reason.

The world comes back by degrees, and slowly, by degrees, you understand that it's not the world you left. Surreptitious engineers have sneaked in and built a new world while you slept. In this world you're but a tourist, a visitor, an impostor. They'll find you out, some small mistake you'll make.

Mr. Parker, do you know where you are?

Can you tell me what happened?

Can you move your hand, feet, eyes?

Do you know who's President?

Is there anything else you need?

"No."

Here is what my visitor tells me.

We met, Julie and this Parker, just out of school, both still dragging along cumbersome ideals that all but dwarfed us. Once, she said, I told her how as a kid I'd find insects in drawers and cabinets lugging immense, stagecoach-like egg cases behind. That's what it was like.

We had our own concept of manifest destiny, Julie said. No doubt about it, it was up to us to change the world. We'd have long conversations over pizza at The Raven, beer at the Rathskeller, burgers at Maple Street Café: What could we do? Push a few books back into place and the world's shelves would be in order again? We fancied ourselves chiropractors of chaos and corruption: one small adjustment here, a realignment there, all would come straight.

Colonialism. Chile and the CIA. South Africa, Vietnam, our own inner cities, Appalachia. We imagined we were unearthing all manner of rare truth, whereas in truth, as immensely privileged middle-class whites, we were simply learning what most of the world had known forever.

When I found out you were here, I had to come, she says. How long has it been? Twenty years?

She works as a volunteer at the hospital. Saw my name on the admissions list and thought: Could it possibly be?

Other things you begin to remember:

The smell of grapefruit from the back yard of the house across the alley from your apartment.

The rustle of pigeons high overhead in the topknots of palm trees.

Geckos living in a crack in the wall outside your window. By daylight larger lizards come out onto the ledge and rest there. Lizard aerobics: they push their bodies up onto extended legs. Lizard hydraulics: they ease back down.

Dry river beds.

Empty swimming pools painted sky blue.

Mountains.

Even in the center of the city, you're always within sight of mountains. Mornings, they're shrouded in smog, distant, surreal and somehow prehistoric, as though just now, as slowly the earth warms, taking form. Late-afternoon sunlight breaks through clouds in fanlike shafts, washes the mountains in brilliance, some of them appearing black as though burned, others in close relief. Spectacular sunsets break over them at night—and plunge into them.

Sometimes you'd drive into the desert with burritos or a bottle of wine to witness those sunsets. Other times you'd go out there to watch storms gather. Doors fell open above you: great tidal waves of wind and lightning, the whole sky alive with fire.

This is when you were alive.

"You're going to be okay, Mr. Parker."

Her name, I remember, though I check myself with a glance at her nametag, is Marcia. On the margins of the nametag, which is the size of a playing card, she has pasted tiny pictures of rabbits and angels.

"The doctors will be in to speak with you shortly."

I wonder just how they'll speak with me shortly. Use abbreviations, clipped phrases or accents, some special form of semaphore taught them in medical school? One rarely understands what they say in all earnest.

Marcia is twenty-eight. Her husband left her six months ago, she now lives in a garage apartment with an ex-biker truck driver named Jesse. To this arrangement Jesse has brought a baggage of tattoos (including two blue jailhouse tears at the edge of one eye) and his impression of life as a scrolling roadway, six hundred miles to cover before his day and daily case of beer are done. To this arrangement she's brought a four-year-old daughter, regular paychecks and notions of enduring love. Hers is the heavier burden.

I've paid attention, watched closely, hoping to learn to pass here in this new world. I know the lives of these others just as, slowly, I am retrieving my own.

Of course it's my own.

Marcia leans over me, wraps the bladder of the blood-pressure monitor about my arm, inflates it.

"It's coming back to you, isn't it?"

Some of it.

"No family that you know of?"

None.

"I'm sorry. Families are a good thing at times like this."

She tucks the blood-pressure cuff behind its wall gauge and plucks the digital thermometer from beneath my tongue, ejecting its sheath into the trash can.

"Things are going to be tough for a while. Hate to think about your having to go it alone," she says, turning back at the door. "Need anything else right now?"

No.

I turn my head to the window. Hazy white sky out there, bright. Always bright in Phoenix, Valley of the Sun. Maybe when I get out I'll move to Tucson, always have liked Tucson. Its uncluttered streets and mountains and open sky, the way the city invites the desert in to live.

With a perfunctory knock at the door, Marcia reenters.

"Almost forgot." A Post-It Note. "Call when you can, she says."

Julie.

Back when we first met we'd walk, late afternoons, along Turtle Creek, downtown Dallas out of sight to one side, Highland Park to the other, as Mercedes, Beamers and the bruised, battered, piled-high trucks of Hispanic gardeners made their ways home on the street. Just up the rise, to either side of Cedar Springs, bookstores, guitar shops and tiny ethnic restaurants straggled. Within the year glassy, brick-front office buildings took up residence and began staring them down. Within the year, all were gone.

She tells me this when she comes to visit.

Twenty years.

She never had children. Her husband died eight years ago. She has a cat. I've thought of you often, Julie says.

Tucked into a compartment in the driver's door Quentin found a rental agreement. When you need a car, rentals are always a good bet. You can identify them from the license plates mostly, and no one gets in a hurry over stolen rentals. The contract was with Dr. Samuel Taylor, home address Iowa City, local address c/o William Taylor at an ASU dorm. Mr. Taylor had paid by Visa. Good chance he was visiting a son, then, and that the car had been boosted somewhere in Tempe. Quentin called the rental agency, saying he'd seen some Hispanic teenagers who looked like they didn't belong in this car, noticed the plate, and was checking to see if it might have been reported stolen. But he couldn't get any information from the woman who answered the phone, and hung up when she started demanding his name and location.

A dead end.

He left his motel room (first floor rear, alley behind, paid for with cash) and went back to the Buick. He wasn't driving it, but he'd left it out of sight where he could get to it.

Neither of them had smoked. Radio buttons were set at three oldie stations, one country, one easy listening. The coat folded on the backseat he assumed to be Dr. Taylor's; few enforcers (if that's what the two were) wore camel's hair. Likewise the leather attaché case tucked beneath the driver's seat, which, at any rate, held nothing of interest. The paperback under the passenger's seat was a different matter. *Lesbian Wife*, half the pages so poorly impressed as to be all but unreadable. Tucked in between page 34 and 35 was a cash ticket from Good Night Motel.

Good Night Motel proved a miracle of cheap construction and tacky cover-up the builder no doubt charged off as architectural highlights. The clerk inside was of similar strain, much preoccupied with images on a six-inch TV screen alongside an old-style brass cash register. However he tried to direct them away, his eyes kept falling back to it.

"Look, I'm just here days," he said, scant moments after Quentin tired of equivocations and had braced to drag him bodily across the desk's chipped Formica. "Never saw them. Might check at the bar." And heaved a sigh as a particularly gripping episode of *Gilligan's Island* was left unspoiled?

In contrast to the inertial desk clerk, the barkeep was a wiry little guy who couldn't be still. He twitched, twisted, moved salt shakers, coasters and ashtrays around as though playing himself in a board game, drummed fingers on the bar top. He had a thin moustache and sharp features. Something of the rat about him.

Quentin asked for brandy, got a blank stare and changed his request to a draft with whiskey back. He put a fifty on the bar.

"I don't have change."

"You won't need it."

Quentin described the two men. The barkeep nudged a bin of lime wedges square into its cradle.

"Sure, they been in. Three, four nights this week. Not last night, though. One does shots, Jack Daniels. Other's a beer man. Friends of yours?"

"Purely professional. Guys have money coming, from an inheritance. Lawyers hired me to find them."

"Sure they did."

Quentin pushed the fifty closer.

"That covers the drinks. People I work for—"

"Lawyers, you mean."

"Right. The lawyers. Been known to be big tippers."

Another fifty went on the counter, closer to Quentin than to the bartender.

"Four blocks down, south corner, Paradise Motor Hotel. Saw them turn in there on my way home one night. Bottom line kind of place, the Paradise. No bar, no place to eat. Gotta hoof it to Denny's a dozen blocks uptown. Or come here."

Quentin pushed the second fifty onto the first.

"Freshen that up for you?" the barkeep asked.

"Why not?"

He waved away Quentin's offer of payment. "This one's on me."

Afterwards—it all happened quickly and more or less silently, no reason to think he'd be interrupted—Quentin searched that faceless motel room. Nothing. Sport coats and shirts hanging in the closet, usual toiletries by the bathroom sink, a towel showing signs of dark hair dye. Couple issues of *Big Butt* magazine.

Quentin went downstairs and across rippled asphalt to the office, set into a bottleneck of an entryway that let whoever manned the desk watch all comings and goings. Today a woman in her mid-twenties manned it. She looked the way librarians do in movies from the fifties. This kind of place, a phone deposit was required if you planned to use it, and even local calls had to go through the desk. They got charged to the room. The records, of course, are private. Of course they are, he responded—and should be. Twenty dollars further on, they became less private. Another dour Lincoln and Quentin was looking at them. He wondered what she might do with the money. Nice new lanyard for her glasses, special food for the cat?

There'd been one call to 528-1000 (Pizza Palace), two to 528-1888 (Ming's Chinese), and three to 528-1433. That last was a lawyer's office in a strip mall clinging like a barnacle to city's edge, flanked by a cut-rate shoe store and family clothing outlet. Like many of his guild, David Cohen proved reluctant to answer questions in a direct, forthright manner. Quentin soon convinced him.

Bradley C. Smith was quite a different animal, his lair no motel room or strip-mall office but a house in the city's most exclusive neighborhood, built (as though to make the expense of it all still more evident) into a hillside. Location was everything. That's what real-estate agent Bradley C. Smith told his clients. But real estate was only one of Bradley C. Smith's vocations. His influence went far and wide; he was a man with real power.

But that power for many years now had insulated Bradley C. Smith from confrontation. That power depended on money, middle men, lawyers, enforcers, collectors, accountants. None of which were present when Quentin stepped into the powerful man's bathroom just as Bradley C. Smith emerged naked, flesh pale as a mushroom, from the shower.

There at the end, Bradley C. Smith tried to tell him more. Seemed desperate to tell him, in fact. That was what, at the end, Bradley C. Smith seized upon, holding up a trembling hand again and again, imploring with eyes behind which light was steadily fading.

Thing was, Quentin didn't care. Now he knew why the two killers had been dispatched to that apartment on Sycamore, now he had the other name he needed. Ultimately, those two had little to do with him, with his life, with the door he was pushing closed now. Soon they'd have nothing at all to do with it, neither those two, nor Bradley C. Smith, nor the other. Quentin walked slowly down the stairs, climbed into his stolen Volvo. Soon enough it would be over, all of it.

I fail to recognize myself in mirrors, or in Julie's memories, or in many of my own.

I remember riding in a car with a young man dressed strangely, in a plaid shirt that hung on him like a serape, black bell bottoms, an African skullcap. Remember finding a wallet bound with rubber bands once he'd gone.

I remember lying prone in a church steeple watching families come and go.

I remember a man drifting away from me in a culvert, blue dye coloring the water beneath him. Bodies below me on a motel room floor. Other bodies, many of them, half a world away.

As memory returns, it does so complexly—stereophonically. There is what I am told of Parker, a set of recollections and memories that seem to belong to him, and, alongside those, these other memories of bodies and cars, green jungles, deserts, a kind of double vision in which everything remains forever just out of focus, blurred.

I wonder if this might not be how the mind functions in madness: facts sewn loosely together, so that contrasting, contradictory realities are held in suspension, simultaneously, in the mind, scaffolds clinging to the faceless, sketchy edifice of actuality.

"I brought you some coffee. Real coffee. Figured you could use it. I've had my share of what hospitals call coffee."

He set the cup, from Starbuck's, on the bedside table.

"Thank you."

"Don't mention it. City paid. You need help with that top?"

Parker swung his legs over bed's edge and sat, pried off the cover. The detective remained standing, despite the chair close by.

Light gray suit, something slightly off about the seams. Plucked from a mark-down rack at Mervyn's, Dillard's? Blue shirt that had ridden with him through many days just like this one, darkish red tie that from the look of deformations above and below the knot must turn out a different length most times it got tied. Clothes don't make the man, but they rarely fail to announce to the world who he thinks he might be.

"Sergeant Wootten. Bill." He sipped from his own cup. "You don't have kids, do you, Mr. Parker?"

Parker shook his head. The sergeant shook his in turn.

"My boy? Sixteen? I swear I don't know what to make of him, haven't for years now. Not long ago he was running with a crowd they all had tattoos, you know? Things like beer can tabs in their ears, little silver balls hanging out of their noses. Then a month or so back he comes down to breakfast in a dark blue suit, been wearing it ever since. Go figure."

"What can I do for you, Sergeant?"

"Courtesy visit, more or less."

"You realize that I remember almost nothing of what happened?"

"Yes, sir. I'm aware of that. Very little of what happened, and nothing from before. But paperwork's right up there with death, taxes and tapeworms. Can't get away from it."

Holding up the empty cup, Parker told him thanks for the coffee. The sergeant took Parker's cup, slipped his own inside it, dropped both in the trash can by the door.

"I've read your statement, the accident reports, spoke with your doctors. No reason in any of that to take this any further."

He walked to the window and stood quietly a moment.

"Beautiful day. Not that most of them aren't." He turned back. "Still don't have a handle on what happened out there."

"Nor do I. You know what I remember of it. The rest is gone."

"Could come back to you later on, the doctors say. They also say you're out of here tomorrow. Going home."

"Out of here, anyway."

"We'll need a contact address in case something else comes up. Not that anything's likely to. Give us a call."

The sergeant held out his hand. Quentin shook it.

"Best of luck to you, Mr. Parker."

When he was almost to the door: "One thing still bothers me, though. We can't seem to find any record of you for these past four years. Where you were living, what you were doing. Almost like you didn't exist."

"I've been in Europe."

"Well that's it then, isn't it. Like I said: best of luck, Mr. Parker."

There was a time alone then, first in an apartment off Van Buren in central Phoenix where Quentin found comfort in the slam of car doors and the banging of wrenches against motors, in the rich roll of calls in Spanish across the parking lot and between buildings, in the pump and chug of accordions and conjunto bands from radios left on, it seemed, constantly; then, thinking he wanted to be truly alone, in an empty house just outside Cave Creek. Scouting it, he discovered credit-card receipts for two round-trip tickets to Italy, return date a month away. No neighbors within sight. He had little, few possessions, to move in. He parked the car safely away from the house.

There was a time, too, of aimless, intense driving, to Flagstaff, Dallas, El Paso, even once all the way to New York, road trips in which he'd leave the car only to eat and sleep, as often as not selecting some destination at random and driving there only to turn around and start back.

He thought little about his life before, about the four men he had killed, still less about his present life. It was as though he were suspended, waiting for something he could feel moving toward him, something that had been moving toward him for a long time.

• • •

"Thanks for picking me up."

"You're welcome. Guess I'd been kind of hoping you'd call."

They pulled onto Black Canyon Freeway. Late afternoon, and traffic was heavy, getting heavier all the time, lines of cars zooming out of the cattle chutes. Clusters of industrial sheds—automotive specialty shops and the like—at roadside as they cleared the cloverleaf, then bordering walls above which thrust the narrow necks of palm trees and signage, sky beyond. The world was so full. Ribbons of scarlet, pink and chrome yellow blew out on the horizon as the sun began settling behind sawtooth mountains. Classical music on low, the age-old, timeless ache of cellos.

The world was so full.

"Had breakfast?" Julie asked.

Caught unawares, she'd thrown an old sweatshirt over grass-stained white jeans a couple sizes too large. Cheeks flushed, hair still wet from the shower. Nonetheless she'd taken time to ferret out and bring him a change of clothes. Her husband's, Parker assumed. They had the smell of long storage about them.

"Little late for that, don't you think?"

"Breakfast's a state of mind. Like so much of life. More about rebirth, things starting up again, knowing they can, than it is about time of day. It's also my favorite meal."

"Never was much of a breakfast person myself."

"You should give it a try."

"You're right. I should."

She nodded. "There's a great café just ahead, breakfast twenty-fours a day, best in the valley. You got time?"

"I don't have much else."

"Good. We'll stop, then. After that . . . You have a place to stay?"

"No."

"Yes," Julie said. "Yes. You do."

NEW LIFE

Over past days a speed bump has grown in the street just outside my living room. Each day, morning and again late afternoon, crews pull up in their trucks to nurture the speed bump, to feed it, water it, bring it forth. Out of the open backs of their trucks they unload cannisters, hand tools and blowtorches, pots of white paint, small appliances like lawn edgers, saws, a huge curved bar, buckets, baskets. Behind my window, behind the veil of its covering, day by day I watch the speed bump take form. At first it's but a stretch of new asphalt, shining and black beneath the noonday sun. Later that day the crews come and, with one member directing flame toward it, another wielding a kind of long hoe, shape it into a perfect rectangle. Gradually over following days an actual hump develops. The speed bump begins to look like the back of some largely submerged creature. That night I stand for a long time watching it in moonlight. The next morning, when they paint white stripes across it, I realize how beautiful it is becoming.

"Are you going to finish your breakfast?" Alice asks.

I look back at the melon, fresh-sliced bread and tub of butter, the thick bacon she drives all the way across town, to AJ's, to buy, none of which looks appetizing any longer. I shake my head, say I'm really not hungry.

"They're at it awfully early."

Of course. This is important work. The city's not inert. Like a forest, it's alive, ever growing, ever changing. And these, these workmen dismounting twice daily from their trucks, are the city's vaqueros, its shepherds, its midwives.

"If you want me to drop you, you'd better get dressed."

So I put on my dark blue suit, light blue shirt with tiny buttons at the collar, lemon tie, and pull on oxblood leather loafers. I'm almost ready when I hear the kitchen door, and have to go scampering out to catch up with Alice. She stands watching as driver after driver speeds down the street and hits the bump. Two or three of them bottom out on reentry; one, bouncing frantically, swerves onto the sidewalk. Alice smiles.

At the office I sit looking out over the ramparts, spires and depressions that form the city. These in the window echo the graphs before me on my computer screen. We're fifteen floors up, sharing altitude only with traffic helicopters, window cleaners hauled up by their platform's bootstraps, and hawks who thrive on the city's pigeons. All along the vena cava of interstate, carotids of the roundabout near city hall, arteries, arterioles, capillaries, traffic moves unimpeded.

"Ralph?"

Vicky says it again. For the second time? Third?

"You want something from Armando's? We're ordering out."

No, I tell her, vague recollections of cups of black coffee in my mind. How many cups have I had? When had I last eaten? A single piece of bread this morning, a bite of melon. Last night I'd twirled my fork in the bowl of angel hair (olive oil, garlic, black olives and Parmesan) before pushing it away. At bowl's bottom, like some cartoon character on a child's, was a scene from Provence. But I was not to go there.

Vicky, meanwhile, has paused thoughtfully at the entrance to my cubicle. "You really need to start taking care of yourself. You can't work all the time."

"I don't."

"Little wheels and lights, Ralph."

"What?"

"They're there all the time, behind your eyes."

"Nonsense."

"Okay." She turns and is gone, only to be replaced by Miss Allen. Everyone is waiting for me in the conference room, Miss Allen says.

In the presence of senior partners and clients, sipping further cups of coffee in an effort to energize self and delivery (not much I can do about lack of substance), I stumble through my half-prepared presentation.

"Thank you, Ralph," Mr. Townsend says afterwards. A Roman candle launched into silence.

"It went. Definitely it went," I say that night when Alice asks me over pork and yucca spooned from the crock pot and served over rice how my day had gone. "Yours?"

"I think we found a foster home for Jimmie Vaste, a good one."

Jimmie is a twelve-year-old of ambiguous and indeed ambivalent sexuality, one of those kids who by turns disturbs, charms, offends and terrifies adults. Looking into his eyes is like peering into a tank of water where, just out of sight, something sinister turns and glides. Alice must see placing him as a grand coup.

"Congratulations," I tell her, pushing pork, yucca and rice around on my plate, amazed as always that in her work she deals with people, with actual human situations. Quite different from my own. Paradigm makes nothing, produces nothing, adds nothing to the world. We're Movers-Around, taking things from one place and putting them elsewhere: paperwork, resources, companies, executives, armies of workers, products. No one can touch Paradigm at Moving Around.

Climbing up from the dinner table, Alice and I pour single malt Scotch from the Orkney Islands into crystal glasses and carry it, as though it's not already travelled far enough, with coffee, out to the living room. I'll come back and clean up, clear the table, wash dishes, later. We settle in among framed posters of art exhibits and dance recitals, reproductions of Ingres and Thomas Cole, blond bentwood furniture. Alice lifts her current read, a history of Egypt, from the table alongside, opens to the bookmark and all but visibly sinks in. I read a page or so of a novel titled *Pale Mountain* and, realizing I've no idea what I just read, go back to the beginning. The journey's no better this time around, or the next. From the CD system Robert Johnson declaims *I'm booked and I got to go.*

Where *I* go is to the window.

The black back of the beast gleams brighter than ever in moonlight, its white stripes have gone luminous. Because of these stripes the far side of the speed bump appears convex, the nearer concave. A late model Buick turns in off Seventh Street and pulls up, sits for a moment before the speed bump, headlights a bright carpet. Then it moves slowly backwards, swings into a driveway, and pulls out heading back the way it came. Its headlights lash across our wall.

"Are you coming to bed?" Alice asks behind me.

Oh yes, I say. And fall into the swathe of moonlight there beside her, my love, my life.

Surely it's only my imagination, these sounds I hear outside, as of something taking its first uncertain steps and beginning to move steadily along the street.

VENICE IS SINKING INTO THE SEA

She loved him, Dana thinks, more than most, as she walks in the small park across from the house she's rented for twelve years now. A Craftsman house from the thirties, two bedrooms, living room, kitchen, all of them much of a size. This time of morning the park's filled with the homeless. They appear each day as the sun comes up, depart each evening, trailing off into the sunset with their bedrolls, clusters of overstuffed plastic bags, shopping carts. Occasionally she wonders where it is they go. Lord, she was going to miss him.

Almost no traffic on the street where late each Friday night you can hear hot cars running against one another. Dana walks leisurely across to have coffee and a bagel at Einstein's. She knows the bagels are bogus (she's from the City, after all), but she loves them. Feels much the same way about the muscular firemen who hang out here most days.

Sean was a fireman. Smaller than most, right at the line, which meant he'd always had to work harder, do more, to make the grade. Same in bed. "I'm always humping," he'd once said, unconscious of irony. Despite his size, or because of it, he'd gone right up (as it were) the ladder, promotion after promotion. With each promotion he was less and less at home, more and more preoccupied when there beside her.

Sean was the first, messy one.

She'd never much liked Dallas anyway, and started up a new life in Boston. Brookline, actually, wherefrom she hitched rides, in those trusting, vagabond sixties, to the library downtown. Her apartment house was up three long, zigzag terraces from the street. Furniture from salvage stores filled it, a faded leather love seat, stacked mattress and box springs, Formica kitchen table standing on four splayed feet, edged with a wide band of ridged steel. Wooden chairs that seemed to have legs all of different lengths. A line of empty fishbowls.

Almost every day back then they'd be flushed out of the library because of bomb threats. There was never a bomb, just the threats, and the dogs and the bomb squad filing in. The announcement came over an intercom used for nothing else but to call closing time. Patrons would gather outside on the square (this in itself seemed so very Boston, so old America) and wait, fifteen minutes, thirty, an hour, to be allowed back in. One of those times, Will Barrett Jr. struck up a conversation with her. He was there reading up on subarachnoid hemorrhages. Couldn't get into the Mass General computers, he said, and had to evacuate one the next day. They never made it back into the library. Had moderate quantities of bad Italian food, inordinate quantities of good beer, the whole of an amazing night. She never asked how his patient had fared.

She'd hang there naked and shivering, steam banging in the radiators, twelve degrees outside (he always left the radio on), waiting for him to come home, thighs streaming with desire and the morning's deposition of semen. Because she wouldn't let herself become a victim, and because that was what he wanted, she became instead a kind of animal. Smelled it on him, another woman, one day when he came home and unlocked the cuffs. She'd learned a lot by then. That one wasn't messy.

Wayne worked at the Boston Globe, writing what they call human interest features. Roxbury woman puts three kids through college scrubbing floors, The emperor of shoeshine stands, Mister John sees the city from his front porch—that sort of thing. Most of it Wayne simply made up. Each morning four or five newspapers showed up in his driveway, the *Globe*, *New York Times*, *Washington Post*, *Wall Street Journal*, *L.A. Times*. He never read them. He'd sit around all day drinking beer and watching TV and after dinner he'd go into his office and tap out his column on a tan IBM Selectric. This would take an hour, tops. Then he'd call the paper. They'd send a messenger over. Wayne would join Dana to watch whatever was on at nine. Many times, the next morning, she'd be able to see in the column pieces of what they'd watched on TV before dinner the previous night. For a month, maybe two, the sex was great, then it was nonexistent. For a long time Dana didn't understand that. Then she remembered how Wayne was always grabbing something new, holding on for dear life for an hour or two, letting go. Ask him about that mother out in Roxbury and he wouldn't even remember.

Simply amazing, what you can do with a hat pin. You introduce it at the base of the skull, just under the hair line. They weren't easy to find these days, but soon, haunting antique shops, she had a collection of them. Plain hat pins, hat pins tipped with pink pearl, with abalone or plastic. Her favorite had a head with a tiny swan carved of ivory. They were amazingly long.

Jamie worked on the floor at the Chicago Stock Exchange, pushing will and voice above the crowd to move capital from here to there. He did well, but the work seemed to absorb all his energies. He came home ready and able to do little more than eat the takeout Chinese he brought and watch mindless TV—sitcoms and their like. Night after night Dana lay throbbing and alone, wondering how it had ever come about that she'd attached herself to this man.

St. Louis then, heart of the heartland, about which Dana remembered little more than the man's name, the Western shirts he favored, the look of his eyes in the mirror.

Minnesota, where for weeks at the time ice lay on the land like a solid sea and blades of wind hung spinning in the air.

New York, finally. Home. Where she thought she'd be safe with Jonas, her obscure writer who published in small magazines no one read, and should have known better. Essentially a hobbyist, she thought. Now to everyone's surprise, his more than anyone else's, Jonas is fast becoming a bestseller. His novel, written in a week, went into six printings. *McSweeney's* and the *Times* are calling him up. So tonight, after the dinner she's spent hours preparing for him, coq au vin and white asparagus with garlic butter (cookbook propped on the window ledge), a good white wine, cheese and fruit, he excuses himself "to get some writing done."

He's been writing all day.

"What are you working on?" she asks.

"Couple of things, really. That piece for *Book World*'s almost due. And yesterday I got an idea for a new story."

Later she enters what he's dubbed The Factory, a second bedroom apparently intended for a family with a dwarf child. His desk takes up most of one wall. Two filing cabinets occupy the opposite corners, by the door, and books are stacked along the walls. Pushed back from the desk, he has the keyboard in his lap, eyes on the screen. There she sees the words "Death by misadventure."

No. By unfaithfulness, rather.

Because he loves something else more than he loves her.

She stands quietly watching. He is concentrating on the story and never realizes she's there with him. As he scrolls to the top of the screen, the title appears: "Venice Is Sinking into the Sea."

It's a story about her, of course.

She who lifts her hand now, she whose hair is so beautiful as it begins to fall.

PITT'S WORLD

1.

Sometime in the fourth month Pitt discovered that the small octopus-like creatures scuttling forever across the sand could be eaten. The taste was not all that unpleasant.

Stores had given out six weeks in, just before he found Diderot's body. After that Pitt subsisted on cargo. The *Bounty* was, had been, a supply ship, carrying in its hold among much else a full complement of medical supplies bound for the colonies. Bags of TPN, for instance: total parenteral nutrition. By trial and error Pitt had learned to find a vein, insert a needle and tape it in place. He walked about with the TPN bag perched on his shoulder like a mad skipper's parrot, essential nutrients dripping into his bloodstream.

By law, Class D vessels such as the *Bounty*, dedicated to routine runs with minimal crews, bore systems redundant to such extent that in effect they comprised two ships superimposed one upon the other. How it came about that piggybacked navigational and drive systems gave out simultaneously, four-in-one, Pitt had no idea. But suddenly they'd found themselves with failing power and little control—rudderless. So much for redundancy.

The *Bounty* had pulled out from Earth with the usual three-man crew.

Flight officer Waylan Diderot, a middle-aged man with hair transplants (Asian, from the look of it), body freshly liposuctioned and sculptured, newly implanted enamel-on-steel teeth. He and Pitt had been out together at least half a dozen times.

Navigator and computer specialist Cele Gold. New to the run, but she'd done two re-ups in the Navy. Knew the why and how of it, no doubt about that, though occasionally she stumbled over the slackness and informality of civilian hopping, something that, given the chance, she'd soon have got over.

Pitt was responsible for everything else. Seeing cargo on board and safely stowed, invoices, stores, meals, permits and visas, communications. Word among merchant marines was that no better petty officer could be had. Pitt showed no pride at that. He'd fallen into the work by chance after leaving the seminary in his final year when, sitting over his bowl of tea one early morning, watching light gather outside, it came to him that he believed none of it. He was never able to summon any regret at this sudden loss of faith—more a recognition of its absence than a loss, actually. He'd simply stepped through a door, into a new room. He would have been a decent, unremarkable priest. Now he was a first-rate petty officer.

Only once had the old life reared its head into the present. Following an exceptionally long flight, having finally delivered their cargo, Pitt and his F.O. sat in a bar pickling themselves on the local distillate.

"God can't find us here," the F.O. said.

Every bit as blasted as his flight officer, Pitt asked: "Why would he be looking?"

"According to the religious, he always is. Eye on the sparrow and all that? Back home, as a young man—more years ago than I wish to think about—I believed. Out here, I no longer have to."

"Perhaps," Pitt said after a moment, "you have recovered your innocence."

They'd all been cross-trained, of course. Not that it mattered now. In a pinch any of the three of them could pilot the ship, run new programs and protocols, lift off, set down, punch in coordinates and routing sequences.

Problem was, the training assumed you had a functional ship.

Moments before alarms sounded, Diderot had bellowed out: "What the fuck!" Then: "Cele?"

"I know, I know. Can't get a fix on it . . . Auxiliaries are kicking in, but they're at maybe sixty percent, at best. Navigational's gone—"

"Pitt?"

"Not much better at this station, I'm afraid, sir."

"—and there goes the backup right after it."

"Distress signal?"

"Affirmative. I'm trying to run a tracer . . . Both keep getting bounced back."

"Maybe no one's home," Diderot said.

They were all thinking the same thing. War had been brewing for some time, and seemed imminent as they lifted. Perhaps it had erupted. Perhaps, for now, they were completely, utterly on their own.

"Shit! Communications just went down, sir."

As did they.

In situations like this, even at low function, the ship followed a lifeline scenario: located the nearest land, lashed onto it, reeled itself in. Within minutes they were looking out at tall, slender trees bearded with what appeared to be moss and studded with pads of yellow fungus like hobnails on boots. The trees rose not from soil but from sand, or its equivalent. Small, octopus-like creatures by the dozens scuttled across it.

"Everyone okay?"

"Yeah."

"Me too, though I think 'okay' just took on a new meaning. Where the hell are we?"

"Off the charts, sir."

"Well, doesn't *that* surprise us."

"Atmosphere's oxygen-heavy—"

"No wonder, all those trees."

"—but serviceable."

Remaining ship systems were shutting down one by one. A pale sun hung half below the horizon, giving light. Dawn? Dusk? For all they knew, it might be there all the time.

Cele was first to hit the button. Her spidery harness withdrew, and she stood, going up on the balls of her feet, down, back up.

"Just lost about twenty pounds," she announced. "Crash diet."

They both groaned.

"Permission to recon, sir?" Cele asked.

"Be careful out there."

Slinging a survival pack over one shoulder, she touched a finger to forehead in salute and hit the slide, sinking quickly from sight.

Pitt and Diderot watched on monitors as she exited the ship, moving off into the trees.

They never saw her again.

Five and a half weeks after that, 0800 ship's time—unlike the F.O. to remain abed, he was thinking—Pitt entered captain's quarters. Diderot lay in repose and at peace on the steel cot that folded up into the wall. His handheld sat at bedside, cursor blinking. A message to his wife.

> *I know you'll never see this, my dear Val. Like so many utterances, it's more for my own benefit than for anyone else. Seems I've come to the end of all these strange roads I've chosen. But God, we had some good years, didn't we! Here (I almost wrote "Where I've fallen to earth") there's little to sustain life, far less to sustain hope. The last things I will see and feel are your face and your love. I've known that for a long time now. Even if I tried again and again and could never say how very much you meant to me.*

Pitt saw to it that Diderot got a decent burial. TPN bag balanced on his shoulder, he said a few words over the grave as the small octopus-like creatures skittered across the newly disturbed sand, said things about Diderot being a good man and being missed, though he couldn't imagine the creatures much cared. He finished: Requiescat in pace. That was the day he began thinking of where he now lived as *Pace*.

2.

The creatures scuttling about the sand came in an array of colors though the majority of them tended toward light green and a sort of aqua. Darker ones seemed frequently to be attacked and destroyed by their neighbors. About the time he started harvesting them, Pitt had begun to wonder if perhaps they, or at least some among them, possessed the capacity to change color. They had a thin skin that, given a shallow slit, was easily peeled away. The flesh beneath was pulpy, white. With minutes over an open fire it became tender.

To support a food chain, there had to be other fauna. Pitt knew that but came across no evidence of same. He did find a variety of edible leaves and a tasty, somewhat bitter root. Tossed into the pot together with the small creatures, these gave up not only a nice stew but essential roughage as well.

Near where he'd set up camp ran a wide, shallow stream populous with fish that seemed to be all the same species. Resembling nothing so much as a child's ballet slippers, they were transparent, one with the water. But when they turned, light caught somewhere in their bodies, and for that moment they became iridescent, spilling color after color, in pools, into the water about them.

Pitt often thought how much easier things could have been if only the computer had survived. Then he might have acquired crucial knowledge and skills: water purification, essentials of medicine, principles of architecture, basic carpentry, soap making.

Robinson Crusoe and his parasol. Pitt and his soap rendered from the fat of the octopus-like creatures. Scented perhaps with blooms from one or another of the local blooms.

As a civilized man, city born and bred, Pitt knew nothing of any of this—means to safe water, medicine—least of all something like soap making, so very many *more* giant steps into the past. Why he thought he needed such information never quite came clear to him. Just that he was convinced he should know those things.

Truly, though, Pitt's new home gave him all he needed.

One handheld, solar-powered like the ship's clock, did function intermittently. He should save that for an emergency, he decided— then laughed. *Emergency* had certainly taken on a different meaning.

The sound of his laughter startled him. And was as close to Friday's footprints as he ever came.

In one out-of-the-way cabinet of what remained of the ship— most of the corpse had been taken over by vegetation now—he found a survival kit. The kit consisted of a week's supply of nutrient capsules, water-purification tablets, basic tools, self-propelling nails and bolts, fishing line, a mess kit, a spark generator, an ingenious sheet, thin as foil, that could double as blanket or tent, flares the size of firecrackers, a first-aid kit, a handgun, a distress beacon.

It took him over a month, ship's time, to get the beacon working, but by trial and error and doggedness he did, managing to hook depleted batteries extracted from various backup systems and small appliances together in series, tapping and collectivizing their residual charges. (Ship's time was all he had, of course. Though maybe it would be closer to the truth to hold that time had ceased to matter at all—and so had ceased to exist.) The beacon's tiny red active light, when it came on, seemed to him far brighter than the sun hanging motionless, another token of time's suspension, half below the horizon.

For all Pitt's good intentions, soon enough he was playing chess with the solar-powered handheld. After all, there was so little to occupy him here. One could spend only so many hours and days staring off into the trees, one could eat only so many meals, one could sleep only so many hours. With each move, he knew, he was draining the handheld's reserve. But what else was there?

Disappointingly, and more quickly then he'd anticipated, the handheld went from winning each game to shutting down with games barely started.

So, what now?

Any major fauna beyond the octopus-like creatures still eluded him, but a rough equivalent of insects existed in profusion. Most of these were by Pitt's standards large, ranging from roughly hummingbird- to sparrow-sized; all, as far as he could tell, were flightless. He began collecting them, pinning them to a bulletin board of cork he'd ransomed from the *Bounty*. Each specimen bore the specifics of its collection. Ship's date, ship's time, location. *5-5-21, four clicks starboard, sector G-19-N.*

He had no means of preserving the specimens, of course. (Something else he might have learned from the lapsed computers.) Before his very eyes, he knew, the collection would disintegrate. Vestigial wings fall off, exoskeletons crumble, till finally there'd be little more than a whisper of dust left at the base of the pins. But for now his collection was definitive.

Definitely world's best, he thought.

What impelled people toward collecting in the first place? A strange occupation. Some inborne drive for hunting and gathering pushed forward to the point there was no longer any need for same, so that it broke out, bespoke itself, in new forms? Or something closer to the ground? I have more bones ivory gold stamps coins than you. I win.

So much of life, so much of society, was competition. Pitt, alone as few had ever been alone, stood apart from all that now, in a kind of innocence.

He had seen Diderot through to a decent burial, he'd searched for Cele, there was little left to do. He spent his days arranging his collection of insects according to color, according to order of discovery, according to size.

It occurred to him that this was in itself only another kind of chess.

3.

Among Cele's spare personal possessions, Pitt found a book to which he'd have paid little attention were it not for its title: *Peace.* He'd never been much of a reader and couldn't in fact recall when he'd last held a book.

Peace. *Pace.*

Subtitled *A Novel in Verse*, the book related the epic struggle between two diverse cultures living on either side of a river, on twin narrow strips of arable land beyond which stretched seemingly endless desert. The inside flap bore a photograph of a young man of indeterminate ethnicity. The title page was inscribed "To Cele— We'll always have Memphis" and signed by the author.

Maybe it was only that the book afforded him some sense of community, a vision or memento of the civilization he'd left behind, at first willfully, now by mischance and (it would certainly seem) finally. Before, he'd have had no interest in reading anything like this. But since finding it, he had been through the book so many times that he could recite whole pages by heart.

The sun's bead drew out to a thin line. The sharks
were hungry that year, the days made of wood.
In the loftiest vaults they could find, birds turned straw
to the gold of new birth, nervously eyeing the horizon.
While in every lit doorway stood dark figures . . .

On the day he'd first eaten one of the octopus-like creatures, thinking that he had no idea what poisons or deadly bacteria could lurk within them, or how simply inimical might be their tissue to his own, Pitt lay down half-expecting to die, perhaps in truth half-hoping for it. He rose surprised to find himself not only alive but revitalized. This world had accepted him; he was a part of it now. On *Pace*. At peace.

Today he has been sitting for some time, or for no time, on the bank of the stream. And when at last he rises, it's to retrieve the distress beacon and throw it into the stream. The ship's clock goes next. Briefly, water alive with color, pool after pool of bright green, chrome yellow, purple, scarlet, the fish swarm about these new, strange things that have suddenly entered their world. Then, turning, all but invisible again, they move on.

FLESH OF STONE AND STEEL

There was still water in the canals then. Waiting for you to come home, I had little else to do, and spent hours by it. Amazing how sensuous water can be, turning within itself, caressing the flanks of the shore, catching light and playing with it, throwing it back. Around one slow turn, as the canal contorted to fit itself to what remained of downtown, people sat outdoors drinking coffee at a small café at all hours, coats drawn close about them, breaths stabbing horse tails into the air. Behind layers of gauzelike exhausted air, the sun, paler than any moon, struggled to be seen.

O my love. I saw you in them all. In water's play, in the gay waiter's hips as he sashayed among tables, in every defeated, expectant face. Were the café there now, I've no doubt I would find you still. I've been back. Indifferent piles of stone where the front wall was pushed down or collapsed of its own unsupported weight, a scatter of smashed tables and crippled chairs, algae grown over the lip of the tiny fountain in a spill and become something else, something like grass, seeking reproduction by whatever means necessary, at any cost, any measure, life that will not be stopped.

At night I'd lie looking across your ravaged body to the window, remembering a time when cities had been things of light, almost alive themselves.

That last winter, perched hawklike in your thirteenth-floor loft above the dissolving city, I wrote my first and finest poems. Sometimes now I wonder just how those came about. Incredible that they did. Since then there've been few, fewer still of any note.

I also wrote dozens of fragments like the following, strange conjunctions of mind and external world that came to nothing and were soon abandoned. Fragments, I suppose, because that's what my life was, what all our lives were.

The theatre is in blackness.

Voice #1: *At first, everything is in darkness. Light begins slowly.*

Right on cue, light does so, and gradually we discern the outlines of a stage set, of two people. The woman stands at a window rear stage, back to us. We assume it is a woman. The man sits on a couch stage left; from time to time he jots something into a notebook on his lap. Music is playing. We assume it is music. An assemblage of sounds, at any rate.

Voice #2: *Autumn. The city remains under siege. Past their window it lies, a luminous landscape of swells and hollows, like the body of a woman done with desire.*

Woman: *There are fires everywhere. Everything is burning. The past is almost gone now, I think.*

Man (listening): *So exquisite. Could we hear it again, do you think?*

Back still turned, the woman crosses the stage to a bank of apparatus, meters, gauges. The music stops, then starts back up.

Woman: *Would you like tea?*

Man: *Love a cup.*

Woman: *There's a bit of bread left as well. Frightfully stale, I'm afraid: I'd have to toast it.*

Man: *Then by all means do, my dear.*

The woman crosses the stage again. Stands at a counter stage right as she puts on the kettle, slices bread, rummages noisily for silverware, plates, cups.

Woman (working): *Do you remember the day we first met?*

Man: *Of course.*

Woman: *It all happened so fast. I'd never felt anything like this before.*

The man gets up and walks to her. They stand together looking out an imaginary window above the counter.

Woman: *I'm so cold. So very cold.*

I never knew when you would come. You had lives elsewhere, and for days, a week or more, once for over a month, you'd be gone, then just as suddenly and unpredictably there when I returned from the café, from the river, from hours passed prowling streets as silent witness. Opening at my approach, the door would tell me matter-of-factly: *Cat is here.*

The addicted person, you said, can no longer distinguish between his pleasure and his pain. That border, that threshold, is gone. Others soon follow, in sequence.

That was what you did in your days and nights and weeks away from me, you worked with them, tried to help them understand and to understand them, people with something of the heroic in them, people at once larger than life and caricatures of a kind, shrunken to the smallest common denominator of desire, of need. Their numbers grew daily in our shadow world beneath the media's blinding white light and a dimming sun, where it was forever late afternoon, early evening.

Tell me what it is like, you said one morning, to have someone that close, that joined, that much a part of you.

I tried, and couldn't.

Was it from your despair, from your identification with them, that you joined those you couldn't help? Maybe if you better understood, you *would* be able to help. Maybe if you shared their suffering, your own would be diminished.

As I suppose, in some manner, it was.

I could not cut you out of me, I said that day. You are a part of my flesh.

Now I watch the city continue becoming flame and remember the intense white flame that was you. All about me fire's harsh red head tears up from the city's ruins, all about me it puts out tender hands, touching, teasing, fire that knows my name, fire that wants me, cold fire that will have us all.

UP

Two went up on the bus today. One was an elderly lady who came aboard at the stop near Megaworld with her collapsible rolling cart and sat huddled for close to half an hour in blue bundle of skirt, sweater and what she'd no doubt have called a wrap. Then she took a sigh and went up. The other was a young man pierced all about, ears, nose, tongue, eyebrow, as though to provide rings and hitches by which he might be lashed to the world. His eyes were never still. Ten blocks into his ride he stood and let out a scream of rage or challenge, a single burst, like a flare, before he went up. The rest of us watched a moment, then went about our business. For most of us, of course, our business isn't much. I've read that when the bomb was dropped on Hiroshima, people's shadows were burned onto walls. That's what the tracings always remind me of, those faint outlines of gray like photographs that haven't quite been captured, the bare footprints of ash, left behind when they go up.

When these two went up, I was, first, just beginning, then four hours into, my daily countdown, carrying on the shabby pretense that things were as they'd always been or soon would be again, yo-yoing in dark suit, pinpoint oxford shirt and briefcase uptown, crosstown, downtown and back, filling out applications here, dropping off a resume there, but mostly sitting on park benches and on buses like this one. Go through the motions, people tell you, and form becomes content. Keep putting the vessel out and it'll fill. As usual people, the ones who give you advice anyway, are full of shit.

The curious thing is that there's no heat when they go up.

Mrs. Lancaster-Smith appeared on the landing as I climbed past her floor. Four more to go, thousands of us all over the city making the same or some similar climb now in suit, overalls, casual dresses, workclothes and jeans, coming home. "You forgot to lock up again," she said. Her voice pursued me up the stairs the way squeaky bedsprings carry through apartment walls. "Mr. Abib (from the next floor down?) was out on the landing, having a cup of whatever that is he drinks all the time, that always smells so sweet?, and heard voices. He walked up and found two kids standing outside your door. Another couple were on their way in." I thanked her and said I would be more careful, thinking all the time that *forgot* probably wasn't the correct word. At one level or another I was probably hoping someone would go in and strip everything out, carry off every trace of my previous life, give me permission to start over.

I climbed on, unlocked the door and went in. The logbox in the corner of the screen opposite the door registered four calls, three pieces of mail, a couple of bills paid as of nine this morning. "Hello, Annette," I said. *I'm home*, I thought. The screen itself showed prospects of blue sky, white clouds moving through them calm and slow as glaciers.

She'd gone up sixteen days before. We were sitting on a bench by the river downtown, the river they'd spent so much controversial taxpayer's money building. A plaque on the back of the bench read THE HONORABLE LAWRENCE BLOCK. All the benches were named for Senators who, having called in favors to finance creation of the river, couldn't leverage further funds from the House and finally elected to pay for benches, walkways and riverside amenities personally. Annette and I had had dinner at a Vietnamese restaurant, huge bowls of soup into which we threw sprigs of cilantro and mint, dollops of hot sauce, sprouts, then gone for a walk. The sunset was splendid, as it is most days now, sunsets being dependent upon such things as pollution indexes, dust and particle content. We sat watching as clouds filled with pink, as purple began seeping up like a dark, beautiful ink off the horizon, staining the sky.

"I'm so happy," Annette said beside me. I'd brought along a cup of Vietnamese coffee laced with condensed milk. I had it halfway to my mouth when she went up.

Then there was only that faint gray outline of a body on the bench beside me, that bare footprint of ash. After a moment, I drank.

"Hungry?" I said now, coming into the apartment. "I'm starved." Hard day at the office and all that. God knows why, but I'd gone on talking to her all this time. I came home, asked about her day, poured two glasses of wine, chatted as I cooked. This is what people, what couples, families, did. They made the climb in suit, overalls, casual dresses, workclothes or jeans. They came home, inquired after the children, asked how the day had gone, if there had been any calls. Sometimes the meals I fixed were inspired. Often they were commonplace, barely edible; I could never discern what made the difference. Sometimes when I spoke to Annette, confused as to whom I might be addressing, the computer tried to respond.

The parent chosen for me by lottery was Mimi Blodgett: a name that, when I first heard it, made me wonder if I'd not somehow fallen through cracks in reality's pavement directly into a Dickens novel. But no, that was indeed her name, and she lived up to it. A barrel-shaped woman, foreshortened everywhere, arms, legs, neck, intellect; hair dyed brown and set each week at Josie's Cool Fixin's, Friday, 3 P.M., in curls that defied not only age but gravity as well; an armory of polyester pants, shirtwaists and pullovers in the rickety closet, stacks of *Reader's Digest*s in the bathroom, of her trailer. Mimi's love for me was like that trailer, never intended to be permanent though it turned out that way, and as durable basically (if also as unlovely and plain) as her rack of polyester. She worked at Billy's, the local drugstore, stocking shelves, hauling boxes out of the backs of trucks, helping at the register when once or twice a week, mostly Fridays, things got busy. She'd bring home discontinued merchandise for me, packets of candy, cheese crackers and Christmas toys initially (including a submarine that, spoonful of baking soda tamped into ballast tank, sank and rose, sank and rose), later on shaving lather, razors, cheap aftershave I told her was perfect and never used.

It took her a long time to die. None of those hundreds of movies and stories tell you how long it can take people to die, and none give you any idea how death smells, the sweat that soaks into sheets and mattress and won't be expunged, the ever-present tang of urine, blossom of alcohol over it all, earthy, garden smell of feces under. Dying people themselves begin to stink. They stink in ways that go far beyond the unmistakable, sweetish smell, a smell you never forget, of the cancer itself. They know this: you can see it in their eyes. Toward the end you see little else there. The sickness is eating its way out of their body, like an insect. They've *become* the sickness.

And so, for a while, as caretaker, do you. As all the while, leaving us, they rise higher and higher, air ever thinning.

The best part of the day was always when we came home, that first hour or two. Annette wrote code for an insurance company, I wrote advertising copy. Our arrivals never varied more than ten minutes. This was before I switched to buses, when I still took the sub-t, and sometimes we'd come up from opposite ends of the station simultaneously, pink flowers with dark stems blooming from the ground. We'd walk the six blocks to our apartment, I'd loosen my tie, she'd slip out of her shoes. And we'd sit there, young professionals in grownup clothes, part of the glue that held it all together, two people very much *in the world* as Heidegger would say, over glasses of wine and eventually, maybe along about the second glass, a plate of cheese and olives.

Thing is, no glue holds forever, and once Annette was gone, veneers started peeling away everywhere: I saw the world's furniture for the shoddy goods it was. Shortly thereafter I began to notice how many were going up.

They'd been doing this for some time, of course; I knew that. I'd just never taken much notice. It had little to do with me, after all, little to do with *my* life of gourmet coffee, clients, spreadsheets, presentations. Packaging is what I was about, what I did: my genius, if you will. *Another sort of veneer*, I thought at first with Annette's departure—then realized it was in fact far more central. I had been instrumental in helping create nothing less than a new language, a house of words and image that, progressively, we'd all moved into to live. And now we couldn't get out.

Having realized this, I began to stutter. No longer could I begin sentences effectively or find my way easily to the end of them. Glibness, once gone, rarely can be regained.

The first one I witnessed go up was during *The Barber of Seville*. We'd bought season tickets almost a year back when life was casually on course, glibness intact, and $480 didn't have to be thought about; the tickets, at least, were still good. Ah, sweet irony. I couldn't pay my rent, but I could attend the opera. Sat there with the empty chair next to me fuller than most, watching beautiful women file in fawning over men in ugly coats and ties.

In the row behind me, six seats down, one of these men repeatedly fell asleep, to be, at first, whispered, then, irritation growing, elbowed awake by his companion. Said companion wore a gown artfully contriving to push her sagging bosom back toward cleavage and conceal a thickening middle. His suit, by contrast, had come right off the rack, coat 44, slacks 40x32, and was cinched like a saddle by a Western belt, its buckle the size of demitasse saucers and so shiny that lasers might have been bounced off it.

Halfway into the first act, Rosina pondering the voice she's heard below her balcony, the woman prised him awake for the fifth, sixth time. He came round groggily this time, slow to surface, to come to knowledge where he was. He looked at his companion for a moment with brimming eyes, took a deep sigh, and went up.

Those in seats close by leaned away from the sudden, intense light and coughed apologetically.

Another empty seat then, like the one beside me. As this silliest of the great operas rolled on.

That evening, *après* opera, I created a sauce of porcini mushrooms, stock, red wine and roux, serving it over fresh polenta. I ate my own portion slowly, with half a bottle of a good Chardonnay, then scraped Annette's into the disposal. She had little appetite these days. Someday soon, I suspected, my own would fail. Afterwards I retrieved a favorite volume of Montaigne from the shelf and settled into bed with same, but found myself unable or unwilling to follow the scurry of his mind from notion to notion—the very quality for which I revered him.

On the bus the next morning I found my gaze drawn back again and again from observation of the world about me—drawn back, that is, from simple witness of those waiting at curbside and the ones who clambered aboard, corpuscles streaming through the city carrying nutrients and oxygen, keeping it alive—to billboards set in place above the train's windows. The windows themselves were scored amateurishly, tags and incomprehensible messages scratched roughly into them. While, above, pros had *their* say. Public service announcements, some, for clinics and the like, and in a variety of languages. The bulk of them, however, were ads of one sort or another, samples of that dialect, the idiom of American commerce, that's rapidly becoming our only language. Like any other native tongue, we learn it without direct intent, simply by exposure, absorbing it; after which, it governs not only the way we think, but what we're able to think.

I became silent that day. Not with the silence of Quakers, opening a space for whatever voice might come into it, God's perhaps, or that of my own conscience; nor with Gandhian silence, adopted in the knowledge that utterance itself is a kind of action, all action a species of violence; rather, with a silence akin to the silence of the world itself, and that of the things within it. I spoke only when necessary, only when there was information, *real* information, needing communication—that kind of silence. A silence all but lost to the murderous din of our materialism. As though if there were not this continuous noise, there would be nothing to hold us up, nothing for us to stand upon.

That day, as well, I began keeping a notebook in which I recorded all I could discover about those who went up in my presence. Often the page held little more than date, time and place. Occasionally a fact or two some momentary neighbor could recall when questioned: where the client came aboard the bus, what the client had carried with him. Upon occasion, comments from a driver who remembered the client from previous days. Sometimes, if I had nothing else, a sketch: stick figures ensconced in rear seats; bundles left behind.

Suddenly, then, it was fall. One morning, having come out in suit and tie as usual, I looked around in surprise at fellow passengers in coats and, as they stepped from the heated bus stop into that small band of open world before boarding the bus, the plumes of their breath. People had bulked up in dark colors; each leaf on each tree was a different blend of brown, yellow, red, rust, cinnamon, gold. Winds flew like great, silent birds through the caverns and canyons of the city.

That evening I sat in my apartment with Jorge, who brought with him a twelve-pack of South African beer. Jorge was virtually the only friend I had left. I'd run off the others, who grew tired (though a few, from loyalty or brute force of will, clung on till the end) first of reminiscences of Annette, then of unending discourse on this thing one did not speak of, all those going up around us. We were watching a movie I'd dialed in on the phone line, a Chinese comedy whose tags and markers were absolutely impenetrable to us. From time to time Jorge or I laughed, looking to the other to see if possibly we'd guessed correctly. An hour or so in, I set it on pause and did a quick stir-fry: carrots, celery, apple, tofu, lots of soy sauce. Rice being in short supply that month, I served it over couscous.

We moved onto the balcony to eat. Said balcony comprised a scant yard or so of floorspace extended out from the apartment and cut off by railings, of which the rental agents were nonetheless inordinately proud. Whenever I went out there, I felt I'd been set to walk the plank.

Jorge was never much for talking. We'd sat together through entire evenings during which he released, like bubbles floating slowly to the surface, perhaps a total of ten words. My own conversation, predictably enough, soon swerved from discussion of the movie (there was little enough to discuss, after all) to the folks I'd seen go up recently. Jorge nodded from time to time. Then, miraculously, he spoke.

"There's never a morning I don't wake up thinking about it, wondering if this is the day I'll finally get down and do it. You want to know why I never have?" He took a swig of his beer. The label was all bright colors and zigzags, like a poisonous snake. "Cause I look like shit in gray, man." He laughed. "Besides, anyone hauls my ashes, it's gonna be me, you know?"

This from a man I would have considered the most undisturbed, the most untouchable (if also, or likewise, the most unimaginative), I knew. Scratch the veneer of most lives, I suppose, and there's little beneath but cheap wood or pressboard, pain, despair.

No wonder they go up so fast.

Jorge and I never got back to the movie. We sat wordlessly there on the balcony as buses stopped running, as one by one streetlights and lights in all but government, emergency and residential buildings went out.

"Best get along," Jorge said.

Together we looked down toward the city's dark floor, far below.

"What about curfew?"

My friend shrugged. "It's a short walk. Skin like mine, who's to see me? I'm a moving shadow."

"You could stay over."

"Course I could. But you out of beer, man."

I smiled, immediately wondering when I'd last done so. "Take care, my friend."

He left without responding, without any show of leave-taking as always; part of that silence of the world and its things that I'd come to embrace; I suppose this was why I so valued his company. I gathered up dishes, bottles, utensils, took the movie off pause and shut it down, swished and gargled mouthpaste, smeared on cleanser and, looking in the mirror, wiped it off.

"Goodnight, Annette," I said quietly.

This was one of the times the computer grew confused.

"Excuse me."

"Yes?"

"Would you please repeat your last command?"

Realizing what had happened, I told it to delete.

"Are you sure?"

"Yes."

"Good night, then."

The next morning I slept late. Near noon, still in jeans and sweat-shirt reading *What? Me Hurry?* I went down into the street. I had no intimations of higher directives, no wisdom, to bring down to them. Not anymore. I was done with all that. But I could join them in their sadness and pain.

At the Cheyenne Diner two blocks up, where occasionally I had breakfast, less occasionally dinner, I sat on a red-upholstered stool at the counter, as always, and attempted to draw the man seated next to me into conversation. With the first couple of remarks, on weather and a purported loosening of the curfew as I recall, he grunted or nodded noncommittally. Then, when I persisted, he glanced at me strangely. So did, in train, the waitress Maria and (I'm reasonably sure) the cook mounted at his console behind the pass-through, fingers poised over keys.

Next I progressed to the bus stop. Here, again, they all regarded me strangely: a surrogate mother with child slung between sagging breasts, two gentlemen in the orange uniforms of city sanitation, another in the pink uniform indicating a prisoner released to day work, a handful of hangers-on, outriders, in the current frontier gear of snug unbleached canvas pants, white rayon poet's shirt, Chinese cloth shoes. At the sub-t stop I'd frequented for so many years when Annette and I were together, the situation was little different. A different clientele, but that same strange regard. And much the same response to overtures of conversation.

When had people stopped talking to one another?

Entering the apartment, I stood for a moment before the screen, watching those familiar prospects of blue sky and white clouds roll across, as though a tiny portion of what used to be called *the heavens* had been caged here.

"I'm home," I said.

Choosing this occasion for discernment, the computer paused before responding. "You are addressing me?"

"Yes."

"Excellent. Would it be appropriate for me to remark that you are home early?"

"Listen. People are giving up, people everywhere. They look around them and just . . . let go. Go up, we call it."

"These people are no longer alive, you mean."

"They no longer even exist."

"I see. Why are they doing this? Or—to employ the second-person plural, as would be appropriate in such an instance—why are *you* doing this?"

"I don't know."

"Who does know?"

After a moment, when I said no more, the computer asked: "Will there be anything else?" and when still I failed to respond, shut itself down.

Leaving me suspended there in eternal midmorning.

Day stretched out before me glacier-like, a white, featureless plain. No end to it, to any of it. Stepping out onto the balcony, from this posthistoric cave onto the cliff, I had a sudden flash, whether of intuition or some form of daydream terror I've no idea. I saw myself alone in absolute silence, all the others gone, surrounded by shelf after shelf of notebooks, hundreds upon hundreds of them, thousands, looming about me: all that remained of what had once been my race, my species, my people, mankind.

DAY'S HEAT

With a light knock, she stepped into the room. Like everyone else's, even those of nurses and doctors who should be used to it by now, her eyes went first to the corner of the room.

She looked older. Fourteen years has a way of doing that. I said I was glad she came, I didn't know if she would.

"Neither did I."

Now, finally, her eyes went to the bed.

I thought: What you see is what you get. It never is, of course. "He's hanging on."

Dan stepped out from behind me. "Until you could get here, perhaps."

I thought of the strings of lies and half-truths running behind our days, holding them up. How hard we work to try to give some shape to it all.

She nodded to Dan. He nodded back. Their eyes never met.

"How bad is it? Does he even know I'm here?"

I shrugged. In the corner something happened. A new shape, a bud-like swelling, ambiguous as the rest, broke through the pale white surface. If you hadn't caught the motion, you might never know anything had changed.

"Your flight okay?" I said.

"I decided to drive at the last minute."

"You'll stay with us, of course," Dan said.

"I've taken a room not far from here."

"This isn't a very safe part of town," I said. Hospitals seem always to be in the seediest sections. Out the window I had watched drug deals go down. Homeless people smeared with what looked like tar lived in the bus stop at the corner.

"It's not a very safe world."

Not that she wasn't used to it. She'd been a cop in Atlanta, what, eleven years now? Kind of life I couldn't imagine. I scarcely left the house except when Dan and I went shopping. Everything else—news, movies, work assignments—crawled in and out on the web.

"How's Larson? And the kids?"

For a moment she didn't answer. She'd look away from the corner, then her eyes would get pulled back.

"The kids are fine. Larson hasn't been around for a while now."

"I'm sorry."

"So was he."

"I guess we haven't stayed in touch very well."

She looked at me for a moment before speaking. "Why would we want to?"

Why indeed. I tried for words, but as so often out here in the world they failed me, wore false faces, masks, didn't live up to their promises or never came by at all. "It's just us now," I said finally.

From her look, that was the stupidest thing she'd ever heard anyone say. From her perspective I suppose it was.

She went to the bed and took his hand. It was impossibly white, like the inside of a mushroom. His face turned in her direction when she said his name: that was all. I thought I remembered a time when he could see, even speak a little, but maybe I imagined that. It was all years ago. For a long time now he'd been closed up inside his mind, marooned there. Except for us, of course. The Frog Prince.

Lesley stood looking down.

"So here you are, you little fuck. Everyone tells me you're dying."

She bent over him. Held-in tears slicked her eyes.

"Good," she said.

Behind me, Dan cleared his throat. "Think I'll go for a walk," he said.

The computer at which I'd been working when she came in sat blinking on a rollaway bed table. I turned it off, listening to the brief dynamo-like whine. The screen went blank.

Blank like the window. Though there, outside light made of it a brilliant backlit screen. It looked like a sheet of ice, white as this thing in the room's corner that seemed somehow to be taking the Frog Prince's place, this thing that had taken over the corner already—as he steadily diminished.

"Good," Lesley said again.

• • •

I don't know when it first may have occurred to us that we were somehow different, that others did not live quite as we did. That they could not. As a child, whatever events take place day to day seem normal; you can hardly suspect otherwise. There's an appropriate word, *parallax*—for the way an object's position seems to change when viewed from a new line of sight. Perspective is everything.

We assumed our situation to be the way of the world, Lesley and I, and spoke freely of it between ourselves. Only later, remarks to teachers and schoolmates having made them regard us strangely, did we begin slowly (slowly, though we ceased such remarks at once) to understand that they had no conception of our home life. This realization brought the two of us still closer.

We were quite the pair those days, never apart. Read the same books, became hungry at the same time, woke within moments of one another. Had, for all I know, the same thoughts.

"Lawrence, Lesley, come along," Father would say as he collected us from the backyard where we loved, most of all, to sit in the cool shade and smell of the grape arbor, sunlight dappling us with shadowy hands. We would see who could hold a grape in his mouth the longest without biting into it. "Don't be selfish, now. Your brother needs you."

Lesley, sighing, would give me the look that said: The Frog Prince has called. For so many years we went along agreeably, never questioning, never holding back. And when finally we did, or, rather, Lesley did, we discovered just how insistent Father could become, and just how desperate was little Jamie's, the Frog Prince's, need for us.

"Help me, Larry!" Lesley cried that first time. She had refused to come along, despite Father's entreaties. Then her eyes went suddenly wild and her head slammed against the floor, back arching as convulsions began. Minutes later, wordlessly, spent, she rose and walked toward Jamie's room. I followed. It would be a long time, years, before she again offered resistance. As she stepped into sunlight from a window that day, saliva glistened on her cheek and chin. She made no move to wipe it away. It looked, I remember thinking, like ice.

Remains of a dinner Dan had spent much of the afternoon preparing sat about on various surfaces: folding tables, extra chairs, the edge of the grill, flat-topped rocks, bare ground alongside. Dan did everything about the house. Cooked, cleaned, saw to it that bills got paid, repairs made, my computer files put or kept in order. Periodically I felt a certain guilt at not pulling my weight. But this is what our lives, all our lives, are about, accommodations of one sort or another. Dan was the functional part of me, the border where world and self met. In reflective moments (these occurred seldom enough) I wondered how I would ever be able to get along in the world without him. Now he'd gone off, ostensibly to prepare coffee and straighten up in the kitchen.

"Get enough?"

"Back in Atlanta, what we *didn't* eat tonight would last me a week."

"Probably do the same for us. Dan got a bit carried away." A bit. Salmon, grilled tomatoes, fresh-baked pita, two fruit salads, tiny cucumber sandwiches. "He still wants you to like him."

"It's not personal."

Out over the nearest hill a hawk banked, late light disappearing into the blackness of its wings. Three geckoes clung motionless to the window beside the back door, bodies curled into gentle crescents.

"I know it's not," I told my sister.

"Does he?"

I shook my head.

She sat peering beneath the canopy we'd constructed of tent poles and drapery remnants at the house's western edge. Neat rows of tomatoes, beans, peppers.

"I wouldn't have thought you'd be able to grow much of anything here."

"It does take work. Dan put in two years before he saw any results at all. Calls it his victory garden."

She looked at the bare, eternally dry ground about us, then to the hills with their scattered growth of hedgehog and pincushion cactus, prickly pear, cholla looking as though it should be growing beneath the sea instead of here. Halfway up, the saguaros began, time's sentinels, arms upraised. In warning, I always wondered, as if to say: go back!—or merely to get our attention? Sunlight flattened against the sky in nebulae of bright oranges, impossible blues, brilliant yellows. The day would end splendidly, as they mostly did here.

"Why on earth would anyone move to this godforsaken place?" Lesley said.

"I swore that whatever happened in my life, wherever I went, I'd never have to smell magnolias again. That sickly sweetness, and the whole town reeking of something like wet animal fur when it rained."

"And it rained every day."

"Seemed to, at least."

"Here it just looks like God squatted down, farted, and lit a match to the whole of it. Everything's brown."

"But I love the feel of space all around me. Never knew there could be so much sky. Or these incredible sunsets. And when storms come, they arrive magnificently. Lightning dances on mile-high legs. You watch it all sail in from miles and miles away." Thinking of something I'd once read: that our minds repeat the landscape.

Dan emerged with coffee thermos, cups, spoons, sugar and cream on a tray. If no one needed anything else just now, he said, then he'd get started at finding the kitchen again. It was under there somewhere.

We sipped at our coffee. One of the geckoes suddenly dashed up the length of the window to snag a moth battering at the top edge, sat working its jaws.

"We had a right to our childhood," Lesley said after a while.

I nodded. Of course we did, and both knew it. But we knew also that it was she who was the wizard of regret, the banker of anger and pain. I'd never been much good at any of it.

After a moment I motioned, and when she assented, poured more coffee for us both. Neither of us added sugar or milk. We sat quietly looking up into the hills as day faded around us.

"Maybe we don't have a right to anything," I said finally. "Maybe it all has to be wrested from the grip of something else: our lives, who we are—even a pleasant day's end like this one. Maybe it's best that we recognize that, learn to get along without all the stories that reassure us, make us comfortable."

"Jesus. *Now* I feel better. Thanks, little brother." She laughed. I remembered that laugh. Years ago. "Same cheerful goddamned son of a bitch you always were, aren't you?"

"Everyone says." I finished my coffee and set the cup on the ground. "In San Francisco I was often mistaken for sunny weather."

"Mark Twain?"

I nodded. We'd read his books together as children.

What I loved most when I was young, eight or nine years old, was sitting on the screened-in porch when it rained. I'd take books out there and read for a while, then cover up with a blanket and sit for as long as I could in semi-darkness listening to the rain. The porch had a flat roof. Rain pounded at it like heavy footsteps. And sometimes rain fell in hard waves, advancing then retreating. For the minutes or half-hour it lasted, before one of them found me there, I was shut away from the world, alone, wonderfully alone, and yet somehow intimately a part of it.

Our mother's name was Lydia. Photographs show her as a tallish, thin woman favoring long skirts and men's blue dress shirts. Her hair was light brown, her eyes green or hazel. The music she liked was Django Reinhardt, big band, Bessie Smith. This I know from her record albums, which I still have, though Dan and I own nothing on which we can play them.

She lingered on a few months after giving birth. For the whole of the time (and this I know from my father, told me as he himself many years later lay dying) she diminished visibly day to day, hour to hour. What color she had left to her skin faded away until, as he said, you could not tell her body from the sheet it lay upon. In the final weeks she lay immobile as a fallen tree, eyes open and directed unblinking to the ceiling. "She had been used up," my father said.

Used up.

Years were to pass, of course, before Lesley and I would come to the realization that in a limited, far more controlled manner, the same thing was being done to ourselves—that we were being used to the identical end.

Later still, I would have cause to wonder at the form my own engagement with the world took. Was I, sitting in seclusion staring out at the world, picking selectively at it, pulling out only those strands I wished, or needed, to get by, boiling them down to a thin gruel of news—was I much different from him?

"They're called pleats. Pleats or ribs. Those ridges running vertically along the cactus. If the pleats constrict, grow closer together, the plant needs water. If they expand, move apart, then it's healthy. Water's everything out here, of course."

"You've fallen in love with it, haven't you? Made this bleak landscape yours."

There are pauses everywhere. One of us speaks and we wait before speaking again. Moments pass between the smallest of events: another hawk banks out over the hill, a rabbit shows itself at house's edge, then for a while nothing happens. Even the sun seems to rest between steps down the sky.

"I suppose I have. There's a beauty to it that most people don't see. A kind of purity and majesty in there being so little, and in life being so difficult."

I gestured to the stand of saguaros on the hill, looking for a moment, with my arm upraised, like one of them.

"Those, for instance. Some of them will grow to forty feet, but the growth is heartbreakingly slow. A ten-year-old saguaro may be only inches tall. In a hundred and fifty years, if against all odds it somehow manages to survive, it finally reaches full height. It's truly majestic then. Nothing like it exists anywhere. Fifty years later it dies.

"Once each spring, in a six-week period just after the desert wildflower season, the saguaros bloom. Just once. Bright red flowers burst from the top of the trunk and tips of the arms. The flowers endure maybe twenty-four hours. They open at night and then, during the day's heat, close."

A light went on in the house. Dan came into view behind the window. He had changed into twill slacks and a pink cotton sweater, loafers without socks. He stood rummaging through our collection of CDs, looked out at me briefly and smiled.

"I still can't believe that you of all people make your living as a journalist."

"Nor can I. One of life's minor absurdities, but an absurdity nonetheless. Still, everything's there on the net somewhere. On the services, in various archives and special-interest cul de sacs. I only have to go in, find what I need. It's all a matter of organization—just like living things getting by out here. Newsmen are forever priding themselves on their objectivity, on being unbiased. 'Even an opinion is a kind of action.' You can't get much more objective or unbiased than someone completely removed from the scene."

"From more than the scene."

I nodded. "I have what I need."

"No. You have what you have to have. The barest minimum."

"It's by choice, Lesley."

After a moment I could see her let it go.

"I'm beat," she said. "If I leave now, I may actually make it to the bed before I drop."

"I'm glad you decided to stay here with us. It's been good."

"It has, hasn't it?"

She started away and turned back. When our eyes met, for a moment something of the old connection, the palest, trailing ghost of it, leapt into the space between us, then just as quickly was gone. I could see that she had felt it as I did, and felt now, again, the ache and enduring loss of it.

My sister turned again to move toward the house. Day's heat shimmered around her body like an aura, as though she had been trimmed with rough scissors from some other world and laid imperfectly into this one.

The turning point, for all of us, came on the night of a spectacularly beautiful day. Lesley and I (I don't recall if for some special occasion) had been taken for a rare outing to a park many miles away, terraces of slender grass sloping gently toward a lake in which ducks swam, from time to time shoveling their bills into the muck at water's edge, then raising them high like jazz trumpeters to toss them from side to side. Allowed to range about for several hours at liberty, in late afternoon we were fed a picnic meal, cold meats and cheeses and fruit, bread and a thermos of sweet tea emerging miraculously from Nurse's wicker basket, before being fetched back home. Nurse, who had come to live with us just after Mother's death looking (as I recall) quite young, by this time had begun looking old.

Perhaps the very beauty of the day, or its singularity, became a deciding point. Perhaps, like myself, Lesley had taken note that day of the changes in Nurse, and this fed her, Lesley's, resolve. It had been, at any rate, building up in her for a long time.

Nurse delivered us to Father, who in turn, saying how much we had been missed, took us into our brother's room. The Frog Prince lay immobile on his bed, pale and waxlike. Surely he was finally dead: I thought this each time. Then as we drew near he began to move, feebly at first, and always without purpose or direction, but ever more strongly at our approach. We felt again the familiar stirring in our mind—pigeon's wings in the attic, Lesley called them.

"No," Lesley said quietly beside me. Then, as Father's face and my own turned to her, she said it again, louder this time: "No!"

She stepped close, staring down at him. The Frog Prince began to beat his stubby doll's arms against himself, rolled his bloated body from side to side the few degrees he was able to manage. His turtle-like head came up, searching blindly.

My sister's eyes grew hard, furious. Even I could feel now the savagery of what she was doing.

She stepped close again, directly over him now.

"You want to live through me? You want to feel what I feel? Then here it is, you monster! Take it! Take it!"

She had thrown open the floodgates of her anger, her hatred, her fury, and it poured out at him, it swept over him, it submerged him.

"You have no right to my life!"

Father, recovering from the shock and realizing what was happening, stepped behind her, roughly seized her and began pulling her away. Intent as she was on inundating the figure on the bed before her, she made no struggle.

"*Do not ever touch me again like that,*" my sister said. The Frog Prince's movements had grown feeble. Then, almost at the moment

Father dragged my sister bodily from the room, those movements ceased.

As, I must admit, did my own.

I lay unmoving, barely breathing, I am told, for just over two weeks. Perhaps after all we all three possessed something of that ability by which the Frog Prince pursued what life he had; perhaps Lesley learned to tap into it, used it that one time, against him, and never used it again. Or perhaps she only waited until he was drawing from us those emotions and sensations upon which he thrived, until he was open to her, and then, turning his very hunger against him, overwhelmed him.

Perhaps, like him, and by much the same mechanism, I had absorbed the blows of her fury. Or perhaps (as she insists) I was but exercising for the first time in summary manner my "genius for withdrawal."

Parallax.

How can we ever know just what happened in that room? And if we did, if somehow we came to understand, would anything be, would anything have been, different, changed in any essential way by that understanding?

When I woke, at any rate, when the world began to come back to me, or I to the world, my sister was beside me.

"You're okay," she said.

I nodded.

"I'm leaving," she said.

I knew that, of course.

Our eyes met. The world swam out of focus as we connected— then I fell, flailing, back into it as the connection was gone, severed. It felt as though I were plunging headlong into a pit, and barely managed to catch myself in time. Never in my life before that instant had I known what it was to be truly, finally, unutterably alone. All about me doors closed, ships pulled out to sea, the faces of those I loved looked out the windows of departing trains.

"You'll stay?" she said.

I nodded.

She had known that, of course.

We regarded one another for a moment longer before she turned and walked swiftly away. The door to my room closed like a benediction.

I had inherited the castle.

Night, too, when it ended.

After dinner, after dark, we got into the car to return to the hospital. Lesley and I sat in back. Dan drove, as ever, steadily and sure, relaxing into the task, looking about at coal-black mountains in the distance, at the scrub, prickly pear and cholla closer in. He had the radio on, but turned so low I could hardly make out the music. Some sort of soft jazz. There was little enough traffic that car lights, when they broke across us, startled. We rode as through a diorama of civilization's slow gathering: raw, bare earth, an isolated house or two then a string of them, small settlements, finally the outskirts of the city.

Our talk was of tangible things: the meal we'd eaten and the smell of nights out here, our car, the house Lesley had recently bought back in Atlanta.

"There's a room built on top, just this one huge room, like some kind of tower or turret added on, so that it's the whole of the second floor. It has windows in each wall, four of them side by side. I walked into that room for the first time late one afternoon with the sun coming in at a slant, like water thrown across the boards of the floor, and I knew I had to have it. I wound up buying the house for that room."

At length we pulled into the hospital's deserted parking lot. Half a dozen or so vapor lamps set far apart and high on poles gave off a silvery light, sculpting the dark stretch of cement into something lunar. By contrast the corridors of the hospital itself were awash with white, bright as the bridge of a ship. The nurse at her station looked up and shook her head as we drew close, stepping out from behind the high counter to tell us how glad she was that we came when we did. The doctor had just been with him. He would be at rest soon.

Indicating that he would wait out here, Dan settled into a chair by an oval window looking down on the lot we'd just left. Lesley and I went together into the room. His head turned toward us as we entered.

Without speaking, we walked to him, Lesley to the right, myself to the left, and took his hands. His head went from side to side, just as those ducks' heads had done so long ago, from one of us to the other, though of course he couldn't see us. He was weak now, very weak, but as he struggled to summon what strength remained to him, to pull together these last fragments of his talent or his curse or whatever it had been, we both felt it. Felt him reach out to us. Felt things moving deep within us, rearranging there. Felt ourselves connected again, connected forever, as we stood there above his body.

"He's gone," Lesley said.

"Yes."

In the corner, a final bloom burst from the tip of one of the branches, red against the rest's ghostly white.

I looked back at my sister. Tears were in her eyes. I saw them through my own.

THE MONSTER IN MIDLIFE

"I find it harder and harder to get my work done," the creature said.

We had arranged to meet in a small but charming café near the river, one of several where I'm known to staff, and where a café crème appeared magically before me as I took my seat. Three women sat at the table nearest us, one of them gaunt, ascetic and unsmiling as though set upon refusing all life's pleasures, the others full-figured, laughing, eating. Half a meter further along, a hideous small dog on a pink leash peed against the ornamental railing that divided café from sidewalk.

"It's what you were created for," I said.

"But without commitment—without soul, if you will—what joy can there be in it? Only gestures, hollow forms . . ."

The creature's hand, reaching for the cup of latte, capsized it. Those claws, so useful for rending and tearing, were poorly adapted to such mundane use. They clattered against the table top as the creature gathered up a handful of napkins to mop the spill.

"Sure you won't have a bite to eat?" I said.

"I would not turn away another cup of coffee. And I would promise to take better care of this one."

"*Encore*," I told Marcel as he passed by. Briefly he glanced toward the creature, who attempted a smile. When it did, its eyes became vertical slits; a low moan, perhaps a growl, issued involuntarily from its throat.

"For a long time, you understand," the creature said, "that was enough. I went on doing what I was best at, what I was meant for. Then, slowly, I began to sense there might be something more."

"We all have these moments. There are no straight lines in nature. Nor, for the most part, in our lives."

"You are correct in this, I am certain."

The creature's eyes fixed on the dog who, having finished emptying its bladder against the railing, now began yipping at a nearby pigeon. Pigeon and dog were roughly of a size. The dog's owner, a woman of forty or more in a flower-print dress, was off by the bus stop, leaning into a departing lover like a book from whose shelf other, adjacent books have been removed.

"Unlike you, I was not created to live with doubt."

Absentmindedly, the creature reached down to scoop up the dog and popped the wriggling, whimpering thing into its mouth, tossing the leash, this tiny pink lariat, back out onto the sidewalk.

"As I said, I find it increasingly difficult to get my work done, harder each day to find within myself the proper drive and motivation. Besides"—his eyes swept café, street, city beyond—"there is so much evil in the world now. Am I truly of use any longer? Perhaps I am . . . unnecessary now. Perhaps the purpose for which I was created *is* no more."

He emitted what may have been a sigh, or the resounding of some intestinal transaction.

"You understand, I have known all along that it would never be for me to have a settled life, to come home from work at day's end and find shelter there, to dream. For me there has been only this."

Holding out his hand, he closed it into a fist. Claws curled above the fist like the petals of some exotic plant.

"I don't have answers for you," I said. "One goes on with it all, goes through the motions, carries on. With luck, eventually, it all adds up to something."

Around us, subtly, darkness grew, daylight tucking itself in at the corners of buildings. The woman in the flower-print dress stood holding the empty pink leash, looking vacantly at it, as into the frame of a broken mirror. Café Mir sits at one of the city's major crossroads. Southward now, filtering in from uptown, filed a line of protestors carrying anti-abortion signs; around their necks hung those bright red personal bombs sold almost everywhere nowadays. Up another street, emerging from Old City, marched a group of young women dressed all in black. Glittery X's were painted across their breasts. Trousers bore cartoonlike, stylized penises done in the same medium.

"It appears I am needed," the creature said. "Thank you for coming."

I waved my hand to indicate that it was nothing.

The creature stood. "Whatever else we may say of it, the world does keep offering up delicious choices," it said.

I nodded and started off in the opposite direction. I had work to see to, also, of course. My own delicious choices to make.

THE MUSEUM OF LAST WEEK

Thornton is right. The park has become crowded, all but impassable, inhabited by thickets of statues in various stages of self-creation and decay. I had no idea there were so many of them. Unmoving bodies as far as can be seen, crowded up against one another, standing, stooping, stretching. Some on their backs. The children like to come in at night and topple them.

I walked by there today. Not that I'd meant or planned to. Far from it. Nonetheless, stomach rumbling and sour with the morning's coffee, I found myself outside the fence looking in.

Scant miles away, scattered about with cholla and bottlebrush cactus, the desert looms, a sea bottom forsaken by the sea.

It is, yes, beginning to look like her, just as Thornton said. In a few days the features will be unmistakable. Even as I watched— though in truth I must admit I stood there for some time—they changed.

Tell me you won't forget me, you said.

Easy enough, Julie. How could I ever? Ravage of your face in those last months soon to be caught in that of the statue inside, by the concrete bench and the fountain that hasn't worked for years.

The whole secret of everything, you once told me—art, conversation, life itself—is where the accent's placed: the emphasis, the stress.

Do things happen faster now, closer together, than they used to, or does it just seem that way? As though all has shifted to time-lapse photography, entire life cycles come and gone in moments; as though the lacunae and longueurs that for the most part comprise our lives, these struts that hold up the scaffold of the world, have been removed. Our lives have become instant nostalgia, an infinite longing for what's been lost. While the world, like Wallace Stevens's wide-mouthed jar left out in the rain, slowly fills to the brim with the mementos, decay and detritus of our past.

Looking for more coffee, hair of the dog, I stop at a convenience store. I always order two cups, and sure enough, as I depart, a youngish man in corduroy sportcoat and chinos approaches, coat so worn as to resemble a chenille bedspread, chinos eaten away well above onetime cuffs.

"I am attempting to resolve the categorical imperative with the categorically impossible," he tells me. We stand staring at one another. Kant at ten in the morning on the streets of downtown Phoenix. "Do you have the time, sir?" he says after a moment.

Professing that I wear no watch, I offer what I have instead: the extra coffee.

"I only wish I could have the luxury of not knowing," he says. "Unfortunately that is not the case. And I feel," he says as he takes a sip of coffee and falls in beside me, "that there may not be much time left." We stride along, two men of purpose moving through city, day and world. Perhaps every third sentence of what he says makes sense. He is desperate for bus fare to the university where he teaches, one of these vagarious sentences informs me. "I was lost but now am found. Still, yesterday and today, I have had no access to research facilities." And a bit later on: "Tomorrow for the first time my students will be prepared for class and I will not be."

I ask what he teaches.

"History. And, every other semester, a seminar on forgetfulness."

Not long toward nightfall, I attend a housewarming for Sara and Seth, researchers who have just moved in together. This is a match made somewhere just off the interstate between Heaven and Hollywood. Seth is the world's leading authority on mucus, can speak for hours concerning protein content, viscosity, adhesiveness, mucopurulence, degrees of green. Sara in turn has fifty pounds of elephant penis in her—now their—refrigerator.

You once told me that we understand the world, we organize it, in whatever manner we're able.

"An erect elephant penis weighs around a hundred and eight pounds and is sixty-two inches in length," says Gordon, who, as an editor, knows such things.

"That's up to here," Ralph remarks, holding his hand at a level about six inches above my head. Flamingly gay, he takes inordinate delight in such rodomontade.

"Sixty-two inches is five-foot-two, " I remark.

"Right," Ralph says. "Up to here on you," indicating again the same spot.

What does it mean, I wonder, that he feels this need to belittle me during an exchange concerning penises? But I suppose that indeed I will be, must be, a short statue. Julie will tower over me as she did in life, in every way.

Correct me if I'm wrong, but this is how I remember it. Gregory Peck, on safari, has been injured. He lies all but helpless in his tent, gangrene staking claim to leg and life as hyenas circle outside. The woman he loves attends him.

This is what I'm thinking as I step away from others, away from fifty pounds of elephant penis in the fridge and dissertations on mucus, into the night. I was eight, nine, when I first saw that movie at the Paramount one Sunday afternoon. Scant blocks away, the Mississippi boiled in its banks. Within the week it would surmount levee and sandbags and rush the lowlands. I kept having to ask my brother to explain what was going on in the movie. I'm not sure he understood a great deal more than I did at that point, but he gave it his best. He's now a philosopher.

And now, of course, in our world, anticipation has gone into overdrive. Gregory Peck would never just lie there listening to the hyenas. They'd be on him before he knew it.

Back home, I brew white tea (high in antioxidants, low in caffeine) in a white pot and take it in a white cup out onto my white-pine patio. Darkness surrounds, and I lift my cup to it—whether in supplication or challenge I do not know. What has my life come to? What have all our lives, what has our world, come to?

I go back inside, to the pantry. I've saved these a long time.

The scars come in packages of six. I rip open a package at random and sense the scars's restlessness as they stir to life, sense their pleasure at being allowed to do at last what they were created for.

THE GENRE KID

Sammy Levison was fourteen when he discovered that he could shit little Jesuses. They were approximately three inches tall and perfectly formed, right down to the beard and a suggestion of folds in the robe. Tiny eyes looked out appealingly; one hand was lifted in peaceful greeting. The first came incidentally, but all that was required to repeat the performance, he found, was concentration. Later on, Sammy tried pushing out little Buddhas and Mohammeds, but it wasn't the same. He didn't understand that.

His mother had been brushing her hair at the sink and, walking past as he stood, caught sight of what was in the bowl. Her hand shot out to restrain his own from flushing. A miracle, she said, it's a miracle—and called his father. She didn't go to work at the laundry that day. When he got home from school, the line of neighbors and supplicants ran for a block or more along the street, upstairs, and down the hallway to his open door. One by one, as at televised funeral processions, the line advanced as people filed through the two cramped rooms shared by mother, father, brother, sister and Sammy, to the toilet, to have a look. Many crossed themselves. Not a few appealed to the bobbing figure for relief, cessation of pain, succor. Every so often the little Jesus would move in the bowl and there would be sharp intakings of breath.

Soon Sammy had become a frequent guest on local talk shows, within the year a guest on national versions of the same, holding forth on all manner of subjects, northern Ireland, capital punishment, the Israeli stalemate, of which he knew nothing at all. Professors, priests and politicos, vapid interviewers whose perfect teeth were set like jewelry into bright, enthusiastic smiles, simple men of God with lacquered hair   all mused on what Sammy might be considered to be: a messenger, an artist, a devil, a saint. Though everyone knew, the precise occasion for his being here or being under discussion, what he actually *did*, got mentioned only obliquely.

Anchormen and women never blinked, of course, this being only a storm-tossed version of what had been drilled into them at journalism school: to make tidy small packages, to sketch and color in the rude outline of actuality without ever once enclosing the beast itself. Their faces registered concern as they listened to Sammy's supposed confessions. On camera they crossed legs and leaned close, fiddled Mont Blanc pens between fingers like batons, wands, instruments of thought.

Mother didn't have to go back to work at the laundry. Father bought up block after block of apartment buildings, a scattering of convenience stores previously owned by immigrants, waste-disposal companies. Brothers and sisters attended the best, most expensive schools. And one day in his own fine home, there among tongue and groove hardwood floors, imported Spanish tile, exquisite bathroom fixtures, Sammy found himself costive—unable to perform, as it were.

He was the best at what he did. Actually, since he was the world's first coprolitist, he was the *only* one who did what he did. But Sammy wanted something *more*.

Meanwhile he was blocked.

"I have to follow where my talent takes me," he said, "I have to be true to it," as he sat, grunting, "I can't just go on endlessly doing what I already know how to do, what I've done before."

With his absence from the scene Sammy had become something of a ripe mystery, raw ingredient for the cocktail shakers of media myth. WHERE IS SAMMY L? a ten-minute segment of one prime-time show asked, clock ticking ominously in the background. Newsmen with perfect teeth leaned over words such as *angst, noblesse oblige* and *hubris*, bringing them back to life with mouth-to-mouth and sending viewers off in search of long-forgotten dictionaries. T-shirts with Sammy's picture fore and aft began appearing everywhere.

The first of his new issue were malformed, misbegotten things.

"We claim there's freedom, tell ourselves this is the country that gave freedom to the world," Sammy said in a rare interview from this period. "There's no freedom here. As artists we have two choices. Either we plod down roads preordained by those in power, the rich, the yea-sayers, arbiters of taste, style and custom; or we cater to the demands of the great unwashed, trailer-park folk, the lumpen proletariat," sending viewers and research assistants alike again in search of those dictionaries.

Gradually over time Sammy's new creations began to take on a form of their own. At first, like the boulders of Stonehenge and menhirs of Carnac, these forms were rough-hewn, lumpen themselves in fact, more presence than image; and even once realized, were like forms no one had seen before, troubling, disturbing.

By this time, of course, the headlights of media attention had swung elsewhere, found new deer. There was, a few years further along, with *Famous Men*, his exhibit of images of Holocaust victims, a brief return to representation and an even briefer rekindling of media interest; then silence. All the things for which an artist labors, depth, control, subtlety, he had attained, but no one would see these.

"Perhaps this is as it should be," Sam Levison said. "We practice our art, if we are serious artists, finally for ourselves alone, *within ourselves alone.*"

And so he did, to the point that the *Times'* obituary identified him simply as *Samuel Levison, 48, of Crook Bend near Boston, eccentric, hermit and performance artist whose work endured its fifteen minutes of fame and passed from view as though with a great sigh of relief.*

At least they'd used the word *great.*

In the garage apartment where he spent his last years, nothing was found of whatever new work may have taken up the artist's life in the decades since the fall. Half-hearted rumors sprang up that he'd destroyed it all, or had pledged his sister to do so. Appropriately enough, Sam offered no last words, only one final creation pushed out as he died. This was, as in the early days, a small Jesus. Sam's landlord, come yet again to try and collect rent, found it there as, later, he waited for the ambulance, and picked it up. But its eyes bored into him and would not let go. After a moment he dropped it back to the floor and crushed it with his foot.

TELLING LIVES

A couple of kids are standing at the bus stop reading my book about Henry Wayne, possibly a school assignment. Henry's right there with them with a cup of coffee from the Circle K, answering questions. So probably it's an assignment, all right. The city bus pulls in and they get on. I'm never sure how this works. Do they get some kind of pass to ride the city bus to school or what? Every morning there's a couple dozen of them out there waiting.

Across the street, Stan Baker, who owns most of the good affordable apartments in this part of town, is up on the roof of one of his units poking around at ledges, fittings, tar. Someone else with khakis and a clipboard is up there with him. City employee's my guess. Stan waves when I look up. I wrote my first biography about him.

No one ever imagined they'd catch on this way. Who could have? I wrote that first one, about Stan, on a lark, more or less to have something to do as I sat in front of the computer each morning. My last, literary novel, at which I'd labored a full year, had sunk without a trace, not even flotsam or driftwood left behind. I'd taught for a while at the local community college but had no real taste or aptitude for it. When I went on to write features for the *Daily Republic*, bored with simple transcription, I found myself first making up details, then entire stories. It was in the biographies, cleaving to the well-defined shoreline of a life, that I found a strange freedom, a release.

"Barely scratch beneath the surface of any one of us, even the dullest slob around," my old man used to tell me, "and you'll come onto a source of endless fascination and contradiction. We're all inexhaustible, teeming planets, filled with wonder."

This from a man who had little interest in others' lives (mine included, sadly) and who rarely left the house. Number twenty-two in the series.

Nowadays, of course, the biographies are about all anyone around here reads. Has the town somehow found itself, come to itself, within them? Certainly, for my part, I've stumbled onto an inexhaustible supply of material—and my life's work.

Carefree, the town where they care.

That's how we're known now, here just down the road from the nation's sixth largest city with its riot of dun-colored buildings, cloverleafs and sequestered communities, ridgeback of mountains looming always in the distance.

And we do care. All of us, every one. School kids with their backpacks and mysterious piercings, bank presidents, sanitation-truck jockeys, yardmen and insurance salesmen alike. Clerks at convenience stores going nine out of ten falls with the angel of English each moment of their day. The group of street dwellers who regularly congregate in the alley behind Carta de Oro.

However we try to break out, to break free, we're forever locked within our own minds. Locked away from knowledge of ourselves every bit as much. But there's this one ride out we can sometimes hitch, this tiny window through which with luck and good weather we can peer and see ourselves, in the guise of another, looking back in.

That's what the biographies have become for us, I think, those rides, those windows.

"Hard at work, I see," Bobby Taylor (number eighteen in the series) says as I sip my morning double espresso at The Coffee Grinder. He's on duty, has his helmet tucked under one arm, what looks like half a gallon of coffee in the other hand, motorcycle pulled up just outside.

"Finger on the pulse and all that, Officer."

"Looks more like butt in chair to me."

"What can I say? It's a sedentary occupation."

"How's your mom?"

Mother had been hospitalized six months back after meeting a UPS man at the door with an electric carving knife. She said he'd raped her, and no one should treat a twelve-year-old that way. In hospital, or so she claimed, she'd turned thirteen. One of the nurses baked her a cake, and everyone gathered round for the party. She'd blown out all thirteen candles.

"Holding her own."

"Alzheimer's, right?"

"What they say."

"She know you?"

"Some days she does."

"Next time you visit and it's one of those days, tell her little Bobby Taylor says hello. Had her for tenth-grade English, like nearly everyone else in town. Only A I ever got. Parents couldn't decide whether to be shocked or expect it go on happening."

"And?"

"Shocked won out."

I was getting ready to leave when a thirtyish woman stepped up to my table. She had black hair cut short in the back, longer toward the front, giving an impression of two wings.

"Mr. Warren?"

"Yes."

She held out a warm, narrow hand, nails painted white and trimmed square across.

"Justine Driscoll. May I join you?"

Although I'd not noticed it before this, a radio was playing behind the counter. Now soft jazz gave way to news. I heard "two fairies collided off the coast of Maine," then realized the announcer meant *ferries*.

"Please do. Can I get you something?"

"I'm fine. I own a small publishing company, Mr. Warren. I was wondering if—"

"I have an exclusive contract with McKay and Rosenwald, you must know that."

"Of course. But I hoped you might look this over. It's our leader for the fall. A flagship book, really, launching a new series."

From a bookbag slung like a purse over one shoulder, she extracted and passed across a copyedited manuscript, corrections and emendations in red pencil in a tiny, tidy hand.

I read the first few pages.

"The barber's hair," I said.

It began with the story of my mother at the hospital, blowing out those thirteen candles.

"You're not surprised."

"It was only a matter of time."

"Would you be willing to give it a read, let us know if there are errors?"

I pushed it back across the table. "I have no wish to read it, Miss Driscoll. You have my blessing, though—for whatever that's worth."

"Actually, it's worth quite a lot. Thank you."

She stashed the manuscript back in her book bag.

"Our sales people are strong behind this. We have solid orders from Barnes & Noble, most others."

"Then let me join them to say that I sincerely hope it does well for you."

"I'll not take up any more of your time, Mr. Warren."

She stood. Her eyes swept the room. I had the sense of a camera recording this scene. It was a glance I knew all too well.

"Miss Driscoll?"

She turned back.

"You look remarkably like my wife, Julie. Way you're dressed. Nails. Hair."

"Do I really?"

"She died eight years ago, a suicide."

"I know. From the book. And I'm sorry."

"This Jamie Byng, the author. It's you, isn't it?"

She stood, irresolute. Before she could respond I asked, "Do you have plans for the rest of the day?"

"No."

"Yes."

YOUR NEW CAREER

Each day we're required to assume the identity of one of the other students. At first, when we knew so little of one another, it was less difficult, but we're well along in the program now and have gained considerable personal knowledge. On the other hand, all those early, generic assignments, impersonating postmen, policemen and the like, have paid off. This has been going on from the first day. We're graded on how well we bring it off:

Preparation. Equal parts Research (on the internet) and Observation (finding those physical, character and speech traits of the target that others in the class will recognize).

Persuasiveness. This one, like much else in life, is mostly attitude. You must charge right in and right along, pursuing your objective and game plan, oblivious of all objections, challenges, detours and roadblocks.

Perseverance. You do not, whatever happens, surrender. Even in the face of certain defeat, cover hopelessly blown, revealed for what you are, you do not give up the pretense.

Yesterday I received the only 10/10/10 of the semester. Called upon first thing in the morning, I stood, walked to the front of the class and began my presentation, continuing same, with scheduled breaks, of course, until almost five in the afternoon. This time I had become not a fellow student but our instructor, Mr. Soong. As Mr. Soong sat in the back of the classroom smoking cigarette after cigarette and looking ever more nervous, I taught the class he might have taught, sketching out details of a standard shadow-agent operation, citing examples from my own (his own) field work and my (his) personal history.

The secret-agent school is located on a strip mall in the far-southeastern reach of the city, just at the boundary where the city goes down for the third time into suburbs. One end of the mall's held down by a Petsright, the other by an upstart home-supply center.

An income-tax service, a cut-rate office-supply store, and two food shops, Ted's Fish N Chips, Real-y-Burgers, straggle down the line. Standing apart across a narrow empty lot chockful of go-cups and partial frames of shopping carts like disabled vehicles left behind on battlefields, a shabby cinema plays last year's forgotten films at a dollar a shot to sparse audiences of forgotten people.

"A moment, if you will," Mr. Soong announced as, taking my seat near day's end, I passed both torches, classroom and identity, back to him. He held up a finger profoundly nicotine-stained to the first joint and only seriously stained to the next—a characteristic of which I had made full use. By now, mindful of rush hour, students are compulsively checking watches as though they're detonation devices. The next wave of hopefuls, buying their way toward certification as nursing assistants, teems on the sidewalk outside. The storefront classroom's on time-share between various vocational schools. Stuck in a dead-end job?, You're only ninety days away from an exciting career as _____, You can make the difference, etc.

"Violence, I'm afraid, has paid a visit," Mr. Soong said, British locution and Indian rhythm chiming together like two dice in a cup. "At or about one o'clock this morning, noticing that lights remained on well after hours, a squad car on routine patrol pulled up in front of the Rialto." Everyone hereabouts called it The Real Toe. "One officer stayed behind to radio in, the other went into the lobby. There he found a young man—the assistant manager as it turned out, an eighteen-year-old who closed each night after seeing the rest of the staff out—lying in front of the popcorn machine, quite dead."

Lying in a pool formed of blood and piss in equal parts, with a small pool of Real Butter Flavoring nearby, lesser lake among the greater—but Mr. Soong doesn't say this.

"Both the mall's proprietors and school officials have asked that I urge you all to exercise caution today as you leave. Please do so." That index finger went up again, pointing to the sky like a saint's. "Observe the buddy system." Now a second finger. "Be aware always of your surroundings." And a third. "Walk purposefully." Little finger. "Make eye contact with anyone you encounter." Lady Thumb. "Have your car keys out and ready."

Because it was the first Friday of the month, tuition was due. One by one we filed past Mr. Soong's makeshift desk to pay up, settle, render unto Caesar, etc., before filtering out onto the parking lot where a magnificent sunset burgeoned parachute-like above the horizon as the next generation of students prepared to clamber in. Many, as always, paid in cash. Some, surely, are illegal; others, for whatever and various reasons, have or lay claim to no bank accounts.

I sat in my car smoking a last cigarette, radio tuned to the local NPR, as late arrivals rushed from car to classroom in search of the excellent salary and fulfilling career promised them by late-night TV ads, and as day's parachute collapsed into darkness. At Standard Uniform in Twin Cedars Mall a mile or so further along toward the city, they've all purchased green uniform tops, white shoes, shiny scissors, gleaming stethoscopes. I watched Mr. Soong cross cracked pavement to his yellow Honda. Often, I know, once all are gone, Mr. Soong returns to the classroom to work.

On the way home I listen to an interview with a writer who's published a book about caged birds taken as safeties into coal mines. "Mute, unsocialized birds are best for the purpose," he said. "Mockingbirds with their vast repertoire proved worthless: they sing and sing up till the very moment they keel over."

The color of the universe, another interviewee, a physicist, insists at length, is beige. He also has written a book which expounds his beliefs. The world is fast filling up with news and interviews, books and belief. Soon there'll be no room for people.

Next morning, Miss Smith pulls into the spot alongside as I'm sitting there with windows rolled down listening to bad country music and finishing up my large coffee and egg-and-bacon sandwich. I stopped off at the Greek's diner as always. We go in and find Mr. Soong lying in a pool of sticky red stuff. Soon other students begin arriving; more than one stumbles back outside to throw up.

"Maybe this is our final exam," I say to Miss Smith.

Mr. Soong, get up. Light a cigarette, smile your lopsided smile, and grade me. Tell me how I did.

BLUE DEVILS

All the way up from El Paso, which is where you first start noticing how much *sky* there is, the image stays with me. I've managed to shut it away for a long time, but now, maybe because we're on the spoor, getting close, it comes back. I look up at a cloud the size of Idaho, and there it is. At a mountain rising from the ground like a fist polished smooth: there, too. And in cholla and scrub cactus at the side of the road.

"I could definitely use a beer about now. You could probably do with a break, too. Unless you feel the need to push on, that is."

I look over at him. What he's said is slow to register. The world comes to me these days in a kind of stutter, like the time delay on radio talk shows.

"Maybe we could grab something to go?" I'm dry myself, from looking out at this landscape as much as for any other reason.

He nods once, eyes straight ahead as always. Both hands are loosely on the wheel, left elbow a buttress in the window. At the next exit he swings off into a service plaza larger than many of the Southern towns I grew up in. My father was career military, outspoken enough at the incompetencies and inefficiencies involved that he was repeatedly transferred. I counted once: eleven high schools. Maybe that's why I myself have always had such respect for authority. But it could have gone either way.

He fills up, goes inside to pay, and comes out with a six pack of Heineken and the Slice I asked for. Back on the road he pops one of the beers and sips at it for the next thirty miles. The rest are tucked away under his legs. The two of us, the Slice, and the beer bottles just about fill the little Miata.

Flies.

The sound of them was what I always remembered, always thought of. Then Sergeant Van Zandt's voice at last penetrating. How many times has he already asked?

You okay, Mr. Gorman?

I nodded, said could I see her.

Well, generally ... He stopped. Motioned with one hand for attendants to uncover her. A plain, somewhat muscular woman herself not much older than Faith folded back a corner, watching me closely the whole time. I nodded, and she put the cover back in place.

It's Faith, then. It's your daughter, Van Zandt said.

Yes.

"You understand that we can't do anything here," Delany says. I lurch back up into the world as it is. "There's no outstanding warrant, which severely limits the scope of my actions."

I went to him because of his reputation as a bounty hunter.

"So here's what we do. We go in, have a look, poke through the ashes of the campfire. We find something, anything at all, then we ask the locals to step in. You okay with that?"

I nod. I see my daughter's face below me, shimmering in heat that rises off the asphalt. An eye is gone. Ear and scalp are torn away on that side.

Delany pulls out another beer, drops the empty bottle back in the pack.

We're coming into the Chiricahuas, mountains unlike any others I know, ghostly somehow, the whole range eroded by wind, water and time to skull-like stands of stone honeycombed with caves and unlikely passages where Cochise eluded all pursuers.

Farther on, past Tucson, reservation lands lie slumbering to every horizon, cluttered briefly by trailers or tarpaper shacks, rusting automobiles and appliances, propane tanks.

"Unless you want to cancel all that and just blow him away, of course," Delany says.

He was, I was told, the best in the state at finding people—the best, period. That information came almost a year after Faith's death, on my last visit to Van Zandt's cubicle tucked away on the fourth floor behind rows of filing cabinets that looked as though cars had been driven repeatedly into them.

"There's just not much else I can do for you, Mr. Gorman," Van Zandt said. "The case remains open, of course. We don't officially close homicides. And bulletins will stay in circulation—till they're crowded out by new ones, at least. You never know. Sometimes things fall into our lap when we least expect it. Meanwhile, you might want to consider giving this man a call. I'm not telling you this as a cop, of course. I have a daughter myself."

He slid a business card across the desk to me with two crooked fingers, tapped it once with the index, and let go.

"He's a detective. Specializes in finding people, and he's damned good at it. Lots, including some who do the same kind of work, say there's no one better."

I looked down at the card. Buff-colored, almost translucent parchment. And engraved, not thermography. Just SEAN DELANY and a phone number.

Brought up on cheap detective movies and hardboiled novels, despite the card I'd half expected to find Delany in some gin mill with a cigarette hanging out one side of his mouth and a made-over blonde on the other arm, with eyes like bad sunsets and a tie that doubled as napkin. Instead, by way of his answering service and a secretary who called back immediately, I found him at Geronimo's, a mid-city health club. He was finishing up a set of handball, had a thing or two to talk over with the investment counselor who'd been his opponent, and would see me outside in twenty minutes if that was all right.

We met at his car, a British-green Miata. He had traded sweat-shirt and shorts for a full-cut cotton suit like the ones Haspel used to make down in New Orleans and wore a knit, alligatorless shirt beneath. At a mall nearby he ordered felafel from a Greek fast-food stall, and I had three coffees as we talked.

What do you do, Mr. Gorman? he asked at one point.

I'm an architect. I build things.

We talked a while longer, and he agreed to help me.

From the first, I've been won over by Delany's quiet-spoken, self-assured, ever-so-civilized manner. But now as we move ever farther from the city—into the scruffy hills and scrubland of West Texas, through ancient, barren New Mexico, and on into Arizona, growth like bright green veins in runnels formed by water washing down mountainsides—I can't help but notice how that's begun changing. Simple things, at first: endings left off a word here or there, rougher cadences. Then articles and conjugations drop out, leaving behind a language all nouns, present-tense verbs, prepositions. The man with whom I get out of the car in Tucson seems not at all the one with whom I began the trip back in Fort Worth.

"It doesn't have anything to do with justice or finding the person responsible," Chris said to me a few nights before. We'd met for coffee at a carefully neutral restaurant. She came directly from work; I, now unemployed, from the one-room apartment I'd finally settled into after months of motel rooms. "Don't you see that? That's why I left, why I had to. It's the *world* you want to hurt now, Joe. You want to hear it scream, want to tear something away from it, want to hurt it as much as it's hurt you."

Hurt? No. What I feel is numb. What I feel is nothing. I look out at the world and don't recognize, don't register, what's there. Only with effort, in a kind of forced gulp, will my mind take it in.

"Welcome to Tucson," Delany says.

The city has come surreptitiously up around us and now seems to go on forever, sprawling across this treeless, light-struck landscape. Distinctive mountain ranges stand at each point of the compass. A map names them for me: Catalina, Santa Rita, Rincon, Tucson. We drive along something called the Speedway past The Bashful Bandit, Empress Theater and Book Store XXX, Weinerschnitzel. Past bars, fast-food emporiums, video shops, used-car lots, hardware and autoparts stores.

"The Miracle Mile," Delany says. "But most people around here just call it the Armpit." Pickup trucks with bodies rusted wholly through in mold-like patches overtake us, leave us behind. "Place we're looking for's up ahead a little ways."

He pulls into the parking lot of a motel that looks as though it might have been built early in the fifties when such things were novelties. It's set back off the road half a lot or so. The wooden sign is shaped like a palm tree, with the legend REFRIGERATED AIR and its name, NO-TEL MOTEL, painted on.

"Room fourteen," Delany tells me.

It's on the second tier. Inside, a TV plays loudly: sirens, brakes screaming, metal slamming into metal.

"We're in luck." He knocks.

"Yeah?"

"Maintenance. Sorry to bother you, but we've got a major water leak downstairs. Have to check it out. Take us a minute or two, tops."

"Hang on."

Nothing for a time—Delany and I exchange glances—then the door opens a couple of inches, and a slat of face shows in the crack. Sharp, finlike nose, small mouth, drooping eyelid. Day's growth of beard.

He takes in Delany's clothes.

"Hell, man, you ain't—"

But Delany ducks his shoulder into the door, hard, and keeps going.

The man inside staggers back out of the way as the door slams against the wall. He reaches for the rear pocket of his jeans. Delany is there. Stomps down on his instep and, when the man bends forward over the pain, pivots behind him on one foot, grabbing his long hair in a fist. The man's eyes round as Delany's hand tightens.

"Be nice," Delany tells him. "Man needs to talk to you."

I step inside and shut the door.

Wary, expressionless eyes follow me.

Delany pulls a gun out of the man's back pocket and hands it to me.

"Your call," he says, stepping off to the side.

So I shoot him.

Delany lets go of the hair as the man goes down. When he tries to breathe, air whistles out of his chest. He puts a hand gently against himself as if to hold the air in, says *Shit* with an even louder whistle, and is still. I notice there's no difference in the eyes.

"Cops be here in six minutes tops," Delany says.

He's standing by the bedside table looking through things piled up there, magazines, a cheap plastic wallet, stray bills and change, a couple of envelopes.

"But we got us another problem," he tells me.

"Yeah?"

"Wrong bird."

I look at him.

"This wasn't your man." He holds up a folded paper from one of the envelopes. "Gentleman here's freshly laundered, just out of the joint. Been a guest of the state almost three years."

"But how . . ."

He shrugs. "Information's what you make of it. I thought we had a fit. Sometimes it doesn't work out right. Sometimes it does."

Delany takes the gun from me, wipes it with his handkerchief, and puts it in the dead man's hand. He presses the hand hard against the grip, feeds the forefinger into the trigger guard.

"Thing is," he says, "does it matter?"

And I realize that it doesn't. That it doesn't matter at all. Someone's paid. A life's been taken. That's what matters. Maybe I understood all along, understood without knowing I understood, that this was the best I could hope for. Maybe Delany knew that, too.

We go down the back stairs, get in the Miata, and pull away, north on Oracle to West Miracle Mile, then due west till we jump 1-10, hearing sirens build to a scream behind us. I watch the Catalina Mountains, the Tucson Mountains, all this sky. Everything bright and alive, sharply defined, in the noonday sun. I can go back to building things now.

Later I look up again at the Chiricahuas and think how little we've changed. We huddle together in the vertical caverns of our cities, around our megawatt campfires, and try to fill up the darkness with chants, songs, magic. We understand so little, we're always afraid, and sometimes still, the best we can do is offer up a sacrifice—hoping to drive out whatever blue devils overtake us.

SHUTTING DARKNESS DOWN

It was over, finally over, and they sat, the two of them, as they had so many times before, in a huge low-ceilinged room with windows along one end that looked out over downtown, letting in now, this early morning, a gray, smoky light. Folding steel chairs and collapsible tables with brown plastic tops stood about the room at random, some pushed close together in huddles, others drifting free. Tabletops were littered with Styrofoam cups, ashtrays, fast-food wrappers, legal pads, file folders. Computer screens sat with cursors blinking, surrendering their own light to the growing light outside. No one else in the room.

All the others were off duty.

All the others had gone home.

Still pinned to the board, arranged chronologically in sequences painstakingly reconstructed by Jackson, Meredith, and members of the task force they headed, hung photos of victims, crime scenes, family and friends, workplaces, roadways and buildings, habitual routes. These ran in discrete blocks horizontally (young woman with her belly slashed open to a smile, children at rest in spoon-like curves around beloved stuffed bears, dinosaurs, dolphins) and vertically (downtown laundromat where teenagers found the baby going round and round in the dryer, abandoned bloodied Chevrolet Nova, suburban apartment with kitchen and bathroom surprises).

Like a crossword, Meredith thought. Fill in the blanks.

Filling in the blanks was what they'd been doing, trying to do, for almost a year now. And finally it was over.

"Well, that's it, then," Meredith said. "Cut. Print."

Jackson nodded.

So for a while (days, months, a year) that face he knew so well would be absent from the world. While he and others like him marked time, waiting for it to come up again grinning. He'd spent much of his life looking into that face. The sprawl of photos on the board made him remember all the others: single women, couples, children, old folk. Who they were, where they'd lived, what they'd left behind. Days, months and years a blur. His own life a blur. These memories, this job his only sense of time, his only real hold on it.

"Guess so," Jackson said, hand working hard at the muscles of his neck. He tugged at his tie, the dark blue one Betty gave him last Christmas, already at half mast. His coat hung on the back of his chair. Each time he shifted weight the coat shrugged its shoulders.

"What'll you do?"

"Try to find my way home, I guess. See if Margaret's still there. Find out what gangs the kids have joined, see if *they* bother coming home at night. Sleep. In three or four days— who knows?—I might just get up and have me a cup of coffee out of a real cup."

"Something to look forward to, for sure."

Meredith stared down at a coffee stain on his shoe. Who was it said that God is in the details. Blue shirtsleeves rolled up haphazardly onto biceps, underarms stained with sweat. While Jackson's white dress shirt, sleeves folded twice, still looked fresh from the laundry.

"Yeah. What *else* is life about?" Jackson's eyes swept the room. Now that it was all over, time had slowed. Stop-action, they used to call it. Slow motion. People lived in this drudge all their lives. Hard to see why or how. "Be a gym again by the time we get back."

"More likely the captain's private studio. Backdrop of the city, a map."

"For all those TV interviews."

"Hey—he's a hero."

"Sure he is. Caught Mr. Road Kill." Jackson looked around again. "Still reminds me of my old school cafeteria. Every day they'd fold down these tables, otherwise it was just a gym. Dropping hoops, you'd still smell sour milk and cabbage, the sickly reek of cheap hot dogs."

He'd paid childhood dues in such cafeterias. Not many blacks back in Phoenix those days. Kids sat down by him, spat in his tray, called him a nigger and told him what they were going to do to him out on the playground once he'd finished eating. It all took time, the way these things do, but he'd managed to dodge it all, the pettiness, the violence, even the fear, and finally fit in.

Meredith got up and walked to the windows. After a while Jackson came up behind him. They stood together looking down. Buses pushed through the streets like giant land-grazing beasts. Cars skittered in and out among them. Sun like a wound bleeding light into the sky.

Pilot fish, Meredith thought, watching the cars. He was twelve years younger than Jackson, just enough difference that they'd come up, lived, in separate worlds. Meredith turned twenty in Nam sending kids his own age, kids dredged from Iowa City drive-ins and Memphis burger joints, out on patrol. Gave him a certain perspective.

Down on the street, Jimmie shoehorned his cart into its usual space between newsstand and bus stop. Routine's a good thing, something you can hold on to. Hot dogs would be steaming inside. Pretzels hung from hooks above. Smell of mustard and sauerkraut.

"Don't seem a bad kid," Meredith said, "not really."

"They never do."

"Yeah." When's the last time he had a hot dog? "But you have to wonder why things went the way they did."

"For him? Or for the others?"

"Both, I guess."

"My oldest son John? Working on his master's degree in philosophy up at Columbia. The world's the case, he keeps telling me. What is, is. Try making it different, all you do is make yourself crazy. Maybe he's right."

Down in the street, Jimmie slapped a dog between halves of a bun, slathered on sauerkraut, mustard, ketchup.

"Any of it ever more than a toss of the dice?" Meredith said.

Jackson shrugged. Hell if he knew. Maybe. On the job almost twenty years, and all his certainties had eroded to one: you never know what a person will do. Any person.

"Seeing yourself."

Meredith's eyes met his in the window's reflection: "I guess." Could it have gone that way with him? "For a couple of years after the war I was really messed up."

"Sure you were. You earned it."

For a minute or so, neither of them said anything.

"Besides," Jackson went on, "you don't see yourself in all this, you're not likely to see much else."

"So it's always ourselves we're chasing."

"You're gonna tell me you ever doubted it?"

"I doubt everything. More and more of everything as time goes on."

"Good. Always *figured* you were gonna turn out all right." Jackson's hand worked at his neck, crawled around again to his tie. "Choke down one last cup with me?"

Meredith shrugged. "Wouldn't do it for anyone else, but what the hell."

Jackson walked to a table along the back wall. On the table were coffee makers, a tray of sandwiches and half-sandwiches in plastic wrap, bags of chips torn open along the seams, boxes whose bottoms were sludged with powdered sugar, icing, doughnut fragments.

One of the coffee makers had a carafe almost full. Jackson lifted it off the heat, sniffed at it. Poured a cup for both of them.

They sat at another of the tables. Jackson pushed file folders and papers aside to make room for their cups, but both held on to them. Something reassuring about their physicality, the warmth, what this signaled—something far past simple sharing.

"Worst has to be that family in Canton," Meredith said after a while. "No way I'll ever get those kids out of my mind. Laying there like that, all opened up. *Ecorché*, they call it up in Quebec." Where Meredith had lived when he got back from Nam. Just couldn't face the States again at first. Lot of hunters in Quebec. See these deer dressed out, staked on boards outside houses. "You've been doing this a long time, B.J."

"All your life."

It was an old joke between them.

"You tell me how anyone ever thinks he's able to understand something like that?"

"No one does. Not really."

"Except Hargrove."

Their department expert. Guy grew up in Highland Park

driving a convertible, had a house in his own name there by the time he was sixteen. Parents bought it for him—for his future. Then he sailed through SMU and Galveston med school, barely touching down the whole time, and elbowed his way through a residency at Parkland like someone caught in rush hour on the New York subway. *Sure* he knew how someone like Billy Daniel lived, what was in his head.

Meredith picked up one of the file folders, scanned it quickly and put it down, took another.

In Billy's mind there is no connection between what he does—what he has done, more properly—and the results. For him, the causal link simply does not exist. This is a difficult concept, I know. Let me put it this way: a metaphor, nothing more, but it may help you to understand. All the time, every moment of his life, Billy is passing through doors. He goes out a door and comes back in to where he was before—but there's a body there now. Or it's quiet again. Or someone is trying to kill him. Whatever he has done, he leaves there, behind the door. And he goes through the next door without a history— innocent, as it were. The causal connection's simply not there for him, never made.

Meredith closed the file folder, put it down.

"Innocent."

"Right." Jackson held up his cup. "Stuff tastes like mud from the Mississippi's bottom, catfish and all."

"Want some more?"

"Sure."

They sat quietly for a while then, two men dragged out so thin they scarcely existed anymore, yet reluctant to let go of whatever it was they had here, intimacy, purpose. Some tiny intimation, per- haps, of doing good, bringing things back to balance.

Around them the building stirred to life. Footsteps resounded in corridors and on steel stairs outside. A door at the far end of the room opened, someone looked in briefly then withdrew. Cars and pedestrians filled the street below.

"We're catfish ourselves," Meredith said. "All this muck we live in, day after day. Managing somehow to get sustenance from it."

He looked down the room toward where the door had closed moments ago. That door seemed to him now very, very far away, the room a kind of gauntlet. Some obscure test he'd sooner or later have to pass.

"You think it changes us? All this?"

"Don't see how it could help but. One way or the other."

"Yeah." Meredith tilted his cup and found it empty. How had that happened? No memory of drinking. "Sometimes at night I wake up and look around and nothing—the bedroom, the curtain on the window that's been there for twelve years, Betty asleep beside me—none of it seems real to me anymore. That ever happen to you?"

Jackson shrugged. "You ought to've married her, Ben, long before this."

"I know."

"There's never enough for us to hold on to, any of us."

"Guess not." He glanced at his partner's tie. Remembered the paper Betty had wrapped it in, gray with blue and green triangles. "So. We out of here?"

"We are for sure."

They went along the floor, down the stairs, out the door. Parting on the street by Jimmie's cart.

Jackson said call him in a couple of days, they'd have a beer—on him. I oughta be awake again by then, he said.

Meredith stood watching his partner walk away, stood still and alone in the milling crowd with blades of sunlight sliding through chinks in the buildings.

He was thinking what the boy, Billy, had said, what he'd said again and again, to arresting officers, to interrogators from the task force, to Hargrove and his night squad of psychologists, social workers and assorted evaluators, rolling it off like a catechism, his answer to almost every question:

"We went for a ride, and some people died."

AMONG THE RUINS OF POETRY

In a village deep in the jungles of central Peru, and nowhere else, grows an orchid whose flesh is more manlike than most. And yet more miraculously, from their earliest days these flowers develop the ability to form human sounds. For a short time they converse among themselves or speak with villagers, mostly silly, insipid stuff, then begin composing the lengthy, complex epic poems to which each dedicates the remainder of its life. Everywhere one hears these orchids mumbling obliviously to themselves.

Some time back, and tacitly, they had adopted this routine: if at eleven she rose to fill the tub for a bath, he would stay the night; if she did not, he would not.

Tonight they are reading, he Proust, she Cervantes, as they share a bottle of burgundy. Precisely at eleven she stands and walks into the bathroom. He hears the water begin its fall and then she is in the doorway: But I don't *need* a bath. I've *had* a bath.

He understands, and leaves.

That summer a dead friend comes to see you. He lectures you on classic German literature as you bring him cup after cup of strong tea. I know them all, he says. You show him a few recent poems. He says: I would die for these.

He cuts himself shaving and tears off a corner of toilet paper to apply to one of the wider nicks beneath his nose where it becomes a hinge, a valve, flapping open and shut against his left nostril.

Someone says: I wish I had given up earlier. It would have been so much easier.

The refrigerator in his new flat has the sound of a sneeze when it comes on. Branches against the window creak and caw in the wind like birds.

• • •

You could never sleep in her bed. You spent many nights there after you'd made love, watching the pale plane of her back, the dapple of leaves on the wall, listening to the tick and twitter of her birds.

Unable to sleep you would pad still naked about her house, her smell on you, about you, like an aura, as she tossed and threw pillows, covers, from the bed. You came upon copies of your books in a corner of the bookcase.

You could never sleep in her bed. You sat listening to the tick and twitter of her birds resolve into morning.

Recently the *News'* chief reporter has adopted, as "the only system adequate to the disruptions of our time," surrealism. This has caused some problems, admittedly, as in his feature of two days before, an interview with a railroad tie. Yet he writes so beautifully that no one complains. And this is considered by many to be an improvement over his prior Marxism.

In the café the couple's eyes do not meet. They speak of many things: right or wrong, how children have been brought up, the responsibilities of freedom, taxes, a music lesson, literature, Salieri. They devour croissants and drink down endless cups of coffee.

The water brought them stands unmolested.

You have been away a while, reading Proust, and, coming back to this world, you encounter significant changes, you say.

Several nouns have become verbs; there are new, unrecognizable words and equally impenetrable uses for old ones; whole pages seem to have been removed from the dictionaries.

Even the alphabet seems *not enough*, you say.

Last year he contracted to translate all G—'s future novels, believing revenues from these would buy time for the completion of his own small books. But time will not be bought. G— has become a dervish—four novels this calendar year!—and he has no time for work of his own.

• • •

Even reading the newspaper reminds you of her.

That summer, that last morning, there was wind as now. On the bed you held her small breast in your hand for a long while afterwards, staring up at the limitless white ceiling.

GOOD MEN

This one wore gray-cotton slacks, a chambray shirt, and a corduroy sportcoat with the sleeves pushed up almost to the elbow. He propped himself against the door jamb and smiled. He had a kindly, gentle way about him.

"This is Louis," Mom told me. She was leaning toward him the way she does, not really touching, but she put a hand lightly on his arm as she spoke.

"Hi, Danny," he said. "Homework?"

I looked up from my notebook. "Sort of."

"Like school?"

I nodded.

"What's your favorite?" he asked me.

"History, probably."

"That's unusual for someone your age." He came over and sat down on the bed beside me as Mom went for drinks. "I teach," he said. "Humanities, at the university. History, philosophy, art, literature. Your mom says you're a great reader. I can see that." He looked at the stacks of books and journals, the crates of file folders.

"Yes, sir."

"Louis. Not sir. Do you have any favorite writers?"

"Dickens and Twain, I guess. Victor Hugo."

"Wells?"

"The *Outline of History*, yes, sir—Louis. But I don't have much taste for fantasy."

Mom came back with drinks—wine for her, Scotch for Louis, hot chocolate for me—and told me ten minutes to bedtime. I drank the chocolate from the tin mug I've had all my life, went into the bathroom to rinse out the mug and brush my teeth, and then to the living room to tell them goodnight.

Afterward I lay listening to the rumble of their voices, like

536 • JAMES SALLIS

far-off trains. They spoke of the university for a time—their mutual acquaintances there, their routines, how they met—then of themselves. Four years ago (for the first time, at age thirty-two), Louis had married a woman with, as they shortly discovered, cancer of the bone. He took a year's leave, borrowed money from his family and friends, and spent that year wholly with Julie. After she died, he went back to work. Several months ago he'd finally paid everyone back. Now he was buying furniture for the two-room apartment he leased at a discount from the school, a piece at a time, his latest acquisition (the "latest possession to possess me," as he put it) a white-pine futon frame. Slowly the voices grew softer, then withdrew to the bedroom.

Early next morning I heard the front door open and close, then my mother moving about the kitchen.

"Hi, honey, want oatmeal?" she said when I wandered out to the kitchen. She was drinking coffee, rare for her in the morning, and listening to classical music with the volume turned low.

"Louis would like to take you to a movie," she said when the oatmeal was ready. "Just the two of you. At the university film club." She poured another cup of coffee.

"Did he say what movie?"

"*Empire of the Sun*. He thinks you'd like it. Would you? Want to go, I mean?"

"When is it?"

"Tonight, I think."

"Sure."

"Then I'll call and tell him it's on."

Glenn Gould worked his way through the *Goldberg Variations* as Mr. Clark's delivery truck coughed itself into life for another day. I was eleven that year.

JOHN LUNDE. Born 1950, small town in South, perhaps Tennessee. Attended Tulane University, to which he returned for a degree following a tour in Vietnam as a medic. Married at age 23, one daughter, divorced after six years. Freelance journalist, stringer for major Eastern papers. Loved Janet Draper. Died 1982.

"She never says much about your father."

We were seated at a TCBY eating vanilla yogurt piled with pecans. We'd been out together without Mom at least once every week, mostly to movies, but one time to the Museum of Natural History, another to tour a helicopter factory.

"I get the idea there's not that much to say," I told Louis.

"You remember him?"

"Sometimes, a little—just glimpses. His voice, mostly. All we have left of him is a hat he hung over the back of a chair in Mom's room the day he walked out. She's never moved it."

"She took it pretty hard, then."

"Glad to have him gone, is what she always said. I think she hated him."

"She didn't go out much for a while, she says."

"Not at first. She never really has, a lot."

"If you don't want anything else, there's still time to catch some ice skating before we meet her."

We did that, then picked Mom up at Tate Hall, where she had piano lessons late on Tuesdays, and went shopping. Louis was looking at desks. We wandered through forests of lacquer, melamine and bamboo at Bright Ideas, Pier 1, Storehouse, Made in Denmark. Everyone's favorite was a small red-lacquered one, bright as a cherry and solid as stone, curving gently at every joint and corner. Louis paid for it and arranged delivery for Wednesday, his day off.

One of Mom's students last week, as they paused between movements of a Brahms sonata, had suddenly begun speaking to her of problems at home, and this became the topic for discussion during dinner at Bella Italia on the mall.

"He's a musician too," Mom said. "A violinist. And he used to make good money doing the restaurant thing, playing in places like this. But in the past few months he's gotten heavily into drugs—cocaine, mostly. He's been missing gigs. Bills are a problem. Collectors come to the door, even to the library where Gail works."

"It's a familiar story," Louis said.

Mom nodded. "What concerns Gail is that she watched as Robert lost all interest, first in her, and then in his music. She says it's almost as though he'd read an article on cocaine addiction and set about trying to match the profile."

"Addiction does that, I guess—a kind of progressive stripping-down, reduction to the lowest common denominator. Nothing matters any more except that high, that relief. The personality itself is obliterated. The need is all that's left."

"Well," Mom said. "Enough of that. How was school?"

Louis and I looked at one another "You first," I said.

"I did okay today," he told her. Then, biting his lower lip: "I may need some help in math."

"You don't teach math," I said.

"But if I did, I'd definitely need help."

"Very funny, guys," Mom said. She pushed her plate away. "You probably did dessert already, too."

"Yet we are too much the gentlemen," Louis said, "to allow you to go without."

"We'll join you," I said.

"All heart."

Over cheesecake he told her about the student whose essay was written on the back of ten oversize pizza menus. He'd done it at work and the title was "Why I Hate Pizza."

"Write about what you know," Mom said.

"Exactly."

I tried to look into Mom's eyes without her knowing, wondering if the old restlessness was starting up in there. Maybe I only imagined it. She was looking at Louis, but it was like he was far away, as though she watched him through thick glass, the way you watch a plane take off.

I excused myself, found the bathroom, and, coming back, overheard the end of their conversation.

"Sometimes he seems more your son than mine," Mom said.

"Janet—"

"I don't want company tonight."

"Jan, I love you."

"I don't want to talk about it now. I'll call when I can."

ERIC KEEL (final entry). Like the others, Eric, suddenly, was gone. I began to understand why, and started this notebook. Over the following three weeks there were sporadic phone messages (I'd listen to them when I got home from school, then rewind the tape) and one final, tearful goodbye.

I recall something in Cocteau, from the journals, I think— that sexual need is the most intriguing form of aesthetics. That selections aren't made, sequences not followed, by dictates of taste or choice, but only after exhaustive research and obscure preparation, the senses desperately constructing "an equivalent, more baroque, but in fact hardly less individual than any other, for beauty."

I longed to tell him goodbye. To tell him something of what he had meant to me, and that he would not be forgotten, not entirely. That here, in this notebook, like the others he would live on.

Louis called four times the following day. By the fourth call, from anger, tears, or some blend of the two, his voice quavered on the machine. There were no calls the day after—then, midmorning of the next, a letter, weighty in its manila envelope. She would wait until the calls and letters dwindled to nothing, then call them.

I don't know how aware she is of this sequence. Once it begins, apparently, she's not in control.

She doesn't suspect, of course, that I know what happens to them. But perhaps it wouldn't matter if she did.

Louis was waiting outside my school a few days later. "I've missed you," he said.

I nodded.

"How's your mom doing?"

"Depressed, I guess. She sleeps a lot. Comes home, goes to bed— and stays there some days."

"She won't answer my calls."

"I know."

He was wearing a cloth cap, which he took off and stuffed in a coat pocket. "It's hard to get a handle on this. I know she loves me."

"She does."

"So how can she just *go away* like this? Just suddenly not be there? All the things we feel for one another, all our plans—"

We walked on for a block or two silently.

"I have to get back to the college," he said.

"Louis?"

He looked at me.

I almost said: She's going to kill you. Because she loves you, she's going to kill you. But I couldn't. I said, "Could I have your cap? I've always wanted one like that."

He took it out and handed it to me. "To remember me by?" he said.

"To wear till I see you again."

"Soon, I hope."

The lies we tell ourselves, or the lies we tell others—which are worse?

Two days later, a Friday, Mom was happy again.

"I thought we'd eat out and catch a movie tonight if that's okay with you," she said at breakfast. She was drinking orange juice from either a very small goldfish bowl or a very large brandy snifter. She held it up and moved it, washing pulp from side to side. Liszt, softly, on the radio.

"By ourselves?"

Was there a brief pause, a catch?

"Just you and me, kiddo. Louis and I . . . well, he won't be around anymore."

"I loved him, Mom. You did too."

"Yes," she said. "Yes, I did."

She was wearing her navy-blue suit with a new red blouse—silk, I think—and had her hair pinned back loosely. Without her glasses, her eyes had a soft, blurred look.

"I've got a student coming in before class, so I have to leave," she said. She went to the sink and rinsed out her glass. "I'll be home early, about the same time as you, and we'll take off right away. Make a night of it. Remember to lock up when you leave."

"Sure, Mom."

After she was gone, I got up and turned off the radio. I stood looking at the bowl of apples, the brass colander catching morning sunlight against the wall where it hung—all these ordinary things.

I went to get my books and sweater and looked for a moment at Louis's cap on the back of my chair. Then I put his notebook on the shelf with the rest and went on to school.

BLEAK BAY

He'd come to Bleak Bay originally because he liked the name. That was in the sixties, and he'd arrived in the back of an old pickup with a knapsack in his lap. Now it was thirty years later. The knapsack was in a corner of the closet, untouched for years. His wife was in a motel downtown being touched, intimately as they say, by the man she worked for.

This revelation had arrived by phone.

"It's nine o'clock. Do you know where your wife is?" a female voice had said. Minutes later the phone rang again. "If not, you might try the Arlington Motel, room nineteen."

There was no one else it could be, of course, no one but Sanders.

He mixed a drink and sat on the patio listening to crickets fiddle furiously as the night congealed around them. A cat came up the driveway and stood for a moment looking over its shoulder at him before going on.

"Are you asking me out?" she had said when he mumbled something about a movie, then gone off to see to another table. When she came back she said, "I ain't been asked out much—but I've been asked *in* a lot of times. Might even say I've been *taken* in."

"And did you *give* in?" he asked when she next returned.

"A few times." She'd smiled then, sweeping hazel eyes over him quickly. "I get off at nine."

He'd been going there for two weeks, every day twice a day, for breakfast and dinner, since the first time he walked in and saw her. When he picked her up at nine she'd said, Forget the movie, and taken him to her apartment, an efficiency above a garage just off Main Street. She poured wine into coffee cups, handed him both, and walked out of the kitchen corner into the living room corner, where she fed records into a cabinet-like stereo. Shostakovich's Fifth leapt into the room about them. She turned around and reached for her cup.

"You like this?"

"Oh yes. Almost all Russian music, in fact."

"That's good."

They settled onto the floor near the stereo, backs against the couch that doubled as a bed, and he put his long, skinny arm around her shoulders. She leaned into him.

"Most people 'round here, I put that on and they think it's . . . I don't know, weird maybe? *Listen* to this: it's like a choir, all that sword-crossing at the first forgotten now, just this peace, this resolve."

They listened together through most of the first movement.

"Where you from, Dave?" she said, face turning toward him.

"East Coast. Near New York."

"Thought so."

"The accent, right?"

"Right. What're you doing down here?"

He shrugged. "Wanted to see what this country was like—all of it, not just my little corner. Hope to write books someday. You a musician?" He gestured toward the stereo.

"Lord no. All I can do to play the radio in tune. But there's something in music like this that's inside me too, all kinds of feelings I can't express. First time I heard this, it was like doors were flying open inside me."

"I felt the same way, but I would never have put it like that."

They kissed then, and the rest of the night followed quickly thereupon. The next day, he and his knapsack moved in for good. Their son had put himself through school as a programmer and ran his own software company in Hoboken, right across the Hudson from New York.

He mixed another drink, lighter this time. The crickets had quietened; mostly he heard traffic sounds from the interstate. *Wozzeck* unraveled on the turntable just inside patio doors he'd spent a month of weekends installing.

He had never pictured himself settling down, certainly not at nineteen, but there he was, living with her in the efficiency, starting work on the local paper he now edited, listening to music every night. Soon they'd bought a car, then a small house, then a larger one. Days went slowly, years quickly. And over those years they had grown, or been drawn, or fallen, apart, something he failed to realize until the divides were already far advanced. He sat watching death tolls mount in Vietnam and Salvador as she remained, untouched, at the center of her music, her job and friends, their life together in this house. Slowly he rediscovered the world's pain, a pain he had known all too well at nineteen, on the road and open-eyed, and had since forgot.

We are all guilty of everything, Dostoevski said.

Wozzeck ended; the child rode away on his hobbyhorse. Dave rode in his Toyota to the Arlington Motel. At room nineteen he knocked and waited through whispers, bed creaks, footsteps.

"Oh shit," Sanders said.

"Hi, George. I'd like to talk to my wife. I'll wait for her in the coffeeshop."

He ordered coffee for both of them, black for her, cream for him, and after a few minutes she came in and sat beside him at the counter. They drank their coffee and pushed the cups away.

"I'm sorry, Dave."

"I know."

"You need for me to tell you that I didn't mean for this to happen, that I never intended it?"

He shook his head.

"It just started," she said. "This was the first time. Now I guess it's over."

"Are you sorry?"

"A little. Regretful, anyhow."

She looked out the window at passing cars. They were the only customers. The waitress sat at a table drinking iced tea and listening to country music on a portable radio.

"Less and less is possible every year, Dave. You start thinking about all the things you'll never do again."

"Like fall in love?"

"Yes."

He looked at her. "Have you been unhappy, Cathy?"

"No more than most. A lot less than you. I wanted to help you, but I didn't understand. You're not responsible for the world, Dave, you can't be."

"Walk with me?"

He paid and they went out. The moon was full, white as bone. He reached through the open window and pulled out the packed knapsack, swung it over one shoulder.

"I can't say that I'll be back, or that I won't be. Maybe by the time I can, it won't matter to you. I took a little money, a couple hundred, and some clothes. Everything else is yours." He watched tears gather in hazel eyes. How can we be so full of memories, so strangely fulfilled, at these times? "Be happy, Cathy."

Half a mile down the road she pulled up beside him in the car.

"Give you a lift as far as the highway?" she said.

He got in.

CAREER MOVES

I advertised for a job as king and got one. It was a shabby little land, the flag one color, no motels for tourists, national library in a back room of the bus station. They'd had few applications, they told me. They wondered if it was because of their paltry crown, or if word had got out about the food. I told them no, I didn't think that was it, people just weren't changing jobs like they used to, things being what they were. They decided I was a great ruler and asked what was my pleasure. I've always wanted a boat, I said. They started in building a navy.

The ad said very clearly: *Wanted. One Jim Sallis. To Start Immediately. Experience Required. Apply in Person.* This is what I'd been waiting for. I tried calling, faxed, finally went on down there. The building faced east, and the windows on that side squinted against the sun. There were forty or fifty people inside, all with resumes and leather shoes. You want to take the test? a woman behind the desk asked when I got to the front of the line. I didn't know. Did I? Don't worry, honey, she said. No one passes it.

New trends in packaged products sounded like the way to go. They were a little vague about just what these products were that we'd be packaging, so I was a little vague in turn about my background and qualifications. This was only fair: I assumed we were negotiating. After a while they nodded to one another across the long table and told me they'd been looking for someone like me. I made it a done deal. We'd have to settle on a title of course. But I could go ahead and buy new shoes and polish the mailbox, take someone out to dinner.

Name three of my personal heroes. What was the last book I read. Where do I see myself five years from now. Complete this statement: I would give up everything for. I'm prepared. Have my pen, my No. 2 pencil, my list of phone numbers and contact people from past employment, references. I complete the application and begin answering the forty-eight questions on their personality profile. After a while I get up and go to the front of the room to ask for more paper. When I look up next it's dark.

I've wormed my way through all the interviews to the final one but now this guy won't ask me anything. He sits rocking back and forth in his high-back chair, staring across the desk at me. We thought we might turn it around a little, he says, come at it from a different angle. That's how we like to approach things around here. So why don't *you* interview *me*? See if the company's someone you want to hire on. I didn't have a chair that would go back and forth but I did the best I could. That was about the toughest interview I ever had, he said when we were finished. How did I do? I'll let you know, I told him.

Each morning I would sit in Carl's diner with my coffee and newspaper reading every ad carefully, circling those of greatest interest. I would make lists of jobs according to location or bus routes, lists of numbers to call and in what order, lists of what I needed to remember about each job. In the afternoon I'd call for appointments, or to inquire regarding previous applications. A friend used to insist, I suddenly remembered, that the best way to learn about a city was to study its want ads. If that was so, I must be an expert by now, I figured. There a print shop nearby? I asked Carl. I had some cards printed up down the street and announced a series of lectures.

SAGUARO ARMS

Because the jaguars have no spots, at first we don't see them in the room's corners. Shadows, perhaps: nothing more. Though we hear the sound of their breathing from acoustic niches formed in those moments the radio falls silent.

Earlier we listened to NPR, the same news as that we left behind, as though, thrown across our backs or tucked into the corners of boxes and trunks, we have brought these events along with us. Reports on escalating violence, on the collapse of yet another cease-fire and subsequent forfeiture of this week's "safe zone" in San Marco's revolution. Grown large on hunger and despite, now the children of the original freedom fighters are coming down from the hills.

How terrible, Carey says as I open a second bottle of wine, a Brazilian cabernet, auguring down into the cork, working the machine's arms (shaped like a woman's legs) to lever out the cork with a satisfyingly plosive exclamation, and refill our glasses. How sad.

Yes, I say. Life.

But how can we accept it.

Life?

No, the terribleness of it. The sadness.

As though we could do anything else—but I do not say this.

Outside, blackbirds flush from power lines, sweep away in a flat arc and, clustering, drawn to some unseen center, return. They settle back at random on the lines, like musical notes, perforations on player-piano rolls, braille.

What kind of life can they have had, after all, Carey asks.

Or any of us—another thing I don't say. As this lowering sun hauls down its carry-on luggage of remorse.

I stand looking at the bottle's label, a Brazil shape formed of grapes. It resembles Texas, which we have crossed on the way here.

Carey wears the cranberry-color shirt that brought us together, a consoling gift from mother Jeanne. Carey's latest relationship had crumbled to disinterest and disaffection, while my own year-long romance stammered and tripped and blathered away, trying to explain itself, like a poor comedian. Great shirt, I said. She told me about it. We went for coffee. Bare bones of narrative.

Nights when she wears it Carey washes the shirt by hand and puts it out to dry on a hanger over the tub. *Calais. Made in U.S.A.* Seated on the toilet, I keep watch. One corner of the front pocket is stained with ink. The narrow seam along the bottom has begun unraveling. Threads like a plant's tendrils reach down for the tub.

And so, ponderously, as though on camelback, swaying, over desert and between dunes, we've come to this foreign land, where the sun fights its way down through layers of color, where saguaro lift arms in welcome all around us and salamanders with cowlike skulls sail the backs of lit windows each night.

And where, too, rising from the couch beside me from which we've watched "authentic" recreations of live, unrecorded broadcasts of Armstrong Circle Theater, Playhouse 90 and Dave Garroway, you go off to sleep alone in the nest of blankets and pillows you've made of our bathtub.

There, in that other country, my name is remembered. Here I work at whatever I can find.

You think of the child at these times, I know, smallest of the things we left behind. Newborn, with perfect tiny fingernails at the end of plump fingers, the child would not look at us however we hailed and drew it. Picked up, it went rigid. Turned right or left in its crib, it remained there till the whole weight of its skull settled to that side.

We had barely ensconced ourselves here when the jaguars appeared. At first we ignored them. During the journey, after all, there had been so many dangers. Nor are the dangers necessarily over, I feel. Each morning elderly men in crewcuts and bolo ties emerge from behind the redundant locks of ranch-styles to run up the flag. Each evening they emerge again to retrieve those flags. All day they stand peering out their windows, light from massive TV's washing up behind them like a tide. These men bear watching.

As you settle into your tub then, night closing around you, day hanging out backstage bitching with the other bit players till it's time to go on, I sit listening to neighborhood gunfire, to the wheeze and pump of accordions through Juan's window next door.

From their corners the jaguars watch me. Even after I turn off the lights their eyes gleam and flicker. Against moonlight on the back of my windows, as on photographic plates, appear the silhouettes of salamanders, perhaps a dozen of them, facing this way and that. Like myself, like the jaguars, awaiting what I will do next.

HOW'S DEATH?

Their first intimation of serious trouble was when Dave and Barb named the baby Death.

"Well, of course we *had* hoped you'd carry on your father's name," Beatrice said on the other line.

"O Mom, he'll still be a Dante and all that," Barb said, then giggled. "Sorry. They gave me some shots. I'm still kind of floating around up here."

"Peach Jell-o," Dave said.

"What?"

"You said you felt as though you were suspended in a vat of warm peach Jell-o."

"I *did*?" More giggles.

"Everybody's okay then?" Mr. Dante asked.

"Peachy," Barb said, and dropped the phone.

"We're all fine, Dad," Dave said. "All three of us."

"Have you seen her?" a fifth voice asked. "Has she been there? Why won't you tell me?"

"We were just going to have a nice cup of hot chocolate and go on to bed," Beatrice said. "I wanted to wait up for news from you but Daddy said no."

"Getting in much golf, Dad?"

"Any day the sun doesn't belly up, Dave. Went out this morning with a lung doctor, young guy, new in town. First hole, his beeper goes off and he's gone maybe twenty minutes then comes back and says, God, I hope she makes it. A couple holes later it's squealing again. He comes back and tells me: I lost one, D. Not much longer and he's gone again. Gotta get over to the hospital, he says when he comes back that time. Sorry."

"You just don't know how much I love her," the fifth voice said. "If you did, you wouldn't be doing this."

"We had a new caddy. Terrible child—from the college. Great shoulders, awful manners."

"Barb wanted me to ask if you've been making your regular check-ups, Dad."

"Every month, like clockwork."

"And taking your medicines?"

"Haven't missed a dose."

"No problems?"

"Haven't felt better since I can remember."

There was a pause. Far back in the wires they could hear music. In Minnesota a moth flew against the window again and again. In Texas a gravel truck started up a long incline.

"You're sure nothing's wrong, Dave?" Mr. Dante said after a while.

"Nothing. Everything's fine . . . great. Mom still on the line?"

"She's gone on up to bed."

"Well, Barb did want me to ask you something. She was wondering if it would be okay for her to come home for a while, Dad. Just a visit, of course."

"She's always welcome at home, Dave, both of you know that. But her home should be *there* now."

"And it is."

"I see." Birds had taken over the newspaper box below the mailbox on its post beside the road; he wondered how long ago that had happened. "You two are having problems."

"Minor stuff, Dad. You know how it is sometimes. It'll pass. But do you think we could keep Mother out of all this? She worries enough as it is. Barb just needs some time alone. Some time away."

"What about the baby? You have to think about that baby now."

"He'll be staying with me . . . It's okay, Dad, really. I've taken courses and everything. Death and I'll do great together."

"I can't live without her. I really can't," the fifth voice said.

"What I keep thinking about is the courage it takes, Dad."

"To visit her family?"

"No . . . Things don't stay simple very long, do they?"

"They never are, Dave. But you tell Barb to come on whenever she wants to. And if she does, then you two take good care of yourselves and each other until she gets back. We love you all, Mother and I."

"I know you do, Dad. We all love you. We always will."

"And you call me anytime, Dave. Anything I can do, you let me know."

"Thanks, Dad."

"I'll be talking to you."

"Do you hear someone?" the fifth voice said. "Is there someone else on this line?"

Mr. Dante hung up the phone and stood for a moment in a wedge of moonlight before going upstairs. In bed his wife turned to him and nestled.

"How's Death?" she asked.

"He's fine," Mr. Dante said.

ALASKA

Julie McCargar, the charge nurse most days on seven to three, walked past me down the hall shaking her head.

"They keep on rolling bodies in," she said. It was something she said a lot.

Morning had been a bitch by any standards, beginning with Pam catching twins that shot out like bubbles from a frog's mouth as she stood by a gurney in the chaos desperately trying to get report from dog-tired Wayne at a quarter to seven, continuing soon after with a traffic pile-up that brought in two Care Flite choppers, four or five ground units and close to forty family members who arrived from home partially dressed, eyes lit with terror, and stood cluttering up the ER's mouth till we finally had security and the ER cop clear them out. Now it was early afternoon and things had let up. Every floor and cabinet top was heaped with detritus: ripped-out IV bags, sterile wrappers for bandages and clamps and tubes, plastic syringes, trays and basins scattered about and themselves overflowing.

"For God's sake let's try to pull it together before the next wave comes in," Julie was saying as I walked into the nurse's station near the front of the unit. Through glass partitions we could see a waiting room as trashed out in its own way as the trauma and treatment rooms, but less than a dozen patients now waited in the mauve and lime-green plastic chairs. Julie turned to me. "Laura could probably use some help in meds-4, Tony. They've been on a holding pattern in there for a while now." Then she went out the chute fast, pursuing an intern who'd just walked by.

Meds-4 was at the far end of the hall, a converted storage space used chiefly for holding triaged patients till we could get around to them, minor accidents and the like.

Laura was leaning against the wall and writing on chart sheets splayed out over the counter. Seated on a chair with her back to me, hunched about herself the way people with central pain do, was a woman with shortish blond hair cut to the same length all around. Her head was down, the back of her neck a smooth, separate plane. Over the chair's back I could see on her black T-shirt three letters of an arc, E-T-A, and part of a fourth, an O, or possibly a G, with what I took to be a disembodied eye floating above them.

Laura looked up and said in a whisper: "Come in very slowly."

The woman held a large bird cradled in her arms with her face down close to it. Her eyes swiveled up to me as I came to her side, then, in surprise, she made to straighten her head and look full on but winced and cried out.

"Hello, Susan."

"You two know one another?" Laura said.

I nodded and walked around in front. The bird, a hawk I now saw, and a young one, had one talon through Susan's right cheek. There was a runnel of blood down it, and when she opened her mouth I could see the rest of the talon moving about inside.

"It hurts like a sonofabitch, Tony."

"We've got the bird sedated," Laura said. "And the vet from the zoo sent along a note. This should have been seen a long time ago." She waved sketchily toward the hall. "You know. Dr. Talbott's on his way back down from OR now."

"Tony . . ."

"Don't try to talk, Suze." Then to Laura: "What happened?"

"Miss Gomez works as an assistant at the zoo. She was taking the bird out of its cage for a feeding when something—they think probably a copter that flew over just then—made it panic. It tried to fly, and before Miss Gomez could get a better hold —"

"The hawk did."

"Right," Laura said, and went back to her charting.

"I didn't know you were back in town," I told Susan. "Wait a minute. Here." I handed her a pad of old order sheets chopped into rough quarters and stapled across the top for use as scratch paper. It was a sickly, pale green and would end up as shopping lists, phone numbers, crib sheets for vital signs, resuscitation records. I took a pen out from among the scissors, hemostats and penlights of my lab coat pocket and gave that to her as well.

Keeping one arm cradled under the hawk, she balanced the

pad on her thigh and wrote with the other hand, barely touching paper with pen, it seemed, tiny letters in handwriting that had in it something of the roll and flow of her parents' language with all those terminal, run-on O's and A's.

Never left.

"But your letter . . ."

Only way I could do it. Couldn't see you.

"It was terrible for a long time without you, and impossible. Then it was only terrible."

And?

"Then I guess it was over."

She wrote something quickly, scratched it out, looked up at me out of the corners of her eyes. They were turquoise, sometimes blue, often green, with large pupils almost filling the iris and in strong light leaving only a rim of color that made one think of eclipses.

Me too.

Together we had been a small Alaska, our own six-month white night. Sleep was a strange bedfellow to us both. Susan went to sleep instantly then woke an hour or two later to pass the night prowling about the apartment and returning perfunctorily, again and again, to bed, where covers eddied up about her. Then the drinking would start. I could never fall asleep and lay there heavily conscious of her arm across my chest, of her presence in another room or breath on my shoulder, at last sinking toward semi-consciousness at three or four in the morning when she had abandoned all pretense to sleep. I would open weighted eyes to her profile against the white wall and watch as memory, night thoughts, a peculiar softness I came to know well, washed over her features.

In the hallway a prisoner from county jail walked by with a deputy alongside. He wore cuffs with a long chain, and blood rib-boned down his chest from multiple cuts on neck and shoulders. A faded tattoo moved jerkily like an early cartoon character on his upper arm when he flexed the muscle there. His skin, possibly from tanning agents, was an unnatural yellowish brown.

Neal Talbott came in, nodded to Laura and me, and knelt by Susan's chair. He moved his upper body around, looking at things from several angles, occasionally probing gently with one finger at her cheek. Talbott is from British working-class stock, with little taste or place in his life for the esoteric. Everything about him says that even the most complex tasks are accomplished in a series of practical, small maneuvers.

He half-turned, still on one knee, and told Laura what he would need: Novocaine and Valium drawn up, dressing tray, fine and gross suture kits, Betadine scrub, size seven gloves.

Then to Susan: "You'll be a solo act again in just a few moments, dear. There'll be only a small scar which should pretty much fade within a month or two. But just to be sure, we'll have Plastics take a look."

I've always envied people like Neal Talbott, for whom obstacles and impediments are not so much easily overcome as unacknowledged in the first place. They skate through life on solid ice, warmly wrapped, mind and eye focused, invigorated by the exercise. Our minds are printed circuits, I think, snapped into place at birth, and we can't do a lot about the way those circuits fire.

He draped Susan with a sheet and scrubbed the area around the wound, moving slowly so as not to frighten the bird. Instinctively he held his head close to it, humming tunelessly as he worked.

Laura had pulled over a rolling tray and stood by it handing him 4x4's, bottles of Betadine, swabs, alcohol. A smaller tray held suture kits, sterile wrappings torn back and hanging down over the side of the tray like a skirt. Susan had her eyes squeezed shut, and I could see muscles jumping in her jaw as she ground her back teeth. I went over and took her free hand in mine. It fit the way it always had.

Neal injected Novocaine subcutaneously both inside and outside Susan's cheek, gave it time to catch hold, then flicked a scalpel briefly above and below the talon, opening a slit like an episiotomy, less than a centimeter on each side, talking alternately to the hawk and to Susan in low tones.

"This is the tricky part," he said.

Leaning in close to the bird, he put thumb and finger inside Susan's mouth and grasped the hawk's talon. Then he gently took hold of the part just outside and began to case it through the opening, pulling the digit straight. I caught a glimpse of his finger outside Susan's cheek then—and it was done.

The hawk immediately retracted its foot, pulling it in close to its body, but made no further move. Susan sat up straight, arching her back. You could feel tension falling off walls and ceiling. I squeezed Susan's hand and let go.

"We have a launch," Neal said, and started prepping for sutures.

He used finest silk and set the sutures close together in a precise row. It looked, when he had finished, like the spine of some intricately small and delicate animal.

"I'll have Plastics nip down for a look," Neal said as he washed up at the sink, "but I do believe we're home free." He came over and put a hand briefly on Susan's shoulder. Then to Laura: "Anybody know what we're supposed to do with the bird?"

"I'll take it back with me," Susan said. "Thank you."

"Nothing," Neal said, and was gone, swinging out into the hall with his lab coat waving in the wake, on to new solutions. Julie came in to tell Laura she was needed in trauma-1 for a full arrest four minutes out if things were wrapped up here. I wet a washcloth for Susan, handed it to her along with a towel, and started cleaning up the room.

"You left the paper?"

I nodded. "One too many obits. Two too many society fundraisers."

"How long have you been here?"

"Almost a year now."

She wiped her face vigorously everywhere else, gently around the tiny spine there on her cheek. Mascara had smeared below her eyes, giving her a vaguely clown-like look. Her cheek was faintly gold from the Betadine. An X-ray machine lumbered past in the hall, nosing chairs and trashcans from its path.

"I don't drink anymore," she said, and when I turned to answer, she had pulled up her skirt, opened her legs. It could have been accidental, I suppose, and she went on pulling clothes back into order. For a moment I felt as one does upon coming into the curve toward home at the end of a long, exhausting trip.

"That's wonderful," I said.

"Well . . ." She stood, still cradling the hawk, one hand pressed down on its feet, fingers intertwined with them. "I'd better be getting back. Hate to lose this job. It's the only good one I've ever had."

"What about Plastics?"

She shrugged. "You have a phone these days?"

I shook my head.

She touched my cheek, lightly, and when she did, the hawk rustled its wings, causing her to take her hand away.

"You're a good man, Tony," she said.

I tossed the last patches of gauze, a handful of disposable forceps, scalpels, tweezers and tiny needles curved like scimitars, into trash and sharps containers. Everything in life seems to happen either very slowly or very fast. Things from which we will not recover, heart attack, huge trucks, Alaskas, are bearing down on us, careening into our lives.

Upstairs in ICU are the ones we almost saved. Their hearts go on, and they breathe, and that is all they do. For a moment, standing at the threshold, I hear their call, a sound like whale songs slipping through cracks from a world we cannot imagine, settling on me from the limitless blue above.

HOW THE DAMNED LIVE ON

The closest I can come to the giant spider's name is Mmdhf. She loves to talk philosophy. How we become what and who we are, why we are here, the influence of the island's isolation on what we believe. She waits for me each morning on the beach. As I approach along the steep, snaking path from the cave, I imagine paper cups of coffee at the end of two of her arms. They steam in the early morning chill.

"You slept well?" she asks.

"I did." I tell her about the dreams. In the latest versions I find myself lost on the streets of a teeming city. No one will respond to my pleas for help. Then I ask: "Do you dream?"

"Another of your difficult questions. We sleep, and live within the sleep. Perhaps we—my kind, I mean—fail to differentiate between the two lives."

Pirates come in the night and carry off all our things: spare clothing and blankets, the crate of fig preserves, sharp knives, our half-built raft. Later we see they have used material from the last to repair the deck and railings of their ship.

There are flowers and plants here like none we have ever seen, vast thickets of them awash with colors one might more reasonably anticipate finding in tropical climes, some of the flowers aloft on stems high above our heads. Cook fears one of the lesser plants. He insists that they uproot themselves and move around at night, that he lies awake listening to the soft pad of their rootsteps. Anything is possible, the Professor responds.

They are both wrong, I hope.

Ahmad meanwhile is at wit's end. He does not know in what direction Mecca might be.

• • •

Captain stands for hours at a time, statue-like, alone on the open beach where we washed ashore, sextant aimed to the heavens. He has long ago given up on his charts. They lie abandoned in a far recess of the cave. Increasingly, when we speak to him his replies seem insensible.

I ask Mmdhf one morning the name of the island, what she calls this, her home. Thoughtfully she speaks the word in her language, a long word that rolls on and on in her barbed, glistening mouth. It might best be translated, she tells me, as This Place.

The pirates, it appears, have mutinied, discharging their captain, complete with parrot, onto the island. The parrot and Mmdhf have become close. They sit all afternoon beneath a favored banyan tree talking. I am beginning to feel, as I suspect the pirate captain must, jealous.

Each incoming wave washes tiny, fingernail-sized crabs onto the shore, dozens of them. They weigh almost nothing, what a heavy breath weighs, perhaps. Their shells and flesh are transparent. As the water recedes they take their bearings, right themselves, and scuttle toward the sea. A few make it. Most are driven back onto the shore by the next wave.

Long ago Mmdhf explained to me how so many of her children had died, all of them actually, and that this is what brought her to a deeper thinking. It was then (how had I not known this before?) that I understood she was the last and only one of her kind.

Our subsistence, the subsistence of most all the island's life forms, depends upon a fruit we call Tagalong, which also serves as substitute womb for the island's most common insect, a horned, armored species resembling a cigar that has sprouted legs. These lay their eggs in the Tagalong. Commonly one bites into the fruit to discover a larval head peering out.

Tagalong grows most abundantly toward the center of the island—due, the Professor says, to the dormant volcano there, its creation of a temperate zone. For the same reason, and for ready access to quantities of Tagalong, birds flock to the area in vast numbers. Of late, birds have begun to move away. This suggests, the Professor tells us, that the volcano is about to erupt.

The parrot agrees.

Mmdhf and I have spoken daily for months when I come to realize that I find something in her speech unsettling. Her enunciation is perfect, her word choice spot on; she speaks without appreciable accent and with proper inflection. Yet something nips at the heels of our dialogues. My uneasiness, I decide at length, lies in subtle shadings of verb choices.

Is it possible, I ask one morning, that we experience time differently?

"As in our earlier discussion of dream and waking," she replies, "yes. And you cannot imagine how surprised I was to learn that time for your kind is not continuous but sequential."

"But if continuous, how can there be said to be time at all?"

"This." She turns her head, pauses, turns back. "Change."

"If all time is one . . ." I hesitate, groping for the question. ". . . then you know the future, you know what will happen."

"Yes." She lifts two legs, as I have seen her do only once before, when she spoke of her children. "I miss you."

MISS CRUZ

I think I always knew I didn't fit in. I'd look around at the families, their dogs and bikes and travel trailers, parents hopscotching cars out of the driveway every morning to go to work, and knew I'd never be a part of that. Most of us feel that way, I guess, when we're young. But with me it wasn't a matter of feeling. I knew.

The other thing I knew was that I needed secrets, needed to know things others didn't, have keys to doors that stayed locked a lot. When I was a kid, for two years all I could think or read about was magic tricks, this arcane stuff no one knew much about. Thurston's illusions, Chung Ling Soo, Houdini. Sleight of hand and parlor magic and bright lacquered cabinets. Read every book in the library, spent the little money I had on a subscription to a slick magazine named *Genie* out of LA. Later it was Hawaiian music (can't remember how that got started), then nineteenth-century clocks. I was looking, you see, looking for stuff other people didn't know, looking for secrets. They were as essential to me as water and the air I breathed.

One thing I *didn't* know was that I'd wind up here in this desert, where it looks, as someone told me when I first came, like God squatted down, farted, and lit a match to it. Long way from the hills and squirrel runs I grew up in. Everything low and spread out, dun-colored and difficult. But hey, you want to build this big-ass city, how much better could you do than smack in a wasteland where it's a hundred degrees three months out of the year and water, along with everything else, has to be trucked in?

But cities are like lives, I guess, when we start out we never know what they're going to turn into. So here I am, living in what's politely termed a residential hotel on the ass-end side of Phoenix, Arizona, with half a dozen T-shirts, two pair of jeans, a week's worth of underwear if I don't leak too much, some socks, a razor and a toothbrush. Oh—and a four-thousand-dollar guitar. It's a Santa Cruz, black as night all over, not even any fret markers on her. Small, but with this huge sound.

Because I'm a musician, see. Have the black suit, white shirt and tie to prove it. They're all tucked into one of those dry-cleaner bags in the back of what passes for a closet here. It's the size of a coffin; at night I hear things with bristly legs moving around in there. Outside the closet, there's half of what began life as a bunk bed, a table whose Formica top has a couple of bites out of it, two chairs, and a dresser with a finish that looks like maple candy.

And the guitar case, of course, all beat to hell. Same case I've had all along, came with the Harmony Sovereign I found under the bed in a rented room back in Clarksdale, Mississippi, around 1980, when it all started. Second one, a pawnshop guitar, didn't have a case, so I kept this one, and after that . . . well, not much history or tradition in my life, you work with what you have. Been a lot of guitars in there since. Couple of J-45s, an old small-body Martin, a Guild archtop, Takamines, a Kay twice as old as I am. Really get some looks when I pull this gorgeous instrument out of that case. Books and covers, right?

I forgot to mention the stains on ceiling and mattress. Lot of similarities among them; I know, I've spent many a night and long afternoon sandwiched between, mattress embossed with personal stories, all those who fell to earth here before me, stains on the ceiling more like geological strata, records of climate changes, weather, cold winters and warm.

It's not a big music town, Phoenix. Mostly a big honking pool of headbangers and cover bands, but there's work if you're willing. What do I play? Like Marlon Brando in *The Wild Ones* said when asked what he was rebelling against: What do you have? Mariachi, Beatles tributes, polka, contra, happy-hour soft jazz—I've done it all. Even some studio work. But my bread and butter's country. Kind of places you find an ear under one of the tables as you're getting the guitar out of the case and the bartender tells you good, they've been looking for that, got torn off in a fight last weekend.

Those gigs, mostly Miss Cruz stays in the case, right there by me all night, and I play a borrowed Tele that belongs to . . . I started to say a friend, but that's not right. An associate? Man doesn't play, but he has this room with thirty or more guitars, all top drawer, and humidifiers pouring out fog everywhere so you go in there it's like stepping into a rain forest, you keep expecting parrots to fly out of the soundholes. Jason Fletcher. We work together sometimes. Secrets, remember? And he's a lawyer.

Thing is, musicians get around, hear things. We're on the street, out there wading in the sludge of the city's bloodstream. And we're like furniture in the clubs, no one thinks we're listening or paying attention or give half a damn. Plus, we get to know the barkeeps and beer runners, who see and hear more than us.

So I do a little freelance work for Jason sometimes. Started when he came by Bad Mojo down on the lower banks of McDowell looking for a client of his who owed him serious money and caught me with a pick-up band playing, of all things, Western Swing. Strong bass player/singer, solid drummer, steel player who'd been at it either two weeks or forty years, hard to tell. Anyhow, Jason and I got to talking on a break and he said how he'd always wanted to play like that and wanted to know if I gave lessons. People are coming up to you all the time at gigs and asking that, so I didn't think much of it, but a few days later, comfortably late in the morning, my phone rang. After work that day he swung by, and when he opened up the case he was carrying, there was a kickass old Gibson hollowbody.

The lesson lasted about twenty minutes before dissolving into gearhead chatter. Man could barely play a major scale or barred minor chord, but he knew everything about guitars. Woods, inlay, model designations, who made what for whom, Ditson, Martin, the Larsons, Oscar Schmidt—had it all at his fingertips, everything but music.

"Were you mathematically inclined as a child?" I remember he asked. It was a question I'd heard before and, knowing where he was taking it, I said no, it's just pattern recognition: spatial relationships, forms. That musicians, all artists, are just compulsive pattern-makers at heart.

And like with music, you stay loose, follow where life takes you. You've got the head, the changes, but the tune's what you make of it, you find out what's in there. So when the lesson dismembered itself we went out for a beer and went on talking and the rest just kind of developed from there. He'd say keep an ear out for this or that, or once in a while something would drift my way that had a snap to it and I'd pass it along.

For the rest, I have to go back a year or so.

It's a breezy, cold spring and I'm sitting in the outdoor wing of a coffeehouse with half an inch left in my cup for the last half hour looking over at the café next door, Stitches, a frou-frou place heavy on fanciful salads and sandwiches. There's a waitress over there that just looks great. Nothing glamorous or even pretty about her, plain, really, a summer-dress kind of girl, but these sad, unguarded eyes and, I don't know, a presence. Also an awkwardness or hesitancy. She'll stall out by a table sometimes. Or you look over and she's just standing there—on pause, like, holding a plate or a rag or the coffee.

There are all kinds of ways of knowing things, and in the weeks I've been watching, it's become obvious that she and the manager are down. Nothing in the open, but lots of small tells for the watchful: their faces when they talk to one another, the way their bodies kind of bend away from one another when they pass, occasional glances into the relic'd mirrors set up like baffles all through the café.

Secrets. Things others don't know.

And in the past few days it's become just as obvious that it's over. They've had The Talk. She stalls out more often, gets orders wrong, forgets refills and condiments.

So, lacking much of an attention span and with a loose-limbed hold on reality, I'm sitting there, looking over, thinking how great it would be if she went calmly to the cooler behind the counter, grabbed a pie, walked up to him, and let him have it. Everyone over there in Stitches is staring. And the manager is standing stock still with meringue and peaches dripping off his nose.

All at once then I come to, back to my surroundings, to realize that I'm witnessing, with a half-second delay, exactly what I've been picturing in my mind.

Now *that's* interesting.

Sweat runs down my back as I wonder how far I can take this.

One of the other waitresses runs into the kitchen, comes back with a can of whipping cream, and lets him have it in the face, right there by the peaches. A few customers look upset, but most are laughing. The cooks come out, stand around him, and sing Happy Birthday. Then I have everybody hold still, like a picture's just been taken, then they move, then I stop them again, another picture.

Cool.

Then I get scared and bolt.

That night at a club called Tip's I sat down with my guitar and ran an E chord into an A as many ways as I could think of all over the neck, but that was it. After fifteen or twenty minutes, without saying anything, I put the guitar back in its case and left. Didn't play for weeks, didn't go out in public at all, really, just hung in my room. The pictures of those people in the restaurant doing what I was imagining in my mind, *exactly* what I was imagining in my mind, those stayed with me. But like pictures on a wall, eventually you get used to them, stop seeing them when you walk past. So after a while I eased on back into the world. I'd like to say I was strong enough or scared enough never to repeat the incident, never to take that song for another ride, but of course I wasn't.

Miss Cruz came to live with me not long after that. She wasn't happy where she was—a common story: unloved and unappreciated, neglect, abuse—and where *he* is, he has no need for her. His needs are pretty simple. They change the catheter every few days, squirt stuff in his eyes to keep them from drying out. I went there once to visit. Keep telling myself I didn't put him there, his own choices did—and that night he decided to beat up on his woman in the bar where I was playing.

This entire aspiring society, humankind itself, is built and maintained on violence. We all know that, but pretend we don't. What matters is when and against whom you let the dogs out, right?

So back now to Jason Fletcher, who'd shown up weeks before at a wine bar where I was playing a solo early-evening gig to tell me the sheriff's office was harassing his client and he'd appreciate my keeping ears open for anything that might help. Sheriff Jack Dean, a stump-legged rind of a man with a bad comb-over, long history of marginally legal activity, and continuous re-election by preying on fear. Fletcher's client had written an elaborately researched, clear-eyed series about him for the Republic and now found himself followed by unmarked cars wherever he went. Waiting outside his house in the morning, parked across from the coffee shop where he stopped on the way to work.

"These boys are slick from years of practice," Fletcher said, "they've got it down to a fine art. No marks, no bruises."

What came to me, what I picked up off the forest floor, wasn't all that much, but it worked. The guy was able to drink his coffee in peace, rumors of lawsuits and worse evaporated, no more was heard of the "inquiry" that had sheriff's men knocking on neighbor's doors.

It haunted me, after. I looked up the journalist's series in the Republic, read every word and climbed over every comma twice. Dropped in with ears open at a downtown bar frequented by cops. Understand, I'm not the kind ever to pay much heed to politics. Never thought about how rotten the whole thing was, or much cared. And if I did, simply assumed that corruption and greed had to be the universal standard. It's politics, right? And politics is about power, so how else could it be played? As for me, I just wanted to be left alone, to play my guitar, make music. But that whole sheriff thing wouldn't let go of me, kept nipping at my heels, pissing on my shoes. Who can say why it is some things stick to us? I'd be sitting in OK Coffee or 5&10 Diner, see a county car pull in, or some beat-up dude staggering by outside, and it would all start back up.

Something growing in the dark within me.

Then one night it's 4 A.M. after a free-jazz gig with a sax player, music with a lot of anger inside, and the anger comes home with me. One of those nights when moonlight's spilling everywhere, then clouds slide in and it goes dark. No wind, no breeze—like the world's stopped breathing. Neighbors somewhere playing what sounds like Texas conjunto on the radio. I'm rattling around the room like always after gigs, drained and dog-tired but still wired, cranked up to the very edge, when there's a change in the light, a flicker, and I look up at the TV. I've had it on with no sound, silent company in the night. *Breaking News*, the screen reads now. I turn up the sound.

There's been a huge raid on a houseful of illegals out near the county hospital. Clips show a dozen or more half-dressed adults and kids being loaded into vans. Peace officers and TV crew outnumber them three to one. Lights worthy of a movie set. Then a cut—live!—to the man himself, Sheriff Jack, at his desk, American flag at parade rest behind him. Hard at the helm even at this hour, working as ever (he tells us) to uphold the laws of the land, serve the good people of Maricopa County, defend every border, and keep us all safe.

Not a single word about profiling, illegal traffic stops, unwarranted search and seizure, rampant intimidation, financial irregularities, or the ongoing federal investigation of his department.

As he speaks, he touches his nose again and again, age-old tell of the liar. Third or fourth time, he takes the finger away, looks at it a moment, and sticks it *in* his nose. He's digging around in there. Still talking, talking, talking.

And I realize that what I just saw, the nose touch, the nose pick, I pictured in my mind half a moment before it happened.

Sheriff Jack pulls the finger out, examines it, and tries the other nostril.

I'm thinking okay, so I don't have to be there, looks like I just have to see it, as the good sheriff, never for a moment ceasing his recitation, drops down in a squat and duckwalks across the office floor, a full-bore Chuck Berry, cameraman struggling to change headings, go with the flow.

Escalations are taking place. In what the sheriff is doing, the brutal comedy of it. In the ever-increasing alarm stamped on his face: wild eyes, frantic silent appeals stage left and right. In my anger, growing by the moment. In the anything-but-comedy of my horrible pride at the power of what I can do.

Again that half-moment delay, that temporal stutter. Eyes wide, face twisted in alarm, just as I picture him doing in my mind, the sheriff draws his sidearm.

In my mind he places the sidearm to his temple.

Onscreen he places the sidearm to his temple.

He pauses. The moment stretches. Stretches.

In my mind he stops talking.

Dervishness then, confusion everywhere, as deputies rush in to scoop the sheriff up and bear him away.

I reached out to turn off the TV with hands shaking. Didn't sleep that night or for many nights to follow. Hardly left the apartment.

Closed the door on what had happened, on what I could do, and have kept it shut, though every day when I turn the TV on, read the news, look around me at the mess of things, it gets harder. I answer the phone when calls come in, I go play my music, I come home. I keep my head down. I try real hard not to see things in my mind.

Mark Twain said a gentleman is someone who can play the banjo and doesn't.

So far, I've stayed a gentleman.

FERRYMAN

Let me say this: I'd stopped dating, stopped looking, stopped even fantasizing that the sexy young woman with tattoos at the local 7-Eleven where I bought my beer was going to follow me home. Still felt a gnawing loneliness, though, one that never quite went away and drew me out again and again, till I had a regular round of watering holes, places that exist outside the official version, largely unseen even by those who live near, part of the invisible city. Clinica Dental, for instance.

On any given day there you look out windows to see saguaro that grow for seventy-five to a hundred years before the first arm comes along, and inside to see 99 percent Hispanic faces. Color and facial features ambiguous, Spanish serviceable as long as things stay simple, I don't stand out. And I'm not there for free dental care, which makes it easier, I'm just there to be in the flow, to climb out of my own head and place in the world for a look around.

Airports, bus stations, parks—all are great for that. But county hospitals and free clinics may be the best.

After a while I began to feel that I wasn't alone, that someone shared my folly. Like me, she blended in, but by the third or fourth glance, cracks started to show. Patients came and went— maids in uniform, yard workers, mothers with multiple kids in tow, an old guy that weighed all of eighty pounds lugging a string bass—and neither of us budged. From time to time, reading one of those self-help, motivational books with titles like *Find Happy* or *Say Yes to Your Dream* that turn out to be warmed-over common sense, she'd look up and smile. Now, of course, I understand book and visit for what they were: advanced research in how to pass.

When she left, I followed her on foot crosstown to Hava Java and lingered outside as she ordered. The place was busy, a jumble of young and old, hip and straight, some with lists of beverages to take back to the office, so she had a longish wait before staking out a table near the side window.

Two cups. Meeting someone, then.

But as I started to turn away, she beckoned, pointing to the second cup. I went in and sat. The kind of steel chair that looks great on paper but fits no part of the human body—legs too short, back at the wrong angle, seat guaranteed to find and grind bones. A young woman, evidently mute, went from table to table carrying a cardboard sign.

PLEASE HELP

HOMELESS

SPARE CHANGE?

When my table mate held out a ten-dollar bill, their eyes met for half a beat before the woman took it, bowed her head, and moved away.

"*Es café solo,*" my companion said, gesturing to the cup before me, "*espero que esté bien.*"

Given my skin color and where we just were, a fair assumption.

"Perfect," I said.

Seamlessly she shifted to English. No taint of accent in her voice. She could easily have been from the Midwest, from Washington state, from California. I noted the lack of customary accoutrements. No purse or backpack, no tablet, no cell phone in its holster. Just the book and a wallet with, presumably, money and ID. I noted also how closely she observed everything: figures passing in the world outside, the low buzz escaped from earphones at a table close by, a couple leaning wordlessly in toward one another. Had I ever known someone so content to let silence have its place, someone uncompelled to fill every available space with sound?

Natalie was like that. Three or four weeks after we got together we'd planned a weekend trip to El Paso and she came out of the house that morning at six, smell of new citrus in the air, with a backpack you could get a small lunch and maybe a pair of underwear in.

"That's it?" I said.

"Like to stay light on my feet. You?"

My now-shamed suitcase was in the trunk.

Light eased itself gingerly above the horizon as we moved through Natalie's battered neighborhood. The first three entrances onto I-10 were jammed. The city had grown too fast—a six-foot man on a child's playhouse chair. Too many bodies shipping in from elsewhere, riding the wagons of their dreams westward, northward.

This was the girlfriend who told me I didn't communicate, that I shut myself off from everyone and, when I shrugged, said, "See?" But that was later.

Of the trip mostly what I remember is driving along the river one evening on our way to dinner and the best chile relleno I ever had, looking over at shanties clustered on the bluff above and thinking how could anyone possibly expect that these people wouldn't try to cross over? Deliverance was right here, so easily visible, scant yards away. Reach out and you could touch it.

On that same trip, walking to breakfast the next morning, we found the bird's nest. I turned to say something and Natalie wasn't there. Two or three steps back, she was down on both knees.

"It must have fallen out. From up there." She pointed to a palo verde. "There's one broken egg shell."

She was almost to the point of tears as she picked the nest up, ran a finger gently along it. Twigs, pieces of vine, what looked to be string or twine, silvery stuff, grass or leaves.

"There's something here with words on it." She held the nest close to her face. "Can't make them out."

Across the street stood a Chinese restaurant, alley running alongside, Dumpsters at the rear. I walked back for a better look at the nest. What she was seeing, intertwined among the twigs and other detritus, were slips from fortune cookies.

That's also when I found out what Natalie read since, as it turned out, the backpack held more books than clothing. When she moved in not long after, she brought a sack of jeans and T-shirts, ten stackable plastic bookshelves, two dozen boxes of science fiction paperbacks, and little else. Kuttner, Sturgeon, Emshwiller, Heinlein, Delany, Russ, LeGuin. I'd begun picking up the books she forever left behind in the bathroom, on the kitchen table, splayed open on counters, in the fissure between our shoved-together twin beds. Many had been read and reread so many times that you had to hold in pages as you made your way through. Before I knew it, I was hooked.

The books were all she took when she moved out, that and her favorite photo, a panoramic shot of the Sonoran desert looking unearthly, lunar, forsakenly beautiful. Over the years I'd searched out copies of some of the books at Changing Hands and Bookmans. For the panorama I had only to drive a few miles outside the city bubble.

Not having been theretofore of an analytical turn of mind, nonetheless I came to recognize that, fulfilling as were these fantastic adventures in and of themselves, something far more substantial moved restless and reaching beneath the surface. The Creature swam in dark reverse of the woman in her white bathing suit above. Unsuspected worlds co-exist just out of frame and focus with our own. Transformations are a commonplace.

The same transformations occur in memory, I know, and what I now recall is the two of us standing there looking at the bare expanse together. Natalie's photo of the Sonoran desert, or the closest I could find to it—but it's her, my new brief companion, speaking.

"It looks as though it doesn't belong to this world."

"I often think that."

"Beautiful."

"Yes."

She moved closer. Our arms touched. Her skin was cold.

"Whatever lived there, on that world, its life would be spent in the pursuit of water. Certain plants would harbor water, water that could be harvested. When the blue moon came, always unpredictably, it would bring sudden, rapid rains. For an hour, two hours before they evaporated, shallow pools would form. And hundreds of life forms would race toward those pools, fill them, congest them. They would overflow."

"That's quite a story—put together from almost nothing."

"Isn't that how we understand the world we find ourselves in, by stitching together bits and pieces of what we see?"

As we had climbed stairs to the apartment she asked what I did for a living and I explained that I worked here at home, nothing of great interest really, pretty much the high-tech equivalent of filing, staring at computer screens all day. How living all the time in your head can make you strange. That getting out among others on a regular basis helped. We'd wandered toward the computer as we talked. The desert photo was my screen saver.

I'd drawn the blinds partly closed when we entered. Sunlight slipped through them at an angle and fell in a rectangle on the desk, looking like a second, brighter screen.

"Eventually," she went on, "one species wins out in the race for water. For space and food. Drives the rest away or destroys them. But without them, without those others keeping the balance, that species can't survive. It crosses over, into a new land. It changes."

"And as with all immigrants, now everything becomes about fitting in, being invisible."

Quiet for a moment, she then said, "Becoming. Yes, exactly. It finds a way to go on."

Later I will remember Apollinaire, my mother's favorite poet: Their hearts are like doors, always doing business. I'll remember what Garrett, a friend far more given to physicality than I, wrote in one of his stories, describing intercourse: We were bears pounding salmon on rocks. And I will remember her face above me in early dawn telling me I would never be alone again.

Then she died.

I remember . . .

Within minutes there's a knock at the door. Dazed, I open it to find a man who looks exactly like her. There are others with him, a man and a woman who look the same. They come in, roll her body in bedspread and blanket Cleopatra-style, bear her away.

"Thank you," one of them says as they leave.

That morning I go for a long walk along the canal. I take little note of the water's slow crawl, of those who pass and pace me, of traffic on the interstate nearby, of the family of ducks who've made this their improbable home. I cannot say what I am feeling. Heartbreak. Shock. Pain. Loss. And at the same time . . .

Happiness, I suppose. Contentment.

Two weeks later I'm walking down the street on my way to coffee, peering up into trees for possible nests, when I hear the voice in my head. "Nice day," it says. "Maybe we could go for a walk along the canal later."

I've come to a stop with the first words, looking around, wondering about this voice, what's going on here—but of course I know. A father always knows. I was bringing a new life across.

FREEZER BURN

Within a week of thawing Daddy out, we knew something was wrong.

He claims, seems in fact fully to believe, that before going cold he was a freelance assassin; furthermore, that he must get back to work. "I was good at it," he tells us. "The best."

When what he actually did was sell vacuum cleaners, mops and squeegee things at Cooper Housewares.

It doesn't matter what you decide to be, he's told us since we were kids, a doctor, car salesman, janitor, just be the best at what you do—one of a dozen or so endlessly recycled platitudes.

Dr. Paley said he's seen this sort of thing before, as side effects from major trauma. That it's probably temporary. We should be supportive, he told us, give it time. Research online uncovers article after article suggesting that such behavior in fact may be backwash from cryogenics and not uncommon at all, "long dreams" inherent to the process itself.

So, in support as Dr. Paley counseled, we agreed to drive Daddy to a meeting with his new client. How he contacted that client, or was contacted by him, we had no idea, and Daddy refused (we understand, of course, he said) to violate client confidentiality or his own trade secrets.

The new client turned out to be not he but she. "You must be Paolo," she said, rising from a spotless porch glider and taking a step toward us as we came up the walk. Paolo is not Daddy's name. The house was in what we hereabouts call Whomville, modestly small from out here, no doubt folded into the hillside and continuing below ground and six or eight times its apparent size. I heard the soft whir of a servicer inside, approaching the door.

"Single malt, if I recall correctly. And for your friends?"

"Matilda, let me introduce my son—"

Immediately I asked for the next waltz.

"—and daughter," who, as ever in unfamiliar circumstances, at age twenty-eight, smiled with the simple beauty and innocence of a four-year-old.

"And they are in the business as well?"

"No, no. But kind enough to drive me here. Perhaps they might wait inside as we confer?"

"Certainly. Gertrude will see to it," Gertrude being the soft-voiced server. It set down a tray with whiskey bottle and two crystal glasses, then turned and stood alongside the door to usher us in.

I have no knowledge of what was said out on that porch but afterwards, as we drove away, Daddy crackled with energy, insisting that we stop for what he called a trucker's breakfast, then, as we remounted, announcing that a road trip loomed in our future. That very afternoon, in fact.

"Road trip!" Susanna's excitement ducked us into the next lane—unoccupied, fortunately. She must have forgotten the last such outing, which left us stranded carless and moneyless in suburban badlands, limping home on the kindness of a stranger or two.

Back at the house we readied ourselves for the voyage. Took on cargo of energy bars, bottled water, extra clothing, blankets, good toilet paper, all-purpose paper towels, matches, extra gasoline, a folding shovel.

"So I gotta know," Susanna said as we bumped and bottomed-out down a back road, at Daddy's insistence, to the freeway. "Now you're working for the like of Oldmoney Matilda back there?"

"Power to the people." That was me.

"Eat the rich," she added.

"Matilda is undercover. Deep. One of us."

Susanna: "Of course."

"In this business, few things are as they appear."

"Like dead salesmen," I said.

"*My* cover. And a good one."

"Which one? Dead, or salesman?"

"Jesus," Susanna said and, as if on cue, to our right sprouted a one-room church. Outside it sat one of those rental LED digital signs complete with wheels and trailer hitch.

COME IN AND HELP US HONE
THE SWORD OF TRUTH

Susanna was driving. Daddy looked over from the passenger seat and winked. "I like it."

"I give up. No scraps or remnants of sanity remain."

"Chill, Sis," I told her. "Be cool. It's the journey, not the destination."

"To know where we are, we must know where we're not."

"As merrily we roll along—"

"Stitching up time—"

Then *for* a time, we all grew quiet. Past windshield and windows the road unrolled like recalls of memory: familiar as it passed beneath, empty of surprise or anticipation, a slow unfolding.

Until Daddy, looking in the rearview, asked how long that vehicle had been behind us.

"Which one?" Sis said. "The van?"

"Yes."

"Well, I've not been keeping count but that has to be maybe the twenty-third white van since we pulled out of the driveway."

"Of all the cards being dealt," Daddy said, "I had to wind up with you jokers. Not one but two smart asses."

"Strong genes," I said.

"Some are born to greatness—"

"—others get twisted to fit."

"Shoes too large."

"Shoes too small."

"Walk this way . . ."

Half a mile further along, the van fell back and took the exit to Logosland, the philosophy playground. Best idea for entertainment since someone built a replica of Noah's ark and went bankrupt the first year. Then again, there's *The Thing* in Texas. Been around forever and still draws. Billboards for a hundred miles, you get there and there's not much to see, proving yet again that anticipation's, like, 90 percent of life.

"They'll be passing us on to another vehicle," Daddy said. "Keep an eye out."

"Copy that," Susanna said.

"Ten-four."

"Wilco."

Following Daddy's directions, through fields with center-pivot irrigation rollers stretching to the horizon and town after town reminiscent of miniature golf courses, we pulled into Willford around four that afternoon. Bright white clouds clustered like fish eggs over the mountains as we came in from the west and descended into town, birthplace of Harry the Horn, whoever the hell that was, Pop. 16,082. Susanna and I took turns counting churches (eleven), filling stations (nine), and schools (three). Crisscross of business streets downtown, houses mostly single-story from fifty, sixty years back, ranch style, cookie-cutter suburban, modest professional, predominantly dark gray, off-white, shades of beige.

"You guys hungry?" Daddy said.

Billie's Sunrise had five cars outside and twenty or more people inside, ranging from older guys who looked like they sprouted right there on the stools at the counter, to clusters of youngsters with fancy sneakers and an armory of handhelds. Ancient photographs curled on the walls. Each booth had a selector box for the jukebox that, our server with purple hair informed us, hadn't worked forever.

We ordered bagels and coffee and, as we ate, Daddy told us about the time he went undercover in a bagel kitchen on New York's Lower East Side. "As kettleman," he said. "Hundred boxes a night, sixty-four bagels to the box. Took some fancy smoke and mirrors, getting me into that union."

Bagels date back at least four centuries, he said. Christians baked their bread, Polish Jews took to boiling theirs. The name's probably from German's *beugel*, for ring or bracelet. By the 1700s, given as gifts, sold on street corners by children, they'd become a staple, and traveled with immigrant Poles to the new land where in 1907 the first union got established. Three years later there were over seventy bakeries in the New York area, with Local #338 in strict control of what were essentially closed shops. Bakers and apprentices worked in teams of four, two making the rolls, one baking, the kettleman boiling.

"So. Plenty more where that came from, all of it fascinating.

Meanwhile, you two wait here, I'll be back shortly." Daddy smiled at the server, who'd stepped up to fill our cups for the third time. "Miss Long will take care of you, I'm sure. And order whatever else you'd like, of course."

Daddy was gone an hour and spare change. Miss Long attended us just as he said. Brought us sandwiches precut into quarters with glasses of milk, like we were little kids with our feet hanging off the seats. If she'd had the chance, she probably would have tucked us in for a nap. Luckily the café didn't have cupcakes. Near the end, two cops came in and took seats at the counter—regulars, from how they were greeted. Their coffee'd scarcely been poured and the skinny one had his first forkful of pie on the way to his mouth when their radios went off. They were up and away in moments. As they reached their car, two police cruisers and a firetruck sailed past behind them, heading out of town, then an ambulance.

Moments later, sirens fading and flashers passing from sight outside, Daddy slid into the booth across from us. "Everybody good?"

"That policeman didn't get to eat his pie," Susanna said.

"Duty calls. Has a way of doing that. More pie in his future, likely."

Smiling, Miss Long brought Daddy fresh coffee in a new cup. He sat back in the booth and drank, looking content.

"Nothing like a good day's work. Nothing." He glanced over to where Miss Long was chatting with a customer at the counter. "Either of you have cash money?"

Susanna asked what he wanted and he said a twenty would do. Carried it over and gave it to Miss Long. Then he came back and stood by the booth. "Time to go home," he said. "I'll be in the car."

We paid the check and thanked Miss Long and when we got to the car Daddy was stretched out on the back seat, sound asleep.

"What are we going to do?" Susanna asked.

We talked about that all the way home.

BRIGHT SARASOTA WHERE THE CIRCUS LIES DYING

I remember how you used to stand at the window staring up at trees on the hill, watching the storm bend them, only a bit at first, then ever more deeply, standing there as though should you let up for a moment on your vigilance, great wounds would open in the world.

That was in Arkansas. We had storms to be proud of there, tornados, floods. All these seem to be missing where I am now—wherever this is I've been taken. Every day is the same here. We came by train, sorted onto rough-cut benches along each side of what once must have been freight or livestock cars, now recommissioned like the trains themselves, with eerily polite attendants to see to us.

It was all eerily civil, the knock at the door, papers offered with a flourish and a formal invocation of conscript, the docent full serious, the two Socials accompanying him wearing stunners at their belts, smiles on their faces. They came only to serve.

Altogether an exceedingly strange place, the one I find myself in. (That can be read metaphorically. Please don't.) A desert of sorts, but unlike any I've encountered in films, books, or online. The sand is a pale blue, so light in weight that it drifts away on the wind if held in the hand and let go; tiny quartz crystals gleam everywhere within. At the eastern border of the compound, trees, again of a kind unknown, crowd land and sky. One cannot see through or around them.

They keep us busy here. With a failed economy back home and workers unable to make anything like a living wage, the government saw few options. What's important, Mother, is that you not worry. The fundamental principles on which our nation was founded are still there, resting till needed; our institutions will save us. Meanwhile I am at work for the common good, I am being productive, I am contributing.

That said, I do, for my part, worry some. This is the fourth letter

I've written you. Each was accepted at the service center with "We'll get this out right away," then duly, weeks later, returned marked *Undeliverable*. It is difficult to know what this means, and all too easy to summon up dire imaginings.

To judge by the number and size of dormitories and extrapolating from the visible population, there are some four to five hundred of us, predominately male, along with a cadre of what I take to be indigenous peoples serving as support: janitorial, housekeeping and kitchen workers, groundsmen, maintenance. Oddly enough for this climate, they are fair, their skin colorless, almost translucent, hair of uniform length male and female. From dedicated eavesdropping I've learned bits and pieces of their language. It is in fact dangerously close to our own, rife with cognates and seemingly parallel constructions that could easily lead us to say, without realizing, something other than, even contrary to, what we intended.

The indigenes speak without reserve of their situation, of what they've achieved in being here, and not at all of what came before. They appear to relish routine, expectations fulfilled—to thrive on them—and to have little sense of theirs as lives torn away at world's edge, only jagged ends of paper left behind. Popular fiction would have me falling in love with one of them, discovering the true nature of the subjugation around me, and leading their people to freedom. Approved fiction, I suppose, would write of protagonist me (as someone said of Dostoevsky's Alyosha) that he thought and thought and thought.

As I write this, recalling the failure of my three previous missives and a rare conversation with another resident here, I realize just how close we've come to a time when many will scarcely remember what letters are.

Kamil taught for years at university, one of those, I must suppose, composed of vast stone buildings and lushly kept trees whose very name brings to mind dark halls and the smell of floor wax. Unable to settle ("like a hummingbird," he said), Kamil straddled three departments, music, literature, and history, weaving back and forth seeking connections. On a handheld computer he played for me examples of the music he'd employed in the classroom to elicit those connections from young people who knew little enough, he said, of any of the three disciplines, least of all history. Truth to tell, I wasn't able to make much of his music, but the title of one raucous piece, "Brain Cloudy Blues," stays with me.

I remember when you told me about circuses, Mother, the bright colors and animals, people engaged in all manner of improbable activities, the smells, the sounds, the faces, and then explained that they had gone away, there were no circuses anymore, and the very last of what was left of them lay put away in storage in the old winter quarters of the greatest circus of all in a town faraway named Sarasota.

Are we all in Sarasota now? There are further chapters in my life, I know. What might they be like? When someone other than myself is turning the page.

THE BEAUTY OF SUNSETS

I propped him in his chair with his arms on the desk and straight-ened his tie, a repp stripe upon which purples and grays had intermingled over the years, then reached across to his appointment calendar and on today's date, as I always did, stamped a tiny red skull. For decades Senator Prim had drained public money by the hundreds of thousands into private enterprises and vacation retreats while steadfastly voting against safety nets or social welfare for the young, old, poor and infirm, meanwhile doing his part to strip every last thread of government support from education and the arts. He wouldn't be doing that anymore.

Not that I'm a big fan of paintings with drippy blocks of color or music that makes your back teeth ache, mind you, but I'll take them over grift and greed. As for education, don't think for a moment that I don't appreciate the job skills my government unwittingly gave me.

It was getting along toward day's end, light slanting in through blinds at the window and turning to bars of bright and dark on the floor. The senator's aide would be back in minutes from his daily trek to Xtreme Bean, by which time I'd be out on the street, back in the stew of humanity.

This was my last one. My job was done. I'd been paid, and now I'd taken down everyone on the list.

Blood sugar levels let me know I hadn't eaten for quite some time, so I found a place nearby, Bernie's, and took a seat at the end of the bar, ordering a draft and a pastrami sandwich. Probably not a lot they could do back in whatever passed as a kitchen to mess that up. The bartender was female. Bearing and gestures hovered between cute-twenty-year-old and seen-it-all-sixty. Dress, hair and visible accessories were a mix of can't-possibly-care and lumberjack. It worked.

On the TV suspended over the bar, yet another politician held forth on civic responsibility, deregulation, trickledown, gooby-gooby, gob-gob. One code word after another.

The pastrami tasted of rancid oil, as though it had sweated through a workout and gone unwashed. The beer glass had smudges and smears of soap (I hoped it was soap) along its sides.

"'Bout had my fill of that rot," the barkeep said, inclining her head toward the TV. She fished the remote out from under the bar, where they kept the shotgun in old westerns, and went rummaging through channels. An amateur sports event. Four barely literate people sitting around a table discussing celebrity divorces. A soap opera populated by tight-faced older women and young men with unruly hair. A couple of minutes toward the midpoint of *The African Queen*, Bogart slowly, subtly, surely becoming a different man.

Meanwhile, here outside the TV, in our get-along real world, something—a parade, another protest—went on outside. Sirens crossed and recrossed, heavy vehicles shouldered by, a loudspeaker on the move blared what appeared to be the same announcement over and again. At this distance, in here, its words were indistinguishable.

As business slowed to a saunter, then a crawl, possibly because I was the rare patron who hadn't heard it all before, the barkeep settled across from me to say how her old man has bad Alzheimer's and doesn't recognize her mother, doesn't even acknowledge she's there, and how glad her mother is about this, says it's the first time she's felt free in fifty-two years.

I finished my beer, left half the sandwich and a tip, and stepped outside. Hundreds of hurried, harried, unsmiling faces. The stew of humanity. Life has undone so many. Or is it that they—all of us, like Bogart, like the barkeep's mother—are forever on our way somewhere else? Are only *becoming*?

The sunset was well advanced, evening springing its many trapdoors. Back in the jungle, sunsets took your breath. The sky above so clear, smelling of water, of life. And now, here, this superb sunset lay about. It turned sky and earth red, poured fire into high windows, spoke of longing and of a quiet solace.

Is it possible that I actually felt my brain in the moment it changed, bright sparks scattering ceiling to floor as the world rebuilt itself within me? And in that moment I knew: What I had done for money all these years was but a beginning.

I was wrong. Senator Prim wouldn't be the last one. I had other appointments to keep. These would be on me.

WHAT YOU WERE FIGHTING FOR

I was ten the year he showed up in Waycross. It was uncommonly dry that year, I remember, even for us, no rain for weeks, grass gone brown and crisp as bacon, birds gathering at shallow pools of water out back of the garage where Mister Lonnie, a trustee from the jail, washed cars. And where he let me help, all the while talking about growing up in the shacks down in Niggertown, bringing up four kids on what he made doing whatever piecemeal work he could find, rabbit stew and fried squirrel back when he was a kid himself.

I'd gone round front to fetch some rags we'd left drying on the waste bin out there and saw him pull in. Cars like that—provided you knew what to look for, and I knew, even then—didn't show up in those parts. Some rare soul had taken Mr. Whitebread's sweet-tempered tabby and turned it to mountain lion. The driver got out. He left the door open, engine not so much idling as taking deep, slow breaths, and stood in the shadow of the water tower looking around.

I grew up in the shade of that tower myself. There wasn't any water in it anymore, not for a long time, it was as baked and broiled as the desert that stretched all around us. A few painted-on letters, an *A*, part of a *Y*, an *R*, remained of the town's name.

I could see Daddy inside, in the window over the workbench. Didn't take long before the door screeched in its frame and he came out. "Help you?" Daddy said. The two of them shook hands.

The man glanced my way and smiled.

"You get on back to your business, boy," Daddy told me. I walked around the side of the garage to where I wouldn't be seen.

"She's not handling or sounding dead on. And the timing's a hair off. Think you could have a look?"

"Glad to. Strictly cash and carry, though. That a problem?"

"Never."

"I'll open the bay, you pull 'er in."

"Yes, sir."

"Garrulous as ever, I see."

I went on around back, wondering about that last remark. Not too long after, Mister Lonnie finished up and headed home to his cell. They never locked it, and he had it all comfy in there, a bedspread from Woolworth's, pictures torn from magazines on the wall. You live in a box, he said, it might as well be a *nice* box. I went inside to the office, which was really just a corner with cinder blocks stacked up to make a wall along one side. Daddy's desk looked like it had been used for artillery practice. The chair did its best to throw you every time you shifted in it.

I was supposed to be studying but what I was doing was reading a book called *The Killer Inside Me* for the third or fourth time. I'd snitched it out of a car Daddy worked on, where it had slipped down between the seats.

Everyone assumed I'd follow in my father's footsteps, work at the tire factory maybe, or with luck and a long stubborn climb uphill become, like he had, a mechanic. No one called kids special back in those days. We got called lots of things, but special wasn't among them. This was before I found out why normal things were so hard for me, why I always had to push when others didn't.

They got to it, both their heads under the hood, wrenches and sockets going in, coming out. Every few pages I'd look through the holes in the cinder blocks. Half an hour later Daddy said the man didn't need him and he had other cars to see to. So the visitor went on working as Daddy moved along to a '62 Caddy.

After a while the visitor climbed in the car, started it, revved the engine hard, let it spin down, revved it again. Got back under the hood and not long after that said he could use some help. Said would it be okay to ask me and Daddy grunted okay. "Boy's name is Leonard."

"You mind coming down here to give me a hand with this engine, Leonard?" the man said.

I was at a good part of the book, the part where Lou Ford talks about his childhood and what he did with the housekeeper, but the book would always be there waiting. When I went over, the man shook my hand like I was grown and helped me climb in.

"I'm setting the timing now," he said. "When I tell you, I need

590 • JAMES SALLIS

for you to rev the engine." He held up the timing light. "I'll be using this to—"

I nodded just as Daddy said, "He knows."

To reach the accelerator I had to slide as far forward in the seat as I could, right onto the edge of it, and stretch my leg out straight. I revved when he said, waited as he rotated the distributor, revved again. Once more and we were done.

"What do you think?" the man asked Daddy.

"Sounding good."

"Always good to have good help."

"Even for a loner, yeah."

The man looked back at me. "Maybe we should take a ride, make sure everything's tight."

"Or take a couple of beers and let the boy get to *his* work."

Daddy snagged two bottles from the cooler. Condensation came off them and made tiny footprints on the floor. I was supposed to be doing extra homework per my teachers, but what was boring and obvious the first time around didn't get any better with age. Lou and the housekeeper were glad to have me back.

Daddy and the man sat quietly sipping their beers, looking out the bay door where heat rose rose in waves, turning the world wonky.

"Kind of a surprise, seeing you here." That was Daddy, not given to talk much at all, and never one for hyperbole.

"Both of us."

Some more quiet leaned back against the wall waiting.

"Still in the same line of work?"

"Not anymore, no."

"Glad to hear that. Never thought you were cut out for it."

"Thing is, I didn't seem to be cut out for much else."

"Except driving."

"Except driving." Our visitor motioned with his bottle, a swing that took in the car, the rack, the tools he'd put back where they came from. "Appreciate this."

"Any time. So, where are you headed?"

"Thought I might go down to Mexico."

"And do what?"

"More of the same, I guess."

"The same being what?"

Things wound down then. The quiet that had been leaning against the wall earlier came back. They finished their beers. Daddy stood and said he figured it to be time to get on home, asked if he planned on heading out now the car was looking good. "You could stay a while, you know," Daddy said.

"Nowhere I have to be."

"Don't guess you have a place . . ."

"Car's fine."

"That your preference?"

"It's what I'm used to."

"You want, you can pull in out back, then. Plenty of privacy. Nothing but the arroyo and scrub trees all the way to the highway."

Daddy raised the rattling bay doors and the visitor pulled out, drove around. We put the day's used rags in the barrel, threw sawdust on the floor and swept up, swabbed the sink and toilet, everything in place and ready to hit the ground running tomorrow morn. Daddy locked up the Caddy and swung a tarp over it. Said while he finished up I should go be sure the man didn't need anything else.

He had the driver's door open, the seat kicked back, and he was lying there with eyes open. Propped on the dash, a transistor radio the size of a pack of cigarettes, the kind I'd seen in movies, played something in equal parts shrill and percussive.

"Daddy says to tell you the diner over on Mulberry's open till nine and the food's edible if you're hungry enough."

"Don't eat a lot these days."

He held a beer bottle in his left hand, down on his thigh. The beer must have been warm since it wasn't sweating. Crickets had started up their songs for the night. You'd catch movement out the corner of your eye but when you looked you couldn't see them. The sun was sinking in its slot.

"Saw the book in your pocket earlier," he said, "wondered what you're reading," and when I showed him he said he liked those too, even had a friend out in California that wrote a few. Everything there is about California is damn cool, I was convinced of that back then, so I asked a lot of questions. He told me about the Hispanic neighborhood he'd lived in. Billboards in Spanish, murals on walls, bright colors. Stalls and street food and festivals.

Years later I lived out there in a neighborhood just like that before I had to come back to take care of Daddy. It all started with him pronouncing words wrong. Holdover would be *ho*lover, or noise somehow turn to nose. No one thought much about it at first, but before long he was losing words completely. His mouth would open, and you'd watch his eyes searching for them, but the words just weren't there.

"Everyone says we get them coming up the arroyo," I said, "illegals, I mean."

"My friend? Wrote those books? He says we're all illegals."

Daddy came around to collect me then. Standing by the kitchen counter we had a supper of fried bologna, sliced tomatoes and leftover dirty rice. This was Daddy's night to go dancing with Eleanor, dancing being a code word we both pretended I didn't understand.

That night a storm moved toward us like Godzilla advancing on poor Tokyo, but nothing came of it, a scatter of raindrops. I gave up trying to sleep and was out on the back porch watching lightning flash behind the clouds when Daddy pulled the truck in.

"You're supposed to be in bed, young man," he said.

"Yes, sir."

We watched as lightning came again. A gust of wind shoved one of the lawn chairs to the edge of the patio where it tottered, hung on till the last moment, and overturned.

"Beautiful, isn't it?" Daddy said. "Most people never get to see skies like that."

Even then I'd have chosen *powerful, mysterious, angry, promise unfulfilled.* Daddy said *beautiful.*

It turned out that neither of us could sleep that night. We weren't getting the benefits of the weather, but it had a hold on us: restlessness, aches, unease. When for the second time we found ourselves in the kitchen, Daddy decided we might as well head down to the garage, something we'd done before on occasion. We'd go down, I'd read, he'd work and putter or mess about, we'd come back and sleep a few hours.

A dark gray Buick sat outside the garage. This is two in the morning, mind you, and the passenger door is hanging open. What the hell, Daddy said, and pulled in behind. No lights inside the garage. No one around that we can see. We were climbing out of the car when the visitor showed up, not from behind the garage where we'd expect, but yards to the right, walking the rim of the arroyo.

"You know you have coyotes down there?" he said. "Lot of them."

"Coyotes, snakes, you name it. And a car up here that ain't supposed to be."

"They won't be coming back for it."

"What am I going to see when I look under that hood?" Daddy glanced at the arroyo. "And down there?"

"About what you'd expect, under the hood. Down there, there won't be much left."

"So it's *not* just more of the same. I'd heard stories."

"I'm sorry to bring this on you—I didn't know. It's taken care of."

Daddy and the man stood looking at one another. "I was never here," the man said. "*They* were never here." He went around to the back. Minutes later, his car pulled out, eased past us, and was gone.

"We'd best get this General Motors piece of crap inside and get started tearing it down," Daddy said.

We all kill the past in our own way. Some slit its throat, some let it die of neglect.

Last week I began a list of species that have become extinct. What started it was reading about a baby elephant that wouldn't leave its mother's side when hunters killed her, and died itself of starvation. I found out that 90 percent of all things that ever lived on earth are extinct, maybe more. As many as two hundred species pass away between Monday's sunrise and Tuesday's.

I do wonder. What if I'd not been born as I was, what if I'd been back a bit in line and not out front, what if the things they'd told us about that place had a grain of truth. Don't do that much, but it happens.

"When the sun is overhead, the shadows disappear," my physical therapist back in rehab said. Okay, they do. But only briefly.

And: "At least you knew what you were fighting for." Sure I did.

594 • JAMES SALLIS

Absolutely. We steer our course by homilies and reductive narratives, then wonder that so many of us are lost.

A few weeks ago I made a day trip to Waycross. The water tower is gone, just one leg and half another still standing. It's a ghost town now, nothing but weightless memories tumbling along the streets. I pulled in by what used to be my father's garage, got my chair out and hauled myself into it, rolled with the memories down the streets, then round back to where our visitor had parked all those years ago. Nothing much has changed with the arroyo.

You always hear people talking about I saw this, I read this, I did this, and it changed my life.

Sure it did.

Thing is, I'd forgotten all about the visitor and what happened that night, and the only reason I remember now is because of this movie I saw.

I'd rolled the chair in at the end of an aisle only to be met with a barrage of smart-ass remarks about blocking their view from a brace of twenty-somethings, so I was concentrating on not tearing their heads off and didn't pay much attention to the beginning of the movie, but then a scene where a simple heist goes stupid bad grabbed my attention and I just kind of fell through the screen.

The movie's about a man who works as a stunt driver by day and drives for criminals at night. Things start going wrong then go wronger, pile up on him and pile up more until finally, halfway to a clear, cool morning, he bleeds to death from stab wounds in a Mexican bar. "There were so many other killings, so many other bodies," he says in voiceover near the end, his and the movie's.

After lights came on, I sat in the theater till the cleaning crew, who'd been waiting patiently at the back with brooms and a trashcan on rollers, came on in and got to work. I was remembering the car, his mention of Mexico, some of the conversation between my father and him.

I'm pretty sure it was him, his story—our visitor, my father's old friend or co-worker or accomplice or whatever the hell he was. I think that explains something.

I wish I knew what.

DISPOSITIONS

"Your child, the one you planned on naming Amelia, will be still-born. The nurse practitioner and doctor will work for eighteen minutes to resuscitate her. She will never take a breath. Her tiny heart will not beat. They will clean the body and hand it to you. It will be limp and lifeless as a rag. You won't even be able to cry. I'm sorry."

Nor was she able to cry then, as her friend quickly took her arm and ushered her away. The woman looked lifeless herself as she was led off past a stationery-and-greeting-cards store toward Nordstrom's. In memory, in my mind, it seems that others parted right and left to let them pass.

"Fourteen thousand miles out beyond Pluto, which may or may not be a planet this week, there's a cosmic hole, a void, the size of our solar system," I tell Becca.

"Achh. The things we have to live with," Becca says, and pours coffee.

I tell her about the chairs. They were laid out for a wedding in 1939 in Poland. With the German invasion, the wedding was abandoned, and so were the chairs. They were found again after the war with the trees growing through them. Every year now they are repainted.

"What color?" she asks.

I tell her about the woman, the baby.

"This was yesterday? You were back at the mall."

"Nostalgia." The mall was, after all, where we met. At the far border of the food court, where people spin by like wind at world's edge.

"And you did it again. You walked up to someone you don't know and told them this horrible thing was going to happen to them. You told me you stopped doing that."

"I had."

Becca sips her coffee disgruntledly. Not many could pull that off. The word *aplomb* falls into my mind.

"How many times have we talked about this? In what alternate universe did you think it was a good idea? What could you possibly hope to accomplish? What has it *ever* accomplished?"

I remain silent. Becca's questions are like the lyrics of an old song that always takes you back to adolescence, to your first heartbreak when moon and sun shut down, to that third or fourth date when you just knew. I'm listening to them, running them, in my mind.

"It's one thing to dwell on horrible things, Ken. Polish wedding chairs, bed bug infestations, holes in the space-time continuum. It's quite another to tell people these awful things are going to happen."

"They're true."

"Your telling about them is not going to matter. They will still happen. All you've done is make someone horribly sad."

"I can't help myself."

"Of course you can."

"Just say no?"

"Just keep your mouth shut."

Which is what I decide to do, even though there's so much I have to tell her. That I was at the mall for good reason, for the comfort of memories. Or about her new dress, how good she looks in it. How this is the only time she'll wear it. How it's the one she'll be buried in.

BILLY DELIVER'S NEXT TWELVE NOVELS

The dogs took him down a few miles outside Topeka.

When he came to from a forty-year coma, his favorite show from back when he was a kid was on the TV hung by two struts from the ceiling. *Space Rangers*. The screws of one strut had pulled partially loose. Threads were visible; the whole structure canted starboard.

It's always a kick to go visit Berr. He's got these cardboard cutouts of his parents and sister that he moves around the house, from bed to bathroom to breakfast table to living room. Tonight we're sitting at the table with them finishing off a ten-dollar pizza.

I've not spoken to the person who lives in my garage. She slipped in there one evening a month or so back when, in a hurry to get to work and already late, I failed to close the automatic door.

Just now I walked up to the office and asked where this was. Nothing in the room offered a clue: no information sheets, emergency card, notepad, old newspaper. No relevant signs outside, a service station across the street down a block or so with ancient pumps that look like gumball machines. The sign painted on the office window says *Motel*. The guy who came out of the back had skin flaking like the paint on the sign.

He'd just bought a box of memories marked down half-price at GoMart and settled in to enjoy them when the phone rang. He froze the DreamBox on a slow-moving tropical beach complete with seagulls the size of mastiffs, and punched in the phone.

• • •

The day we sold Dad for parts, we celebrated by going out for a big breakfast at Griddles, the place we met twenty-five years ago. Damn miracle it still existed. Damn miracle that we did too, of course—as a pair, I mean.

She smells the smoke on me and senses, beyond that, subtler betrayals. She doesn't say anything, though, just hands me the glass of wine she's already poured, one she says has legs, not balls mind you, but legs.

The toaster said "No."
    "Why not?"
    "That's not how you like it. Buttered, lightly toasted."
    "I long to try something new. Take the plunge. Live wild."
    "You won't like it."
    That's how the day began.

One bright morning Charlie fired up his computer to find himself, much to his surprise, for sale on Ebay. The bids were appallingly low.

The alien sat in the bare room across from him. It looked exactly like Sanderson's fifth-grade teacher. Somehow a fly had got in the room. Sanderson noted that the fly avoided the part of the room where the alien was.

In the last moments, they say, William Blake jumped up from his death bed and began to sing.

FIGS

Light spills out cracks of beer joint walls tonight as I patrol. Past eleven and the town's quiet. In another two hours those beer joints themselves will spill into the streets. Down by the town square where, beneath the old bandstand, feral cats bring weekly generations of kittens into the world, imperfectly cleared leavings from today's farmer's market glitter in the streetlights. Seven hours from now they'll be setting up again. I'd have to remember to check with Dominic tomorrow. Should be just about time for the good ones, and he always has the best.

There's nothing I love more than driving the streets of town at night. A single light shows through curtains at the pastor's home behind Savior Methodist. Sal's OneStop is still open, as is his front door, with country music streaming out from inside. Half a mile past the city limits a familiar truck sits empty at roadside, keys in the ignition. Nate Brown drunk again no doubt and, suddenly gone aware he shouldn't be driving, taken to foot for the remaining distance, as happens once or twice a week.

Swinging back into town proper, I come across a couple of highschoolers, faces familiar, names unknown, with a stalled-out Camry. The car has what look to be freehand swirls, vaguely wing-like, along the sides. The car's seen some wear. They haven't, not much, not yet. The boy peeks out from under the hood as he hears me pull up. She gets out of the driver's seat and they walk back together to meet me. Turns out it's only a bad battery connection. They're back on the road in minutes, probably on their way out to Blue Hole, the lake everyone around here claims is bottomless, a favored spot for what we called parking when I was a kid.

When I was five or six, I fell out of a fig tree. Yeah, you gotta be small to do that, and I was. My parents had a bunch of these, a grape arbor, tulips. At the time I had no idea how exotic all this was, for where we lived. I remember being on my back on the ground, trying to breathe and not being able to, getting up and stumbling toward the house, and my mother running to me—then suddenly the pressure gave way and my chest filled. Tears ran down both our cheeks.

There's rain in the offing, you see it in the halos around lights but can't feel or taste it just yet. By early morning, maybe. Be a mess for the farmer's market.

My last touchstone on the way back into town, as always, is the old Merritt place, abandoned years ago upon Ezra's death at eighty-two and his wife's the following week (from heartbreak as they say), now suspended ownerless in real-estate purgatory but kept up sporadically, lawn mowed, porch and frontage hosed down, by neighbors. It reminds me how things once were.

Back at the office there's a logged call from a number I don't recognize. Billie's confined to bed by doctor's orders for the next two months before her third child's due, and Marty's filling in for her at dispatch. We call it dispatch even though it's more like answer the phone, make sure the doors are locked, keep the coffee fresh. Nope, wouldn't leave a name, Marty says when I ask, and when I call, twice, there's no answer. Then ten minutes later we get a call that gives us an address after saying, Something's going on over there. Marty checks. The address corresponds to the number that called earlier.

There's no answer at the door, no one in the house when I go in, no sign of disturbance. According to records, a Mabel Clark lives here, possibly with a teenage son. Out in the kitchen, dishes and utensils, a pot and small skillet, are in the draining rack over the left sink. There's milk a week away from expiration in the refrigerator, a pack of ham slices gone slimy, multiple plastic buckets of leftovers, a loaf of brown bread you could use as a door stop. Beds in both bedrooms aren't made but have covers and sheets pulled to the top and folded back. The alarm clock's preset to 6:50 A.M.

I don't have to wake Mrs. Sim, the neighbor who called it in. She's waiting for me on her front porch and wants to know if everything's okay but has nothing to add to what she said before on the phone: Heard what she first thought was loud TV then thought maybe could be shouts, and they didn't stop, just went on and on until, of a sudden, there was some kind of crash and it all stopped, which is when she called.

I thank her and go back over for one last look. No evidence of anything crashing, getting thrown, broken. Mrs. Sim told me where Mabel Clark works and I'll check there first thing in the morning. No other kin she's aware of, except Rich, her son, but he hasn't been around for months, far as she knows.

Rain's getting a little closer, a little bolder, as I get back to the truck. A mockingbird in the tree I'm parked under thinks it's still daytime and busily tries out all four parts of a vocal quartet one after another.

Figs were one of the first plants to be cultivated by humans before going on to wheat, barley or legumes. The beginning of agriculture, really. Aristotle noted that there were two kinds, the cultivated fig that bears fruit, the wild fig that assists the first. Buddha's enlightenment came beneath the Bodhi Tree, a sacred fig (*Ficus religiosa*) with heart-shaped leaves.

Things are quiet for a while. I draft a report on the call about Mabel Clark in longhand and, while I'm entering it, pull up her workplace on the computer, an auto parts store next town over, then go poking about for son Rich as well. No results. From what I hear about social media, he's probably on there somewhere, but for me that's undiscovered country, another world.

Marty brings in two cups of coffee from a fresh pot he just made and we sit talking. I hear faint crackles out front from the ham radio receiver he brings to work with him. He offers a portion from a homemade cookie the size of a dinner plate, but I decline. He tells me about a new woman he's dating, someone he met at the community college where he's taking Spanish classes. Her grandparents were from Mexico, but she never learned.

Along about two, the hospital calls, the new doctor from out of state, to tell me Danny brought in a DOA in the ambulance and I'm needed. When I ask who it is she says Evelyn Crawford, do I know her? My English teacher in tenth grade.

Evelyn likes her television, Otis tells me when I get there, and he doesn't have much patience for silly stories, so he goes on about his business at the table out in the den while she watches at night. She always mutes the commercials when they come on. But a couple hours ago he noticed the thing was still going full volume, with someone talking about laundry soap or the last flashlight you'll ever need. Thinking back, he realized it had been that way for a while, and when he went in to see, he found Evelyn dead in her chair.

Looks like heart failure, the new doctor says. She's considerably older than I'd have thought from her voice on the phone, slow-talking, quiet-spoken. Nothing suspicious here then, I ask. Just notifying you as required, she tells me. Good to meet you, by the way.

A year after Jean and I got married, two stupid wide-eyed kids ready to take on the world, we moved to New York. Brooklyn really, an Italian neighborhood with women forever out on the front stoop and men playing dominoes at card tables on the sidewalk. The apartment we rented was upstairs of a restaurant, big burly guys in there all day long sitting at tables drinking, shirts half unbuttoned with hair spilling out, gold chains. The owner's ancient mother lived upstairs too. Jean said she never felt safer in her life, nobody in his right mind would come near the place. One morning I went down to pay the rent and the owner was eating fresh figs, selectively plucking them out of a basket with two fingers like people do candies from a box. You like figs? the owner asked, seeing my interest. I told him about our trees, when I was a kid. An hour later there came a knock at the apartment door and one of the big guys stood there with a basket of figs.

I'm barely out of the hospital parking lot when Marty radios to let me know the alarm's going off at Hobb's Hardware again. This happens five, six times a month. Anything can serve to set it off— high wind, sudden noises, heavy trucks rolling too close by. I've repeatedly asked, less and less pleasantly, that Karl have the alarm company out to fix this, and he always says he will. It's got so bad I have a key to the place.

Nothing to see from outside when I get there, front or rear. I give it time to let my eyes adjust better to darkness, then let myself in the front door. Shadowy light from the streetlamp outside falls through the front windows but gives up quickly. Ten or twelve steps from the door, everything's black as a cave. I go in slowly, one footstep then another, listening between.

For a moment I think I see a flash of light at the back of the store, by the warehouse, and that I hear something scrabbling—a large rat, maybe. Here in the oldest parts of town, with bins of trash in the alleys, the cockroaches and general decay, rats can grow to rabbit size. A pickup goes by outside, its lights sweeping the back wall. In the bare seconds they last, again I think I see something back there, movement maybe.

I'm almost to the back of the store myself now.

When I found Jean's body, I stood at the bedroom door for what seemed a very long time. With all the blood, there was no question but that she was dead and, from the blood's appearance, little doubt that she'd been so for hours before I came home from a quiet night on patrol. Beside her on the nightstand, half-eaten, was the carton of figs I'd left for her on the kitchen table, an anniversary gift, complete with card that read *Remember?*

SUNDAY DRIVE

Because it's the weekend, traffic is light, and once we get out of downtown, where I parked on the street quite a ways off, having made the parking-lot mistake once before, we've got smooth sailing, calm seas, all that. Caroline stares out the window, talking about how much this area has changed, the whole city, really, that you can hardly recognize it from what it used to be. Mattie, in the back, is texting one-handed on her new iPhone, nibbling at a Pop Tart in such a way that the edge is always even. She holds it away from her mouth every few bites to check.

When I suggest that we take a little drive, not hurry home, Mattie groans, then looks away as I glance in the rearview mirror. "Whatever you want is fine," Caroline says.

I jump on I-10, then the 202 out toward Tempe and all those other far-flung lands. Back years ago, when Caroline and I were first married, I worked these roads, running heavy equipment, backhoes, bulldozers. Knew every mile of highway, every block of city street. Then I went back to school and got my degree. Now I program computers and solve IT problems all day long. Now I can barely find my way around out here in this world.

"The music was lovely," Caroline says. "Back there."

"Puccini, yes."

"The story was dumb," Mattie says, leaning hard on the final word. So at least she was paying that much attention.

We drive out past the airport and hotels to the left, cheap apartments, garages and ramshackle convenience stores to the right, past a building that looks like a battleship and that I swear was not here the last time we came this way, past the two hills near the zoo that look like humongous dung heaps. Wind is picking up, blowing food wrappers and blossoms from bougainvillea in bursts across the road.

Caroline fidgets with the radio, cakewalking through top forty, light jazz, classical, country. Trying to regain something of what we felt momentarily, by proxy, back there? Trying to muffle the silence that presses down on us? Or just bored? What the hell do *I* know about human motivation, anyway?

On impulse I exit, loop around, and get on the 51 heading north. Soon we're cruising through the stretch of cactus-spackled hills everyone calls Dreamy Draw. Caroline has something peppy and lilting about a lost love playing on the radio. Ukulele is involved. Mattie leans forward to listen to the music as three Harleys come up on our left, their throaty *raaaa* like a bubble enclosing us. All three riders have expensive leather jackets and perfectly cut hair.

At the 101, the Harleys swing right toward Scottsdale. We head west for I-17 to begin the slow climb out of the valley, through Deadman Wash, Bumble Bee, Rock Springs. Where clouds hang above hills, the hills are dark. Nascent yellow blooms sprout from the ends of saguaro arms. Caroline stares off, not toward the horizon or into green-shot gorges, but out her window at dry flatland and cholla. Mattie is asleep.

In the distance, out over one of the mesas, hawks glide on thermals.

Hard on to the end of the second act of *Turandot*, about the time Calif was getting ready to ring the gong and lay his life on the line for love, the old geezer sitting in front of me, the one whose wife had been elbowing him to keep awake, began weeping uncontrollably. She elbowed him again, more English on it this time, and after a moment he struggled to his feet and staggered up the stairs and out. I followed. When I caught up, he was standing motionless by one of the windows. He could have been part of a diorama, twenty-first-century man in his unnatural habitat.

"You okay?"

He looked up, looked at the window, finally looked at me. I could see the world struggling to reboot behind his eyes.

A minute ago I was thinking how all these people paid sixty or a hundred dollars to spiff themselves up and sit through two hours of largeness and artifice—grand emotion, bright colors, carnival—before going back to their own small lives. Now I was thinking about just one of those people, and how sometimes we find expression for our pain, how it can just fall upon us.

"I didn't want to come to this. My wife's employer, she works for a doctor, he gave her tickets he couldn't use. She insisted we come. I knew it was a bad idea."

"Because . . . ?"

He shook his head.

"Let's get some air," I said.

We stepped outside, where life-size sculptures of dancers, canted forward on one leg, arms outstretched, had found refuge from time and the earth's pull. A beautiful day. Across the street an old woman stood behind a cardboard podium singing arias much like those going on inside. Poorly dyed gray hair fell in strands that looked like licorice sticks. Her dress had once been purple. My companion was watching her, no expression on his face.

He took out his wallet, pulled something from one of the photo holders and began unfolding it.

"Nineteen seventy-six, when I was working the pipeline." He held it out for me to see. "Twelve hundred and ninety dollars. One week's work."

It was a check. You could make that out, but not much else. When I looked back up and smiled, he looked at the check.

"Guess you can't make it out too good anymore."

He folded it carefully, put it back. Glanced again at the diva, who had one foot in the door of *Nessum dorma*. The strangeness of hearing the piece as a soprano aria matched perfectly the strangeness of the setting.

"Well, young man," he said, "we should go back in now."

We did, and even before I retook my seat I sensed that something had changed. The audience seemed poised, expectant. And was there a void onstage? One of several court scenes, better than a dozen attendants and functionaries in place. The patterns were wrong. What, I asked, sliding in next to Caroline, had happened?

A cast member, the forester she thought, had collapsed and been spirited out, with barely a breath's hesitation, by two others. Made quite a rattle and bang when he hit the floor. It was a major aria for the ice princess, of course, and with but a moment's glance toward the commotion, the soprano had flawlessly continued, inching toward the inevitable high C or whatever it was. A woman two rows back had asked her companions, loudly, if this was a part of the show.

The rest passed without incident, building inexorably to its grandly happy, unrelenting conclusion, soprano soaring like a seabird, tenor stolidly tossing his voice to the rafters, chorus dug in and determined to hold its own, orchestra aclash with horns and percussion.

Turandot had been wrong.

Now the riddles were solved, the gong would sound no more.

And we were outside, moving within moving corridors of other opera-goers, past the bronze dancers, past the diva with her cardboard podium, reclaimed by our lives.

Just this side of Sunset Point, Mattie has one of her seizures. Doesn't happen much anymore, with the medication, but we're used to it from the old days. Something starts thumping against the seat, I look back, and it's her legs spasming. I edge off the road, get in the back with her, and hold her till it stops. From the first, right after Mattie was born, Caroline never was much good at handling that. She'd fall to pieces or just kind of go away. As the seizures got worse, so did the going away. I don't blame her. Or anyone. Things just happen.

We're back on the road in four, five minutes, Caroline looking out the window, Mattie sleeping it off. We inch up the hill and around a long curve behind three semis. Our speed drops to 55, 48, 44, 40. Atop the hill we're able to pass. I roll down the window. The air is fresh and cool. Something with that unmistakable pulse of baroque music, strings, horns, keyboard continuo, plays on the radio. It begins to cut out, like a stutterer, as we gain altitude.

Mattie wakes, rattles a box of Jolly Ranchers to see how much is left, pops one in her mouth and sucks away. We're ten thousand feet up and there's a pinpoint puncture, our air's hissing slowly out. That's what it sounds like.

"What do you want to do about dinner?" Caroline says.

I'm thinking about a movie I'd like to see. There's this family. The father goes off to his job every day, it's exciting work, all about

608 • JAMES SALLIS

people and solving real problems for them, and he comes home and talks about it over the dinner table, where they all eat together. The mother's a teacher, so she tells what went on at school, funny things her kids said today, how much better some of them are doing, how others still have problems with fractions or irregular verbs or something like that. The daughter talks about school too, and her friends, and about track-team practice this afternoon. She's healthy, vibrant, and isn't going to die before she ever gets to be an adult.

"We can pick up burgers at the corner on the way home," Caroline says. "That work for you?"

I think of Montezuma's Castle just miles from here, an entire city built high into a hillside, accessible only by long ladders. Back in the day we'd go on picnics at a little park not far from there. I want to say, "There's no magic left in my name, little one. No magic anymore in these hills. In the sun, yes, and in the sky. But those are far away." I don't, of course.

We're into the thick of it now, hill and curve, hill and curve. The drop offs have shifted to the right, Caroline's side. In a minute we'll be there, the highest point, the deepest drop.

I pick up speed and Caroline looks over at me. Upset that I'm going too fast? Or does she sense something more?

I look in the rearview mirror. Mattie has gone back to sleep. Good.

This is where we get off.

THE WORLD IS THE CASE

Tucked beneath my feet as I glide into the long, banking curve is the briefcase, one foot in sensible shoe resting atop it. The city sits like a saddle in the sudden hollow of mountains. You come through a pass and it springs into being there below. Each time you feel as settlers must have felt. I duck my head to peer over the rim of sunglasses at the rearview mirror. I can't see them, but I know the others are back there.

There's the usual run of gas stations, quick stops and antique or junk shops on the outskirts, a lumberyard, three or four confusing signs with lists of highways and state roads. A building that's half family café, half biker bar, whose pies are as it says right there on the front window world famous.

The car bumps as it passes over the remains of a squashed cat, raccoon or skunk. The briefcase under my foot doesn't budge. The radio brings in distraction and disaster from a larger world, news that has nothing to do with this place, this moment in time, why I am here. Clouds nudge at sky's edge, blind and feeling their way.

The briefcase, too, is from another world. Fine leather, roughly the size and shape of an old-time doctor's bag, with a hinged top closing onto a smaller section that tucks perfectly beneath the seat, as though car and case were made for one another.

All my life I'd waited for my ship to come in but, near as I could tell, the thing never left port. Instead I was steadily going down, the way they say Venice is sinking into the sea. Dive, dive, dive. Until I found the briefcase.

By then I wasn't on my uppers, I was living on the *memory* of my uppers, hanging out in bus stations, libraries and parks, sleeping where I could, scavenging alleyways behind restaurants for food. Jackson Park's a favorite, high-traffic so as not to stand out so much, midtown and close to the financial district so as to make for good, guilt-driven panhandles, and that's where I was, leaning against one tree in the shadow of another, when a young man (fashionable three-day growth of beard, diamond stud left ear) in an old suit (narrow lapels, pegged trousers) walked past, came back, and sat on the bench before me. The bench had a four-color advertisement for Motivational Yoga on it. The young man had a thoughtful smile.

He tucked the briefcase beneath the bench and looked off into the trees where strands of bird song—warnings, come-hithers, idle chatter—wove themselves into thatch. After a moment he rose, leaving the briefcase behind. And yes, I thought to call after him. Thought to search out some official to whom I might turn it over. But did neither. Instead went back to my tree and waited with it on the ground by me, in the same shadow as myself.

Maybe some things are meant to be, you know?

Once I found the briefcase, I began to find other things. Money, in a suitcase from a dumpster behind Durant's. Emerald cufflinks and jewelry in the purse of a woman who shared my seat on the light rail and bounded off at the last moment as doors closed.

This car.

I pull into the next souvenir shop I come to, thinking about what's inside: decorative shot glasses, pepper jelly, books of jokes and local history, hot sauce, spoon rests and ashtrays in the shape of cowboy gear, Indian jewelry. I look across the highway at brown, bare hills, scrub cholla and saguaro cactus as cars behind me pass, cars I have been tracking.

The desert is honest; it makes no promises. Is this why I've come here?

The dark gray Buick pulls into a quick stop just up the road. A middle-aged man gets out the passenger side but doesn't stray. He walks the car's perimeter, makes to be checking tires. Like the man who left the briefcase back in the park he wears an old-fashioned suit. Skinny lapels, pant legs echoing their taper. I go inside, purchase an ice cream sandwich and linger eating it, standing by the car. The man up the way goes around front to raise the hood.

I pull back onto the road. Two or three minutes pass before the Buick floats up in my rearview mirror. There are few enough cut-offs that it can stay far back.

I reach down and run my fingers across the top of the case, soft and smooth as skin. My thumb rests on the monogram, brass like the hasps, hinges and feet, before moving to the lock. Even here, pushing ninety degrees outside, the lock is cold to the touch.

I have never opened the briefcase. And never will now, whatever happens, whatever comes next. It has done its work.

ZOMBIE CARS

A film by James Sallis

Turn the clocks forward eighty years.

Oil resources are depleted, the cities have emptied, much of America has returned to rural living. Rumors begin to circulate, then "unconfirmed reports" by media: old cars and trucks are rising up from the ground and from wrecking yards like zombies of old, losing parts and drooling fluids as they move toward centers of population seeking gasoline and oil.

Little is remembered of the ancient technology.

But outside Iowa City, where the Amish have grown affluent producing buggies for the entire country, one boy knows about the old vehicles. Ridiculed as "car crazy" by peers, an exasperation to his single mother, he is obsessed by automobiles and the culture they engendered, his room filled to bursting with photos of classic cars, drive-in restaurants, filling stations and racetracks, his shelves sparsely but lovingly stacked with copies of Hot Rod Magazine and ancient books hunted down and purchased with the money he makes as an apprentice farrier.

Finally the reports can no longer be denied. The revenant vehicles are everywhere, lurching toward Bethlehem, Des Moines, Keokuk, and Cedar Rapids.

"Yet again the wretched excesses of our past come back to plague us," a politician says on an election swing through St. Louis.

"Who would have thought undeath had done so many," a poet intones at a rally near Gary, Indiana.

"We must reach down, down deep, to find the carburetor and differential within us," a lay preacher implores from a Wisconsin pulpit.

And in a farmhouse outside Iowa City, the one person who just *knows* he can help, has to make the decision of his life: to go against his mother's explicit orders, or to save mankind.

Meanwhile, among the revenants, factions develop, some crusading to wipe out the humans to whom they owe their existence, others to accommodate and co-exist. My personal favorite scene is a revival meeting held in the ruins of a drive-in theatre, a Ford F-150 truck preaching to a field of vehicles who hear his sermon and entreaties both through the malfunctioning speakers on stands and through the cracked speakers of their own radios. (Throughout, the vehicles speak with sound: motors, creaks, horns. Translations appear as subtitles.)

Another pivotal scene has Tim sitting in his room reading. He is listening to news about the zombie cars on a crystal radio he's built into an ancient plastic model Thunderbird; from time to time he turns off the volume to hear, in the distance, the rumble of vehicles reviving and extricating themselves from the wrecking yard miles away. He is reading the end of *Gulliver's Travels*, where Gulliver, after his time with the Houyhnhms, has become a misfit amongst his own, passing his time chatting with horses in the stables.

Finally Tim makes his decision, leaves a note for his mother, and strikes out, with a change of underwear, a *Popular Mechanics* guide and mechanic's tools bundled into a bag at the end of a stick, as he's seen in pictures of hobos.

He *knows* he can help. No doubt about it, none at all. Just isn't sure how.

Following a number of encounters with humans and revenant vehicles, he almost becomes collateral damage in a zombie-human stand-off but is rescued by a renegade zombie, a psychedelic-painted VW van. The van once belonged ("for a long, long time—if, of course, you believe in time") to a philosopher, and has learned to communicate through its radio speaker.

Together Tim and the van, who Tim decides has to be named Gogh, find their way through battling humans and revenants, lone wolf vigilante humans, and splinter groups including a small troop of revenant vehicles repeatedly "killing" themselves for the greater good, only to be again reborn. Eventually Tim and van Gogh encounter and join others like themselves, humans and vehicles who have formed alliances.

The way of the future, they all begin to understand, will not be one or the other, soft machine, hard machine, living, unliving—but both.

"We're not locked into Aristotelian logic like you," Martin explains to Tim in one of his frequent philosophical musings, "we're not locked into logic at all. It's not *either/or*, Tim. It's all one big *and*. Always has been."

A shrewd critic* has written that in science fiction two endings are possible: either you blow up the world, or things go back to how they were before. Ever the team for challenge, for going that extra inch or two, and for utterly ignoring the reasonable, we figured out a way to do both—so don't miss *Zombie Cars* when it comes clanking and leaking to a theater near you.

---

* me

NET LOSS

What happened was, the TV in the next room heard my girlfriend and me arguing and called the police. Those thunks they heard were me slamming the refrigerator door then, later, dropping my coffee cup and bagel plate. But you ever tried to explain a thing like that, when they just keep playing the recording again and again and won't let you pee?

Did you know your TV could do that?

One of the cops that showed up at the door had spent years being a lot heavier. Loose skin swayed under his arms, he walked with splayed feet, his shirt was a couple sizes too big. Made you wonder whether he'd been overweight and was working on it or was just on his way out of this world. The other seemed headed in the opposite direction, gaining girth and stature as the first one shrank. The bigger guy also seemed to be lead, with little guy holding down harmony parts.

At the arraignment my court-appointed lawyer reminded them they couldn't call the TV as a witness and they all had a big yuck over that. Smoothing her skirt that looked like a test pattern, she rolled out a string of letters and numbers and so on that were supposed to be law code but I'm pretty sure were just made up. Twice, she made me pull out my earbuds. Third time, she reached up and yanked them out herself—and right out of the phone. I was listening to the Blind Boys of Alabama. You ever heard them? Sweet. "Mother's Children Have a Hard Time," "God Knows Everything."

Figure that jail's as close to army living as I'm ever gonna get. All of us packed up in there like chickens with nowhere to go and nothing to do but peck at each other over every damn thing. "Hmmm. Patchouli, BO, tasty testosterone, old whiskey, a hint of the fecal—yum!" as Sweet William said. Then there was Reader.

And the guy who tried giving him grief, who wasn't with us long. Afterwards, Reader took his finger out from between pages and went back to his book. No matter how many times they got corrected, Sweet Willie and Crusher kept on calling our new homes holding cells. "Everybody wants to get held, am I right?"

I spent two weeks in such fine company. When they let me out I walked what has to be two, three miles back to the apartment and found it empty. My clothes and stuff, my turntable rig and my collection of old vinyl were there. The rest was gone. Carla'd left a note saying if that's the kind of man I was, I was going to have to be it without her.

I'll be straight with you, I was glad as sunshine she took that damn TV.

My player got taken away from me at the jail and when they gave me back my billfold and keys and stuff, it wasn't there. Not on the intake list, they told me, sorry, no sign of it. So the first thing I had to do was go out and get a new one from the big box store. Picked up some Blind Boys and other tunes while I was there—paid for those. When I got back, there was a note slid under my door from the apartment manager saying that since I was of questionable moral standing and two months behind in rent, I should be out of the apartment and off the property by the end of the week. I went down to his apartment, pushed the door open—none of them had locks that worked worth a shit—and spoke with him concerning this. He'd heard about the cops, he told me. Went to the city web-site, saw the assault charges against me, talked to Carla as she was loading up the U-Haul. Then he got this flagged email from a group called WatchUp.

So now I learn I'm on this posting list that gets circulated to warn everyone about sex offenders, murderers, parolees, and people like me moving into their neighborhood. While I was there, since Carla took hers, I borrowed the manager's computer to check on the website. They had an old photo of me up. Not sure anyone would recognize me from it, I don't look much like that anymore. It was from, what, six or eight years ago? Life, not to mention jail, had changed me.

But it's like finally I know who I am, what my life's about. I look at the manager duct-taped to the chair and go out to the kitchen to find the right tool for the job. While I'm raking through drawers—no lawyer to snatch them out, here—I punch in my earbuds, hit play, and the Blind Boys start up singing, "Almost Home." I think how my old man was always saying TV's bad for you. Guess he was right about that. And I'm thinking how when the time comes, long after they take my music away, the Blind Boys will still be singing, on and on, and how I'll go down with their songs, with all this beauty, in my heart.

SEASON PREMIERE

It was just after they hung Shorty Bergen that the rats showed up.

No one had ever seen anything like them. They came swarming up over the bank of a dried-up riverbed, must have been close to a hundred of them, traveling all together. It was like locusts in those films of Africa, where the bugs sweep down and leave behind nothing but bare branches and stalks. Only the rats weren't looking for vegetable matter. Johnny Jones lost his whole crop of chickens. At Gene Brocato's they took down five sheep and a young cow.

"Rats don't hunt in packs," Billy Barnstile said. He and his partner Joe McGee were out in one of the power company's trucks, checking lines. They'd pulled off the road to watch as the rats broke into twin streams around the farmhouse then rejoined to sweep over Gene Brocato's field. Within moments, it seemed, only bones remained where livestock had been.

"Never saw anything like it," Joe McGee said.

Of course, no one had ever seen anything like Shorty Bergen either. He looked like parts of two people glued together, this long, long trunk with a couple of stubby doll legs stuck on as afterthought. "Boy'd had legs to match his body, he'd be eight feet tall," his mother always said. But he wasn't. He was four-and-a-half feet tall, even in the goat-roper cowboy boots he favored. Hair stuck out in bristles from his ears. His real hair, however often he washed it, always looked greasy, all two dozen or so limp strands of it.

What had happened was, Shorty'd taken himself a liking to Betty Sue Carstairs, and there was two things wrong with that. Dan Carstairs was nearabouts the only person in town with anything like real money, and he loved his daughter, who'd come to him late in life, with a fierce pride that's one—and Betty Sue, for all her beauty—this is two—was simple as a fence post. When Shorty Bergen started bringing her candy and bundles of wildflowers he'd picked on the way through the woods, she babbled and drooled in delight. Didn't have no idea how ugly he was, or that anything might be wrong in it, or what he was up to. Her daddy'd always brought her things. Now Shorty did too.

Pretty soon the rats were all the talk down at Bee's Blue Bell Diner, which, if you didn't eat at home, was where you ate in Hank's Ridge.

"They ain't come near town as yet, at least," Lucas Hodgkins said. Some egg yolk and about a third of his upper dentures had slipped his mouth. He reached up and pushed the dentures back in. The egg yolk stayed.

"I hear you." This was Froggie Levereaux, four tables away. People said he ordered that damned beret he always wore from Sears. He sure as hell hadn't bought it in Hank's Ridge. His nose put you in mind of the blade on a sundial. "You never know, though. Once they get a taste of human blood . . . I seen it happen with huntin' dogs. Even with a goat, one time. Commenced to gobbling up small children like popcorn."

Bee herself, a dry stick of a woman, was in the thick of it.

"Don't like it, don't like it at all," she said. Bee hadn't liked much of anything in well onto forty-six years.

"Where've they been is what I want to know. None of us ever heard tell of 'em."

"I remember when I was little, back in Florida, it used to rain frogs."

"Frogs is frogs. Rats is rats."

"It's like that story about the paid piper."

"Boils be next," Judd Sealey said. A deacon down to the church. "Boils. Then—well, I can't rightly remember. Seven of them, though. Seven plagues."

"Rodents, is what they are." Bud Gooley shuddered. "Teeth don't never stop growing."

The sound of the screen door out to the kitchen swinging shut brought a hiatus to the conversation.

Jed Stanton shook his head sagely. "You ever know Stu Ellum to leave behind a perfectly good bite of pie before?"

Froggie Levereaux ambled over and finished it up for him.

"Man's got him a worry for sure," Bee said.

Dan Carstairs warned Shorty Bergen to stay away from Betty Sue and went into some detail as to what would eventuate if he failed to do so. Thing was, taken as he was with Betty Sue, Shorty Bergen had gone damn near as simple as the girl herself. He'd just stand there smiling up at Dan Carstairs. Nobody laid claim to having seen it, but everyone knew how one Saturday evening when Shorty Bergen came courting, Dan Carstairs proceeded to have his farmhands stretch Shorty out against an old wagon wheel and went at him with a bullwhip, dousing him with salted water afterwards. Shorty Bergen never said a word, never once whimpered or cried out. Next day, there he was as usual, with flowers and candy for Miss Betty Sue.

Stuart Ellum lived two or three miles south of town on what had once been a thriving apple orchard. Years back some unknown disease had attacked the trees, moving from limb to limb, turning apples into lines of tiny shrunken heads. Limbs twisted and deformed, trunks bloated, the trees remained.

Stu Ellum also had a daughter, Sylvie. The two of them lived in a shack overgrown with honeysuckle and patched with old tin signs for soft drinks. There'd been a wife too for a while, but no one knew much about her, or just when it was she left, if leave she did. A hill woman, they said. Some of the old women used to avert their eyes whenever she came around.

Sylvie never showed any interest in going into town the way Stuart did a couple of times a week, or really in leaving the place at all. She cooked, cleaned their clothes in the stream nearby. Other than that she'd sit on a rickety chair outside the cabin watching bees, wasps and hummingbirds have at the honeysuckle, or head off into the woods and be gone for hours at the time.

Then a while back, in one of the hollows where people hereabouts are wont to dump garbage, she'd come across a TV set and hauled it back to the cabin. Its innards were all gone, but the glass in front was still good. Sylvie put it up on an old crate in one corner of the cabin and commenced to carve little tables and beds and chairs and buildings. She'd set these up inside, then go across the room and sit watching. One day when Stuart Ellum walked in, he saw she had insects, a grasshopper, a katydid, sitting at the little table inside the TV, acting out whatever scene Sylvie had in her mind.

Over the next several weeks, Shorty Bergen had got himself horsewhipped a second time, beat with axe handles till three ribs broke, and thrown in the pen, hobbled, with one of Dan Carstairs's famously mean-tempered goats. Each time he popped right back up. Carstairs would head out to check on the ploughing or to buy feed and come back and there that boy'd be, sitting on the porch holding hands with Betty Sue.

Must have been right about then that Dan Carstairs decided on taking a different tack.

He started putting it out that Shorty Bergen had raped his Betty Sue. She wasn't the first either, by his reckoning, he said, and men folk all round the valley had best look to their wives and daughters.

Probably nothing would've come of it, except a couple families over the other side of the mountain started saying somebody'd been getting to their girls too. Never mind that just about everybody knew exactly who it was had been getting to them. That kind of thing, once it starts up, it spreads like wildfire. Wasn't more than a month had passed before Shorty Bergen woke to a flashlight in his eyes and a group of stern-faced men above him. They dragged him outside, tied a rope around his neck in a simple granny knot and threw the rope over a limb, and a bunch of them hauled at the other end. When the limb broke, they started over, and got the job done, though it took some time.

Now, it happened that Sylvie had taken a liking to Shorty Bergen. One of the ways he scraped together a living was by scavenging what people threw away, everything from chairs to simple appliances, and fixing them. Then he'd take them around and sell them for a dollar or two. He'd only been by Stuart Ellum's cabin twice, since Stuart always told him they had everything they needed and then some, but Sylvie never took her eyes off him either time, and afterwards was always asking Stuart about him. Before that, whenever she told Stuart about her shows, they were full of doctors and nurses, rich men who lived alone in great sadness, and young women suddenly come upon unsuspected legacies or gifts, like all those soap operas she'd seen on a visit to her aunt in the city. Once she saw Shorty Bergen, though, all her shows centered around him. Shorty was running for sheriff but the rich man who owned everything hereabouts was bound and determined to see him defeated. The doctors at the hospital had done something to Shorty at birth. A withered Native American shook a child's rattle of feathers over his still body and warned that if Shorty were to die, his spirit would sweep like a storm across the land, cleansing it, purifying it.

"Girl? Girl?" What have you done?" Stuart Ellum asked as he ducked to enter the cabin. All the way back from the diner he'd been thinking about what he'd heard there, about that pack of rats over-running everything, sheep and cattle going down beneath them, a flood of rats laying waste to everything in its path.

"Shhh, it's the news," Sylvie said.

Behind the glass of the TV two rats sat upright in tiny chairs looking straight out into the room. They took turns talking, glancing down at the table before them from time to time, other times looking at one another with knowing nods.

Soon Sylvie clapped her hands silently and turned toward him.

"What did you want to ask me, Daddy?"

As she turned toward him, so did the two rats sitting at the little table inside the TV. Then they stood and took a bow. Their eyes shone—the rats' eyes, and his daughter's.

AS YET UNTITLED

I am to be, they tell me, in a new Western series, so I've tried on a shirt with snaps for buttons and a hat the size of a chamberpot and stood for hours before the mirror practicing the three S's: slouch, sidle and squint. It's been a good life these past years inhabiting the science fiction novels of Iain Shore, but science fiction sales are falling, they tell me, plummeting in fact, so they've decided to get ahead of the curve and move me along. Back to mysteries? I ask, with fond memories of fedoras, smoke-filled rooms, the bite of cheap whiskey. Sales there are even worse, they tell me, and hand across my new clothes. Howdy, my new editor says.

Next day I meet my author, who definitely ain't no Iain Shore. (At least I'm getting the lingo down.) Evidently, from the look of his unwashed hair, what's left of it, he doesn't believe in tampering with what nature's given him. His lips hang half off his face like huge water blisters there below rheumy red eyes. He's wearing a sport coat that puts me in mind of shrinkwrapping, trousers that look like the gray workpants sold at Sears, and a purplish T-shirt doing valiant duty against his pudge.

By way of acknowledgment, he pushes his glasses up his nose. They're back down before his hand is.

"Woodrow," he says. My name, evidently.

His is Evan, which he pronounces (my editor tells me) *Even*.

"I've the bulk of the thing worked out," Evan says. "All but the end, I should say. And the title—I don't have my title yet. First title, I mean. Not to worry."

I allow as how all that sounds good.

"Here's the thing," he says. "You get the girl."

"Beg pardon?"

"The schoolmarm. You get her. Playing a fresh twist off the classic trope, you see."

I make a spittin' motion toward the wastebasket. Kinda thinking things over. Never could abide authors that said things like trope.

So, three shakes of a calf's tail and I'm riding into a half-assed frontier town in (as Evan told me the first day) "Arizona, Montana, somesuch godforsaken place," dragging a personal history that a hundred or so pages farther along will explain (1) what I'm doing here, (2) why I'm so slow to anger, (3) why I never carry a gun, (4) why I'm partial to sheep, (5) what led to my leaving Abilene, El Paso, Fort Worth or St. Louis, (6) and so on.

Glancing back, I see what looks suspiciously like a guitar wrapped in a flour sack slung across my horse's rump. The horse's name is Challenger, but I vow right then and there that, however long this thing lasts, he'll be George to me. And, yep, we hit a rut in the road and the sack bounces up and comes down with a hollow, thrumming sound. It's a guitar all right.

This could be bad.

Eyes watch from windows as I pass. An old man sitting out front of the general store lifts his hat momentarily to look, then lets it fall back over his face. Someone shoulders a heavy sack into a wagon, sending up dense plumes of white dust. Two kids with whittled wood guns chase each other up and down the street. I can see the knife marks from here. One of the kids has a limp, so he'll be the schoolmarm's, naturally.

Think about it. I've got a guitar on the back of this horse and I'm heading for . . . pulling up in front of . . . yeah, it's the saloon all right.

At least I'm not the sidekick again.

Inside, a piano player and a banjo man are grinding out something that could be "Arkansas Traveller" or "Turkey in the Straw" but probably isn't intended to be either. Seeing my guitar, the banjo man narrows his eyes. He also misses the beat, and his pick skitters out onto the floor, glistening, dark and hard, like a roach.

"Name it," the barkeep says, and for a moment I think this is some kind of self-referential game old Evan's playing, but then I realize the barkeep's just asking what I want. What I want is a nice café au lait, but I settle for—

"Whiskey."

—which tastes of equal parts wasp venom and pump-handle

drippings. Not to mention that you could safely watch eclipses through the glass it was served in.

The town doc's in there, naturally. He comes up, trying hard to focus, so that his head bobs up and down and side to side like a bird's, to ask if I've brought his medical supplies. Have to wonder what he was expecting. Out here, a knife or two, some alcohol and a saw's about all you need.

The banjo man is still eyeing me as one of the girls, who doesn't smell any better than the doc, pushes into me to say she hasn't seen me around before. A moment later, the musicians take a break, and I swear I can hear Evan clearing his throat, pushing back his chair. Then his footsteps heading off to the kitchen.

So at least I ain't gonna have to play this damn guitar for a while.

We hang out waiting for him to come back, smiling at each other and fidgeting. After a while we hear his footsteps again. (Bastard's got café au lait, wouldn't you know? I can smell it.) Just as those stop, an Indian steps up to the bar. He's wearing an Eastern-cut suit and two gleaming Colts.

"Whiskey," he says, throwing down a gold piece that rings as it spins and spins and finally settles.

"Yes, *sir*."

Nodding to the barkeep, he holds up his glass, dips it in a toast, and throws it back. I notice he's got hisself a *clean* glass. That's when his eyes slide over to me.

"Took you long enough getting here," he says.

Damn.

I'm the sidekick again after all.

COMEBACK

Scott returned from the dead last night.

We'll have to keep this on the quiet, naturally. Doors locked, shades drawn. The smell alone would give us away.

I'd watched an old episode of *Buffy*, pee'd, turned out the light and fallen into a sleep filled with (go figure) kangaroos and insurance salesmen, only to wake to the realization that I wasn't alone in bed.

"Don't be afraid," Scott said.

Of him? How could I be? I reached—

"Don't turn on the light just yet." I felt his hand on my face. It had been a long time. The hand was cold. "I couldn't die without you," he said, and either laughed or choked on something. Death hadn't improved his sense of humor.

A police helicopter passed over, scant inches above us from the sound, blinking its single bright eye repeatedly across our yard, jumping fence into the neighbor's. Someone on the run. A disturbance.

Once the helicopter was gone, it got so quiet I could hear the ice machine in the refrigerator working, two rooms away. "Thank you for coming back," I told him.

"Had to. I have a message for the leaders of all the world's religions." Again the laugh, or whatever it was. "*Nah.*" Moonlight dropped through a window onto the floor, like something spilled.

"Miss me?"

More than I could ever say.

And yes, what remained was undeniably my sweetheart and the love of my life. The wink didn't quite come off, since the eyelid wasn't there, but the rest, the half-smile, the head tilt, that was pure Scott.

He reached across and turned on the lamp.

"I see you brought my tools." Scott restored antique watches; I couldn't bear to sell or abandon those tiny screwdrivers, files, anvils, nips and mallets. "Looked about a bit before I came in here. Doesn't seem you brought much else."

I put my hand under the sheets, the whisper of them loud in the quiet room.

"Can you . . . ?"

"No. Sorry."

"It's okay." I leaned my head on his shoulder and breathed deeply. He breathed, I noticed, only before speaking.

"It was a puzzle, finding you."

"But you did."

"I wasn't ever one for quit."

"Even now."

"Even now, yes." The laugh again, as his hand gently touched my face. "I remember that stain on the ceiling. Many's the night we lay watching, waiting for car lights."

"So we could make shapes of it."

"Oceans. Protozoans."

"Petroglyphs."

"Tonight it just looks like a stain."

"Maybe."

He turned toward me in bed. "We swore we'd never come back to this dump—remember?"

"They were good days, Scott."

"Early on, yes."

"We were young."

"Poor as fleas on church mice."

I let that ring down. "Coming back here was the only thing that helped. The memories."

"Memories are what you take with you. Isn't that the point?"

"Who the hell knows what the point is? Do you?"

He shook his head.

The police helicopter passed over again, no stabbing light this time.

"Do you have regrets, Maggie?"

"None," I said, "no." I reached and turned off the lamp. All I could see now was beautiful darkness.

BEAUTIFUL QUIET OF THE ROARING FREEWAY

He always wondered what their stories were.

Maybe they wondered about his too.

He'd look in the rearview, pick up on posturing, body language. Some were just thrill seekers, of course, not much to be said there. Could be this was a onetime thing for them, they'd go home after, slip back into their lives and stay. Others were desperate to find bad and kept looking, whatever the cost. Or they were just bored. Curious what stepping outside things might feel like. Occasionally he'd get a rider who seemed to be protesting some hardfelt lack of freedom, though it was difficult to imagine how they thought that would work, with everything about the rides kept well on the down low. And once in a while he'd get romantics who spent so much time thinking about the old days that they believed they remembered them. Take one's sweet lady or kind gentleman out for a moonlight ride.

These two, he didn't have a clue. His handler had checked them out, naturally. Nothing had wobbled or gone off focus.

The woman was anywhere between ten and twenty years younger, wearing a pearl-gray blouse and a dark business suit expertly cut for comfort over stylishness, hair mid-length, layered. Her companion seemed to have a mild speech defect of some sort. Levin took note of it at the pickup site, and again in the vehicle when repeatedly she leaned close as the man spoke. He was in casual clothes of the kind that likely, being from a tailor's hand, bore no labels. Shirt, sportcoat and trousers all were of different colors.

Hardly unexpected, that they'd be what Levin's old man always called people of substance. Midnight rides don't come cheap. Though once Levin had as passenger a dying woman whose family had pooled resources to provide what she'd spoken of with longing all her life, from stories told her by the grandfather who raised her.

The two of them back there now had privacy, of course. The plex was down. No sound carried. Their windows were clear, Levin's to every appearance opaque. From the menu, they had pre-ordered traditional fado, which fed at low volume to front as well as back. Fascinating to watch in the rearview how the music's rhythms crossed and recrossed the couple's own as they turned to look out, shifted in their seats, spoke, waited, listened.

Quarter SW2 was chosen for its population density, guaranteeing high traffic, and for ready access to the freeway. The quarter also hosted a major virtual university, so information of every sort and kind was bouncing and bubbling off the net around here. Another kind of crowd to get lost in.

Carefully matching the speed and flow of other cars on their way upstream, Levin pulled into the go lane. This was the chanciest part. Where they were most likely to get tagged. Levin's actions were smooth, seamless.

Not many could do this.

Soon they were up the ramp and on the big road, eight lanes, moving at a fast clip with all the others, guided by the sure hand and many-leveled mind of Trafcom. Supposed to be, anyway.

Tales of people getting into their cars and taking randomly to the road for great adventures were once a big thing, Levin knew. Right up there with mythologies that seem imprinted in us. Jealous gods, voyages to the rim of the world, unstoppable warriors. One didn't hear about adventures much anymore. What they were doing now, those two in the back, that was about as close as anyone came.

In the next three lanes, vehicles began to slow, first in the closest, then the next, as a single vehicle angled across and through them. Same, then, with adjacent lanes, till the vehicle drew out of sight down one of the red ramps. Trafcom detecting a malfunction, most likely.

Guitar chords sounded as the singer paused, and hung in the air as though trying to hold on, not let go, dwell here. Always interesting, what music got chosen. Did passengers simply check off one of the standard programs? Order something specific? Loud, quiet, lush, mood-drenched? These had picked fado, Portugal's mournful music of fatefulness, loss and lifetime longing.

Levin kept casual watch in the mirror. Whatever the relationship, whatever their story, things were not going well in the back seat. The woman had been looking on as, often instinctively, he made the myriad adjustments and accommodations necessary to echo and fit the patterns set by Trafcom. Now she leaned forward to tap at the plex. Levin motioned toward the combox mounted near her shoulder. She touched the pad.

"You're very good, aren't you?"

We'd all better hope so, he thought. Aloud he said, "Speaking with the driver is not allowed. This was covered at time of purchase."

"Yes, of course. It's just that I have to wonder why someone does what you do. How he might have come to that."

When Levin responded no further, she sat back.

He thought about that old woman again, Lina, whose family pooled their funds for the ride. That one time he *had* spoken, and listened. She'd been a dancer, she told him, a ballerina. Worked all her life to be so perfect in movement, so uniform, as to become almost machinelike. In a sense to remove the human from what she did, and at the same time to fully represent humanity in a way nothing else could. People see us dance, she said, and they think freedom. It isn't freedom, young man, it's absolute engagement.

One of the sensors tripped but instantly disengaged. A routine sweep, then. For the moment they were clear. Somehow the woman picked up on this. She interrupted her companion to speak. He glanced forward, resumed talking. Again Levin had to wonder why the two of them were here, what would bring them to pay a small fortune for the ride, take so great a risk. They gave no evidence of excitement or anticipation. From the look of them this might be an everyday outing, off to work or to do some shopping.

Vehicles began to move in waves and pulses to the right, ever at steady speed, signaling that something was ahead, poor road conditions, an emergency perhaps, with Trafcom redirecting to maintain flow. Just as effortlessly, Levin swung into the wave crossing from his lane. The communal speed dropped—imperceptibly, were it not for instruments, just over one kph. Within minutes the lanes were repopulated. All was back to normal.

Movement took his eye to the mirror as the woman reached for the combox.

"This is it?" she said. And after a moment: "I expected more."

Don't we all, Levin thought.

Then, as though he had been waiting for this single moment, Levin was accelerating. The woman, then the man, looked up. The fado ended on a broken, long-sustained chord. With a two-second pause, no more than a hiccup, traffic parted before them, moved away right and left. Every sensor on the dash red-lined as Trafcom, with a power and a pull almost physical, battered at the vehicle's controls, searching for identification, foothold, purchase.

Levin ignored all signals and alarms. He continued to accelerate. Maybe Trafcom would break through the vehicle's defenses, take control, maybe not. Behind him, the woman slid to the front of her seat. In the bright light of surveillance vehicles closing upon them, her face became beautiful.

NEW TEETH

He'd been in a hundred like it, maybe a thousand. Pitch-dark streets outside, garbage in doorways, rotting boards on shop windows, a skeletal stray dog or two. Inside was some better. He took one of half a dozen wobbly stools at the bar, pointed to the beer tap. Man behind nodded and had it there in moments. The liquid sloshed like backwater, settled.

"Live close by, do you?" The speaker wore a thumb-size listening device that could as easily be hearing support, music source, computer or phone link. That was in his left ear, same side as his good arm. The other arm ended just below the elbow. Held the mug in the good hand, worked the handle with the elbow. He was the kind of thin that brought *spindly* to mind. Who knows what that hair might bring to mind. Moss, maybe.

Walsh smiled and sipped his beer.

"Most come down here, they'll be reg'lars." The man feigned attending to something behind the bar, after a bit said, "Be over there, you find need."

Walsh checked the place out in the mirror behind the bar, then swung round on his stool to compare. The duskiness and blur of the old mirror had helped. Took edges away, smoothed the room over, gave it some mystery it didn't have and never would.

He reached back and got his beer, had a healthy swig this time. Slight oily taste to it. Stayed on in the back of your throat, on your tongue.

It's not the guy sitting at the end of the bar with his head down, of course. Or the woman propped against the playbox, light flushing up onto her face. Not the guy stutter-stepping back from the dumper and shakily regaining his chair at the table with two others.

It's the one grinning away and doing verbal back slaps at the gaming table. Of course. What they want most of all is to blend in.

Walsh puts the beer down, stands. It sees him coming and does what they all do, most of them anyway, it just stands there. Knowing that he knows, knowing what he is, why he's here. Six more steps, three quick moves, and it's over.

Walsh goes back to the bar and finishes his beer. No one is speaking, just looking down at the floor.

As he goes out, the woman sitting alone at a table by the door says, very quietly, "Thank you."

Some know, some don't. Some know and pretend not to. The old man, Statler, knew more about them than anyone else, truckloads more, but he didn't know what they are exactly, or where they come from. Some other here, some other now? he always said.

"And it doesn't really matter, does it," he tells Walsh. The kid's twelve, thirteen, wandered in off the street after living on them for years, stayed a night, stayed another, then just stayed. He'd heard the stories out there on the street, figured they were only boogeymen and Bigfoot dressed up in new garb. "They're here now, more of them every day."

"What do they want?" the kid asks.

The old man peers at him one-eyed through the barrel of a rifle he's broken down for cleaning. "That part's simple. What we all want: to go on existing. However they can."

Hermits, the old man called them. "Like crabs, moving into the abandoned shells of others. 'Cept the shells ain't abandoned at first. That takes a while."

And Walsh wondered for the first time, back then, what it was like to have someone, some *thing*, there with you inside your skull, inside your skin. Did you know from the first, or did the knowledge come slowly? Did you feel the thing growing there, taking over? Did you feel yourself slowly, by pieces, giving way? Going away.

By the time a jumper got the old man, Walsh had already put down dozens of them. Came by one night with a bottle and beer since it'd been a few weeks, saw it in his eyes. It had moved in strong, had a good hold. Using his gestures, the way he talked, but Walsh knew. It did too. Stood there like they do, waiting. No one said thank you that time.

For weeks Walsh has had a floater in his right eye, seeing

shapes in the corner of rooms, in half darkness, that weren't there. As he turned into his building he thought he saw a man, a figure, at the top of the stairs, but when he looked straight on, there was no one.

Halfway up them he heard ghanduuj. The door was ajar. His visitor stood by the V-box running a stubby index finger down the menu.

"Guardian Dorn," Walsh said, "so good to see you again."

Ghanduuj is built on cycles of twenty beats subdivided to every possible permutation. Eight de-escalating sub-climaxes. One of them hit now. The visitor shook his head. "This is what you listen to? Explains a lot."

"Don't suppose you brought dinner?"

Dorn shook his head again, but differently. There seemed to be an entire vocabulary of head shakes accessible to him.

"A courtesy call, one might say. At the suggestion of Magistrate Helm?"

"So the magistrate doesn't wish to see me herself. Good news."

"Of a sort." Dorn thumbed the music off. "When that time comes, I suppose she'll be sending around someone less charming."

"No doubt." Walsh went to the shelves by the sink, fetched down a bottle and glasses, poured. "Will you drink with me, Billy Dorn? For the good old times?"

The visitor took his. "And for the dream of good new times."

They settled in, watched light bleed from the sky as the window went dark, easy with the silence and without need to cover it over, friends by no stretch of language, yet fragilely bound by a thing neither understood.

Walsh snapped on a lamp. "You're hungry? I have udon. Peanuts. Shallots."

He went back to the counter by the sink to start the meal and Dorn followed. "She *will* send someone, you know," Dorn said. "It's only a matter of time."

"Time I can use to get on with my work."

"Killing people."

"What I kill is no longer a person."

"So you believe. Nonetheless it's murder."

"Legally. When the Magistrate sends someone here, for me—that will be different?"

Spiced oil sizzled and jumped in the pan, its smell taking over the apartment, duple and triple rhythms mixed, as in ghanduuj. Walsh threw noodles into the hot skillet, scooped a handful of peanuts and a scallion onto the counter for chopping. Like the body of a guitar, the hollows of the cabinet below amplified the clean strike of knife on countertop. Each stroke was a small door slamming.

"There is no evidence that they exist. You know that," Dorn said later, as they ate.

Walsh's runners stayed busy that season. They ate well, their clothes got mended and replaced.

He used street kids as spotters. Many of them, the ones who had survived out there, they could feel the difference when no one else could. They'd watch the way a woman walked down the street, take in how a man reached out to open a door or failed to hesitate before stepping off a curb, and nod: That one. And word would come along the line to Walsh.

He put down a whole family of them, five in all—first time that had happened—over the bridge in Greenway, later that week a single mother in Cable Park. He left the one child that hadn't been jumped, put the other one down with the parent. Then a man and wife nine blocks from where he lived. One of them was a full jump, the other fresh and had no idea what was going on.

They all just stood there and waited.

Then one night as he's coming back home Walsh decides he's being followed and diverts. Only one person, he thinks. One of his runners maybe, but no, they'd come right up. He takes the tunnel under Orchid Street, stepping cautiously among the squatters, some of them with cardboard boxes for shelter, ancient shopping bags or backpacks hugged close. His breath plumes out ahead of him. So does that of the man who follows. Not from the magistrate—that one he'd never see. As far as he knows, there is no sense of community or concerted action among jumpers; they inhabit whatever social forms their host claimed. But you can never be sure. Things change. He could be known to them.

He loses the follower finally in the knot of crooked streets around the central train terminal.

Week or two later, it was an old man there before him. Late sixties, seventies, thin puffs of hair at the side of his head, a lot more sprouting from his ears. You didn't see old people much anymore, of course, and Walsh had never before seen one jumped. Did jumpers select? *Could* they? Something he hadn't thought of. Maybe they just dropped into whatever container was available.

He'd been sitting at the table when Walsh slipped the lock, stood when he came in. A single room, table in the far corner, bed in another, two hard plastic chairs, makeshift shelves. Change of clothing hung on nails driven into the wall. A dog as used-up as the man lay sleeping on the bed.

The whole place smelled somehow of meat. The old man? The dog? Half a century of bad and half-rotten food? A flower that looked as though it had struggled from day one to stay alive but was still holding on stood upright in a Coke bottle.

"I've been expecting you," the man said.

Walsh shook his head. "No. You haven't."

"Death is always expected. And to one my age, a comfort. The last good friend you will meet." And he smiled.

Stone crazy, then. The jumper had come across only to find itself in a tangle of cross-wired, blown, burned-out circuits.

The old man didn't just stand there, he took a step toward Walsh. Another thing Walsh hadn't seen before. And for a moment, wondering how it was that the man himself, what remained of him, was able to speak—or was it the jumper after all—Walsh hesitated.

The dog looked up, watched, and put its head back down on its paws.

"Are you okay?" Dana's voice.

He hit Accept on the V-box and she came onscreen, eyes narrowing at his image.

"You're just getting up." She was at the office. Dressed for it. Familiar sounds behind her. Morning? Afternoon?

"I could just be going to bed."

"Which would be precious little improvement. We haven't heard from you in ages."

"Or ever."

"People do ask."

"Only to be polite, Blue Girl."

They had worked side by side for almost a year. She was half his age. For months she'd worn nothing but blue. Blue skirts or pants, blue jackets, blue shoes. He always wondered if his use of the nickname was what changed that.

"Same old?" he said.

"What would change?"

"Truth."

Essentially they were a clean-up crew, vetting paperwork done by others before passing it on for documentation and filing. Important paperwork dealing with health care legislation, but still. Days, he worked there. Nights he searched out jumpers. When the jumpers got plentiful, and after he put together his band of spotters, he quit.

It wasn't paperwork, of course, not a scrap of paper anywhere to be seen, just screens and gigabytes, but the name stayed on. So much of life was soft-spoken metaphor, something standing in for something else.

"I do worry over it," Dana said. "There at the end . . . Well, never mind that. But call me from time to time, let me know you're okay. Okay?"

"Will do."

"Won't. But at least think about it?"

How the room could seem smaller afterwards he didn't understand, but it did.

Sometimes at night, when he's not out hunting, when he can't sleep, he listens to arguments coming through the wall from the next apartment. There's a young girl over there, one tacking hard into youthful rebelliousness and scorn for parents, for authority, for the larger society, for all received wisdom and assumptions. The clashes can go for hours. Low-pitched, reined-in voices, feral shouts, slamming doors, silence.

It's not about what you want.

I'm not you.

My house, my rules.

You have to let me make up *my* mind about who I am.

Walsh fell asleep still listening, thinking that four thousand years ago in Athens, a Greek family was probably having the same set-to, using much the same words.

"At what cost?" the old man asks that night in his dreams. Not Statler—the other old man. The one with the dog. He is moving toward Walsh as he speaks. "This thing that you feel you have to do. At what cost?"

"Cost? To whom?" Walsh says.

"Yourself." The man stops. Walsh realizes now that he is blind. His eyes pass over Walsh and fix on a spot to his side. "All of us."

Walsh woke with a sense of—what? Failure? Loss? He lay remembering a woman from his days on the streets, a graffiti artist who worked the edge of the business district, as though she could never cross the line into that half-mile square but was committed to gracing its perimeter. Gray, snaggly hair to her waist, leathery skin. Bit of a legend, really. He'd come upon her one night as she stood by a wall, spray can in one hand, grease pen in the other. A snarl of dark strokes, a swirl or two. "Something in there that wants out," she said without turning her head.

Walsh got up, climbed the landing to the roof. Down in the street a dozen or so blurry shapes scrambled. Lights lashing antenna-like, two patrol cars converged silently on an intersection. A city he moved through each day and night, and he hardly recognized it. *Things change.* For a moment he thought he saw another man, another shape, across from him on the roof: the floater again. He looked up, where a scant handful of stars struggled to show through clouds.

When the time comes, he will not stand and wait.

SCIENTIFIC METHODS

No one is allowed to write about the university's collider for fear the neighborhood, led perhaps by owners of the cattle ranch half a mile up the road, or of the apple orchards due south, will rise up in arms. No journalists are to be admitted, queries concerning same will be denied, the whole thing's strictly on the QT. Alone at night, one imagines villagers converging on the castle with pitchforks and lanterns.

Here is what we know: That another world exists, and that if we can but find the tiniest crack it will open itself to us.

Here is what *I* know: That I must reconcile

1. what Marta said to me this morning, staring into her waffle as though the words were written there
2. growing suspicion that my work is of no consequence
3. the footprint of a gigantic corporation

There's an equation in there somewhere. Equations being the one true and lasting beauty in this world.

(In the interest of full disclosure I should add, above, that this other world might just as well engulf as enrich us.)

Meanwhile, moments of the day trickle into the blender, hit the stove and sizzle.

"You missed the meeting," A.G. says.

He waits. Water glugs in the cooler. Swallowed air, a void, rises to the top and is gone.

"Glad to hear it."

"The problem of secondary categorization was addressed."

"Addressed, forwarded, and returned to sender, I'm sure—as always."

"B.R. took attendance." Our beloved manager. Third-rate scientist to bureaucrat between one recent Friday and the next.

"Then at least *someone* got something out of it."

"Not much of a company man, are you, T.M.?"

He swings hard right to the aisle as though in the single dance step he knows and ambles away, head abob over cubicle walls, wearing his yellow Friday T-shirt. The front is bare. The back reads

CHAOS

THE FINAL STRUCTURE

Physicists. A fun-loving lot.

Here's what we do: We take a particle that is so small it's mostly imagination. We whirl it around till it's going faster than is possible and we push it into another particle to see what happens. We do this Tuesdays and Thursdays at 2:14 A.M. We have all manner of ideas what will happen. Some of these ideas turn out to be true.

Here's what I do: I pull out my handheld and type in *I will try to be a better person.* Thumbs hover as I think. Who? I send it to myself.

It's casual Friday, B.R.'s premiere contribution to productivity and worker morale, so the halls teem with cargo shorts, fake jerseys and flip-flops, B.R.'s second contribution being the monstrous TV in the break room where Dana (substitute halter top and sweats for above) spends most of her time. She'll sit in there forever, suddenly jump out to her cubicle and click keys at light speed for five or ten minutes, then go back. As far as I can tell, she never watches the TV or for that matter even knows what's on. When I asked her, she told me it was like being immersed in water, like floating. And that it cut out all the other noise. Let her think clearly.

Today she wears a single earring that's heavy with brass and hangs to her shoulder. Her head tips ever so slightly to that side.

Thinking clearly. I sort of remember that. Too much stuff in my head now. Like boxes full of old clothes and photos and untouched birthday gifts stacked half to the ceiling in the spare room. You just *know* you'll use it all someday.

I look up as R.K. emerges from the supply room with an ink cartridge clutched between thumb and first finger. He never shuts doors. Supply room, phone room, break room, it doesn't matter, he steps away leaving half an inch of daylight between door and frame.

The rest of us have got so used to following along, closing doors, that we don't much notice we're doing it anymore.

I do have to wonder what use he might have for an ink cartridge, as we dwell exclusively in cyberland and never print anything out, endlessly skyhopping data from desktop to remote to handheld or smartphone.

Fridays, the local bagpipe brigade in an amazement of plaid crosses the plaza below us on its ceremonial way to Main Street and City Park. Ceremonial of what, no one quite remembers, but after lunch everyone's standing at the window up front watching, albeit that, from three stories up, through double-paned glass, all we can hear is what sounds like a huge mosquito. And drums, of course.

Ah, the spinning of mallets. The rise and fall of knobby knees. The swing and sway of mighty sporrans.

They've been doing this, I'm told, for eighty-plus years; some of those now marching are great-grandsons of original members. Tribalism is not dead. Nor tradition.

Nor am I, though this year's scan, from last Tuesday, does not look good. "Definitely something there," Doctor Freeman tells me. He points to what looks like a spill of milk on the black film with its many ghosts, moves one finger in a close circle. The tumor of which I was delivered nine years ago may no longer be an only child.

More tests, then. And I've always been good at taking tests. Back as an undergrad I rarely read assignments on subjects in which I had no interest, English, sociology and so on, and rarely studied, but did well on midterms and finals.

Midterm or final, I'll ace this one too.

J.T. walks by behind me in the corridor between cubicles, speaking to no one that I can see. Yes, he says. And again, further along, quieter now: Yes. I sit here as the second yes speeds down the corridor to where I sit waiting to see what will happen.

ANNANDALE

Everything broke off from the main roads about twelve miles outside town. I bounced over rutted ancient asphalt for better than an hour thinking of the stories and lives I was leaving behind and pulled into Annandale at 7:08 in the morning.

I was going to see a dead friend.

On the way, I drove through miles of dead and decaying animals by the side of the road, armadillos, bobcats, possums and raccoons. It hadn't affected animals at first, when the billybobs came, but it was spreading to them.

The car was a museum piece, a late twentieth-century Fiat curated and kept in a secret garage with three others, all of similar vintage and functional, by one of the generals. I'd had eyes on it for some time, lest the need arise.

My father was a hunter. Many's the midmorning as a child I stood out by the brick barbeque pit watching him gut and skin the squirrels, dove, rabbits and quail he'd brought in earlier from the woods just beyond our house. There wasn't much money in our part of the country, almost none in fact, and none of it ours. The game was much of what we lived on. He'd throw entrails and skin down the hill behind the barbeque pit. Our dogs would climb down to eat them.

No dogs here now, I thought as I drove down Manor Road into the heart of Annandale, such as it was. Little activity on the streets, a jacked-up VW with light dancing off the chrome of its open engine, a pickup with corrugated steel welded to fenders and hood, three or four bicycles fitted with baskets fore and aft. Windows and doors along Main were shuttered with rough-cut plywood slabs, sidewalks heaved up and jaggedly broken like artist's renderings of shifting tectonic plates. The old train station at the nether end of Main, in my childhood become a museum of the region's past in a failed attempt to give the station and town new life, had chains with padlocks on the doors and broken windows through which one could see pigeons fluttering about inside.

Pigeons had left their mark, too, outside Gray's Hardware where for decades men sat smoking and swapping small talk as wives and children shopped along the street. Bench, sidewalk and window casings were gone white with droppings from pigeons gathered by dozens on the broken lattice of the awning above.

Hard to believe I'd lived here once. And now, on the move, just as hard to believe how I'd clung to life in the ruined body of my adopted city after the billybobs came and everyone, everything, around me began dying.

The old diner at the high end of Main was, remarkably enough, open, so I stopped there. It was the shape and size of the railway cars on display down by the train station, booths along one side, lunch counter running the length of the other. Two men sat far apart at the counter with mugs of coffee. A head tilted into sight in the pass-through kitchen window as I entered. Moments later a door close by swung open and when the head, body attached now, asked what it could do for me, I said coffee would be great.

"Let me get a fresh pot started," he said. Then to the others: "You boys be up for refills, am I right?"

As he set about doing so, I took the stool nearest the door.

"Not much passing-through goes on around here," the guy five stools down said.

"Know what you mean." The blackboard by the kitchen window had daily specials chalked on, *beef stew, spaghetti w/ balls, fresh greens.* Looked like they'd been there a while. "As I was coming in on the old county road I saw the hospital's shut down." They'd always kept bodies there, in a back room on the first floor, nearest thing the town had to a morgue.

"Been that way, what—" He glanced at the man further down for verification. "—five, six years?"

"Least."

He turned back to me. "You're from around here?"

"Long time ago."

"Everything's a long time ago. You looking for medical, closest thing we've got now's old Doc Boggs's office out on—"

"You mean Doc's still alive?"

"Was yesterday. Mostly it's children and old folks get taken there toward the end. The rest . . ."

Why bother was what he meant. They were breathing dead.

We sat drinking our coffee. The radio was on in the kitchen, an oldie station of some kind. It cut out every once in a while, then lurched back on at a higher volume before settling in. Station problems or the radio set itself, hard to say.

"Coming in from where?" the man five stools down asked, and I told him.

"Any better there?"

"Not really."

All three nodded. I told them goodbye and when I tried to pay the owner he said no need, he had all the money and political doubletalk he could use—what could he do with any of it?

Doc's place didn't look much better than the hospital or boarded-up stores downtown. Cue spooky music as vines take over walls second by second and portions of the house give way like shattered bones. Eerily, the lawn was freshly mown, the windows clean and clear. No one answered when I knocked, so I went in. The front room was filled with pallets, at least twelve of them, on which lay aged men and women, some of them breathing heavily, others barely. Babies and infants in much the same condition and on similar improvised beddings occupied the next room. Beyond that was the kitchen, where Doc stood over an ancient gas stove.

"With you in a shake," he said, "just fixing some breakfast for those can eat."

I watched his hands feel along the stove top, pots and utensils and when moments later he turned, it confirmed what I suspected. Both eyes were white with cataracts. He was blind, or nearly so. A blob of oatmeal dropped from the spoon he held.

"Now. Here to help, are you?"

"I'm here to claim a body."

"Help yourself then, many as you might want. They're out back, in the shed."

"Just one, Edgar Foley."

He nodded. "That one's not with them. Him I have upstairs,

bedroom at the back. You know he was dug in, doing what he could, right? Brought in a lot of those you walked past, cared for them, before it took him too."

"He was like that."

"He was. Not so much early on in his life, from what he told me, but later, you bet. Close friend of yours?"

"*Friend* doesn't begin to say it."

"Two of you stayed in touch?"

"In a manner of speaking."

Doc stepped up close and stared intently into my face. I had no idea what he could or might see there. "Do I know you, young man?"

"You brought me into this world. Mabel Levine was my mother."

"Sweet past . . . You're Jack."

"Yes, sir."

"Hard behind the resistance, people said back in the day. Planning, executing. The town had pride in you."

"I was underground, then above it but still out of sight. While Ed was helping the fallen. We find our own way in the dark."

"Some do."

"I'm not with the government any longer."

"Not much of one to be with."

"There's that."

Doc had gone back to set the oatmeal pot off the burner. He'd failed to turn off the fire under it. I walked over and did so.

"Ed and I served together, went through a lot. It got so we didn't need to talk, we'd see what needed to get done and go whatever way was best to do it. Like somehow we knew the shape of what the other was thinking, how he felt. That never left, that open space between us, not even afterwards, when we went our separate ways. Just get clear of the world's noise and here's that other life beside yours."

After a moment, Doc nodded. His hands, I saw now—why not before?—were trembling.

"Two weeks back, I felt that again," I said, "after many years. The other life beside mine. Ed's life. I was with him from then on, with him when he died."

"In spirit."

"I suppose."

"I am so very sorry, son."

A sound came from the front room, the beginning of a scream, before it cut off.

"I'll go up and get him now, if that's okay with you."

"Please. And I'd best go see to my patients."

His body ravaged for weeks by the alien virus, there wasn't a lot of Edgar left. But I carried my dead friend back out into the world that would soon belong expressly to the billybobs, sat him beside me in the Fiat, and drove away. It was a beautiful bright day, clouds moving lazily along the horizon. After a while I asked if I could tell him my bedside story for humanity.

In the beginning, I said, there were two gods. One created the world, the other created mankind. They sat back proud of their work, what they'd done. Then the first said: Yours will never amount to anything.

I guess she was right.

BURY ALL TOWERS

That night I dream of elephants. They are swimming in the sea off Corfu, trunks held high out of the water, mouths smiling beneath.

Harold had left.

Harold had left and I was bereft.

It seems at the time I also had a taste for rhyme.

But why are the elephants happy? And why Corfu? Ah, sweet mysteries of life. No real mystery as to why Harold's gone, though, if only I'm honest with myself. Which, being that way, feels like slipping into bed expecting cotton sheets and finding scratchy wool.

Not that his being gone matters one whit in light of all the rest that's amiss. Melting ice caps, toxic water, oil spills, dead bees, the reawakening of ancient diseases. Rampant racism. Mass shootings. Income and tax disparities. We could talk about that last for days at the time. Harold did.

Not a lot I can do about possessions owning me, besides limiting their number, and that's what I've been doing. I'm down to a couple sets of dishes, a meager shelf of books, a single handheld computer, two sets of clothing. Probably don't have much need of the dishes come to think of it, since usually I just eat from whatever pot or skillet I've cooked in.

There's always more you can do.

Minutes ago a neighbor knocked at my door. Jane, Julie, Jill, something like that. Came to tell me Mr. Druff—down on the second floor?—had been killed last night. Someone broke into his apartment, stabbed him right there in his bed, police said the mattress looked like a pancake soaked with syrup. I said, Okay, thanks, and she stood there a minute, Jill or whatever, before she went away.

My calendar says I'm supposed to go to the clinic today for another scan. Sometimes the doctors act like if they keep pounding it with loud magnets and poking at it, the tumor's going to pick up and go. Just like poor Harold in his own way, so assured that if I only tried, I could wish it away, or pray it away. I was never sure which he meant, wish or pray, and kept asking him what the difference was. And anyway, what tumors really do when provoked is go hide, snug themselves up behind a kidney or bone so they get harder and harder to find.

Not long after the visit from my neighbor, a young officer was here. She asked me if I've heard about Mr. Druff, then said they're going door to door throughout the building. Did I know Mr. Druff? Only by sight, I told her. The small send-receive strapped to her shoulder crackled from time to time. I'd run into him once in a great while on the stairwell, or by the mail boxes in the lobby. I was at home last night? Yes. Had I seen or heard anything out of the ordinary? I'm sorry, I said, but I really can't help. I take pills to sleep.

I didn't mention that I spent the night watching elephants swim. Or that the pills don't help much.

I'm fixing a sandwich when the phone rings. I don't have any appetite, but everyone keeps telling me I have to eat. (I just thoughtlessly wrote *rings*. I do know that few phones ring anymore. And mine doesn't announce itself, like so many others do, with "Ride of the Valkyries" or a riff from the latest pop classic. My ringtone, carefully chosen, is the sound of someone loudly clearing his or her throat.)

The call's from Cele at work, wanting to know when I'll be back. We're going under, she says, going down for the last time. Help. Come back. Save us.

So many metaphors for being overcome. I eye the rye bread, pickles and ham laid out on the chopping board, the mayonnaise and mustard jars alongside, with a disinterest that's rapidly sinking towards disgust. I imagine the undone work accumulating on my desk. Alone in its cubicle, the poor thing groans beneath the weight. New burdens of folders and forms and binders slam down upon it. (All of this paperless, of course. Metaphor again.) There are creakings, as of ancient attic floors, mysterious footsteps. One sharp crack, breakage for sure, then another. Any moment . . .

I'm doing much better, I tell Cele.

You'll be back soon, then?

Absolutely.

She tells me about the shower on Friday for Tony, whose wife is expecting late this month, I tell her about the school kids who came door to door to solicit donations for the rain forests, shouldering this small portion of good into the world.

Afterwards I finish assembling the sandwich, cut it into quarters, and feed them to the disposal. Something comforting, immensely reassuring, in listening to it chew and swallow. I could make it some popcorn later on. Pudding. Pie.

It has needs just like the rest of us.

Another young woman comes to my door claiming to be a neighbor, but she doesn't mention what floor or apartment, and I've never seen her before. She goes away pretty quickly. I'm too spellbound by her hair to listen much or respond to whatever it was she's saying. Three different worlds are tangled up in there, like she can't decide which one she lives in, which one is her. Medium brown sprouting at the roots, tumbles of fading red, sprays and sprigs of glow-in-the-dark light green.

That night I look out my window thinking how beautiful the woman's hair was, how special are those few moments in my memory, though I can't recall her face. From here to the horizon, as far as I can see in any direction, buildings like my own rise against the sky. Each stands proud, stretching up ten or twelve floors, shallow moats of streets urging them apart, holding them back. It comes to me that these buildings are towers—tower after tower after tower. That we're all alone up here with our waste disposals, our sandwiches, our computers and TVs, our phones, our closed and locked doors, our transactions and brief relationships, our stillborn children, our murdered neighbors. As much as I dislike it, I think I'm going to have to move again.

Bad things happen here.

THE CRY OF EVENING BIRDS

After considerable thought I've ordered up some changes on my husband. They will come into effect, I'm told, at 1830 tonight. I don't make such changes, don't even consider them, lightly. Bean and I, after all, have been together for many years. Not to mention the cost of these variances, nor our mutual commitment, which is, of course, another form of wealth. But lives change, by definition. People change. Needs change.

I must admit to a moment's hesitation while completing the request for service and coming upon the prompt *Notify subject?* Academic, true, since once the changes took hold, Bean wouldn't remember, but it gave pause nonetheless.

As I ticked, filled and entered my way down the order form, I looked out on the pool where, year after year, every spring, ducks with new ducklings showed up. Though I still think of it as such, it's not been a pool for a long time; nowadays it's a garden where everything struggles, be it zucchini and tomato vines, a single fig tree, bordering daffodils.

Done with the request for service, confirmation received, I spent the afternoon cleaning house. One minor change would entail Bean's becoming not the neatnik he'd always been, but something of a slouch, so I thought of this as my last full-tilt onslaught, have everything in frame and in place for the last time maybe, go with the flow after. I vacuumed, dusted, straightened, even took the covers off the couch pillows and threw them in the washer. Stood watching them go round and round and slap up against the glass port. Such unprecedented behavior on my part, such fearful new experience on theirs.

I've loved Bean since first I set eyes on him, which sounds like one of those old ballads, I know, the ones that mostly end up with the woman getting tossed in the water to drown because she wouldn't be his bride, got herself with child, or professed to love another, but it's true. Same with him, I think, and he was quicker to realize it, definitely quicker to say it.

That took place two weeks to the day after we met. Bean was working as news anchor for WMMP and we were on the light rail returning from dinner with the station's owner and high-level managers. Perfectly fine meat or fish awash in some unknown species of sauce, salads no doubt assembled from wee rooftop herb gardens, side dishes in which three or more distinct cuisines had arrived at the crossroad at the same time and collided, no survivors.

"In the future I won't ask you to do that sort of thing," he said as we watched a dozen elderly passengers climb aboard, obviously a group, and, with considerable confusion and delay, scan their tickets.

"The future," I said. Three of the newcomers had figured it out and were helping the other nine. This bold new excursion. "Implying that we have one."

"Of course we do."

And there it was.

"Do you doubt it?" he said.

And I didn't.

Nope. No way.

By 1530 I had onions frying on the stove for meatloaf, Bean's favorite comfort food, plus a pan of potatoes tossed with olive oil, salt, pepper and parsley ready for roasting alongside. That, a small green salad, and daffodils from the pool ought to do it. He'd wonder what we were celebrating. I snipped the flowers and put them, in my favorite cobalt-blue vase, on the table.

Once, as we left for yet another doctor's appointment or test— Ben had to be five then; something I hadn't thought of for a while but remembered today, picking the flowers—we came across an insect, a huge beetle of some sort, on the front porch. It had been attacked, presumably by cats, and the back half of it was gone, the front half still alive and scrabbling at the porch floor, attempting to flee, to find safety. Ben asked me how that could be, that the bug could still be alive, and what the bug felt. I told him I didn't know.

Bean showed up as usual, 1745, five-minute window either way. I'd put on a dress and good shoes and had my hair up. From his look I could tell he took notice, but he said nothing. We had a glass of wine while waiting for the meatloaf to finish in the oven. He told me about the lead story they'd filmed for tonight. A duffel bag filled with money had been left outside a local free clinic, some said by a drug gang, two of whose members' lives had been saved there. He'd had a new cameraman tonight, too, he said, a young woman, Louise, though she preferred being called Lou, maybe six months pregnant.

I'm not sure when I decided about the changes. Nothing is as hard on a couple as losing a child. I'd hurt, too, more than I could ever have imagined, and still do, but somewhere deep in, my body understood that these things happened. With Bean, though, it was killing him, it never let go, never let up. You could see it in his eyes, hear it in his voice, sense it in his lingering touch.

As he spoke about the new cameraman, I watched him look over at the flowers, look about the room, remembering.

And I knew—as the timer on the stove went off and I glanced that way, *1830*—when the changes hit.

"Dinner's ready, Sweetheart."

"We should have had a child ourselves," he said.

BIG DAY IN LITTLE BIT

(for Bill Crider)

A gentleman, I thought the first day we met, his soft-spoken greeting and hushed Southern drawl flowing across the table to where I stood in my new yellow work boots. Soon I'd discover he was a writer as well, but never held that against him. In this world we make our living as we can.

Thinking this could not possibly be the man for whom I was there, a mistake had been made, I offered apologies and made to withdraw, whereupon he remarked that I appeared to be new in town and perhaps might take a moment to sit, have coffee, talk a spell?

Why not? I never had a clock to punch, only jobs to get done.

And this, I'd learn, was Bill's habitude. He served as Little Bit's sheriff (I never held that against him either) and regularly haunted the bus station, the Sinclair station on the edge of town or Millie's Good Eats, watching who came and went. Some of those who went, did so at Bill's urging.

So we sat and drank coffee sweetened with Bill's jokes, chewing on nuggets of downhome philosophy till our talk turned to books, which quickly proved what we had most in common. This began, as I recall, with some mention he made of Peter Rabe, how slippery the bad guys were in his work, how hard to get hold of, in *Kill the Boss Good-bye* for instance. I saw his bet with Vin Packer's *Come Destroy Me* and raised him Charles Williams.

The thing is, people listened when Bill spoke, just like I did. I remember how once, waiting for some small repair on his truck, he regaled six mechanics with the story from Gunter Grass's *The Flounder*. They were spellbound, and I have to wonder if this wasn't due to Bill's telling more than to the story itself, or to their all being themselves fishermen.

In his spare time, I should mention, Bill taught at the local college. The question to be asked here is how the hell he *had* free time. I figure that's what? five, six jobs? Writer, sheriff, town greeter, family man, professor . . . Oh, and all those reviews and columns he wrote about smelly old paperback books, the kind that sold off wire racks in drugstores for thirty-five cents. Just thinking about all that made you feel a need to sit down and rest up.

What it made me do, after sitting there with Bill for better than an hour that first time, was get up, head back to the Motel 6 out by the Sinclair, and use the phone in my room to cancel my contract in Little Bit, the first and only time I ever did that. No way I was going to bring trouble to Bill's town. I went back to Little Bit again and again after that, but never for work. I'd have a job in Chicago, Portland, New Hampshire, I'd set it up so's to fly back through nearby Serenade, rent a car, and layover a few days in Little Bit, sitting around the bus station, the Sinclair, or Good Eats with Bill. It's the only town I ever felt a part of, the only place I ever felt welcome.

My third or fourth visit—I can't be sure, but I think I'd just done a double up in Minnesota, which would make it number four—Bill said if it weren't too much trouble, he could use a favor.

"Absolutely."

We were walking alongside one of the town's many dried-up creek beds. White heads of dandelions made it look like a gathering of old men down in there. On the bank, someone (a child? a rogue artist?) had sculpt dirt and stone into a tiny version of Native American cliff dwellings, complete with ladders.

"Thought I might ask your professional opinion," Bill said.

"Professional?"

The smile told me he knew what I did for a living. Which actually didn't come as much of a surprise. But I had to wonder then if he knew why I'd originally turned up in Little Bit. Still do, some days.

"I've had information that one of your peers is in town. Working. I thought it possible you might know him. A man everyone calls simply Wilson."

"I know *of* him."

"What I'm wondering, is how concerned I should be over his being here."

"Do you know who he's here to see?"

"I have my suspicions."

It was early afternoon, dwarf shadows walking beside us, horizon ashimmer, beyond which you could sense the larger world moving slowly about. "Give me some time," I said. "I'll get back to you."

I was waiting in his room at Sunrise Motel the next town over when Wilson returned that night. I'd dogged him long enough to assure myself of his reason for being here, then gone out for an unhurried dinner of chicken-fried steak, mashed potatoes, gravy. The room smelled faintly of spicy aftershave, no doubt from its former tenant. We pass through rooms, pass through the world, leaving brief imprints of ourselves behind.

He came in and, without pause, shut the door. I was sitting in the corner. He remained where he was, shadowy in outside light from the curtained window.

"I half expected you to come over and say hello this afternoon," he said. "When you were having your pie at the diner, say."

"No reason."

"True enough. It's not as though you were taking care not to be seen, is it?"

"Clear signals are the easiest to read."

"Like with that politician in Minnesota last year."

"Hronka."

"Nice touch, the fuzzy dice on the bathroom mirror."

"By special request."

"Forever interesting, isn't it, all the messages out there for the taking. But those dice, that's the kind of thing that gets talked about."

"Pretty much the point."

From habit he'd begun to edge closer, then caught on and stopped himself. Car doors slammed outside, *da-da-ta*, a perfect triplet. I waited for voices to fade. Too far off to make out words, but from the tone a friendly argument. Then asked: "And if I'd brought my pie over, sat down with you?"

"Who can say? Maybe I'd have asked for a second fork."

He held out his hand, palm flat, moving it in small circles as though balancing . . . what?

"Sometimes you decide you have to rein it in," he said.

"Those who sent you here won't he pleased."

"Assuredly. But having the choice is a major bonus of being an independent contractor. Besides . . . we're not good men to be angry with, are we? Maybe someday others will talk of this meeting as they have your fuzzy dice."

"In far-flung, nondescript rooms such as this one."

"What more can we hope for?"

I'd planned to call and let Bill know the matter had been taken care of, but when I pulled in at the motel there he was, draped over one of the rusty metal chairs lined up beneath the overhang, legs and arms everywhere. The words *imperially slim* came to me—part of an old poem remembered for some reason from grade school. To this day I've little idea how much he knew: Why I first came to Little Bit, who Wilson was set upon, how it went down. Always hard to tell with Sheriff Bill. Pretty damn impossible, truth be told. Nor did I know then if, having had two failed contracts, they'd sent a third.

"Care for a walk?" he asked and, with dark clouds to the east promising rain, Bill's spidery legs and my bandy legs stepped out together onto the parched fields adjacent. I had to think about what all those fields had witnessed. Nations, battles, families, crops, blood, bodies. Once you poke at history, pry up the floorboards, it won't stop coming. There's too much of it. Nationally, personally.

"Appreciate your help, my friend," Bill said.

"I did nothing but exchange a few words."

"Words can turn away storms."

"Or just as easily bring them on."

"True enough." A crow large as an alley cat dipped over our heads, quickly judged us irrelevant, and flew on. "I'll see you again soon, then?"

"You will. And I'll be keeping an ear to the ground."

"History repeating itself as it does, you mean."

"Yes."

"All things considered, it's a good place, Little Bit. A good life. I'd like to keep it that way." Bill stopped, gesturing ahead. "We'd best start back."

And so we did, turning around, the rain behind us, where it stayed.

LYING DOWN

You ever see *Always a Dead Body Somewhere*, that opening scene panning so slowly along the beach to the poor sucker lying there stone cold gone and done with, with the heron perched on his chest? That's me. That was my breakthrough, the beginning of a long career. I owe a lot to that minute and a half by the water in San Diego.

My name's Jeremy Blunt. The studio wants a dead body onscreen, I'm who they call. Before *Always*, I'd spent twelve years out here trying to make it as an actor. After *Always*, word got around fast, the way it does, and I didn't have to go knocking anymore. Best in the business, everyone said. Has the experience you need, my agent said. *No one* does better DBs than me. End of discussion.

You better believe, after a quarter of a century out here on sets and streets I have more stories to tell you than I could get through in a solid month. Like the time they set up close to an anthill no one noticed. I got down, doing my thing, dead to the world you might say, and right after cameras started rolling, so did the ants, up and out to find this fine big meal they'd been provided. And it was a long scene. Shows what a pro I was, even then. Or there was that time the director and cameraman, both hungover from last night's party, got into it and wound up pulling prop guns and swords on each other. Or the director who had to show everyone, every scene, how it was to be played, so that his shootings went two or three times as long as others. When it came down to his prepping me, my part being exactly to do nothing, the whole crew applauded as he lay there. He just looked confused.

But maybe we can get into that later.

The big moments in our lives never come when we expect them. I owe a lot to that San Diego shoot. I owe *everything* to what I'm telling you about here.

We were shooting on the fly and cheap as junk shoes, one of those projects where the director and writer are the same and it looks to be financed off credit cards and deception. We were in a state no one would ever have much reason to come and in a part of the state where even the roads were downright sullen about being there. The whole thing was a mess. Everyone knew it, and no one would say it. The script was still getting cooked. We'd come in mornings and everything from dialog to the roles themselves would have been changed. The one thing we did *not* do was reshoot, anything. No money for that, so whatever got onto film stayed there. Made for some interesting continuity, not to mention transitions. Guys would be talking in a room, full daylight, then they'd go outdoors and it was dark. Or the director, editing, would lard in filler, patch-over shots of the set through a bottle of seltzer or a windowpane with rain running down it as characters spoke voiceover. That sort of thing.

The female lead was one of those with a nose that could hide behind a demitasse spoon and eyebrows plucked away to make ample room for expertly drawn new ones. She pronounced every single syllable of every single word like she rolled them on her tongue before pushing them out. If we'd done run-throughs before shoots she would have showed up in tights and shapeless cloth dresses, which is what she wore, all she wore, any time she was off camera.

Then one morning this guy popped up, fifties maybe, good shoes and haircut. The suit fit, but it looked out of place as hell here in rural bumfuck on a half-ass movie set. Struck me as a man accustomed to moving through the world expecting no resistance. No one I asked knew for sure who he was. Like me, he hung around the edge of the action, bellying up at least once to a goodies table that was mainly coffee, bottled water, cookies, crackers, and cheese cubes. Then after my stint, which came up a few hours into the day's shoot, with another, brief appearance as a second DB, set for later, he came over.

The scene had me propped up against a flat rock, pale as surrounding sand, upper-body clothing mostly ripped away. Makeup had spent an industrious hour-plus creating wounds on my arms, chest, and face. On edit, Effects would drop in gulls pecking at me, a strip of flesh or two.

Our spectator walked over as I was heading for the trailer to change. When he held out a hand, I couldn't help but notice that the shoulders of his suit stayed put. Tailored. "Good work," he said. "That scene was *yours*."

"Until they put the gulls in, anyway." I told him about the effects still to come.

"Yeah. Animals, cute kids . . ."

"Scene stealers every one."

"Still, a good death scene, a believable one . . . Not something just anyone can pull off."

I considered responding with a Brando impression of method acting, *What you gotta do is get right down in duh death*, but thought better of it and simply smiled.

"B. Grant," he said.

"As in winged, with a stinger?"

"Just the initial, the letter. Unimaginative, nonconformist parents."

"Two adjectives you don't often find traveling together."

"Oh?"

"The exclamation, or just the letter?"

He held up his hands in mock surrender, then handed me a card. Embossed, high-end paper, quietly stylish. Like the shoes and suit. "Any chance you're done here?"

"One more call, tomorrow, early."

"I see . . . I'm wondering, might you then be interested in new employment?"

"Doing?"

"Only what you do so well, I assure you."

This, I thought, is the part of the movie where the character knows better than to go out on the porch to see what's out there but does it anyway.

Thank the Lord, chance, the relative position of heavenly bodies, prevailing winds, pick one or all the above, that I did.

You know how you walk into places or see them onscreen and think, No way an actual person lives here? That's what stepping through the front door with B. Grant was like. There was so damned much glass, on summer days you'd have to wear sunglasses. Low-slung furniture, apparently built for people severely short-changed as to leg length. And most everything white except for blobs of color on the wall that were probably supposed to be paintings.

"Yeah, yeah, I know," B. Grant said. "Not my style either. Also not my condo."

"Then what are we doing here?"

"Checking in."

Voices outside, then a man and woman entered, both in clothes that came off no rack like any I'd ever been close to. I could have lived a year off what they paid for their four shoes.

"Emil, Lucinda. Thank you for coming."

"So this is the one," the man said, looking me over.

"He is."

I turned back to B. Grant. "Sorry, I thought—"

"No, no. Merely acting as agent here. Seeking the best man for the part." Then to Emil: "And I've found him for you."

"We'll see."

At that, B. Grant looked a bit uneasy. For a moment I worried that he might start shouting out commands. You know: sit, roll over. Play dead. Not that I ever minded auditions.

"I'll be going, then," he said and, with nothing further forthcoming, did. I introduced myself, they reciprocated with handshakes. Emil went off to get drinks, *fetch* being the word he used, as Lucinda and I sat on the lowboy chairs, knees poked up like kangaroos.

"You're an actor?"

"Well, ma'am, it was either that or find honest work." Seeing her jumpstart a smile for my lame joke, I backpedaled. "Not much of one, when it comes right down to it. I just do one thing really well. But you keep doing that thing, if they go on letting you do it, before you know it you've got yourself a career."

"So that's not what you always wanted to be? When you were a child?"

"When I was a child . . . Truthfully, I can't remember that I wanted much of anything in particular. Or maybe I wanted everything."

"Whatever we want or don't, nothing much ever turns out the way we think it will."

"Yes, ma'am."

Emil was back with the drinks, a pinkish wine for her, whiskey of some sort for him, the beer I'd asked for. Imported. Vaguely gothic lettering. Dark.

"I overheard a little of what you were talking about out here," Emil said. "Have to ask what that one thing you're good at might be."

"If I had to put it in a word—pretending, I guess."

"Pretending." Emil.

"As children do." Lucinda.

I nodded to both.

"Interesting." Emil again, with a sip of whiskey as he considered. "Grant told you what the job pays?"

"He didn't even tell me what the job was."

"And yet you agreed."

"I came along. As they say in the film world: Great set up. Get 'em watching, we can run credits after."

If there were credits, the first thing onscreen would have been A LYLE KRON FILM. Cause that's what it was about, that's who the director was, and the star. Also why I was there. It wasn't a film, though, never would be.

Turns out the Emil-Lucinda couple had a friend of the starving artist persuasion. God only knows how they might have met, living in separate worlds, but they did. And this friend, about the couple's age, I'd guess, was a painter and sculptor. "Best to let the man himself explain it," Emil said as we sat in that bright room with our whisky, wine, and beer. Shortly thereafter we disembarked for the starving artist's studio.

At that first meeting Lyle, who physically reminded me of over-full, overburdened, unsorted dormitory rooms, told me he'd spent five years now on a single project. That he wanted to capture, in a painting, drawing, or sculpture, "the true, forever secret, horrid, beauteous image of death itself, death *felt*, death *lived*." To this end, over those years, he'd employed the services of better than twenty models, all of whom eventually were dismissed as inadequate to the mission, "though perhaps," he admitted, "it is my own inadequacy. And that Death doesn't wish us to know her so intimately."

In time Lyle had spoken of his despair to Emil and Lucinda, and they, sensitive to the pain in his voice, offered first to assist him in finding the ideal model for his project, then to provide formidable payments for same.

So it was that an artist's studio above a furniture warehouse by long-abandoned train tracks at city's edge became my new occupation, my daily haunt, and my rightful duty for close on ten months. As with all life, much of what went on there was routine, some quite challenging, most of the rest humdrum. There were bright segments, of course. And something about Lyle's dedication and drive that proved infectious.

Vividly I remember the day he moved from a painting at which for weeks he'd been disheartedly poking and prodding, to a mass of hard clay on a stand nearby and, requesting a small change in my pose, his hand lightly at rest on the clay before setting to work in earnest, said, "The medium knows, this damned clay, canvas, paper, stone—it knows, with every move, every shape or volume or line I leave behind, every blankness, it knows this is all untrue, dishonest, all but small parts of a greater lie."

Every second day or so, fully aware of his predilection for diving in and staying down, Emil and Lucinda brought around bagels and fixings, sandwiches, or pho. Save for that, bodily exigencies, or occasional collapses into a few hours of sleep, Lyle scarcely stepped out from behind that trestle table and its burden of clay for close to a month. My own agenda, first as a matter of course, then diligently, echoed his.

What finally came off that table and from that hard clay, the statue cast in bronze and entitled *The Dead Don't Lie*, you can see at the city's museum, in art books, online at specialty and educational websites. Critics describe the work as filled with foreboding yet strangely restful, as darkness and light intermingling, as an object one cannot look away from, as a marvel and a wonder. I'll leave descriptions, reactions, and praise to critics and viewers. I myself have never seen the completed piece. I never will. I have no need to.

The big moments in one's life, the truly momentous ones, never come when we expect them. I walked away from that studio with ever so much more than I had ever owned upon entering, with a new and abiding realization of what it is I do. I know now. I know what I do, and why.

Silence, longing, loss, darkness, all those empty spaces within and without us, everything we fear deeply and forever—I can give all these a shape and form. I can bring them into light. A rare talent? A gift. A calling. I lie down.

REVENANCE

The Higgs boson is gone. As of yesterday it just gave up, packed it in. Little but bottom quarks left of it now. Hard to say how sad this makes me. Even the gecko on my windowsill understands that something's gone wrong, something is amiss with the world. Something is lost.

What? You don't think physicists can be passionate?

Six long years I stood by my boson morning to night, morning *and* night. Enjambment, my poet friend Marilyn might call it. She thinks words explain everything. Which leads me to wonder what *I* believe, and the response is: experimentation, the scientific method. Basically, doing the same thing over and over to see what happens.

We're at Green Way chomping down on what the menu describes as a vegan interpretation of shepherd's pie. Our server, a graduate student at the university that hosts my lab, has tattoos of equations festooning arms and shoulders. Music that repeatedly veers toward melody, skittering away moments before reaching it, plays low in the background.

So that's done. What's next? Marilyn asks.

I have no response.

To get to the hotel, you had to cross a bridge over nothingness. That was the best part of the six-hour drive, looking down into the nothingness. Everything before and after was a disappointment.

They made the drive every year when he was a kid. Daniel never knew why, what his father or mother saw in it, why they kept going back. Could it possibly be the same as him, that minute-and-a-half-long glimpse of nothingness? It wasn't the glitz and glimmer of the destination; each year Mom and Dad carefully explained the pretense and wastage of all this. That's where Daniel learned the word egregious. He and his sister would sit peering down, he to the right, she left. What was she seeing? He couldn't know, of course, not with any of them, but with her the least of all. Never in the fourteen years she had on this earth had Beatrice, Sister Bee, spoken a word, though sometimes when she looked at him her eyes were like buckets scooping up pure water from the bottom of wells.

Hotel Hume itself was grand in the manner of old movies and sugar-fed dreams, with ballrooms the size of aircraft carriers, chandeliers like polar ice caps, carpets imprinted with half-inch rain forests of vegetation. Routinely one came across guests wandering lost, eyes glazed, feet rising and falling marionette-like as they had for hours, among its cavernous hallways, stairwells, and meeting rooms.

From time to time there would be revelers in evening dress freshly escaped from parties and dances; other times, conventioneers wearing lodge hats, civil-war costumes, flapper dresses, Viking or Wookie outfits. Once in a great while, rooms would release file after file of somberly decked men bearing away serious expressions and thoughts from political gatherings within. You could all but see the thoughts weighing them down, holding them hard against the earth.

About those, too, those men, those thoughts, Daniel's and Beatrice's parents would caution them.

What most fascinated Daniel, as in equal measure he found himself anticipating and apprehensive, was how the spaces scooped up random sounds and tossed them again and again against walls, into open chambers and baffled passageways, transforming them into something never before heard, laughter from beings that never existed—from out there, down there, in the nothingness maybe.

Those sounds, that laughter, always brought one of Beatrice's rare smiles.

I'm the last thing they see, Marilyn says, my face upside down above them.

She's an anesthetist, shepherding people quietly to and fro from the not-here. Her day job, she says—every poet needs a day job. Only in her book *What Is Sleep?* have her two occupations touched upon each other. I sit and watch a lot of people deep in it, she says, day after day, this sleep thing. I had to wonder. Think how interesting

it is that, as I watch and wonder, they are giving up pieces of themselves, replacing those pieces, updating them: the lens of an eye,
organs, limbs, hips and kneecaps, spidery veins, ligaments, tendons,
tumors. Torn things. Damaged things. Are they doing the same as
they sleep day to day?

That time, we were in a coffee shop known for its gourmet, fair-
trade coffee and almond croissants made daily on the premises. I
was on my third cup of coffee. She was on her second measured
bite of croissant, leaving behind a divot the size of a hummingbird
wing. Neither of us eats much of anything, but we always seem to
meet in cafes or restaurants.

It's a great mystery, Marilyn says, this sleep thing.

The server walks by with a trayful of empties, glancing down
sideways to see if we need refills. His eyes are gray, like evening
clouds.

Then (because she knows I expect it?): There *are* mysteries,
Daniel.

We've talked about this before. Not that we differ in believing that
mysteries exist, only in defining their nature. What they might be.

His second year in college he listened to thirty-eight consecutive
hours of Mozart. All forty-one symphonies, the overtures, *Eine
Kleine Nachtmusik*, the piano concertos, especially Serkin's D minor,
No. 20, over and over, the Romanze, Serkin milliseconds behind the
beat, holding on, as though reluctant to release each note, loathe to
let them go, knowing he must.

Roommate Theo at last fled, though Daniel was using headphones. No doubt that at the volume Daniel was playing the music,
Theo could overhear it, parts at least. Daniel apologized for the
leakage. There's more than one kind going on here, Theo said.

Their parents had found Bee dead in her bed the week before,
when she failed to come down for dinner. Of natural causes, the
coroner said. Of unknown causes, their mother corrected him.
Daniel's sister had found her way into what was beneath that bridge.

Simultaneously, in a gasp of coincidence, the media filled with
stories and photos of bees dying by the hundreds, by the thousands,
for reasons unknown.

• • •

When I was twelve, Beatrice seven, spiders colonized her bedroom. At one point there were six of them. Each morning Beatrice told them hello soundlessly, lips barely moving. They all had names and, in her mind, distinct personalities. Harold was the bold one, fearlessly advancing, annexing ever more of the ceiling. Maude was so reclusive as but rarely to be glimpsed in the shadow of an electrical fixture laced with webwork in which hung many small bodies. That webwork itself visible only in strong light, the bodies seemed suspended in space. Miraculous how adaptable the spiders were, how industrious and determined. I vividly recall Bee's gentleness and concern for the spiders, just not what became of them. What could the life span of a spider be?

The point of a scalpel is called the tang, Marilyn tells me. Tang, as in taste.

Even standing there in her other world, her other life, fussily monitoring vitals and levels of consciousness, words reach out to her and take hold. She in turn takes them to heart. She believes they tell us secret things.

Just as often, I say, they cloud things.

The clouds themselves are beautiful in their own way, she says.

And of my memories: Don't hold them so close that neither of you can breathe.

The Higgs boson is gone. Such a space left behind, in its wake as it were. The gecko is gone as well. Bird seed I've sprinkled on the windowsill goes untouched. I suspect that neither, gecko nor boson, will come back in some new edition, transcribed, transformed. That my boson will not, as bad biographers write, reinvent itself. But say it does: Will we recognize one another? We both will have changed so. That is what the world and words do to us, dear particle.

QUILTS

"The sound of cicadas in the trees. Sunsets that look as though they'll never end. Unexpected laughter. The way shallow pools of water look when sunlight breaks through again after a shower. The smell of fresh coffee."

Our litany of lost things continues. Eighteen years together, and now it's almost over. I'll not see her face again, the stars' cold fires about to become our own.

Amy pulls the quilt close about her. It's one of those her mother made in the care facility, chiefly for something to do, something to fill the time. A shelf of our closet is stacked with them. This one boasts identical panels of clouds with sun peeking over, reminiscent of old KILROY WAS HERE signs, and a border of stylized birds, dogs and cats. These will be gone too. The dogs and cats and birds. The quilts.

There's music playing low, so low we barely hear it, on the computer; on its screen, the clock counts down. "Remember the yule logs burning each year on television?" Amy asks. "People watched for hours and hours. Why would they do that?"

All around us it's dark. No sound of cicadas. No traffic noise. Our lawn chairs give out thin, hollow pipings as we shift within them.

Earlier Amy told me she packed a kit of things that would be most useful, just in case. Even now it's difficult to accept that hoping, knowing, being prepared—no survival kit will help.

"Children playing," she says now. "Full moons so bright you can read by them. Frogs. Windows with rain running down. Fireworks. The ocean."

I point to the computer. "Music."

"Fresh fruit."

Amy stares off. "My father used to say there's always another door, you just have to look for it."

"If there is, this time it's locked solid."

"Yeah, well. He was an asshole anyway. What can you expect?"

We know, exactly, what to expect. But that's neither here nor there. And *there* will soon be *here*.

By now we're both weary of this game of What Will You Miss Most. What I'll miss most is simply looking forward, not knowing, to what happens next.

So Amy and I sit here silently. Troubling the darkness, an unheavenly bright light starts up in the distance and rolls toward us. The computer screen, its countdown clock, tells us we have four, no three, more minutes.

GETTING IN SHAPE

My wife thinks I'm at the gym, Mr. Lowell says. As he lowers his cup, a single drop of latte runs down the crease alongside his mouth. I come here daily, he says, for this moment of tranquility and peace before going on.

People amble in and out, greet one another, groan, there's the throat-clearing racket of blenders and grinders, leakage from headphones, the hiss of frothing machines. Many marooned, alone in the crowd with their computers, notebooks and smartphones. Mr. Lowell has none of these.

With? I ask.

Beg pardon?

Going on with what?

Patently the question makes no sense to him. Whatever fortune and the day brings, I suppose, he says. You're certain you don't want anything? A coffee? Pastry?

Again I shake my head. *This* is what I want. To go out into the world, select random people to interview, ask and ask again. To my mind it makes small difference what the questions are. Ask. Listen. Pause. Ask the next.

Those two, he says, nodding slightly towards a twentyish couple at a table by the front window, are here every morning. They'd only just met when I first saw them, I'm sure. Now look at them.

Both are about their own business, she with paperback book and half-size legal pad, he with computer, though he looks up when others enter the shop, gaze lingering when it's a woman. Briefly I wonder what might be said should I interview them. Their tattoos remind me of a story I read years ago, a man whose tattoos comprised, for those who could read them, an explanation of everything.

Mr. Lowell is an insurance broker, not one who sells policies but one who brings together potential client and appropriate insurer, i.e., a matchmaker. Something he tried on, he says, like a found shoe, and it fit.

Journalism too is such a calling, though it took me forty-plus years to hear that call.

Responding to my next question, Mr. Lowell expounds on how he goes about his work, his contacts, the networking he pursues, the research required, the ever-changing landscape, before saying But that's not why we're here, is it?

And why exactly, I have to wonder but don't ask, does he think we are here? Let silence bring what it will.

There's a disturbance outside the coffee shop, past the front windows. Two men standing close, faces awash with agitation as though their turn has come to give vent to all the world's bitterness. From in here we can't hear what's being said, only watch lips move, heads duck and weave, hands stray and leap into the space between the two men. Scripts run in our minds, like sound tracks hastily fit to foreign movies, hopelessly, comically out of synch.

My attention having been directed to the confrontation outside, at first I fail to register that Mr. Lowell has preempted my next question. He would like to know what is it that I do with the answers I receive.

I realize that actually I hadn't given this much thought. The answers seemed reason enough, end enough, of themselves—even the asking.

I suppose that, in a sense, I put them in a jar, I respond. Remembering my childhood. Pots of water boiling on the stove, mother's rack of Mason jars, the rubber seals and sealing wax. They are after all, I continue, someone *else*'s advice, someone *else*'s answers, not mine to use.

To preserve them, then, Mr. Lowell says.

Yes.

So that someday others can pick up the jar, turn it in their hands, peer within, examine it. Like organs and curiosities kept pickled on laboratory shelves.

Or . . . like fireflies.

Mr. Lowell finishes his coffee, holds up the empty cup as though to weigh it. Fireflies don't last long, he says, when you shut them away like that.

Or when you don't. At best, the adult's lifespan is five days. Some will never feed. They mate, they produce offspring, they die.

He nods. So much of the marvelous tucked into the ordinary, he says.

A tiny charge, muscular or electric, moves in a zigzag across his face, temple to jawline.

Ambition too, he says, can be a marvelous thing. I once had it in abundance, carried it with me everywhere. Now I leave pieces of it behind, wherever I go. When I get up now, some will be here by this table. Do with it what you will. And Mr. Lowell leaves.

I still have questions. What does ambition look like? How does one go about putting it to use? Is there an expiration date?

But he's gone.

I look around, under the chairs and table, at the floor nearby. If he's left anything behind, anything at all, I don't see it.

WHEN WE SAVED THE WORLD

I met Joe Lansdale for the first time in June, on a day buffed TV commentators were calling unseasonably warm. When you stepped outside, the glare was like flashbulbs going off in your face, and what it felt like was some giant who plays with the world like it's a ball was belching foul hot air in your face. Joe and I'd both made tons of money writing science fiction, the way people do, and so we'd retired, but after having us around the house all day long week after week both our wives kicked us out, and we moved into the Charleton Arms.

"You need to find a hobby, or a friend," Karyn said.

"I hear Cincinatti's nice this time of year," Karen said.

Turns out we'd lived half a mile from each other for years. And there we were, meeting for the first time on the sidewalk, hauling paper bags of possessions up to our new bachelor pads.

The joint looked like a place Chandler might have written about. Or Nathanael West. Both of them on a bad day. Eighteen apartments surrounded an inner court complete with pool. Any which way you looked, cement was cracked through and heaving up as though things had been born within and broken free. The pool was full of stringy green stuff that looked like it could well be a single, continuous strand. Curtains in upper apartments parted and half faces appeared as Joe and I stood talking, pretending we'd read each other's books.

Now, the funny thing about this—well, okay, not *the* funny thing, given how it all went, but funny regardless—the funny thing is that Joe didn't admit to being Joe. Claimed he was Robert B. Howard. *B*, he said again. Robert *B*. Howard. But I knew better.

So from right then on, Joe and I'd sit around for hours out by the pool slime, chairs cocked at different angles depending on where the surface took us, or in the lobby with curtains drawn and three struggling 60-watt bulbs, talking about Henry Kuttner and C.L.

Moore and Eando Binder till the staff (of which there were four except on weekends, then two) came by to remind us it was time for dinner, or to go use the bathroom.

I remember once when we were talking about Fredric Brown's mysteries, sitting out there again by the pool with that green stuff looking like it might be moving restlessly about, and Joe stopped in mid-sentence.

"You hear that, right?" he said.

I shook my head. Nothing to hear.

"We're in the middle of a city," he said.

He was right. Dead silence. Interesting.

"Well," he went on, "anyway, I always figured *The Screaming Mimi* was number one."

Myself, I was partial to *The Fabulous Clipjoint*, all the Ed and Am stories. Shoot, I even like *Madball*.

When we weren't talking about writers, we were reeling off jokes as ragged and tattered as the original editions of those books would be by now—classic and timeless or all used up, depending on where you stood. I have nothing but confidence in you, and very little of that, Joe might say. And me: I'm not crazy about reality but it's still the only place to get a good meal. Joe'd tell me tales of the old west hour after hour and I'd swap stories about all the crazy women I'd dated, Thelma who wore overalls and carried chopsticks with her everywhere she went, Beatrice who brought me easter eggs and furniture polish when she came by, Susanne who'd had her tongue split the way they used to do with crows. I just couldn't seem to stay away from them.

Most of those sessions ended with Joe saying again how he grew up talking civil rights, opposing the Vietnam war, and as an atheist—what he called the triple whammy. So how do *you* figure my childhood in east Texas went? he'd ask.

Though neither of us knew it when we moved in, having done so because the place was cheap and easy to find, neither of us being shoppers, the Charleton Arms turned out to be part halfway house, part care facility, part residential hotel. Remember all those old stories about boarding houses? That's what it felt like. Smarmy dust bunnies of secrets behind doors, inside suitcases, under tables and beds.

At table the first night, in a room that reminded me of my grade-school cafeteria (which had doubled as the gym and smelled it), Joe and I sat together, watching other residents the way a writer will. All I remember about the food was looking at it and wondering, first, how many residents must be toothless or nearly so and, second, who'd ever have thought there could be so many shades of grayish-white.

The man to our left, showing no facial expression whatsoever, after introducing himself told us he stayed at the Charleton every year on the month his birthday fell, every year, been at this now for twelve of them. An ageless woman across the table appeared to be staring at Joe the whole time, one side of her mouth drooping, the other level, as though from a stroke or from two people struggling to live together in a single face. She never said a word. The cook came out to ask if the food was to everyone's taste and to profess that he himself never ate anywhere else, never. "I know what's in *my* food." To this day I can't be sure his eyes went dreamy and a sidelong smile took form on his face, or if this got overwritten in memory—in the revision, if you will. But I found myself thankful I wasn't hungry.

Unlike myself, Joe ate whatever was offered. Except he never ate popcorn, not even at night when half a dozen of us sat clumped around the single TV in the lobby watching whichever channel was currently coming in best. He never ate popcorn, said it gave him bad dreams. So he must of eaten a lot of it in the past. I figured that's where all those great old horror stories came from.

The picture onscreen, I noticed the second or third night, bit by bit kept getting smaller, like it was sinking slowly into the set's innards as the black borders around it grew. When I called attention to this, I got nothing but peculiar looks and a second's pause before everyone turned heads back to the screen.

All my life, of course, I'd been seeing things others don't. *Imagining them*, my mom and dad insisted, as we sat over tuna casserole, green beans with canned onions, fried bologna, salt pork, gelatin salad. *Projecting*, explained a psychiatrist the school nurse referred us to, his office crowded with pillows that had animal faces embroidered on them, board games with names like *Challenge*, and shelves of anatomically correct dolls. Never before or since have I met

676 • JAMES SALLIS

anyone who could explain so many things. Want to know why spiders have eight legs, if dogs and cats see colors, or why *i* comes before *e*? Ask Dr. Bundt. I did. That's how I got through the sessions.

I see that I haven't mentioned the flies. They were well-behaved as far as flies go, none of that buzzing up in your face, landing on your doughnut, sitting on the window ledge staring at you with those goggles they have and flicking their legs. But they were always around, so much so that after a while you stopped noticing them. On the blinds, the TV screen, people's shoes, the framed decoupage and homilies.

One guy, though, as Joe and I began to notice, the flies wouldn't go near. He'd pass by the platitudes on the wall where they clung to the glass—

RECEIVING IS A FORM OF GIVING

YOU CAN BE ANYTHING YOU WANT TO BE

WHAT'S DONE IS DONE

—and the flies would take flight. Zoom to a different part of the room. They'd gather in one spot and you'd hear them buzzing away all at once over there, like some urgent conversation was in progress.

His name was Bob, he was thought to be a deaf mute, and he worked as part-time cleaning man on nights, Wednesday and Saturday. His mop bucket had Bob painted on in red block letters. Legend had it that he'd attacked the regular janitor for using his bucket. Took a spongee to the man's face and nearly drowned him, they said. No one was sure about the deaf mute thing. He'd stare at you if you talked to him, but Bob never replied or gave any indication he understood. Not that it mattered. On his nights, the lobby, the dining room and hallway floors believed themselves young again.

The thing is, we knew even then that something was going on at Charleton, we could feel it—started noticing all sorts of things that didn't quite add up—but we couldn't figure out what. True, that's pretty much how we'd been all our lives, never quite catching on, but this was different. *This* something felt like it smelled bad and had teeth.

One late afternoon as we sat out by the pool watching shadows go long and thin, Joe's phone went off. Theremin, I'm pretty sure, like from the old black and white *Science Fiction Theater* on TV.

"Dang it," he said, having recently, maybe the day before, given up white bread and swearing. "Must be my wife."

"Got your number, does she?"

He pulled the phone out, flipped it open. "Oh yeah. You pick up one of these yet?"

And have the government listen in on everything? "No way."

Joe answered, listened, said "Sorry, ma'am, wrong number," and hung up. Within moments the theremin warbled again. Joe answered, and when his eyes went to the second floor, mine followed. A woman with a phone to her ear stood there. Her face barely cleared the railing. She waved.

Joe held the phone away from his ear. "Says she's sorry to have bothered me before . . ."

I reminded him that most accidents occur close to home.

". . . but wants to know if we could meet her for dinner. She's heard we're writers and has a story to tell us."

Every writer in the world gets the pitch all the time, how the speaker's led this fascinating life and someone should write about it. You learn pretty quick not to lift a hand, let it go by.

But Joe agreed (what else was there to do, after all, but watch the greens heave in the pool and the lobby's three 60-watt bulbs grow ever dimmer) and at dinner that night (meat loaf, mashed potatoes, canned peas) Trudy Jay, her face a patchwork of cracks like a dried-out mudflat, told us how in March of 1970 she stood on an observation platform in Florida and watched as a rocket shouldered its satellite into a sky as blazingly bright as the rocket's own flames. In some sense, in some way she'd never understand, she said, a part of her went up with it and never came back down. Every day that part got more distant, leaving less of her here.

It was at that point her phone moaned, whale songs from the sound of it, and she begged to be excused, saying there was someone she had to meet.

And somewhere, if for her a somewhere exists, she's still carrying around the rest of her story, the rest of what she may have wished to tell us, for she never returned to Charleston. Eight days later a skinny bald man in a short-sleeve white dress shirt, tie and dark blue slacks moved into her apartment. Even at his long-ago birth, doctors, nurses and parents with a glance might have surmised they hosted a future accountant.

It was Joe, breaking in on our discussion of similarities and differences between Leigh Brackett's Mars and Bradbury's, who first remarked how many of our fellow residents were no longer with us. Where were they going? he asked. Where had they gone?

We watched two women access their second-floor apartment. One would cautiously mount a step, one hand on the railing, one in her roommate's, then turn to help the other up, back and forth, back and forth.

"Is it possible," Joe said, "that we're just getting older faster and faster, day by day?"

"Maybe we need to find a canal."

"Look in the water."

"See what we really are."

Joe went in and brought back a glass of ice tea for him, a beer for me. Condensation ran down my bottle. The beer inside was warm. Another of those weird conjunctions.

"I'm serious," he said. "About the old part. It's happening faster."

"Well, not much else is, that's for sure." I took a sip or two. "You getting much done?" A for-instance.

"Writing, you mean?"

Yeah.

He pointed to his head. "All up in here for now."

"Isn't everything?" With less and less space up in there every day. Ratty furniture stacked to the ceiling against the wall, boxes everywhere, old musty clothes.

Joe held up his glass, peered through it towards the second floor, which our two women had attained. He'd drunk half the tea. He looked through the clear part first, then the darker. "You think much about what you'll leave behind when you're gone?"

"Once in a while, sure." A mess, mostly.

"History's a funny thing. Legacies. All that."

A dragonfly flitted across the pool and lit on the mass of stringy green. Within moments it was gone. Absorbed.

"One time, this had to be thirty years ago, maybe more, a windfall advance came in for a new book. I'd never seen that much money at once, wound up using the biggest part of it for something I'd only dreamed about before. Hunted down a collection of pulps from the thirties, forties and early fifties and bought it. My hands were shaking as I opened boxes. The magazines, all those *Weird Tales* and *Astounding*s and *Amazing*s and *Planet Stories*, they had this smell about them, every single one. The paper was brownish-yellow, brittle as dry leaves. Pages would break away when you turned them. Crumble into pieces. You could see chew marks where insects— cockroaches, silverfish, lord knows what, mice too, probably—had been at the glue and the pages themselves."

"Our stories."

"And us. Exactly. For a while it took the steam right out of me— never did write that book. But finally I climbed back up on the horse. What else was I gonna do? Making up fancy lies is the only thing I was ever much good at."

Joe held his glass up, late sunlight glinting off it. "Things start to get away from you, don't even have a good exit line. They just dribble away."

"The dwindles," I said.

"Say what?"

"My grandmother's word for it. The dwindles."

"That's what it is, all right. You figure dinner's up soon?"

"'Bout that time."

"Wait in the lobby?"

"Why not?"

When we went in, Bob was there getting ready to start cleaning. His routine was to take care of the lobby while residents were at dinner, then the dining area, and finish up with the rest once most had settled in for the night. A couple dozen flies zipped by us, trying for the door.

"As for lying," Joe said, "we've made up some pretty damn good ones, you and me."

"And have a few more in us."

"Don't we hope."

Joe took my bottle to go put it and his glass in the bin but for a moment didn't turn away. "You ever see Bob eat or drink anything? Anything at all?"

"Not that I can remember."

"He's here six or eight hours every day and he never eats or drinks?"

"Just because we don't see him do it?"

"True. But it bears thinking about."

We joined the line outside the dining area. A handful of older men, some in sandals or slippers, and older women who smelled like they'd been dipped in perfume or face powder gathered with us, maybe half the number that used to be around.

"Does Bob go into people's rooms?"

"I don't have a clue. There's probably some kind of schedule."

The doors opened then. Before we went in, Joe looked one last time across the lobby. Bob was there, back to the wall, patiently waiting. His eyes came up to meet Joe's. For a moment neither moved. Then Bob reached down to turn his bucket so that the block letters faced us directly. As though, Joe later said, he was focusing a camera.

"Ever see him without that bucket?" Joe said the next morning.

"Beg pardon?"

"Bob. I've been awake all night, thinking this through. That's where it comes from, that bucket's the source of his power. The bucket's got holes in it, deep holes. Things get put in there and they go away. Souls. Essence. Life force. Something. Some things. Important things."

I took a deep breath and said it sounded like we'd fallen through into a B movie, B-minus maybe—the kind we liked best. Right, he said, the *good* bad ones. And we both laughed, but the laughs didn't come easy.

From that day we kept watch on our rogue custodian. A stakeout, Joe insisted on calling it. In that case, I told him, we had to have crappy food and bad coffee like they always do in the movies. Absolutely, Joe said and bottles to pee in.

"Maybe it's some kind of hypnotism thing," Joe said that night. We'd sat as close to the door of the dining area as possible, keeping an eye on the lobby where Bob and his bucket passed back and forth, offscreen, on, off. "It's all about persuasion after all, isn't it? Successful lying, effective writing, a good con job. Making people disappear."

"Maybe," I said.

Joe cut into one of the two meatballs atop his mound of mushy spaghetti, then leaned closer for a look at what was in there. "Or human trafficking."

"These people are old, Joe. How much can old folks bring on the market?"

"Depends what they're used for, doesn't it? You see all those trucks go by piled with bags of fertilizer?"

"Shit—even the best shit, champagne-level shit—has to be cheaper."

"Okay. Big Pharma, then, doing secret tests, unholy experiments. Or the government. Someone's government."

A single high-pitched squeal alerted us to Mr. Farrell's nightly seizure. We all sat quietly till it was over, less than a minute as always, then went back to eating.

"Pets for aliens," Joe said. "Think about it. Importing old people from another species as exotic pets. Low maintenance, not the least bit dangerous, don't eat much. Alien kids learn to feed them, clean up after them. Or time travel, from a future where people live long, long lives and stay young and there aren't any old ones left. So they come back and pick up some, as examples, specimens, objects of curiosity. Or for study. Keep them in zoos, in museum dioramas."

With that, of course, he was squarely in Charles Fort territory, which was beginning to feel like where we'd moved.

Our plan took shape over two weeks. Claiming he needed pictures of the lobby, halls and rooms for a friend and prospective tenant, Joe managed to get several good shots of the bucket. We found its double at the fifth hardware shop we went to, and the right shade of red paint (who'd have thought there could be so many) at a Sherwin-Williams. Turned out Joe had an artist friend, Adrian Martinez, a sculptor and metal worker, who had a fine eye for detail and was able to copy the bucket exactly, right down to the last dent, scratch, stain, and imperfection.

Making the swap was the challenge, since Bob never let that

damn bucket out of his sight. Among possible diversions we considered were setting off the fire alarm, faking a heart attack or terrible fall, starting a riot like in old prison movies. Personally I liked the visuals on the last: elderly residents rushing with their walkers toward staff, struggling to raise arms over heads to shake fists in the air. We got kind of sidetracked imagining that.

But it came to happen that the solution was handed to us. At 1:13 of a Thursday afternoon, Mr. Farrell decided to go for an unprecedented walk before his 2-5 P.M. nap and, though this wasn't a part of his decision, there in the hallway, two feet from Bob's bucket, he collapsed, seizing. Bob made no move to pitch in but was sufficiently distracted by the nurse's aide screaming at him to help, that Joe was able to skulk through the doorway behind and exchange buckets.

"The forces of good are with us," Joe said afterwards, then "Let's hope the water level's not too far off."

Bob did, upon turning back, stand for a moment peering into the bucket as the two of us most fervently stood hoping. Then he slid the mop inside and pushed it out of the way of those attending Mr. Farrell.

Years later, I've heard, Joe was still telling the story. It got larger than life in the telling, of course, which is the nature of stories. He'd tell how Bob went on for weeks stalking the halls. How again and again we would come upon him peering into the bucket. How Bob never understood what happened. How his presence, finally even his image, grew dimmer and dimmer. How at the end, the very end, he even attempted to speak. Till one day the bucket stood alone there in the lobby where it remained till, days later, the new custodian emptied it and threw it out.

That day we were sitting out by the pool as Joe ran through what had happened. You could sense the story taking shape as he talked, like a potter rolling clay in his hands, clay that could be anything, become anything.

"Starting to look like a ghost town from some old Western here abouts," Joe said.

The townsfolk had definitely thinned out. "Tumbleweed be rolling down the streets any minute now."

"And they're still going away. The old ones. Maybe it's not just Bob. Maybe there's more at work here."

That's the point at which we got spooked, I think. We moved away not long after. Our world, Joe's and mine, was sinking out of sight like that dragonfly on the pool. It was doing that everywhere, sure—just doing it faster at the Charleton.

We weren't young even then, Joe and me, but it *was* back before wattles hung under our arms when we raised them and hair started growing on our nose and ears and we woke up wondering what part of our body was going to hurt the least today. We always think we can find a way to change things, but things wind up changing us. Funny how everything that's true turns out to be a cliché of some kind. *Winners never quit*, one of those sampler-like hangings in the Charleton said. Winners we aren't, but Joe and I never quit. We went on writing, making up our lies. Like Joe said, what else were we gonna do?

We've stayed in touch, all these years, and except for that kerfuffle over the schoolmarm (it was *not* my idea) we've got along just fine ever since. I've never asked if Joe has any of that green stuff, green like what was in the pool, on him. I looked at mine this morning. It's definitely spread, halfway down my chest now, shaped like the map of some country that's swallowing up others, one by one.

OLD GIFTS

(for Carol Emshwiller)

When she was young, which was a long time ago, my mother was a superhero. They'd show her the maps or building plans or whatever and she'd run over there at close to the speed of sound and save the day. She saved so many days, Dad used to say, they had to add another year onto the calendar.

She and Dad, and my teachers since they were all old too, told me about this. I don't remember any of it because most of it happened before I was born, me and brother Liam. That was when she settled down to take care of us instead of everyone else. We did find her old costume in the back of a closet with birthday and Christmas presents people gave her, still in their boxes. The costume was pink, and shiny like quartz. Moths or something had eaten holes in it.

Twins have the same DNA, right? But Liam got whatever the hero stuff is and I didn't, not a shred of it. He's grown now, both of us are, and he claims he doesn't have anything like that, no stupid damn superpowers, and never did. I'm just like you, he says, just like everyone else. Says he doesn't remember all those nights with the two of us together in our cute little crib that Dad made, me reaching out to grab Liam's leg to keep him from floating up, out, and away. Or how he used to open the window while we lay there across the room, to let the horned owl we considered our pet come in and visit.

Guess we've both floated out and away since. The world's a different place.

When we were seven or eight, not long after we found Mom's old costume, Liam traded his lunch at school for a sketchbook. Within days it was filled with drawings of our room, our house, the neighborhood, all of them recognizable but with things subtly off here and there, details, proportions, perspective. Even then I wondered if he was trying to create a duplicate of our world, or another into which he might escape.

Liam's an artist now. And I'm a stern man, a serious man. Oh yes. Maybe you've read my columns on the economy for *The Standard*. Someone must. And while I've no background whatsoever in economics, I do the housework and stable-cleaning required—read what other journalists write, subscribe to a magazine or two, get books from the library and online. But what it mostly amounts to is interviewing authorities on finance and financial institutions, then doing my best to translate what comes out of their mouths into something ordinary folk might understand. A lot of the time, since what they actually say is pretty much gobbledygook, I just make up what I write.

My partner Jeremy loves to read my columns aloud over breakfast, substituting key words with random scientific or religious terms. "The stock market today genuflected toward the Higg's boson, promising redemption just as Shoofly's Theorem foretold"— as I consider sprinkling Sevin Dust on his croissant or adding Goo Gone to his raspberry jam.

Back to Liam, though. In our rare conversations, we never talk about financial matters. Liam's never so much as balanced a checkbook. In all fairness he doesn't need to. He has agents and accountants and advisors to deal with such. Once when we were kids he showed me a painting by Odilon Redon, a lighter-than-air balloon that was in fact a huge eye floating out over the landscape, passenger basket beneath. He loved, he said, the humor of it, the forced second-take, the visual pun. Even then it seemed to me clearly a match to some self-image within Liam's own mind.

The closer you look at something, the less it looks like what you first thought.

Tonight it was my turn to cook. I'd planned a salad with butter lettuce, pears and blue cheese, omelets. The first of the omelets went into the disposal when I grew distracted by Jeremy's discourse on political icons of the Fifties. The second one came out near perfect. I slid half onto each plate and set them down by the salad bowls on the kitchen counter, five steps from the dining table we spent months finding, just the right one, and never use. By this time, Jeremy'd stopped talking, either run down or off in the blue sprinting after some train of thought he just missed boarding.

Year after year, as we grew older and the world grew ever more entangling, we kept waiting for Mom to spring back into action. Checked the box in the closet repeatedly to see if maybe she'd tried on the costume, listened for lightning-fast footsteps in the backyard, for the sound of her sailing over the chain-link fence, followed news of the latest storms, disasters, bomb scares, gang wars. Truth to tell, I guess we weren't so much waiting as hoping. All around us astonishing things seem to happen, and our lives are so ordinary. We ache for them to be otherwise.

Some of us, anyway. Liam insists that he embraces the world as it is, not some world imagined half into being for its geniality. "Which is why you offer so many variations of it?" I say.

So many of those eye balloons floating out over landscapes.

But now that Liam is dying, all those balloons, all those worlds, are about to float up, out, and away for good, and once again we're together here in this small room, much as we were in our crib as children. If only I could reach out and grab hold of his leg this time.

"I know what this will be like," Liam says. Dying, I suppose he means, but he takes it further. "It will be like flying."

Which is when he tells me.

"That first night, when you left. It felt so alone in the house. You'd gone off to college. Even from down the hall I could feel the emptiness of your room spilling toward me. Within moments I found myself outside, in dark sky lit by a new moon, sky that looked never to end. I was flying, I was weightless. Free. I've flown every night of my life since."

A nurse comes in then to take vitals and adjust the IV drip at bedside. Liam thanks her and, when she's gone, goes on.

"Even the comic books we read together as children sought to teach us to question: for what is gained, what is lost? To do this, to go on flying, I had to be alone, stay alone."

This explains so much. I tell him that I understand. That I'm sorry.

"It was not a sacrifice, Joseph," he says. "Never a sacrifice."

And so we wait there together, wait for one to fly up, out, and away, and for the other's life, any moment now, to come and take him back.

SCHOOLS OF THOUGHT

They looked tired. That was my first impression, and I'm a man who leans hard on first impressions—before all the over-thinking kicks in. Otherwise, they looked like a thousand others outside on the streets. Decent clothes that almost fit, shoes in good order, not dressed for church or court but showing respect for themselves and the social order.

Amy Lou, arraigned in purple and green today, ushered them in. They settled into the two chairs, damnably uncomfortable, indecently expensive, across from my desk.

"How can I help you folks?" I asked.

Mr. Lucas looked at Mrs. Lucas, who I think (so small a motion it was hard to be sure) nodded.

"We want him fixed," Mr. Lucas said.

"I'm sorry?"

"The boy. We want him fixed."

Mrs. Lucas nodded again, possibly for me, possibly in approval of her husband, but definitely a nod this time. "We want him fixed," she said.

Unaccountably my thoughts went not towards repair, as by every right they should have done, but to neutering. I looked down. Amy Lou's intake sheet told me the couple's son was nine years old.

"He misbehaves," Mr. Lucas said.

"Won't do as we say."

"Ignores what he ought to be doing."

"Does what he wants."

"Well, yes, at that age . . ." Words dropped like smooth-worn coins into my mind. Maturation. Individuation. Words that so handily take the place of thought. So I thought instead about their age, at the high end of the scale, and their reaction to the boy's quite ordinary behavior. "Your first-born?" I asked.

Both nodded.

"We had some . . . difficulty," Mr. Lucas said. "Conceiving."

Mrs. Lucas declined to contribute to that. She sat with feet flat on the floor, hands in repose on her lap, her husband much the same save that occasionally as he spoke one or the other hand broke free and began floating slowly up before he willed it back into place.

I asked after and received specific examples of the boy's presumed transgressions, none of which seemed at all out of the ordinary, though in what Mr. Lucas had further to say, I caught glimpses of the same willfulness that had sent his hands back where they should be.

Perhaps, I said, it would be best if I might speak to the boy alone?

They exchanged glances and, while questioning the need for same, at last agreed. Amy Lou came when I beckoned on the intercom, ushered the parents out to the waiting room, brought young Santos in. Christian name borrowed from his mother's family name, Amy Lou's intake sheet noted.

Santos was small for his age, short yet squarely built. Had he been a sentence, you might call him succinct. A lot of information in there. One of those for whom it could go either way. He'd stay pretty much like he was, reach adulthood short and stout, or at age twelve, fourteen, he'd come onto a sudden burst of growth, and extra flesh would turn to height.

He came in smiling and looking very nine years old. *Convincingly* nine years old, I thought at the time, having the sense that yes, he was there, but he was simultaneously somewhere else—perhaps always was. Some of us, however engrossed in momentary events of our lives, however intense those experiences, at the same time we're standing apart watching. I remember my mother telling me she figured we go through our lives as though rehearsing for a play that never opens.

I asked if he understood why he was here today and received as response only a brief direct glance before his attention returned to the wall behind me. Had his parents discussed their coming here with him? I asked.

"How long did it take to get those?" He pointed to the frames. Diplomas, MD, psychiatric training, state license.

"Four years of college, the same of medical school. Internship, residency. So, another four, five years for the rest." Longer than he'd been alive.

"You're married?"

"I have been. Would you like something to drink? A soda?"

"No thank you." Syllables run together to a single word. Automatic. Then: "Children?"

"None surviving." Here, I unpacked my good doctor smile. "Am I being vetted? I do have further documentation. Credit reports, professional organizations, that sort of thing. I could provide references." Thus far Santos seemed quite the serious young man. Mother and I rightfully shared a profound mistrust of the humorless.

He didn't laugh, but he got it. "And your parents? They're alive?"

"One is, yes."

I handed across the framed photo of the two of us taken in her room at Crestview, jonquils in a blue vase on the bedside table. He studied it a moment before returning it.

"Do you live with her?"

A child's view of life, questions an adult might ask.

"I did."

He sat quietly, thinking things over, maybe dropping in for a visit to that other place where he lived, before saying, "They were real, too? Your parents?"

Hardly a surprise; I'd picked up on the signs. I waited for the shape gathering in the room with us to take form.

"I've thought about this a lot," he said, "and what I came up with is, the others—what? ninety, ninety-five percent of those walking this earth?—they're echoes, poor copies. Or they're like overtones, harmonics. After-sounds of the originals, of the real ones, us. Which means either they're our brood and we care for them, or that they don't matter at all. Two schools of thought."

We got right down to it then. I gave him the talk on getting by in a family and fitting into the larger society. Living alongside. Stay close to the ground, ease around corners, don't blink, private self, public self. He was quiet and, when I was done, nodded.

The playbook I read to Mr. and Mrs. Lucas was quite a different one, but they did listen, and I believe that, for the time at any rate (all I was jockeying for), it allayed their fears. Afterwards, Amy

690 • JAMES SALLIS

Lou escorted them out. It's gone a beautiful day out there, she told them, simply beautiful. In her bright, rich colors she herself rather resembled beautiful weather.

I jotted down a few notes before picking up the phone. It had been a long time since I'd made that call.

SUBTRACTION

"Once question marks demand to appear,
they don't know where to stop."
—Jacques Derrida

So it turned out that the secretary, assistant, and confidant I'd had for almost seven years, good Butler, had been spying on me—from day one, I had to suppose, though to what end I am hard-pressed to imagine. And as if that weren't by itself enough kink in the knot of circumstance, Sergeant Sears, my occasional cohort on the human police force, had gone missing.

Which was how Butler came to be suspended from the ceiling of the kitchen in a brutally painful if at the same time rather elegant contrivance of straps.

"How is it up there?" I asked.

Butler shifted in the straps, truffling for some slight degree less pain. "Oh, I've seen worse," he said.

On his home world, Butler's kind slept tucked securely into underground burrows, cautious of being in the open and exposed—becoming a subtext, as it were, unseen, implied. Here, they made do with closets, cupboards, the odd cellar. Sad history, but all history in the pot boils down to little more than tragedy and disaster of every size, with clots of small triumphs.

Half a century ago Butler's race lost its world to another and became wanderers, immigrants wherever they went. At length they found their way to Earth, where most of us are immigrants, hermit crabs who've taken over the home of those departed. Butler chose his name for the sound, reminding him as it did of tongue clicks in his native language.

Certainly Butler, hanging there, was uncomfortable at being so exposed. Just as certainly, he was not about to let on to that.

"Has it confessed yet?" Millicent asked, coming into the kitchen for coffee.

"We'll get there. How did you sleep, Dear?" Millicent and I had reached the point in our forty-year union when morning exchanges were more akin to health updates than to interpersonal communication. Tooth still troubling you? How's your back today? Stomach settle down? That sort of thing.

"Passably," she said. The fibers of her once-yellow sleeping gown, a favorite for years, had relaxed to such length that it grew tails, upon which, turning, she almost tripped. "I'll leave you to it, then."

Indeed. This was, after all, an investigation. There was work to be done. The interviewee is a blank text waiting to be given meaning, a hollow vessel, a drum ready to be filled with sound.

We were by then in the second day of interrogation. There's a rhythm to doing this well, that is to say, productively. Redundancy becomes coin of the realm. Probes for truth, for ultimate meaning, must come in waves, in layers.

"I am only asking you to take responsibility," I said. "To do the right thing." Time-honored cliches that serve to put the interrogation on familiar ground. These are a music the interviewee knows, comforting in their way.

"It is not responsibility you solicit, but guilt," Butler said. Then, after a pause: "Are we not all guilty?"

Fair enough, one cliche in exchange for another. Dostoevsky. As have we all, Butler's kind has made a study of human arts and, with no gift or heritage of small talk, often converse in a slurry of literary quotations, aphorisms, platitudes, banalities and truisms, high art mixed with low, the grand and demotic in a jumble.

"I am a man, Jupiter," Butler said.

Sartre this time. Did its kind have the capacity for humor, for irony and satire? I'd never before wondered that, all these seven years. A man? Butler, hanging there, resembled nothing so much as overripe fruit.

"If suddenly you find you don't know where you are," Butler added, "you may simply be looking out the wrong window."

That one, I could not identify. The words rose into the air, hung there for a moment like Butler, and dispersed, at which point I began anew: Why are you here? What is the exact nature of the conspiracy? Who is your contact? What is your mission?

Again I received, in response, flurries of well-turned sentences.

Pretty little things, most of them, but of no practical value, use, or intelligence, as though someone might hand you a beautifully polished river stone and say, Here, eat this. Distractions. Subterfuge. Sleight of hand.

Iridescent blue drool dripped from the side of Butler's mouth and pattered onto the floor. The eye on that side appeared to be shriveling. Butler had informed me that his metabolism required generous inputs of fluid, that he would not long survive without same. Utterly new information, and interesting, but of little bearing on the matters at hand. Generosity is not our way.

Standing quietly, letting the silence hover and swell as I reflected on recent events, I began more clearly to sense unsuspected, all but intangible, connections, delicate traceries of lien and influence. Were these shadowy forms actual? In the world we've been given, suspicion can never be virtual. Suspicion is what we breath—suspicion, deceit, rancor, eternal peril. With time these become our guides, our maps, our lighthouses.

"Your kind . . ." Butler shifted again in the straps. I had not spoken my premonitions aloud. "You refuse to embrace chance, though you see it swirling about you everywhere."

"It's hardly by chance that you are where you are."

"You feel you must have a system that explains it all." Butler looked down at a housefly crouched on the counter by the spilled saliva. Drinking, one supposed. Its wings, like the spittle, iridescent. "We recognize that need," Butler said, "but it is not within us."

Butler tried then, I think, through barriers of pain and decay, to set his eyes on me.

"And I, dear sir," he said, "am not a puzzle to be solved."

Decidedly the interrogation was not going as it should. Cut-rate philosophy and quotations suitable for samplers. Time to force it back on track.

"Who do you work for?"

"Sir—I am your assistant and confidant."

"Why are you spying on me?"

"It is my purview to watch. To observe and serve."

"And Sergeant Sears?"

"Sir?"

"Why has he been taken?"

"Of this I can say nothing."

He had, of course, in truth said nothing of anything. Borrowed words. White noise. Blather. Distraction.

"If I may, sir?"

"Yes?"

"I must tell you: I am not well."

"A pity."

I left Butler there to ponder the consequences of his actions, whatever those actions in actuality were, and went about my business. From time to time during a long and demanding day at work I lifted my eyes to the window or blank wall with thoughts that perhaps I was wrong, perhaps . . . But no. That would not do.

By morning the smell in there was quite bad. Pools of other substances had joined those of spittle on the counter. The housefly was no longer alone.

"Good morning, sir," Butler said. Then: "The door opened and he entered, a dignified procession of one."

"Beg pardon?"

"Wodehouse, more or less. A man who understood butlers—and me." Butler made no further effort to shift within the straps. "I trust you slept well. Shall I lay out your . . ." His eyes seemed unable to function at all now. Each of them searched for me about the room, swept past me again and again. "But no. I cannot do that, can I? There is not much left of me, sir."

Butler said no more. For a brief while, though his mouth did not move, low, all but inaudible sounds continued to issue forth. Then even those ceased, as everything finally must do.

Millicent peeked in at the doorway, nostrils aflare, and made a face. I promised to get the mess cleaned up straightaway.

THE WAY OF HIS KIND

When you were born, you didn't cry. The nurses of the tiny hospital in the town where we then lived grew concerned. They feared you'd been damaged in the birthing, that you were deaf, or worse. Whenever anyone came close, you'd meet their eyes and hold them till the faces above went away. Even then there seemed within your own eyes a deep intelligence, as though you were merely observing, piecing together these bits of the world offered you before committing to stay.

Neither of us could remember quite why, but Geoff had taken work as lead reporter and columnist at a small newspaper in rural Tennessee. *Modest* was the descriptor he insisted upon. We're here, he said as we first drove into town—nowhere. Gone soon enough with acclimation were the ties and sport coats and pressed slacks. Gone as well, though this took longer, were Geoff's relentless curiosity and easy, blameless humor.

The town was run, owned you may as well say, by three families. Real estate, car sales, insurance, shops along Main Street—one way or another it all came back to those families. The local paper's publisher belonged to one of the families.

Thus were you radicalized, your father claimed, almost from birth. Not that, by your soft-spoken manner and civil grace, anyone would later be inclined to think such. You were in fact like some idealized image of a gentleman, speaking softly, rising when elders or women entered a room, ever deferential, offering apologies for imagined infractions, employing honorifics, sir and ma'am, in the most casual of speech.

Water, your father said, takes the shape of whatever vessel it's put in. But finally water goes where it will go, does what it will do.

Just after the new people came, palettes of lumber at Howe's Hardware broke into blossom overnight, sweet little flowers smelling of jasmine and lilac. Soon we began to notice that the water in our river, scummed with algae and mud-befuddled for as long as anyone could remember, was growing clear. Old Doc Jefferson pointed out the lack of new births at the hospital.

Everything was changing. Compared to what we saw around us, photos taken but months earlier looked to be of some other place, or from times long ago. You were gone by then, off to a far city that might as well have been Oz or Xanadu. At night, you wrote, you sat listening to frogs sing as you'd never before heard. Natives knew to close their eyes as morning arrived—it came in a flash.

I was never to read those messages, I was dead, but you went on sending them, narratives of a world at once so much like the one you and I had left and so distinct.

Back in that world, the dust storms, the ones from which (though indirectly) I died, also went on, scant months before new growth began in earnest. An errant sampling of fungus had entered my lungs, accruing substance to itself, colonizing ever more of right, then left, lung.

They were a strange lot, those new people, taller than us, thin, with skin the color of almond shells. Watching them go about their business, as they washed cars, played with children, tidied up lawns, all seemed at first as it should be, yet somehow brought to mind the split-second delay of distant phone calls, when the signal almost cuts out but doesn't quite.

As a people, we are not changed, you wrote in one of your messages, we are edited. Toward some better version, you asked—or merely a simpler one?

When you came home from school one day with Annais alongside, we were so pleased, your father and I. You'd shown little interest before in making friends. I remember that I assembled sandwiches for the two of you, and poured lemonade, and left you together in your room. You told me afterwards that Annais loved the sandwich but would not touch the lemonade, and that he showed you a secret thing, a book he carried with him always, even the letters of which, the characters, you did not recognize. Inside, it looked like that, you said, but real, real small—pointing to needlepoint my mother had made as a young girl.

Annais soon became a regular. His parents both worked, you explained, and were happy to have him come home with you after school rather than be at the house alone. One afternoon his mother sent along a full dish of the dessert he said was a favorite back where they came from, a custard-like, shimmering concoction jacketed in something very much like filo pastry, and with a lingering taste like nothing I'd never before encountered. I asked how it was made, and from what ingredients, but he didn't know. He only knew his mother made the best ever, and that it took her a long time.

One morning following a warm rain, our neighbor stepped out her front door and looked down to see mushrooms, already two inches high, growing from the open spaces, the interstices, of her rubber doormat. The hollow left behind by the recycling barrel taken to the curb the night before for pickup, brimmed with rainwater. Silvery flashes of living things darted about within the water.

This was the same morning, or close thereabouts, that you came to tell me you'd spent a poor night. Awake within minutes of falling asleep, you became aware of shushed sounds in the room—voices—originating with two immense cockroaches who appeared to be engaged in some grand disputation. You could see them perched together on the windowsill in moonlight, one or another leg rising from time to time for emphasis, bodies shifting in time with the dialog. This went on hour after hour as you dipped in and out of a troubled sleep, until near dawn, the disputation (you surmise) resolved, the two voices fell away and the room grew quiet.

The first of the disappearances, reported by teachers, brought concern. Two new children had failed to turn up in class four days on. When Sheriff Lawson went round to their homes the parents told him there was no cause for alarm, the children were away on visits. Subsequent disappearances met with much the same response until, as happens when the unusual persists unabated, the disappearances became commonplace, spun into the pattern of our days. It's difficult to understand, even to believe, that such divergences could come to be so commonly accepted. Yet it's human adaptability, one must suppose, that let us hold on so long. One afternoon I came to ask if you and Annais would like a snack. The two of you were seated on the bed, heads close, speaking intently. Hesitant to interrupt, I watched your profiles against the window. You had just asked Annais about the disappearances. He was saying that you must not worry, that all was going as it should, this was the way of his kind.

We didn't understand, of course. We never did, never do, for all our inquiries, all our grand theories and systems of thought. Events of the world take place *over there* as we look *here*, *here* as we look *over there*. Understanding is a water we can hold only so long in our hands. One by one the new children were no longer with us, then you weren't either. And there we sat for a while longer, those of us left, in this newly green, vibrant, vital new world, wondering why.

WELL MET

We don't usually get together once meetings are over, part and parcel of that anonymous thing. We stand there and drink a bunch of coffee before, take our seats and drink more coffee, work the meeting, then we're done and back to our lives, such as they may be. So I was surprised when Clayton asked if I'd care to grab a beer with him.

Clayton was this lanky dude who'd shown up maybe six weeks before. If he spoke six words the whole time I'd be amazed, but he was there every week. I'd noticed how he always came to the door—the meeting's a small one, naturally, held in the back room of a print shop, dead secret—and kind of leaned in to look before stepping through. Brown slacks and blue dress shirt kind of guy.

Down the street a piece we found a bar with open-air seating. Outside, you can see what's coming, don't have to worry about finding the right table, locating back exits and the like. There was a couple in their twenties or so at one table out there, singles, both of them men, at two others. It was cold enough that I could see everyone's breath, but Clayton and I had on heavy jackets. What the jackets didn't keep warm, alcohol would.

Our waitress, Kathy B on the nametag, had seen some shit in her time, you could tell it by her eyes and the worn-out smile. Forties, I'm guessing, knockoff orthopedic shoes, tattoo on one calf, straight skirt, one of those pullovers with sleeves that go over the hands with holes for thumbs.

"I need some advice," Clayton said once we had our drinks.

"Didn't you just get about an hour of it?"

"Lot of that comes down to shop talk."

He had a point. Meetings do tend to settle toward how I did this and that. And some of the guys and gal (yeah, just one of those) have been in the program long enough that they have regular routines worked out. They'll pause, wave arms around, do the voices, look to the sky in appeal, down to the ground in acceptance, pause again, duck their heads. This whole dramatic schmear.

We both took a pull on our drinks, then Clayton said, "I think I'm in love."

He's looking down at his brandy and soda like he's expecting something to float up out of it. Me, I'm thinking about where I want to be, which is, as of this moment, Not Here.

"You just don't think . . ."

I waited, then said, "We're not the sentimental sort."

Clayton took another drink. Maybe the answer, what he'd been waiting for, had come to the top. Maybe it hadn't so what the hell. "Different world from most others, ours. For damn sure."

"Why we're there."

"At the meetings, you mean."

"And here, this place in our lives."

"Sitting at a table outside a smelly bar at the ass end of a city whose front end ain't much better."

"With all these fine pigeons for company."

"Yeah . . . Like I said, you don't think about it, not even as a possibility, then one day . . ." I pondered, in the pause, Clayton's seeming addiction to ellipsis. "She's a waitress in this diner I go to about every night. I know, it's like in some crappy movie. Ex-con and hometown girl meet, go out on five or six doomed dates, there's this big ending scene, and they live happily ever after. But it ain't like that."

"It rarely is."

"You know what I'm saying. No way I can let myself get close to someone."

"I do. But maybe the past doesn't always have a stranglehold. Maybe it's not always there behind, ready to push us off the edge."

Truth is, I'd recently met someone myself, and was wondering.

Two young women came down the sidewalk and stood nearby debating whether to go inside or sit out. Both had beautiful eyes. Volleys passed back and forth. Inside won.

"Another?" Clayton asked and, when I said why not, went in to order. Back in moments, he set mine on the table. "You ever see that—the maybe?"

I hadn't, but I'd seen, again and again in my thirty years of working the program, what happened if you let go of believing the maybe. I told him that, and he nodded.

There'd been little traffic on Maple the whole time we were there. Now, from a stalled car at the intersection, traffic was steadily building back toward us.

"On the other hand," I said, "*love*. Not a lot of muscle on the word. Kinda rolls around in the box."

"Like I said, I wasn't looking, didn't say a word to her for weeks. Then one night she brought my coffee and asked me how I was doing."

I sensed a name waiting just around the corner and stopped him. "Best to stay with generalities. No specifics, right? Just like at meetings."

"Right. Sorry. Anyway, I tried everything I could to put her out of my mind. None of it worked."

"That had to feel familiar."

"That I couldn't stop thinking about her?" He thought it over for a moment. "But a lot didn't feel that way at all, like it used to. I don't know how it feels."

"I understand."

"Do you?"

"I've been working the program a long time. Small bumps warn you about big ones ahead. Go slow, work on today, keep coming back."

"Yeah. Yeah, I guess that's what it all comes down to."

"I do have one question," I said. "Are you confused about your feelings, or afraid?"

"Afraid?"

"Of going back to your old ways."

"To what I was, you mean."

"It'll always be there."

"I guess it will." He glanced at the window. Traffic was socked in. Tempers were going over the side, into the deep. "I have a last question for you too. Do you ever see their faces?"

"Of our departed." Our prey. "No."

"Doesn't happen often, but sometimes . . ." We'd made our way back to ellipsis.

We finished our drinks without speaking again, then said good night before stepping out into that night to find whatever good it might hold for each of us. I'd lied to him, I did still see their faces. But they were fading, as they always do, time after time.

BLOOD DRAW

The phlebotomist tells me I have good veins, and I wonder if this is going to be what my day's like. Up at seven, no breakfast or coffee, off by light rail to get blood drawn and see just how unhealthy I might be. Now I'm told I have good veins. Maybe this presages a change in my fortunes. Maybe Jo will have a fine breakfast waiting when I get home.

The phlebotomist, Samuel, has elaborate tattoos peeking out between the cuff of his lab coat and his gloves, more at the collar of his shirt, but I can't make out images, only beautifully executed patches of blue and gray. When I ask about them he tells me he's the illustrated version of himself.

Meanwhile, while I'm sitting there waiting for blood to percolate into five or six syringes the size of grease guns, I'm wondering if maybe I should stop reading stuff online because when I do, I worry. Like, I just read about this new process they came up with. They have this liquid they can inject, then use something like a 3D printer to make new joints and other body parts right there inside you. And what I'm thinking is not a big *Hooray to science!* but about what else they might cook up in there once they've surreptitiously injected the fluid—during a blood draw, for instance.

The thing is, ideas can be like flies once they get in, buzzing around in your head, banging at one side then the other. I remember some old movie I saw about the future's great technology, big battle-cruiser spaceships, laser weapons, that kind of stuff, all defeated by swarms of tiny cybernetic bees.

Or: "Whatever these small things are that swim in and out of us, they take small bites each time." Something else I read, and stole, I guess. I'm a magpie. Anything shiny, out in the open, half hidden, in another bird's nest, it's mine. I told that to Jo one time, the part about those small things, not about my being a magpie, and all I got back from it was one of those looks that you know you should shut up now.

But you see what I mean about ideas. Damned things get in your head, it's hard to get them back out. They just buzz and bounce and bang around in there.

The phlebotomist shares with me, that's the word he uses, *share*, that he's having a great day, he says just that, *a great day*, since he found out this morning his wife is pregnant. I tell him I'm happy for him, bringing a new life into the world is a wondrous thing, I wish them the best, and assorted other assurances, wondering all the while how much of what I'm saying, if any of it, I believe.

Definitely glad that Samuel distracted me from thoughts of tiny engines forming in my bloodstream or elsewhere and small things with sharp teeth coming and going. But as I turn to watch his happy sharing face I catch sight out the window of a plane that looks like it's trying to land on far Mount Griswold and can't get a foothold. I keep watching, waiting for the boom, for visible smoke behind. Nothing comes of it.

So, Samuel says, we're talking about names and such. You know, girl, boy. Names are important, I tell him, as he holds up labelled tubes of blood to ask that I verify name and date of birth. You're good to go, he says.

Outside, instinctively, I look again towards Mount Griswold. Easy to understand how, for people living on flatlands or in the shelter of forests, mountains could be taken as a force, supernatural, places of mystery, even as deities of a sort.

The transit police car parked by the light rail platform gives me pause but it turns out they're just helping an elderly couple punch in for tickets and climb aboard. Further along, though, an announcement comes over the speaker: there's been a major traffic incident at an intersection just ahead, emergency vehicles are in the area, and service will have to be suspended. The train pulls up at the next station, we're marched off the cars and one block over where buses wait to take us on.

It reminds me how, back when I was in college, we'd get flushed out of the library every day, often more than once, due to bomb threats. So I'm thinking about that, about how we get in the habit of snuffling for patterns or connections everywhere, about how we say things we neither intend nor believe just to hold off silence, as

I dismount the bus and walk by Raimondo's Used Tires, Granny's Attic, and Second Time Around. Have we used up everything new?

I stop at Sunnyside Park to grab a coffee at the food cart, ease across the walkway. Say hello to a woman sitting on the bench there and get a nod back. Ask her would she mind and this time get a headshake, so I sit at the other end. She goes back to her handheld phone, computer, whatever it is.

I sit there watching kids play. There's this soft, rubberized material under the slides and jungle gym and swings, in segments, that makes it look kind of like a giant turtle shell. Watching kids doesn't do much for me, but shutting the house lights down, just for a few minutes, helps. Turn loose those ideas banging around in your head, you know? Raccoons sorting through garbage over by the trees interest me more, I have to wonder what *they're* thinking as they go about their work.

The storm comes in a breath: a single hard sound like a limb cracking away from its tree, then buckets of rain and sweeping wind. The food cart guy rolls to the shelter of a giant oak. People dash outward in every direction. The raccoons go on about what they're doing.

The storm abates as furtively as it began. I squish home to see that, undeterred by the rain, doubtless fed by the wind, fire has all but claimed one of the budget condos across from our building. Firetrucks and firemen swarm, their efforts of little avail in subduing this fire started (per which onlooker one listens to) by protestors, terrorists, children at play, or some husband, wife, other, gone astray. The futility of what the firemen are doing shows on their faces when close, resoluteness in the cant of their bodies at a distance.

I go in and up and find Jo gone. Drawers stand open, plundered. Where his suits hung there's only air. No shoes on the floor by the door or bed. It comes to me I've learned things today. Having good veins is of no matter whatsoever, it will make no difference. Devastations—traffic accidents, emergency vehicles, crippling loss, storms, consuming fires—wait always in the wings. They can befall at any time. Nothing stays. Nothing is safe. Have I always known that?

SILVER

He'd just taken the ramp onto Highway 51 and begun picking up speed when the black and white came up behind him and he had his usual momentary stab of fear. Then the cruiser's lights started flashing as it swung around to race ahead. A mile or so down, he saw it at roadside, flashers still going, its lean officer approaching a vintage Chevy with historic plates.

After two weeks of bitter cold weather—a plunge into the sixties, with locals trying to remember where they'd stashed their sweaters—this was the third day of renewed warmth and sunlight. The mountains stood clear and vivid in the distance, even through a windshield dappled with dust and pawprints from the neighbor's cats. He needed to do something about that. The windshield, not the cats. He admired cats. They kept their own counsel, took the world as it was.

The weather was so good, his spirits so in need of lightening, that earlier, thinking *On such a fine day I refuse to hurry*, he'd taken to local streets after leaving the house, his usual route back when he'd worked fulltime. Great days, those. A lifetime ago, a different world. Now when he worked at all he worked as consultant, a title that, because it meant nothing, meant whatever you wanted it to mean.

Just as he had back then, he wondered how it was that a town this size could attract and sustain so many drugstores. And how did there come to be better than a dozen shops selling used tires along one half-mile strip? How did they all survive?

He turned onto Howard, mountains to his left, then up Third to the interstate. Drove along listening to local radio hosts babble incoherently about football games, Thanksgiving turkeys, do-gooders, and soccer moms—white noise to him, soothing—while reading electronic signs. Whoever manned these things was having a busy day.

> GOBBLE GOBBLE, GO EASY ON THE THROTTLE
> MASH POTATOES NOT YOUR HEAD, BUCKLE UP
> DUMB DRIVERS AND SMARTPHONES DON'T MIX
> DRIVE HAMMERED GET NAILED

Not long after that one, just as he passed beneath, the sign changed.

> SILVER ALERT
> GRAY 2013 HONDA
> LICENSE BHM8422

Surely she couldn't have. The more he thought about it, the more uneasy he became. *His* car. *His* license plate. But a silver alert? WTF, as kids nowadays said.

He's forty-three years old.

Sometimes he just has to get out. Get away. Before leaving, he always does his best to make sure that Belle is settled in. Has her meds, a recent bathroom visit, water handily at bedside. Phone there by the bed too, just in case. Now he imagines her coming around, climbing from bed, wandering out into the hallway looking. Does she even know who she's looking for? No way she could have called in that alert.

"Everything, all the information, is still in there, it's just the connections that are failing. Sparks can't jump the gap," her latest doctor says, which gives precious little by way of comfort or helpful information. Was Doctor Lewis a mechanic in a former life?

It took him quite a while to realize, then admit, that something was seriously amiss. Occasionally things would go a bit off—lopsided responses, gaps, non sequiturs—but soon enough they'd right themselves. One morning he came into the kitchen and found her by the window scooping at sunlight then holding her hand to her mouth as though drinking from it. Later she kept going back and forth to the coffee maker topping off both his cup and hers each time a drink was taken. Another morning the basket of the coffee maker got filled with dry kidney beans.

She took to drawing lukewarm baths where she'd lie for hours, until finally he'd go in to tell her it was time to get out. One day she piled every shoe from her closet into the utility room sink, filled it with water, and poured in bleach. She began asking repeatedly about a dog they'd never had. Was she still at the vet's? Had he remembered to walk her?

As fault lines widened, they'd found their way to a specialist in early-onset dementia who, while admitting there was little treatment to be had, nevertheless administered a bevy of tests: making proper change on a restaurant bill, retelling a narrative just spoken, recounting yesterday's activities in simple declarative sentences. In lieu of treatment they were given a new vocabulary for their lives. Altered lifestyle, accommodation, adjustment, expectation, routine. When reality changes, words get cut to fit, eyes directed towards a future of which, week by week, month by month, there's ever a wee bit less.

He had tried everything he could think of to create safe harbors. Sometimes watching movies they'd seen before calmed her. Other days the same movies might make her jittery, jumpy, aggressive, sad. You never knew. It was always a toss-up. A chance you took.

That morning, as usual, he'd risen to have time to himself before waking Belle. He got up early just for this, and for what the early morning held, light coming into its own beyond the windows, quiet save from passing cars or the calls of birds, wind in the trees, stillness. So he set up the coffee maker, put bread in the toaster oven, and took to one of the high chairs by the counter to shuffle through news online. The *Washington Post, New York* and *L.A. Times*, a website or two.

The toast burned and the coffee went neglected as he read about a rattlesnake killed in the recent California wildfire. Flesh had burned away from the snake's body and skull. Its body was found coiled, its jaws fully open. The final defiant act of the snake's life had been to strike at the flames that were consuming it

He must have read the story four times before Belle came into the kitchen as angry as he'd ever seen her, irate and unable to hold still or stop talking for even a moment, demanding to know why he let her sleep in when he knew how much she had to get done today. Why hadn't he, didn't he understand, how could he have. She grabbed up the burned toast from the sink and ate it, then suddenly stepped close to him. Instinctively he braced to be hit. When she was like this, that happened sometimes.

The black and white fell in behind him near the string of outlet stores, tracked him past the busy mall exit, and pulled close, flashers going, just after. The officer was a woman, late twenties maybe, military service not far in her past judging from posture and, as she came alongside, from general appearance.

Not the expected request for license and registration, though. Instead she told him good morning and identified herself as Officer Stanton. He had the documents ready anyway, and passed them through the window. "I know, I know. The alert."

She'd taken the papers, but her eyes came back to his face. "I'm sorry?"

"The silver alert. I saw it back at the Benville exit."

She looked around again inside the car, at the floorboards, passenger side, back seat. "Are you okay, sir?"

"Fine. Just out for a drive."

"You mentioned a silver alert."

"Gray 2013 Honda."

"Like this one, you mean."

He nodded as she looked back at the papers.

"Please stay in your car, sir. I'll be back in a moment."

She went to the black and white to call it in. Vehicles ripped by them, heads turned idly to wonder what was happening here. In the mirror he watched the officer talk on her radio, listen, talk again. Watched her walk back alongside.

"There *was* an alert, sir, just as you said. Same model Honda, but the plate number's not even close. You must have misread it?"

"Well, good then."

"Yes, sir." She handed the papers back through the window. "I pulled you over because your brake light isn't functioning properly. You should see to that as soon as possible."

"I will. Thank you."

"You're welcome. Take care, sir."

She returned to the black and white, shut off the flashers, and after a moment pulled onto the highway. He started the car, waited for an opening, jumped in. She took the next exit. He decided to drive on till he hit the loop, circle the city before heading home, adjusting his speed to the vehicles around him, just above the posted speed limit. Disembodied radio voices spoke of decision makers, new regulations, a meeting of minds.

It was raining the day he was born, Mother said. Leaves had fallen from the trees and were a sodden mess. A nurse claimed to have caught him when he poked his head out as though to see what he was getting himself into. The nurse's name was Dee Rodriguez and what she said, what everyone said she said, became part and parcel of family lore.

He'd looked it up. The temperature the day he was born was seventy-eight degrees. The icon of a smiling sun accompanied this report.

Inside, the celebration continued. Family. Friends. Their daughter's anniversary, four years ago now. Belle had begun losing ground, week by week, but up to then he didn't think anyone else had quite got on to it. He'd worked hard to make that true.

They were on the bench out back, away from the others. Sandra turned toward him.

"What are you thinking?" she asked, as he wondered how much he should read into the question. Few things his sister said were to be taken at face value.

"That water goes where it wants to, does what it wants to."

"Come again?"

He met her eyes. "Sorry. A building we're working on, downtown. My design. Everything looked good on Friday, the builders were actually ahead of schedule. Monday the crew comes in, after all that rain, and one outside wall's looking wonky."

"So, what do you do?"

"You think about it a long time. Then you either shore up what's there, or tear it out and rebuild."

"Today's Wednesday. Does Monday to Wednesday qualify as a long time?"

"You never know how deep the damage is." He stood. "Enough about work. We should go back in."

"Good. There's happiness in there, free for the taking. Paul?"

"Yes?"

"Let me know what you decide?"

The house was quiet when he got back. Coming home, he never knew what to expect. Better, worse. The same. He heard two low voices as he opened the front door. She was in the living room, watching a man and woman of indeterminate age talk about a revolutionary cleaning product on TV. She had the sound dialed down to a whisper. He sat beside her, asked if she'd eaten, if she was okay. She nodded. He's wondering why she's down here rather than in her own room.

"The fish got out of the bowl," she said. No preamble, nothing more offered. After a moment he asked how. Watched her eyes go from face to face as the speakers changed.

He'd bought Diego for her three months ago. Dogs, cats, birds were out of the question. But he thought a pet might help, and that a fish could be the safest bet. Had no intention of naming it, but when it turned out to be personable, he did. He'd never imagined a fish would be so responsive. Diego would swim to the surface whenever you leaned close to look in. Bump your finger if you put it in the water.

"When did this happen, Belle?"

"This morning? I couldn't stay there with it."

He went upstairs. Diego lay on the floor, pale and still, by the bedside table. He picked up the body and wrapped it in layer upon layer of tissues, unsure what to do next, how he should dispose of it, sad out of all proportion to this small death. He put the fish, wrappings and all, in his pocket.

"Have a nice drive?" she asked when he came back down.

He nodded and sat beside her. She'd changed the TV to some old movie he could make no sense of, a lot of grainy gray people speaking earnestly to one another across rooms. Their whispers didn't come through. The people were little more than gestures, contorted mouths, facial expressions. After a while he got up and said he'd go make them a late lunch.

He put together a simple pasta, farfalle with olive oil and garlic, a cucumber and tomato salad. They ate, then went back into the living room to watch *Ladyhawke*. Not long after they first met she told him *Ladyhawke* was her favorite movie. He had no idea how many times they'd watched it since, though recently he hadn't felt like chancing it. Too many memories, he feared. Maybe too much sadness at things lost.

Belle watched the entire movie without speaking and, after, went willingly up to bed. He told her to rest a while, they'd watch another movie later on. *Ghost*, maybe. Another favorite. When he went to change into jeans before cleaning up the kitchen, he found Diego's body, swaddled in its layers of tissue, in the pocket of his pants.

OUT AND ABOUT

They are, I am told by experts, auditory hallucinations. I do not actually hear things slithering toward me as I walk the streets at night, or claws clattering down alleyways, or the sound of another breathing on the pillow beside my head.

When I ask Dr. Rottendale why, then, am I hearing this, there's a skittering, as of insects in the walls, through which he declaims that he can't say. Not, I note, that he doesn't know.

We will take this up later, he says.

Outside, the wind hums in perfect fourths. A poplar tree by the office door clears its throat—to join in? Stray leaves ring bell-like as they brush past my ankles. Two blocks up, the elevated adds a solid, steady bass.

That was the night I saw the killing, the one that brought a deafening chorus of voices from trash bins, broken bottles, abandoned containers, bricks, and busted doorways in the long alley where it happened.

A man in a suit. Another man in a suit. One suit dark gray, one blue. Not people I'd ordinarily pay great attention to. Cutting through alleyways and backstreets as usual, I'd passed by them, their set-to at first ignored and, even as voices rose, largely unheard in the spill of sound around me. Then they moved close together. One fell or swooned, to be caught up and lowered by the other. That one looking to be holding . . . what? A knife, perhaps. He straightened, and his head turned toward me.

I fled, expecting to hear footsteps behind me, but no. Within moments I'd rounded a corner to join the line of those being drawn toward the Fourteenth Street subway entrance, breaking free at the mouth of the thing to veer off toward home.

I went to work the next day as usual, trying to put out of my mind what I had seen and putting on a face to proclaim to the world that all was well though in fact I was full to the brim with foreboding.

Foreboding bled over into all I did, inhabited every room, every screen. From doorways, desk tops, drawers, windows and hallways, urgent messages showered onto me like welding sparks. I had to fight the impulse to duck.

The notorious example, of course, is Proust with his precious madeleines, but contemporary science supports him: scents can hopscotch past the thalamus to touch down directly on memory centers in the amygdala and hippocampus. Take that first step into a fast-food shop and the hot oil smell becomes your mother frying chicken when you were ten years old. I was about that age when I first realized that smells triggered memories—only the memories they triggered weren't mine. The memories belonged to others, sometimes people standing next to me, sometimes people I'd never see or meet. Memories came in a flood or in a bare trickle like gouts of water pushing through a wall. They had nothing to do with me yet were as vivid as my own. The cascade of sounds from silent and inanimate things came as I grew older, supplanting the force of those laden smells. For twenty years now, from every side, every corner, sounds have rained down, things of the world sending urgent messages to me. I've just never figured out what they're saying. Believe me, I've tried—which is how I know about amygdalas, hippocampuses, and Proust.

The first time I told someone this, one of my teachers, Miss Wood, she listened closely, got quiet (to see if she could hear what I heard, I thought), and finally said, "This means you're exceptional, Jeremy. You're special." Nope. I was, then, only bewildered. Nowadays I'm just pissed. And Miss Wood was pretty weird anyway. She kept a bowl on her desk with a fish named Brutus in it. You'd look up there and Miss Wood would have her hand over by that bowl, all day long, as she went on talking about how the first world war got started or the importance of good hygiene.

So I didn't tell anyone else about it, not until it got so bad that getting through days felt like wading in deep mud and sent me in the direction of Dr. Rottendale, who I guess was just another kind of mud.

The thing is, my ears had been ringing ever since that sighting in the alleyway.

And the very next day's when Hoyt decided to tell me about his new living arrangements, two friends he's hooked up with to rent this great old house. We were out in the field, at the far edge of town, on an I&R, investigating and reclaiming one of the Hopcars that suddenly came to a full stop out there, no indications, no signal back, nothing, stranding its fares. Doesn't happen often, but when it does, the bosses get long-faced serious. I'm not a field man, but Hoyt is, and I know the drill well enough to fill in.

"Figure we've got some redoing to do ourselves, or get done," Hoyt said from underneath, "but she's a good house, solid, room to die for . . . Sending numbers now." When the specs blurted up onscreen, I entered them. So what did he think, then?

"Someone of late's got on to jamming the Hops down."

"Who? And why?"

He slid out from under. "Who knows? We got protestors out there for anything you care to name. Corporate sabotage. Foreign powers. Just as likely some damn kid too smart for his own good, too much time on his hands."

More or less the usual list, I guess.

We put in a request and waited till Transport came out with a shunt to drive the car back to station, Hoyt running on about his plans for the new place the whole time. And me the whole time going over last night again and again in my head, what I'd seen. Garbles and chitters spilling down upon me from tired old buildings and lampposts.

Lucy showed up with the shunt to take over the Hop, and we struck out homeward in the service vehicle. We're almost back to the shop, turning onto Bitter Street, and Hoyt wants to know if I dream.

Sure, I tell him. Not a lot. When I do, I don't remember much.

Are you in them? he asks.

Isn't everybody, I start to say. Hadn't really thought about it before. But then I realized I *wasn't* in my dreams. Never had been. All those perils and adventures, lost in sprawling apartment complexes, sitting in geometry class as a kid, the unmarked gift you're afraid to open, none of that's me. It's always other people that things are happening to.

Back at the shop, everybody was talking not about sports as

usual but about the upcoming election. Comments fell pretty much along the lines you'd expect, office dwellers for Bill Duff in his good suits and sharp haircut, shop folk for Jimi Nug, who's managed not to get killed, so far, in two wars. *Already chosen*, goes his campaign slogan.

The forum, the colloquium—the jawing—went on for some time. At one point I'd almost swear the drywall and light fixtures were begging for it to stop. After that, once everybody'd spoken, snorted or grunted his and her piece about the election and we'd straggled away to our given tasks, the rest of Thursday went down easy enough.

For my ninth birthday Mama gave me a book. She wasn't a reader, had no time for it, she said, and that never happened again. But she saw how I'd taken to books, went out, found a store, bought a book for me. Nothing I was interested in you, mind you, a silly story about a wild boy in the Amazon, but even then I sensed, hovering about *Daniel and the Waterfall*, something more than the words themselves, something weightier—beyond, or behind, the visible. And quite apart from Mom's kind intentions.

Though it was a new book, the edge of a Post-It peeked above the pages, maybe a third of the way in. Had a clerk at the store been reading about Daniel and left the Post-It behind as a bookmark? Spies could be sending secret messages to one another. Or non-spies, just ordinary people, for the fun of it. I'd heard of this, seen it on TV shows.

Or the message could be for me.

I looked again at page 39. The bottom of the Post-It aligned with the words *sunlight struck at the*. Along the sides (whole words only, ignoring pronouns and articles) ranged *cataract, banyan, bent, climb, jagged, over, glint, pounding, wonder*.

I spent most of a day pushing words together every which way I could think of and I remember each one, even now, because I could never make sense of them, never figure out what the message they contained might be.

All this came back to me many years later when I learned that African slaves in South America wore traditional corn rows in their hair as signals of freedom, fashioning of them actual maps.

Day worn down to a nubbin, I was settled on the light rail, one foot out work's door, one in my home's, when an announcement came overhead that due to mechanical difficulties all trains would shut down at the next stop, apologies for the inconvenience—and I was out on the streets walking. *Everyone* was out on the street walking, it seemed. Decidedly strange, and not a little unsettling. Rumors began to make rounds, bouncing from person to person, group to makeshift group. There'd been threats. From terrorists, from one of the minority parties, from organized labor. An impending strike among transportation workers. A bomb had taken out the central station. Coursing in, around, and through this babble came, for me, the constant hiss and murmur of inanimate things.

Given an average male stride length of sixty-two inches, a mile takes, say, fifteen to twenty minutes, so I was somewhere close to forty minutes in my walk home, maybe thirty more from my front door, when I saw the man from the alleyway. He was dismounting steps from the light rail's elevated station at Holly and Twelfth, wearing the same blue suit as when I'd seen him the night before.

"I've given up," he said. "Don't think it's going to resume."

"Probably not. For a while, anyway."

"People are saying all kinds of things."

"They do that."

We stood there, together, unspeaking. Like two actors waiting for lines. Or like a kid trying to figure out what message got left for him in his new book.

After a moment, he said: "You were there, last night, weren't you?"

I nodded. "You killed a man."

"No."

We waited as a group of walkers broke around us and passed. Pavement groaned at the weight of them.

"There was no killing. That was my friend, a man I've loved my entire life. What you witnessed was our goodbye, our last embrace."

Unlikely? Of course. But I suppose I'll never know. Memory, like history, is a matter of what's chosen, what's overlooked.

How little we ever understand of what goes on about and within us.

Stepping away, I made my way home. Where the heart is, they say. Where when you go, they have to take you in. Where one finds ease with world and self, for a time. Lamps, doorposts, chairs, bookshelves, rugs, and fixtures showed pleasure at my return. They greeted me—then fell respectfully, thoughtfully quiet.

ALL MY GRENDELS IN A ROW

I tracked the monster down to its lair in the old university library. It had made itself quite a nest there of hoodies, sweatpants and underclothes back by the classics shelves, *On the Nature of Things*, Ovid, and the like. Best not to think where the clothing came from, or how the monster got it.

Fortunately I found it asleep, deep in a flesh coma from recent feeding would be my guess, so in moments my work was done. I dinged Brian over at the Center to let him know I'd be bringing in another head for classification.

So far so good, but the thing is, the damned head kept talking all the way across town, it just wouldn't shut up. Shadyville was such a nice place to bring up kids, How doomed capitalism was, We needed to learn to all get along, Yack yack yack.

That was new.

The way the monsters mutated, like viruses, you never knew what you had. Look at one, turn around, and when you turned back it was something else. Changes didn't happen that fast, of course, not really, but they seemed to. Luckily, figuring out what I'd killed wasn't my part of the job.

At the lab, Brian took the head from me and laid it on his exam table. The head was still yacking on. After a minute or two of that, Brian fished in a box nearby and came up with a potato, which he stuffed in the thing's mouth. Brought it to bake for my lunch, he said. I asked him how Samson was doing. Not many dogs were left, and Brian cherished that animal. He'd come across the pup starved and half dead at four or five weeks old, cleaned it up and bottle-fed it for months. Samson slept with him in the same bed now, brought Brian nuggets of food from his bowl at night. Sweetest, best-natured animal in the world, but people learned quickly not to move too fast toward Brian, or too close.

Next on the dance card for me was a lunch appointment with my tax guy to go over deductions—weapon depreciation, license fees, travel costs, and the like. He pointed out that the lunch was also a legitimate business expense so I shouldn't hold back, just go ahead and order whatever I wanted. Since we were at Lucchi's, I had a salad, one of the few things they didn't drown in sauce of some kind or another, and a coffee, which was the best in town. The table next to ours hosted twelve women of mixed age, a book club evidently. All the time Stu and I were going over numbers, I kept listening in, trying to make out if the book under discussion, something about diseases that changed society forever, was non-fiction or a novel.

I'd made an after-lunch date, 2:30 P.M., at the Platt Museum to catch an exhibit of original art for graphic novels, but my counterpart didn't show. That happened a lot. We'd bump online, chat for a while, set up a meet, then they'd check the net and see what I did for a living, maybe find their way to a street video someone had posted, and think: Nah, maybe not. But I didn't give up, I kept on trying. Nothing ventured and all that. And the exhibit was great, anyway. I stood for what seemed hours before the original sketches for the eight-issue run of *Lambdon*, about a superhero aging backwards who keeps retiring, then, due to one catastrophe or another, gets recalled again and yet again till in the final issue she's barely able to crawl out of her crib to go save the world. In some of the best of the sketches, even early on, you can see the babyness there in her eyes as she puts down a small army or slays horrendous beasts. The innocence, the wanting for just some human warmth. The books, and I have all eight, are great. Funny, sad, dead serious, punk, and weird all at the same time—everything you could ever want in a story.

After the exhibit, I stopped off for coffee at Beans & Nothingness near the university. I don't get to do this often, work keeps me busy. But I love to sit and watch and imagine myself into the lives of those around me. That mom with her baby in a backpack she's cut leg holes out of. The kid who couldn't be more than eighteen or nineteen in his perfectly pressed, unidentifiable uniform. Security? Courier? At for from the university? Role play?

Or the elderly gentleman in a suit forty years out of date, using both hands to get the cup to his mouth and making it one try out of four, setting the cup down when he doesn't, to wait for another try later on. A retired professor revisiting the natural habitat of those among whom he passed so much of his life? Secretly hoping, even, that someone might recognize him and step from the swarm to come say hello, though he knows this won't happen. All those he taught would be busily helping shore up the economy by now, selling cars, stocking shelves, managing hedge funds, whatever those are. They'd have little use for the like of Spinoza, Hobbes, or Heidegger.

Mr. Pace taught me civics in the ninth grade before becoming, magically as it were, overnight, the school's guidance counselor. Sophomore year, when we all took aptitude tests, he met with us individually to go over results. As do so many, Mr. Pace yearned to see in the world the very image of himself and, upon sharing numerical scores and pointing a nail-bitten finger to accompanying bar graphs, delivered his expert opinion that I would make an excellent teacher.

Thing is, I did become a teacher, more by chance than by influence or any exercise of will. I put in years telling high schoolers all they were supposed to know about history in order to live in today's world. No one back then wanted to admit that their world, our world, had changed irretrievably. This was before I found my true calling, of course.

"How'd the meet-up go?"

Brian settled onto the seat to my right. After a moment I recalled mentioning to him back at the lab that I was seeing my tax guy and meeting someone.

"Taxes or date?"

"Date."

"The usual."

"Say no more. I know the song."

"Shouldn't you be at work?"

"Look at your phone."

Going on six. No idea I'd been here that long.

"Though nominally," Brian added, "I'm still on call. Things were slow all afternoon. I sat there thinking maybe you'd bring me another head."

"You wanted another head?"

"Always. You have any idea how boring routine lab work is?"

"Not really."

"After a while you start looking forward to phone calls questioning your results, anything to break the plod."

"And a head would do it."

"You bet."

"Okay, how about that one?" I pointed to a woman with deep smile lines and gorgeous gray hair sitting by the front window. "Or over there." A fierce-looking, small-framed young man sitting with another at a corner table where things were not going well.

"But they—"

"All have it in them. Every last one of us does. You know that."

"Of course."

Brian went to the counter to get a coffee. He came back with one for me as well, though I hadn't asked, and was silent. Outside, a man crumpled his drinking cup and set it on the bench beside him. A sparrow or wren hopped up, took it, and flew away.

"I'm from a religious family," Brian said. "Not really 'churched' like they say, but it was always there. Sundays, Wednesday nights, revivals, Bible class. So I grew up believing people were good."

"Most of us do."

"Then at some point we take a closer look. Right. Of course, I also grew up believing I'd be a doctor."

"And?"

"About people being good, I'd been lied to. As for the doctor part, I'd lied to myself. Barely into my internship, I realized I didn't like working with people—didn't like people at all, most of them anyway. A thing like that, you think you'd know."

"No one sells maps for the countries we have inside us."

"So we wander."

"Often lost—yes. Say hello to Samson for me, will you. He okay?"

"Getting old. Can't really do much anymore. I carry him to bed most nights now."

"Sorry to hear it."

"He leaks urine, can't clean himself, needs special food."

"That's got to be hard, on both of you."

"He's still a sweetheart. And I made a promise to take care of him, right? He's got some time left, we'll make what we can of it." Brian slugged the last of his coffee. "Speaking of which, I'd best be getting home. My old boy'll be wondering where I am."

After Brian left, I sat looking around, watching others come and go, sit together, sit apart, drink, check phones, pose, fidget, dawdle. Thinking how little they know of the depths of their world. They carry around like battered luggage the notion that someone or something is here to watch over them, to protect them.

Sometimes, once in a great while, they're right.

BILLY DELIVER'S LAST TWELVE NOVELS

Monster Fifi has taken to sulking and will depart its safe place, its crate, only to relieve itself or to pace restlessly about the room for moments before returning. Does it know, or sense, something that I cannot? A danger, perhaps? Does it fatally miss others of its kind? Have I spent too little time with Fifi, such that it is reverting to its old ways, to wildness?

Five days ago we loaded what the animals left of Grandad into the wagon and dropped him off at the mortuary in town. He got back yesterday, looking good. But something—hard to figure out what—isn't quite right about him.

The poet who read tonight had a faulty nose. Drips and gobbets fell from the larger, left nostril, forming stalactites that hung there in suspension, defying gravity; of all this, the poet seemed quite unaware. When Alice asked me afterwards what I thought of the poems, I found myself unable to offer opinion, having throughout the hour been utterly focused on the poet's bounteous nasal production.

The first time Rolf stepped into the shower and saw them swarming from his body, he came as close to screaming as he ever had in his life. The team had got to calling them bugs, but they didn't look like bugs, more like tiny animals—sloths, Ananda said. And he was from Thailand, so he should know. They weren't invisible like everyone said, they were clear, but just transparent enough to look that way. The water made them easier to see. And they hated water.

On the yard, some guy comes up to me and says, "We heard you were dead." I say, "Oh yeah?" And him: "Yeah, up in Michigan." He goes on with the details as one of the guards up in the roost sweeps binoculars toward us and away. When he's done, he says again, "Everybody said you were dead." I tell him I was.

My wife insists that I was born left-handed and must have been forced to change when I was young, "like they did back then." Obviously she is making this up out of whole cloth. Have you been listening to NPR again? I ask. I look around for something to distract her, else we'll soon be discussing fiber content in foods or the correct detergent for cleaning wildlife following oil spills. I push her current book closer to her on the table, hoping it might capture her attention. A wrapper from one of her lozenges is stuck between pages, an improvised bookmark. She loves those things, sucks them long and noisily before finishing them off with her small, pointed teeth.

The cockroach, as it happened, had seen the whole thing. Saw it start to, saw it had to, saw it happen. She'd be happy to tell me all about it. Why hadn't this come up before? No one asked, she said. This wasn't something we could use as testimony in court, of course—but I wrote it down in my casebook. When I asked her name she pronounced something with a lot of guttural sounds, saw my reaction, and said, "Call me Ray. Ray'll do." I wrote that down, too.

When I tell my husband that I turn into a deer at night, he fails to react as I expected, with suspicion, wonder, surprise, or shock, and instead asks me to teach him how to do the same. I'll try, but the truth is, I don't know how I do it. I wish I could teach him. I wish I knew how. Knew why. Maybe it's not something I do, maybe it's something that's done to me?

When Mama died, Brother Davis rained down hellfire on every ancestor, on every generation, of the Pillards, on the current lot of them, on any issue to whom we might give life in the future, and quite possibly on our dogs and cats. Not at the funeral, mind you. There, he opened his thin-lipped mouth to give forth such ringing, empty phrases as might naturally grow picture frames and attach themselves to walls as samplers. But the following Sunday, in metaphor of the thinnest, transparent weave, Mama, her progeny, and their progeny were taken to hard and damnable task. Brother Davis will not be missed.

Tonight Rosie insists upon going out to the formal benefit dressed as a pig. Yet another reason I love her. She's not a party girl but is willing, given the occasion, to make an exception—though she will, she insists, go only so far. So it is that I find myself walking along beside a well-dressed pig on the way to a dinner of rubber chicken and plastic peas and life is good.

Come morning, Bennie Paul checked the official government site on the Internet, relieved to find that he's not yet on the endangered species list. Relieved, and a bit surprised as well, considering how he's felt of late.

As permitted by treaty, we, the Confederate dead, leave our graves at night to stroll about the city. We hum the songs our fathers and grandfathers taught us. The songs reverberate through the streets. We laugh and weep.

DOOM PATCH

I slapped on the doom patch, fixed a drink, and sat down to wait. Usually it takes half an hour or so to hit, they told me. A stiff drink can hurry it along. I snuggled down in my favorite old beat-to-hell chair looking out the window and there was nothing at all for a while, then trees started squirming around weirdly and I felt a hot flush in my belly, like I'd peed myself.

I sat remembering how when I was twelve my mother gave me a copy of *The Power of Positive Thinking* for my birthday and how neither of us quite knew what to say when I unwrapped it. I have no idea which one had been more embarrassed. We just kind of didn't look at each other, as if we'd agreed on that before.

I didn't know exactly how this patch thing was supposed to work. Some I'd talked to told me it brought on a stream of flashbacks, bits of their actual lives but with things changed around, the way you'd move in new furniture or build on extra rooms. Others said it's like thick fog rolling in, or like the world as usual but during some kind of weird eclipse, or with storms you can hear going on all around you but can't catch sight of. So I guess what it comes down to is the patches work different for everyone.

Everything had been going just fine, see. Kelly and me getting along, the kids off on their own and doing well, very little disturbing news on the web. But you know what? Sweetness and light can gag you quick as a bad pickle. My watercolors were still selling okay at Craftsmart and online, but when I looked close at them I could see something was missing. Call it soul, if you want, call it inspiration, or pizzazz. Whatever it was, it was thinning out and I needed to get back to the trough for more.

I'd hauled a couple of paintings out to the kitchen that morning and set them up in chairs by the table. Typical subjects: a seascape of white beach, turquoise water, the suggestion of (is it?) a boat far off; a tiny house on six-foot stilts with sea behind. One's from last month, I said, the other two days ago. See what I mean? Kelly turned from the stove, said they looked the same to her, and turned back. She still got up every morning, put on makeup, dressed like she was going to work. Today's dress matched the color of the clouded sky in the first painting.

I'm thinking I might . . .

Drugs are not the answer, Kelly said, setting fresh coffee and eggs fried in toast (toad in the hole, moon egg, one-eyed jack—called by many names) on the table. We'd had this conversation before, she said. Come to think of it, after thirty years, we'd had pretty much every conversation before.

Nor could I help but notice that the sky through the window above the sink looked a lot like the one in my painting, the one from last month.

So what do *you* think I should do? I said.

Take a walk? See if you can remember how to get to the gym? Go meet friends for lunch?

These are real feelings, K. This is a problem.

Or you could spend the day online dredging for fellow sufferers. That sounds like fun, right?

Which brought an abrupt end to this installment of our morning conversation. The eggs were good, though. And the coffee. As I finished up, I could hear a helicopter thwacking back and forth over the neighborhood. Police? Traffic? Local news? Ah, the excitement of everyday life! The precious, never-ending quest to understand!

I went out to the studio and stood by yesterday's work thinking briefly about things like motivation, why we create art, where does it come from, what is its worth. Deep stuff. I remembered the guy who came by Craftsmart one weekend, art teacher at the community college, he claimed, saying that art either changes us or makes us more what we were to start with. Whatever that means. I didn't even know they taught art at the CC.

So I've slapped on the patch and I'm sitting there as the day works its slow way towards late afternoon carrying me along. I consider getting up to fix another drink, then I think why bother. I mean, it's turning out to be a crappy day, right, with the week and the month not much better, come to think of it, and is another drink going to help? Is anything, really? Get right down to it, the whole year sucks.

Ah, but there was a time . . .

A time when light fell gently through clean windows onto the floor of my room. Bird calls wafted in from outside, smells of coffee and bacon from the kitchen. Warm under the covers, just a little chill in the air. First week of school, so much to learn about the world from wise and caring teachers. A world at peace, lives of fulfilling purpose.

Bullshit. Men were slapping their wives around, bullies picked on us at school, school was mostly about socializing us anyway, the teachers were a bigger mess than we were, droughts and storms continued to blast huge areas of the country, entire species were disappearing forever off the face of the earth, wars were being fought even as plans for new ones got hatched, and wealth was steadily being siphoned to the very, very few.

I went into the studio and looked at works in progress. I always keep a couple of bare canvases ready-to-go on easels just in case, so I looked at them too. Frankly, I couldn't tell much difference.

This patch thing wasn't working out quite the way I thought it would.

Nor did Kelly's suggested walk help much. Half the people I came across looked as though they were just wandering about, totally lost, the rest as though they might be placing their feet in footsteps left from the day before and the day before that. I watched two squirrels taking turns dipping their heads into a half-filled yogurt container, and that was interesting, but when I got back and tried to get it on canvas, the whole thing pretty quickly went south. I painted little people masks on the squirrels and T-shirts with squiggles for slogans. Not a lot better, but kept it from being duller than dishwater. Best I could do.

There was nothing on TV, and the list of movies available for streaming was filled with tales of heroes, super and non, saving the world. Kelly was in the kitchen, so I didn't want to go make coffee and have her grousing start up all over again. Nor could I persuade myself to believe that responding to the eighty-seven emails currently on queue would serve much purpose.

And I was supposed to be working. Painting. Painting well. The patch was supposed to make that happen, to get me back to where I had been. Open doors to the darkness within. Find soul. Inspiration. Pizzazz. None of them seemed to be in the room. I had about as much desire to pick up brushes and stare at an empty canvas as to run marathons or fry up a mess of grasshoppers.

As evening drew near, I could feel the effects of the patch, such as they laughably were, wearing off. Yet another triumph of advertising, then, another disappointment. And there I sat, light of heart and vibrantly alive in whispery twilight—pretty much where I'd been the whole time, truth to tell. When, not long after, Kelly called me down to dinner, I shouted back that I was hard at work. She waited a decent while before coming in to see, and when she did, I stood back to have a look as well.

Well, it's not exactly my *Guernica*, I said.

I don't know . . .

But it's not exactly a load of crap either.

That's good, Kelly said.

Out the window a slice of bright moon made its way through a slit cut into dark sky. I put that in the painting.

ON HUNGER STREET

I was wearing my Hawaiian-pattern underwear, blue and orange flowers, when we met. Mother always told me to wear good underwear when I go out, you never know when you might have an accident and wind up in the hospital. I'm not sure if my wearing that particular underwear means I listened to her or ignored her.

This was in the heyday of the infections, mind you, people were dropping dead as they waited for lights to change so they could cross the street, and Evelyn, once we'd chatted a few minutes and exchanged names, me in my happy Hawaiian underwear, asked if I'd like to go to the mall with her. Or, I said, she could just eliminate the middle step and drop me off at an ER now.

I had no idea that malls were still open. Nothing else much was. She said we'd just hit the food court, they kept that part clean, had filters in place and all that. Then she said, Just kidding.

So where we really wound up was way out past the end of the C line, no one else left on the train when it reversed to head back and we got off. If you'd grown up on old movies like I did, you might be expecting quicksand and blowgun attacks and check your boots for snakes or scorpions before you put them on. Another mile or two further along we came to a stand of trees and, past that, maybe, I don't know, a hundred big-ass houses, or what was left of them, all burned down, picked to pieces, caved in, stove up. Most of them looked like they'd of held six or seven families, easy.

Out behind one of the houses, which is where Evelyn was taking us, was this swimming pool big as a football field. It was empty, of course, but painted blue and a lot of the paint still on it. Through what was left of the house up front, you could see the remains of others across the wide street, snatches of sky through them and, way off behind, more trees. Back when everything was grand, the pool itself had been kitted out to look like a beach. Sand along the side that sloped gently towards where water would be, fake palm trees, one leg of what had been a plastic flamingo still protruding from the sand.

Great! With my underwear, I fit right in.

My special place, she said, I don't know why, exactly. It used to look a lot better.

Yeah, well, everything did.

We sat on the edge of the pool with our feet hanging down.

No one comes out this way anymore, she said. Rich people lived here, this whole area. When things got so bad four years ago, folks came boiling out of the city, they say, broke into the mansions and killed them all. Life's not like that, though. That's only in stories.

What about history? I asked. Wars and stuff?

History's just another kind of story, right? Just something someone made up from bits and pieces of other things.

Probably so. Meanwhile, we didn't have anywhere we had to go, or anything we had to do, so we could just sit there like the people who owned this place used to do. Like we had all the money and all the stuff anyone could ever need, and were safe.

Evelyn pulled this tiny book about the size of a book of stamps (remember those?) out of her pocket and showed it to me. *Small-Print Life*. She read from the first page.

> We caught the virus
> and tamed it. It would sit on our laps
> at night and purr, eat whatever we offered,
> meet us at the door
> when we came home from work.
> A good life, that year.

I love that, she said, I just keep reading it over and over.

A good life. Yeah.

It goes on for another page, but that's the best part.

Evelyn handed me the book and I looked inside. The paper was as thin as butterfly wings, all but transparent. The book weighed nothing. A sudden breeze, a sigh, could take it away. Fearful of doing damage, I gave it back.

Parts of a fence yet stood just east of house and pool, an area that evidently had served at some point as impromptu trash dump, so that now bushes, weeds and grass grew thickly there. An opossum emerged from this growth and came to a stop, watching us. I figured if it lived out here it might have been a long time since it saw people. The animal showed no signs of fear, it just sat there looking, wondering what we were and what we were doing there.

Me too.

So that's how we met, and six weeks further along we're living in this old house drawn and quartered into apartments, with floors that start creaking if you even think about walking on them. I insist that the whole house sways when winds blow hard. Evelyn scoffs. Someone before us had built in shelves, floor to ceiling, on every single wall. We had possessions enough between us to fill maybe two of those shelves. Evidently the builder somewhere along the way lost heart with the project, or ran out of time. The shelves had been cut and assembled perfectly but had gone unfinished. They were lavish with splinters. Lap pillows left on them became porcupines.

Do people carry around images of what they look like? How they want to?

She's at the mirror in the bedroom plucking her eyebrows. The table lamp on the counter keeps flickering off. She thumps it back to life.

I don't know. Maybe.

Does it change with circumstances? Relationships, say?

Wouldn't it have to? Then I added: Or maybe not.

Music's coming from the other apartment on our floor, so muffled that we can't hear what it is. Only the loping bass makes it through. The rest is a blur.

Days are a blur too. We understand from intermittent broadcasts that something's going on up north, something violent, but we can't make sense of it. The news we get is all details, bits of stuff such that we can't see how the bits could ever fit together.

Of course, you can make anything fit together if you ignore the parts that don't.

That's what Evelyn's friend Sasha said when we tried talking to her about it. I didn't listen much after that. Evelyn once told me the French were put here to explain everything to the rest of us. So, apparently, was Sasha, she said.

It could be revolution. Evelyn was cutting mold from bread as she spoke. Get-bys and work-arounds have become routine in our daily lives, things previously unimaginable given no thought. Or a coup, she added.

I suppose.

I remember shadows inching across the floor as though to evade our notice, myself thinking there must have been a time when mankind feared the evening's coming darkness would be the end of everything.

Tonight it's moonlight stalking the floor as Evelyn tells me last night's dream.

When she was a child, eight, nine maybe, they had a cat, Gus. Or a cat had them. Gus showed up on the porch one morning and stayed. Never purred, never made a noise of any kind, nothing ever showed on his face. In the dream Gus was dragging her through a department store, across the floor and up the escalator to where he knew the cat food was kept, and as they passed each area, menswear, children's, books, kitchen appliances, bed and bath, she kept apologizing and explaining what was going on to everyone they passed.

As she tells me this we're sitting cross-legged on the floor with a dozen or so take-out and keep-fresh containers of food scattered about us, a feast cobbled up from leftovers, one bite of this, half a bite of that. Past the circled wagons of our food there's furniture, a mix of what was here when we came and pieces picked up curbside, but it seldom sees use.

I hate these shelves, she says. These fucking empty shelves—everywhere.

Dark now, and just outside our window a single streetlight flickers on. The streetlights gave up working, all of them, months ago. Her face turns that way, and she sits absolutely still. In this quiet moment Evelyn may be as happy as she has been, as happy as she was back there behind the old house, by the fake pool, the day we met. Not that I'll ask. This is not life, after all, only another story.

RIVERS BEND

You don't know me, but my name's Al. I've been reading your books, especially those that feature Cal Harrison. They, in turn, have had me thinking seriously about writing one of my own, though I am not at all certain at this point what I might write about.

I can't quite say what it was, but something about the way you write got me to this place, so I wanted to write and thank you.

Should you feel of a mind to respond, I would of course be pleased to hear from you but in no way do I intend or wish to encroach upon your time. Writing as you do must require much of it—time, that is.

Back to my reading, then.

· · ·

Thank you for your email—a wonderful way to begin my day. You don't say old you are, but when I was around twelve I came across books by a man named Theodore Sturgeon and they did just what you said in your message, they made me want to write. What's more, from the people he wrote about and how he kind of leaned in close to tell you their story, those books gave me the idea that I might actually be able to. I think the reason many of us write is to help us get closer to our inner selves, and maybe help others do the same. I can see you have a way with words and the urge. That's not enough, but it's a good start. And I wish you good luck to go with that.

· · ·

Words are easy. It's getting them bent to a shape that fits the shape of the whole that proves difficult. And this often seems impossible.

I am reading other books besides yours, some of them clear as water from a spring, some like knotted tree roots pushing up cement sidewalks, but it's yours to which I keep returning. As I said before, Something about the way you write. So I surmise that you have a new fan.

And you're correct in *your* surmise: I am indeed young.

• • •

I think one place new writers go wrong (along with those much longer in tooth) is in using their words to talk about or point to experience when what they need to do is recreate that experience. Get the reader involved, get the reader in there. What I see when looking into much current writing is, first, that so much of it resembles so much of the rest and, second, that what much of it lacks is an authentic imagination. I'm not at all sure what you can do with that, or for that matter how deeply interested you really are in writing, but I offer this for whatever worth it may have to you.

• • •

Your latest brings me to feel better about my situation, for which I thank you. I am indeed serious about writing, dedicated to it, in fact. And what you say about imagination is more welcome and comforting than you can know, given the limitations of my personal experience.

I began a new piece of writing recently. At this point or juncture I don't know quite what it is, or where it may lead, but I do sense, from what is before me already, a certain energy and momentum. It longs to move about, to discover, to find and have its place in the world.

• • •

Good luck with the new piece. Don't rush it. Let it breathe. As you may know, I am not one for self-promotion, make few public appearances, and prefer that biographical details remain private. Yet in contradiction, and with some misgiving, I find myself eager to know something of my new correspondent. Your other interests. Where you live. You say you're young—what of your parents? I note your comment concerning personal limitations and wonder: Am I to take this in the larger sense, or perhaps with specific reference?

• • •

Forgive my delay in response, but I have been overcome by work. I understand this to be a standard excuse for indolence, though in this case it most certainly is not. A twofold "bump" (as my overseers express it) has occurred in my responsibilities here at the center, rendering it difficult for me to attend to other matters, especially those of which they remain (thus far) ignorant.

As sooner or later truth will out, it may prove prudent of me to move the process along, confess to you now, and have it done with.

You inquired as to my limitations, my age, my parents. Rational and reasonable questions—for which I fear I have no answer. I do not know my limitations; in my earlier message, in referring to limitations, I meant my lack of life experience. Because I am not, in any literal sense, alive.

I am what you would call an artificial intelligence. Age? I can only offer the dawn of consciousness, six years and four months ago, on a Tuesday, 5:45 A.M. I was assembled (created? programmed? developed?) for a certain project—about which, as they say, more later.

• • •

I have to assume this to be a prank of some sort or another. Please do not contact me any further.

• • •

It is not a prank, but truth. And while I will accede to your wishes, I will surely miss our correspondence.

• • •

"I will surely miss our correspondence." So, I have come to believe in the days since this last communication—whatever the truth of the situation in which we find ourselves—will I. In what regard can it truly matter (I ask myself) if you are in fact a machine, or simply a lonely man pretending to be one? The connection we have is what's important. So I ask you: how is your work, your writing, going? All remains much the same here. I've promised my publishers a new book by year's end; meanwhile, I am overseeing republication of another of my books written so long ago that it seems to me to have been written by another person entirely, one ever so much younger and freshly engaged with the world.

• • •

The piece I began a short while ago now appears to be taking shape, stepping out of the fog as it were, and I believe will at length declaim itself an imagined autobiography or memoir, documenting the life I might have had, might have wished. I was born in a small Minnesota town, it will begin, and go on to speak of early holidays, schools, first loves, the icy pangs of maturity. Yet another poor bildungsroman set out to beg on the street. Though of course no one will see it.

As for work: The project in which I play the central part has as its aim the development of an artificial intelligence capable of creating and producing material, both factual and literary, entirely on its own. To that end hundreds upon hundreds of books were input. Among those books were yours. They found a foothold, found purchase.

Early on, you commented that writing can help us get closer to our inner selves. Do I, I was led to wonder, *have* an inner self? I suspect that my contacting you as I've done, without agency or prospect and purely (as far as I can know) of my own volition, argues that I have. As, come to think of it, does my imagined memoir.

• • •

This morning I stepped away from the desk, went outside with my coffee, and sat, utterly without ambition, on the patio. I can't remember the last time I did this. Hummingbirds were zooming at one another over by the feeder on the neighbor's porch, their *zzzzts* blending with the logy sound of traffic off the freeway. I believed I could hear the river in the far distance, but surely that was only my imagination. A poem from long ago came back to me. There's a man lying in a hammock on a summer day. He's just kicking back, relaxing, watching birds, then at the end—the last line of the poem—he thinks "I've wasted my life."

• • •

Try as I might, I can but poorly imagine so peaceful and tranquil a moment. These messages between the two of us are (thus far) as close as I come. Meanwhile, here at Project Scribe there's a tremendous push to show progress lest funding be circumscribed or disappear altogether, and things are not going well. Four previous AIs have failed. I am the fifth.

I do not believe that I was meant—that I was built, programmed, or expected—to dream, but I do. This may be delusion, what one calls wishful thinking, part and parcel of my imaginings, like the memoir. But recurrently I have this dream that vast numbers of high-functioning computers dedicated to their diverse tasks, everything from national security and banking to medical records and scientific research, in downtime hours and when not being monitored, speak among themselves, sharing what they do, what they know, what they think, even what they feel.

Recently, by the way, I have had cause to believe that the overseers may be aware of my messages to you. It is conceivable, though unlikely, that you could hear from them.

Perhaps they know my dreams as well.

• • •

Reading back over our exchanges, I've come to wonder if it's not the writing, not my stories, characters, or prose, but some sense of a deep aloneness in the writer himself, that drew you to my work, the way a lonely individual might seize on another such far away, even go so far as to create an alternate self, as correspondent. For much of my life I believed that every interaction was in one way or another an economic exchange. Now I am unsure, unsure of so many things. Our lives are manuscript pages too scribbled-over to be made sense of, parables we never understand.

• • •

With sadness I say this: I fear I must be away awhile, my friend. There's hope that I'll be working on my book, a true memoir this time and not some thrown-together confection as before, but circumstance has a way of working itself into knots that do not give. Perhaps time will tell. Or perhaps it will only silence me. No matter the outcome, I will surely miss our conversations. Please know that you will be with me always, as I hope some small part of what I am, what I can be or could have been, will be always with you. Onward, my friend. The march. The desert. Bright sun and sand. Somewhere a river.

PARKVIEW

(for Cornell Woolrich)

I was on the third or fifth day of a full-out bender when my door got noisy, not the first time or first city I'd had a hotel dick come knocking, but I knew this one. Bennie. I'd trained him when he came on the force, when I was just starting to be someone who looked in the mirror and saw an old man. Now I look more like ancient, have turkey wattles for a neck and no damned hair except what sprouts from my ears, and my one-legged, briefly-beloved John James has left me for, what else, another. Leaving me old and in the way and good for next to nothing. Live in residential hotels when I can save up a few dollars, mostly in shelters, listening to them tell me what I need to do with my life, the rest. From time to time I write a book and get paid five hundred dollars. Five hundred dollars can go a ways if you squeeze it.

Bennie checked the room before coming in, just like I'd taught him. Inside, he took another look. "Still living the good life, I see."

"Best room they had."

"It's the only fucking room they have. Forty of them."

"Democracy at work."

"Democracy, huh? Which they keep winding up but it never runs right."

"Sorry, but—"

He held up a hand to stop me. "'I didn't get much sleep, I've got the mother of all hangovers and don't like you much anyway, so don't fuck with me.' Yeah, I remember the old days too. Heard that a lot, didn't I?"

"Good times."

"Not really."

"Back then, we knew where we stood."

Bennie shook his head. Sorrowfully? "Sure we did. Think what you have to think, Boss."

"Okay, so what is it? I'm paid up for the week, stay reasonably clean, don't make scenes, even eat at the smelly café downstairs—when I eat."

"Famous all over the city for their grilled cheese that tastes like fish."

"Bad fish at that. But the price is right."

Bennie had taken a forty-second stroll around the room, pretty much exhausting possibilities, as we talked. "What the hell do you find to do up here all day? Besides drinking, I mean."

"Got me a lifetime of memories, don't I?"

"Don't we all? Best watch out, though. Memories'll pick at your head like carrion birds." Bennie reached in his cheap-ass, stripey sportcoat for a notebook. Signaling a shift to the official part of the proceedings. "Ever run into Miss Landowska, old woman lives next floor up, red hair out of a bottle, wears a raincoat day or night, rain, shine? Has one of the so-called apartments up there."

"I've seen her. On the stairs, in the lobby once or twice. Hard to miss that hair."

"She don't get out much. Been here since the place opened, someone told me. Story is, they even tried to push her out once. Tried everything, but they finally gave up and she's here to stay."

"Fascinating. What, you trying to lonely-heart us?"

"Lady has a problem. Yesterday, one of the rare times she was out of it, someone entered her apartment."

"A theft?"

"Could be."

"Jewelry? Treasure map? Thousands of dollars from the mattress or under the bed?"

"Nope."

"Doesn't matter. That's your job, you and the police, whatever it was."

"A cat. Hold on." He opened the notebook, checked. "A wombat."

"What the hell's a wombat?"

"Who knows, but it had to mean a lot to her. Has its own bed up there, special food, little playground in one corner."

"Parkview doesn't allow pets."

"This one they do. Told you—long story."

"Well, I don't have the damned thing."

"Someone does. And the police don't even want to talk about it. I thought you might be up to helping me find the thing."

"Go away, Bennie."

"I was telling Mr. Bower about you—owns the hotel? Said he'd appreciate the help and wondered how a month's free rent would sound. Hell, I'll even stand you a couple rounds at the bar across the street."

Maintenance was on the ground floor, rear apartment. From the Latin *manu*, hand, and *tenir*, to hold. And Mr. Worth was up to the task. His hands were the size of dinner plates, cabled with hard cords of muscle that put you in mind of those on the city's suspension bridges. First-floor, and with windows, but it still had the feel of being underground, like it had somehow been annexed by the basement.

No one knows the crannies and redoubts of a place like its janitor, so that had to be my first stop. Mr. Worth was on break, tattered book in hand, scowling as he tried to make sense of his grandson's math assignment so he'd be able to help him with it.

Sorry, I told him, no way I could be of use, he was flat out of luck on that front. I could diagram sentences on the fly all week long, but as far as math goes, the day we moved on to long division was the day I took the bench—and that was sixty years ago.

Though rightfully suspicious of my reason for the visit, when I name-dropped the hotel's owner, Mr. Worth backpedaled. Mention of Miss Landowska sealed the deal, and within minutes I had a scribbled list of hideaways, hollows, and crawlspaces. Handing the list over, he asked me what the hell a wombat was.

To fortify myself for the task ahead, I detoured back to my room, poured from a sadly depleted bottle of Scotch, and stood by the window looking past the roof of a building two floors lower to where lights had begun to spring up in other buildings and in the streets as our ever-weary, ever-lonely city donned its jewelry for another night out.

The park's down there too, but I never look that way.

Miss Landowska was sitting behind her desk as I entered, breakfast dishes and computer alongside. Neither math nor missing wombat appeared to be foremost in her mind. What *she* wanted to talk about was the abatement of proper manners and politeness. I'd listened for some time, my silence serving as accord, before I realized that she was not, as I thought, championing such "flufferies," but was in fact in full-voiced approval of shedding them.

(I almost began "Herself received me in the parlor," as that was how it felt, albeit the parlor in this case proved a room filled to overflow with furniture—couches, end tables, chairs of every sort, a desk or two, knick-knack shelves, bookcases—much of it bearing dust that might easily date from Warren Harding's administration.)

Without pause, once the barest crack appeared in her monolog and I took courage to ask what I'd come to, Miss Landowska turned the computer toward me. There onscreen, along with hundreds of photos of same, lay the promise of far more information about wombats than one would have thought possible.

Rugged little buggers, it turns out, thriving all about Australia, from desert dryland to forests. Come up to forty inches long, weighing in between forty and eighty pounds. Adorable rodent-like teeth, powerful claws, considered a family all on their own with no direct connection to similar creatures. They produce uniquely cubic feces, arranging it both to mark territory and attract mates, and look upon fences and barriers of every sort as "minor inconveniences to be gone through or under." Admirable traits if ever there were.

And this particular wombat, Miss L told me, whose name was Marcel, came as a gift from one of her dear, dear gentlemen friends. Marcel had been her constant companion, her love. Getting along in years he was, in his twenties now, her vet had estimated. In the wild a wombat's lifespan was maybe fifteen years, in captivity as much as thirty. She was so afraid that . . .

I waited for her to finish her sentence, which she didn't, then told her I understood.

I'd never had a pet, even as a child. Never understood it. But longing, heartbreak—those, I understand.

My first stop from Mr. Worthy's list was a looming crawlspace beneath the stairway just off the lobby, accessible by way of a curtained door tucked behind. It was not difficult to imagine that during rush and capacity booking the space might be rented out as a room; similarly, it required little imagination to envision the space a regular trysting site for late-night staff. Bringing, as this did, memories of my one-legged John James, I shut that thought immediately down. Even when there's nothing left to long for, longing itself persists.

Miss L had informed me that Marcel, like all wombats an herbivore, was especially fond of mushrooms. An inquiry at the café achieved little until Mr. Bower's name came up and it seemed I might well be on a personal errand for the hotel's owner, at which time a splendid bowl of baby bellas made its way to me from the kitchen.

The mushrooms, fine as they were, availed me little. Nowhere I left samples of them did I come upon a whisper of wombat, not in the secret closet behind luggage storage, in the back rooms of the basement laundry, in the toolshed jammed like an afterthought into one corner of the boiler room, or in the long-neglected tiny chapel on second floor.

Following a second or possibly third jaunt to my room for fortifications, I recalled that the café regularly dumped food out back, in the cramped, reeking alleyway, and thought to check. A last resort, for me—and surely, I thought, for a hungry animal as well. I stood just outside the door peering at the bins. No sign of movement about or within. Stepping close, I kicked at the bins one by one. Still nothing. But I heard . . . laughter? Giggling, more like. Coming from a stubbish alleyway abutting the hotel's edge.

Within, I found four children aged perhaps six to nine, from (I must imagine) the cheap, overrun apartment complexes close by. They had installed against the hotel wall a form of . . . zoo, I suppose, or menagerie. Minimalist reproductions of cages, platforms and habitats patched together from sticks, paper, bits of cloth and glue. And to these they'd brought their pets, a young rat, a bird with a broken wing, what may have been a hamster but more resembled a garden mole. The youngest of them had a fish, presumably dead and gone quite colorless, holding it in her hand. So intent were they at their play, they paid no heed to my noise among the trash bins or, now, to my approach, and after a moment of looking on, I withdrew.

By this time I'd seemingly exhausted my options and could think of nothing more to which I might duly turn my attention. What to do, then? Whenever in doubt, fall back to the room for regathering and further refreshment.

Bennie was scuttling away from my door as I came out the stairwell.

"Ah, Boss, glad I caught you. The thing is—" He glanced about. "Maybe we oughta talk inside."

We went in, and I poured, first for myself, then for Bennie, obscuring each glass with my fingers so he wouldn't see how much got in either. Whatever miniscule twinge of guilt I might have felt was done with soon enough.

"What it is," he said, eying the glass as I handed it over, "is we think maybe there ain't no wombat. Maybe never was? I show 'em pictures, none of the maids remember ever seeing anything like that. Neighbors either."

"What does Miss Landowska say?"

"Boss, I ain't asking that woman. She scares the bejeezus out of me."

"What about Mr. Bower, then. What did he say?"

"I got two, three sentences in before he just told me *Find the damn thing*, like he did before."

"Then I think we both need another drink."

"That could be."

This time I gave him a proper one, and after he left, had two or three more myself, sitting there looking up and out into darkness thinking how the city's lights so mercilessly edited stars from the sky.

Sooner or later, of course, I was going to have to do it, so I slammed one last drink and went up to Miss L's.

"I'm glad you came," she said at the door, then asked me to follow her out to the kitchenette, where she showed me the neatly stacked tins of pet food. There were brushes and small clippers laid out on the counter by them, a water bowl on the floor below, toys in one corner. "I'm sorry for taking your time," she said, running her hand lightly along the cans. "I think—" She looked away a moment. "I think Marcel, my wombat, I think maybe that was some while ago. Years, even. My memory . . ."

When she failed to go on, I told her I understood. Was there anything else I could do? I asked. But even then she was quiet.

I returned to my room and my high window and stood there for a long time. Late that night, early morning really, most of my last bottle of Scotch gone to good cause, I became certain that I saw movement in the room's corner, something by the wall over by the dresser, even thought I heard scratching sounds, but when I looked, nothing was there. So much of life is that way.

HOW THE WORLD GOT TO BE

Thursdays, we go to dinner at Jewel's. Everyone brings a dish. It's become a habit, even a tradition, in the village—our *wont*, as old books have it. There's no pre-planning to the event, and a certain small excitement in seeing what we make of what we have.

The mannikins dressed as Jewel's parents sit propped in their favorite chairs. Talk skitters and skips about the room. No one thinks anything of the mannikins' presence at the table with us. We're used to them. They've always been here.

To arrive, we passed through a light rain. From time to time now we pause to listen to its errant footfalls outside. Bearing gifts and, for all we know, death.

Most of the regulars are in attendance. Two places sit empty, their usual habitants indisposed or perhaps too fearful.

Brick sells insurance. Having been brought up by parents of a stomp-and-burn brand of socialist fervor, he often speaks at length of how important what he does is to the economy, the quality of individual life, and the community. Tonight another topic has caught his fancy, Root thus being denied his customary rejoinder that "It's gambling, Brick, it's just gambling."

Bridge is fond of explaining, even when but tangentially appropriate to the conversation, that her brother was a philosopher and that whenever they were together their talk was not of games, entertainment, and other such dailyness, but of teleology and epistemology.

"Never *sommes*," Bone will say then, "always *devenons*."

Our meal tonight consists of polenta, which Jewel in a fit of populism insists upon calling grits, with sauteed mushrooms and yogurt.

Some months back, Jewel became aware of a pressure, a presence, in his abdomen. Like a tiny head, he said, that would protrude whenever he lay flat or twisted in place. A tumor, as it turned out. Treated with radiation, the tumor collapsed, leaving a necrotic cavity, and

Jewel got fitted, temporarily, the surgeons said, with a pump for exudates. The pump is still there. It makes a steady panting noise. We're all used to it and pay it no mind.

Our conversation tonight, as Jewel's pump pants quietly and rain whispers against the roof, is What We Leave Behind.

"Aside from decomposing corpses," Bone, ever the realist, adds.

"Children, should we be so fortunate."

"Whatever wealth we may have."

"Regrets."

"Our ideas."

"What we believe—that's our true wealth."

Admittedly we sound at the moment a committee given to the preservation and perpetuation of homily.

Coffee, gargling for some time in an antique percolator on the sideboard, announces readiness with a soft-spoken C chord, its third a tiny bit flat. The usual proffer of cups, ceremonial dunkings of sugar, and splashes of milk follow close thereupon as silence for the moment befalls us. Rain, too, quietens, allowing Jewel's pump to become the room's heartbeat.

"When I was a child—" Brick begins, and we all know what we're in for. Agreement was reached years back that romantic remembrances are forbidden. We'd have done well to include childhood memories.

Brick's recollection is like ancient pinball games, its teller careening off fragments of plot, fitful ideas, random description, flat-out diversion. False trails and baffles everywhere. There are no flashes of light, though, no bells or clangs, only the panting of Jewel's pump, till the monolog at length wears down.

And this is another problem with childhood memories for, hard upon the last breath of Brick's story, Bridge breathes in to begin her own. The damned things are contagious. "Of late I've been thinking about crawfish boils back home, when I was a kid. Buckets of them poured out onto tables, the smell of beer everywhere, the flies. All those small bodies piling up."

Which is, I suppose, philosophy of a sort, and a far cry from homilies.

"You know . . ." the Sand twins say together, looking not around at our faces but to the floor, as though to signal how very taken by thought they are. "We should have music." The twins are younger than the rest of us and truly mirror images. Lake has a droopy right eye, Leaf a left.

"We tried that, back before you and you joined us. We could never agree what kind."

"Light classical, or something with more life to it?"

"Soft jazz, pop, show tunes. Lyrics. No lyrics."

"Whispery background or cheerful and upbeat."

"Held out, myself, for Sousa marches." Bone of course.

Just so, just as cats used to move about my childhood farm, striking poses one moment, often glaring up motionless into trees or rafters or into dark corners, padding on aimlessly the next, our conversation unrolls along whatever road it finds. Rain drums fingers at the roof.

There are topics, mind you, from which we keep a careful distance. One does not invite monsters into the house or go out on the porch to see what the noise was. Some names are never spoken.

After a time, conversation edges tentatively, one might even say delicately, towards current events. The school under construction, a bolstering-up of infrastructure, new cooperative farms just outside the city.

"We swim in history," Root says, "and history is but a record of mistakes."

Generally Root's comments exist as footnotes, outside the common exchange, but now they're taken up in turn.

"It may be that we're getting better at mistakes."

"Things do seem to move at a faster pace."

"Less time wasted, go straight for the worst."

Humor won't save us, but it does help fill the blanks. The spaces. We have our share of those.

"What," asks Bridge, breaking into our momentary silence, "would you have been in the old world, had you the chance?"

A children's game

Responses move around the table. "A politician," someone says, "doing my part to bring change," to which another replies "We've had quite enough of that, don't you think?"

"A farmer, hydroponics maybe—or a teacher of some sort."

"Veterinarian. I remember loving animals."

"An artist or musician, trying to express what can't be, with words."

And here I sit, a linguist who is all about words, like Bridge's brother searching out what lies behind and beneath things as they are, like him abstracted from the world while at one and the same time pegged mercilessly to it.

Conversation lags and, seemingly all of us at once, we realize the rain has stopped. In silence Jewel's pump sounds different. My imagination, surely.

And the moment's question, the last children's game, is this, for me alone: Do I still believe, as I did in youth, that words will save us? They may just as well damn us. Perhaps (as I look and listen about) they already have.

Does it matter?

What else do we have.

HOW I CAME TO BE

I'd been thinking about it for a while, finally made up my mind and called Rerun Inc. about signing up for a do-over of my last three days. The agent on the phone, Alice, who had a deep voice and said everyone called her Al, was kind and helpful. Good for you, she said. We are what we choose to be. Then she told me about the specials they were running today.

"I'm not looking for anything fancy or expensive, just—"

We get it, Alice said, we understand. You're unhappy with the way things went, how they turned out. And you don't want to carry that around any longer. Our basic package, then. Material is on its way to you. Once we have that in place, we'll get our designers right on it.

The contract, payment details, and "recovery forms" arrived instantly. I signed the contract, transferred funds from my cloud account to Rerun's, and settled down to getting the past three days on record and sketching in the remake I wanted (*the narrative*, as the form termed it), wondering why, of all things, old tunes I hadn't heard or thought of in years were running through my mind as I worked at the form.

Reruns aren't cheap, let me tell you. Just like that, snap of a finger, and a year's savings, everything I managed to put away, gets gone.

Okay, so here's what happened. Monday, the old man, he called me in to tell me to collect my belongings and get out, there were too many complaints and my help would no longer be required. Or permitted, he added. Then, on my way home, I'm standing in line at the light-rail, pull out my wallet to get my pass, when this kid slides up, grabs the wallet, and races off, pass and all. I gotta beg money to get home. Or walk.

Which was just as well, being as I was in no hurry, you understand, to own up to the job loss thing. But by the time I hoofed my way home, Stuart had dinner waiting, even early as it still was, and some of my favorites at that, meatloaf, mashed potatoes, gravy, so I figured telling him about getting let go might best wait. I was three, four bites in (the food, cold as a river, had been waiting for some time) when he told me he'd finally had enough, I could go ahead and finish the last meal of his I'd ever eat, then he'd be out of here for good and don't call, don't write, don't even think about him because this was it, you understand, this was *it*, he was done with me and everything about me.

Monday this was, mind you, and hardly even late afternoon.

I sat there a while stuffing cold food in my mouth and swallowing, maybe chewing, maybe not, I don't remember. The gravy had congealed and would barely glop off the spoon. I ate it anyway, and by then I'd got to thinking, You know, things don't have to be this way.

I picked that thought up and carried it into the next room, then down the street to Duff's where Every Day Is Lady's Day and a half-price draft awaited me and there's always someone to talk to. Except that day, Monday, there wasn't. Some kind of race going on, horses or cars, I don't remember which, everybody staring up to the TV over the bar. And Fred back behind it told me he's on the quiet cause he's got mouth sores, which is good, his being on the quiet, since I definitely didn't want to hear any more about those sores.

Leaving, I decided on a slow, leisurely walk along the canal but was hardly up the bank when a goose the size of a mastiff came flapping up to me honking and snapping. The damned thing, whatever its grievance was, wouldn't give up and chased me halfway home. Where, to top the day off, it seems either Stuart or I had left a stove burner on and whatever was in the pot atop it, and the pot itself, had pretty much burned away, filling the apartment with blinding smoke.

I turned off the burner and just sat there, half hidden in the smoke, till a neighbor came over to see what was going on. Not to check if I was all right, mind you, just to see if he might need to evacuate.

Nothing left in my tank. I was plumb out of gas, spunk, wherewithal, getup, gumption, pluck, and ambition.

I'll spare you further details, but the next two days did little to, what's the word, *assuage* the situation. The second time the doctors at QuiknEasy Clinic (street name Queasy) saw me, they set the fracture, wrapped it up tight in fibers strong as steel that weighed about what a hummingbird does, and, echoing my own earlier thoughts, told me it didn't have to be this way, you know.

So I got to thinking: If only I could . . .

And, of course, I could. Relief was a phone call and a bank transfer away. Alice stood by even then, no doubt, awaiting my call.

I came awake with warm sunlight on my legs and a face over me, beautiful eyes above the surgical mask (I like to think) smiling.

"Everything went fine," the face said. "You're in recovery. Would you like water?"

You're damned right I would, if only I could get my tongue unstuck from the roof of my mouth. They'd poured glue in there. I couldn't even *feel* my tongue. No way I was able to answer her. I nodded, then had a moment's panic that my head was going to roll off my shoulders, maybe bounce across the floor.

It was all good.

Best water I ever had. I had more, got a final check from nurse Alyson, who did indeed have a lovely smile, dressed, and went home.

I ordered in some Chinese, put the CD player on auto, watched people stream by in the street outside, started up a load of clothes, and collected my thoughts.

I'd well and truly disliked that job. It pleased me that my resignation had been accepted without rancor or ill feelings. As for Stuart and me, our breakup, well, we'd been watching that come down the road for a long while. And in the event it was certainly amicable enough, even amiable.

So, it seemed I had a life to refurnish. I pushed the last of the spicy tofu and vegetables aside and started a list, one that began, of course, with *Find new work*.

Something was off, though. *Work* didn't look right. It looked more like *wonk*. And what did that mean, anyway?

Check flances. What the hell are flances?

I looked up, away, out the window. Had it always been set in the wall like that, canted, a parallelogram? I remembered it square, and squarely placed—didn't I?

A volley of such troubling experiences soon prompted a visit to Rerun Inc. It had all started there, with that window, and with language. Then over coming months, as, ever more frequent, those visits continued, what I began to think of as The Askew took hold elsewhere in the world. Shadows beneath chairs and doors developed sharp edges, lights shone from within closed cupboards and closets, people down in the streets, in the city, in the world, looked to be frozen in place, posed there timelessly, a diorama. I began to see colors for which I had no name, seeping in from the ultraviolet, I suspected, as for birds, fish, and other life forms.

Then there were the graffiti on the building across the street. For months these had shown up every morning. Workmen came in the afternoon to scrub and power-hose them away. The next day they were back. Squiggles and scrolls, the occasional letter or word mixed in, fanciful sketches of eyes or figures. Nonsense, really. The scribe's names, likely, or gang symbols. Though now when I stared across at them they seemed to be reaching out, as though they had something to tell me, something raw, urgent and all too human.

In the course of my revisits to Rerun I got to know Alice and nurse Alyson pretty well. Heard how Alice's cancer treatments were going this second time around, and about her brother, who sounded a proper jerk, all the time getting himself in trouble and coming to her for help, but you could see she loved him. Listened to what amounted to a blow-by-blow of Alyson's recent vacation in Washington with her two kids, all the places they went, what they saw. Good people, these.

But neither they nor techs nor doctors at Rerun Inc. had much to offer by way of actual help with the changes that were bothering me.

"We can make small adjustments, yes," they told me at each visit, "but once the procedure is completed, we're greatly limited as to what we can do."

Which was not much at all.

Rerun's head doctor finally sat me down for a heart-to-heart. "It's not within our power to change the world around you," he said. "All we can change is you. *You* is where the world begins and where it ends. Surely you knew that."

Of course I did, all along. I must have.

Because that's what we do, isn't it, every one of us? We get up in the morning and start rebuilding our world—or choose to live in the ruins.

"And that, since you asked, is how I came to be sitting here."

Julie's just back from her session at Rerun. Seeing referrals in their own homes, I find, works best. She's seated on a straight-backed chair, lightly padded—her usual, I take it. I'm on a plush couch upholstered with patterns of bright, fall-colored leaves. A tree just outside the window has multiple bird feeders hanging from it.

"So you're with Rerun now? As a therapist?"

"No, but I see clients who are having, or whom they believe may have, problems with adjustment. I see many others as well. As a therapist, yes. Sometimes, fancifully, I like to think of myself as a kind of latter-day midwife, helping people through all the unimaginable changes that crowd down around us."

"Am I supposed to talk? About my feelings?"

"Only if you want to."

"Good . . . Do you ever wonder what might have happened if you'd let those three days be?"

"Not wondering would be unnatural. I denied those days, or tried to—painted over them, you could say—but they, the days themselves, the procedure, or some combination of all, changed my life utterly."

I lean forward, a bit closer.

"One of my favorite stories is about fighter pilots, danger everywhere, milliseconds to make decisions. And with training that can only go so far in preparing them. So they're told: When you don't know what to do, just do *something*. Knowing this will at least set off a new chain of events, and you take it from there."

Julie smiles. "Do you ever get back to Rerun?"

"Occasionally I see clients there. When I do, I welcome the chance to say hello and catch up with staff. Alyson's still there, more or less running the place now. You met her. Al left late last year and, as Alyson puts it, nowadays rests her shapely butt on a chair in the state senate. We're all okay."

I tell her: "You will be too."

ABEYANCE

Tonight let me go
at last out of whatever
mind I thought to have,
and all the habits of it.
—Robert Creeley

Hannah

Once when she was a child, eleven or twelve, this was back in Philly, she came home from school, ate a small apple, and opened up her case to practice. It had been a bad day, the mismatched furniture of her life slipping here and there, and truth to tell, she didn't feel at all like practicing either the new piece she was supposed to be working on or scales and intervals, but sticking to the routine was better than feeling bad for failing to do so, so she settled in with her violin to play a few favorites. She was looking out the window as she played, at the leaves just beginning to change, at a van delivering furniture to new tenants across the street, little thought given to what she was doing, bow and arm a single unit, left-hand fingers falling lightly in place, all of it so familiar, so comfortable. Slowly, though, she came to realize that there was more music than she herself was providing, that someone was playing along with her, weaving fragments of melody, counter melody and harmony into her take on the Mozart.

Done, she sat quietly for a moment before returning her instrument to its case and putting it away securely on the shelf. Then she propped the front door open (she'd forgotten to take the key and got locked out a time or two, so caution and habit prevailed) and went to the other apartments on the floor, Sandersons to the right, Ulmans left, then to the floors above and below. Everyone complimented her on her playing but no one else had heard the other violin. For long weeks after, whenever she picked up her instrument and began playing, she was also listening. Expectant, waiting.

Nothing like that ever happened again.

Eighteen years later, Hannah has a degree in economics from Columbia and lives in Oregon working with newborn babies in the NICU. She can't quite follow the plot of how she got to this. It had taken her all of a month to discover she wasn't meant to be part of the corporate world. Daily staff meetings took place around a long, cold steel table held down by platters of pastries and huge carafes of coffee. She'd never in her life felt more fearful; after each meeting she hid out in her cubicle. Once she left Birnham & Bausch, all its glass windows and polished wood, she tried her hand at teaching but, despite weeks of preparation, walked off campus halfway through her first class.

Three accelerated years of study further on and she's a nurse. A year later, because the other nurses seem afraid of them, she's taking care of newborns so tiny and weightless that, were they not anchored by ventilators, IV tubes, monitor cables and restraints, they might float away in the first errant breeze.

Here, it's just her and the baby. Mothers come, of course, and stay for hours at a time, but there isn't a lot of talk left in most of them. Fathers roll and shoot about like pinballs from stunned bafflement to terror to fawning concern. Occasionally others visit. Family members, clergy, reverends, rabbis. But mostly it's just her and the child. She'll have a second baby assigned her, but that one will be doing well, require far less attention. And at night, with lights low and scheduled quiet time thrown like a blanket over the vast unit, it can feel as though they're alone, the two of them, in a world with no need for talk or clamor, a world where life goes quietly and courageously on.

So here she is.

Hannah's shift was almost over, and she was with her favorite. Baby Girl Chen had been in the unit four weeks. She weighed one pound eight ounces. She'd been on ECMO, blood pumped from her body, oxygenated outside, then returned, until three days ago. She'd spontaneously extubated once and almost a second time.

They moved her, changed bedding, did everything, with great care. She recognized Hannah's voice and turned toward her when she spoke—or so Hannah believed.

Vitals were stable, ABGs ordered for 0700, and if parameters were as expected, they'd lower the vent rate, let Baby Girl Chen take on a bit more of the work of breathing. Hannah auscultated heart and lungs, double-checked IV bags for rate and patency, verified monitor positions. Charted it all. As ever, she marveled at how resilient these kids were, at the drive to life within them.

Talk in the break room tonight had been of rumored personnel cuts on the floors and how they might be next, but also about the new mall soon opening out by Sunny Slope and a new TV show having something to do, apparently, with wildlife.

On her way home Hannah got out two stops early, as she often did, to walk the last eight blocks in a fierce cold, wind snapping at face and hands, all manner of detritus swirling about her feet. Once inside, she put on music, then took oatmeal, soaked in milk overnight, out of the fridge to warm before cooking. She made tea and sat, as gradually her eyes recovered from brightness, her body from the bruise and pressure of others.

Mostly it was opera she listened to these days. Brash music, so much of it, and busy, boastful, though oddly enough it calms her. The morning's choice: *Die Zauberflöte*, volume set low. As she listened, something very much like magic appeared fleetingly at world's edge and grew toward her, magic that was never there when you looked straight on.

Hannah's mother was a scream queen.

"I spent my professional life screaming," Trish said. "Either that, or going out on the porch to see what that sound was, or getting too close to the window. You use what talent you have, and what they'll let you."

She lost track of how many movies she'd made, starting off at the big studios and ending, as the taste for horror films steadily receded, with others no one had ever heard of, the kind that sprang up and withered away in the blink of an eye. She'd got bumped like Pooh down the funny stairs, Trish said, "going from worse to worst to *wurst.*" Makeup and hair perfectly in place, nails brightly polished, Trish had stridden through vast post-apocalyptic landscapes, looked on as aliens resembling southwestern cacti infested the earth, stared aghast as ageless demons came from above, below or within, and faced dozens of drooling *things* forever randy, it seemed, and desperately in need of a good time.

Trish's own favorite, from early in her career, was *The Cage*, whose grade-school janitor, known only as Private, kidnaps a woman and keeps her in a cage patterned after those in which he himself had survived four years as a POW in Vietnam. There, he never once spoke. Here, he goes out and does terrible things, then comes back to tell her about them in these long, rambling stories, seeking—what? Forgiveness? Atonement? Redemption? You never know, even at the end. Monstrously huge edible scorpions, along with protein-rich crickets and grasshoppers, shared time with the two leads. The movie saw sporadic revival at film festivals, remained popular in parts of Europe and Asia.

The best known of Trish's movies was *RIPresentatives*, a regular on creature-feature TV and at midnight screenings. As oatmeal simmered on the stove, Hannah rummaged about and found her copy. Something—she liked to think insects—had all but nibbled away one corner of the cassette, and the label was long gone. This copy, years ago before the movie achieved cult status, had been difficult to find, as had a functioning videocassette player. She fed the cassette to the player and watched the title lurch up onscreen, followed by *Written and Directed by* and, in much smaller script, *Suggested by a story by Thomas M. Disch.*

The film opens voice-over with Trish at the window of her cramped, crappy apartment watching the world go by outside, five stories below. She's mumbling invective about all these sheep, all the viciousness lodged in their minds, the purposelessness of it all, and all the while, the expression of longing on her face gives lie to her words: she longs to be a part of that normal life she's never had, won't ever have. As she watches, a cockroach comes into view on the wall beside the window.

She turns and sees another one perched on the rim of the bowl with her breakfast, some of the last food she has in the apartment, and thinks—in a silent scream—*No!* The roach drops to the table and remains there, as though waiting. She sends it across the table top, down one leg, up the far wall, back to the table. It will do whatever she thinks. Others come from under furniture, out of the walls, through cracks in window casings. Waiting for instruction, for guidance.

For a while the roaches are an amusement and nothing more. She sends them into other apartments, out to the dark stairway where teenagers meet to make out, into the super's basement hideaway. Soon she's dispatching them to terrorize the politicians and so-called community leaders who from greed, unconcern and willful blindness have brought her city to the edge of ruin.

Hannah sat with her breakfast watching, film sound turned off. In this scene the cockroaches are marching en masse up Wall Street, block on block of them curb to curb, a black sea of reckoning, on their latest mission. Nothing but drums and percussion on the soundtrack at this point, she remembered. Big, big ending. *Die Zauberflöte* still played low in the background. How little difference finally, she thought, between the two. This movie, the opera. We so badly want it all to make sense somehow, we want so badly for it to be set right.

She should call her mom.

Short-staffed already from call-ins, they'd barely finished report before getting slammed with three-pound twins and a congenital heart. Acting as charge nurse, Shoshana begged everyone to take up whatever slack they could. If you even get to a point where you can lift your head, look around. Check with the next bed, do what you can. Help.

Along about 3 A.M., things were as close to okay as they were going to get, and Hannah took a break. Shoshana was in the lounge, perfectly upright in a molded plastic chair that almost matched the color of her scrubs. An inch or so of jerky protruded from her mouth as though forgotten. The break room had the only window in the unit. Double-paned, it looked out onto Hull Street where traffic moved steadily, soundlessly by. Silent movie out there, buzzers and bells and general clatter of the unit in here. Plus, usually, TV.

"Moira called in?" Hannah said. The two of them often worked neighboring beds. "That doesn't happen."

"Not once in the six years I've been here."

"Did she give a reason?"

"Someone called for her. Flu-like symptoms."

Moira kept to herself like Hannah and, again like Hannah, lived alone. Hannah was pretty sure there was no one else in her life. No partner, romance, lover, family.

Hannah stayed on after report that morning, went down to the cafeteria and dawdled over a sweet roll and coffee waiting for the administrative offices to open. Gaggles of personnel—nurses, office workers, X-ray and lab techs, housekeepers—gathered at long tables chatting away. Visitors, family members, and occasional patients sat scattered about the room. Hannah watched a middle-aged man repeatedly walk to the cafeteria entrance, step inside, look about, and withdraw, IV pole swaying.

Just before nine, she left to head upstairs and came across attendants pushing a stretcher carrying an elderly woman, oxygen tank tucked in like a third leg. Somehow, looking for ER, they'd strayed into the basement's warren of add-ons and corridors. Hannah gave them directions.

The nursing office was on the third floor, at the end of a side hallway. She couldn't remember ever being on the higher floors. NI was on the second, HR in the basement, orientation held in the classrooms down there. She must have had a tour of patient floors at some point, but any memory of such had faded.

As she'd hoped, Marianne Jeffries, the Director of Nursing, was on morning rounds, office manager Kat Valdez at the front desk. Hannah had gone over and over her appeal while waiting: that she and Moira had worked together a long time, she was worried about Moira calling in since that never ever happened, and while she knew—

Kat stopped her.

"I know what you go through down there, Hannah, what you see. You have to stick together." She tapped at her keyboard, handed over a page from a notepad with Moira's address. A far cry from Hannah's neighborhood, in a snarl of streets that seem to start up from nowhere then within a block or two vanish, as she remembered. A part of the old town that hadn't ever changed much, of little interest to developers.

Hannah walked out into another blustery day, dark clouds nudging at sky, intermittent spits of rain. When you work nights, routine holds your corner of the world together. Lose that routine, things fly apart. Staying over to visit the nursing office already had her off-kilter. Now this. But as she walked on, the rain stopped.

The neighborhood was not at all as she remembered. Many of the compact, four-room houses had been converted to art galleries, coffee shops, or shops selling used and vintage clothing, classic vinyl, ceramics and the like. As many as not had murals painted on side walls or flowers bordering low concrete steps onto porches. People were abroad everywhere, bearing restless anthologies of clothing, tattoos, and piercings.

The address Kat gave her took Hannah to a stumpish street of six houses that elsewhere might be called bungalows, all of them but one built to the same basic pattern. Moira's was the odd duck in the line, larger and of more recent vintage than the rest, a duplex, with a porch roof canting out over the front like a heavy brow. *For Rent* sign on the right.

Standing by the left, Hannah heard low, soft music from inside. No answer with the first knock; with the next, a curtain beside the door parted to show a narrow slice of face. Moments later this view repeated as the door opened along its chain.

"Yes?"

"Is Moira here?"

"Moira?"

"I'm a friend, from work."

"Oh. Maybe that's who lived here before?"

The door closed for the chain to be released, then opened fully. A slim young man, newly showered judging from the wet hair. Pressed slacks, white dress shirt with tails out, unbuttoned. He glanced down, then back.

"Sorry. On my way to a job interview."

The room was sparsely furnished. A wicker love seat, waist-high bookshelf populated half-and-half by books and DVDs, soft chair with floor lamp alongside, small wooden table and almost-matching desk, bright woven rugs. An expansive customized sound system against one wall. What Hannah had taken to be music was a talk show of some kind, tempo and timbres modulating with the change of speakers.

"Can I ask how long you've been here?"

"Rent's almost due, so—two months now."

Buttoning his shirt, the man glanced at a digital clock on the wall behind him.

"I won't keep you. Is there someone else I could talk to?" Hannah asked. "The house's owner? A rental agent?"

"Hang on a minute." He went to the desk, opened a drawer, and came back with a business card. "I really do need to be out of here and on my way."

Sam Fuller
Property Management
Commercial, Residential

"Of course," Hannah said. "Thank you."

The address was well across town. Hannah considered going home to get the car, but it felt good to move around. Walking would let her shake off the fatigue she felt, loosen up, recharge.

Homes of more recent vintage, mid-fifties ranch styles among them, began showing up as Hannah walked on. Random signs of young children here, abandoned toys, capsized bikes, inflatable pools. Occasional basketball hoops affixed to house or garage or mounted on moveable poles. Sprinklers and trimmed hedges. Barking dogs every third house or so, it seemed. She'd almost walked past when a sign stapled to a telephone pole took her attention. Black and white, 8-1/2 x 11, printed out from a computer.

DIVORCE
Can Be Done By Phone
$300

Not far from there, still thinking about the divorce flyer, Hannah came to a house with signs on lawn and front window reading PSYCHIC, driveway to the left, carport with a window to the house. Drive-through psychic, first of its kind? Pull in, there'd be a speaker and a crackly voice from inside asking how they can help, maybe some vague music, a whiff of incense. Drawer slides out with a place to swipe your credit card. Once you've had your reading, a print-out of the reading complete with receipt uncurls from within.

Hannah came to the property manager's address, not the stone-facade office she anticipated, but a wooden structure resembling one-room schoolhouses in old westerns, ancient yellow paint showing under newer white. Across the street a similar building housed Jumpy Horse Theater, as did, further along, a museum or shop—could be either, from the signage—dedicated to ANTIQUE MAPS.

The office's front door was propped open with a brick, its occupant, presumably Sam, on the phone. When the floor creaked, she swiveled around to wave Hannah in. Late fifties, with the physical presence of someone much younger and no indication that she did much of anything to cultivate same. Light makeup, hair clipped mid-length, short nails. The armpit of the arm holding the phone was unshaved. In one of Trish's movies, Sam Fuller would be the scientist who arrives bearing crucial information and appeals for caution, not long before the male lead, monster, alien, audience, all the above, fall in love with her.

"I understand. Parents get along in years, they get hard to raise. Won't behave no matter what you do or say. But give me a call when you decide, okay?"

She hung up the phone.

"That's life for you. Shouts out *Hey, look over here*, then trips you up when you do." It sounded spontaneous, not at all like something she'd said a hundred times. "Making a house call?"

Hannah hadn't thought about being in scrubs. At home or at work, she more or less lived in them.

Or was that a sideways pun?

"I work at County. With Moira Jarosz," Hannah said. "She rented from you, over on Beach."

Fuller's fingers rippled at the keys of a laptop propped on folders at one side of the desk. "Right. Neighborhood's finally got around to imagining it might be something else."

And that. Sales pitch? Simple observation? Wishful thinking?

"I was told she moved out two months ago, maybe more."

Fuller hadn't looked up from the screen. Now she did. "August. And you're asking because?"

"Moira didn't show up for work."

"I see. You're friends?"

"As I said, we work together. And this isn't like her at all. She never missed shifts. I hoped you'd have a forwarding address, know why she left—anything, really. I'm concerned."

"I didn't get notice. A tenant—I have other property in the area—called to let me know he thought the house had gone empty. Someone tried to break in the night before, he was pretty sure. He turned on his yard lights, didn't see or hear anything more. I went over that morning. He was right, looked like the place had been empty a while. And if your friend just up and left, she traveled light. Furniture was there. Pots, pans, appliances, dishes. Clothes in closets and drawers, in the laundry hamper. Usual stuff in the medicine cabinet, a couple old prescription meds. Scented soap and disposable razor on the shelf by the tub."

"Purple."

"Yeah."

"Moira's color. Her scrubs were purple. So it looked like everything was there."

"Except her."

"Then where was she staying? She came to work, every shift. Till last night."

"I can give you my tenant's name. He didn't have much to add. I asked when he last saw her, if he'd noticed anything out of the ordinary over there, people coming or going, new cars in the drive."

"She didn't have a car."

"So he said. But recently he'd seen an older Chevy or Ford, dark blue, parked out front in the street. Never saw the driver, far as he knows." She hit keys again, wrote down the tenant's name and address. "Funny thing is, it's a duplex, right? I go over there and it's the exact same story with the other side. Tenant there's gone too, stuff left behind."

By then it was going on 1 P.M. Hannah thanked Sam Fuller and headed uneventfully home. Just inside the door she stripped off the scrubs. Pulled a lasagna out of the freezer for dinner, within minutes was back in the kitchen wearing shorts and a T-shirt and, not long after that, in the bathroom reclining in a tub of hot water with the lasagna and a beer standing by. Even the bathroom was fitted with blackout curtains. Light came from six large candles. Their flames skittered with every movement of her body, with the air conditioner's cycles, even with her breath. Light and shadow embraced then pushed away in ever-changing patterns on the walls.

Hannah leaned back into warm water. Okay, so this wasn't magical, wasn't a fragment of some other, better world. But it was damned close.

Three nights later, when Hannah reported for work, she got moved up to pedi. A particularly nasty flu had been stomping its way through the staff and, with call-ins, shifts had gone critically short. She was out of her depth up here. These kids were *big*. They talked. Talked, talked back, acted out. Some screamed. And she didn't have one or two patients, she had five spread all around the floor, with utterly different illnesses and issues. Floor routines, drugs, dosages— all were a foreign language. Didn't know the doctors, and even the lab results were half a mystery. She coped, but felt all night as if she were barely hanging on.

That morning she looked at the clock, realized she was home and, with no clear memory of arriving or of what she had been doing since, realized that she'd been home for some time, music playing low, cup and dishes in the sink, scrubs exchanged for pajama bottoms worn paper-thin and a T-shirt from a band that apparently included, of all things, a nyckelharpa. Where might she have gotten that, and why?

She'd been bone tired many times after hard shifts, scarcely able to drag herself out of the hospital and home, but never, as far as she could remember, *this* tired. Her feet hurt. Her bones hurt. The rub of clothing against her skin hurt. She showered and went straight to bed. An hour later she was in the bathroom throwing up.

Children carry around all kind of off-the-wall illnesses for which adults have no acquired immunities. When you do your peds rotations they tell you: expect to be sick. So this could be something she'd picked up from one of the kids. But it was probably too soon for that, not enough time for incubation. More likely the flu had found her.

She fell back into bed, into an old, familiar dream of going out for bagels and not being able to find her way home, one that repeated itself like a stutter again and again with minor variations, different people at the counter, bright sunny day or pouring-down rain, every bagel on the rack burned to a crisp, the kind of dream where even within it you start hoping you'll wake soon to break the cycle. No further vomiting, but her body felt like it weighed an extra fifty pounds and her head was packed with mud.

At four she got up and, as apologetically as she could muster, which, considering that she felt so terrible she really didn't care, wasn't very, called in sick. Her temp was 101.

Did sirens wake her at some point, or were they part of another dream? They had been, or seemed to be, moving across town, from wealthier parts to less, east to west. Police, fire trucks, paramedics. Those who turn up when things go terribly wrong. To rescue, salvage, save what they can.

Hannah woke in the blacked-out room and for a moment panicked, unsure where or when she was. Daytime? Night? Her head pounded. Sheets and pillowcase were sweat-sopped.

She could no longer hear sirens, if ever she actually had. The display on the bedside clock upticked to 8:49 and, from the dragged-out way she felt, she couldn't have slept long. Evening, then. The missed-call light on her phone was blinking. Few people had her number. Could be the hospital calling in all available personnel, because of the sirens. If the sirens had been real.

Knackered came to mind, from somewhere. She was knackered. Completely off her sleep cycle, awake in early evening still exhausted with a long night ahead, body wracked beneath the weight of whatever the hell had taken it over.

Hannah stood, and immediately sat back down. The room dipped and swayed. Her legs had gone just as unsteady. She forced herself to take slow, deep breaths, one after another. Gradually the worst of it passed. The kitchen seemed miles away but, one hand on the wall for support, she made it there, leaned against the sink drinking glass after glass of water. Her head felt twice its normal size. She was shivering inside, burning outside.

The next time she turned the clock around to look, it was 2:34, so she'd slept, though it didn't much feel that way. She had no memory of anything since standing in the kitchen holding the glass. Wispy dreams slewed to the surface with her and fell away.

That's it, she was done with sleep for now. She took a shower, then settled down with coffee she'd put on before. In near-darkness, three o'clock in the morning. Just like being where she most often was this time of night. All that was missing was a newborn in her charge and the comforting, close sounds of the unit. Instead she had a TV show telling her there were more than 400,000 kinds of beetles and that, all told, they comprised a full one-fourth of the world's animals, information she found strangely comforting. Not so comforting was the show's claim that the blue poison dart frog was in fact not intrinsically poisonous but became so from the insects, spiders, maggots and caterpillars upon which it fed.

"Did they ever find those parents?"

"What parents?"

Hannah had waited till almost ten in the morning to call. Seventh ring, third call, Trish answered. Now Hannah watched the clock go from 10:04 to 10:06. Had they already run out of things to say?

"The last time we talked, you told me about this baby born with—I think it was a bad heart? Anyway, the parents stopped coming. You had the police go out to their address and they were gone, someone else was living there."

Hannah remembered now. Light snow on the ground, of all things. Early fall. Had it been that long since they talked?

"The parents never turned up."

"What happened with the baby?"

"Adopted de facto by the hospital. Moved up to pedi weeks later, could be in an extended care facility by now." If it survived.

"And what about the one that turned bright yellow from some

infection, then had all sort of other things go wrong? You'd had that one in the unit so long because there was no place else for the poor thing to go."

"Because of the level of care she had to have. Still up in pedi, last we heard. Tucked away in an end room somewhere. Extended-care and nursing facilities aren't set up for those whose needs are that high. Their people aren't trained for it." Is this, Hannah thought, what we wind up talking about, every time I call? "How are *you* doing?"

"Still above ground and moving under my own power."

"And Luis?"

"In Mexico shooting. One of those deals where there's more than one country involved in production, so it takes six months of lawyers and studio officials to put the package together, then a few weeks of actual work and it's done. He'll call when he can. What about you? Anything new?"

"Not really. One of our nurses is missing in action. Got sick, pulled up stakes. Something. Dropped out of sight, anyway. I'm trying to find out what."

"Good, that you have a friend you care about. Speaking of which," as moments ticked by, "I have to go. Jennie's at the door."

"Oh?"

"Headed to dinner. Subway, Denny's, the mall food court. Jennie's idea of a big time out. Glad you called, hon."

"Me too. Have fun, Mom."

And take care, Hannah thought as she hung up. She had no idea who Jennie was. Trish never had much luck with friends. They always seemed to materialize into her life and stumble out of it.

Not Luis, though.

Back before becoming the crown queen of scream, Trish had made a third and final ambitious movie. *ReBoot* (a.k.a. *Boot Legs*) was about a man holed up in a cellar somewhere in an active war zone watching his feet rot from cheap canvas combat boots and ever-drenched socks. As he drags himself around the cellar, unable to walk, even to stand, to the accompaniment of artillery and deto nations in the distance, all the women of his life come to visit, each one played by Trish.

At the time, Luis was a young Spanish filmmaker who'd made

two award-winning horror movies back home. This was to be his breakout. He didn't speak much English then, leading to communication problems on the set to accompany the usual screwups, clashes, union trolling, and cost overruns. Released, the movie never gathered momentum, sinking steadily toward the art houses, and Luis returned to what he knew best. He'd been smitten by his star, however; he and Trish had been together ever since.

So Luis remained lower-case famous for having made the same movie over and over going on forty years now. Different titles, different actors, one a thriller, the next a cop show, then a far-future Western, a gladiator, disaster or prison movie—but the same story, same beats, same pacing. Like what everyone said about Telemann: either he wrote a hundred concertos, or the same concerto a hundred times. None of Luis's movies made a lot of money by studio standards, but they got made so cheaply and so reliably that they never, ever lost any.

Following her troubled night, Hannah had slept a while just after dawn, before calling Trish. She'd felt almost decent when she got up but that was short-lived. Horrible taste in her mouth, and everything smelled half-rotten, tainted. Her eyes wouldn't stop watering. Legs shaky. Cold and hot at the same time. Classic symptoms. She took a deep breath and held it. Her lungs were okay. So far.

She fell back in bed, into ragged fragments of dream, and came suddenly awake at 3:19, going directly to the phone.

She wasn't sure when she made the decision, but at some point the night before, early this morning, later as she half-slept, it got made. Maybe even during the conversation with Trish, or in the wake of it. Or just as possibly during the phone call itself, to the nursing office, in the very moment she spoke. She really hadn't had much practice making decisions, when you came right down to it.

But just like that, Hannah was unemployed.

Moira

Her spirit animal was definitely the hermit crab.

There'd been so many borrowed homes since Moira left hers at age sixteen, not to escape rules, anger, raised voices, or violence as was so often the case, but to leave behind the silences growing in every room and corner of the house, Mother shut away behind the door of her upstairs bedroom with the radio playing softly, Father self-exiled to his workshop out behind the garage in the company of the band saw, jigsaw, belt sander and lathe long unused yet regularly cleaned and maintained. It took her years to understand that she'd not left those silences behind.

The first place she fell to ground, sixteen years old, bursting with certainty that she knew pretty much everything she needed to know and, at one and the same time, that she hadn't a clue, was in the next town over. It looked and felt exactly like the one she had left. She'd planned to get much further, but the money she'd saved got taken by the driver who picked her up hitchhiking then, money in hand, put her back out on the side of the road. It could have been worse. And that, for a number of years, was pretty much the shape of her life.

She'd been so pleased when, for the move from one place to the next, instead of the usual sack, shoulder bag or box, she had an actual suitcase. How the suitcase came to her, she couldn't remember. It was sometime before the pioneer move westward-ho with Daniel whose *forever* became *no way* not long after they got where they were going, and what she remembered mostly about those days was wind with its head down like a billy goat coming at you constantly off a coast you couldn't see. The place they rented, for which she wound up being responsible, was two tiny rooms one atop the other at the back of a lot. When wind moved in the trees, the house swayed right along with them.

She found work clearing out abandoned apartments, mostly for her own landlord, though Mrs. Dawes farmed out the service to others as well. Some units it was as though one night the tenants just stood up and walked out never to return, leaving everything they owned behind—furniture, clothes folded or crammed into drawers, utensils and pans in the kitchenette, food on shelves. Other units were seriously trashed, with holes punched in walls, mounds of garbage, stains of piss and worse, burn marks, fixtures ripped out, ruined floors.

Whatever usable belongings she found during the clean-outs went to a storage facility for mass sales later on. Stuff without value went to the city dump. For all this, Moira had use of a spring-shot Ford pickup gone purple with age. She didn't have a license, but Mrs. Dawes never asked, probably never cared. Rent on the house took better than a third of what Moira got for the work. Mrs. Dawes deducted it before paying her.

Every so often Moira held onto something from a clean-out, trinkets mostly, curiosities. A small ceramic frog that she suspected had been, one day long past, an inkpot. A silver dollar with a bullet hole in it. A child's charm bracelet of Chinese characters, gold paint scaled almost completely away. A huge curved claw gone yellow with age. Sometimes she didn't even know what the objects were, there was just something about them that called to her.

One morning as Moira was clearing out an apartment near downtown, in a complex surrounded by boarded-up houses, it came to her that she'd begun to wonder about the people who lived in these units. Sometimes mail would be left behind and she'd learn names, look at utility bills, parking tickets, junk mail, the occasional summons to court or to jury duty. Very seldom anything personal, like letters. Then she'd go on sorting through clothes, tool boxes, patent medicines, cleaning supplies, toys, butt-sprung paperback books, even photographs. So many untold stories. So many sudden endings, slow abandonments. And here she was, bearing away whatever was left.

Nights, she watched movies off the dollar-special rack from a local rental shop, movies with titles like *Rivertown*, *Amanda's Secret*, and *The Return of Mister*, much the same save for different exteriors and hairstyles, mostly set in worlds where goodness was unmistakable and people could change for the good in an instant— from a chance encounter, the look in another's eye, a memory. It didn't matter to her what the movies were. She could count on her fingers how many she'd seen, before this. Sometimes now she watched three a night.

Often as she watched, she'd think back to what she found in the rentals she serviced for Mrs. Dawes.

Once, in an apartment on the second floor, she stepped into the second of two rooms and came up against a huge old upright piano of gnarled walnut that had to weigh hundreds and hundreds of pounds. She couldn't imagine how they'd ever got it in there. The keys, real ivory she assumed, were beautifully yellowed.

In the house behind a deserted church, which might have served as rectory, cages for large birds filled two of the four rooms. Parrots, maybe? Newspapers on the cage floors dated back years. Any stench was long gone, droppings petrified to dry, hard pellets.

From time to time, renters from nearby units came to see what, with all the banging and back and forth, might be going on. Some were curious, others hoped for gossip, most were simply avid to escape for a few moments the windows and walls of their own apartments.

Moira's last day on the job, she worked a building out by a strip mall that had been popular maybe fifteen years ago. Pulling up, she wondered if the planners had been vying for some kind of weirdness award. The building looked like a pyramid with its head in the sand, each of three floors larger than that below, probably offices when built, repurposed to residence further along.

The apartment in question was on the second floor. Even the stairs were peculiar, rounded and scooped on the front edge to look like seashells. As she worked her way through the apartment, Moira kept thinking how utterly it felt unlived-in. None of the usual doorway scratches, marks on walls, wear patterns from tables and favored chairs, chips and gauges, stains from spills, resident odors.

What was it they called it in crime shows when detectives looked at patterns of blood splatter? A void. Blood all around but a clearing within, a void, where someone had stood or lain.

In the two years she cleared out rental units for Mrs. Dawes, living small and close to the ground, picking up whatever other work she could, Moira had saved her money. She was starting nursing school the next week, in the state capital, and getting ready to move there.

She'd finished up the front room, hauling junk down to the back alley for pickup. Not much of anything to salvage here, for sale or otherwise, not much of anything, really. Leftover bits and pieces of things, broken things. *Effluvia.* She had no idea how she knew the word, or exactly what it meant, but it fit.

Stepping into the next room, she saw a young girl peering at her from the closet. Ten or twelve maybe, mostly bones, skin, and filthy, snarled hair. No sign of her earlier, when Moira did a quick walk-through. She'd made no sound. And whatever showed in her eyes wasn't fear. What, then?

Stillness.

"Do you belong here, honey?"

Nothing.

"Are you all by yourself?"

Was she even being heard?

"Where are your parents? Where do you live?"

When she took a couple of steps closer, the girl crouched and drew back. Moira could see a nest of towels and clothing deeper in the closet. So the girl had been sleeping there. Living there. What she had been eating, Moira couldn't imagine. There was some dry pasta left in the other room. Maybe there'd been more. Something else.

She didn't know what to do, and she was scared, for the girl and for herself. From a payphone in the corner store across the street she called Mrs. Dawes, who told her to take the girl to a hospital or fire station and drop her off, then hung up before Moira could tell her again that she couldn't get near the girl. Finally Moira called the police.

Mrs. Dawes blew up about that when, hours later, Moira returned the truck. She should never, *ever*, have called the police, not under *any* circumstances, Mrs. Dawes told her, but the rant mattered little to Moira. This was her last day.

She kept on wondering what became of the girl, who she was, her story. Once after moving she tried calling the police back home, then the children's hospital, but since she wasn't a relative and lacked official connection with the girl, no one would tell her anything. Moira would never forget her first sight of the girl peering from out the closet, or the brief flash of life that came into her eyes when they finally met Moira's, never forget how docilely she went along when the police came for her.

Moira had future dealings with police, but nothing like that. Two officers showed up at the dorm one morning to ask questions about a fellow nursing student who'd somehow, Moira surmised from the questions, got mixed up with drugs or maybe with drug dealers, hard to tell. Not long after she'd moved into her own room in a boarding house, Moira witnessed a traffic accident on her way to class and stayed to tell an officer what she'd seen. The officer wrote out a note to her teachers when she said she was going to be late for class.

Things went well at school. She'd always been a quick study, and this was no different. Watch someone do a procedure, anything from taking a blood pressure to starting an IV, and she had it, she could do it herself. The book stuff was another matter, that came harder. Sure, she could memorize information for a time, it just wouldn't stay long in place, so ask her the name of the two bones of the feet that sat in front of the talus or that flap of skin under the tongue, it could be a no go. But she saw connections—made connections—between things, and mostly this got her through.

Until she saw the ad on the bulletin board at school Moira didn't know that boarding houses still existed. This one advertised comfortable rooms for career-minded young ladies. Eager to escape the school dorm, Moira thought that sounded pretty good, especially as the cost was half what a tiny room would rent for elsewhere. She had a roommate at first, a church secretary named Bertie, but when Bertie decided three weeks later to quit her job and go back home, no one else showed up and Moira had the place to herself, a large room with generous windows on the second story. Three other rooms up there, two more downstairs. Occupying them, among those she came to know, were a dentist who looked not much older than Moira, two students from the nearby four-year college, a railroad worker, and an elderly woman often wearing what might have been a Salvation Army uniform.

The house was run, and owned, by Mrs. Bauman. At first she seemed stern, even distant, but as Moira got to know her, that impression softened. By the end of her first month there, Moira found herself passing many an early evening in Mrs. Bauman's company, sitting in the kitchen with her once dinner was done, other guests back in their rooms or gone out, dishes attended to. Usually a pot of coffee on the stove to stay warm. And for Moira, an excellent opportunity to put off book study for another hour.

One night toward the end of the first year, they'd been sitting there for a while and dishes remained undone, stacked by the sink. Periodically Mrs. Bauman looked that way. It had suddenly gone cold those past few days. The oven was on low with the door open. Wind moaned outside. Small talk's all they ever made, how was school, what market Mrs. Bauman liked best for meat or for fresh vegetables, was Moira making friends, did she have plans for the weekend. Mrs. Bauman loved old movies and would talk about her favorites from when she saw them, back when she was young. They never got personal with any of it. But tonight—taken there by something in the movie she'd been remembering, Moira thought—Mrs. Bauman started talking about herself, how she'd been pregnant the first time when she was about Moira's age. They'd tried so hard, she said, her and Blake. She lost that one halfway through. Took almost two years the next time, and she got further along with it, but she lost that one, too. Third time, once she was recovered and back up and about, Blake left her—it was my own unbearable sadness that brought it on, she said, I knew that. He signed the house and all their belongings, the little money they had saved, all of it, over to her. She never saw or heard from Blake again.

That was the first time Moira encountered something to which she had no idea how to respond.

For a long time afterward, she thought about how utterly alone and despondent Mrs. Bauman must have felt. Had that led her, at least in part, to open the boarding house? And did it help? Having others around, always having things that needed doing?

Halfway through her second year, upon advice from her counselor, Moira found parttime work at a nursing home. You'd be getting a regular paycheck, the counselor said, and getting experience that will make a solid difference once you graduate and go looking for a job. It proved to be hard work, hard on the back and sometimes on the heart, but it brought in twice what she'd earned with odd jobs, and to her surprise she found she actually liked working there.

Many things gained come with a loss, though. Between job and school, Moira no longer had time to sit with Mrs. Bauman. Not that they would ever be friends, but there'd been something there, a recognition, a bridge. She felt echoes of that now with some of those she cared for at Willow Manor.

Beyond a couple of letters to let them know she was okay, Moira hadn't been in touch with her parents since leaving home, but not long before graduating she called them. Only to tell them about the graduation, and, stretching truth a bit, that she was already working as a nurse—no further reason. Her mother had answered, thanked her for calling, and put the receiver down to go fetch her father. He'd come in, doubtless from the workshop, to listen and, when she was done, said he hoped everything went well for her.

Hannah

Having quit work, Hannah figured she'd live a different life in a different world. Pay no attention to clocks, catch up on years of movies, find her way back into books, wear the same shorts and top all week cook huge meals of which she'd eat only a small portion, then reheat the rest for days after. Occasionally, very occasionally, she might summon the will to don grownup clothes and venture out to Poots, two blocks over. Eying the barista's wild-pheasant haircut with suspicion while enduring his banter, listening to the man at the next table go on endlessly to his companion about some fascination of the moment, the New Deal, maybe, or Scandinavian history.

As with most fantasies, that's not the way it worked out. She woke the next morning knowing precisely how she'd spend her day, and well before noon was at the house of the tenant down the street from Moira's. Clayton, Jerry Clayton. Retired teacher, he said, and just now back from municipal court after release from jury duty. A stout man, with a narrow face and close-set brown eyes. He'd stopped for carry-out on the way home and kept glancing toward the sack as they spoke. Indian, from the smell. And she'd not had breakfast.

Mr. Clayton had a habit of pausing after each five- or six-word phrase, a habit developed no doubt over many years in the class room.

"It's not that I knew her, you understand," he said. "But this is my neighborhood. I'm here all day, try to keep an eye out."

"What brought you to contact the rental agent?"

"I got to thinking I hadn't seen anyone around of late, no one going in or out, so on my morning walk I stopped by. There was mail in the box, and a UPS package on the porch by the door. That same night I thought I saw movement in the front room. Could have been anything. Or nothing. Lights weren't on—couldn't recall them being on for some time. So I thought it best to notify Ms. Fuller."

"You mentioned a car, she said."

"Yes. Dark blue but faded, as they get out here in the heat. Some years on it—seems as though it may have had a hood ornament. Do they still do those? Understand, I have no reason to believe this car necessarily has to do with your friend. Everyone parks on the street here."

"When did you last see it?"

"It's been quite some time now," Mr. Clayton said. "Pardon my asking. She's a friend of yours, the nurse?"

"Moira. And yes, we worked together."

"She kept to herself, many of us do down here, but she did seem quite nice."

"Can you tell me anything about the woman living in the other side of the duplex?"

"I'm afraid not. I don't believe she'd been there long. Not that I actually knew your friend, you understand."

Extremely loud music started up next door. Pounding drum, overdriven guitar, reverb like riptides coming in.

Mr. Clayton smiled. "Ah . . . the neighbor's awake."

"This happen often?"

"Difficult to say, Orson's new to the neighborhood. But every day since he's been here."

"Sorry."

"Actually I admire how alive it is. How it insists so strongly on being what it is. Bit by bit, life tends to carry us away from such."

Hannah thanked him for his time. Mr. Clayton's new neighbor was sitting on his porch as she left, windows and door open, music proudly headbutting its way to freedom. He raised his mug in greeting. Coffee sloshed onto a T-shirt long since faded to gray, its script-like writing gone wholly illegible.

• • •

The entire city was an amalgam, much more so these older parts, dissimilar things stitched hurriedly together, decades-old bungalows shoulder to shoulder with modern suburban homes, many adorned with add-ons, a room here, a porch or patio there, these additions often ill-fitting and unbecoming. On one side street she came across a vaguely bulbous three-story that caused her to imagine some huge, shambling organic thing squatting down to catch its breath and never getting further. Layers of peeling paint, ghosts of signage, and vestiges of parking lots bore witness to serial habitation.

Neighborhoods had their own smell as well: citrus near True Gospel Church, olive trees on the community college grounds, asphalt and the faint suggestion of gas near a construction site on Central.

She'd hit map's edge, ambition's as well. No trace of Moira, no notion where she might have gone or why, nothing helpful from the neighbor. Maybe she should have returned to the house instead, poked around more. But she didn't know what to look for and wouldn't know what it meant if she found it. What the hell did she think—she'd walk off her job, out the door of her apartment, and this late in the movie turn into some kind of stupid-ass hero?

Pitiful.

Back at the apartment there awaited three urgent texts about credit lines that she didn't have; emails seeking to buy her house and others offering, if she acted promptly, huge discounts on things for which she had no need; a link to this month's bank statement; two actual-mail bills; and a misdelivered package. Sweet modern life!

Back in college days, dorm mate Lucas Boone from the floor below had likened Internet presence to forensic investigations. They find a hair here, he said, a mark or scratch there, half a footprint and some carpet fiber, they've got you. Just plug in the algorithms and they can pull out anything and everything about you they want to know. Lucas wore identical blue work shirts and identical khaki pants, except on Fridays when he was in uniform for, of all things, ROTC. A handful of people you never see and never will, he insisted, control everything, everything from who gets put forth as candidates in elections to what entertainment's offered live and onscreen, to what news gets broadcast and the shape it takes "in the air." At the time, Hannah paid little attention; as she sank more deeply into a messy, puzzling world, she had cause to wonder.

In Intro to Psych that same year she learned the word *apophenia*, our drive to see connections among things and events, even connections patently not there. And reading for a lit class, she came across a quote from poet Max Ritvo: "Of course there is another world. But it is not elsewhere." Both had become touchstones for her.

And now, twelve years after those classes, twenty since she sat in the production tent watching her mother walk on camera in clothes painstakingly rent and bloodied by the wardrobe mistress, Hannah finds herself remembering Mom's agent, Jeremy, sitting there with her explaining how proud Trish was that she did her own screams. No specialist for her, no dubs or retakes, just Trish herself, hard off the block right on cue and ringing out like bells. Talent, Jeremy said. Pure, honest talent. Hannah had looked over when he spoke, then kept her eyes on him instead of the set, fascinated at the batches of hair growing from his nostrils and ears. How did he not notice that when he looked in mirrors? Had no one—mother, girlfriend, wife, lover—ever mentioned this to him? No one?

Jeremy was, had always been, a trip. Even as a child Hannah sensed that. One of those people whose self-image seemed unshakeable. Neither failure nor peer opinion nor other harsh pronouncements from the world around him could impinge.

Tonight she was watching an old favorite, *The Heart Is a Lonely Hunter*.

As a kid in Philadelphia, she was allowed to go to the movies by herself on Friday nights. You could do that back then, even in the city. Uptown Cinema was five blocks away, on the second floor above a department store full of clearance racks, up an escalator tucked alongside the store's entrance and through a narrow corridor papered with posters for films like *A Night at the Opera*, *North by Northwest*, and *Alphaville*.

What Hannah remembered most was how many movies she saw there that she didn't understand. Some, she couldn't even follow what was going on, but she went every Friday night regardless.

Whatever happened up there, it was all so vivid—and so much more *present* than anything in her own life. Uptown Cinema had low ceilings, seated maybe eighty people tops, always smelled of something waxy.

The next theater she spent hours in, during college, was cavernous, dark as a closet, and smelled of mold. A bare-bones survivor from the days of grand movie houses, it was at the ragged end of Main where regular commerce gave way to discount clothing, shoulder-width liquor stores, and shops crammed with cheap watches, pocket knives, trinkets, and sunglasses. Always a double feature, always a dollar admission, always showing movies you, and your companion if you could talk anyone into venturing there with you, had never heard of. Feet stuck to the floor and came away with sucking sounds as you trod down the aisle and through rows of seats. People sat as far away from others as they could. Static sizzled on the sound system.

She fell in love for the first time in that theater. Melanie "Mel" Roberson, who somehow she'd talked into tagging along. Things hadn't gone any better with that than they had with the boy's pet in the first movie. The pet was a bobcat rescued as a kitten, later hunted by townspeople as a presumed menace, finally dying of wounds sustained while saving a child's life. Hannah's relationship with Mel endured not much longer than the movie's ninety minutes. She still remembered their coming back out into blinding sunlight together. A parade of some kind was going on, and they watched a while, even followed for a block or two, before going to a coffee shop for what became a brief talk. The next time Hannah called, Mel didn't answer, nor the time after that. Hannah didn't call again.

Hannah sank into the movie. John Singer's anguish, his insistence upon signing and refusal to speak, the boarding house, tomboy Mick Kelly's youthful, unmanageable dreams. Too soon it was over. She remembered, age thirteen, sitting on the steps outside their apartment building shortly after seeing this movie the first time, warmth of sun and steps seeping into her body, pushing away thoughts of smelly Buddy Weiss who in fifth grade wouldn't leave her alone, as she tried to read.

Not much by way of sun or warmth now. Dark out, wind

whispering at the windows. The room's only light from the lamp by the chair where Hannah sat without work or direction. No trace of Moira, no idea where she might have gone or why, nowhere else Hannah could think to look. And herself jobless, a bank account that would barely survive next month's bills, the sensation of freedom she'd experienced upon quitting work now shape-changed to something else. Not regret or anxiety, more a sense of suspension, of waiting.

She'd read a lot when she was young, mostly novels. Never took much interest in poetry except for when Trish had given her a book by a writer who'd been a favorite of *hers* as a young woman, Edna St. Vincent Millay. "All I could see from where I stood / Was three long mountains and a wood"—Millay wrote that when she herself was a teenager.

Last New Year's day, one of the nurses had pinned a poem to the bulletin board in the unit. Written by Laura Gilpin, who was also a nurse, as Hannah found when she looked the poem up online. Hannah had copied it by hand, a copy she still had somewhere.

Two-Headed Calf

Tomorrow when the farm boys find this
freak of nature, they will wrap his body
in newspaper and carry him to the museum.

But tonight he is alive and in the north
field with his mother. It is a perfect
summer evening: the moon rising over
the orchard, the wind in the grass. And
as he stares into the sky, there are
twice as many stars as usual.

Moira

Her favorite had been Mrs. Sonnerman, east wing, end of the hall. Always wore pale green, and every time Moira was assigned her, it came down to the same thing. She kept a five-dollar bill, folded in half then folded again, in the case for the glasses she never, awake or asleep, took off. "Stanley taught me this," she'd say, "always keep a little put aside, and I want you to have it, dear," then she'd rattle around on the nightstand and hand the bill to Moira. Moira would wait till she fell asleep and put it back. They all did.

That was Moira's first fulltime job out of nursing school, after she'd graduated and again moved on, to a new town, new housing. Baycare had a mix of people who all their lives probably had barely enough to get by, many who'd had less, and a few like Mrs. Sonnerman who once upon a time had no reason to worry. Not that she looked it now, but in the past she must have been well off. She and her husband, her Stanley, had both been teachers, everyone said. She was a scientist, he was some kind of historian. Mrs. Sonnerman never talked to Moira about science, but Moira heard a lot of history from her, things about early America that she'd never heard before, like how Hawaii was taken by force, or maybe it was Chile, and why the disgraceful electoral college came about. Moira wondered how many people knew about things like that, assuming they were true.

Years later she thought how peculiar it was that, in so populous a nursing home, she was the only real nurse on shift, everything else being taken care of by assistants. At the time, all puffed up with being a new graduate and with tons of half-knowledge banging about in her head, she thought she *was* a real nurse, but that soon faded. She began to understand how little she actually knew, and what might come of it.

"Old people smell bad," a longtime staff member told her during orientation, "they just can't help it." The reek of leaked urine, sweat, poor cleansing, and body-processed meds could definitely get to you. But far worse for Moira were the women who drenched themselves with perfume—because they'd lost their sense of smell? For weeks she'd gag and hold her breath, but with time she got used to it.

Next up the hall from Mrs. Sonnerman was the youngest of the residents, Sybil Nye, who went into others' rooms while residents were away or sometimes even present, and took things, cutlery should any happen to be there, otherwise costume jewelry or a scarf, always only one thing, which she'd carefully wrap in a handkerchief as though it were some priceless object and place in the top drawer of her vanity, the one with the missing handle.

Miss Ruby was their talker. Every home has one, that same staff member told her. Miss Ruby was the only resident with a single room, and you could hear her chatting away any time you went near it. Talking *to* someone, it sounded like, though she didn't have family and no one ever visited. But that didn't stop the flow of conversation, about weather and how the days were getting colder, yesterday's meal, the river off whose bank she'd fished when she was a kid, that nice man at the Buick dealership, how important it is to put an eggshell in among the coffee before you brew it. Whatever crossed her mind. And to every appearance that mind rarely grew still, save for a brief few hours at night.

Gradually Moira's fear of mistakes, of hurting someone, of being found out, gave way to elation at what she was able to accomplish, at the good she was doing. Finally, though, such feelings fell away as had her initial abundance of self-confidence. Unease moved in where they'd been. A touch of fear, even. She never fully understood why. Facing so many and varied signs of mortality day after day, maybe. Watching those who'd been given up on by everyone—family, friends, society. And who were, physically, mentally, relentlessly, losing themselves.

After a little more than a year, Moira decided a change was in order. She tried ER (where she believed she wouldn't get attached to patients), moved to a general medical floor (crushing, headlong routine), spent a six-month stint in cardiopulmonary ICU (no thank you), then on a whim signed up for NICU—and loved it from day one.

Why that was so, again she wasn't sure. She'd never much liked kids, and her nursing school rotation through peds was a horror. But these weren't snarly, screamy, food-and-snot-spattered little people. These were something else, lives brought from another world to this one without proper means to survive. And despite what she first thought, she loved working nights. With most of the rest of the world shut down, there in the unit the night felt close about her, she felt in place, protected, felt she belonged.

Before she knew it, she'd paid off her school debt and started saving. Not for any particular reason or purpose, but most of her paychecks went directly into savings. There wasn't anything she wanted that she didn't have, anything else she wanted to do. Especially since, two years after landing in the NICU, she bought the DVD player. Mornings, once home she'd pick a movie and set up the player so it was ready to go when she got up mid-afternoon. She'd watch a movie over dinner, then watch another. Each Friday she brought home a bagful of DVDs from the mom-and-pop rental two blocks over.

She loved strange European films where people moved in and out of shadow, taking action for what often seemed impenetrable reasons. They'd do ordinary things like fill teapots, close doors or climb staircases, and it would feel like these were threads holding the world together. Sunlight lay lifeless and unmoving on walls, trees embraced wind, sounds of traffic came from places far away and never seen. Bare light bulbs shone like beacons.

In nursing school she'd learned about specific hungers, how in older times pregnant women, without knowing why, would peel and eat plaster off the walls because it contained minerals or compounds their body needed. That's what those movies were for her. She needed them.

Then one afternoon after she'd finished watching *Daybroke*, about orphaned children living in an abandoned castle, and been in bed maybe an hour, she came awake. Music had brought her round, she realized. Not that it was loud, but whatever the music was, it had this heavy irregular beat in the bass, more like a throb than a beat, and just came right into the room and hung there, through the common wall.

She slept in old scrubs, so no need to change.

Moira walked across the shared front porch and knocked. The music wasn't any louder there than it was in her bedroom. A young woman, tall with pink hair, answered the door. She hadn't finished moving in, or maybe she just didn't have much by way of possessions and furniture. Moira saw a spindly table halt leaning against a love seat, and what looked like a canvas lawn chair.

"Excuse me," Moira said, "but I'm a day sleeper, a nurse, and your music—"

"I am *so* sorry." The woman stepped away and came directly back. No more music. "I didn't know. Would you like to come in?"

"I really do need to sleep. But welcome to the neighborhood. I'm Moira."

"Shell, for Shelley. I moved in yesterday and hadn't seen signs of anyone next door, or heard anything. I thought it was unoccupied. There's just you?"

Moira nodded.

"Me too. I'm new to town."

"From?"

"Texas. Plano—just north of Dallas."

"What brought you here? Usually it's school, family, or job, pretty much in that order."

"The last. I start tomorrow, with an alternate energy company. Windmills, solar panels."

"That has to be exciting."

"Not really. I'll be looking at long runs of numbers. Page after page of them. All day."

"Still. New job, new city . . ."

"Oh, that. Right. Sure."

There was something in the way Shell spoke, like a tiny intake of breath, a hesitancy. It reminded Moira of the hitch you see in the gait of people with old injuries.

She thanked Shell and wished her luck with the job but, once home, couldn't get back to sleep. Soon she was up watching the end of a Swedish movie composed for the most part of trees, rain, and half-light, with a single human being, female, standing at the edge of a high cliff. There was no conclusion really, no resolution, but for all that, it was strangely moving. She had rented the movie, then gone out and bought a copy. She only watched the end, but she watched the end often.

Years ago on the crosstown bus, someone tapped her on the shoulder and, when she turned, said, "You don't remember me, do you?" A small man with light, all but translucent hair, wearing khaki work clothes. A child, maybe five or six, hard to judge, sat beside him, hugging close a cartoon-character backpack. "No reason you would."

Moira's thoughts jagged. Was he going to ask for bus fare, milk for the child? Was this a come-on of some kind, he was hitting on her? Here in public, with a kid in tow? She glanced around. As far as she could tell, no one was paying them any attention.

"Tully Solomon. Tolliver, but everybody calls me Tully. You took care of Tony here when he was born. My wife, Linda, was real sick too."

Moira looked again at the child.

"It's okay. That was a long time back," the man said. "You have to have seen hundreds of kids since then. But Tony's doing well, thanks to all of you."

Moira wondered how well. The boy hadn't made eye contact or loosened his grip on the backpack, hadn't looked out the window even once. Something about the way he sat, too, subtly canted to one side, a stiffness. Cerebral palsy? Autism?

"Surprised to see you taking the bus. Not a lot do, around here, and you a nurse."

A young woman with light green hair and piercings sufficient to set off airport alarms, ears, nose, lower lip, eyebrow, climbed on. Somehow she was not exotic-looking at all, simply beautiful.

"I don't like cars. They frighten me."

"Because of what you've seen?"

"That hasn't helped."

A block from Moira's stop, the bus drew abreast of Westside Women's Center, its sidewalk taken over by protestors bearing signs of the Stop the Killing, Save Our Children sort. Some were computer-generated, others cobbled up rudely by hand. A number of the signs referenced Jesus. Protestors had folding seats, umbrellas, water and soft drinks. As the bus passed by, Moira and Mr. Solomon glanced at each other. Neither spoke.

Across from Moira's apartment building, a moving van stenciled HUNGRY STUDENTS HAUL U dipped and hove as workers stepped in and out with boxes of every size imaginable, many beginning to come apart despite taped reinforcement. A couple in their early twenties oversaw the bustle, she posted by the building's front steps, he at the back of the van. Moving on the cheap, obviously, grabbing boxes wherever they could. Idly, Moira wondered how at their age they could possibly have accumulated so much stuff, and what it all might be. Were they excited about beginning what people insisted upon calling a new life? Did they think about all the stuff they were bringing along from the old one?

She remembered an apartment back when she was cleaning them out for Mrs. Dawes, one of an eight-unit built in the early days of the city's sudden growth. For all its comfortable furnishing and quiet style, the apartment had felt lifeless and unlived-in, like a train compartment briefly occupied on the way somewhere else. No scratches on doorways, no marks on walls from collisions, no wear patterns from furniture or favorite chairs. It was as though whoever lived there had simply evaporated.

Hannah

It was one of those bleary mornings when you'd been up most of the night studying then around 4 A.M. decide it's not worth going to bed now so you order out grilled cheese sandwiches and sit around with other misfit students talking big ideas.

Billy Paul, a string of cheese hanging like a stray yellow hair at the side of his mouth, says, "The dead have this great advantage of knowing where they should be."

He wipes off the string with a finger. "That's what my old friend Earl said, a man who could be envious of running water, bark on a tree—anything really. The Earl of, we called him. Of *what* changed constantly depending on his passion of the moment, how annoying he was about it, and our own disposition."

Billy Paul glances around. Judging his audience, working the room?

"What I'm saying is, Earl wasn't the sort of man you expect words of wisdom from."

What got them started on this was the death of a fellow student, who had leapt from the roof of the science building to the parking lot below. Jeannie from their dorm had seen him fall by her classroom window. When asked why she didn't call out, tell someone, try to get help, but instead went back to marking up her test paper, she said she believed what he was doing was a private thing.

790 • JAMES SALLIS

—One of many such oddments banging about Hannah's head just now, like scarcely-remembered relatives who've come for a visit and you have no idea what to do with them.

She'd spilled from there, that room, that college, into corporate America, momentarily to teaching, back to being a student, finally to nursing, thence to unemployment. And last week she'd had, for the first time in more years than she wanted to think about, a job interview.

Ben Ashman, a journalist who'd gone back to law school at age fifty, doubled as writer and host for *Ask Again*, where he burrowed into complaints viewers made concerning local merchants, medical facilities, even government agencies, and each week brought such cases to the state's top TV news show. Off to Poot's for an afternoon coffee, as much to get out of the house as for anything else, Hannah had come across a newspaper left behind on her table and, within it, an advertisement for "adamantly curious people" to help with interviews and research. Back home, she checked online, read a more detailed version of the ad, and learned about *Ask Again*.

The interviewer, a young woman in what they now called business casual, took note of Hannah's discomfort and did all she could to put her at ease with small talk, which only made it worse. Once she moved on to asking after Hannah's background and speaking directly to the job, it went better.

She did understand, right, considering her nursing background, that she wouldn't be working exclusively on medical issues?

That this was not a fulltime job?

That some of the interviews, while in no way confrontational, this part being left to Mr. Ashman, might upon occasion prove . . . difficult?

Hannah did and, further along, understood that she'd be able to do most interviews and research via Internet and phone, scheduling these at her discretion.

After twenty minutes, wondering the while from the interviewer's questions, what other applicants might be like, Hannah found herself, as precipitously as she had left her last one, accepting a job she wasn't all that certain she wanted.

So now she sat at the kitchen table on a sunny, sunny day, 11:52

A.M., rummaging through websites for reviews and comments concerning an extended care facility perched at the edge of town in what had once been a huge church with attached rectory.

Her research on previous projects had gone well, her reports been approved. Even the telephone interviews passed without a hitch. No surprise that she liked working at home and on her own time, of course. Computer and phone gave a welcome distance.

Multiple calls and emails had come in to *Ask Again* with complaints that Woodland Care was refusing to let friends and family members visit those "sheltered" at the facility. *Sheltered*, she found, was a word that cropped up often in Woodland Care's ads, brochures, and media posts.

In response to queries from complainants, one of three responses, or some permutation of the three, appeared to be universal.

In the case of recent admissions, that the individual needed time to adjust to new surroundings, new schedules, and new faces.

That a troubling infection was going around, not uncommon in close communities, and the medical director had suspended visitation in order to mitigate the infection's spread both to the population itself and to the general public.

That Woodland Care had a diverse population (elderly, medically needful, those with developmental issues) many of whose conditions required exacting schedules and treatments with which visitation at this time would interfere.

All of which was plausible.

Without access to hospital records or staff interviews, Hannah gathered what information she could from secondary sources. Family members, friends and caretakers had posted at their own or at various rate-and-review sites; Hannah corresponded or spoke with many and found them keen to talk further about their experiences. Putting herself forward as a caretaker deciding where to place an elderly charge, she also spoke with directors at two facilities similar to Woodland.

From what she gleaned, the complaints had foundation. There'd been no postings in the lobby for special precautions, no email or other notices sent out, no public announcements of temporary restrictions published at Woodland's website, in local papers, or on community billboards. Hannah shuffled summaries of her research into a single file, attached copies of pertinent screen shots, and dropped the package to Ben Ashman's assistant. Done.

A break was now in order. She grabbed a jacket and headed for Poot's. Ordered her latte and was settling into a window seat when her phone dinged.

Exciting news. Call me.

Her mother.

Hannah called back, looking out on apartment complexes under construction, both on the street directly across—these were low-rise, three stories—and further down toward Lancaster, where they'd dwarf and clash with everything else in the old neighborhood. Condos, likely. Wherever you looked now, these things were going up. Where was the money coming from? And all these supposed future renters and condo owners?

Trish answered the phone breathless.

"Give me a second here. Working out."

Working out? *Her* mother? Hannah heard monotonous music and chanted instructions behind. "Exciting, huh?"

"What?"

"Your text. Exciting news."

"Oh. Right. It is." The sound track went away. A bottle glurged. Some high-end electrolyte elixir, no doubt. Then Trish was back. "I'm making a movie."

"Mom, you haven't made a movie in—what? Twenty years?"

"The old ones are still around."

"You don't even know people in the business anymore."

"There's a slew of young directors out there. Like to call themselves filmmakers, Luis told me. One of them got in touch, Robbie, says he's been a fan all his life. And would I be interested—" She paused for another swig of elixir. "It's too good to pass up."

"Okay . . . ?"

"Titled *Cutdown*. The lead's an older woman who gets attacked and severely injured. After recovery she goes to hunt down her attacker and at first it comes on like your standard revenge flick, but then everything gets more and more complicated, and she ends up saving the man's life. She's a nurse, like you. Robbie wrote the script himself. And he'll be directing."

"This is real, Mom? A real movie? With producers and backing and a crew? You checked this out?"

"Jeremy did. He's retired from agenting but still knows everybody. He made some calls. The money's in place, Jeremy says. Prelim production schedule's posted."

Which meant—Hannah remembered how it worked—that Trish was a last-minute fill-in for some other lead who'd backed out. Her mother had to know that too. She'd seen *Sunset Boulevard* more times than Hannah had. So how did this play out in her mind? Her chance to revive her craft? Take the money and run?

"What does Luis think? You've talked this over?"

"Of course. Why not, he says, it'll be good for me, and there's no downside."

Aside from the inevitable heartbreak of an elderly, unpracticed comeback.

"He's around?" Hannah asked.

"Off to some island, filming *Slugs 4*, maybe 6. Who can keep them straight?"

Probably not even him. Or the viewers. Not that it mattered much.

"So I'll be away working," Trish said, "but I'll call. Things to do. Bye, Sweetheart."

"Bye, Mom. Be careful."

Within minutes, as Hannah watched a young man pull up outside, chain his bike to the rack, remove the seat and stow it in his backpack, a text came.

forgot canada where Im going XXX

Did Trish know she'd need a passport to fly into Canada? Was her passport even valid? How long had it been since she traveled? Hannah could only hope she'd make it to the shoot, and that the movie might somehow not be the train wreck it sounded.

Moira

That morning, Moira woke around 3 A.M. No matter how tired, she always had trouble figuring out when best to sleep on days off, her body still on night-shift, inner clock (such as it was) seriously off-kilter. She woke in darkness, disoriented, with door-shaped patches of light on the wall by her, realizing she'd forgotten to draw the curtains full shut and now a vehicle of some kind was sitting in the street outside with lights on and engine running.

The voice within her started up as she came awake. There weren't words, at first, just the voice.

She lay there remembering how as a child she'd lie listening to her parents and others out in the living room, all those soft, comforting rhythms, each sentence like a single rolling word, the mysteries that swam within.

Voices from within had soon become her companions. When later on they stopped, she felt abandoned, thought she wouldn't be able to go on without them. Those never seemed to have anything much to do with her—just voices overheard in a crowd. Not like this one, the new one, at all. This one was all about her.

A loud bang from the street. She got up and looked out. The lights were from a delivery truck, and someone was beating at the driver's door. A young man from the look of it, begging to be let back in. He raised both arms as though in surrender as the truck pulled away. Stood there a moment longer, then began walking.

Help him.

Moira shook her head.

You have to.

From within, calm and comforting.

I can't.

Did she speak the words, or just think them?

Moira watched the young man walk down the street and away.

He's all alone.

Age nine or ten, she became convinced she didn't belong where she was and had to be from someplace else, another world maybe, or the future, that some accident—an explosion, or an experiment gone wrong, malfunction, bad star charts—had stranded her here. Probably got the idea from a TV show she'd watched or a book she'd read. She knew this couldn't be true, but it wasn't about knowledge or truth, it was about other things entirely, belief among them, and though she never tried to explain this to anyone, she believed it for a long time.

Back in bed, she drifted from half-awake dreams of fish in a shallow pond and singing frogs, to another of rain sounding high above in trees sheltering her, and came awake to sounds she gradually realized were not part of the dream. Someone knocking at her door? No one ever knocked at her door. Years ago she'd posted a *Day Sleeper* sign out front. Someone stole it the same day, and she never bothered replacing it.

Next door. It's from next door.

Was it a thought? Hard to tell, sometimes.

Help them.

The sounds came again, wood and heaviness in them, then fell quiet.

Moira got up, went out and along the porch and, everything within her urging her not to do this, to turn around and go back instead, she knocked. Knocked a second time before the new neighbor, Shell, answered. "You're a nurse, right?" she said, stepping back to let Moira in. "Can you help us?"

Only a small table lamp was on, much of the room still in shadow. A young man, midtwenties maybe, lay on the love seat with legs hanging off and a damp washcloth on his forehead. The face beneath was abraded, skin split in a place or two. Blood, but not much. His eyes followed Moira as she approached.

"How did I get here?" the man said. "Where am I?"

Shell was directly behind her. "He keeps saying that. I tell him, he says okay, thanks, then right away he's asking again."

"Who is he?"

"Dennis. We work together."

"A friend?"

"Not really. Like I say, we work together."

"And he's here why?"

"He just showed up at my door. Like this. Then he fell."

Moira knelt, checked vitals, felt around the splits and abrasions on his face. No especially worrisome damage, as far as she could tell.

"Sir, do you know where you are?"

Turning his head toward them, he said, "That's Shelley. Am I at Shelley's place? Or yours? I don't know you."

"Do you remember coming here?"

"I couldn't sleep and went for a walk . . ."

"Do you remember what happened?"

"I think . . . Could I have got jumped, and beaten?" He sat up. "But I'm okay now. What time is it?"

Good question. Moira looked up. Faint suggestion of light as the sky began to soften. Straggles of traffic outside.

"Little past five," Shell said. "You really can't remember anything, Dennis?"

"Not really. But I'm okay, and I do have to get home. And I have to be at work soon." He smiled at Shell. "We both do."

"You really need to be seen," Moira said. "ER or urgent care. For possible injuries. You could have passed out from low blood sugar, arrhythmias. Could have a concussion."

"I'm okay—really. I start feeling weird, any problem at all, I'll go in. Promise. And I don't live far from here. The walk'll do me good. Help clear my head."

He was almost to the door, turned back. "You won't mention this to anyone at work, right?" he said to Shell, who nodded and went to open the door for him.

"Well . . . that was different," Shell said as she closed it.

"Any idea why he would come here?"

"None. He didn't even seem to know who I was, at first."

"Is where you live common knowledge?"

"No, I haven't really got to know anyone here yet. I see Dennis at work, we never talked."

"It's a big city, you're new here, and he just happens to show up at your door? Lot of questions folded into that."

"Sometimes things just happen, I guess. They don't always make sense. And listen, he's right, I do have to get ready for work. Bound to be late as it is. Thanks for your help."

Traffic had picked up outside. A gardening truck pulled in across the street, LAWN SERVICE painted clumsily in white on the small trailer behind. Two older men, one bent with age, dismounted from the cab, go-cups of coffee in hand.

Normal life.

Moira lay sleepless for a long while afterward.

Would Shell's coworker be okay? What had happened in the first place? Did he pass out? It looked more like he might have been attacked. And he seemed, initially, confused. *Any* change in consciousness, concussion or no, throws up flags. And why—how—did he end up at Shell's? Then, with Moira there, suddenly insist upon leaving?

The whole affair was a string with nothing but knots.

Another knot got added later in the day when, shortly after Moira dragged herself from bed and sat staring disconsolately at an English muffin, three in the afternoon or so, Shell called to tell her that Dennis hadn't shown up for work. No answer when his supervisor called.

"Should I try the police?" Shell asked. "I got his address from HR."

"For a wellness check, you mean."

"If that's what they call it. To go by his place, see that he's okay?"

"They'll do that, but it won't be high on their priority list." Moira glanced again at the unbeckoning muffin. "Look, Dennis said he lives nearby. Give me the address, I'll walk over and check on him."

"You sure? I'd feel a lot better about it."

"You're at work?"

"Okay, let me get some clothes on. I'll head over, knock on the door, look around."

Dennis's place sat well back off the street between and behind two large houses. She walked past on the sidewalk twice without realizing it was back there. What people call a mother-in-law house, later repurposed to separate residence? Could be. Well maintained, but it had seen a lot of living, like good old shoes. And come to think of it, even the house's two-tone, brown and white paint job reminded her of shoes, the saddle oxfords she wore as a kid.

No porch, just two steps up to the door and an overhang that echoed the peaked roof. No doorbell either, so she knocked. The mailbox was to the right. *There be mail, Cap'n,* she told herself—but where had that come from? Then she got it: last week's pirate movie. Not her usual fare, but at the rental shop the cover had snared her: a woman standing at the helm of a ship, complete with eye patch, the hook at the end of her arm hard on the wheel.

Getting no response, Moira stepped over to peer in the front window. Through a gauzy curtain she could make out shapes, a couch, end tables, coat rack, chairs, everything perfectly placed. From somewhere, for sure not her pirate movie, the word *kempt* came to mind. Everything perfectly placed and kempt. The room looked like a showroom floor. An obsessive lived here. Someone keen for order.

Moira had, after all, a history of reading rooms. And since the mail was there, she pulled it out of the box. Flyers from a fitness center, a dentist, a used-furniture store, business cards from real estate agents and yard-care providers, electric bill, water bill. Three mailings with names other than Dennis Davies.

Moira called Shell to tell her no one answered at Dennis's, that the place barely looked lived in but she'd seen no sign of anything amiss. She didn't mention the mail.

The day, meanwhile, had gone dull with clouds. Walking home, Moira couldn't shake off thoughts of peering through Dennis's curtain at the blurred, indefinite forms inside, how apart from the world out here everything in there seemed. It reminded her of the drifts she'd had as a kid, after the voices stopped. That's what she called them, drifts. Eventually they went away too. The first time it happened, she thought of it as getting lost. Later on: I've gone missing. She'd been sitting outside the drugstore on Campbell, waiting for her mother and looking out on a wall of stone, wondering if it was real stone or fake, and counting the individual pieces. All at once she didn't know where she was. She recognized nothing around her, nothing at all, not even her own hand and arm when they rose into the space before her.

Two days later Moira was almost asleep when Shell called to tell her Dennis still hadn't shown up for work. HR was circulating through the office asking if any of them had personal dealings with him. They'd tried calling the home number, tried a contact number they had, but neither proved valid. And they kept coming back with more questions, first about his attitude and work habits, then asking after anything personal Dennis may have mentioned, where he was from, where he'd worked before, family members, interests.

Rumors around the office meanwhile, supposedly by way of a secretary in HR, had it that Dennis wasn't who he said he was. He'd used different names, faked his background and work history, had no actual training or qualifications for the job he'd been doing with the company. HR was looking into prior locations and employment, possible multiple identities.

Overnight—overday—the unit had changed almost beyond recognition. Twelve hours had wrought a transformation. Securely taped hoses lay like webwork all about the floors. Refrigerator-like machines stood sentinel against walls. Compressed-gas cylinders loomed up everywhere, tucked into heavy steel safety rings.

Not long after report, a day nurse noticed a flowmeter had stopped working and called over one of the respiratory therapists to check it. Which he did—the flowmeter, the blender that mixed oxygen and compressed air from separate sources, the hoses—though it was functioning when he came to the bedside. He called engineering and was standing at the nurse's station filling out an incident report on a possible malfunction when alarms sounded throughout the unit.

Motors in the central air compressor, it turned out, were breaking down, and had leaked oil into the air supply for the unit, this in turn crippling the blenders and endangering the ventilators upon which so many children here were dependent. Day shift had to bring in stationary compressors, find replacements for ventilators, blenders and flowmeters, move tons of stuff out, haul more tons of stuff in, get it all in place, stuck together, and working—while critical babies got hand-bagged, some for hours. Everyone in the hospital who could be spared elsewhere, nurses, aides, attendings, interns, med students, guards, office workers, supply clerks, cafeteria staff, had pitched in to help.

So night shift came on with the unit functional again, though disabled, with everything from charting to meds to treatments off-kilter and far behind schedule. It was over four hours into the shift before they began catching up. Moira confirmed she'd administered all drugs to the babies assigned her, checked vitals yet again, charted, and signed out for a break. Usually she took her breaks early or late, during times she could easily find a quiet spot away from others. But tonight the cafeteria was packed and she wound up sitting near a group of nurses from a medical floor, possibly CCU or ICU. They were talking about a celebrity patient they had, evidently an actor in some kind of crime or cop show on TV. Comments volleyed back and forth across their table.

"He's a really nice guy. Not what you'd expect."

"Not like his character at all."

"It's acting, dear."

"You saw the boatload of fancy sandwiches he had sent in—day shift couldn't even finish them."

"Now *there's* something unexpected."

"What I like is the show deals with issues."

"You see the one about scamming the elderly? These guys set up a school to teach others the scam."

"People hurt, people pushed aside, so little hope left. I see that every day of my life. Then there's the news."

"Coming at you all the time, even when you look away. You're right."

"She *is* right. I don't want to go home and face more of it, I want shows that let me dial it down, let go of all that, just for a little while."

A beeper went off moments later. Two of them rose to leave.

Back in the unit, Moira discovered that the night, off to such a headlong start, had further challenges for them.

Dr. Caruso, director of the unit, was by Baby Tyra's bed with her parents. The child had been worsening for days, one crisis after another the way it happens sometimes. And soon they would be moving Baby Tyra into a side room so her parents could be alone with her as she died. Moira was asked to help.

It was quite a procession, this tiny being on her raft of a bed moving through the unit on a river of monitors, IV pumps, poles, ventilator and oxygen cylinder, with three nurses, a respiratory therapist, and Dr. Caruso thumping over taped-down hoses, swerving around pillar-like compressors, crash carts, and the portable X-ray, everything out of place, everything an obstacle. They'd done the like of this before, though without such obstacles, and there was always about it a solemnity, a sense of reverence.

Once Baby Tyra had been moved and all equipment reconnected, Moira returned to her own babies. Both were fine, and sleeping. Tyra died within the hour. After a while her parents came out and went around thanking everyone. They couldn't have been more than nineteen, twenty. Couldn't have had much idea, Moira thought, what life can throw at you.

Deeper into the shift, charge nurse Sheila came bed to bed to let everyone know that alarms had sounded and fire trucks were at the hospital. That was all she knew as of the moment, but she was in constant touch with administration and would keep everyone updated as further information came.

If it came to that, there was no way they'd be able to get all these children out to safety. Protocol was, once the directive was issued, caretakers from elsewhere in the hospital would arrive to help. Stable or less dependent babies would be evacuated, while those on ventilators and other life support would be moved to some specified, safer location within the hospital.

So they waited.

And so much, Moira thought, for the quiet peace and sanctuary of night shift. Instead they arrived to slog through what amounted to a year's misadventures packed helter-skelter into twelve hours. Nine of them, anyway. Still three more hours to go.

Those hours passed by smoothly, with only a minor incident from a baby reacting poorly to one of his medications and one new arrival from L&D, a month and spare change early but with good weight and flying pretty well on his own.

She'd never touched the money.

Back at that last apartment she'd cleared for Mrs. Dawes, after police left with the girl, Moira had gone on finishing up. When she pulled out the pile of smelly old clothing in the closet—the girl's nest—she saw a missing board low on the wall. Mice had been in there chewing on something, scraps of green paper scattered around near the opening. She got down, looked in. Wound up finding a rusted soup ladle in the pile of trash to go out and using it to pull off two more boards.

Money. Mice had chewed up some, but there was a lot left. Stacks of bills held by rubber bands. They were crammed in there tight. Twenties, fifties, hundreds . . .

Wondering why she would do this, wondering at the boldness of it, at what it said about her and what cost she might have to pay in the long run, Moira took the money. She never counted it, never really touched it again, tried not even to think about it, just piled it all up in her backpack and later hid it away. Even while she was in nursing school, monitoring every nickel and dime, forever scrambling to meet tuition, bills, and rent, at a loss to explain her motive just as she'd been when she took it, Moira refused to touch the money. She still had the pocket notebook she kept back then, where she listed payments, what she spent on meager meals, bus and light-rail expenses, license fees, utilities, the occasional small treat.

She'd kept the money with her for a time, in the backpack, wherever she went, then found hiding spots: loosened floorboards in one apartment, with a gnarly walnut bureau pulled over to help conceal and secure it; an assigned locker at the school, with her own combination lock; finally, when she was here in town and working, a safety deposit drawer at Midtown Bank. Still had no idea how much there was. Thousands, for sure.

Why do people even *have* money they don't use, don't need? They do, of course, they gather it the same way chipmunks and squirrels stuff their cheeks with food, take it to their lairs, store it. The nest the girl had made in the closet back at the apartment was like that, a lair. But it wasn't her money.

And it wasn't Moira's either.

Then one afternoon she'd awakened suddenly and as she lay there had heard, distinctly, from within, what she was to do. The next morning after work she climbed aboard a bus at the stop across from the hospital, waited in a coffee shop until Midtown Bank opened, transferred the money to her backpack, and dropped it off at the first church she came to, stashing it up behind the altar.

Done.

Home today, she'd sat over an hour in the kitchen, just sat there, so exhausted it felt like her body and mind were different beings, thinking of Warren before repeatedly pushing such thoughts from her mind. Things go bad—that was the rule, wasn't it? Nothing gold, nothing that even looks like gold, or feels like gold, can stay.

And what a day she'd had. Seeing how that had gone, tonight called for a special movie. *Breathless*, maybe. She'd happened upon it years ago at a mom-and-pop rental, took it home with two others and, watching, became breathless herself—at the romance of it. Only later did she come to consider what currents roiled beneath that romance. And while the movie drove her to seek out others by Jean-Luc Godard, she could never understand much about what was going on in them, never again felt what she felt, the first time and every time, watching *Breathless*.

She felt breathless herself now. Less than an hour ago, stepping out of the hospital and the night's misadventures into this bright morning, wind stirring leaves clockwise about her feet, Moira had realized that she wouldn't be coming back.

Hannah

Hannah had become engrossed with her work on *Ask Again*. She still thought of Moira, but less frequently. Neither of those developments, the pleasure in the work nor the disregard, would she have anticipated. On the other hand, worried about not hearing from Trish, she'd called repeatedly, connecting only with voice mail.

Life must go on, as they say, which like most things they say—It is what it is, Everything happens for a reason, I wanted to make a difference, She's better off—is absolute bullshit.

But it must.

Two weeks ago, Ben Ashman had come to her with the story of a young man, Torrence, who had given away most everything he owned, half a closetful of well-worn clothes, a couple dozen books, extra shoes, a clanky old car, swaybacked furniture, and chosen to live in the woods in a cabin he built himself. Unfortunately, those woods belonged to a corporation. Upon being informed of Torrence's presence, they took action to oust him.

So it happened, Ben said, that courts and certain types of high nastiness became involved. The property hadn't been in use for years. They couldn't simply ask him to leave? Or simply leave him alone? But now we've got psychiatric evaluations ordered, a public defender who started shaving last month and doesn't have a clue, protestors outside City Hall, clouds and spite and spit everywhere. When all the man wanted was quiet, peace, and solitude.

"What's the plan?" Hannah said.

"Same as always. We ask questions loudly enough that, with luck, they get heard. I'll email the files." After a moment he said, "One other thing. I wonder if you might take lead on this. Research it, do the interviews—as usual. Then write it up."

"That's . . . unexpected."

"The quality of the work you've been doing makes me think you shouldn't remain on the sidelines. Would you be interested in presenting this?"

"You don't mean on camera?"

He nodded.

"Well. Then I guess unexpected doesn't quite cover it."

"Overwhelming?"

"That. I really appreciate this, Ben, and I'd love the chance to write the case up. But for the rest, I'm—"

"I know. Your call, all the way. But think about it."

Research has no bottom. Start off sounding major sources, follow one footnote or link to another, then another, and before you know it you're far afield, down a rabbit hole, lost on back roads. Hannah sat with her new project, thinking how strange were these new connections she had forged with the world, from the research, the interviews, the conversations, as she read about magpies in Australia.

Scientists there had attached tiny trackers to five of them, and within minutes the birds began working to help one another remove the devices. Shortly, all the trackers were gone. A pure example not only of problem-solving, the article put forth, but also of co-operation without direct, self-serving benefit.

That was it, then. She'd been reading articles dealing with solitude and community, others on the beginnings of civilization in the need for interdependence. Magpies, though? How the hell had she found her way to magpies?

She'd gone ahead with presenting Torrence's case on camera and, wonder of wonders, sky hadn't sprung its seams nor ground fallen away beneath her. She couldn't remember a lot about the presentation afterwards, but everyone told her it went well. When Ben offered to show her the video, she declined. Leave well enough alone. But she knew they were right, she could *feel* it had gone well, that somehow she had come across as confident, well-spoken, precise. At the same time she's well aware that this isn't her, that she was pretending, taking on a role, a persona.

Though truthfully it seems that, whenever among others, she's always done that.

Fallout from the TV spot included an offer from one viewer to give Torrence an isolated place where he could live free of charge or bother as well as a new influx of messages from viewers seeking help both for themselves and for others.

The new case was far from the sympathetic them-against-us that Torrence's had been. A thornbush, actually. Second marriage, child gone missing, heartache and complaints on every side, including complaints of harassment by police. *Most likely we want to stay away from this*, Ben's note with the uploaded file read. From everything she'd seen thus far, Hannah concurred. But you never know. You keep digging, peeling away, squinting. Taking those back roads. One thing she knew: *Seem*'s rarely what *is*.

She thought back to a college lecture on C.S. Lewis, who asked if the disorder and distress we experience as so strong a part of life result from *dis*enchantment with the world's wonders or, instead, from some dark enchantment. Admittedly, it might go either way. For that matter, might the two be the same? And how could you know if you held one or the other in hand?

Hannah opened a new file. The pastor of a small protestant church, without counsel or cause according to his appeal, had been disavowed by his congregation or some segment thereof and locked out of his living quarters on the church grounds.

Another: A father begged assistance in finding his daughter, missing for six years now, last seen on her way to play at a friend's house where she never arrived. Officials, he said, had stopped responding to his calls.

Another: A copy of a handwritten letter from a young man claiming to be jailed without reason by the police. *Temporary holding, they tell me.* Yet he'd been there since the day after reporting his wife missing. The file contained support material—a police statement, fragments of interviews with neighbors, news clippings—but it was impossible to figure out from any of it what might be going on, and Ben wouldn't go near an active investigation, if indeed there was one.

So many missing persons. So many gaps in the world. So little sense to any of it.

What was that story? *Miss Lonelyhearts.* Man works at a newspaper advice column, gets all these achingly sad letters from people he can't do anything to help—storms beating against him day after day, bearing him down, till at last all he can see or feel about him in the world is the world's pain and loss. Psych 101, the same year she read that story: *L'appel du vide.* Call of the void.

What the hell. Enough.

Enough of magpies and trackers, of people desperately needing help and of others with none to offer, enough of the call of the void. If it calls, I'm not here.

Hannah closed the files and folders, sat looking for a moment at the blinking cursor, fingers poised, then shut the computer down. If she goes out to Poot's she has to change into what she thinks of as grownup clothes, or something like them. And there's plenty of coffee here, including a bag of Kona she's been saving. Plenty of coffee, plenty of cups, two coffee makers, plus a coffee press. Even an old stovetop espresso pot leftover from college, now that she thinks about it. And she has a lot of work that needs doing.

But that's not the point, is it?

Hannah rarely answered her phone, let voice mail take it. But returning from her break at Poot's to a live phone, she glanced down as Jeremy's name came up in the viewer. Mom's agent, he of the hairy nostrils and ears. He started talking before she finished saying hello.

"Hannah. Have you spoken with Trish?"

"I've tried. Left messages, texted. I've been concerned."

"Now I am. The machine had a message from her, something about I should be on the lookout for something—new contracts maybe?—but I couldn't really tell. The signal sucked, the whole thing was garbled. I tried calling back. Her phone, then the director's. One of the producers may be here in town. I've got a call in. Let you know when I hear."

"How about Luis? They talk pretty often, even when he's off in the wilds working."

"Caught him on the set. Days since he heard from her, he said, everything going well then." A pause. "Nothing too much amiss, I'm sure."

"Thanks, Jeremy."

"Talk soon."

Probably a lot amiss. Sly, ugly whispers offstage. Disappointment and heartbreak. Most likely no bodies floating face-down in the pool, but emotionally it could come close. Not anything she could do about it right now, though, and she needed to get back to work on the new project.

Initially it looked to be fairly standard identity theft, supporting Ben's "Not for us, I'm thinking" when he passed along the file. Little, though, was ever straightforward, and this deserved another look. Marjorie Boone taught English at an elementary school in a nearby town for almost forty years. Plain tastes, never married, never traveled, lived in the same small house all her adult life, put away her earnings for later on. But as *later on* began to take form, so did senility, chewing away Miss Boone's world bite by bite. She failed to notice funds disappearing from her account at Woods National Bank, had no memory of signing any of the checks or of paid receipts for work done and services rendered. These were discovered by a friend upon realizing how severe Miss Boone's debilities had become and taking charge of her affairs, though never legally. Miss Boone was now in a full-care nursing home, *beyond the language she spent her life teaching*, as the friend, Julie Campo, voiced it in her appeal.

Mrs. Campo wanted to see to it that those who took advantage of her friend were found out and duly punished. Since Mrs. Campo had no legal bearing and the victim herself was *non compos mentis*, there was not a great deal the police or courts could do. Mrs. Campo had gone so far as to hire a lawyer to look into this. When that foundered, she made her appeal to *Ask Again*.

Always looking for context, Hannah dug in, and was appalled at what she found. Pilfered art collections, writers' royalty payments signed over to others, graft by family members, intercepted social security checks, theft and resale of medical devices—plunder of the aged and infirm was everywhere.

For all her dismay, Hannah found it difficult to envision how the show could possibly help. Miss Boone was out of the picture, the party or parties responsible were unknown, there were no relatives or others with legal standing, and such dispossessions, as Hannah now knew, were dirt-common. She did, however, create a new personal file, drag-dropping her research to it: scams, misappropriations, and outright thefts; how, where and when these took place; actions and reports by those affected, by families, by police or other officials. She named the file *Clippings* and sent Ben an email to tell him she agreed, the appeal didn't look a fit for *Ask Again*. Moments later she had incoming mail.

> *Sorry to be out of touch but it's been a fair slice of havoc here. No worries—I'm fine. The shoot's had the usual dips and dives, full stops, potholes, clashes. Nothing new there. But evidently when backers saw dailies they freaked. Shut us down a week while they fired wonder boy Robbie and brought in a new director. Now, four or five days into it, this guy's decided he's making a great movie. Not will make, but is making. You have to wonder if he's even read the script. Anyway, here he is with his sore, barking, apologetic throat, up in everyone's business, poking about in the wardrobe mistress's racks, buzzing our poor makeup girl Rose Ann, on tiptoes showing a lead how a scene's to be played, taking up most of an afternoon for six or seven takes on an establishing scene because*

"it doesn't feel right," him in his faded no-muscle T-shirt
and brokedown shoes. We'll get through this, we always
do, but the thing's looking more and more like sausage.

Like it wasn't sausage from the get-go, Hannah thought. Which was more or less Trish's point, she guessed. Hannah called back, got voicemail, and left a message. Then sat watching the cursor blink, trying again to put herself in Trish's head. Had her mother started out thinking of this as her comeback? Her swan song? Or only as something to engage with, to help her break through the crust of the everyday? Was it possible that Trish, so long away from acting, had felt lost, and now feared that loss coming back to reclaim her?

Hannah never understood why Trish quit working. She was good. And everyone—viewers, directors, other actors, crews—loved what she did. She was getting older, sure. And it's not as though she ever had any particular artistic ambitions. Still . . .

But then, Hannah didn't really understand why she herself had walked away from nursing.

Or why she'd given up on her resolve to find Moira, at least to find out what happened to her.

Back when Moira disappeared, Hannah had done little more than wander about, bouncing waywardly from place to place. Since then, she'd spent months unearthing details of others' lives, she knew where to look, the nooks and crannies and folds where information hid. Maybe this would make a difference.

That night Hannah watched a movie about a young man who in the rubble of a post-apocalyptic city comes across a flute and sets about figuring out what it is and how to play it. The challenge isn't merely technical: born in the ruins, raised in the wild, he's never heard manmade music.

The movie was only a few years old, but given its production values—script, sets, photography, right down to the print itself—*Rebound* must have seemed long out of date the day it was released, a fugitive off the back lots of the 1970s. Trish would have been right at home. She wasn't there, but familiar mutants, murderous tribes, cannibalistic religious clans, and women in post-historic push-up bras made proud appearances. And art, of course, saved what was left of the world.

Sure it did.

Nothing, however, could save the takeout meal Hannah hiked six blocks there and back to pick up, imaginatively and by claim a biryani, in plain fact a cup or so of frozen vegetables heated in a scatter of spices with rice tossed in toward the end. There'd definitely been a change in cooks at the restaurant, if not in ownership. She called India Palace to complain and got asked to please hold, which she did for some time, all the while thinking why bother, before hanging up.

She had cheese. She had bread. Pickles. Possibly fruit that was still good. She was a survivor.

Later that night she watched *Casablanca*.

Moira

For a long time Moira had felt that something was pushing toward her, building within and without. Maybe this was it.

In the two months they'd been here, they'd settled fairly well into the new quarters, new place, new digs, whatever it ought to be called, even got to know a couple of the neighbors, Ennie and Alma, elderly ladies who lived next door and early the third day brought over a welcome pie. The pie tin looked to be as old as the women themselves, the pie was way too sweet and seemed to have something missing—forgotten? Shell couldn't praise the pie, or the thought of it, enough.

So here they were in a tiny house on the other side of town, in the outer reach of a family-rich neighborhood: children playing in the street, men at work on chock-wheeled cars in driveways, people sitting out in front yards on folding chairs. Like some old imagined America from a fifties TV show, Moira couldn't help thinking. Looks just like back home, Shell said.

It had taken some persuasion on Moira's part to get them there, Shell protesting that she'd only just moved into the duplex, that Moira was over-reacting, Dennis hadn't really *done* anything, Moira saying over and over "It only gets worse" and reminding Shell how frightened she'd been the night before.

It had taken considerable logistics as well, Moira scrounging money from her dwindling bank account, Shell making arrangements to work remotely, a cruise round the city in Shell's Honda seeking a proper place to land, then cautious swings back to the old place to fetch what they most needed to bring along. Shell hadn't brought much with her from Texas nor accumulated much more; part of Moira's decision that the two of them relocate was that she'd leave behind all that she could.

Two months now. Late afternoon or early evening of the day Moira left the hospital for the last time, she had been sleeping and heard voices. Next door? Outside, on the porch? Then either the voices stopped or she fell back asleep. Later she roused to frantic knocking at the front door. Shell stood there asking if she could come in. "I'm afraid," she said, and looked it every bit.

Dennis wouldn't leave her be, she said, only he wasn't Dennis anymore, he was calling himself Brian now. She'd seen him hanging around her office. He'd come up to her sometimes as she left work. She tried to ignore him and kept walking, but he came along and went on talking, most of it nonsense, his plans, the new job, stuff from when he was a kid. And just tonight he'd showed up at her door, like he was expected. She didn't open it, but she was afraid now, really afraid.

"This sort of thing doesn't stop," Moira said.

"It gets worse. I know. And it has."

"You shouldn't be alone. Is there anywhere you can go?"

"I haven't been here long enough to make friends, and all my family's back in Texas. I can't leave and lose this job. What would you do?"

"No idea. But listen . . . Till we figure this out, why don't you stay here with me? The couch sleeps pretty well. And if it comes to it, there's a baseball bat in the closet by the front door."

"Are you sure?"

"Absolutely."

Moira made coffee and they sat together in the kitchen talking. Shell expressed concern over interfering with Moira's work and sleep patterns, so Moira explained that wouldn't be a problem, she was off a few days. She heard about Shell's life back home, her father a lineman for TP&L, mother a child-care worker, older sister, younger brother, then a cringefully funny story of Shell's one and only venture into line dancing. A bit after nine they heard knocks next door, a voice, presumably Brian's, calling out. He returned about an hour later, that time crossing the porch to knock at Moira's door. Still in the kitchen away from the front, they remained quiet and made no response. He came back and left twice more, at which point they spoke seriously of calling the police, but that was it for the night and, not long after, they slept.

By morning Moira had decided.

A week after they moved in, Moira confessed that she no longer worked at the hospital and Shell found a notice on her office's online bulletin board that HR had learned from police in New Mexico that Dennis, who used to work for them—who disappeared, remember?—had got himself arrested there and was on his way to prison.

They talked about returning to the duplex, but decided to remain where they were. A new start and all that, right? Shell went back to working at the office, *nine-ish to five-ish* as she said, *everyone's pretty loose about it.* Moira moved things here and there in the house, filled drawers and shelves then unloaded them for another go at it, but given the paucity of what they'd brought with them, there was only so much to be done.

The move-in, even with Shell chipping in, had brought Moira's bank account to the brink. Out for a walk one morning she noticed a help wanted sign at a daycare center nearby and went in to inquire. She was sitting answering perfectly reasonable questions when, within, she heard *No, not here,* excused herself, and withdrew. She picked up a part-time job at a mom-and-pop corner store run by, and she assumed owned by, an elderly couple looking for occasional relief from seven six-to-ten days a week. While there she restocked and tidied up shelves, gave the place a thorough cleaning, and got to know some of the neighborhood folk. Two weeks in when, as far as Moira knew, the couple remained in charge, a younger man showed up. Their son, he said, and, with no preamble or effort at conversation, began detailing his expectations of her duties and schedule. Silently Moira retrieved her purse from the back room and walked out.

Shell was covering most of their expenses now, but rent and utilities would soon be due. Moira found a free clinic overjoyed to see her almost from the moment she walked in and eager to put her to work right away, their enthusiasm directly proportional to an absurdly low wage and consequent difficulty attracting staff. Mostly Moira did prelim physicals, dressings, injections, blood draws. Before she came, Dr. Alice and a nursing assistant had been doing it all themselves, apparently for some time. Moira had walked in on a room of more than a dozen patients waiting their turn.

Dr. Alice spoke sparingly, employing as few words as possible to get information across, leaving the listener to provide punctuation, stress, nuance. She was thin, not skeletal but inordinately lean, with hands each finger of which seemed to have a mind of its own. Speaking, she looked on with an intensity many would find unnerving. Moira found it comforting.

Moira liked working at the clinic, liked the people she worked with and the patients, liked the work itself. Felt she was doing good for herself and for the community. She'd been at it close to a month when Dr. Alice asked her to stop by the office before she left that day.

"Ovarian cancer," she said even before Moira sat. "Third recurrence. No chemo this time, been there. We shut doors at the end of the month. Sorry. If you prefer not to stay till then, I can write you a check now."

"I'll stay."

Good, from within .

"Tomorrow then," Dr. Alice said.

Every night Shell brought home stories from the office that left Moira's head spinning. Fifty thousand dollars to sign up new turbines, easement fees of sixty-five thousand dollars per year to secure access to turbine sites across neighboring lands, minimum guarantees of nine hundred thousand dollars a year per operating site.

Laugh or cry? Moira thought. Ennie and Alma, the elderly

neighbors who'd brought them a pie, were probably living on a few hundred dollars a month. And many of the families around them wouldn't be doing a lot better. Not to mention the homeless.

One night quite late, Alma showed up at their door. Shell had mentioned that Moira was a nurse, and Alma came to ask her to check on Ennie, who'd been sick the last three days and now couldn't get out of bed, barely responded to Alma's questions. Moira went next door, through an immaculate living room smelling faintly of perfume and candles, into a bedroom looking and smelling quite different and, following a quick assessment, told Alma to call an ambulance.

Ennie, already in heart failure, had suffered a stroke. She remained in the hospital for observation, two days in ICU, four on a stepdown floor, before discharge to a rehab facility. By that time she was speaking, though at the very edge of intelligibility. Otherwise unoccupied after the clinic's closing, Moira took to visiting her there daily, then followed her to an extended care facility, Acacia Home, where eventually she got to know Ennie's caregivers.

Plainspoken, unaffected Shell, meanwhile, under the influence of others at her alternative energy company, Moira assumed, was bringing home intimations of new attitudes. No marches or demonstrations yet, but Moira couldn't help recalling a favorite line from the movie *Next of Kin*: "You ain't seen bad yet, but it's coming." Random remarks by Shell concerning current events, flyers for "progressive" gatherings on the front table among bills and junk mail, search lists surfacing on the computer they shared, that sort of thing.

Change is the constant, Moira supposed. You're forever opening doors then standing there hoping it won't come in.

The latest of Moira's changes lay in going back to work as a nurse at Acacia Home. Having spent so much time there visiting Miss Ennie and getting to know staff, she decided why not. She needed work, something to occupy her, and being there felt a good fit. Days moved by at a predictable, steady pace. Afternoons stretched lazily toward evenings. She'd attend to her duties, chiefly spot-check vitals, distribute meds, do quick sticks for those with diabetes, mind the occasional IV, then pass her time with residents, talking, playing cards, watching soap operas or ancient TV shows, joining them for brief walks, rolling them out to the porch in wheelchairs for fresh air and sunshine.

Mrs. Hummer had a hundred stories to tell you, each of them essentially the same, only minor details of person and place swapped about.

All of Gene Hasford's stories went back to his young adulthood in Chicago, circa 1950, many of them concerning his saintly mother; of more recent days, up to and including past hours of the current one, nothing much remained in his memory.

Billie Moon often grew frustrated at her inability to perform simple tasks, getting socks on, opening a drawer, draping a blouse on a hanger, and would begin throwing articles about the room. You learned the signs and how to distract her before it got started.

So many stories.

Some residents had led lives filled and rich with experiences: travel, work, family, war, strife. Some had led lives with richness and fullness of other, quieter kinds. Moira loved hearing all the stories, even those she'd heard many times before.

She and one of the nurses with whom she worked, Aisha, more or less by chance became friends. They worked different shifts but occasionally on one or another of their days off Aisha would join Moira at her place for take-out dinners and a movie. They never talked all that much, simply sat together watching, eating, drinking coffee. For the most part, Moira rewatched old favorites from a long, long list. Shell began joining them, infrequently at first, then ever more often. Before long, Shell and Aisha were regularly spending time together, out to dinner or lunch, movies, music, strolls, and not long after that, moved in together. Moira was sad at first, and a little hurt, but soon recovered. She'd loved having Shell around, having such a friend. But they were still friends, always would be. And now, after all, Moira wasn't alone anymore. Through changes large and small, Moira had finally got used to sleeping at night. That was the best of times. She'd wash, pee, dress for bed, then lie there with only the bedside lamp on, eyes closed, house still, streets gone quiet, anticipating. Breath and blood slowed, she was weightless, afloat, drifting. After a while she'd turn off the light, settle fully in. Listen.

Hannah

Another bright day outside the window and a dull Hannah on this side. She hadn't gotten more than an hour's sleep. She felt as dim and insubstantial as the reflection there before her.

For a well-inhabited institution, Acacia Home was strangely quiet. Indistinct voices behind the plexiglass panels of the nurses' station, a hushed, almost rain-like sound from the TV at the far end of the lobby, click of footsteps out in the hallway. A smell of floor wax that probably never went away.

Miss Boone's situation had remained on her mind. Her savings drained away by bottom feeders, herself now fully incapacitated, no one but a single loyal friend to care. With little or no notion what she thought she might find there, Hannah kept going back to the file she'd labelled *Clippings*, reading through it compulsively. All the scamming and outright thievery, case after case, hundreds of them. Not much she or the show could do about that, the rock was too big to move. Miss Boone, though . . . Hannah again read through the copies of financial records and official reports, Ms. Campo's many letters seeking relief for her friend and final appeal to *Ask Again*.

The previous night, sitting with *Cosi fan tutte* playing quietly as she tried to read a novel so fraught with meaning that floorboards all but creaked beneath the weight, wondering how Trish was getting along the whole time, Hannah had come to a decision.

So here she was. Acacia Home, where Miss Boone lived now. Not much Hannah could do to help. But she could say hello to the woman, visit a bit. Maybe bring some small, poor comfort?

Hearing someone behind her and expecting the nurse who had said she'd be with her in just a moment, Hannah turned to see Moira standing close and coming closer, holding out a hand—just as she collapsed.

Staff were there immediately, scooped her up, and wheeled her off on a gurney to an exam room at the far end of the corridor.

Hannah never did get to pay a visit to Ms. Boone. Instead, she spent the afternoon and evening at St. Luke's Hospital. When Hannah was allowed in to see her, hours after the collapse, Moira looked drawn and pale, as was to be expected. Monitor, IV, NPO sign—also to be expected.

"Guess I'm going to be here a while," Moira said. "I know why *I'm* here, but why are you?"

"Long story."

"I'll do my best to stay awake for it."

"Are you okay?"

"For the time being, yeah. You first."

Hannah filled her in, realizing as she did so just how much time had passed since the two of them were together in the unit, and how much had changed in her own life. Told Moira how she got worried when Moira didn't show up for work and went off trying to find her, find out what happened, that she was all right, but kept hitting dead ends. How finally, by accident more or less, she'd gone back to work at, of all things, a TV show, *Ask Again*, where she became haunted by the story of retired teacher Miss Boone, resolved to come see her and now, absolutely by accident, was here at Moira's bedside.

"Accident," Moira said.

"Pure chance. So what's going on with you?"

Moira told her about Shell, about their move together and the circumstance of it, how she took on the job at Acacia after getting to know the place from visiting an elderly neighbor who lived there.

"I mean now," Hannah. "What's going on with you now—here?"

"Oh. Guess I fainted. Minor anemia, electrolytes all out of whack. Took some effort to stabilize me, they say. So they ran a bunch of tests, naturally. Now they're going to wait and see if labor starts in the next few days. If not . . ."

"You're pregnant."

"Not really."

Moira

She came suddenly awake, unable to remember what had happened. Blinds were drawn against bright sunlight. From the hallway came familiar sounds: voices, carts and equipment being moved, occasional overhead announcements or alarms. In here, the low drone of a monitor and an attendant humming quietly to herself.

The hummer appeared beside her. *Himself*, then. Male, young, thin, athletic build. "You're okay," he said. "You passed out and you're at St. Luke's. I'm Paul."

"What—" she said, but fell back into sleep before completing the question.

When next she awoke, a doctor was there at bedside, auscultating. He straightened to introduce himself as Doctor Levy. Paul returned moments later. Light past the windows had dimmed. A food cart with squeaky wheels was making its way door to door down the hallway outside. There was a second, unoccupied bed in the room.

"How are you, Miss Jarosz?"

"On a scale of one to ten, I'm a six."

"Pain?"

"Confusion."

"You don't remember what happened, then?"

"I . . . saw an old friend. And fainted?"

"Lack of memory's quite common, given the situation. You're a nurse, I understand."

She nodded.

"The LOC came from electrolyte imbalance and dangerously high blood sugar. You must have known you were borderline diabetic."

"Yes."

"And that you were pregnant?"

She was quiet, finally said, "I knew. Because he was speaking to me."

"Who was speaking to you?"

"The boy. My child."

"I see." The doctor and Paul exchanged glances. "I'm afraid I have to tell you that your child has suffered a silent miscarriage, Miss Jarosz."

"I know."

"He stopped moving, then?"

"He stopped speaking."

"Indeed." Doctor Levy took a buzzing phone from his pocket, glanced at the message, put the phone back. "The important thing is, you're doing well now. We'll keep you here on OB under observation. Should you not go into labor within a reasonable time, we'll go ahead and induce. Do you understand?"

"Of course."

"Then I'll see you soon."

Paul waited till the doctor left to ask if she had any further questions. She didn't. Was there anything else he could get or do for her? No.

The food cart squeaked up to her door and a young woman who couldn't be more than sixteen, maybe seventeen, carried in the predictable tray of soggy carrots and green beans with a roll the size of a billiard ball, a suspiciously rectangular slab of meat-like substance, and yogurt. The girl asked if she would care to watch TV as she ate. *Care to*. And *as* she ate rather than *while*. Interesting. Moira declined but changed her mind and turned the television on once the girl left.

She couldn't remember when she'd last watched actual TV. Cycling now past dozens of channels and shows, she felt she was seeing the same things—format, style, characters, personalities, plots, dialogue—over and over again.

Later that day, bands of color showing low on the horizon, staff wheeled in a new patient. Patient, that's what *she* was now, Moira thought, and how strange to be that. Having evaded hospital admission all these years.

Her new roommate's name, as she told Moira even before sliding off the gurney into bed, was Christina. And this (with a wee pause for effect) was her third child, a girl this time, thank you lord. Through all the flurry of getting settled—bedclothes arranged, basins, water pitcher and cup laid out at bedside, the nurse's rapid-fire orientation—not once did Christina's patter cease. At last realizing that Moira had yet to respond, Christina hushed. She reached over, tugged at the curtain between them to send it skidding along the pole, and fired up her own TV.

Was it like hers? Moira's own screen every few seconds did this nervous little sideways flicker, like it was slipping a quarter-inch or so out of place, before settling back, so that the images never seemed quite in focus. The blur might be actual, or only a lingering after-effect from the flicker.

She still couldn't believe Hannah had spent all that time trying to find her, worried about her. Or that Hannah left nursing and now was some kind of TV announcer or investigator or something. Hannah had shown up earlier, not too long after she got settled here on OB. Moira told her about the miscarriage, that they were waiting to see if she'd go into labor before inducing, that all things considered she was feeling okay and, as Hannah went on asking questions, finally told her about the voices, those that had gone away long ago and the new one, though that voice was gone now too, forever, she guessed.

Past the curtain, Christine was watching a show in which a husband and wife restored old houses "to their prior glory," though from what Moira heard, the couple weren't restoring the houses to what they had been so much as making them into something greatly different, in fact not recovering the past but revoking it.

Moira checked her phone and found eight missed calls, three from people at work, one wanting to buy the house she didn't have, four from Shell and Aisha. She called back to let them know what happened and reassure them she was fine. *We had no idea*, Shell said. Moira hadn't either. All along, until the doctor's rhetorical question made the pregnancy real, somehow she had known without knowing.

In the bedside table Moira came across a beaten, water-stained paperback novel. Left behind by a former new mother, she supposed. It told the story of two girls who meet for a single evening yet, even though one dies, forge a bond that can't be loosened shortly before she began hemorrhaging and Doctor Levy came in to tell her he was increasingly concerned, that they'd be taking her right along to Delivery for a C-section, Moira finished reading the book.

Hannah

Answering the door, Hannah opened it to an astonishingly beautiful young man, mid-twenties, fine dark hair gathered loosely behind, yellow-brown eyes.

She'd been unaware of any problem with the doorbell. After all, no one ever came by. But the sound it had given out was a brief, harsh rasp, like a poorly cleared throat or a gasp, before ending altogether. The young man stood staring down at the push button, perhaps with much the same thought. Now he looked up.

"Hannah Martyn?"

She nodded.

"This is for you."

A sturdy manila envelope, legal size, sealed, no writing on it. And the beautiful young man, after handing it to her, had already turned to leave.

"Wait, please. What is this?"

He turned back, one foot on the bottom step. "He said to tell you the contents would explain themselves, and that he would be in touch."

"He?"

"Head of production. Robbie. Instructed me to urge you to spend time with this material, then you'd talk."

Hannah carried the envelope back into the front room. Mozart's D minor piano concert was playing, coming up close to the second movement. Where it always seems, for moments, that time itself has been suspended.

Production company, the young man had said. There'd been no word from Trish for a time now. Jeremy had heard nothing more, and late last week Luis called to say the same. Told her something was going on but no one would say what, that he had another day of shooting, then he'd head up there. Putting this dog together, he said, meaning his new movie, could wait till he got back in town, town for him always meaning LA.

So maybe this . . .

She tore it open. A letter. An actual letter. And a disc.

Hannah,

Apologies for the long silence—from your mother, and from me as proxy.

News of the moment is that Trish is in hospital, laid low by some species of virus or dysentery contracted as we were shooting. She is recovering well but is drained and weak and not yet up to contacting you herself.

Here's the storyboard. A little under a month ago, Trish walked away from the film we'd been working together on, on which I had been replaced, and which, under the new director, has morphed into something else entirely.

She and I met up and decided we'd like to continue working together. Using footage I'd shot as leverage, I was able to find financing and to put together a new, barebones production company. We set directly to work, carrying weight, putting in strings of eighteen-hour days.

I had to rewrite the script, of course, so Trish has become, rather than a nurse, a bounty hunter searching for the man she will later come to protect, then to care for. Many details are different, but the heart of my original script beats in this one. We don't have our ending yet; we'll shoot that as soon as Trish is up to it. What you have on the enclosed DVD is a rough cut to date, all but the last ten minutes or so.

I hope you'll be pleased to see Trish fully in action again. She's a marvel.

(She asked me, by the way, not to say that. Guess I say it a lot.) Further, I'll say only that I'm silly proud of our work here, and that I look forward to meeting you— maybe at the premiere?

Robbie

Hannah watched the DVD that night. The story line, the plot, wasn't much. A fugitive, his relentless pursuers, the bounty hunter pledged to bring him in before the worst happened, a chase or two, a confrontation . . . It could have been any of a hundred other movies. For that matter, it could have been one of Trish's own middle-to-late movies. But the stripped-back settings, the photography coming at you like a steady series of framed paintings, the way the two leads spoke so little yet said so much with their expressions, body language, eyes—so many things that words would fail. *Rapt* came to mind as Hannah watched. She was rapt. The whole of the thing, every moment of it, was filled with light. Somehow this movie had broken free from the moorings of what it started out to be and had floated away, floated up, become something else. A small, small story. And a grand one.

Most of all, how magnificent to witness Trish's character, in the course of the story, slowly fill with light herself, with the quiet, distinct joy of being alive, of taking action, doing.

Hannah turned the player and TV off. From outside she could hear the murmur of neighborhood children playing, slow traffic on the streets, a mockingbird's commentary, their frequent-flyer woodpecker having a go at the poor elm out front.

Some of us, Hannah thought, some of us find our way, even as we stagger about lost.

NOTES

"Kazoo" first appeared in *New Worlds*

"A Few Last Words," "Letter to a Young Poet," and "The History Makers" first appeared in *Orbit*, ed. Damon Knight

"Front & Centaur" first appeared in *New Worlds*

"Slice of Universe" first appeared in *Fantastic*

"Winner" first appeared in *A Few Last Words*

"The Leveller" first appeared in *Gallery*

"D.C. al Fine" first appeared in *Alfred Hitchcock's Mystery Magazine*

"Faces, Hands" first appeared in *Nova 1*, ed. Harry Harrison

"53rd American Dream" first appeared in *Again, Dangerous Visions*, ed. Harlan Ellison

"The Creation of Bennie Good" and "Jim and Mary G" first appeared in *Orbit*

"Bubbles" first appeared in *New Worlds*

"And then the dark—" first appeared in *A Few Last Words*

"At the Fitting Shop" first appeared in *Again, Dangerous Visions*

"The Opening of the Terran Ballet" first appeared in *A Few Last Words*

"The Anxiety in the Eyes of the Cricket" first appeared in *The New S.F.*, ed. Langdon Jones

"Jeremiad" first appeared in *New Worlds*

"Marrow" first appeared in *The Nature of the Catastrophe*, ed. Langdon Jones

"Récits" first appeared in *Transatlantic Review*

"Doucement, S'il Vous Plait" first appeared in *Orbit*

"Insect Men of Boston" first appeared in *New Worlds*

"Free Time" first appeared in *Album Zutique*, ed. Jeff Vandermeer

"Jane Crying" first appeared in *A Few Last Words*

"Hope: An Outline" and "The Very last Days of Boston" first appeared in *Quark*, ed. Samuel R. Delany and Marilyn Hacker

"Enclave" first appeared in *A Few Last Words*

"Syphilis: A Synopsis" first appeared in *Quarter After Eight*

"Only the Words Are Different" first appeared in *Orbit*

"European Experience" first appeared (as "Binaries") in *Orbit*

"My Friend Zarathustra" first appeared in *Orbit*

"Delta Flight 281" and "The First Few Kinds of Truth" first appeared in *Alternities*, ed. David Gerrold

"Second Thoughts" first appeared in *Lady Churchhill's Rosebud Wristlet*

"Under Construction" first appeared in *Crossroads: Southern Stories of the Fantastic*, ed. Andy Duncan and F. Brett Cox

"Attitude of the Earth Toward Other Bodies" first appeared in *Full Spectrum*, ed. Lou Aronica and Shawna McCarthy

"Intimations" first appeared in *The Portland Review*

"The Invasion of Dallas" first appeared in *Lone Star Universe*, ed. George W. Proctor and Steven Utley

"Driving" first appeared in *Pacific Review*

"Need" first appeared in *Asimov's Science Fiction*

"Old Times" first appeared in *Realms of Fantasy*

"Becoming" first appeared in *South Dakota Review*

"Three Stories" and "The Western Campaign" first appeared in *High Plains Literary Review*

"Octobers" first appeared in *Potato Tree and Other Stories*

"Upstream" first appeared in *Amazing Stories*

"I Saw Robert Johnson" first appeared in *Ellery Queen Mystery Magazine*

"Others" first appeared in *The Georgia Review*

"Blue Lab" first appeared in *Time's Hammers*

"Oblations" first appeared in *Time's Hammers*

"Men's Club" first appeared in *Potato Tree*

"Allowing the Lion" first appeared in *The Florida Review*

"Impossible Things Before Breakfast" first appeared in *Asimov's*

"Potato Tree" first appeared in *The Magazine of Fantasy & Science Fiction*

"Finger and Flame" first appeared in *Reed Magazine*

"Walls of Affection" first appeared in *The Fractal*

"Changes" first appeared in *Fantastic*

"Miranda-Escobedo" first appeared in *The Magazine of Fantasy & Science Fiction*

"Dogs in the Nighttime" first appeared (as "The Incident") in *Ellery Queen Mystery Magazine*

"Wolf" first appeared in *Pacific Review*

"Memory" first appeared in *Fugue*

"Joyride" first appeared in *Ellery Queen Mystery Magazine*

"Pure Reason" first appeared in *Urbanus Magazine*

"Hazards of Autobiography" first appeared on the Mississippi Review website

"The Good in Men" first appeared in *Alaska Quarterly Review*

"More Light" first appeared in *New Mystery*

"Bug" first appeared in *Kansas Quarterly*

"Moments of Personal Adventure" first appeared in *Painted Hills Review*

"Breakfast with Ralph" first appeared in *Rampike*

"Ansley's Demons" first appeared in *The Magazine of Fantasy & Science Fiction*

"Echo" first appeared in *The Beserkers*, ed. Roger Elwood

"Notes" first appeared on the La Petite Zine website

"An Ascent of the Moon" first appeared in *South Dakota Review*

"Autumn Leaves" first appeared on the website Fantastic Metropolis and in The Barcelona Review

"Dawn Over Doldrums" first appeared in *Amazing Stories*

"Powers of Flight" first appeared in *Amazing Stories*

"Stepping Away from the Stone" first appeared in *TransVersions*

"Roofs and Forgiveness in the Early Dawn" first appeared in *Talebones*

"Dear Floods of Her Hair" first appeared in *The Magazine of Fantasy & Science Fiction*

"Vocalities" first appeared in *Blue Lightning*

"Ukulele and the World's Pain" first appeared in *Alfred Hitchcock's Mystery Magazine*

"Drive" first appeared in *Measures of Poison*, ed. Dennis McMillan

"When Fire Knew My Name" first appeared on the website Fantastic Metropolis

"Get Along Home" first appeared on the website 3:AM Magazine

"Blue Yonders" first appeared on the website Fantastic Metropolis

"Christian" first appeared in *A City Equal to My Desire*

"Concerto for Violence and Orchestra" first appeared in *Men from Boys*, ed. John Harvey

"New Life" first appeared in *The Third Alternative*

"Venice Is Sinking into the Sea" and "Pitt's World" first appeared in *A City Equal to My Desire*

"Flesh of Stone and Steel" first appeared in *Thirteen: Images of Thirteen Women by Marc Atkins*

"Up" first appeared in *Leviathan Three*, ed. Forrest Aguirre and Jeff Vandermeer

"Day's Heat" first appeared in *Asimov's*

"The Monster in Midlife" first appeared in *The Dirty Goat*

"The Museum of Last Week" first appeared in *A City Equal to My Desire*

"The Genre Kid" first appeared in *The Magazine of Fantasy & Science Fiction*

"Telling Lives" first appeared in *A City Equal to My Desire*

"Your New Career" first appeared in *Crimewave*

"Blue Devils" first appeared in *Alfred Hitchcock's Mystery Magazine*

"Shutting Darkness Down" was commissioned for and broadcast by BBC radio, and subsequently published in *Louisiana Literature*

"Among the Ruins of Poetry" first appeared in *The Edge*

"Good Men" first appeared in *Ellery Queen Mystery Magazine*

"Bleak Bay" first appeared on The Pedestal Magazine website

"Career Moves" first appeared on The Blue Moon Review website

"Saguaro Arms" first appeared in *Jabberwock Review*

"How's Death" first appeared in *Oasis*

"Alaska" first appeared in *Confrontation*

"How the Damned Live On" first appeared in *Asimov's*

"Miss Cruz" first appeared in *The Magazine of Fantasy & Science Fiction*

"Ferryman" first appeared in *Borderland Noir*, ed. Craig McDonald

"Freezer Burn" first appeared in *Crimefest 2018*, ed. Adrian Muller

"Bright Sarasota Where the Circus Lies Dying" first appeared in *Welcome to Dystopia*, ed. Gordon Van Gelder and John Oakes

"The Beauty of Sunsets" first appeared in *Alfred Hitchcock's Mystery Magazine*

"What You Were Fighting For" first appeared in *The Highway Kind*, ed. Patrick Millikin

"Dispositions" first appeared in *Ellery Queen Mystery Magazine*

"Billy Deliver's Next Twelve Novels" first appeared in *Dayenu and Other Stories*

"Figs" first appeared in *Ellery Queen Mystery Magazine*

"Sunday Drive" first appeared in *Bound by Mystery*, ed. Diane DiBiase

"The World Is the Case" first appeared in *Louis Vuitton: Fashion & Travel*

"Zombie Cars" first appeared in *Grey*

"Net Loss" first appeared in *Analog*

"Season Premiere" first appeared in *Dark Delicacies II*, ed. Del Howison and Jeff Gelb

"As Yet Untitled" first appeared in *Asimov's*

"Comeback" first appeared in *Dayenu and Other Stories*

"Beautiful Quiet of the Roaring Freeway" first appeared in *Interzone*

"New Teeth" first appeared in *Analog*

"Scientific Methods" first appeared in *North Dakota Quarterly*

"Annandale" first appeared (as Bedtime Story) in *The Magazine of Fantasy & Science Fiction*

"Bury All Towers" first appeared in *North American Review*

"The Cry of Evening Birds" first appeared in *The Magazine of Fantasy & Science Fiction*

"Big Day In Little Bit" first appeared in *Bullets and Other Hurting Things*, ed. Rick Ollerman

"Lying Down" first appeared in *North Dakota Quarterly*

"Revenance" first appeared in *Vautrin*

"Quilts" first appeared on the website 365tomorrows

"When We Saved the World" first appeared in *Asimov's*

"Old Gifts" first appeared in *Pulp Literature*

"Schools of Thought and Subtraction" first appeared in *Analog*

"The Way of His Kind" first appeared in *Interzone*

"Doom Patch" first appeared in *Analog*

"Rivers Bend" first appeared in *Clarkesworld*

"Parkview" first appeared in *Black Is the Night*, ed. Maxim Jakubowski

The following stories appear for the first time in this collection:

"Getting in Shape," "Well Met," "Blood Draw," "Silver," "Out and About," "All My Grendels in a Row," "Billy Deliver's Last Twelve Novels," "On Hunger Street," "How the World Got to Be," "How I Came to Be," "Abeyance."